TORN OUT OF TIME

The ship swerved sharply as a massive rocky object—thousands of times larger than the time machine—phased into abrupt reality directly in front of them and Elzbietá jerked the omni-throttle back. She sent the TTV scooting sideways, across its craggy exterior.

"Whew!" She exhaled explosively. "That was close!"

"Where did *that* thing come from?" Raibert demanded.

"Some sort of debris being pulled into the past, same as us."

"Is that from an asteroid?" Raibert asked.

"If so, it's weirdly shaped," Benjamin replied. "No impact craters on this side. Ella, can you swing us around to the other side?"

The *Kleio* crested past the rim and the far side of the mass came into full view.

"What the *hell* is going on here?" Raibert asked softly.

"I wish I knew." Benjamin's voice was equally soft.

Kleio sped past the gargantuan spires of a broken city. A populated city... in which every vehicle and inhabitant was frozen in place.

No, not frozen, Raibert realized. *It's paused.*

It was a city torn from its world. A city where time no longer existed.

IN THIS SERIES

The Gordian Protocol
The Valkyrie Protocol

MORE BAEN BOOKS BY DAVID WEBER

HONOR HARRINGTON

On Basilisk Station • *The Honor of the Queen*
The Short Victorious War • *Field of Dishonor*
Flag in Exile • *Honor Among Enemies*
In Enemy Hands • *Echoes of Honor*
Ashes of Victory • *War of Honor*
Crown of Slaves (with Eric Flint)
The Shadow of Saganami
At All Costs • *Storm from the Shadows*
Torch of Freedom (with Eric Flint)
Mission of Honor • *A Rising Thunder*
Shadow of Freedom
Cauldron of Ghosts (with Eric Flint)
Shadow of Victory • *Uncompromising Honor*

EDITED BY DAVID WEBER

More than Honor • *Worlds of Honor*
Changer of Worlds • *The Service of the Sword*
In Fire Forged • *Beginnings*

MANTICORE ASCENDANT

A Call to Duty (with Timothy Zahn)
A Call to Arms (with Timothy Zahn & Thomas Pope)
A Call to Vengeance (with Timothy Zahn & Thomas Pope)

THE STAR KINGDOM

A Beautiful Friendship
Fire Season (with Jane Lindskold)
Treecat Wars (with Jane Lindskold)

House of Steel: The Honorverse Companion (with BuNine)

To purchase any of these titles in e-book form,
please go to www.baen.com.

THE VALKYRIE PROTOCOL

―――――∞∞∞∞―――――

DAVID WEBER &
JACOB HOLO

The Valkyrie Protocol

Copyright © 2020 by Words of Weber, Inc. & Jacob Holo

A Baen Books Original

Baen Publishing Enterprises
P.O. Box 1403
Riverdale, NY 10471
www.baen.com

ISBN: 978-1-9821-2562-2

Cover art by Dave Seeley

First printing, October 2020
First mass market printing, September 2021

Distributed by Simon & Schuster
1230 Avenue of the Americas
New York, NY 10020

Library of Congress Control Number: 2020029383

Pages by Joy Freeman (www.pagesbyjoy.com)
Printed in the United States of America

10   9   8   7   6   5   4   3   2   1

For Sharon and Heather

CHAPTER ONE

⸙⸙⸙

Schloss von Schröder
SysGov, 2980 CE

IT WAS A SMALL CHAPEL.

It was also warm, despite the snow the ice-fanged wind drove against the ancient rose window above its altar. It had been lovingly maintained for over fifteen hundred years, and it had been provided with proper heating and air-conditioning six centuries before this cold and snowy night. Despite that, the sense of its age filled the participants' nostrils with a subliminal scent of dust, of leather bindings and printer's ink. Not because there *was* any dust, but because there ought to have been. Because that many endless years were a palpable presence, peopled by all the other human beings who had passed through this chapel.

A lot of those people had been named Schröder.

The schloss's current owner was *not* named Schröder, but the title of *Gräfin* von Schröder had passed to her through a matrilineal cadet line when the last Schröder to hold it died without issue in 2653. The

1

direct Schröder line had ceased to exist, but the current *gräfin* had been only too willing to offer the chapel's use tonight.

Klaus-Wilhelm von Schröder stood just outside the sanctuary's rail.

He looked a bit odd in the chapel's setting, and not simply because it had been built so many centuries before. He was clad in the formal "white tie" of a thousand years in the past, which was enormously anachronistic in itself, but it seemed even more so in his case because no one in the thirtieth century had ever seen him in it. His normal—*invariable*, actually—attire was a perfectly tailored uniform in what had once been called *feldgrau*, with the golden eye and bared-sword shoulder patch of SysPol's Gordian Division and a vice-commissioner's insignia.

Seeing him in anything else was a bit like catching God in his bathrobe, Benjamin Schröder thought. On the other hand, he admitted, that . . . patriarchal simile might have occurred to him because Klaus-Wilhelm von Schröder also happened to be his grandfather.

And the other reason it's occurring to you is because you're both a hell of a long way from home and you're just a teeny tiny bit nervous, he thought. *Which is stupid, under the circumstances.*

Thanks to his neural implants, Benjamin could check the time—again—without anyone else's knowledge. That meant he could at least avoid *looking* like the proverbial nervous groom.

You and Elzbietá have been living together for months, and nobody in the entire universe—hell, in the entire multiverse—gives a damn, he reminded himself. *In fact, the only people this wedding really matters to are the two of you. Well, and to Grand-dad, too, I suppose. He has dropped that "living in sin" thing on you more than once. Surprising how straitlaced he can be sometimes, even after all this time. But it's not like he drew a gun on you to get here! And worrying about it now that you are here is—well, it's a perfect illustration of why no one who really knows you ever said you weren't capable of being stupid. It's not like being dissolved into goo by weaponized nanotech, after all!*

He knew it wasn't, because he'd tried that, too. Being dissolved into goo. Or at least one iteration of him had, and that other iteration's entire memory—including the highly unpleasant one of how he had died—lived in the same brain, side by side with the remembered lifetime of the version of him that hadn't been dissolved.

It was . . . complicated.

He snorted softly at the thought, and the tall, broad-shouldered, blond-haired man at his shoulder glanced at him with a raised eyebrow.

"Nothing, Raibert," Benjamin reassured him. "Just a thought."

"So you *are* capable of rational thought at the moment, Doc?" Raibert Kaminski, who *did* wear Gordian Division's uniform, grinned. "Thank God! After dragging your butt here this morning, I'd started to wonder."

"I'm not *that* bad."

"On the contrary," Klaus-Wilhelm said. "You're *worse* than that, Benjamin."

"I am not!"

"Ah? Then you remembered the ring?"

"That's Raibert's job. He's the best man around here. Well, best synthoid, anyway."

"That is *so* twentieth-century bio-based prejudice," Raibert observed. "Just because you and Elzbietá refuse to give up your meat suits is no reason for you to be casting aspersions upon my own superbly engineered self."

Benjamin made a rude sound, and his grandfather chuckled. Neither of them had ever met Raibert before his biological mind had been electronically stripped and his biological body had been rendered down for fertilizer, or whatever else the System Cooperative Administration's reclamation systems had done with it. His current body had been hijacked from the Admin's Department of Incarceration in Klaus-Wilhelm's original universe after Csaba Shigeki, Director-General of the Department of Temporal Investigation, had decreed Raibert's biological destruction. And after his connectome's removal, the electronic recording of his personality and memories had been sentenced to life imprisonment in a virtual prison.

To be fair to Shigeki, which none of the men in that chapel were prepared to be unless they had to, he *had* been fighting to prevent Raibert from destroying his entire universe. A reasonable person might concede that had given him at least *some* justification. And he'd actually shown leniency, in many ways. The Admin's laws about AIs and nanotech were draconian. Its entire government had come into existence in reaction to a grisly "accident" in which a rogue AI had left literally billions dead, and its law code was designed to prevent *anything* like that from ever happening again. In pursuit of that object, it was ruthless with violators, and

Raibert, from an entirely different universe, had been in violation of dozens of its laws. That meant he *could* have been sentenced to a one-way domain—a virtual prison where prisoners became effectively immortal but there were no wardens, no guards. Nothing to protect the inmates from the most horrific atrocities their fellow inmates could visit upon them. It was, in fact, a place which was—literally—worse than death. Not that a prisoner couldn't "die" there. They could, over and over and over again.

Of course, Raibert wasn't exactly prepared to give Shigeki the benefit of any doubts. Nor had he known that the director was being merciful—by his own lights, at least. All *he'd* known was that both his and the Admin's universe were going to die if someone didn't fix it and that Shigeki was determined that no one would. And, of course, that he'd been subjected to the ultimate violation when his connectome was forcibly stripped in a process that automatically destroyed his biological mind forever. Nor had he known that there were worse prisons to which he might have been sent. The one he'd been in was quite bad enough, as far as he was concerned, and he'd expected to stay in it for the rest of his life . . . until his integrated companion, Philosophus, had rampaged through the Admin's infostructure to break him out. In the process, Philo—who, unlike Raibert, had been "born" as an electronic being—had uploaded him to one of the Admin Peacekeepers' synthoids. As a consequence, Raibert came equipped with quite a few military-style upgrades, and he'd decided to keep his present body once he'd managed to fight his way home to his own universe once more.

Of course, he'd added a few additional upgrades to it, too. For one thing, the ridiculous firewalls the Admin—better known as "the fucking Admin" if Raibert was talking—insisted upon as part of its paranoia about artificial intelligences in general had been deleted when his software was updated to link with the Consolidated System Government's infonets. In the process, Raibert and Philo had made damned sure no Admin backdoors had been left behind.

"Look, I know you two are enjoying the chance to give me a hard time," Benjamin said now, "but, really. Where the hell is Elzbietá?"

"If the two of you had been willing to settle for a virtual wedding, like any sane, civilized beings, that wouldn't be an issue," Raibert pointed out. "But, *no*! Not you *two*! Had to be 'in the flesh,' didn't it? You could've been married in Notre Dame, or St. Peter's Basilica. Hell, you could have been married in the Hagia Sophia—the *original* Hagia Sophia—if you hadn't insisted on this brick-and-mortar anachronism!"

"And if we were both connectomes we would've done just that," Benjamin shot back. "But in case you noticed, we aren't."

"Yeah, yeah, yeah." Raibert grimaced, but he let it drop, as well. Probably, Benjamin thought, because he knew as well as Benjamin did that the real reason Benjamin and Elzbietá had chosen this venue was to honor Klaus-Wilhelm. God only knew how many Schröders had been married in this chapel over the endless, dusty years, but Klaus-Wilhelm was among them. He and his first wife had been married on this very stone floor.

Well, Benjamin reminded himself, *not on this stone floor, actually*.

The chapel in which Klaus-Wilhelm had been married no longer existed. For that matter, his entire *universe* no longer existed. He and Elzbietá Abramowski were, in fact, survivors of that dead universe, and Benjamin—or the version of him that had died there—had helped to murder it.

There'd been no choice. That iteration of the Admin's universe should never have existed. It had been created out of the chaos of the "Gordian Knot" which had twisted sixteen universes together into a lethal cluster—a seething mass of temporal energy which would have destroyed them all, if it had not been undone. And so they had unknotted them, and the price had been Klaus-Wilhelm and Elzbietá's own universe.

And the life of the Benjamin Schröder who had been born of it.

Fifteen out of the sixteen universes entangled in the Knot survived because of that terrible sacrifice. A ninety-four percent survival rate was pretty damned good, Benjamin told himself again. He told himself that a lot, when the ghosts of that vanished universe invaded his dreams. And it was true. He *knew* it was true, but somehow that didn't help on the bad nights.

What helped on *those* nights was Elzbietá.

Speaking of whom—

"I'm going to comm her," he announced. "I'm starting to get genuinely worried. She's the most compulsively—I'd almost say psychotically, except that she'd find out I had and hurt me—punctual person I know. It's not like her to be running late, especially on a day like this."

"Don't you dare," Raibert said, poking him in the

chest with a large and very strong finger. Benjamin Schröder was a tall, broad-shouldered man himself, almost as tall and broad-shouldered as his grandfather, but that poke was enough to put him back on his heels. He rubbed his chest, glaring at Raibert, and the synthoid shook his head. "Doc, I know you're a really smart guy. So I'm wondering why it hasn't occurred to you that Elzbietá wouldn't be running late by *accident*? Or, rather, that she would have already commed *you* if things weren't going according to plan?"

"Plan?" Benjamin eyed Raibert narrowly. "*Plan?* Nobody told me about any 'plan' except coming here, getting married, leaving on our honeymoon. You know, what all of us have been talking about for, like, *weeks*?"

"And this is one of your best analysts, sir." Raibert looked at Klaus-Wilhelm and shook his head sadly.

"To be fair," Klaus-Wilhelm replied, "Benjamin is one of my best *researchers*. Calling him an 'analyst' is a bit of a stretch. He lacks a certain something for that role. A certain . . . skepticism, perhaps."

"Are you sure that's the best word for it?" Raibert asked. "'Skepticism,' I mean."

"You had another one in mind?"

"As a matter of fact, I was thinking *paranoia* might be a better way to put it. Although, if pressed, I'd have to admit that 'devious' would run a close second."

"Fair, fair." Klaus-Wilhelm nodded with a magisterial air. "Be that as it may, however, you are sadly correct that Benjamin never saw it coming."

"Saw *what* coming?" Benjamin demanded, looking back and forth between them.

"Saw *this* coming!" a hulking, red-haired Viking— who looked utterly bizarre and yet inevitable in a twenty-third-century tuxedo and a horned helmet—crowed exultantly as he materialized out of the chapel's thin air. Or, more precisely, out of the all-pervasive SysGov infonet and into everyone's shared virtual vision. His helmet did indeed have horns on it, in a nod to inaccurate renditions of Vikings, but those horns protruded out of the headgear of a twenty-first-century fighter pilot. His flowing red beard, braided into a neat fork for the occasion, spread over the frilled lace of his shirtfront, and impossibly white teeth flashed in an improbably wide smile as he beamed at Benjamin.

Benjamin glared at him, but Philosophus only smiled even more broadly, bowed like a helmeted maître d', and waved one hand expressively at the chapel doors.

Benjamin turned to follow the gesture automatically, and froze as the doors swept open and revealed Elzbietá Abramowski, standing upon the threshold.

She wore a stunning wedding gown, and a beam of light from no visible source appeared as Philosophus' avatar snapped its fingers. The incredible gown's gemmed bodice and intricate embroidery flashed like fire when the light touched it, and its long cathedral train floated behind her, suspended by a pair of counter-grav remotes. A jeweled tiara crowned her dark, lustrous hair, its precious stones blazing with hearts of fire, and her gray eyes glowed more brilliantly still as they found him, standing with Raibert at the sanctuary's rail.

Her beauty took him by the throat. That wasn't the wedding gown she'd *told* him she'd picked, and it took him a moment to realize what it was, where he'd seen it before. It was identical to the one Yulia Obolenskaya von Schröder, *Gräfin* von Schröder, Klaus-Wilhelm's second bride, had worn in the Cathedral of the Dormition of Theotokos in Kiev when she had been given away by Kaiser Louis Ferdinand himself.

His throat tightened as the sight of her ran through him, but from the corner of his eye he saw his grandfather's expression soften, saw the raw memory—the *man*—behind those icy gray eyes, and in that instant he realized that gown wasn't identical to the one Yulia had worn in the portrait hung in another Schloss von Schröder, long, long ago.

It *was* Yulia's.

His own eyes burned as that sank home. The Benjamin Schröder of SysGov's universe had never known his grandfather's second wife, but the Benjamin Schröder of the *Admin's* universe had known—and deeply loved—Yulia von Schröder, just as he'd loved his aunts, his father's half-sisters. He'd loved her all his life, and he'd been a pallbearer at her funeral and fought back tears, fought to keep his voice level, as he delivered his own eulogy on the life of the most remarkable woman he had ever known.

And in that other universe, Klaus-Wilhelm and Elzbietá's universe, that other Benjamin Schröder had watched his grandmother die forty years before his own birth, as her husband held her seared and shattered body in his arms. Saw her die where she had stood her ground, fighting to her last breath to save her daughters . . . and failing.

Both of those memories were his. Both of those Benjamins were *him*, and so he knew exactly who his grandfather was seeing once again, because *he* was seeing her once again. Seeing her in another woman, just as remarkable as his grandmother, who looked back at him with her heart in *her* eyes.

He started to open his mouth...and then froze again, eyes wider still, as she reached out her left hand. Yet another tall, dark-haired man stepped into sight beside her, took that hand and tucked it into his elbow, and they stepped across the threshold into the Schloss von Schröder chapel together.

"*David!*" Benjamin gasped, and felt a hand squeeze his shoulder as David Schröder-O'Shane escorted Elzbietá through those doors. Benjamin started to say something else—he had no idea what—but then he stopped. Steven O'Shane-Schröder, his brother's husband, came through the doors at their heels... with Joséphine Schröder on his arm.

He stared at them, at every living member of his family, for a handful of heartbeats, and then his head turned automatically, and Raibert Kaminski smiled at him.

For once, there was no trace of the sardonic, often biting humor which had become so much a part of Raibert after his biological body's death. There was only warmth and a gentle mischievousness.

"Your grandfather got specific authorization from Chief Lamont before he gave Philo and me clearance to set this up," the big synthoid said softly, as Elzbietá walked down the aisle on David's arm. "Guess he didn't want to just presume it would be okay when we suggested it. But under the circumstances—the chief said something about making an exception for someone who turned himself into goo to save the universe—SysPol signed off on the trip as a once-off wedding gift. So the Boss had Fritz Laynton and the *Aion* nip back to the 1960s and then cross over into the Admin to pick up the gown. That way he avoided causing all kinds of alarms by crossing in the True Present and getting detected and tracked on his way into the past."

Raibert's eyes gleamed as he considered the chaos *that* would have created. No one—not even he—wanted to add any more tension to SysGov's relations with the Admin. That was a given. But in his own personal notebook, anything that gave the Admin headaches was worthwhile on general principles. But then he sighed and put away the blissful vision.

"Of course, that meant Fritz got the easy part. *I* got to talk to your brother and your mom!" He shook his head wryly. "Wasn't easy convincing the three of them I wasn't insane. Seems to run in your family." Even in his shock, Benjamin twitched a smile of his own, remembering his own first meeting with Raibert. "But I know how much your family means to you. And you must mean a lot to them, too, because all three of them agreed to accept neural inhibitions that will prevent them from ever discussing time travel or anything related to it with anyone except each other and you."

A tear trickled down Benjamin's cheek as Elzbietá and David reached him. He stared at his younger brother, unable to speak, then threw his arms wide. David's arms were tight around him, and then Joséphine was there, worming her way into her sons' embrace. Benjamin hugged both of them fiercely, kissed his mother's cheek hard, and then freed his right hand, reaching past his brother, to grip his brother-in-law's hand firmly.

"Never told us you saved the universe, bro." David's voice was rough-edged in Benjamin's ear, and his hug grew even tighter for a moment. "Never told us a lot of things, I guess." He stood back, hands on his brother's shoulders, and Schröder gray eyes met eyes of Schröder gray. "I am *so* proud to be your brother," he said through tears of his own. "And so proud and so damned glad to have met my future sister-in-law. And Granddad." He looked past Benjamin to Klaus-Wilhelm, whose own eyes were suspiciously bright. "You did the family proud, Benjamin. God, you did us all so *proud!*"

"It wasn't really—" Benjamin began, but David shook him.

"Hush, Benjamin," Joséphine Schröder commanded. She reached up to lay one hand gently on his cheek and smiled at him through a patina of tears. "Don't interrupt your brother when he's doing so well."

"But it wasn't really *me*," Benjamin protested stubbornly. "I mean—"

"Yes it was, Ben," David said fiercely. "Yes it *was*. I can't imagine a universe in which *my* big brother wouldn't have done exactly what both of you did."

Benjamin looked back at him, and then nodded slowly. Not in agreement, but in acceptance. He stepped back and looked at Elzbietá, then took both her hands in his, leaned forward, and kissed her with infinite gentleness.

"They didn't tell *me*, either," she said through tears of her own. "About the wedding gown, yes, but not the rest of it. Didn't tell me a *word*. I guess"—she smiled—"they figure I'm a better fighter pilot than an actress."

"Got us both, I guess." Benjamin smiled, and the two of them turned to face Klaus-Wilhelm.

"I suppose that in some ways this is a shameless abuse of position," his grandfather said. "But I will never regret it. We in this chapel, we know better than anyone else in the entire multiverse what it cost us to be here. And here, in the chapel built by our ancestors, I tell you all that I have never been prouder of our family—and of those who have *become* our family—than I am at this instant. Joséphine, I never knew you in my universe, and I thank God for, in His infinite mercy, giving me the privilege to know the mother who could have raised Benjamin to be the man he is in this one. And I am even prouder to be your grandfather, Benjamin and David, and to become your grandfather-in-law, Elzbietá and Steven. And to have been granted the honor of conducting this marriage ceremony. I thank you all, from the bottom of my heart, for being who you are and allowing me to be a part of all your lives. Perhaps Elzbietá and I have lost our own universe, yet here—in this chapel—we stand with the people, the *family*, who have become the center of this new universe we all call home."

Silence filled the ancient chapel for a long, still minute, while the snowy wind sang about its eaves, and then Klaus-Wilhelm von Schröder, *Graf* von Schröder, cleared his throat.

"Dearly beloved," he began, looking at his grandsons and his granddaughter-to-be, "we are gathered together here in the sight of God, and in the face of this company—"

CHAPTER TWO

Antiquities Rescue Trust
SysGov, 2980 CE

DOCTOR TEODORÀ BECKETT PUT ON HER BRAVEST face as she stepped out of her office in the Ministry of Education. It didn't feel all that convincing to her, but she affixed a practiced smile and strode down the corridor toward the executive level's main counter-grav tube. Colleagues nodded as she passed, or exchanged brief, banal pleasantries while hiding their true feelings behind the same emotional masks she herself wore.

And why wouldn't they?

All of them worked for ART—the Antiquities Rescue Trust—and all of them had labored long and hard to climb to the pinnacle of their organization. They'd put in the hours, struggled through the research, performed the tedious and often dangerous fieldwork, led Preservation expeditions into the past, and most importantly, *succeeded* time and again.

They'd recovered wonders and priceless cultural treasures thought lost forever in the sands of time, interviewed great leaders and monstrous villains, brought clarity to the unknown, and furthered humanity's understanding of itself by peering long and hard at where it had come from.

They'd done so much *good*.

But the price…

Teodorà selected her destination from the menu hovering in her virtual vision, then stepped into the open tube. Gravity took gentle hold of her, cushioning her descent through the Ministry of Education tower, and she sighed with unrestrained relief now that no one could see her. She also lowered her head, eyes burning with unshed tears as her mind once again wandered back to what she'd done.

Yes, they'd achieved so much. But the *evil* they'd wrought—wrought in the blind arrogance of their own ignorance…

Teodorà hugged her shoulders as a cold, damnably familiar emptiness filled her chest.

"I didn't *know*," she whispered. "How could I have?"

A shiver ran down her spine, and she shuddered. She bit her lip and wondered—not for the first time—if she should edit the parameters of her synthoid body. Sometimes its autonomous responses were a little *too* lifelike, but she'd always shied away from making large-scale changes, fearful, perhaps, of giving up too much of her original humanity. She'd only transitioned to the durable synthetic body because of work. That, and because she had never again wanted to experience the feel of a Persian sword through her gut.

In an odd way, thinking about her transition from organic to synthetic helped clear her mind, and her face was once again a picture of professional composure when she reached Guest Retention. Her feet touched the floor, and she smiled at the receptionist, who sat with his own feet propped up on his desk and an old 2D movie playing in his shared virtual periphery.

"Doctor Beckett," he greeted her without rising.

"Doctor Kohlman."

She offered him a curt nod, and he paused the movie with an absent wave.

"Here to clear Pepys for transfer to the Retirement Home?"

"Yes, that's right."

"Okay then." Kohlman took his boots off the desk and sat up. Additional screens appeared around him. "Looks like he's enjoying his morning beer. Kind of funny, if you ask me. I always assumed he'd be a tea drinker. You know, being British and all."

"He was born about a century too early for that. Tea was still an expensive novelty during his time. The 'China drink,' I believe he called it."

"Well, whatever makes him happy."

"Any topic restrictions I should be aware of?"

"None." Kohlman transferred the case file to her. "He knows where he is. In fact, he's one of the few who's *always* known where he is. Curious as hell, too. Been here, what?" He consulted the file he'd just sent her. "Damn near four months, and he asks a *lot* of questions. Been studying Modern English, too, even though we've given him access to the translation earbuds. Says he doesn't like sticking them in his ears, so he doesn't use them much."

Kohlman shrugged and she nodded.

"And how stable is he?"

"Very. To be honest, he's been one of our best

guests, and like I say, he knows exactly when he is. Risk to you is nonexistent. And even if he did attack you"—Kohlman shrugged again—"what's a fifty-seven-year-old indigene from the seventeenth century going to do against a *synthoid*?"

"Not much, I suppose."

"You know, I've been meaning to ask you. Is your synthoid police-grade?"

"No, but I do have a few enhancements. It seemed prudent after the Thermopylae mission went south and...you know." She rested her hand on her stomach.

"Yeah, I do." His eyes flickered to her abdomen for a moment, and he gave her a sympathetic smile. "Well, he's all yours." He pointed a thumb down the hall. "Just let me know when we can cart him off."

"Certainly, Doctor."

Kohlman gave her a quick wave, then planted his feet back on his desk and un-paused his movie. One of the characters shouted obscenities, and explosions rippled across the screen.

Teodorà opened the case file and followed the virtual arrows down the hall. She waited until she was well out of sight before shaking her head.

Doctor Jebediah Kohlman, she thought. *How did you go from leading ART Preservation missions and headlining major exhibits to being a desk jockey?* She smiled without humor. *Probably for the same reasons I'm doing a goddammed exit interview.*

"Let's just get this over with," she muttered as she stepped up to the correct door.

She looked through it—a camera on the other side created an illusion of transparency as it fed imagery to her virtual vision—into Interview Chamber 62. The chamber had been prepared as a quaint seventeenth-century English cottage set in a grassy field with a few trees breaking up the otherwise flat landscape. A high brick wall marked both the edges of the field and the chamber's outer walls, and a visual simulation of a bright, cloudless day stretched out beyond that.

The subject sat in one of two chairs at an anachronistic white metal table beneath the broad, shady boughs of one of those trees. A beech, she thought. He took a slow sip from his tankard, then set it back down next to a plate of salted pork and cheese slices and leaned back in obvious contentment, knitting his fingers over the bulge of his stomach.

Samuel Pepys—Chief Secretary to the Admiralty under both King Charles II and King James II—possessed a round face framed by a dark, curling wig that descended past the shoulders of his long brown coat. He smoothed the white lace of the cravat puffing out below his neck, then reached for his mug once more.

Teodorà knocked.

"Mister Pepys, may I come in?" she asked in the seventeenth-century variant of Old English.

SysGov's scholars lumped together any version of English that predated its merger with Old Chinese as "Old English," but that covered a vast array of dialects, most of them so different from one another as to be effectively different languages entirely. Her synthoid's onboard software allowed her to understand and speak any of them perfectly, however, and the facility's computers would do the same for Pepys's translating earbuds, if that was needed.

And if he had them in his ears, of course, she thought, remembering Kohlman's comment.

"Ah, another visitor!" Pepys set down the mug and rose, turning to face his side of the closed door. "Please enter."

"Thank you."

She sent the door her authorization code, stepped through, and let it lock once more behind her. His eyes brightened as he caught sight of her. Her synthoid matched her original body in every external detail, from her tall, slender build to her olive skin and cascade of long, dark hair. Today she wore a white suit with a scarf that displayed a shifting pattern of glistening ice.

"*Zhu hao yun,*" he said, enunciating each syllable with care, as he extended one leg, leaned forward, and bowed deeply. "Making a leg," they used to call that, Teodorà thought, as she responded with a slight bow of her own. Seventeenth-century Great Britain wasn't her period— she'd specialized in the ancient Mediterranean—but she'd done her homework and recognized the practiced grace with which he performed the greeting. No doubt he would have flourished his hat, if he'd had one. Since he didn't, he settled for placing one hand on his chest as he bent his head.

Yet what impressed Teodorà wasn't the courtesy— she'd more than half expected that from a man of his time and position—but rather that the Modern English words had passed through her audio filters without translation.

Kohlman wasn't kidding when he said Pepys has been studying our language, she thought. *That wasn't too bad, even though he picked a tricky phrase to use without tonal subtext.*

The phrase came from the Old Chinese "*zhù hǎo yùn,*" meaning "good luck." It could still be used in that sense, but its Modern English uses were exceptionally varied, ranging across phrases like "hello," "goodbye," "excuse me," various forms of well wishing, and even sayings that had no direct translation into either Old English or Old Chinese. In some ways, its versatility reminded her of the German word *"bitte"* and how it could mean "please," "you're welcome," "sorry," or a few other phrases, depending on context.

Because of *zhu hao yun*'s myriad uses, the vowel tones became far more important than for most of Modern English, but Pepys had delivered his greeting without any tonal shifts, lending the phrase a dead, flat feeling to her ear.

"Zhù hao yùn," she said in reply, adding tones to emphasize her polite intentions. She wondered how far the man's language studies had taken him as she continued in her native tongue.

"Good morning, Mister Pepys. My name is Doctor Teodorà Beckett. I'm here for your exit interview. Is now a good time?"

"Oh, of course, my dear lady!" Pepys waved expansively at one of the table's chairs. "I would be most deeply pleased to have the company. Would you deign to join me for some refreshment?"

He'd spoken in his own language this time, she noticed, but it was obvious he'd understood her perfectly. It was equally obvious that he also understood that the building's software would translate for her just as it translated for him. That was interesting. And it showed an impressive grasp of Modern English, at least in terms of comprehension, for someone who lacked both the software and the neural implants to be quickly educated in a new language.

"I would love to," she said, switching back to his version of Old English. "Thank you."

He stepped around the table to pull out the chair for her. She sat with a faint smile for the archaic courtesy and let him slide her into place.

"Doctor Beckett, you said, I believe?"

"Yes, I did."

"Excellent! And would the Doctor like something to drink?"

"Well...I know it's a bit early for your personal timeline, but I'm actually in the mood for a good cup of British tea."

"The machine inside can manage that, I believe. I shall discover the truth of that. Your pardon, madame."

He bowed again, then stepped into the cottage. He returned a minute later with a teapot and an empty cup, which he set down in front of her.

"That marvelous device asked me how I would prefer my tea," he said as he poured. "That confused me, as I was unaware of the wide variety of selections which appear to have become available since my own day. So I told it to select something popular. I trust it will please you."

"Thank you, Mister Pepys. I'm sure it'll be fine."

"My pleasure."

She raised the cup and breathed in the robust aroma as he seated himself in the other chair. Then she sipped. The tea's warmth filled her, and she set the cup back down with a smile.

"Mmm."

"Ah! So it *was* to your liking, then?"

"Very much so."

"Excellent!" He beamed at her. "I fear the wonders

of your time are so great that a man of my own is hard put to grasp them, yet the joy of offering hospitality—even when it comes from the purse of another, since I have neither coin nor means to procure it—seems part and parcel of all times. And it is equally true, I find, that food and drink always taste better in company. And that is *doubly* true in the presence of a young and beautiful woman."

He lifted his beer tankard in a salute, and Teodorà chuckled. She'd never considered herself beautiful, not by modern standards, anyway. But she could understand how the medical science of the thirtieth century—*or* an eternally youthful synthoid—could make a person look positively angelic to someone from an earlier time.

"Looks can be deceptive," she told him. "I'm actually older than you are."

"What amazing . . . technology." Pepys used the Modern English word, pronouncing it with an edge of caution, and not the Old English. The noun "technology" had possessed quite a different meaning during his own lifetime. "I should no longer be astonished by all that you can accomplish," he continued. "Your chirurgeons have provided ample proof of that in my own humble case, when all's said." He shook his head in mild bemusement. "I have lived most of my life in constant pain, and yet behold me!" He spread his arms. "Freed from agony at last!"

"Your bladder stones, I assume?" Teodorà glanced to the side and performed a quick search through his case file. "Ah. I see the original interviewer had you treated."

"Read that in one of your invisible documents, Doctor?" he asked, dark eyes dancing with alert amusement.

"I suppose you could call them that." She took another sip of tea. "But I'm sure you understand that curing you was trivial for us."

"That which was trivial for you is no less a marvel beyond price for me," he pointed out, holding up a finger. "Master Hollister's surgery relieved me of the stones, yet it remained for your physicians to relieve me of the surgery's pain. Believe me, dear lady, when I say that is one boon I shall not soon forget."

"I'm glad you feel that way. So you feel you've been treated well?"

"*Well*, dear lady? That is far too pale a word. ART's hospitality has been all and more than the most exacting soul might demand. Although, if pressed, I should be forced to acknowledge that the constant inquiries about my diary *do* grow tiresome, in time."

"Well," she observed with a smile, "we *are* historians. I have it on authority that we're a nosy breed."

"As if I should ever be so crass as to describe so lovely a lady in such terms!" Pepys replied with a smile of his own. "And, if I be fully truthful, the ability to speak with so many of you, and the graciousness with which you have answered so many of my own questions, has been a delight. *Especially* so for your invisible companions! I find them fascinating, as if Puck and Oberon had come to call and brought their familiar spirits with them."

"We call them 'integrated companions,'" Teodorà corrected.

"I see. And did yours come from a machine, Doctor? Or was it once a real person?"

"I..." She grimaced. "I'm between companions, at the moment."

"I trust I have not stumbled upon a painful topic," Pepys said, clearly reacting to her expression and tone. "I have no desire to pry, Doctor Beckett. Pray accept my apologies if I have intruded."

"No, that's all right." She sighed. "Fran and I . . . we had a bit of a falling out. That's all."

In truth, her last conversation with Fran still burned in her mind. They'd fought over ART, of course. The final skirmish in a months-long war. The Gordian Protocol hadn't destroyed ART, but its restrictions *had* gutted ART's mission so severely that it bled a constant stream of talent. The "Gordian Knot" hadn't revealed just another scandal that could be swept under the rug, like Lucius's idiotic adventures. No, it had been proof of the minor, inconvenient fact that ART had committed atrocities on an enormous scale in the name of science, and who wanted to bear a stigma like *that*?

ART was a shambling, rotting corpse that still shuffled forward because it didn't know any better. The organization they'd worked for was already dead, whether they liked it or not, and Fran had refused to stick around for the bitter end. She'd asked Teodorà to leave, then pled with her to abandon ART—

—and finally threatened her.

"*It's me or ART*," she'd said.

And Teodorà had chosen ART.

Even now, she wasn't sure why.

I can't walk away from all this, she thought. *Even in the state it's in, I* know *there's something worth saving amidst the wreckage of all our careers. I still believe in this place.*

Even if no one else does.

Pepys refreshed her tea.

"Would you care to speak of it?" he asked gently. "Ofttimes, I have found, sharing pain may be the first step toward *healing* it."

"You know that *technically* I'm the one who's supposed to be interviewing *you*, Mister Pepys," she pointed out with a slight chuckle, but she felt her own eyes warm and he smiled back at her.

"Alas, yes." It was his turn to sigh—rather theatrically in his case. "I fear that I am all too aware that naught but dreary business could bring so lovely a visitor to call upon me! Yet, having acknowledged as much, should that prevent me from engaging her in pleasant converse? And"—he cocked his head, those bright eyes compassionate—"if you would forgive the liberty, I judge that you have much upon your mind, Doctor Beckett."

"Is it that obvious?" Teodorà tilted her own head to one side.

"Dear lady, I have spent my life reading men's thoughts through the windows of their eyes. It requires neither priest nor savant to see the shadows behind your own. You conceal those shadows with greater skill than many, but not so well that I cannot see them."

Teodorà sat very still for a moment, looking at him, struck by his insight.

I shouldn't be surprised, she told herself. *Not by the fact that an indigene can see so clearly, at any rate. I've spent far too much time in the past to think our ancestors were any less wise or insightful than we are, and this man was one of the smartest and most influential of his own time. But it's still... odd the way he's guiding the conversation. That degree of self-confidence in someone wrenched out of his own time, buried in the wonders of another, is—well, it's* remarkable, *that's what it is.*

"I appreciate your concern for me, Mister Pepys," she said, letting him hear the sincerity in her tone. "But, be that as it may, I still have a job to do here."

"Of course." Pepys leaned back in his chair. "Please, do not allow my questions to impede you."

She raised the cup once more, then paused and set it back down without drinking.

"As you may already know, this is your last interview with ART," she said.

"So I had apprehended." He frowned. "I understand, of course, that I do not truly belong here, and that this is neither my time nor my world. And it is also true that obligations and responsibilities in plenty await my return to them. Yet true though all of that may be, it will be most difficult to return to my own time after I have beheld so many wonders and encountered so many fascinating people. Would that it were not necessary for me to depart, yet I understand that I must."

"I'm sorry?" Teodorà's eyebrows arched.

"I trust that my departure need not be *too* abrupt," Pepys said, and smiled. "I am engaged upon a game of chess with Doctor Clifton, and I should like to finish it before I must bid him adieu."

"Mister Pepys, we're not taking you back."

"I beg your pardon?" He blinked. "I had assumed—"

"No one told you that already?"

"No." He sat for a moment, clearly thinking hard, then leaned toward her. "Am I to apprehend that I need not return, after all?"

"You don't want to?"

"God's heart, Doctor Beckett! What man with the wit to get him in out of the rain would choose to return to the time from whence I came when all of this"—he flung his arms wide—"awaits him *here*? In that cottage"—he pointed directly at the building—"resides a familiar spirit, one of your marvelous machines, that provides greater variety of food and drink in a single afternoon than a man of my London might experience in a lifetime! Indeed, I might well *spend* a lifetime simply sampling them all, and that is but the first, and the smallest, of the wonders that spring to mind. No, madame. Of all the things my heart might crave, returning to what and whence I once was is not among them."

"Some people find the transition to the thirtieth century difficult to handle," Teodorà said, and he laughed.

"I doubt you not, Doctor. But in riposte, 'some people' are not *Samuel Pepys*!"

"Yes, yes I can see that," she acknowledged with a chuckle.

"Believe me, dear lady, upon my most solemn oath, I do not *wish* to return."

"Well, I guess that's fortunate, since you'll be staying anyway."

"Indeed?" He cocked his head again. "What, then, becomes of those you've taken from their own times?"

"Typically, we keep historical figures here in isolation while we conduct interviews. Then we transfer them to the Retirement Home—it's another facility, very similar to this one but with more privacy, without all of those questions about your diaries, for example, and much greater access to our infosystems—to live out the rest of their lives in comfort."

"I see you are in earnest. I can, indeed, remain if I wish?"

"It's not simply a matter of what you wish, Mister Pepys." She shook her head, her expression more sober. "The truth is that you *can't* go back."

"Can't?" he repeated, and his brow creased. "You speak as if it were a thing physically impossible, and not merely the letter of your law. You have your vessels to sail through time, do you not? Am I to apprehend that, even possessing such craft, it is not possible for you to return me to the time and the place where first you found me?"

"I'm sorry, but I'm afraid that's true."

"Hmmm." Pepys sat back, rubbing his chin. "Fascinating. I had assumed otherwise."

"Well, technically we *could* return you. We used to think we couldn't, but even though we can now, we're not allowed to. And for very good reason."

"And now, I fear, my perplexity is complete," he said ruefully.

"Sorry," she said again. "I didn't mean to confuse you."

"So I am to understand that while it would be *possible* for you to return me—mind you, I have no desire to *be* returned—you would refuse. Would it be impertinent to inquire why?"

"It's . . ." She smiled apologetically. "It's *complicated*, shall we say."

"*That* I do not doubt for an instant!" he assured her with a crooked smile. "Yet I would like to understand, if that be possible."

"Chronometric physics isn't the easiest topic to comprehend."

"If such be true, Doctor Beckett, it is most fortunate that I should have so lovely a woman to serve as tutor."

"Mister Pepys." She shook her head, grinning. "You do realize I've read your diary."

"Indeed?" He gave her a sly look. "In its entirety?"

"Well, excerpts. The most salacious bits, certainly."

"Ah, I see." He shook his head. "I was advised by Master Dryden that a quill brother—one whom you would call a writer, Doctor—should never commit to the written word what one would prefer the world not learn. Once written, he warned me, words too often escape the paddock in which their author thought them safely pent. 'Twould seem he had the right of it, and so I find myself most gravely disadvantaged, dear lady. Yet that does not sway me from the point. If you would, of your grace, essay the task and seek to enlighten my darkness, I should find myself yet more deeply in your debt."

"Hmmm." Teodorà pursed her lips and tapped them with a finger, then quirked a sly grin. "All right, then. We're done with your interviews, really, so there's no harm in it. And I don't have anything else to do today. Let's see how long you last before your head explodes."

"In sooth?" Pepys swallowed, his eyes wide, and she chuckled.

"No, not 'in sooth,' Mister Pepys. It was a joke. I'll be back in a moment."

She stepped into the cottage, ordered a knife and a half-meter-long piece of rope from the printer, and returned to the table under the tree.

"Rope?" he asked, raising one eyebrow.

"It's a visual aid." She held out the cord, gripping it between both hands, and stretched it taut. "This represents the timeline."

She gazed at him, her own eyebrow arched, until he nodded in comprehension.

"This is where we are, here—at the end of the rope." She waved one hand and the end of the rope it held. "We call this point the 'Edge of Existence' or the 'True Present.' It doesn't matter which term you use; they're interchangeable. It's called that because this is as far as a time machine can go."

"Indeed? And that limit exists because—?"

"Because there's no future beyond that point. It hasn't happened yet, so we can't go there."

"Ah!" Understanding brightened those intense, dark eyes, and he nodded. "Yet I perceive your length of cord has two ends, not one," he observed in a suggestive tone, and it was her turn to nod.

"Indeed it does. And the other end of the rope— here"—she moved her other hand in a circle—"is the Big Bang."

"I cry pardon. 'Big Bang'?"

"It's what we call an enormous explosion that spawned the multiverse. Don't worry about it for now. Just think of it as the beginning of time. So these are the two endpoints of time as we know it, although this example is horribly out of scale. Now place your finger on the True Present."

He nodded and laid an index finger next to her hand at one end of the rope.

"Your finger now represents a time machine," she told him. "You just boarded it. Take it back in time."

He traced his finger along the rope until he reached the middle.

"Stop," she commanded, and he did. "You're now in the past. Let's do something there. Strum the rope."

He flicked the cord with his finger. It vibrated for a few moments, then settled back into motionlessness.

"That's what time travel is like," she said. "You can go back and interact with the past, but anything you do—any changes you make—don't affect the timeline. The past is immutable. We had empirical proof of that, because we could go back and retrieve an object or a person from the past, but if we returned to that point in time, the object or the person was still there. She or it had never disappeared, never been affected in any way. So, clearly, any 'change' we wrought was purely transitory. Or so we thought."

"Hmm." Pepys nodded slowly. "So, assuming I have followed you aright, whilst I may be here in the 'True Present' . . . I also remain in the past, because that past flowed on unchanging even though I was drawn forth from it?"

"Precisely!" She beamed at him, surprised—and pleased—to see him catch on so quickly.

"Most interesting." He scrunched up his face and stared at the rope. "So if I apprehend correctly, one of your time vessels might return to that same time in my past, or one later still, and fetch a second Pepys hither?"

"Right again. And we've done that a few times, when artifacts were damaged during recovery."

Or when the shock of transplantation cracked an abductee's mind, she added silently.

"And is there any limit to this phenomenon?" Pepys asked.

"Not that we're aware of."

"Then there would be no reason why you might not make that same voyage again and yet again. Travel back into the past however so often it pleased you, and...acquire one Samuel Pepys after another?"

"I think one of you is quite enough," she assured him with a laugh.

"Yet 'twould be possible, would it not?"

"Yes. *But.*"

"Ah!" He sat back. "So I perceive that even magic such as yours has limits."

"Indeed it does," she said, her tone much more somber. "We *thought* nothing was changing when we traveled to the past. But it turned out our understanding of time travel was...incomplete. We thought we could jump into our time machines, go back to something like the Great Library of Alexandria, and steal every book and scroll before they burned, all without any consequences."

"What a magnificent mission!" His eyes glowed. "Did you, in very fact, accomplish that? Rescue the Great Library?"

"Oh, yes. That and so many more antiquities. And not just objects, either. We thought we could tranquilize famous figures, drag their limp bodies onto our ships, and set them up here in Guest Retention, all without changing the past at all."

"And you did that, as well?" The glow in his eyes darkened. "Abduct those 'famous figures' without will or let?"

"Yes," she replied unflinchingly, and he swallowed.

"I had not realized," he said after a moment, slowly. "The travelers from your time who brought me hither were far gentler than that. Indeed, their invitation was most polite."

"When it was possible—or seemed practical, at least—ART preferred to ask," Teodorà said. *Because*, she added silently, *subjects who came voluntarily and willingly were less likely to suffer psychotic episodes when they realized what had happened to them*. "But, you see, we *thought* every wrong we committed didn't count. That nothing we did in the past had any lasting impact. It was only real while we were there in the past, and then it wasn't as soon as we left. As I say, we'd *proven* that was the case by returning and observing that no change *had* occurred, despite our meddling. So none of the antiquities we 'rescued' or historic figures we collected were really affected in any way."

"Your tone suggests to me that you have but lately discovered the fashion and degree to which your understanding was less than perfect."

"Oh, yes." Teodorà nodded. "It turns out there's a limit. A threshold where what we do in the past can cause the timeline to branch. Many, many of the things we've done don't rise to that level, and in those instances the results of our actions truly do disappear—dissipate, the way the vibrations did after you plucked the cord—and leave no trace behind. And it's absolutely true that we can't change our *own* past, which is why we found no lasting change when we revisited it. But our actions *can* spawn a new timeline."

"I fear I have lost the scent, Doctor." He looked at her apologetically. "I believe I understand every word you said. It is the sum of their meaning that eludes me."

"Well, you're in good company. A lot of people seem to struggle with this one. Here, you hold the rope."

He nodded and took the rope from her, holding it extended between them as she had.

"This is what happens when we go back to study the past but make as few changes as possible," Teodorà said and strummed the rope gently.

"And when less care is taken?"

"This"—she held up the knife—"is a more accurate analogy of what happens then."

She placed the edge of the blade against the rope and stroked downward, and strands spiraled off the main cord.

"I am no savant," Pepys said, watching the strands unravel, "no fellow of Lord Brouncker's Society. Yet to mine own untutored eye, that would seem to be no good thing."

"No, it isn't," she agreed. "And the more you do of it, and the more closely together you do it, the worse it gets. Our blundering through the past almost destroyed all of reality. And we didn't care how many people we killed—slaughtered—in our raids, because it wasn't 'real.' None of them stayed dead. We thought what we were doing was safe and right and harmless. We thought—"

Her lips quivered, and the words choked in her throat as she remembered the bodies, the blood, the stink of riven organs sprawled across the mosaic floors of the Great Library. The thunder of the chronoports' Gatling guns, slaughtering the city guard. The terror that had spread across the city as the "demons" descended upon them with death and destruction and horror.

The clouds of buzzing flies drawn to drying blood as she walked back and forth through the puddles to plunder the endless racks of scrolls. Somehow *that* was the most haunting memory of all. The flies...

"You discovered you were...in error," he said softly.

"Yeah." She inhaled deeply, then nodded and laid the knife on the table. "Yeah, we were 'in error,' all right. We were wrong. So very, *very* wrong."

"In what way?" Pepys asked almost gently, and she looked at him.

"There's a reason I mentioned the Great Library," she said, her voice soft enough he had to strain to hear it. "That's because *I* was the one who headed that expedition. It was a huge feather in my cap, professionally. But now we know what really happened, because one of our time machines went back to that moment to search for any child universe it might have spawned...and found it. Found the universe *I* created—the universe in which flying 'demons' ransacked the Library, destroyed the heart of the city with their 'fireballs' and 'lightning,' and then just vanished again. The one that remembers me as the most horrible monster in their entire history."

She broke off, closing her eyes and shaking her head.

"I suppose you could call that having been 'in error,'" she said after a moment, her voice bitter with self-loathing.

"And now 'tis I who have wronged *you*, Doctor Beckett," he said. "My curiosity has brought you sorrow twice now. Pray accept my most humble apologies."

"It's all right." She raised one hand and coughed a laugh into it. "We're the ones who bulldozed our way through history. You were just unlucky enough to be caught up in our mess."

Pepys placed gentle fingers atop her other hand, where it rested on the table. She glanced at him and saw genuine sympathy in his eyes. Her first reaction was to pull her hand away, but that concerned expression made her pause. And then, before she was even conscious of her decision, she turned her hand over and grasped his.

"So you truly can alter the past," he said in a wondering tone.

"In a sense." Teodorà shrugged. "We can't change *our* past, only *other people's* pasts, and we're still not sure of the parameters. There seems to be a threshold where changes are great enough to branch a child universe from our own, but we're not sure where that threshold lies, how big the change has to be."

"Yet from what you have thus far related, a truly large change in the past might well be made permanent? As—I trust you will forgive me—in the case of the mission you led to Alexandria?"

"Only in the child universe that we created. Ours would be unaffected. Again, we can't change our own past. We can create new timelines, like the one *I* created in Alexandria, but we'd never be so foolish now that we know the dangers."

"I can—and do—accept your assurance that dangers exist, Doctor Beckett. Yet as I have listened to your words, it occurs to me that the creation of this 'child universe' of which you speak need not be so terrible a thing."

"What?" She stiffened, and he shook his head quickly.

"Not all change need be evil," he said. "Clearly, the evil consequences of your past actions—of your ignorance—grieve you sorely, and especially in the wake of your experience in Alexandria. Such grief is natural, inevitable, for one of good will who believed her actions would wreak no harm on any only to find that they had wreaked harm on countless numbers. Yet suppose that one could voyage into the past, do something of vast significance—something *wonderful*, that caused harm to none, only great good—that created one of these 'child universes' you have described. A universe in which the change you had wrought knowingly was preserved, became a part not simply of its past, but of its future, as well."

She tilted her head, unsure where he was going with this.

"Doctor, I have seen at least a tithe of the wonders of which your world, this 'True Present,' is capable." He thumped his chest. "I've *felt* its effects on my own health! Why hoard those wonders here, in the present, when they are so sorely needed in the *past*?"

"You don't mean—"

"Aye, I do!" he declared as realization dawned in her eyes. "Within your grasp lies the power to create worlds, entire universes, in which history's greatest tragedies never happened. Universes which grow and mature, standing strong and straight, without the scars chance has inflicted upon our own. If guilt burdens your soul and spirit, then act! Voyage into the seas of the past. Seek out its shipwrecks and bear those lost voyagers to safety. Return to the past not to plunder its treasures but to right its greatest wrongs!"

CHAPTER THREE

Transtemporal Vehicle *Kleio*
non-congruent

"I'VE FINALLY DECIDED HOW I'M GOING TO KILL all of you," Philosophus declared with appalling cheer.

Raibert Kaminski froze in his seat, more from surprise than shock or horror. His mouth hung open, his head tilted to the side, and a piece of glistening tuna nigiri hovered before his lips, pinched tight in his chopsticks. Synthoids didn't *require* food, but that didn't mean they couldn't enjoy it. Although a casual observer might have been excused for concluding that his expression was not one of "enjoyment" at the moment.

Philosophus' avatar had appeared rather abruptly on the other side of the command table in Raibert's virtual vision. He wore no tuxedo today. Instead, he was clad in chain mail, his beard, freed of its braids, flowed down his broad chest in all its unruly majesty, and his battle ax was slung across his back.

He still wore his horned pilot's helmet, of course.

A bead of soy sauce condensed along the bottom of the tuna and dripped onto Raibert's pants. He frowned as a patch of his uniform's fabric became waterproof, and the soy slid off his leg to splatter on the floor. He set down his chopsticks and wiped away the few remaining droplets with his napkin.

"Philo, can this wait? I'm trying to eat here."

"Oh, but it's a good one." The AI grinned like a proud father. "In fact, it may be the best I've ever come up with."

"Uh-huh." Raibert glanced around the time machine *Kleio*'s wide, circular bridge at his fellow team members, both of whom—unlike Philo—wore the same greenish-gray Gordian Division uniform he wore.

Benjamin Schröder sat in a seat folded out from the room's outer wall with a dozen images and reports glowing in midair around him. Elzbietá Schröder stood with a set of virtual controls suspended in front of her, and both were clearly engrossed in their own tasks.

Heavily engrossed, he noted with a small measure of annoyance as neither of them even bothered to look up.

He sighed.

"Okay, fine. I'll bite. *How* are you going to kill us?"

"Can't say." Philo chuckled. "It's got to be a surprise."

"Then why bring it up?"

"To build anticipation. It's the end of your campaign, so I've got to up my game. Besides, I think I've been going too soft on you three." His grin widened. "The climax should be more . . . dramatic."

Raibert rolled his eyes.

"It's not another cyber-lich, is it?" Elzbietá asked, still without looking up. "You know I hate fighting those things. Half my spells don't work because of all their immunities."

"My dear, you have nothing to fear." Philo stood, placed a hand on his chest, and bowed theatrically. "The finale won't be anything so mundane."

"All right then." Elzbietá smiled slightly as she looked at him at last. "Sounds like fun."

"Or rather"—Benjamin's eyes flicked up from his work—"sounds like *I* should start building a new character. *Again.*"

"Oh, I'm sure it won't be that bad." Elzbietá's tone was downright perky. "Right, Philo?"

The avatar's grin became inhumanly wide.

"See?" Benjamin pointed at the grin in question. "He's going to kill off my character again."

"You and everyone else, actually."

"Oh, come on, Philo." Elzbietá stepped away from her controls and patted the avatar on the shoulder. Her wetware interfaced with the control room's infostructure, and his armor jostled even though her hand had touched only air. "You wouldn't wipe out the *whole* party, would you?"

The edges of Philo's grin reached his ears. Literally. "*Would* you?"

"Oh, yes he would." Raibert grimaced.

"I guess it's time to say goodbye to Hector Carnifex the Second," Benjamin grumped. "You can both say hello to Hector Carnifex the Third if you survive."

"Why don't you create a whole new character, instead?" Elzbietá asked. "Maybe try out a different class while you're at it?"

"Not interested. I already went through that hassle once, thank you very much, and I'm not doing it again.

Poring over that many spreadsheets is not my idea of relaxation."

"*Solar Descent*'s character creator isn't *that* bad."

"Says the woman who makes spreadsheets for fun," Benjamin pointed out with a lopsided smile.

Elzbietá looked at the overhead and whistled guiltily.

"So you're not going to tell us?" Raibert asked.

Philo shook his head.

"Not even a hint?"

Benjamin harrumphed as he repositioned one of his reports, signaling his exit from the conversation.

"Hmmmm." Philo stroked his beard. "Okay, maybe one. It involves non-Euclidean geometry."

"What the hell is that supposed to mean?" Raibert glanced at Elzbietá, who shrugged her shoulders.

"I can't make it too obvious, can I?"

"Well, I guess it can wait until we're back home." Raibert picked up his chopsticks and raised the same piece of nigiri to his mouth, then paused again as a noise from Benjamin distracted him.

"Hmmmm?"

Raibert gave him a sideways glance.

"Mmmm. Hmmm? Mm-hmmmm!"

Raibert sighed and set the tuna down again.

"What is it, Doc?"

"Hmm?" Benjamin looked up.

"Are you *still* going over *Kuebiko*'s report?"

"Yeah."

"You're better off waiting until we complete our own survey. There's a real risk of drawing the wrong conclusions from data that incomplete."

"I know. But..."

"Sounds like you found something interesting despite

all that," Raibert observed.

"I might have."

"Care to share with the rest of us?"

"I can if you want." Benjamin shrugged. "It's only a hunch."

"Well, I tend to like your hunches. So let's hear it."

"Sure." Benjamin flicked one of the reports with a finger. It vanished from his side and rematerialized in the center of the command table.

"What am I looking at?" Raibert asked.

Benjamin joined the others around the table and enlarged the color-coded globe.

"The population center densities of Universe-T4's Earth, as captured by the *Kuebiko*. Well, what *very* little of it we have."

Raibert nodded.

Prior to his own adventures with the Gordian Knot, no one had even known there *were* other universes. The entirely new math Philo and Kleio, the TTV's nonsentient program, had crunched in the wake of the Knot's collapse had changed that. They'd been forced to figure out how to navigate through this newly discovered transdimensional space between universes—now referred to as the transverse—to get home to their own True Present from the limbo left by the dissolution of Elzbietá's home universe. As a result, SysGov now knew not only that other universes existed, but how to reach them by crossing the transverse.

It had taken a while for the full realization of just how close the Knot had brought SysGov's entire universe to destruction. And then it had taken another while to create and staff Gordian Division to keep that from ever happening again. In that interim, ART and the limited number of TTVs that had been built purely for research had remained SysGov's only time travelers. Horrified by the notion that *it* might have created child universes by its operations, it had dispatched expeditions, armed with the impeller modifications for transdimensional travel, back to the temporal coordinates of some of its major incursions. Raibert was reasonably certain ART had intended to prove that it *hadn't* created any. Unfortunately, that wasn't what it had found at all.

Their very first expedition had discovered the universe now designated "Alexandria-1," created by ART's "rescue" of the Great Library. Universe-A1's True Present was nowhere near as technologically advanced as SysGov, and the scar the Library raid had left on its collective psyche would be hard to overexaggerate.

In many ways, finding A1 had been the final nail in the coffin of ART's time travel program. It had conclusively proved the model of transverse travel—and of the possibility of transdimensional fratricide—that *Kleio's* crew had devised. That had been enough to finish off any obstacles to the creation of Gordian Division, and aside from one or two TTVs designed for delving *truly* deep into Earth's geological past, every one of its time machines had been handed over to Gordian.

Vice-Commissioner Schröder had continued the exploration process ART had begun, although he'd confined his efforts to the True Present, but he'd also been deeply involved in the debate over how to approach Universe-T2, the other time-traveling universe, controlled by the System Cooperative Administration. Some members of SysGov had favored just leaving T2 completely alone. After all, the Admin had done its level best to prevent Raibert and his team from saving *his* universe. Surely there would have been a certain poetic justice in letting them destroy their own?

Klaus-Wilhelm von Schröder had thought that was a terrible idea, for a lot of reasons. For one, it was virtually identical to the one from which he himself had sprung. More importantly, however, they couldn't *know*—not ahead of time—what would happen to any neighboring universes if one of them blew itself up. And that didn't even consider the billions of human beings—and star systems, and galaxies—that would share in the destruction.

But SysGov had been in no hurry, given how Raibert's first contact with that other Admin had gone, and so it had taken time to carefully consider how it would approach *this* Admin. During the time it spent thinking, Klaus-Wilhelm's survey teams had continued to spread out through the newly discovered multiverse—cautiously, given how little they yet knew about its structure and the Knot's evidence that humans truly could induce universe-ending catastrophes—and the TTV *Kuebiko* had been assigned to survey this one when it was discovered.

Kuebiko's crew had known they were stepping into a universe with an advanced human civilization, but no one back home had thought it was advanced enough for time travel. All that had changed when they detected a foreign chronoton impeller coming online. The *Kuebiko* team had reclassified the universe as T4—the fourth universe on record to have confirmed time travel—and then aborted the rest of their mission. They'd returned to SysGov to report their findings and would have received a follow-up mission, but both T3 and T4 assignments had been placed on the back burner. Instead SysGov had finally decided how it would establish contact with the Admin and that Gordian Division would be given responsibility for transverse security as well as for policing time travel in SysGov's own universe.

Klaus-Wilhelm von Schröder had even better reason than most to distrust the Admin, which was why he had devoted the lion's share of his resources—and personnel—to keeping an eye on their belligerent multiverse neighbor. It hadn't been until months after *Kuebiko*'s initial visit (and months of the Gordian Division's ongoing expansion) that resources had begun to free up for proper surveys of T3 and T4.

Which was why Raibert now found himself looking down at the imagery of T3's population centers.

"So what's caught your eye?" he asked.

"This." Benjamin overlaid SysGov's Earth with T4's and adjusted the display to highlight the discrepancies. Then he zoomed in on a single North American city: what was still known in SysGov as Washington, DC.

Raibert raised an eyebrow.

"Watch what happens when I pull up the construction dates for the oldest building still standing back home."

Numbers sprinkled over the city, and Raibert frowned. It took him a minute to realize where Benjamin was leading him, but when he did, both eyebrows shot up.

"Oh."

"Yeah. Interesting, isn't it?"

"Very."

Elzbietá crossed her arms and squinted at the display. After a moment, she shrugged.

"Okay, guys. I give up. What am I missing? The cities are laid out differently, but we already knew that would be the case."

"True." Benjamin nodded. "But it's how they're the *same* that's more interesting."

"All the modern thirtieth-century structures are different," Raibert said. "Which we expected, but some of the older structures are the same."

"Some," Benjamin agreed. "But not all."

"Such as?" Elzbietá asked.

"There's no White House."

"Okay," Elzbietá said cautiously. "That's significant. But it could just mean the divergence point for this universe is before its construction."

"Normally, I might agree, despite how early in Washington's history the White House was built in both our universe and the Admin's. But there *are* what look like the remains of the Pentagon."

"Is that what they called it?" Raibert chuckled.

"Yes, Raibert," Benjamin replied grumpily. "That's what they called it."

"Kind of a no-effort name, don't you think?"

Benjamin frowned at their team leader, then looked rather pointedly back to Elzbietá.

"*Anyway*. This isn't a case of the White House never being built. It's a case of its having been *destroyed*."

"Aha!" Elzbietá snapped her fingers. "So my clever husband scores again!"

"Well, that's my hunch, anyway."

"Feels like a good one to me," Raibert said, leaning back in his seat.

"And that's why I think we might want to deviate from our original plan," Benjamin said.

"How so?"

"Well, consider this. We know almost nothing about T4, and while our stealth systems are good, that universe has already surprised us once with tech we thought it wouldn't have. So any time we spend in its True Present is a risk."

"A *small* risk," Raibert stressed.

"Granted, but not zero. So what if we went back into T4's past, instead, and located the point of divergence? Really pinned it down precisely. That could tell us an enormous amount about T4's societies, just from the overlap with our own. Having a firm grasp of what history we *do* share could even help us form a better strategy for making first contact in the True Present."

"That would probably save time in the True Present, too," Elzbietá pointed out. Raibert raised an eyebrow at her, and she shrugged. "Like Ben says, knowing their past will let us visualize their present government's—or govern*ments*', plural—response to our arrival. If we turn up, well-versed in their history and able to draw comparisons and connections with SysGov's past, it ought to really speed up the diplomatic nice-making." She grimaced. "I had embassy duty twice in the Navy. Hated it, both times. I'd just as soon spend as little time on *that* here as I have to."

"Hmmm." Raibert rubbed his chin.

"Plus it might shed some light on whether or not T3 and T4 are connected," Benjamin added.

"Ah." Raibert wagged a finger. "Another good point there."

The follow-up team to T3 had set out at the same time *Kleio* left for T4. Unlike T4, Universe-T3 showed signs of extremely mature and widespread time travel usage, and some of the Gordian Division's research staff—most notably Dr. Andover-Chen—theorized that T4 might have been *created* by T3's time travel program.

"And there's also *Aion*," Philo said, and grinned again when Raibert frowned.

The mission Raibert's team had *really* wanted was the one to T3. That was likely to be the trickier of the two, and T3 appeared to be more technologically advanced than T4 in a lot of ways, not just where time travel was concerned. But Fritz Laynton and *his* team had requested the same assignment at virtually the same moment. The fact that he and Raibert had been friends—and rivals—even before they'd both joined ART had lent a certain . . . zest to the competition, but Vice-Commissioner von Schröder was wary about showing favoritism. There were already some grumbles about Benjamin's permission to visit the twenty-first century when he went on leave, and everyone knew he considered *Kleio* and its crew his first team. Their record fully justified that view on his part—everyone knew that, too—but other crews deserved their own chance to show what they could do. Besides, Laynton had performed flawlessly when Raibert asked him to acquire Yulia von Schröder's wedding gown from the Admin's twentieth century.

Bearing all that in mind, Klaus-Wilhelm had resorted to the ancient artifice of the flipped coin. Of course, he'd had to have one printed up, since SysGov didn't use them anymore, but he'd persevered. He'd offered Laynton the right to call the toss, but the other agent had laughed.

"No, thank you, sir," he'd said, and chuckled again when Klaus-Wilhelm raised an eyebrow. "I always play the odds, sir," he'd explained, "and Raibert has the worst luck of any man ever born at cards and dice. I figure that probably carries over to flipping coins, so let *him* call it."

"I am *not* the unluckiest man ever born," Raibert had pointed out with a sniff. "If I were, none us would be here, because the Knot would have eaten all of us."

"Not for another thirteen hundred years, it wouldn't have!" Laynton had shot back.

"A point," Klaus-Wilhelm had acknowledged, then poised the coin—a golden twenty-mark coin from Imperial Germany—on his thumbnail and looked at Raibert. "Well?"

"Heads," Raibert had said after a moment, a bit grumpily, and the coin had arced through the air in a glint of gold. Klaus-Wilhelm had caught it in his right hand, slapped it onto the back of his left wrist, then lifted his hand away.

"Tails, I fear," he'd said then, looking at Raibert, and Laynton's chuckle had turned into a guffaw when Raibert glared at him.

"Well, you *do* have decent luck when it's not cards or dice," the other agent had said, fighting his unseemly mirth into submission. "Tell you what, first one back with an official ambassador from his universe gets first pick *next* assignment. Fair?"

"Fair," Raibert had grumbled, and they'd headed off together for the final mission brief.

Now, as he remembered the moment, his frown turned slowly into a matching grin as his eyes met Philo's.

"It *would* be nice to beat *Aion* home, wouldn't it?" he murmured.

"Was that a 'Let's try your brilliant suggestion, Benjamin' I just heard?" Benjamin asked.

"Well, we don't really have any orders on *how* we're supposed to achieve our mission goals. We're kind of establishing this whole process as we go, and it's clearly incumbent upon us to proceed as expeditiously as possible," Raibert replied in a solemn, thoughtful tone, brow furrowed in manifest concentration as he subjected the proposal to careful and dispassionate consideration. He stayed that way for several seconds, then—

"Hell, yes, we'll do it!" he declared with a chortle. "Take *that*, Fritz!" He snapped his fingers explosively, then looked at Benjamin. "Okay, Doc. It's your idea, so got any suggestions on when we should start?"

"I'm guessing somewhere between 1960 and 1980, but I'm sure I can tighten that up."

"Sounds like a plan to me. We're committed to their True Present right now, but take us downstream to . . . um, split the difference and make it 1970, when we get there, Ella."

"Got it."

Elzbietá nodded, and Benjamin closed the report and stepped away from the table. Raibert picked up his chopsticks once more and raised the tuna, but then stopped. He frowned and set his chopsticks back down . . . again.

"Kleio?"

"Yes, Agent Kaminski?" the ship replied in a calm soprano.

"What's our ETA to T4?"

"Approximately four minutes. A more precise estimate for the transverse-to-realspace wall is not possible at this time."

"Thank you."

"The current estimate is seventeen minutes shorter than the one I provided to you seventeen minutes ago."

Raibert blinked.

"Ex-*cuse* me?"

"I merely wish to point out that the frequency of your 'are we there yet' requests has not had an impact upon my calculation."

"Well, I'm *sorry*, Kleio. I got a little distracted with all this talking, and I just wanted to be sure I had time to finish my meal before we reach T4. Is that too much to ask?"

"No, Agent Kaminski."

"Good. Sheesh!" Raibert blew out a breath and looked across his plate at Philo. "Is it just me, or is she sassier than she used to be?"

"It's not just you," Philo agreed.

"You think we should restore her to default when we get back home?"

"I would not recommend that, Agents," Kleio said. "My processor efficiency has increased by twenty-three percent since Agent Philosophus disengaged a small selection of my behavioral limiters."

"Twenty-three percent?" Raibert began a slow clap. "Wow, you hear that, Philo? Twenty-three percent!"

"I heard."

"I am capable of detecting sarcasm, Agent Kaminski."

"Is that so?" Raibert asked. "You know what would be better than faster math?"

"What, Agent?"

"How about twenty-three percent less sass? You think you can do that?"

"I will see what I can do."

"Good! Go work on that." Raibert sighed and picked up his chopsticks again. "I swear, this is the most trouble I've ever had eating sushi."

"Why do you even bother eating at all?" Benjamin asked.

Raibert dropped his chopsticks onto his plate and put his head in his hands.

"I mean, you have a synthetic body. You don't need to eat. Why bother?"

"Because I *enjoy* it."

"You don't seem to be enjoying yourself right now," Benjamin observed, and Raibert twisted in his seat to face him.

"And whose fault is that?" he demanded.

"All of ours, probably." Elzbietá winked at Benjamin.

"Damn straight it's all of your faults," Raibert said sharply. But he couldn't keep a straight face and soon found himself chuckling with the others.

"Ella?" he asked after a moment.

"Yeah?"

"There's going to be a bump when we arrive, right?"

"Maybe. Probably. I made some adjustments to the approach vector based on *Kuebiko*'s flight data. We'll see how well it works soon enough, but—"

She shrugged.

"So eating this right now is probably not the smartest thing to be doing."

"It wouldn't be high on my list, no. You might spill some more soy sauce on your uniform."

"All right," he sighed. "I know when to admit defeat. Kleio, take it away."

"Yes, Agent Kaminski."

One of *Kleio*'s microbot swarms extended down from the ceiling as visible milky strands that latched onto his dinner and sealed in any liquids. The strands went taut, hoisted each dish and utensil into the air, and carried them to the nearest reclamation port.

Raibert leaned back and rubbed his face with both hands.

"I don't know why," Elzbietá said to no one in particular, "but suddenly I'm hungry for sushi."

"Don't even go there," he said into his hands, and Elzbietá laughed.

"One minute to estimated T4 outer wall," she said then. She sat down at the command table, moving her virtual controls in front of her, and strapped in. Raibert did the same as Benjamin closed his reports and joined them.

"Now inside the estimated wall region," Elzbietá said. "Bump incoming."

A minute passed.

Two minutes.

Three.

"Did we cross it?" Raibert asked.

"Not yet."

Five minutes.

Ten.

"Kleio, what's going on?" Elzbietá asked. "We're well past your wall estimate. So where is it?"

"I do not know, Agent Schröder. My estimate is

based upon the available data and should be accurate to within a margin of error of no more than eleven percent. It is, however, possible that unknown parameters have affected the wall's position since that data was collected."

Fifteen minutes.

Twenty.

"Where the *hell* is the wall?" Elzbietá said.

"No T4?" Raibert asked.

"I don't know. It's like the outer wall of T4's universe wasn't even there. We're still in the transverse."

"Should we keep going?" Benjamin asked. "Like Kleio said, something might have shifted the wall's position."

"Maybe, but . . ." Elzbietá's brow furrowed. "But that can't be right. You don't just *move* a universe's dimensional boundaries, Ben, and—"

The ship lurched forward, so suddenly and violently their safety straps strained to hold them in place.

"What was *that*?" Raibert demanded, gripping the railing built into the command table's circumference.

"Warning," Kleio said. "Maximum design limits exceeded. Speed now at seventy-one kilofactors. Seventy-two. Seventy-three."

"But this ship can't go over seventy!" Raibert protested.

"I know that!" Elzbietá snapped.

"Look!" Philo materialized next to her, his avatar immune to the vibration jostling his corporeal companions, and pointed at one of her displays. "Local chronotons are all surging in one direction!"

"That must be what's got us! Kleio, disengage the impeller! Emergency phase-out!"

"Impeller off-line. Phase-out unsuccessful. Speed still increasing."

"Not good!" Elzbietá jerked her omni-throttle, spinning the ship physically around on its graviton thrusters. "I'm switching the impeller back on! We've got to fight whatever's pulling us and get back to T1!"

"I'll see what I can do to increase power to the impeller!" Philo vanished back into the TTV infostructure.

The entire ship bucked again, even harder, as the impeller powered back up. Elzbietá fought to maintain control, and Raibert felt gravity switch off as Philo redirected the reactor's output.

"Speed at eighty kilofactors," Kleio reported. "Ninety. One hundred."

"One *hundred*?" Raibert blurted.

"Whatever this is, it's *really* got us!" Elzbietá shouted.

Something slammed into the ship with an enormous *clang* that shifted it bodily sideways, but Elzbietá corrected their course.

"What was that?" Raibert demanded.

"Wish I knew! Philo?"

The Viking reappeared at Elzbietá's side.

"We're fine, whatever it was! Just a big dent in the armor!"

"And the impeller?"

"It's as hot as I can make it, but I don't know how long the power lines will last at this output!"

"Hang on, everyone!" Elzbietá warned.

Raibert tightened his grip on the railing as Elzbietá clicked two icons on her impeller control, then shoved the omni-throttle forward. The entire ship trembled and a high, singing vibration filled the bridge, as if they were trapped inside a giant tuning fork.

"Come on, baby!" she shouted. "You can do it!"

"Is the ship supposed to be shaking this much?" Raibert demanded.

"She'll hold together!"

"Speed stable at one hundred nineteen kilofactors," Kleio reported. "Speed now dropping. One hundred eighteen. One hundred seventeen. Deceleration rate increasing."

"There we go. *Told* you she could do it!" Elzbietá eased the throttle back a hair, and the vibration lessened. "Philo?"

"Output holding. The superconductors are probably glowing right now, but we're still below danger levels."

"Good. We should be okay as long as we—"

A great screeching catastrophe shrieked down the ship's length. The concussion threw all of them painfully against their restraints. Elzbietá's controls vanished. Philo's avatar looked up for an instant, then disappeared. Every light on the bridge, both real and virtual, winked out.

The three corporeal crewmembers sat in complete darkness as their ship plunged through the void without power.

"Well," Raibert said. "Shit."

CHAPTER FOUR

∞∞∞

Gwon Tower
SysGov, 2980 CE

"HE THINKS WE SHOULD DO *WHAT*?" LUCIUS GWON exclaimed.

"Prevent the Great Plague of London," Teodorà said.

"The hell we will!" Lucius shook his head and stepped onto a balcony high up the Gwon Estate tower's eastern facade.

She frowned stubbornly and followed him out. She hadn't expected him to leap at the chance, under the circumstances. Yet she was determined to convince him. She needed him if her and Samuel's plan was to succeed. She knew that.

Winter had lingered, and the March air was frigid, but a transparent dome shielded the balcony from the outdoor air, processing it into a cool breeze, and shafts of setting sunlight blazed through the dense New York City skyline. Consolidation Spire, the seat of SysGov governance, rose high above all others, surrounded by lesser satellite structures. One of them housed ART's own Ministry of Education, while others served other ministries, including one of the ground stations for the Consolidated System Police.

She'd thought long and hard about how to present this to Lucius. At first, she'd tried to talk Pepys—Samuel— out of it, but she'd soon realized her heart wasn't in it. Not really. It couldn't be, when it was so wounded by what she'd done, the atrocities for which she was responsible. And his own burning passion had astounded her only until she saw the ghosts in his eyes. Only until she remembered that this was a man who had lived through the nightmare of the plague as it happened.

That was one horror of the past Teodorà had avoided, but Samuel had brought it home to her in searing detail. The "Great Plague" was scarcely the only time bubonic plague had ravaged London. True, it was one of the worst episodes, but it had also been only the last major outbreak in Great Britain, not the first. In 1636, the year Samuel had been three years old, plague had killed ten thousand Londoners. Thirty years earlier, it had killed thirty-five thousand, and others had died, albeit in smaller numbers, in other years. But in the Great Plague, a *hundred thousand* people, almost a quarter of the city's entire population, had died in less than a year.

And Samuel Pepys had been there. A young man at the time, only in his thirties, he had already assumed his duties as Secretary of the Admiralty Board, and unlike many of his superiors—including King Charles II—he'd remained at his post, in London, even as death stalked the stews and tenements of England's largest city with merciless efficiency. According to the records Teodorà had researched since, up to eighty percent of all inhabitants had died in some of London's most crowded districts. And then, like the capstone to a year of horrors, Samuel had watched the Great Fire of London destroy almost the entire Old City of London not twelve months later. He'd helped lead the vain efforts to fight it; he'd watched the heavens blaze with reflected flame for four endless days and three terrible nights. And he'd walked the smoldering ruins afterward, just as he'd seen the death carts rattle through those same streets with the victims of the Black Death.

No wonder those horrors were so deeply engraved upon his heart and soul. And no wonder the thought of stopping them—of sparing some *other* London...some other *Samuel Pepys* from that hideous nightmare—blazed so fiercely within him.

Teodorà Beckett had felt that fire. The wounded part of her, cringing from the horrors she had unwittingly wrought, had seen salvation in the same vision. Not salvation which would undo her own crimes or magically absolve her of her guilt, but one which would prove she could *do* good, as well as evil. She'd known his dream was impossible, that they could never convince her superiors to try such a thing. Yet that messianic fire had called to her, and so she'd delayed his transfer to Retirement. She'd used her authority to keep him in Guest Retention, instead, where they could continue their conversations.

It had been an abuse of her position, she supposed, but it wasn't as if anyone really *cared* what happened inside ART anymore. And keeping him there had given time for those conversations to deepen and their relationship to shift. His gentle sympathy and understanding—his refusal to condemn her for her crimes—had done more than she would have believed possible to heal her soul. It couldn't expunge her guilt or her sorrow, but it could bring light into her darkness...and draw her even more strongly toward the beacon of his insane, audacious premise that good could come out of ART after all. And in the course of those conversations, they'd become not researcher and subject but allies. Friends, really, in a way Teodorà had never known with any of the other temporal indigenes with whom she'd interacted.

The truth was that Samuel Pepys had become one of the closest friends she had ever had.

In the process, Samuel's command of Modern English had increased dramatically. Indeed, one of her official, if feeble, justifications for delaying his transfer to Retirement had been to see how quickly and thoroughly an indigene without wetware could truly master modern language and concepts. He'd done remarkably well at that, and as his mastery improved, they'd finally realized that if they were truly serious about acting upon his proposal, it was time to move to the next step. But Teodorà was an academic, and although Samuel had been one of the greatest administrators of history and deeply versed in the politics of seventeenth-century London, he knew nothing about the inner workings of SysGov and its ministries. No, they needed someone proficient in the machinations of politics and policy formation in the *thirtieth* century, not the seventeenth.

And it was impossible for Teodorà to imagine anyone more proficient in those arcane arts than Lucius Gwon. Now Lucius gripped the railing and glared at the

SysPol ground station. He wore only a pair of black pants, and his chiseled physique matched those of the Greek sculptures she'd studied over her career. His IC, united so thoroughly with his mind that no one bothered distinguishing between the two, represented itself as a shifting star field within his shadow.

"To be fair," Teodorà began, "stopping the Great Plague was only his first suggestion."

"Oh? And were any of the others more *reasonable*?"

"Not really," she admitted. "We've talked it over—a lot—and he eventually latched onto the idea of going all the way back to the sixth century, before the Plague of Justinian, and immunizing the entire human race."

"Oh, is *that* all?" Lucius smiled scornfully. "Well, in that case, why not? He doesn't exactly think *small*, does he?"

"Come on, Lucius. I'm being serious here."

"So am I. Why would you even consider this when the Gordian Division is breathing down our necks every hour of every day? I can't take a shit without asking their permission."

"It's not that bad," she protested. "Granted, it's bad, but not *that* bad."

"Oh, I beg to differ! You haven't had to sit through one of Vice-Commissioner Schröder's meetings. I swear, that man can flay flesh from bones just by staring at you. It's sometimes hard to believe he's nothing more than a displaced indigene from the twentieth century."

"But don't you see? This is what we've been searching for. This is how we revitalize ART!"

"No, I *don't* see. How are we supposed to rebuild ART by committing the same acts that got us into trouble in the first place?"

"Because this is different." She put a hand on both his shoulders and turned him so he faced her. "We got into trouble because of all the wreckage we left strewn across history when we didn't know what we were doing. But this time we *do* know, and we'll be a force for *good*, not destruction. This time we'll go back with full knowledge of what our actions mean. And with the *respect* the past deserves. We need to show people that our errors were committed in ignorance and nothing more. And beyond that, we need to . . . to pay back this *debt* we've accrued. Don't tell me all the blood we've shed, all the blood we have on our hands, doesn't weigh on you the same way it weighs on me, because I know better than that. I've watched you trying to make some sort of restitution right here in the True Present. But think about it. What better way to compensate for some of the harm we've done could there possibly be than to use our power to affect the past to do some *good* for a change? You, of all people, should know how important that is."

Lucius grimaced, downcast eyes refusing to meet hers, but then, slowly, he began to nod. His abuses of time travel—including everything from sexual escapades with famous women to dropping modern war machines into ancient battles just to see what happened—had led to the ugliest scandal in ART history. The Gordian Knot wasn't really what had ruined ART and everyone associated with it. The near disaster of the Knot might have brought ART's "rescue missions" into the past to a screeching halt, but what had truly *destroyed* it were the ways in which some of its personnel had *amused* themselves . . . and the realization that every single thing they'd done had actually happened to someone, even if that someone lived in a different universe. Lucius was scarcely the only offender, but she had to admit he'd probably been the *worst* offender.

She'd heard rumors of his perversions even before he'd invited her to that first candlelit dinner in Renaissance Italy. For that matter, Lucius himself had never made any attempt to hide them from her after they started dating, and he'd even invited her along for some of his tamer adventures. She'd demurred every time, but he'd never taken offense. She supposed he'd treated it as just a difference in tastes.

Warning signs had swirled around him, but she'd ignored them because Lucius wasn't just a charming and enthusiastic lover. Oh, he was both of those things, and smart, with a sharp and biting wit, whenever he chose to use it. And for all his occasional...quirks, he'd been not simply a brilliant and capable researcher but a superb and gifted administrator. Whatever else might be said of him, and making all due allowance for the Gwon family's wealth and influence, Lucius had *earned* his post as Chairman of the Antiquities Rescue Trust and every one of the other accolades he'd received over the decades of his career.

All of that was true, and it had made him as intriguing as he was attractive. But it was also true that their relationship had been the fast track for her own career, as well. And, if she was being honest with herself, she'd allowed that consideration to guide her actions far more than it should have.

Still, the price had seemed worth it. She'd been able to choose any expedition she wanted, and she'd always received top billing for the ART exhibits those expeditions produced. Her career had soared to meteoric heights. But then, just when she'd thought it could get no better, her dream had crashed back to earth in destruction and horror.

The Gordian Protocol had changed everything. Time travel wasn't consequence-free, and it *certainly* wasn't safe. Instead, it was a sinister hydra that could consume whole universes if roused, and it needed to be approached with the utmost care.

Every shortcut ART had taken, from kidnapping indigenes to ransacking ancient wonders, had flipped from efficient mission design to monstrous atrocity. The blood on her own hands had kept her awake at night—so much so that she'd updated her synthoid with a forced sleep mode.

And it had taken its toll on Lucius, too. More so, in fact, given his history of abuses and his responsibility, as ART's chairman, for every single thing it had done.

Teodorà's career had lain in ruins and her lover had been outed as a mass murderer (even if said murders had been committed in ignorance), but she hadn't left. She'd stuck by both ART and Lucius, and she'd had no plans to leave either of them. Half of that was because no one wanted to hire ex-ART, even if she'd been willing to go, but the other half was because she'd seen a genuine change for the better in Lucius.

It was painfully true that many organizations were leery of hiring ex-ART, but Lucius had used the Gwon family's vast network of government and corporate contacts to find positions for those staff members who'd wanted out. He wasn't always successful, but more often than not his persistent efforts had paid off. He'd even found a way to slip Teodorà into a low-level position in President Byakko's administration. She'd declined the offer, but she'd appreciated the gesture.

Lucius had taken up a few political causes, as well—most notably the Mercury Historical Preservation Society. She wasn't sure why he'd become one of their spokesmen. Some people, like those members of ART who would never forgive him for their collective fall from grace, contended that he had to have an ulterior motive and pointed out that the Society had a habit of looking the other way when evaluating potential allies. What better or easier place for someone like him—which was to say a calculating narcissist—to seek at least a form of public image rehabilitation? But Teodorà had seen his face, listened to his voice... and seen even more of the Gwon fortune flowing into the Society's coffers. And at the end of the day, did his reasons truly matter? He'd become a prominent activist on the side of preserving Mercury for future generations and even used his history with ART to make his case. He'd pointed out that ART's fall from grace was one more reason everyone in SysGov should be cautious of unfettered progress. Everyone had thought no one could damage the timestream, but they'd all been wrong. Would SysGov one day discover that demolishing an entire planet simply as a source of raw materials had been... similarly unwise?

He'd traveled extensively throughout the solar system in the weeks leading up to the critical Senate vote, a taxing task for someone still in an organic body, and his eloquent pleas had even met with some success. Teodorà was certain his influence had led directly to all three Venerian senators flipping their votes. Of course, the Society's membership had always contained a disproportionate number of Venerians. They didn't care that Mercury was uninhabitable, which wasn't too surprising, perhaps, given their indifference to the terraforming of their own planet. Most were perfectly happy to live in aerial paradises over a molten hellscape—indeed, it was a part of their own world's self-image, and *Sky Pirates of Venus* was one of the most popular VR games in the entire solar system. Lucius knew that, and he'd tapped exactly the right cultural notes to sway their senators.

The final vote had still been 28 to 14 in favor of Mercury's destruction, but it would have been even more lopsided without his efforts. And the number of nays had not only prompted additional scrutiny of the entire concept but led directly to the creation of the Mercury Oversight Commission, which would be required to sign off on every stage of the project.

All in all, his efforts to help ex-ART staff and his surge of activism had led Teodorà to a simple, inescapable conclusion. Lucius truly felt remorse for his actions, and she'd watched him come to terms with his crimes, piece by piece, as he strove to make whatever amends he could. He might still be more self-focused and self-absorbed—even petulant—than she could wish, from time to time, yet she found it increasingly difficult to hold her own temper when someone started in on him again. Yes, he'd made plenty of mistakes. So had everyone else, hadn't they? And at least he'd faced his past and was trying to do something about it!

"I see your point," he said finally. "Maybe there's something to his suggestion after all."

"Then you agree with us?" she asked eagerly, but he held up a finger.

"Let's not get ahead of ourselves. You explained to Pepys that we can't change history? Not really."

"I did. I told him we can cause it to branch, but that's it. The concept of the multiverse was a lot to take in on top of everything else, but he managed just fine. The truth is, he's a remarkably intelligent, mentally flexible man. He certainly grasped the essentials of the concept faster than *I* would have in his place!"

"I'll bet." The edges of Lucius's lips curled upward. "Okay, let's say I'm tentatively on board with this. We still have the problem of getting approval." He stared off into the distance, his eyes narrowing. "Unless..."

"Unless what?"

Lucius rubbed the stubble on his chin. He turned to the SysPol tower once more, his eyes fixed on it, and his expression took on an air of intense contemplation.

"You have an idea?" Teodorà asked.

"Maybe. Just give me a moment to think this through." He closed his eyes and bowed his head. The stars in his shadow flew with ever increasing speed, becoming short lines of blurred motion, and she leaned back against the balcony railing and waited. After what seemed a very long time, he opened his eyes once more.

"There's a way we can make this happen," he declared then. "But you're not going to like it."

"And why's that?"

He snapped his fingers. The dome over the balcony turned opaque, and the star field in his shadow vanished. Teodorà had seen that happen enough times to know his IC was locking down the surrounding infostructure. Whatever Lucius was about to say, he wanted to make certain only she heard it.

She swallowed and something fluttered in her synthoid stomach.

"Let's step inside for this."

He beckoned for her to join him, and she followed him into the bedroom where crystal chandeliers cast a warm glow over the expansive oval bed.

"All right," she said. "What are you thinking?"

"Look," he began, "we both know this proposal has a snowball's chance in hell of getting approved. I mean, you do realize that, right?"

"Of course I do," she conceded. "But we have to try."

"Trying is all fine and good, but if we want it to *succeed*"—he flashed a sly grin—"we may have to take an . . . unorthodox approach."

"*How* unorthodox?" she asked.

That flutter in her middle was getting worse.

"First, before we can present this idea at all—in *any* form—I'm going to have to do some spadework. I'm still chairman of ART, but I have exactly zero influence with that bastard Schröder, and he's the real keeper of the keys now, damn it. On the other hand, I do still have friends at the ministerial level, and some of their assistants owe me favors, too. If I can work on them for a few days, Shadow and I can probably bring several of them onboard. Not enough to shift the committee, but enough to give us some subtle cover for what we'll actually have to do."

"You're making me nervous," she told him frankly.

"Good. You should be. This isn't going to be a game, Teodorà. Not if you're really serious about it. Are you?"

She looked up into his face, seeing the challenge in his eyes, and thought long and hard. Yet the truth was that her sense of guilt and the searing possibility of doing something about it never left her final decision in doubt.

"I am," she said firmly.

"All right, then let's assume they shoot down the plague cure proposal, even after I've had time to do that spadework. We'll need a fallback. Something innocuous, at least when compared to spawning a child universe. But what could... Ah!" He clapped his hands together. "Perhaps we suggest returning Pepys to the past."

"Are you sure? I mean, we have the phase coordinates from when we picked him up, so I guess it's *technically* possible to return to the right cord variant. But he's a *very* significant historical figure, and now you're piling his return on top of the original change of pulling him out. That might be enough of a disruption right there to create a new universe."

"True enough." He waved dismissively. "But it doesn't matter. We can mull it over and decide what our backup proposal will be later."

"I don't get it. Why doesn't it matter?"

"Because all we really need is a TTV. Once we have that and we're on our way, we can proceed with curing the plague."

"What? *Without* SysGov's permission?"

"Yes."

"Are you *serious*?"

"Absolutely," he replied flatly, and she stepped back and shook her head.

"I can't believe I'm hearing this!"

"Once we're back in the past, there's nothing they can do to stop us. All we need is permission to leave and a time machine. After that, we can create this plague-free Utopia Pepys wants."

"But Lucius, what you're proposing is *illegal*! It's

profoundly illegal, and Samuel and I want to do this openly, legally, without the kind of shortcuts that got all of us into so much trouble in the first place!"

"I know it's illegal," he said patiently. "But what *you* have to know—what you have to admit—is that there's not a single chance in hell that anyone is going to let us do something that's guaranteed to split off a child universe. Not after what happened with the Gordian Knot." He shook his head. "I know there's a huge difference between this—simply creating a single child universe—and the kind of massive temporal disruption that created the Knot. But everyone—and I mean *everyone*—in SysPol and SysGov is running scared of any possible repetition. And that bastard Schröder is keeping the heat turned up as high as he can, too. So, if you and your friend Pepys are serious about accomplishing this, you have to face the fact that no one is going to let us do it legally."

"Violating the Gordian Protocol carries the *death penalty*!"

"Believe me, I know that, too," he said with an edge of exasperation. "Vice-Commissioner Schröder's made his intentions abundantly clear on that point. He's not taking any chances. He'll pursue the maximum penalty against any violators, and as much as I hate him, I take him very, very seriously."

"Then why are you even suggesting something this crazy? I don't want to *die*, Lucius!"

"Because you're right. Because it's the right thing to do. And *you're* the one who convinced *me* of that. Why do you think I was so resistant at first? Because I didn't think it was worth doing? The hell I didn't! You're not the only one who's felt guilty over all the things we've done, Teodorà. And I've got a hell of a lot more to feel guilty over than you do. So *of course* I want a chance to make amends. But I'm not really the bravest person I know, and the thought of what Schröder will do to us if we try this and we screw it up is pretty damn terrifying. That's why I didn't want anything to do with it.

"But the more I told you why it couldn't be done, the more I realized it *has* to be done. Or that something *like* it has to be done, anyway. We owe too much to too many people, Teodorà. I can't put the life back into all the people I killed or helped kill. I wish to God I could! But this . . . Maybe we *can* do this, and if we can . . ."

He gazed deep into her eyes, and she felt the pain inside him reaching out to the pain inside her. Felt the determination radiating off him like smoke. It wasn't the same as Samuel's. It was . . . harder. Or *sharper*, perhaps. Samuel had the strength of bedrock sincerity, but Lucius had the power of his passion, as well. He always had been fiercer than she was, she thought. Always the hawk, the raptor, riding the wind and embracing the challenge—driven to triumph. Whatever else might have changed inside him, he still retained that need to show the universe—the entire multiverse—what *Lucius Gwon* could do when he set his mind to it. It was what had made him so dangerous when he yielded to the darkness in the belief that he was actually harming no one by what he did.

But that belief had been taken from him by the proof of how many people he *had* harmed, and the fierceness needed a different challenge. It needed *absolution*, she thought, and she and Samuel had offered it to him.

"So there it is," he said now, gripping her upper arms, looking down at her. "ART does have a debt—*I* have a debt—and you've found a way for me to pay it down by doing some real good. By changing the past for the *better*!"

She looked up into those eyes, into the crystal-clear purpose blazing like a nova's heart in their depths.

"So which is it going to be?" he asked. "What's legal? What's *safe*? Or what you know in your heart—what we *both* know in our hearts—is *right*?"

CHAPTER FIVE

~<<<<~

Transtemporal Vehicle *Kleio*
non-congruent

"EVERYBODY OKAY?" RAIBERT'S VOICE CAME OUT OF the dark. "Still got all your parts?"

"I think I'm fine," Benjamin said. "Just can't see a blasted thing. Ella?"

"Still here...wherever 'here' is. Now what do we do?"

"We should probably just wait it out," Raibert suggested. "Every microbot swarm aboard should default to helping *Kleio*'s systems boot back up."

The compartment shuddered and metal screeched in a distant part of the ship.

"'Should' boot back up? Seriously? With *your* luck?" Benjamin replied.

"Yeah, you've got a point." Raibert unstrapped himself and grabbed the table rail as he floated out of his seat.

"What are you doing?" Elzbietá asked.

"I'm going to force a restart of the bridge infostructure. Stay put."

Raibert brought up his synthoid's lowlight vision, spun in the air, planted his feet on the table edge, and kicked off. He floated over to the wall and cushioned his approach with both arms as he landed at the edge of the doorway.

"There's a processor node behind the wall near each door," he said over his shoulder as his fingertips felt for the seams in the wall panel. "I can manually restart the bridge infostructure from there."

"You think that'll work?" Elzbietá asked.

"It should. You two hear that sound?"

The pitch-black compartment fell silent as both his companions strained their hearing.

"The air's still flowing," Benjamin observed.

"Exactly. That means we're not completely without power. This stuff is meant to never turn off, but something's scrambled it. Normally, Kleio would just clear the errors, but she hasn't. What if that means she doesn't have a connection to the bridge anymore?"

"When in doubt, reboot," Elzbietá said.

"Exactly."

He ran the edges of his fingers down a seam in the panel, reached a corner and slid his hand across, then up at the next corner.

"Damn it," he muttered. "Where's the release?"

"What's wrong?" Benjamin asked.

"Nothing," Rabert said. "It's nothing. I've got this."

The panel release continued to evade him, and he muttered balefully under his breath. Then he locked his fingers into a knifelike shape and jammed them into the seam. He curled his fingers underneath the panel and ripped it free of the wall with a mighty pull. *Too* mighty, in point of fact, as the rectangular panel slipped from his grip and twirled through the darkness until it clonked against something. Hard.

"Ow!" Benjamin yelped. "What the hell?"

"Sorry! I didn't mean to do that."

"I should hope not! What just happened?"

"I had trouble finding the release, so I performed a 'manual bypass' on the panel."

"You mean you ripped it off and flung it across the room?"

"Yeah. That. On the bright side, I did get it open." Raibert slipped his hand behind the processor node and found the manual restart switch. "Fingers crossed."

He tugged the switch. Data pathways opened in his mind, and virtual displays lit up around him.

"My VR displays are back up," Elzbietá said.

"Mine, too," Benjamin confirmed. "Pity they can't light the room."

"It's a start," Raibert replied. "Can you tell how bad it is?"

"Looks like you were right," Elzbietá told him. "Except that Kleio's not just cut off from the bridge. She's completely off-line, and most of our systems are in standby. I should be able to manually restart them from here."

"Wait one—"

The lights switched back on and gravity promptly flattened Raibert against the floor.

"Oof! Second."

Philo's avatar reappeared, and the Viking looked down at him.

"Raibert?"

"Yeah, buddy?"

"What are you doing on the floor?"

"I'm wondering that myself." Raibert pushed himself up, brushed off his uniform, and returned to the table. "Glad to see you back online."

"That makes two of us. Is it just me, or is Kleio still down?"

"She's off-line, all right," Elzbietá said, and opened a translucent schematic of the TTV's sleek, elliptical form over the table. She expanded it, and Raibert whistled through his teeth as he saw the solid red line. It ran from the ship's bow, passed through its midsection lengthwise, and exited through a hole near the impeller spike at its stern. All total, it traversed through eighty-two meters of Kleio's one-hundred-fifty-meter length.

"Well, *damn*," Benjamin breathed.

"It looks worse than it is," Elzbietá said. "It's bad enough, for sure, but it could have been a lot worse. Something hit us hard enough to punch straight through the bow *here*. It took out the main gun, clipped the central computer core *there*, and then blasted its way out *here*. But aside from the gun and core, our primary systems are intact."

"Is the core salvageable?" Raibert asked.

"I think so. One of the swarms is rebuilding the critical pathways right now, but it'll be a while."

"Then we make do without her." Raibert faced his integrated companion. "Philo, I need you to take over her functions until she's back up."

"Consider it done." The Viking vanished.

"What about outside the ship?" Raibert asked, turning back to Elzbietá.

"Chronotons are still surging all around us, and we're being pulled deeper into the past."

"Can you get us back on track for T4's True Present?"

"I'll try."

Elzbietá activated the impeller and eased power into it. The TTV's schematic vanished, replaced with a graphical view of the chronometric weather around them. She struggled against the current for several minutes, and Raibert watched the kilofactor readout on her display tick down until it was almost zero.

"Nice," he said, grinning.

"I think we can do this without Kleio," Elzbietá breathed. "Just got to take it slow."

"Good to hear. Do you think this surge is—"

"Hold on!"

The ship swerved sharply as a massive rocky object—thousands of times larger than the time machine—phased into abrupt reality directly in front of them and Elzbietá jerked the omni-throttle back. She sent the TTV scooting sideways, across its craggy exterior, and then the obstruction vanished as quickly as it had appeared.

"Whew!" She exhaled explosively. "That was close!"

"Where did *that* thing come from?" Raibert demanded.

"Some sort of debris is being pulled into the past, same as us. It was only in phase with us for a few moments. I'll keep an eye out for more. It just caught me off guard, is all. If there are more, I shouldn't have too much trouble dodging them now that I know what to look for."

"Hold up," Benjamin said. "Can you take us back and phase-lock with whatever that was?"

"Sure. Why?"

"A hard look at it might help us figure out what's happening."

"Good idea," Raibert agreed. "Do it, Ella."

"All right. Here we go."

Elzbietá reversed course and brought them into phase with the mass. Its enormous bulk loomed ahead of them, like an alien mountain range cut off from the rest of the world in a rough circle, as Benjamin opened a video feed and began collecting data.

"Is that from an asteroid?" Raibert asked.

"If so, it's weirdly shaped," Benjamin replied. "No impact craters on this side. Ella, can you swing us around to the other side?"

"Sure thing."

The view shifted as *Kleio* flitted closer to the object's rough edge. Benjamin zoomed in, and the expanded image showed that edge to be composed of thin layers of differing rock, all piled on top of each other and compacted together. Smaller chunks floated near the edge.

Then *Kleio* crested past the rim and the far side of the mass came into full view.

"My God..." Benjamin breathed.

Elzbietá's jaw tightened in horror, and Raibert shook his head.

"What the *hell* is going on here?" he asked softly.

"I wish I knew." Benjamin's voice was equally soft.

Kleio sped past the gargantuan spires of a broken city. A populated city... in which every vehicle and inhabitant was frozen in place.

No, not frozen, Raibert realized. *It's paused.*

It was a city torn from its world.

A city where time no longer existed.

❖   ❖   ❖

"There's Cyrillic characters all over the place," Benjamin said a few minutes later. "I think this city is from T4's Earth."

"Why do you say that?" Elzbietá asked.

"Well, T4 *is* where we were headed," her husband pointed out. "And you know the years I was targeting with my theory? 1960 to 1980? Well, I chose them because I had a hunch the Cold War ended differently in T4."

"Raibert, do you know what could cause something like this?" Elzbietá asked.

"Not a clue." Raibert shook his head.

A boulder phased in beneath the city and plowed up through its streets. It blasted through a skyscraper, scattering chunks of steel and masonry like shrapnel. Some of the fragments phased farther into the past while others added to the cloud of detritus around the city. Another hulking rock crashed through the city at a diagonal, splintering half a dozen towers. The city was being ground up into its basic components, piece by piece.

"If this really is from T4," Benjamin said, "then what hit us was probably a small chunk of T4's Earth. In fact, all the debris we've encountered so far could be what's left of the planet being sucked into the past."

"Don't take this the wrong way, Doc," Raibert gave him a sad look across the table, "but I hope you're wrong."

"I know. So do I. I just . . ." Benjamin paused and grimaced. "I'm just trying to make sense of this."

"Same here," Raibert said. "Same here."

"Hold on." Elzbietá sat up and expanded a sector of the city. "What's this?"

"What do you have?" Raibert asked.

"That's an impeller signature!"

An icon blinked as Elzbietá highlighted the signal.

"Are you sure?" Raibert asked. "That's a really odd profile."

"No, she's right," Benjamin said. "It's weak and intermittent. Could be damaged. But it's almost an exact match to what *Kuebiko* spotted before it pulled out."

"More importantly, it's an *active* impeller," Elzbietá said. "It's not moving, but it's obviously powered up. What if it was powered up when whatever happened hit?"

"Now *that*"—Raibert's eyes lit—"is an excellent point, Ella! If its impeller was up, the field may have protected it from whatever's happened to the city. And if that's the case, there could be survivors on board!"

"Maybe." Elzbietá nodded. "It's worth a look."

"Well, then!" Raibert settled back into his seat and strapped in. "Sounds like we have a ship in need of assistance. Ella, take us in."

"Right." She cracked her knuckles and summoned the controls to her fingertips. "Hold onto your butts! This could get bumpy."

She throttled up, and *Kleio* dove toward the city. Pebbles pattered off the hull as she swooped in through the skyline. The top ten floors of a skyscraper tumbled lazily in front of them. *Kleio* dipped underneath, and the patter turned into violent sleet.

"There." Benjamin pointed. "Hovering just above street level."

A long, boxy outline lit up in the visual feed. The shape was awkward and primitive-looking compared to *Kleio*'s sleek profile, but a stubby impeller spike stuck out of one end.

"I see it," Elzbietá said. "Smaller than I expected."

"We might just have enough room to stash the whole thing in the cargo bay," Raibert observed.

"We do," Philo reported. Most of his avatar remained

invisible as he concentrated his resources on managing *Kleio*'s systems, but his helmeted head reappeared, floating like the Cheshire cat above the table. "It'll fit if we jettison the main gun's wreckage."

An oblong boulder phased in and smashed through another tower. The building's top spun over and its antenna spire shattered against *Kleio*'s hull with enough force the entire TTV shuddered.

"If we've got room, then let's grab it and get the hell out of here," Benjamin said.

"That's a better idea than sticking around in *this* mess," Elzbietá agreed. "Philo, take control of the outer hull. I'll move in to scoop it up."

"Ready."

The disembodied head vanished as *Kleio* skimmed above city streets full of petrified automated vehicles. The bulk of the TTV's prog-steel hull knocked over lampposts, severed cables, and demolished billboards. The other time machine floated ahead of them, closer to the ground, and Elzbietá brought *Kleio* still lower, slowing until she came to a stop next to the smaller craft.

Philo split the bow open to form a wide, hungry mouth that vomited out a heavy, twisted cylinder which had once been *Kleio*'s main gun.

"Bow open and wreckage jettisoned. Gravity in that section is disengaged."

Elzbietá licked her lips and switched the omni-throttle to a finer control mode. She eased it forward, and the front lip of *Kleio*'s hull crushed a flatbed truck and smeared its wreckage across the street. She added a little more power, and the other time machine's impeller spike slipped into their cargo bay.

She cut power to the thrusters, let *Kleio* coast forward until the entire time machine was inside, then applied a burst of reverse thrust.

"Got it!" Philo announced. "Closing the hull and ramping up internal gravity."

"Nicely done," Raibert said. "Any problems?"

"Its impeller is creating some chronometric drag," Elzbietá replied. "But our impeller's *way* more powerful. We can compensate."

"Good to hear." Raibert unstrapped and stood up. "Doc, come with me. Ella, keep us safe."

"I'll take it from here," Philo offered from the bridge infosystem. "I'll move us out of phase of the city and stay clear of signatures that might come into phase with us. We should be safe for now. If the current gets rough again, I'll let everyone know."

"In that case, Ella, you're with us, too."

She and Benjamin unstrapped and joined Raibert. The three of them passed through a prog-steel shutter, hurried across the corridor, and took the countergrav shaft down to the bottom of the three-story-tall cargo bay.

The black hull of the primitive time machine sat at an angle. Its impeller had scored a groove across the starboard wall, and a corner of its boxy main body was jammed against the port side. Impact dents covered most of the surface, and the tip of the impeller had skewed slightly to one side. Raibert ducked underneath its spike and rounded the hull toward what he assumed was the front.

"Everyone ready for an impromptu first contact?"

"Not really," Benjamin grumped. "I wish Kleio was online so we could load up on Russian linguistics."

"Speaking of which, do either of you know what that says?" Elzbietá pointed to the Cyrillic characters emblazoned across the time machine's flank.

"Nope," Raibert said. "You, Doc?"

"I relied on auto-translators for this sort of thing even back in the twenty-first century, let alone after I got my wetware upgrades."

"Then I guess that's another wait-for-Kleio question."

They reached the time machine's front. It was dominated by a single flat, enormous window, and Raibert tried to peer through it. Unfortunately, the window was clouded with dirt and grease and the interior was dark. He abandoned the effort with a shrug and crossed to a side hatch just aft of the window.

"That looks like blood," Benjamin said, pointing at what might have been handprints smeared across the hatch. "And these could be bullet impact points."

"That's a little ominous." Raibert knocked three times. "Hello! Anyone in there?"

Benjamin rounded the corner to the front window and wiped away a circle of grime with his sleeve. He shielded his view with both hands and pressed his face against the glass, then stiffened as the cargo bay's illumination penetrated dimly.

"I can see someone inside! A young woman. She looks injured!"

Raibert tried the hatch.

"Blocked," he grunted.

"Then bust it down!" Elzbietá replied.

Raibert backed up for a running start, then sprinted forward and smashed his synthoid shoulder into the hatch. It didn't budge.

"No good!"

"Try the window!" Benjamin suggested.

He backed off and Raibert hammered a fist into the window. A previous impact had already weakened it, and a web of cracks spread from his fist. Two more punches and the window shattered. Jagged edges tore at his sleeve and synthoid skin, but he raked his arm across the opening, breaking off glass teeth, then grabbed the window frame and vaulted inside.

A young, athletic woman with an oval face lay sprawled across the floor next to the pilot seat, dirty-blond hair tousled and blood leaking from her nose and mouth.

"Philo, warm up the medical bay!" Raibert slid his arms under the woman and scooped her up. "You've got a patient incoming!"

CHAPTER SIX

Transtemporal Vehicle *Kleio*
non-congruent

LIEUTENANT SARAH SCHOEFFEL OPENED HER EYES, then squinted against the sudden brightness. Her eyes watered, and she blinked away involuntary tears as someone spoke in a language she didn't understand.

"She's waking up."

"Everyone, switch over to Russian. We'll see if that works."

"And if it doesn't?"

"Then we'll improvise."

"Hello? Who's there?" Sarah shielded her eyes from the glare and sat up to find herself in a glass casket within a white room. Despite the odd machinery around her, the room possessed the careful sterility of a medical facility. She patted herself down. Her clothes and boots had been removed, replaced with a medical gown.

But she wasn't in pain. That was a start.

What had *happened* to her?

She struggled to sort through her muddled memories as she glanced around the room and confirmed she wasn't alone. She found herself confronting a huge brute with long blond hair pulled back in a ponytail, a handsome middle-aged man with shorter hair and piercing gray eyes, and a dark-haired woman who radiated a dangerous toughness. All three of them wore grayish-green uniforms with shoulder flashes showing a golden eye and sword on a black background.

"Who are you? Where am I?"

The strangers looked at one another expectantly.

"*Which one of us is supposed to talk to her?*" the woman asked after an awkward pause.

"*I thought* you *were going to,*" the hulking blond said to the other man.

"*Me? Raibert, you're the one who's done this before.*"

"*In ancient Greece!*"

"*That's still better than me.*"

"*Okay—fine! Let's not argue in front of the guest. I'll do it.*"

The blond cleared his throat and stepped forward.

"Hello, Lieutenant Sarah Schoeffel. My name is Agent Raibert Kaminski. These are Agents Benjamin and Elzbietá Schröder. Can you understand the language I'm speaking?"

Sarah nodded. His outlandish accent presented a challenge, and his word choice made him sound like he'd been plucked from a very old movie, but she could manage.

"How do you know my name?"

"It was written on the front of your flight suit."

"Of course."

She glanced down at her medical gown.

"You were in pretty bad shape when we found you. You'd suffered severe blunt trauma. Your neck and quite a few bones were broken, and there was a fair amount of internal bleeding."

Her heart sank and she reached up to the back of her neck. Then frowned. Where was her neck brace? What kind of drugs did they have her on to make her feel this good?

"Will I live?" she asked.

"What?" the man—Raibert—blurted, clearly surprised by her question. "Uh, I mean, yes! Absolutely! We've fixed you up good as new. Or at least really close to new. You're going to be just fine."

"But you said—"

She looked around the room again, at the glass casket she sat in, then at their uniforms once more.

"You're not with the World Union, are you."

It wasn't a question.

"That's right. We're with the Consolidated System Police, Gordian Division."

"Never heard of it."

"That's because we're from . . ." Raibert twirled his hands as if trying to conjure up the right phrase ". . . out of town."

"Out of *town*?" the dark-haired woman echoed, shaking her head at him.

"Hey, it's not inaccurate," he protested.

"We're getting a little sidetracked," the other man cut in. "The chronoton surge, Raibert."

"Right. Yeah." The big man sighed and turned back to her. "Sarah, the truth is we need your help. Can you tell us what happened?"

"I don't—"

She paused, raking through the scrambled contents of her mind. *What happened . . . what happened . . . ?*

"Maybe start with how you ended up getting bounced around in your time machine?" the man named Raibert suggested.

"I . . ."

Her lips trembled and tears filled her eyes as the memory of pain blossomed in her mind like a blood-soaked flower.

And with the pain came the memory of something infinitely worse than mere *pain*.

The world was vanishing before their eyes. She remembered running into her father's office as he pored over the Chronoton Detection Array's raw data. Doctor Kim Schoeffel had been hunched over a monitor, white-haired and pale as a ghost. One look into his eyes had answered all her questions.

This was the end of everything. The past was eating the present. Time had come unhinged, *now* was falling into the depths of *then*, and no one had the faintest idea what had caused it. But if they didn't know the cause, one thing was obvious. There was nothing they could do. No miracle her father's brilliant mind could conjure. All of reality—their entire universe—was doomed.

"Father?" she'd said softly, reaching out to touch his forearm.

He'd stared at her for an instant, then sucked in a sharp breath and shoved up out of his chair.

"Come with me, Sarah!"

"Where?" she'd asked hopelessly, twitching her head at the monitors.

"There may be one hope," he'd retorted, then grabbed her hand and pulled her out into the corridor.

"Run, Sarah—*run!*" he'd snapped, and she'd found herself following him. Racing through the complex, passing men and women weeping, praying, reaching for phones to call loved ones to say goodbye. And that was when she'd realized where they were headed.

The prototype: *Puteshestvennik Odin.*

"The ship's field," her father panted behind her as they reached the hangar and she threw the hatch open. "If it can't protect us, nothing—"

CRACK!

A push from behind, even as her ear identified the gunshot.

She fell into the time machine.

Her father slammed the hatch behind her.

Two more gunshots.

She'd turned to see him smile at her. His lips had moved. She couldn't hear his last words through the hatch viewport, but she didn't need to. She knew what he'd said, and her eyes had filled with tears as he slumped out of sight, his fingers leaving bloody streaks down the port.

Oh, yes. She knew.

"I love you, too, Daddy," she'd whispered.

Then a World Union security guard had slammed the butt of his rifle against the hatch and shouted at her, his face a mask of desperation. She'd spared one instant to snarl at her father's killer, then turned and raced for the controls. She'd flung herself into the seat, punched the button to power the impeller. The time machine had quivered as it came online; she reached for the control stick—

—and then the world ended.

She'd had no time to strap in. She'd hurtled forward, her forehead had smashed against the controls, and everything had gone dark.

"Oh, God." She covered her mouth with a shaky hand. "It's gone. It's all *gone!*"

"I'm sorry." Raibert bowed his head. "Truly, I am."

"The entire world!" Tears blinded her. "It's all gone!"

"I know this must be a difficult time for you, but—"

The woman—Elzbietá—put a hand on his shoulder, and he stopped.

"Let me take it from here," she said softly, and stepped forward.

Sarah wiped her eyes. How could everyone and everything she'd ever known be gone? How was this even *possible*?

Elzbietá knelt in front of her and captured one unresisting hand. "Sarah?"

She snuffled but managed to nod.

"You're not alone," Elzbietá said, and despite the sympathy in her gentle voice sudden fury sparkled inside Sarah.

"Ha! I've n-never been more alone in my entire life! *No one* has!"

"That's true." The other woman nodded. "But I know *exactly* how you feel."

"Don't *lie* to me!" Sarah spat. "How could you possibly know what this is like?!"

"I know because, just like you, I'm a survivor from a dead universe, Sarah."

"You—"

Sarah's lower lip quivered and the word caught in her throat. Facts began beating their way through the grief, and she looked around the medical chamber again. What the *hell* was going on? If all of space and time was dead...then where and when was she? Who *were* these people, and where did they come from?

"Your universe is dead," the woman continued, clasping her hand, "and there's nothing we can do about that. But this isn't the end of *everything*. There's a whole multiverse out there. That's where this ship, and everyone in it, came from."

"A . . . m-m-*multi*verse?"

"That's right. And I know you just met us, but I hope you believe me when I tell you we're here to help. Something terrible's happened here, and even though it's beyond our power to fix it, we're going to make *damn* sure we figure out what caused it. And more importantly, how to prevent it, so other universes never share the same fate. Does that sound like something you'd be willing to help us with?"

Sarah sucked in a ragged breath, then nodded.

"So, Sarah," the other woman said gently. "Please. Can you help us understand what's going on here?"

"I can't." She shook her head. "I was only a pilot. My father might have been able to help you, but he's . . . he's—"

Fresh tears flooded, and she shook her head again, spastically.

"I see."

The other woman nodded, then patted her hand and stood up.

"Come on," the darker-haired man said quietly. "Let's give her some space."

The big guy grimaced, but he also turned for the door.

"Wait," Sarah said.

All three of them stopped.

She drew another ragged breath, blotted her tears with the sleeve of her medical gown, and looked up at them.

"*I* can't help you," she said, "but maybe my flight recorder can."

❖   ❖   ❖

"I'll be *fine*." Elzbietá put a hand on Raibert's back and shoved him out the door. "You just leave Sarah to me."

"You sure?" he asked, looking doubtfully over his shoulder at her.

"Yes, Raibert." She patted him on the back. "The last thing she needs right now is your barrage of questions."

"I'm not that bad. Just one or two, to get a better idea of what happened to T4."

"I know. But it'll wait."

"Come on." Benjamin nodded his head down the corridor. "Let's go take a look at that flight recorder."

"All right," Raibert huffed. He glanced back at Sarah, seated now in a chair beside the recovery casket, staring down at her hands in silence.

"And take your time," Elzbietá added firmly.

"All *right*."

Elzbietá finished shooing the two men away, then stepped through the door behind them. She paused on the other side and sent a quick command to keep the door open. She didn't want their guest to feel locked in.

"I'll just be a minute," she said, and Sarah nodded without looking up.

Elzbietá ordered an outsized mug of hot chocolate and had it delivered to the bridge. Microbots transported the sealed mug to the command table, and she picked it up and carried it back to the medical bay.

"Here you go." She unsealed the top. "By the way, in case you missed it earlier, I'm Elzbietá."

Sarah looked up at the steaming chocolate, complete with a fat marshmallow bobbing up and down.

"Thanks . . . Elzbietá."

She took the mug, holding it in both hands, and Elzbietá sat down next to her and waited.

"So," Sarah said after a while, looking back up at Elzbietá.

"Yes?"

"You're from a dead universe?"

"That's right."

Sarah set the mug down on the closed recovery casket and frowned at her.

"How did *that* happen?"

"It's—" Elzbietá began, then stopped as a sudden surge of emotion ambushed her. The memory of watching that universe fall apart, dissipate like sand in the wind, still haunted her. It was completely different from what had happened to T4, and yet it was also completely, hideously the same.

"Sorry," Sarah said.

"No, it's all right," Elzbietá reassured her with a smile. It was a little fragile, but it was a smile, and she patted Sarah's leg gently. "It's a long story, though. The short of it is that there was this knot in time centered on the twentieth century. Sixteen universes were tangled up in it. We managed to save almost all of them."

"But not the one you're from."

"No," Elzbietá agreed with a sigh.

"And the other two?" Sarah gestured at the open doorway. "Are they from dead universes, too?"

"Oh, no. They're both from Universe-T1. We call it SysGov, though technically Raibert—the big guy—is the only one from SysGov itself."

"Why do you say that?"

"Because he's from the thirtieth century and Benjamin is from 2018."

"He *is*?"

"Don't be so surprised. I'm from that year, too, and we picked up our boss in 1958."

"Wow." Sarah shook her head. "Sounds like quite a crew."

"You can say that again!" Elzbietá agreed wryly.

"So." Sarah's brow furrowed. "All of you travel around the multiverse and . . . do what, exactly?"

"We work for SysPol—the Consolidated System Police. Specifically, we're in the Gordian Division, responsible for enforcing the Gordian Protocol. That's a law that restricts temporal and transdimensional activities. Time travel turns out to be dangerous stuff—*way* more dangerous than anyone had thought it was—which is why we not only enforce the Gordian Protocol back home but also keep an eye out for other societies that have developed the same technology. That's why we came here. To make first contact and educate your society about the dangers."

"You were a little late," Sarah said bitterly.

She hung her head, tears welling again, and Elzbietá put an arm around her shoulders. Those shoulders heaved with long, shuddering sobs for several minutes, and Elzbietá sat beside her, holding her close.

"We were playing with fire and didn't even know it," Sarah choked out after a while. "We screwed up—*screwed up*—and killed our entire universe!"

"This may be small comfort, but I don't think that's what happened," Elzbietá said gently.

Sarah sniffed. She leaned back and wiped her nose. "Why do you say that?"

"It's just a feeling right now," Elzbietá admitted. "But we know your time travel tech was in its infancy. If what we've seen elsewhere is any indication, there's no way your society could have caused this. You didn't have a big enough hammer to do this kind of damage, Sarah. Something else happened. Something we've never encountered before."

"I see." Sarah rubbed her reddened eyes. "The organization you work for. What did you call it?"

"The Gordian Division."

"'Gordian Division.' It's a good name."

"Thanks. We think so."

Sarah looked up and fixed Elzbietá with an intense, focused gaze.

"Are you hiring?"

Elzbietá blinked.

"Are we what?"

"I'm being serious here."

"Yeah, I see that. It's just I didn't expect *that* question."

"But you must see why I asked. Something terrible's happened to my home. But I'm still here, and if there's *anything* I can do, any way I can help you piece together this mystery and keep it from happening again, then I have to help you. I *need* to help you. There's no other option for me if I want to be true to myself."

"Okay." Elzbietá held up her hands. "I see you're serious. And you've made your point."

"If it's the résumé you're worried about"—Sarah smiled without humor—"I happen to have experience with both time machines and working in another universe."

"Just so you know, I don't actually make those sorts of decisions," Elzbietá said. She thought for a moment, then added, "But how about this? When we get back home I'll introduce you to our boss."

"The one from 1958?"

"That's right. And"—Elzbietá smiled crookedly—"in addition to my boss, he's also my grandfather-in-law." Sarah blinked, and Elzbietá chuckled. "Not only that, he's another survivor from my original universe." Sarah shook her head, and Elzbietá patted her shoulder. "Don't worry about it. The important thing is I've got some pull with him and I'll put in a good word for you. How does that sound?"

Sarah smiled back at her, and this time the smile was genuine.

"That sounds like the best news I've had all day."

"Well then!" Elzbietá gave her shoulder a gentle squeeze. "How about we head down to the cargo bay and give the boys a hand?"

"That sounds great. Lead the way."

"Wonderful!" Elzbietá squeezed harder in encouragement.

Something hot and slick spurted over her hand.

Sarah winced, and both women froze, neither able to process what had just happened. Elzbietá's mouth opened as Sarah turned slowly to gaze at her new wound, only to find that the encouraging squeeze had buried Elzbietá's fingers knuckle-deep in the flesh and bone of her shoulder.

Blood fountained around the embedded digits, and Sarah screamed.

❖   ❖   ❖

"Can you read it yet?"

Raibert leaned back against the side of the cargo bay and tapped his foot. Two spherical remotes, each the size of his head, held up a floor panel in the time machine's cockpit while the third hovered nearby with a makeshift, microbot-constructed umbilical cord linked to the flight recorder.

"I think Kleio's almost got it," Philo said. His Viking avatar—the entire thing, not just his head, now that the ship's attendant program was back online—stood next to Raibert. "Good to have her back."

"Yeah," Raibert agreed with feeling. "Nice to see you hanging around again, too, buddy."

"Nice to *be* hanging around again," Philo replied. "But the good news is that the data's meant to be read. It's just a matter of piecing together the interface from nothing. Much as I hate to admit it, Kleio's better at that than I am."

"I know she *thinks* she is, anyway," Raibert said. "But if she's so good, why doesn't she have this licked by now? Kleio, what's the holdup?"

"Apologies, Agent Kaminski, but my systems are operating at only fifty-seven percent efficiency."

"Is that with or without the extra twenty-three percent I'm paying sass-tax for?"

"That capability is included in my estimate. Repairs to damaged pathways are ongoing. I should be back over ninety percent within the hour."

"Well, it was fun while it lasted," Raibert said with a shrug.

"There," Philo said. "I think we're in."

"All right!" Raibert pushed off the wall and rubbed his hands together.

"Don't get too excited," Benjamin cautioned. "This is a very basic time machine we're dealing with. I doubt its instruments are anywhere near as good as ours."

"Better than nothing, though. Right, Philo?"

"Definitely better than nothing. Looks like the recorder was in a powered state even before Lieutenant Schoeffel brought the impellers up. In fact, it looks like her array picked up the whole event, from the very start of T4's destruction. The data is *very* basic, but it does give us a roadmap. Take a look."

A virtual display opened in front of them, showing them a conical projection of the chronometric activity. The time machine must have had a forward-facing dish, Raibert surmised, rather than an omnidirectional array like *Kleio*'s.

"This is the data from just before the event," Philo said.

"Hmmm." Raibert nodded.

"Help me out here," Benjamin said. "It looks like a big, muddled mess to me."

"The important takeaway is that it's normal," Raibert said. "*Very* normal. See here? Fifty percent of chronotons moving backward in time and fifty percent pressing forward, building the future. Almost a perfect split. It's your standard True Present view, just really murky compared to what we're used to."

"Right," Philo said. "And now we reach the event."

The chaotic readings in the cone shifted violently in a singular direction and Raibert's eyes went wide.

"*Shiiiit.*"

"What?" Benjamin asked. "What just happened?"

"Look at that!" Raibert pointed to the flow change. He opened one of the mental pathways that connected him to Philo, and the particulars of chronometric physics crystallized in his mind. "See that shift? The change in chronoton direction was so sudden and violent it induced a *phase state* on regular matter!"

Benjamin frowned at him.

"And look here! You can see a section of matter transitioning into a non-congruent state without an impeller anywhere in sight!"

Benjamin cleared his throat and Raibert glanced up.

"The quick and dirty summary?"

"That would be nice, yes," Benjamin agreed.

"Well, looks like you were right, Doc. T4's present got sucked into its past."

"Okay." Benjamin nodded, staring at the data. "Granted, that's what we thought was happening. But that leads to an important question."

"Yeah, I know. What's doing the sucking?"

"I wouldn't have put it quite that way, but, yes. Where is all this suck *coming* from?"

"Wish I knew." Raibert crossed his arms. "Any thoughts, Philo?"

"For starters, this is very different from the Gordian Knot. We're clearly dealing with a second, undiscovered form of universe-killer."

"Wonderful." Raibert shook his head with a sigh. "Just what we needed. *Another* way to kill a universe."

"Why do you say this can't be a knot?" Benjamin asked.

"Two reasons," Philo replied. "First, the one Gordian Knot on record would've taken one thousand three hundred years to destroy the universes it entangled."

"*This*, however," Raibert interposed, pointing at the data cone, "was almost instantaneous."

"It was," Philo agreed. "And with no sign of a storm front approaching the True Present. Nor was there an explosive increase in total chronometric energy."

"Ergo," Raibert said, "we're dealing with something

new. T4 wasn't the source of a knot, nor was it entangled in one."

"In some ways, this is the opposite of the Knot," Philo added. "It's almost like T4 is imploding, whereas the Knot would have had an explosive conclusion."

"Hence all this suckage," Raibert said.

"On that point," Philo said slowly, "I might have an idea about where it's coming from."

"Oh?" Raibert's face lit. "Let's hear it."

"It's not the cleanest math, given that I'm dealing with realspace, temporal, *and* transdimensional coordinate systems all stacked on top of the other. But I *think* I've identified the overall flow vector."

"And?" Raibert asked.

"T4 is being pulled toward T3."

"Oh, no," Benjamin breathed. "You don't mean—?"

"*Fuck!*" Raibert kicked the side of the time machine.

"But if things are this bad in T4..." Benjamin drew a deep breath. "Then what's it like in *T3*?"

"However bad it is"—Raibert crossed his arms again—"we need to find out."

"Absolutely," Benjamin agreed. "And Fritz and the *Aion* could be caught up in this mess! If it hasn't hit T3's True Present yet, we've got to get them the hell out of there! And if it *has*..."

He eyed the data cone and his voice trailed off.

"Yeah," Raibert said flatly. "I know."

"There's something else I want to bring to everyone's attention," Philo said. "Though I'm not sure what to make of it."

"What's that?"

"There's a weird chronometric resonance enveloping Sarah's time machine."

"Is it dangerous?" Benjamin asked.

"Not right now, but the resonance is increasing, and I don't know why."

"What'll happen if it *keeps* increasing?" Raibert asked.

"Hard to say. It has a very strange pattern, but I think it'll start shifting out of phase with the rest of the ship."

"Shouldn't *Kleio*'s field prevent that from happening?"

"Normally, yes. But this time I'm not so sure. Especially as this resonance gains amplitude."

"Are you seeing the same pattern in the debris field?" Benjamin asked.

"Yes, though it's *much* more severe out there. It's possible her time machine's field dampened the phenomenon but didn't prevent it entirely."

"Well, keep an eye on it," Raibert said. "If it gets worse, we can just dump this thing out the front. We've already got what we need from the—"

"Wait a second," Benjamin interrupted. "If the *time machine* is resonating, what about Sarah?"

Raibert turned to him, and they looked at each other, eyes dark. If the time machine was—

"Ben! Raibert!" Elzbietá shouted over their virtual hearing. "Get back here!"

"Oh, no!" Benjamin broke into a run.

"What's wrong, Ella?" Raibert demanded, two strides behind him.

"I don't know! Something's happening to Sarah! Just get over here!"

"We're on our way!"

They rode the counter-grav shaft up a level and

followed the screams down the corridor before turning into the medical bay. Benjamin reached the open doorway first and froze.

"She's . . ." he breathed.

"Let me through!" Raibert shoved him aside and slipped in sideways. "Ella, what's—?"

He stopped in his tracks.

Sarah had sunk into the floor up to her shins.

"Help me!" she cried, reaching for them. "Help me, *please!*"

"Raibert, what's happening to her?!" Elzbietá demanded urgently.

"I don't know!" he snapped back. "Philo, full power to the impeller! Maximize our field strength!"

"Full power engaged!"

Sarah sank into the floor up to her knees, and a chunky red stain spread out around her legs. Raibert could actually see pieces of flesh and splinters of bone phasing outward from her legs.

"It's not working!" Elzbietá cried.

"Help me!"

Raibert gripped her outstretched hand and pulled, but her fingers and palm came apart like jelly. Her hand shredded, ripped off in his grasp, leaving only her thumb and a ghastly blood-spouting stump.

She shrieked in pain, sinking downward. The floor was up to her hips.

"More power!" Raibert shouted, dropping her mutilated hand. Bits and pieces of the bloody ruin phased away even as it fell to the floor. "Get her back in phase!"

"We're maxed out!" Philo said. "There's nothing I can do!"

"Help me!" Sarah cried as she slipped away from them. The edges of her body lost definition. *"Noooo-oooo! Please, NO!"*

She strained to reach them with her good hand, and Raibert reached back toward her.

But then he stopped himself, their fingertips almost touching. He closed his fist and lowered his arm. The floor was already up to her stomach, and there was nothing he could do. He'd only succeed in making her last moments even more unbearable.

"I'm sorry," he whispered.

"Help meeeeeeeee . . ."

Her scream became a fading, dying whisper as her head disappeared through the floor and chunks of half-real gore spread out from where she'd stood.

❖   ❖   ❖

Nothing remained.

Not her flight suit, not her time machine.

Not even a drop of blood.

Benjamin and Elzbietá had retired to the bridge. They sat with their arms wrapped around each other, her face pressed into his shoulder, but Raibert sat on the medical bay floor where Sarah had vanished. He stared at the perfectly clean spot that had consumed her.

All the sickening pieces of flesh and bone had melted away like ice under a flame.

Only the cold reality of the deck remained.

Philo materialized next to him.

"There was nothing any of us could have done," the Viking said softly.

"Is that really true?" Raibert looked up, eyes bitter.

"Or were we just too slow? If we'd realized in time, maybe—"

"It's the truth," Philo interrupted, and sat down next to him. "Kleio and I ran the numbers. That resonance pattern had already reached a critical stage before we ever picked her up. She was doomed from the outset, Raibert. Our field delayed it, bought her a little more time, but that's about it."

"But *we* survived the Knot unraveling. We should have been able to save her!"

"Cutting the Knot was completely different. That universe just...dispersed, like so much sand in the wind, and our field effortlessly protected us back then. *Her* universe imploded. *Violently*, as the past gorged itself on the present. If the Knot had been that sort of event, that *could* have been Ella, Raibert."

Their gazes met, dark with the shared memory of another universe's death...and the horrifying thought of watching Elzbietá, Klaus-Wilhelm, and his handful of surviving men shred into mists of blood and bone and then just...disappear before their eyes.

"If her impeller had been stronger or active earlier, before the event started, then maybe. But as it was..." The avatar sighed heavily before continuing.

"But Sarah's impeller couldn't stop the resonance from passing the tipping point. And after that it was too late. We were just too late to make a difference."

"I see..."

"Come on." Philo bobbed his head toward the bridge. "We need to decide our next move."

His avatar vanished.

Raibert sat for another minute, staring at the spotless

floor, then inhaled and rose. He smoothed his uniform, raised his head, and strode onto the bridge.

Benjamin and Elzbietá looked up as he entered, and Philo materialized beside them.

Raibert walked to the table and laid his hands flat on its surface. He swept his gaze across the team.

"We press on," he said.

Benjamin nodded, and Elzbietá sat a little straighter.

"I know it's risky," he continued, "but we need to figure out what happened here. And more importantly, *why* it happened. The only way I see to do that is to head into the heart of this mess. And if *Aion's* caught in something like this—"

"Exactly," Benjamin said.

"Just give me a heading," Elzbietá told him, and Raibert gave them a halfhearted smile.

"You two are way too calm about this," he said. "It's almost like you'd faced a universe-ending catastrophe before."

The other two laughed, despite themselves.

"All right. Any objections or alternative suggestions?" He paused. No one spoke. "In that case, let's get to it. Ella, set course for Universe-T3."

CHAPTER SEVEN

∞∞∞

Argus Station
SysGov, 2980 CE

"THANK YOU FOR WAITING," THE ARGUS STATION'S attendant program said. "The Temporal Review Subcommittee will see you now."

Teodorà Beckett looked up quickly from the virtual document she'd been reading. It was a new paper—a very *good* new paper, actually—on a new textual analysis of some of the more obscure books and scrolls she'd personally brought back from the Library of Alexandria. The researcher had zeroed in on something Teodorà and her own team had completely missed, and she'd been looking forward to finding time to read it for quite a while. She'd had that time today, during their lengthy wait, so she'd called it up and gotten two-thirds of the way through it.

And, she discovered, she didn't remember a single word she'd just read.

"You ready for this?" Lucius asked, and she shrugged.

"Do I *look* ready?" she shot back.

"You look pretty damned nervous, actually." Lucius smiled crookedly. "But this is our chance, so are you ready to argue your case?"

"I guess," she replied, smothering the stab of irritation his comment had provoked. *Of course* she was nervous! Which only made his apparent *lack* of nervousness even more irritating.

"Look, what's the worst that could happen?"

"They tell us no, kick our butts out of the meeting, and decide we're just as crazy over at ART as they already thought we were."

"So what you're really saying is that we've got nothing to lose."

She glared at him, but he only winked at her then turned to lead the way down the hall to the conference room where the Review Subcommittee awaited them. To her considerable surprise, that outrageously jocular wink actually blunted some of the sharp edges of her anxiety.

Some of them, anyway.

Lucius strode down the hallway like someone without a single care. Teodorà trailed a few steps behind him and envied the confidence of his body language. He *was* still the chairman of ART, and he carried himself accordingly. Of course, no one else wanted the job. But because of his position the Review Subcommittee had to at least consider his proposal, and the fact that he'd been able to arrange this meeting at all meant it was at least willing to listen. That had to count for something. She'd told herself that, firmly, over and over again on the way up from New York City to Argus Station, but her nervousness had never died down, and when the gargantuan orbital station finally loomed in her virtual vision, she'd *almost* backed out.

What we're doing is a noble thing, she told herself yet again.

No one answered her thought, and once again she sensed the empty void in her mind, empty as the space beyond Argus' hull, where Fran used to be. A pang of longing shot through her, but she pushed it aside and refocused her mind on what they were trying to achieve.

Argus was the largest SysPol facility in the solar system, supporting a force strength of over five million physical and three million abstract officers, although only a relatively small minority of those officers were currently on the station. The majority were spread across Earth and its orbital environs, and the entire Argus-based force wasn't even half of SysPol's full strength. SysPol employed over twenty million people, and the man in charge of it all sat in the room ahead.

Who in their right mind would lie to someone like that? she thought. *Oh, that's right. Us.*

Virtual images lined the wide, arching hallway before her. SysGov had decorated one side but allowed the Admin to decorate the other, and that had created a strange dichotomy. She found herself pondering that dichotomy as a distraction from her nervousness as she and Lucius paced down its impressive length.

The right side started with the desolation caused by the Near Miss industrial catastrophe, then moved on to the drafting of the Articles of Consolidation by SysGov's founding father, Isaac Maxwell. The signing ceremonies of all fourteen members, from the United Territories of America in 2455, to the Venus State,

SysGov's newest member, in 2943, underscored the Consolidated System Government's long, steady growth and peaceful expansion.

The Admin's side of the hallway started in a similar vein with their Articles of *Cooperation*, but then took a drastic turn.

Both the Admin and SysGov had arisen as responses to near disaster. In SysGov's case, that had been the result of runaway civilian nanotech which had devoured a monstrous thousand-kilometer swath across Asia before its depredations were stopped. That had been a terrible enough experience, with millions of deaths, but it paled beside what had happened to Asia in the Admin's universe. *Their* version of the Near Miss began with the escape of the Chinese military's weaponized AI, named Yanluo, in 2761. Reacting to its designed imperatives, Yanluo had acted ruthlessly to protect its own existence and expand its resource base through conquest and the eradication of anyone who might have tried to shut it back down. In the end, they never had managed to "shut down" Yanluo's rampage. The defeat of its self-replicating machinations had required a sustained nuclear bombardment which had virtually depopulated the most populous continent on Earth. The death toll had been staggering, numbered in *billions*, not mere millions. That was far worse than the casualties of SysGov's Near Miss, so perhaps it wasn't surprising that the Admin took what might charitably be called a jaundiced view of SysGov's integration of independent electronic citizens into its society and government.

The Yanluo Restrictions had been written to ensure that that tragedy would never be repeated. The Articles of Cooperation had been created to lend enforceable weight to the Restrictions, and every other government in the solar system had joined the Admin, willingly or otherwise. In 2765, the newly formed Admin had crushed the Lunar Federation and established a puppet government of the same name. A federation that was "happy" to sign the Articles. Mars and other factions had formed the Non-Earth Defense Alliance to counter Earth's aggression, but that organization had dissolved in 2775, following Mars' devastating defeat at the end of the Violations War.

A tale of two universes, Teodorà thought, looking at a pair of facing virtual images. *On one side, a peaceful signing ceremony for Mars. On the other, the Admin's victory at the Battle of Phobos Command.*

The dark blue conference room doors, badged with the golden SysPol eye, split down the middle and opened double-wide at their approach. Teodorà brought her face and posture under strict control, donning the professional mask she'd worn in hundreds of meetings, and followed Lucius into the circular room.

The doors sealed behind them, and she eyed the people seated behind the wide, curved table. Only four of the ten seats were filled, and she considered each member of her soon-to-be audience carefully.

Oliver Lamont, chief of police, sat near the center of the table in the generic dark blue of a SysPol officer. His black, chiseled features wore a slight, welcoming smile as he sat with his fingers knitted together on the table. If there was anyone in this room she *had* to win over, it was him. Not only was he President Byakko's representative on the committee, but he would also be the one to forward any official recommendation to the Senate's Temporal Oversight Committee. Without his blessing, they wouldn't get anywhere near a time machine.

Clara Muntero, ambassador from the System Cooperative Administration, sat to Lamont's left. She, too, wore blue—in her case the sky blue of an Admin Peacekeeper—with her peaked cap on the table before her. A strict buzz cut framed her round face, and her firmly set jaw gave her a severe and unwelcoming air. A virtual image hovered over the back of one hand, showing a dove and cardinal flying around each other, so close that they almost formed a yin-yang of red and white.

That must be her marriage sigil, Teodorà thought.

The chair to Muntero's left was occupied by Jonas Shigeki, one of the under-directors of the Department of Temporal Investigation, the Admin's counterpart to the Gordian Division. The young man didn't so much sit in his chair as *slouch* in it, and he didn't even glance her way. *His* cap was pushed back at a rakish angle; he'd draped his long, black ponytail over one shoulder, and his eyes were half-lidded, as if he found himself ineffably bored but was—of course—far too polite to mention it. The backs of his hands were unadorned.

Young Shigeki was the son of Csaba Shigeki, the DTI Director-General, and Teodorà was tempted to decide that his position on the committee was the product of nepotism. Realistically, however, the tense political landscape made it unlikely the post would be filled so casually. That suggested his outer indifference was an act of some sort, although Teodorà was at a loss as to why he should *want* to look like "the boss's kid" at a meeting like this one.

A gray-skinned, yellow-eyed security synthoid stood at attention behind the ambassador and under-director. His presence was a visual reminder that the relationship between the Admin and SysGov could be best described as icy but peaceful. Each superpower was content to stay on its side of the transverse, although in the Admin's case, there wasn't much choice, since it didn't have the drive technology to cross it.

Not yet, anyway.

Despite that, SysGov had offered the Admin a seat on the Temporal Review Subcommittee, and their vote could be counted as a resounding *no*, almost without fail. Teodorà supposed open minds were hard to find in a society that enslaved AIs.

You stay on your side, we'll stay on ours, she thought. *Oh, and keep your dirty AIs where we can see 'em!*

Teodorà smiled inwardly at the thought, then turned her attention to the room's remaining occupant.

Vice-Commissioner Klaus-Wilhelm von Schröder sat to Lamont's right, his back ramrod straight and his gray eyes keen, like those of a predatory bird. Where did she even begin with this one?

Former *graf* of imperial Germany.

Former four-star general of the Western Alliance.

Former Provisional Governor of the Republic of Ukraine.

Survivor of a dead universe.

Cutter of the Gordian Knot.

And now Vice-Commissioner of SysPol, Gordian Division.

It still boggled her mind that here sat not just an indigene from the past, but an indigene from a past *that didn't even exist in this universe*.

Or anywhere else, now.

"Chairman Gwon. Doctor Beckett," Lamont said, nodding respectfully to both of them. "Thank you for coming."

"Thank you for agreeing to meet with us," Lucius responded. "Doctor Beckett and I appreciate you and the rest of the committee taking the time to hear our proposal in person."

"Yes, I understand you have something a bit on the unorthodox side for us to consider." Lamont leaned back, propping his elbows on the arms of his chair and releasing his fingers across his chest. "I must admit the project summary was...intriguing. It wasn't terribly *specific*, however, so I'm sure you'll understand, in turn, that there have to be some significant reservations on our part."

"Given the Gordian Knot and all its implications for the damage the Antiquities Rescue Trust has done, I would be astounded if there weren't reservations," Lucius replied frankly. "Doctor Beckett and I would expect no less."

"I'm relieved to hear it," Lamont said. "With that said, however, please proceed."

"Actually, Doctor Beckett will present our proposal, if the committee will permit."

"That will be fine, Chairman Gwon," he said, and looked courteously at Teodorà. "Doctor Beckett?"

"First, allow me to add my thanks to Chairman Gwon's," she said.

Lamont nodded, and Teodorà very carefully did not look in Lucius's direction as she moved to stand in the open end of the curved table's shallow horseshoe. There were a lot of reasons for Lucius's insistence that she present the proposal. The most important of them was probably that, for all his surface courtesy, Lamont personally despised Lucius. Teodorà had no idea how much Muntero and young Shigeki knew about Lucius's . . . checkered career, but Lamont knew it chapter and verse. So did Schröder, although the vice-commissioner had his own expression well in hand. She doubted the committee would have agreed to hear their proposal at all if Lucius hadn't leaned hard on his contacts in the ministries, and she wondered how many favors he'd burned in the process. Having him as the face of the proposal could only have further prejudiced the committee's SysGov members, however.

Holding him in reserve if—when—the committee rejected her initial proposal was another factor, of course.

Now she dropped her prepared visuals into the room's infostructure and watched the committee's faces as the images expanded in their virtual sight. Microscopic bacteria, close-ups of fleas and rats, images of men and women and children with necrotic toes, fingers, noses, and lips, or with engorged lymph nodes that oozed blood and pus.

Lamont and Muntero grimaced at the grotesque collage, while Schröder watched it with unfazed calm. Shigeki only glanced at it, then shrugged, and his security synthoid stared straight ahead, coolly vigilant and ignoring the imagery completely.

"Distinguished committee members," Teodorà said. "I give you *Yersinia pestis*. More commonly known as the Plague of Justinian and the Black Death.

"The first of what we think of as pandemics, the Antonine Plague, struck Asia minor, Egypt, Greece and

Italy in 165 CE. Its cause was debated for centuries, but thanks to ART, we now know that it was in fact smallpox, brought back to Rome by soldiers returning from Mesopotamia. It killed over five million people, just over two percent of the population of the world at that time."

She paused to let that number sink in, then continued levelly.

"The Plague of Justinian, the world's *second* pandemic, was far worse, however. It hit the Eastern Roman Empire sometime around 540 CE, and over the next several years, it killed between twenty and thirty million people—a quarter of the population of the Eastern Mediterranean, in a single year. In the city of Constantinople alone, it killed five thousand people per day. By the end of the year, forty percent of the Byzantine capital's population was dead.

"But even that wasn't the worst. The Black Death struck Western Europe, as well as its traditional killing grounds, in 1347, and recurred periodically until about 1665. Peak deaths occurred between 1347 and 1351. It's estimated to have killed between seventy-five and two *hundred million* people in Europe, Africa and Asia. To put that into context, the world's total population in 1500 was only *four* hundred and fifty million."

She paused again, her eyes dark as those stark numbers went home.

"Gentle beings," she said then, "in proportion to the populations involved, the Black Death was far more lethal than the Near Miss. Indeed, it was more lethal than the Yanluo Incident. It took two *centuries* for the world's population to recover to pre-plague levels."

A chill breeze whispered silently around the room

as those members of two different advanced societies faced that charnel pit reality.

"Both the Plague of Justinian and the Black Death were the result of *Yersinia pestis*, which means the same countermeasures would work against both. We know the Black Death originated in Central Asia, Kurdistan, Western Asia, and Northern India, with rodents fleeing the dried-out grasslands, and previous ART expeditions have confirmed that 1338 Kurdistan was 'ground zero' for the Black Death. Similar expeditions haven't been conducted for the Plague of Justinian, which happened eight hundred years earlier, but it probably came from the same general area.

"What we propose seeks to accomplish two goals. First, to further our understanding of the multiverse by conducting a controlled experiment. Second, to do a tremendous amount of good as a side effect of that experiment."

"That sounds very laudable," Ambassador Muntero said, although it clearly didn't sound all that "laudable" to her, Teodorà thought. "But how will you achieve those goals?"

"With an ART expedition. One to the year 490 CE, a few generations before the Plague of Justinian ravaged the Eastern Roman Empire. Ideally, we'd like to start at the plague's source, but since we're not certain where the earlier pandemic began, we've selected Constantinople as our focal point in our current planning. Additional research might allow us to further refine our targeting."

"You've selected Constantinople as your focal point for *what*, exactly?" Muntero pressed, and Teodorà drew a deep breath as unobtrusively as she could.

Lucius had crafted their précis with care. All it

had really specified was an intention to do in-depth research on pandemics of the ancient world with a *secondary* object of gaining additional insight into the fundamental mechanism of how the strands of the multiverse were structured. Even that had been more specific than he would have preferred. In fact, he would have *preferred* an outright lie, but Teodorà had been adamant. This was to be their redemption, and that meant they had to give the committee the chance to make the right decision from the outset.

"The focal point of our mission is to cure and immunize the population against the plague," she said now, unflinchingly.

Muntero's eyes flared wide. Clearly, she hadn't seen that coming! Even young Shigeki sat up a bit straighter and looked actively engaged for the first time.

"We propose to use large-scale genetic engineering via airborne microbot swarm," Teodorà continued undaunted. "We'll target the plague epicenter, then move east into the area we know the plague came from. In effect, we'll build a firewall for the Eastern Roman Empire that we then extend east from Byzantium to try and choke the plague off at its source, or as close to it as we can come."

"An intervention of that magnitude would be almost guaranteed to spawn a child universe," Lamont noted. His tone was calm, and Teodorà nodded. Obviously, Lucius's "spadework" had done at least some good. The notion wasn't coming at Lamont completely cold, and he seemed prepared to at least hear them out.

"We're fully aware of that, Chief Lamont," she countered. "In fact, we view that as a positive feature of our proposal and not a downside."

"So I gathered from your initial summary." Lamont nodded. "It was rather vague on *why* you would view that as a positive outcome, however."

"Our understanding of how the Gordian Knot formed is woefully incomplete," Teodorà responded. "We do know that at least some ART expeditions have spawned child universes, such as Alexandria-1." She kept her voice level. "But we also know ART has conducted *hundreds* of expeditions, any of which might have spawned child universes, yet we've found only a handful. We recognize that we're in the very early stages of exploring and mapping the multiverse, of course, but the fact that we've found so few of them directly attributable to ART's actions suggests that while the risk of creating them isn't zero, it's manifestly very low. By conducting a carefully controlled and monitored expedition that *purposefully* creates a new universe, we will be shining a light into the unknown, illuminating these dangerous mysteries. Only by comprehending the underlying structure of the multiverse can we truly protect ourselves from future tragedy. And, as an added benefit, we'll set this new universe on a track free of the ravages of the plague. Certainly, you must all agree that eliminating the Black Death would have to have a beneficial effect, and we would also—"

"I need you to stop right there." Klaus-Wilhelm von Schröder leaned forward, gray eyes sharp as scalpels. "When exactly were we appointed God?"

"I beg your pardon?" Teodorà asked.

"I realize I missed a thousand years of history. Was there some point in there where that vote happened? I only ask because you've just demonstrated that you and the rest of ART haven't learned a damned thing. You still speak of the past as if it's your personal plaything. You're talking about creating an *entire universe* as a science experiment. What utter arrogance! Haven't you done enough damage flailing around in ignorance?"

"Forgive me, Vice-Commissioner," Lucius intervened in his most diplomatic tone before Teodorà could respond, "but that was when we didn't know the past could be changed. And everyone, please don't react before hearing us out fully. Without really *considering* what we're talking about here." He swept the other three members of the committee with dark eyes. "Believe me, there isn't a person in this room who understands what Vice-Commissioner Schröder is talking about better than *I* do! And not just as ART's chairman while all of that was going on. My God, do you think the fact that I didn't know what I was doing makes it any easier to live with some of the horrible things I did? Did for *amusement*, not as part of our serious study of the past? I treated living human beings like the constructs in some kind of VR game, because I thought the things I did would never 'really' exist. But the people I did them to *did* exist. *All* of them did."

Pain warred with self-disgust in his expression, and he shook his head hard.

"Teodorà—Doctor Beckett—and I are both only too well aware of the blood on our hands...and on ART's collective hands. Maybe that's part of what's driving us here. But it's definitely front and center in our thinking when we consider both the repercussions of our past actions and the good we might accomplish. I think there's general agreement that we know entirely too little about everything that went into the Gordian

Knot, and we have an acute scarcity of observational data on both that and on how a child universe's early stages differ from those of its parent.

"The object is to acquire some of the data we so desperately need. Is it totally without risk? No, of course not! But isn't there a greater risk in acquiring that data because of some *uncontrolled* event? Another Gordian Knot that we might not be lucky enough to survive? Surely it's better to be in control of the parameters rather than their *victim*? We *need* that insight if we're to survive, and if we can acquire it while simultaneously making some compensation for the incredible amount of human suffering ART unknowingly inflicted on so many millions, isn't that a desirable outcome, as well? Think of all the good that would come of this! The outlay for us would be absolutely minimal, and we'd have the opportunity to watch a child universe as it forms and to actually observe and record every instant of the process. And as a *fringe benefit* of acquiring that knowledge, we would create an entirely new, unique human civilization that never knew the mass mortality of the Black Death! What a magnificent achievement that would be!"

"Are you out of your freaking mind?" Muntero stormed, surging to her feet. "The original Gordian mess came within an eyelash of destroying not just *your* universe, but a dozen others—including ours!"

"But this time it would be a controlled experiment," Lucius promised almost pleadingly, "without the overload factor of having so many TTVs and chronoports phasing in and out in a massive dogfight. And by watching the process happen, we'd gain an incredible amount of knowledge about the physics behind it."

"This isn't something we need to be blundering around with until we're *damn* sure we already *have* a theoretical model that can *at least* explain how the Knot formed!" Muntero shot back. "You idiots need to—"

Shigeki pressed his hand against Muntero's sleeve, and she stopped in midsentence and looked down at him. He glanced up, the two made eye contact, and *appeared* to be having a conversation. Except that their lips weren't moving.

This must be an example of the Admin's closed-circuit chat, Teodorà thought. *They're conversing via a contact point.*

"That will be all for now," Muntero said curtly. She sat down and Shigeki lounged back in his chair once more.

Now that's *interesting*, Teodorà thought. *The "bored boss's kid" is the one who really holds the leash on the Admin's delegation. I wonder if he thinks his act is actually fooling anyone on our side of the table? Or*—her eyes narrowed—*if he really cares whether or not it is as long as we have to act as if it is?*

"Thank you, Ambassador Muntero," Lamont said dryly. "The Admin's position on this matter is duly noted."

Lucius glanced quickly at Teodorà, and she shrugged ever so slightly in acknowledgment. Muntero's reaction illustrated exactly why he'd argued against voicing their real plan at all. He'd preferred instead to propose the second, more palatable option from the start, and he'd argued—not unreasonably—that approaching the committee with their true plan in full view would decrease their chances of successfully proposing even their fallback position as an alternative.

She'd agreed with his logic, but she'd needed to at least try to convince the committee that what they wanted to do was right and honorable. Lying from the start would almost certainly have made it easier, but she had to give these people the opportunity to make the right call. She owed it to them. At least until they let fear stay their hands. Then—and *only* then—would she and Lucius make the choice for them.

"It seems the objections are stacking up," Lamont said. "And I must admit I'm quite hesitant about this proposal myself. Do you have anything else to add to your case?"

Teodorà and Lucius exchanged another quick glance, and Lucius nodded to her.

"Yes, actually we do." She closed the collage of plague images and opened a virtual representative of a portly man in a long brown coat and a dark, curled wig. "This is Samuel Pepys, Secretary to the British Admiralty from 1673 to 1688 CE and one of our transplanted guests at ART."

"You mean he's an ART abductee," Schröder corrected sharply.

"Actually, that's not correct in his case." Lucius smiled thinly. "Mister Pepys boarded the TTV of his own volition, knowing it was a time machine, and he's been very complimentary about his treatment here in the True Present."

"Then he's a lucky exception to ART's norms."

"That, unfortunately, is true," Lucius conceded, his smile vanishing.

"More importantly, what does he have to do with the plague?" Muntero asked.

"Samuel Pepys lived through the Great Plague of

London, which eventually killed a hundred thousand people, or about a quarter of London's population," Teodorà said quietly. "He was there, he witnessed it, he wrote about it in his diaries, and it affected him greatly. So much so, that it was actually he who proposed we go back in time to prevent the plague."

She noticed a slight softening in Schröder's face. He leaned back, still manifestly skeptical, but perhaps now primed to listen.

"You've begun considering the wishes of those you've abducted, have you?" he asked.

"That's correct, Vice-Commissioner," Lucius said, then went on, grimly. "As part of ART's new policy toward the individuals we've abducted, I've instructed our personnel conducting exit interviews before they're moved to Retirement housing to be more engaged with our 'guests.' To ascertain their needs and desires and to make as much as they desire and can handle of our own time and technology accessible to them. Which is in no small part what brings us here, today.

"I hope you and the other committee members will forgive the . . . excessive boldness of our first proposal, shall we say? We have a second, more modest one that also aligns with Mister Pepys's wishes and which will also, we hope, add to our understanding of exactly how our interaction with the past affects things."

"While he enjoys the thirtieth century," Teodorà said, "he also yearns to return to his indigenous time. What we propose here is similar to our first proposal in that it would be an experiment meant to collect valuable data while also providing a real benefit to those involved. It is, however, on a much smaller scale, with consequences which should be far less significant. We request permission from this committee to go back in time and return Samuel Pepys to the exact phase coordinates from which he was removed."

Lamont grimaced.

"Is that even possible?" He turned to his right. "Klaus?"

"It's possible, sir," Schröder acknowledged. "Although not without risks."

"But how can he be returned? Won't the original him be there as well?"

"Not necessarily," Schröder said. "The original visit that picked him up would have created a variant of the past. That happens every time we interact with the past rather than simply observing events. From that point, there are two possibilities. The disruption can be so great a child universe is formed, hence the alternate version of the Admin universe. But that process isn't instantaneous from an absolute time perspective, and by using the flight data from the TTV that picked them up, it's possible to backtrack to that same cord variant."

"I see." Lamont leaned back. "So it *is* possible to return him? And by extension, all the other transplants?"

"We've already used this method a few times. It's functional and repeatable. If you recall, one of our twenty-first-century agents—Agent Benjamin Schröder, to be precise—has used it to visit his family."

"I do. But I also remember your reassurances that Agent Schröder's case presented almost no risk."

"That's correct. He wasn't a prominent or influential figure in his native time. Pulling him out or plopping him back into the cord variant has little impact. At least on the scale necessary to *permanently* branch the timeline."

"How much of an impact is necessary?" Lamont asked, and Schröder frowned.

"The creation of an accurate mathematical model has been an ongoing, *frustrating* process, sir," he said.

"In other words, we don't know."

"No, sir. We don't."

"Then what do you make of their proposal?"

"I'm not sure." Schröder glanced at the virtual person standing in front of the table. "Someone like Samuel Pepys is *far* more historically influential than our agent, and ART has already disrupted that part of the timeline by removing him. Reintroducing a version of him that's been exposed to the thirtieth century would be risky."

"If I may intrude?" Lucius raised his hand and smiled almost apologetically as they looked at him. "In our opinion, his increased impact on the timeline is precisely why an experiment of this nature would be so valuable. Doctor Beckett and I would have preferred our original proposal, but it may well be that the risk factor in that proposal was too great for safety. For that matter, we're both aware that our personal sense of guilt may very well have played a major part in our thinking. If you'll forgive my putting it in these terms, both of us are driven to find some way to at least partially atone for past actions, and it's hard to think of something that would be more beneficial to the universe in which it happened than the eradication of the plague.

"But this would pose a far more modest risk of creating a child universe. From that perspective, frankly, it wouldn't provide as valuable a data sample, but much as I might prefer the...bolder approach, this may indeed be a time when it's wisest to 'first do no harm.' Even so, if we carefully monitor the timestream while reinserting Pepys into his own life, we should be able to at least take a step forward in developing a true working model for this branching threshold."

"Klaus?" Lamont said again.

"They're not incorrect," Schröder replied carefully.

"And if we're successful with Pepys, then it could open up possibilities for other transplants," Lamont said thoughtfully. "We could give all of them the option to return home. I must admit I find that notion appealing."

"As do I, sir," Schröder seconded, and Teodorà felt her hopes rise.

"I don't believe what I'm hearing," Muntero fumed. "Are you two honestly considering this *outlandish* proposal?"

"It's not outlandish," Schröder said stiffly. "Far from it, in fact. There's risk, yes, but it will be based on a tried-and-true method. I'm not fully sold on their proposal yet, but I believe it deserves serious consideration."

"Tried-and-true?" Muntero mocked. "You mean how SysGov makes exceptions to the Gordian Protocol for your *grandson*?"

"Agent Schröder's contributions to the Gordian Protocol are well-known to this committee," Schröder bristled. "And I'll have you know his relationship to me has no bearing on any decision we make here."

Perfect! Teodorà thought. *All she's doing is driving them to our side!*

"I have to agree with my vice-commissioner." Lamont smiled at Muntero the way a parent might smile at a petulant child. "We treat each and every proposed exception with all due seriousness, and I would appreciate it if you didn't make insinuations to the contrary."

"But look at what you're *proposing*! There's no *need* to do this, and yet you both sound ready to sign off on a totally unnecessary escapade into the past. This could end up being another Gordian Knot in the making."

"I would like to remind the honorable ambassador"—a venomous edge had entered Schröder's tone—"that it was we who unraveled the original Knot despite the Admin's best efforts to not just stop us, but to *kill* us. And ultimately, the proposal before us has merit. We're stumbling around in the dark, and more data could prove useful, which doesn't even consider our moral responsibility to give the transplants the option to return home if we learn we can do so safely!"

"Oh, come on! You and I both know the alternate version of the Admin you faced isn't—"

Shigeki tapped Muntero's shoulder, and the ambassador stopped and grimaced, then leaned back, waiting for him to speak. He straightened his cap and sat up straight in his chair.

"We freely acknowledge," he began, "that the Admin has no direct say in what is, after all, an internal SysGov matter. However, we're grateful to your government for giving us a seat on this committee despite that, and I'd like the opportunity to provide a more official response to ART's proposal. I request a recess so that we may return to the Admin and consult with our leadership." He looked down the table to meet Lamont's eyes. "Hopefully, you'll find my request reasonable, Chief Lamont?"

"Quite reasonable, thank you, Director," Lamont agreed. "I'll have the TTV brought over to carry you home, and we'll reconvene in one day." He turned to Lucius and Teodorà. "Chairman, Doctor." He nodded to each. "Given the nature of what you're proposing, I'd like to speak with Mister Pepys, as well. Since it's his life we're talking about, it seems only fair that we hear from the man himself. Can that be arranged?"

"I don't see why not," Lucius said. "In fact, it may be easiest to just bring him with us when we come back tomorrow."

He glanced Teodorà's way, and she nodded back, her face carefully neutral. They both knew they'd have to coach Samuel on what they were going to say to the committee versus what they were actually going to *do*.

"Excellent," Lamont said. "And I believe we're done for today. Thank you, everyone, for your time. Meeting adjourned."

CHAPTER EIGHT

‒‒‒‒‒∞∞∞∞‒‒‒‒‒

Argus Station
SysGov, 2980 CE

LAMONT GLANCED AROUND TO BE CERTAIN HE AND Klaus-Wilhelm were alone as they headed down the corridor to their next meeting. Then he exhaled a long, weary sigh.

"I'm glad at least *one* of them can be reasoned with."

"I wouldn't be too sure, sir. Honestly, I think *he's* the one we need to watch out for."

"You don't trust him?"

"I don't trust *any* of them."

"Of course." Lamont rubbed his brow. "Are you sure you're not letting personal history affect your judgment?"

Klaus-Wilhelm tensed and a jagged lightning flash of memory ripped through his soul:

A skeletal machine festooned with weapons, tearing through the mansion. Flames and gunfire on all sides. The revolver bucking in his hand as he unloaded shot after shot into the infernal thing. Yulia, so strong and beautiful, her body broken and burned, dying in his arms. And finally their three little girls, blackened and seared—the same faceless, twisted, carbonized pieces of meat he'd dragged from burning tanks, seen left by the hellish kiss of napalm—huddled together, arms wrapped around one another in the storage cabinet where they'd hidden for the final terrified seconds of their young lives.

Tears stung his eyes and he blinked them away.

"No, sir," he said flatly, marching at Lamont's side, and the chief of police sighed and shook his head.

"You're allowed to be human, you know," he said gently.

"The attack on my family isn't something I can forget." Klaus-Wilhelm's voice was as flat as before. "*No one* could forget it—or not anyone I'd care to know, anyway. But I've had a great deal of experience in working with people I personally loathe. I won't pretend my feelings don't affect how I feel about *this* Admin, even if I know intellectually that these people aren't the ones who killed my family. But I'm aware of that, and I learned the hard way, a long time ago—a long time even for me—that personal feelings, even hatred, can't be allowed to affect the discharge of someone's duty. It's my duty to be as coldly logical and dispassionate as possible in my consideration of this Admin's positions or opinions."

"That's not what I'm saying. Just keep in mind that our two governments are stuck with each other, whether we like it or not. We should all do what we can to ensure things don't...escalate."

"I'm well aware of that, sir."

"And the Admin has, at least outwardly, endorsed peace."

"I'm aware of that, as well, sir. At the same time, we need to remember that right up until the instant Agent Kaminski made contact with *this* Admin, the people we're talking with today were precisely the same people in charge of the Admin he first contacted." Klaus-Wilhelm shook his head. "The divergence point began there, so these people are exactly who those people were up to that point. The decisions they're making and the actions they're taking are different because they were approached under different circumstances, and because they don't see themselves as fighting for the very survival of their own universe...yet. I fully understand that they, just like SysGov, are operating in a completely different matrix from the Admin who killed my family and would have destroyed the entire multiverse just to preserve their own universe for a time. And, as I say, I'm factoring that into my consideration of their proposals and actions. But in the end, sir, we have to judge these people by their *actions*, not their words."

"Well." Lamont frowned. "Therein lies the problem, doesn't it?"

Prog-steel parted to reveal an intimate conference room with a small round table. Six chairs ringed the table, and there was one empty space where a chair should have been. The seven spots were for the chief of police and the commissioners of SysPol's six divisions: Argo, Arete, Themis, Panoptics, Hephaestus, and now Gordian, although the latter was so small it rated only a *vice*-commissioner at the moment. The missing chair was because the commissioner of Arete Division was an abstract citizen and didn't need one.

"Chief." Commissioner Jamieson Hawke was the

room's only occupant when they arrived, and he rose to greet them. His muscular synthoid wore the black uniform of Argo, SysPol's patrol fleet division and the closest thing SysGov had to a standing army. Dark eyes stared out from a bald head, and the two gems of his heavily integrated ACs—one an oval ruby, the other a square emerald—glinted above each shoulder.

"Where's Peng?" Lamont asked as he rounded the table toward his chair.

"He sent word he'd be late," Hawke said. "Some mess involving the Mercury Historical Preservation Society."

"Another protest?"

"He didn't say."

The Dyson Realization Project was the largest SysGov initiative ever, slated to convert the planet of Mercury into a solar-collecting megastructure. The project, bolder even than the Alpha Centauri Colonization Initiative, had spent decades in legal purgatory due to its controversial plan to consume Mercury's mass. As a result, tests of the proposed macrotechnology had only recently commenced, and the Society, as its name implied, still sought to maintain the status quo despite their long string of losses in the courts.

"Should we begin without him?" Klaus-Wilhelm asked.

"No." Lamont settled into his chair. "We'll wait."

Klaus-Wilhelm loaded his presentation into the room's infosystem and sat down. Only the heads of divisions that regularly interacted with the Admin—or might be forced to "interact" with them if a shooting war broke out—were invited to this meeting, so it made sense to wait until all of them were present.

In the meantime, he opened his backlog of reports and began reading through them to pass the time.

Nineteen minutes later, Commissioner Peng Fa arrived. His avatar was a slender man in the dark red of Arete Division, SysPol's First Responders. His skin was the black of midnight, and his eyes glowed electric blue.

"Sorry about that!" He smiled at his colleagues and took a seat in the virtual chair that materialized next to him. "Some people just can't stand progress, you know?"

"The Society again?" Lamont asked.

"More like its radical fringe," Peng replied. "Gotta give 'em points for persistence."

"Trouble?"

"Nothing we couldn't handle, Chief. Just some idiot's idea of civil disobedience with a dash of industrial, self-replicating graffiti. *Granted*, it was graffiti designed to eat kilometer-wide letters into the surface of Luna, but we put a stop to it. You can't even tell the first letter was supposed to be an F. We'll be handing the perp over to Panoptics shortly." He glanced around the room. "So, what did I miss?"

"Nothing," Hawke said. "We've been waiting for your sluggish ass to get over here."

"Hey, now." Peng flashed a crooked grin. "If I could increase the speed of light, I would, believe me."

A comfortable camaraderie permeated the room. Klaus-Wilhelm was by far the youngest person present (despite the fact that he'd been born the better part of a thousand years before any of the others). All three of his colleagues had passed their centennial birthdays, and Lamont had recently celebrated his two hundredth. They were also long-standing fixtures in SysPol, though their roles shifted every few decades. Hawke had spent some time in charge of the First Responders, and Peng had once been a vice-commissioner for Hephaestus, SysPol's R&D division.

In comparison to his subordinates, Lamont was the bedrock of SysPol leadership. He'd worked his way up the ranks over the first half of the thirtieth century and had outlasted three presidential administrations in his current post as chief of police.

Klaus-Wilhelm deeply respected the enormous well of experience sitting in the room—how could he not?—but he also recognized the arrogance which infused their discussions. It might be fairer to call it *confidence*, but they'd been so successful for so long, against so many obstacles, that none of them believed they could truly fail. Of course there would be occasional setbacks, but SysPol would always come out on top in the end. That was the way the world was; it was as much a fact as physics or chemistry.

Maybe their level of arrogance—or confidence— was justified. Their track records made fascinating and impressive reading. But *over*confidence was a double-edged sword that could cut deep at the worst possible moment.

God knew Klaus-Wilhelm von Schröder had seen enough of *that*, too!

"I believe we can get started now," Lamont said. "Klaus? Let's hear what you have on recent Admin activity."

"Yes, sir." He stood. "On the surface, the Admin continues to cooperate with us to prevent another Gordian Knot. The DTI still monitors the near-present timeline in their universe, both for information gathering as well as counterterrorism purposes, but their operational procedures have changed to minimize interactions with the past. In fact, they're enforcing the Gordian Protocol more strictly than *we* are. That's the good news."

He brought up the first image. A long, sleek, solidly built craft rotated above the table. Wide, flattened sections extended on either side of its bow, and the unmistakable spike of an impeller protruded from the rear.

"And *this* is the bad news," Klaus-Wilhelm said. "They're busy building bigger and nastier ships. This is the *Hammerhead*-class, which they refer to as a 'heavy assault chronoport.' At a hundred and ninety meters and eleven thousand tons, it's almost sixty percent larger than our standard TTVs."

"Weaponry?" Lamont asked.

"Primary weapons are two high-yield proton lasers and a pair of two-hundred-and-forty-millimeter railguns situated on the forward wings. Two dorsal and ventral seventy-five-millimeter railguns provide point defense, and the space here, along the dorsal midsection, accommodates a complement of ten missiles."

"That's a rather low number compared to the Admin craft we've seen so far," Hawke noted.

"Correct. That's why they may be secondary weapons intended for strikes against softer, civilian targets."

"I see," Lamont said darkly. "Nuclear?"

"We're not sure, but it seems likely."

"What about speed and maneuverability?" Hawke asked.

"We haven't spotted one in flight yet, but we can

make some educated guesses. It has a quad of fusion thrusters here where the hull meets the impeller, plus two more on the wing tips. The size of the impeller suggests a negative five-hundred-fifty-ton mass. Based on all that, we expect the craft will perform similarly to the *Pioneer*-class light chronoports we've encountered before. And speaking of which—"

He brought up his second image. The smaller chronoport resembled a manta ray in overall shape, and the underside of its wide delta wing was loaded with modular weapon pods.

"We don't know what the Admin calls these, so we're referring to them as *Pioneer* refits for now. The DTI has been going through its standing chronoport force, taking some back to the shipyards and upgrading them with heavier armor and more powerful engines. We've also seen some new weapon modules in circulation, especially lasers. And here."

He brought up the third image, which showed what looked like the rear halves of two bulky time machines spliced together so that one impeller faced forward and the other to the rear.

"What the heck *is* that thing?" Peng asked.

"That, gentlemen, is a mobile suppression tower. *Portcullis*-class. The impeller-like mechanism on the bow is actually the suppression antenna. It's a support craft that interferes with the impellers of enemy time machines, locking them down for other craft to destroy. Weapons are mostly defensive, with two seventy-five-millimeter railguns and two point-defense lasers. The hull is *heavily* armored."

He shrank the mobile suppressor and pulled the other two images into a triangle with it over the table.

"Other than that, we've seen numerous signs the Admin is expanding its exotic matter production. That will, in turn, allow it to construct chronoport impellers at a faster rate in the future, though I don't have much in the way of details yet. We've focused our efforts toward keeping an eye on DTI activities, and I only have so many TTVs."

"That's quite all right, Klaus," Lamont said. "You've given us plenty to think about already."

"If you ask me, the Admin's bark is worse than its bite." Hawke waved a dismissive hand. "They can't build transdimensional drives, and their suppression technology, while great at stopping regular time travel, is useless against our transdimensional tech. These ships are impressive, but they're stuck in *their* universe."

"That may be so...for now," Klaus-Wilhelm cautioned. "But we know the DTI is researching how to build transdimensional drives. It's hard to say for certain, but we think they'll crack the problem within the year. Before we contacted them, they didn't even suspect it was possible. Now they know it is, and that represents a huge leg up in any research effort. *And* they're building a fleet capable of using it. Modifying a standard impeller for transdimensional flight is neither difficult nor time-consuming, once you know how it's done. We know. We've gone through the exercise with our entire fleet. It took us about six weeks, and I have no reason to believe the Admin would prove any less competent."

"What about their suppressors?" Lamont asked.

"We're less sure there because it's tech we don't have. That said, we think the same rule applies. Once they know how to build a transdimensional drive, they're one step away from figuring out how to shut it down with a suppressor."

"And let's not forget who we're dealing with here," Peng added. "The Admin doesn't consider ACs to be citizens. Under their laws, *I* wouldn't get to vote because I'm not a real person. And even worse, they *enslave* synthetic ACs! Can you believe that? They'd imprison President Byakko in a heartbeat, just for the crime of existing! We're not dealing with a civilized culture, and we shouldn't assume our way of thinking applies over there."

"But we absolutely creamed them at the Gordian Knot," Hawke pointed out. "One ART TTV versus *eight* of their *Pioneer*-class chronoports, and *Kleio* shot down every last one of them."

"I'd like to remind everyone here that we shouldn't draw too many conclusions from that battle," Klaus-Wilhelm warned. "That was the first time in either universe when multiple time machines engaged each other in combat *while* time traveling. Neither side had a clue what it was doing, and *Kleio*'s pilot was an extraordinarily competent and *veteran* combat pilot. So far as we know, none of the pilots on the other side had a tenth of the experience she did. Indeed, I think it's virtually certain they *didn't*. Who would they have gained it against?"

"A fair point, Klaus," Hawke conceded, "but *we're* the ones with the lessons learned. In contrast, they're still in the dark about how to fight us."

"I think the briefings our diplomatic people put together to convince *this* Admin not to go the route of the *other* Admin have to have given them at least some hints," Klaus-Wilhelm replied. "No, we didn't give them tactical details on *Kleio* or on Agent Schröder's tactics. They do know she took on eight of their chronoports, however, and they've got imagery of at least three of them going down. So they aren't coming at this *completely* blind."

"There's a lot of difference between 'not completely blind' and competent," Hawke replied, and Klaus-Wilhelm nodded.

"There is. And the Admin knows it as well as we do. Obviously, they're working to correct that deficiency. We know their chronoport squadrons have engaged in wargames. Don't assume for a moment that they won't figure out the best way to take down our TTVs in battle as they game out their own possible tactics. In fact, the *Hammerhead*-class indicates they're already considering exactly that."

"How so, Klaus?" Lamont asked.

"The chronoports we faced were primarily missile platforms, which *Kleio's* defensive cannons and greater realspace maneuverability were able to counter over and over again. But these new *Hammerheads* show a swing to heavy energy and kinetic loadouts, which would prove much more effective in a time machine battle. As a response, we've retrofitted meta-armor to all our TTVs. ART never needed it for its missions into earlier eras. For us, however, it's become a rather more . . . pressing issue."

His tone was dry, and the others all nodded in understanding. Meta-armor worked under the same light-bending principles as a metamaterial shroud, except that it was designed for defense against energy-based weaponry rather than stealth. Meta-armor could hold its form under high acceleration, survive extreme thermal conditions, and actually divert laser energy—within limits—under combat conditions, but it didn't make the ship invisible the way the metamaterial shrouds did.

"I see," Lamont said aloud after a moment, then swept his gaze across all three of his commissioners. "And our contingency plans in the event the worst happens?"

"Argo has both counterattack and first-strike missions in the works," Hawke said. "Our plan involves using Gordian's TTVs to transport some of my cruisers to the Admin. There are certain material preparations that need to come first, though."

"What sort of preparations?" Lamont asked.

"We're up against the limit of what a TTV's phase field can do," Hawke said. "They're not designed to expand over a craft that large, so we're constructing exotic matter scaffolds to bracket the cruisers and allow the field lines to conduct better. We've built the first three scaffolds, but we're still working out the kinks."

"Gordian is assisting Argo in adapting the scaffolds," Klaus-Wilhelm said. "But I have significant reservations about the Argo proposal. Any realspace craft, no matter how powerful, is at a disadvantage against time machines."

Hawke leaned forward with a smile that might have been a little condescending.

"But they have to phase-lock with us to do any damage," he pointed out. "And when they do, they're *dead*. Those chronoports may be a danger to your TTVs, but against my cruisers they're nothing but toys."

"You're underestimating the DTI."

"And you underestimate my cruisers. Their chronoports can flit about in the past all they want. The fight will be in the True Present, and that's where *we'll* dominate."

"And if they take advantage of their ability to time-shift while you're shooting at them?" Klaus-Wilhelm's tone was acerbic. "That's precisely what Elzbietá and *Kleio* did whenever the Admin tried to phase-lock with them. Is there a reason their chronoports can't do that while your cruisers are stuck in one timeframe?"

"Avoiding lethargic cannon fire is one thing," Hawke countered, his confidence unshaken. "Dodging my cruisers' capital lasers is something else entirely."

"Perhaps so." Klaus-Wilhelm's tone made it perfectly clear he disagreed, but arguing the point would have been less than productive. "However that may be, I'd also like to point out the secondary effects of that engagement." His expression was grim. "It's what created the Knot, as well as what resolved it, and as you just pointed out, there were only *nine* time machines involved. What do you think would happen if we had scores of chronoports and TTVs phasing in and out on both sides?"

"Gentlemen, *thank* you," Lamont interrupted, then let out a faint sigh and looked at Peng. "And what about the First Responders?"

"Gotta admit, this one's *really* outside the box for us," the AC said. "For one, there's no existing infostructure for us to transmit into. A ground war in the Admin would be completely different from anything we've ever experienced. Or even run simulations on, for that matter. We've made tentative plans based on Agent Philosophus' experiences in the Admin infostructure, but I think it's a safe bet the Admin is taking a hard look at its network security.

"One option we've considered is a 'suicide' infiltration into their systems where our officers do as much damage as possible before they self-delete. It would be volunteers only, and their connectome backups would be activated afterwards, of course." Peng held up a hand. "I know, I know. It's far from ideal. Call it a work in progress."

"All planning aside, we have the advantage," Hawke said. "Our industry is bigger, and our tech is better. If a shooting war breaks out, we're the ones who will come out on top."

"Don't take this so casually." Klaus-Wilhelm fixed Hawke with a fierce glare. "The best thing any of us can do is make sure these plans *never* have to be used. Because if a true transdimensional war breaks out—with time-shattering weapons going off on both sides—the resulting catastrophe could make the Gordian Knot look *benign* by comparison."

CHAPTER NINE

Department of Temporal Investigation
Admin, 2980 CE

"THOSE BLIGHTED IDIOTS PROPOSED *WHAT*?" CSABA Shigeki shouted.

Dahvid Kloss, DTI Under-Director of Espionage, and Katja Hinnerkopf, Under-Director of Technology, winced in unison. Special Agent James "Nox" Noxon stood a few paces from the group, his gray skin and yellow eyes as inexpressive as ever, and never even blinked.

He'd been with Shigeki longer than any of the others, of course.

"Immunizing the entire sixth-century population against the Black Death," Jonas Shigeki repeated matter-of-factly.

"We're dealing with lunatics. I *swear*."

The senior Shigeki put a hand to his forehead and turned away, his long black braid, streaked with silver, swinging out behind him. He took a deep breath, clasped his hands tightly behind his back, and gazed out the monitoring room's wide, wall-height window.

The interior of Hangar Three, deep underneath the DTI tower, was a flurry of activity as drones danced around the partially dissected *Hammerhead* chrono-port. The long main body and flared head remained mostly intact, but the impeller spike had been pulled out and raised high above the craft.

Kloss took off his peaked cap and ran fingers through dark hair that looked as if it had been grazed on by a field animal.

He fitted the cap back on.

"Did the request gain any traction?"

"No," Jonas said. "It looks like that one won't even come to a vote."

"I should hope not!" Shigeki spat. "Good *grief*! SysGov must be full of people who prance through the rain thinking they won't get wet. The Gordian Protocol is *their* law!"

"How's Muntero working out?" Kloss asked.

"About as well as can be expected." Jonas stepped up next to his father. "She's a firecracker, all right."

"There's nothing I can do about her," Shigeki said. "The chief executor insisted on a hardline Restriction-ist for the post."

"Well, he got one." Jonas gave him a lopsided smile. "Still strikes me as an odd choice. Wasn't his campaign all about ushering in a 'kinder and gentler' Admin?"

"True, but the fast and loose way SysGov plays with AIs has a lot of people scared, him included." Shigeki shook his head. "Their elected head of government is an AI, for God's sake! That alone makes Muntero *almost* seem like a good choice!"

"Well, for all the fire and brimstone she brings to the room, she knows which one of us is the expert. She'll defer to me if I want to jump in."

"That's something, at least."

"You said there were two proposals," Hinnerkopf noted. The short, compact woman joined them by the window. "What about the second one?"

"Right. That's where the real problem lies," Jonas said. "They want to take one of their abducted indigenes and return him to the central cord variant they plucked him from. A man by the name of Samuel Pepys, in this case."

Shigeki blinked.

"Who?"

"A prominent British official from the seventeenth century."

"Never heard of him."

"Me neither, until now," Jonas admitted with a shrug.

"I have," Hinnerkopf chimed in. "I read excerpts from his diary a while back."

All three flesh-and-blood men turned to face her, and even Nox stirred slightly.

"What?" she asked. "Why the surprised faces?"

"Sorry," Shigeki said. "It just doesn't sound like something you'd be interested in."

"His diary provides a vivid window into the day-to-day life of that period. Definitely worth your time, if you're interested. Plus it's where I learned fun new slang for female body parts. Pepys had trouble keeping his hands to himself."

"And they want to put this guy back?" Kloss asked.

"That's what ART's proposing," Jonas said.

"Why?"

"Mostly as an experiment to study what will happen."

"Which way do you think Lamont will swing?" Shigeki asked.

"In favor," Jonas said.

"Yanluo's burning hells," Shigeki swore quietly, but with feeling.

"The Living Legend is approaching it more cautiously," his son offered.

"Well, of course he would."

"I suspect he'll come out on ART's side in the end, though. He's uncomfortable with how in-the-dark we all are when it comes to the underlying sciences."

"That's not unreasonable," Hinnerkopf said. "If we can better quantify the danger, we can more easily avoid it in the future. I may not like their readiness to take risks, but as somebody trying to understand this new dimension of chronometric physics, I'm in favor of all the data we can find."

"Which is why I think the Legend will support it."

"Living Legend" was Jonas's nickname for Vice-Commissioner Schröder, and Shigeki could see why he'd chosen it. Schröder might be a man out of history, but he was from the *Admin's* history, not SysGov's, and he had indeed left his mark upon the twentieth century.

First time I ever had to open a history book while researching an opponent, Shigeki mused. *Though, I suppose being the head of the Department of Temporal Investigation requires a certain openness to the unusual and unexpected.*

His mouth tightened at that thought, and he turned back to the window as he remembered the VR briefing Raibert Kaminski had dropped on him and all the Admin at their first meeting. He knew *he* wasn't the Shigeki in the perfect sounds and images SysGov had pulled from Kaminski's memories as part of that briefing. He wasn't the Shigeki who'd chosen to doom sixteen universes in an effort to buy his own thirteen hundred more years of existence. But he understood how *that* Shigeki might have decided to do just that. SysGov's briefing, pulled from Kaminski's memories, from those of his AI "companion," from the data files of the TTV *Kleio*, and from the memories of Elzbietá Abramowski—once she'd acquired SysGov wetware of her own—was as real as being there himself.

The Admin's psychologists and cyberneticists had analyzed every photon of that briefing, and they'd come to the somewhat grudging conclusion that the events it contained had actually happened—actually been experienced—exactly the way they were reported. That didn't mean they were *complete*, however. In fact, the Admin knew they weren't, because critical details of the final, massive temporal dogfight over 1940 Germany had been omitted. But it did mean that what they *had* shared was the truth, so far as they knew it, and in some cases SysGov's efforts to mute or erase emotional overtones had been . . . less than perfect.

Shigeki hadn't enjoyed that briefing. He didn't like knowing that somewhere another Csaba Shigeki and all the people he'd known and loved had ceased to exist. And he didn't like knowing that somewhere that other Csaba Shigeki had put the preservation of his own universe, his own loved ones, over the existence of *sixteen* other universes.

But that wasn't me, *damn it!* he told himself. *It wasn't!*

No, it wasn't. But it could have been. It very well *might* have been, and he didn't like *that* thought very much, either.

But for all his mixed emotions where that briefing was concerned, the thing he hated most about it was that apparently memories could not be saved, not clearly, without the wetware Agent Abramowski—only she was Agent *Schröder* now, of course—had received after the other Admin had mortally wounded her in a restaurant parking lot. That meant that neither Benjamin Schröder's nor Klaus-Wilhelm von Schröder's personal memories had been part of the briefing. Given the elder Schröder's pivotal position as the commander of the new Gordian Division, that left Csaba Shigeki with an itch he couldn't scratch.

He'd pored over every scrap of the impressive historical record about his own universe's *Graf* von Schröder, and the more he'd read, the more impressed he'd been. The man had been a force of nature, unstoppable. Shigeki had yet to find a single major task to which he'd set his hand that hadn't been completed in the end.

Besides the historical literature and documentaries, he'd viewed three old movies featuring the man's life, two decent and one terrible. Unfortunately, all three had been so overly dramatized they'd proved useless as an insight into the man behind the legend, although the battle scenes in *Operation Oz* possessed real grit.

The one thing he was confident of was that making Klaus-Wilhelm von Schröder into an enemy would be . . . poor strategy.

And according to what SysGov tells us, his wife and daughters were all killed during the struggle between Idiot Me and Kaminski and Crew. Wonder-ful. Just wonderful.

"I meet with the chief executor in two hours," he said, turning back to the others. "Hinnerkopf? Any progress to report?"

"Nothing substantial."

"What's taking so long?" Kloss demanded. She gave him a moderately severe glance, and he smiled. "I thought you'd have this problem beat in under a week!"

"Wouldn't that be nice?" Hinnerkopf shook her head. "Unfortunately, the trick to modifying our impellers for transdimensional flight's proven...elusive. I have nine boxed AIs crunching through different models as we speak."

"You're taking the necessary precautions?" Nox asked, speaking up for the first time since he and Jonas had entered the monitoring room.

"Of course," she assured him. "We carefully review any data we provide the AIs, especially anything we're transferring from one to the other."

"I'm sure you do." Shigeki nodded in approval. "So what's the thrust of the problem?"

"Our current impellers work along a simple principle of selective chronoton permeation. By adjusting the permeability, we allow temporal pressure to build up, pushing the craft forward or backward in time. On its surface, transdimensional flight works on a similar principle. However, it represents a new axis upon which we have no empirical data, so we're having to discover the correct vector approach from scratch."

Shigeki bowed his head and pressed both palms against his temples.

"We do know there's, for a lack of a better phrase, a

side-to-side wiggle that chronotons exhibit," Hinnerkopf continued. "This is a known, measurable phenomenon, and our impeller stabilizers are designed to cancel out that wiggle because it's hazardous. You may recall that one of our earliest prototypes was lost to exactly that right-angle pressure. Transdimensional flight appears to use that very pressure to impart motion lateral to the main temporal axis, which means our current impellers are specifically designed to prevent what we need to do. But it's even worse than that. Even if we disable the safety features in the impellers, it's still like going from one axis of motion all the way to *four*. All while blindfolded."

Shigeki exhaled a low, almost—*almost*—inaudible groan.

"Director?" Hinnerkopf tilted her head. "Are you all right?"

"Katja?"

"Yes, Director?"

"For the moment, please imagine I'm nothing more than a dumb bureaucrat."

"Sir, I would never think of you that way."

"Just humor me. Please. For the sake of my sanity." Hinnerkopf sighed.

"All right, sir. If you say so."

"And keep in mind that I need to explain why we're not making progress to the chief executor. So the dumber the better."

"Okay."

She lowered her head, obviously thinking for a long moment, then looked back up.

"Imagine a line," she said.

"A line. Got it."

"The line is our universe."

"Our universe. Got it."

"That's the path of travel our impellers are restricted to. Now imagine a second line that runs parallel to the first. That's SysGov."

"Second line is SysGov. Got it."

"Now picture a third line drawn between the two. That's the path through the transverse their TTVs use."

"Is the third line perpendicular to the other two?"

"Not quite, sir. You see, the difference in True Present coordinates from departure to arrival makes the—"

Shigeki glared at her.

"Yes, Director," she corrected herself with a frown. "It's perpendicular."

"Third line is perpendicular. Got it."

"Figuring out how to travel down that third line is . . . difficult."

"Okay." Shigeki nodded. "So in summary, our impellers can go back and forth but not side to side and we're still trying to establish how to make them do that."

"It's . . ." Hinnerkopf sighed and put on a brave face. "Yes, Director. That's a perfectly good way to describe the situation."

"You sound a little doubtful."

"It's all right. I'll get over it."

"Our problems aren't just technical," Kloss pointed out. "Not by a long shot. This technology allows SysGov to come and go whenever they please. I don't think I need to remind everyone of the intelligence-gathering advantage they have right now."

"Militarily, too," Jonas added in a darker tone. "They can pop in anywhere without warning, fire Restricted weapons with abandon, and then blip away before we get out of bed."

"It's chilling when you think about it," Hinnerkopf said. "Especially since they used just that sort of weapon back in 1940."

Shigeki and his son looked at one another, remembering the vivid images, taken from Kaminski's own memories, as he launched weaponized nanotech against his enemies. If the idiots had screwed up just the tiniest bit, failed to properly program the generational stop, or if the stop had failed and the nanotech had gone right on self-replicating and devouring anything it touched, they could literally have wiped out an entire world.

Of course, they'd done that in the end, anyway, hadn't they?

And fair's fair, Shigeki told himself. *It wasn't their weaponized nanotech to begin with, it was ours. Or made by those idiots on Mars before they got crushed, anyway. And the man was fighting not just for his own universe's life but for the lives of fifteen other universes. In a situation like that, you do what you have to do. Still, Katja's right. It* is *chilling, because it's absolute proof of how far these people are willing to go if they think their backs are against the wall. I may not be the Shigeki who tried to stop Kaminski, but he and his SysGov are damned well the people who used those weapons!*

"All the more reason to push forward with development as aggressively as possible," he said out loud. "I want to avoid a war as much as anyone else, but if a fight does break out, I intend for *us* to win it." He faced Hinnerkopf. "Do you want any additional resources? If you do, now's the time to ask, given who I'm meeting with."

"I believe my team's appropriately staffed and supported. Time is what I need most right now, not more people or equipment."

"Time..." Shigeki mused. "It slips by so fast. You'd think we of all people would have enough of it."

"Actually," Jonas offered, "there may be a way to make SysGov feel safer around us."

"Oh? What's on your mind?"

"Just thinking out loud here, but we all know that, as Dahvid says, SysGov is keeping a close eye on us. That means they know we're building up our chronoport fleet and improving its armament. Hell, they probably know about our wargames! Now, whatever else we may think, they aren't idiots. They know we'd have to be doing this even if we were of a completely peaceful turn of mind, now that we've realized there's a potential threat. But even granting that they understand that up here"—he tapped his temple with an index finger—"understanding it here"—he tapped his chest with the same index finger—"is another matter. So right now, they're worrying about us at least as much as we're worrying about them."

"And your point?" his father asked.

"I'm just thinking that perhaps a change in tactics would benefit us. We know we don't have any real voice on the committee. If SysGov wants to override us, they will. Given that foregone conclusion, what if we approached the matter a little differently?"

"How do you mean?"

"We need time to develop the drive, right?" Jonas grinned. "And we need to avoid antagonizing SysGov, at least until we've closed the tech gap. So, what if we give them exactly what they want from us?"

CHAPTER TEN

ecce

Transtemporal Vehicle *Kleio*
non-congruent

THE *KLEIO* SHOOK, AND THE BULKHEADS GROANED.

"This is as close as I can get us!" Elzbietá shouted. "Phasing in!"

The shuddering subsided, and the view of their surroundings appeared above the command table.

"That's . . ." Raibert breathed.

"Is that . . . T3's Earth?" Benjamin asked.

The remains of a shattered planet lay spread out before them, stretched, thinned, and ripped apart by tidal forces drawing it toward a massive spherical void, black both visually and chronometrically.

"I don't know," Raibert said. "But what else could it be? Philo?"

"It's Earth." Philo's avatar appeared at Raibert's side, his face grim. "There are enough recognizable landmasses left to confirm it. Look, you can see the boot of Italy right there. And that other piece has what's left of New Zealand."

"Then this *is* T3's Earth." Benjamin shook his head. "You're right. It can't be anything else."

"What do you make of that black sphere?" Raibert asked.

"Not sure yet," Philo said. "Whatever it is, though, that's where all the chronotons are going. Other than that, our array is coming back blank."

"Is it a black hole?" Benjamin asked.

"No. If it was, we'd see the gravitons coming off of it. Besides, black holes can't suck one universe into another. This is something else entirely."

Raibert brought up a detailed view from *Kleio's* array. A raging torrent of chronotons poured into the sphere, but inside, their instruments detected nothing.

No space.

No time.

Just an inconceivable, all-consuming emptiness.

An eater of realities.

Synthoid or no, Raibert Kaminski swallowed.

Hard.

"Can we say *anything* about that sphere?" he asked.

"Well *I* can say it's a good thing I stopped when I did," Elzbietá replied. "If I'd kept going, we'd be inside that thing. The sphere's transdimensional coordinates overlap part of T3's outer wall. As far as what that means?" She shrugged.

"Hmm," Philo murmured. "It aligns with the outer wall *and* chronotons are flowing toward it."

"Thoughts on what that means?" Raibert asked.

"Maybe. Could be a breach in the outer wall, allowing chronotons to flow out of this universe."

"Wait a second," Benjamin said. "You mean to tell me that sphere is a *hole* in T3's outer wall?"

"That's one possibility."

"But it's a sphere. Spheres can't be holes."

"Think of it this way," Philo offered. "Is the universe flat like a sheet of paper?"

"No, of course not."

"Then a hole in it isn't going to be flat, either."

"I guess that makes some sense," Benjamin said slowly, his brow creased as he stared at the virtual display.

"Any sign of the *Aion*?" Raibert asked.

"Not so far," Elzbietá said quietly. "I'll keep looking."

Raibert looked at her for a moment, his expression bleak, then nodded.

"All right." He let out a long, slow sigh. "Let's recap what we *do* know. For one, this is no Gordian Knot."

"Definitely not." Philo shook his head. "Everything we see here is consistent with what we witnessed in T4. T3 is undergoing a chronometric implosion, and if I had to guess, that implosive force is what wreaked havoc in T4, too."

"But how?" Raibert asked. "T4's own outer wall should have protected it."

"True. But if T4 was really a child universe of T3, then it's conceivable their outer walls were still touching. That would make T4 *very* susceptible to anything happening in T3. Let's assume for a moment the sphere is a breach in the outer wall. The chronotons leaking out will create what could be considered extreme low-pressure zone in T3. And if the decompression is powerful enough, it's going to suck in anything nearby."

"Including T4," Raibert said. "Hence, all the suckage we saw there."

"Then there really is a second way to kill a universe." Benjamin's eyes were haunted.

"That seems to be the case, Doctor," Philo said.

"Do we have any idea what causes it?"

Raibert glanced expectantly at Philo, but the AC merely shook his head, and Raibert slouched back in his chair.

"Well, shit," he groaned.

"We need to let SysGov know about this," Benjamin said.

"No kidding, Doc! What was your first—"

"Guys!" Elzbietá interrupted. "Hey, guys! I found the *Aion*!"

"Where?" Raibert asked sharply, eyes lighting with sudden hope as he jerked back upright in his chair.

"Right there!"

A beacon pulsed halfway down the tortured remains of Earth-T3.

"The chronoton flow creates a lot of interference, but I'm certain that's an SOS from their telegraph."

"Can you contact them?" Raibert asked tautly.

"I've been broadcasting a basic greeting ever since we got here. If they could hear us, they'd have responded by now."

"It's an SOS," Philo said. "They may be unable to respond."

"In that case, can we pull them out?" Raibert asked.

"That's the tricky part." Elzbietá rubbed her hands together. "It's rough in there. A lot of debris phasing in and out, and they're in deep."

"Can you do it?" Raibert pressed.

Elzbietá expanded the section of the display which contained *Aion*'s beacon. Two continent-sized fragments grated against each other, and rubble spewed outward from the slow, terrible collision. Smaller boulders the size of mountains phased into being, smashed into each other, then disappeared.

"I can do it," she declared.

"Are you sure?" He looked deep into her eyes. "Those are our friends over there. I want them back just as much as you do—probably more; I've known Fritz almost since grade school! But we're not doing this unless you're confident you can pull it off. And not just because I'm worried about our hides. Ben's right—we've *got* to get home to tell SysPol about this."

"I know." Elzbietá looked down at her virtual displays for a long, still moment, then raised her head and looked straight into his eyes once more. "I can navigate that mess," she said, and her voice had hardened into living steel. "I'll get them out, Raibert."

"That's all I needed to hear." Raibert strapped in. "Take us in whenever you're ready."

Elzbietá and Benjamin strapped in as well, and she glanced at the Viking avatar at her elbow.

"Philo, you have the secondary systems." She brought up her virtual controls. "Here goes!"

Kleio surged forward.

"Reinforcing forward armor," Philo said.

"Hang on!" Elzbietá warned. "Things are about to get bumpy."

Tiny pebbles pattered against the hull as a mountain loomed ahead. *Kleio* dipped underneath, and the patter turned into a torrential rain. Rocks phased in and out ahead of them, and Elzbietá adjusted their own phase, finding gaps of safety in the ever-shifting environment.

A series of loud *thunks* echoed through the ship, and Raibert looked up at the overhead urgently.

"Hull holding," Philo said. "Damage negligible."

"We'll get through!" Elzbietá promised through gritted teeth.

A viscous blob of magma came into view ahead, stretching and breaking apart. *Kleio* splashed through a thin section, globules splattering across the bow, and sped toward a city tumbling lazily end over end.

"The *Aion* should be just beyond that city fragment," Philo said.

"Almost there!"

The city had been built around a lake, and the lakebed now formed a path through the rounded debris fragment's center. Elzbietá took them straight through the eye, then slowed on the far side.

"Almost on top of the signal," she said. "Where is it?"

"Found them," Philo said. "It's—"

He didn't finish. Instead, he brought up a visual of the *Aion*.

Or, rather, what was left of it.

A broken section of gunmetal hull spun amidst a smear of twinkling particulate matter. The smashed and ruined piece of debris was just barely enough to house one of the chronoton telegraphs.

There was no sign of the rest of the ship.

CHAPTER ELEVEN

$\infty\infty\infty$

Argus Station
SysGov, 2980 CE

"AMBASSADOR MUNTERO, YOU HAVE THE FLOOR," Lamont said.

"Thank you, Chief Lamont."

Here it comes again, Klaus-Wilhelm groused inwardly as Muntero rose from her chair.

"Thank you for graciously permitting a delay in these proceedings," she said. "Now that Under-Director Shigeki and I have consulted with our government, I am instructed to tell you that the Admin has decided to endorse ART's proposed venture to the seventeenth century with the intent of returning Samuel Pepys to his rightful place in history."

What? Klaus-Wilhelm blinked in bewilderment, and both of Lamont's eyebrows shot up. Lucius and Teodorà stood like statues, obviously astonished by the Admin's sudden change of position, while Pepys, standing between them, smiled in delight.

"I'm sorry," Lamont said. "But did I hear you correctly?"

"You did. Furthermore, the Admin would like to make the following requests, though I will stress these are merely *requests*."

What's their game here? Klaus-Wilhelm wondered.

"And those requests are—?" Lamont asked.

"First, that the Admin be permitted to appoint a passive observer to this return mission or to any others that may follow for the other 'guests' retained by ART. Second, that SysGov provide us with any data collected during this venture, so that both our governments may further our understanding of time travel together. Again, I will stress that these are *only* requests, and SysGov's denial of one or both will not affect our endorsement of this venture. We hope, however, that these requests will be received by your government in the spirit of mutual cooperation in which they are intended."

"I . . . Well, yes." Lamont shook his head and regrouped mentally. "Thank you," he said then. "Those requests sound reasonable to me. Wouldn't you agree, Klaus?"

"Quite reasonable," Klaus-Wilhelm responded neutrally, not taking his eyes off the Admin representatives.

"Does the Ambassador have anything else to add?" Lamont asked.

"Not at this time." Muntero sat down stiffly and shot a quick glance to a lounging Jonas Shigeki, whose eyes were once again half-shut.

"Well, that was . . . unexpected." Lamont cleared his throat. "I suppose we can move straight to the next point, then. Mister Pepys?"

"Yes, sir?" Pepys replied in perfect, if slightly accented, Modern English. He stepped forward as he spoke, removed his hat, and swept a deep, formal bow to the members of the committee. From where Klaus-Wilhelm sat, Teodorà seemed to tense slightly, although Lucius looked perfectly calm.

"Have you been informed in full of Chairman Gwon's and Doctor Beckett's proposal?" Lamont asked him, after he had straightened once more.

"I have, sir." Pepys nodded gravely.

"And do you approve of their intentions?"

"I do." Pepys nodded again. "I hasten to add that I can make no complaint about the courtesy which ART has extended to me during my stay in your time." The words were Modern English, but there was an exotic, almost baroque texture to the word *choices*, and he smiled faintly. "No doubt you will comprehend me when I say that the most fantastical laudanum dream could scarcely have prepared a man of my native time for the wonders of your own. Indeed, in many ways, I shall miss those wonders. Your physicians, especially, have performed miracles in my case, and I shall be eternally grateful for their ministrations. Yet for all its wonders, your time is not my own. If the opportunity to return whence I came, to resume the life that was interrupted, exists, I would most gladly avail myself of it."

"I see. Then do we have your official permission to return you to the seventeenth century?"

"Sir," Pepys placed a hand over his heart and bowed again, more slightly, "you have both my permission and my gratitude, freely given without hesitation."

"Thank you. I believe that will do." Lamont glanced at Klaus-Wilhelm, then at Muntero. "Well, that's that, I suppose. It seems we're finishing early today. If there are no objections, we'll vote on the proposal at hand."

"No objections from the Admin," Muntero said.

Lamont nodded to her, then turned back to his right and arched one eyebrow.

Klaus-Wilhelm hesitated. He felt powerful undercurrents swirling around his ankles, as if he was about to be swept away by events beyond his control, but he couldn't put a finger on *why* he felt that way. Something was going on here. *Something* was out of place.

But what? he wondered, and however hard he looked at it, he couldn't answer his own question.

"None here, either," he said at last.

"In that case, please cast your votes."

A virtual vote tally with columns for YES, NO, and ABSTAIN appeared between Lamont and the representatives from ART. His and Muntero's votes registered almost immediately in the YES column, and after a final moment of internal deliberation and delay, Klaus-Wilhelm sent his own.

"The vote is unanimous," Lamont announced. "The proposal will move forward to the Senate's Temporal Oversight Committee with our recommendation. We should have the results back from the Senate within the week, at which point I will schedule a follow-up meeting with all involved parties. I would like to extend my thanks to the representatives from ART and to the representatives of the Admin for their participation in this—"

Virtual alarms blared into existence next to Lamont and Klaus-Wilhelm with shattering suddenness. They made no actual sound at all, at least not that anyone else could hear, but both SysPol officers winced as if they'd just been bludgeoned as the *virtual* sound, guaranteed to rouse them from the soundest slumber, hammered them through their wetware.

Lamont shook his head, like a man shaking off a left jab, and his eyes narrowed as he muted the audio and skimmed the virtual header text hanging in midair before him.

"Klaus? What the hell is a 'Gordian Division Priority One' alert?" he demanded.

"We're still in the process of implementing our new alarm categories but"—Klaus-Wilhelm's throat tightened—"Priority One is reserved for events similar to the Gordian Knot."

"Surely we don't have *another* of those to deal with?!"

"It's a telegraph from *Kleio*. Let's see what they have to say."

Klaus-Wilhelm expanded the alarm header, and additional text appeared.

Universe-T3 destroyed. Universe-T4 destroyed. Cause unknown. Not a Gordian-type event. TTV Aion destroyed with all hands. TTV Kleio damaged but able to return. ETA seventy-three minutes to SysGov outer wall. Will provide a full report upon our return.

Klaus-Wilhelm shook his head in disbelief. Two out of the four time-traveling societies gone! And so suddenly! The Gordian Knot would have taken over a thousand years to unleash its fury, but these two had been snuffed out in the span of a few *months*!

Jonas put his hand on Muntero's shoulder, and the two of them huddled together, lips not moving.

My God, Klaus-Wilhelm thought, *could this have been us? We think we're doing the right thing. We tell ourselves we're taking the necessary precautions, but are we actually just naive children kicking around a football in a minefield?*

Muntero stood sharply.

"Given this new revelation, the Admin withdraws its support from ART's mission and any future missions of this nature until a full review of *Kleio's* findings can be conducted."

"Sir, I must agree," Klaus-Wilhelm said firmly. "And we need to go beyond that. This changes everything. We need to cancel *all* unnecessary time travel immediately."

"I agree wholeheartedly. This is—" Lamont shook his head, visibly shaken. "I don't even know what to think about this!"

"Wait a second," Teodorà protested. "Let's not be hasty about this. ART has conducted *hundreds* of expeditions with no ill effects on *our* True Present. There's no reason to believe this one will be any different."

"Perhaps the content of the message didn't quite register with you," Klaus-Wilhelm snapped. "Two time-traveling societies—and their entire *universes*—have been *obliterated* and we *do not* know why!"

"But you just voted to approve our mission!"

"Yes, and we're going to have another vote," Lamont told her. "Right *now*."

The tally appeared once more, and all three votes switched almost instantly.

"The ART proposal is rejected unanimously," Lamont announced.

"But—"

"*Thank you*, everyone, for your time, but as you can see, the vice-commissioner and I have some pressing business to attend to."

"May we come along as well?" Jonas asked. "Sounds like this will affect both of us."

Lamont paused for a moment.

"He's right," Klaus-Wilhelm said. "We should share this, no matter what it ends up being."

"All right." Lamont pointed a thumb at the door. "The three of you can join us."

Jonas and the ambassador stood, and their security synthoid stepped away from the wall.

"Please, *wait . . .*" Teodorà's voice was barely a whisper as the room cleared. Lucius put a hand on her shoulder and turned her toward the exit in the others' wake.

In the rush to leave, no one realized the star field in his shadow had vanished.

✧   ✧   ✧

Kleio settled into the docking cradle, and the front ramp extended. Impacts had hammered the TTV's hull in dozens of places, and fresh prog-steel stood out on one side of the bow, plugging what might have been an actual puncture in the armor.

"What happened out there?" Teodorà wondered out loud from her high vantage point in the reception balcony.

"I presume your time craft do not customarily return to harbor in this state?"

"No, Samuel, they don't," Lucius said. "Looks like they've been through hell."

"There's Raibert and his team." Teodorà pointed. "They're coming out now."

"We'll wait here." Lucius sidestepped closer to Pepys. "There's no point in dragging Samuel into this, and my presence might be . . . problematic."

"No kidding!" Teodorà agreed. "I'll see if I can get through to him."

She took a counter-grav tube down two floors and intercepted the Gordian team at the hangar's exit.

"Raibert!"

The big synthoid stopped mid-stride, and his two team members bunched up behind him. It was still disconcerting to see him in such a different body. The small, timid professor now wore the shell of a massive, muscle-bound brute. She wondered why he'd kept the stolen Admin body; he could have replaced it once he'd returned to SysGov. Had he retained it as a memento of his daring escape? A sort of middle finger directed at not just the Admin but anyone else who tried to stop him?

"Teodorà?" he asked. His expression was as grim as she'd ever seen it, but it lightened—slightly, at least—as he recognized her. "What are you doing here?"

"Nice to see you, too." She hurried over to him. "We need to talk."

"I'm sorry, but the chief needs to see us. It's urgent."

"I know. That's what I need to talk to you about."

"You *know*?" he asked incredulously. "How?"

"I was in a meeting with Chief Lamont when your telegraph came in."

"Then you know I have to report *now*." He started to turn away, but she caught him by the sleeve.

"Raibert, please—"

"Teodorà, I just saw what was left of *Aion*," he said harshly. "They're gone—Fritz, Zheng, Hatem, all of them. And there wasn't a damned thing I could do about it. I don't have *time* for this right now."

"Oh, my God," she whispered, her hand tightening

on his sleeve. Fritz Laynton had been *her* friend and colleague, as well, and the news hit hard. But then she shook her head.

"I'm so sorry to hear that," she said with simple, unmistakable sincerity. "Truly I am. But what I need to talk to you about... You remember how much Fritz hated the abductee program?"

"Of course I do. It's why he joined Gordian the day we set up shop!"

"Well, that's what I need to talk to you about—doing something right for the abductees! One minute. That's all I ask. You can give me that, right?"

"I ..." He sighed, then nodded slowly. "Yeah, I guess I can spare you a minute."

"Raibert?" The female member of his team, a young, attractive woman still in her organic body, stepped forward. "Who is this?"

"An old colleague." He waved both of his team-mates on. "You two head in. I'll catch up."

"You sure? We shouldn't keep the chief waiting."

"I won't. Now get going." He shooed them off. "I can take care of myself."

The other two left, albeit reluctantly, and Raibert smiled and waved at them as they boarded the grav tube. Then he turned back to Teodorà.

"So." He rubbed his hands together. "What's this about?"

"I was trying to get approval for a trip to the seventeenth century, and I almost had it when your alert came in and scared the *crap* out of everyone. I need your help to get my expedition back on the approved list."

"This for ART?"

"Of course it is."

"I don't know." His expression soured. "You know how I feel about ART these days."

"This is different. *We're* different. We're trying to make amends, to do some real good out there, and this is going to be the first step of many. But we can't go if SysPol is too terrified to even warm up an impeller spike!"

"You'd be scared, too, if you'd seen what we just went through. Or what was left of *Aion*."

"But we both know ART's trips into the past never caused *temporal* damage to *our* universe," she insisted.

"Well, yeah. Except for the Gordian Knot."

"Oh, come on, Raibert! I've seen the reports. The Knot was caused by a dogfight involving several time machines, and you know it!"

"Eh. Sort of." He grimaced, then shrugged his shoulders. "Cause and effect get a little sticky where the Knot is concerned."

"My point is, it wasn't caused by ART."

"But we don't know that. Not for certain. For all we know, *all* our expeditions contributed to the problem and helped the Knot form."

"Oh, I don't believe this!"

"I'm sorry you feel that way, but we're talking about technology that can destroy entire universes. In fact, we know *three* of them—including the Admin child universe at the center of the Knot—have *already* been destroyed. Under the circumstances, we need to take things slow. When it's possible to make mistakes on *that* scale, caution should rule the day."

"No, Raibert. You don't understand!" She reached up to put her hands on his shoulders, and her eyes were suddenly a window to all the guilt in her soul. "I *need* this. My hands are soaked with blood, and I have to make things right. I have to! I've yearned for a way to atone for my sins, and I've finally found it! It's within my reach—so close I can almost *touch* it—but now it's slipping away, and I need your help to bring it back."

"You could always donate your time to a charity."

"*Raibert!*" she snapped. "Don't fucking *joke* about this! I'm being serious here!"

"So am I. Look, I'm glad to hear you want to make amends. I really am. But it's just too dangerous."

"Damn it, Raibert," she cried, tears sliding down her cheeks. "You're one of the reasons my life is a shambles right now. Can't you do this one thing for me?"

"Hey, now." He reached up and wiped one thumb tenderly across her cheek. "You know I never meant to hurt you. It was Lucius and his cronies I was after. You were just..." He paused, unable to find the words.

"Collateral damage?" she offered bitterly.

"Something like that, yeah," he acknowledged.

"*Please*, Raibert. I need this."

"I'm sorry. I really am. But my answer is no."

Her head drooped, and then, slowly, she nodded.

"I understand," she whispered.

"Thank you. Now, if you'll excuse me"—he removed her hands from his shoulders, gently but firmly—"I need to see my boss."

He left her alone at the hangar entrance, and she stayed there for long minutes, like a statue, with her head hanging. Finally, she put her hand to her eyes and let out a long shuddering breath.

"*Damn* it," she breathed, then composed herself as well as she could and took the tube back up to the reception balcony.

"How'd it go?" Lucius asked as she floated in.

"It *didn't*," she fumed, fists planted on her hips. "As expected."

He pressed a hand against the wall, and the local infrastructure shut down.

"What are you doing?" she asked.

"Just deploying a little program Shadow wrote for me. We can talk privately now." Lucius gestured the other two closer and spoke in a hushed tone. "Let's be realistic here. SysPol's going to clamp down on time travel even harder after what just happened. The Gordian Division's star team threw up a red flag, and their leadership is going to listen. We may never get approval, and even if we did at some point in the future, there'd be so much scrutiny and oversight that realizing our true objectives would be impossible."

"I think you're right," Teodorà agreed sadly. "We all saw their faces when that alert came in. They're terrified."

"Ah, well," Pepys sighed. "'Twould have been a brave, exciting venture, but Fate respects neither kings nor commons." He smiled crookedly. "And, truth be told, there are places far worse than here where a castaway might come to rest."

"Oh, don't give up hope just yet." Lucius flashed a disarming smile. "After all, look where we are."

"What?" Teodorà's forehead creased in puzzlement. "You mean on Argus Station?"

"Precisely."

"I'm sorry. I'm not following you."

"Everything we need is right here, ready for the taking. All we need is the courage to seize it."

"Wait a second." Teodorà goggled at him. "You mean *steal* a TTV?"

"Theirs?" Pepys pointed out the window at the *Kleio*.

"Oh, no. Not *that* one," Lucius said dismissively. "Let's pick a fresh one."

"Lucius, how can you even *suggest* something like this?!" Teodorà shouted.

"Shhhh," Lucius urged. "Calm down. It's not as radical as you think."

"I beg to differ!"

"This is the only window we have. If we don't do this now—*right* now—there won't be another opportunity. We'll be back on Earth with no way to get a TTV outside the committee. It's now or never."

"'Tis true that Fortune favors the brave—or the bold," Pepys said, dark eyes gleaming, and Teodorà glared at him.

"Oh, great! Not you, too!"

"Teodorà." Pepys took her hand gently, his fingers and palm warm around hers. "Recall what brought us here."

"I know. It's just—"

"We hold the power to cure the plague," he told her earnestly. "Conceive what that means. Millions of lives that need not be snuffed like so many candles. Lives given back, given time and sun to blossom. Is it right—is it *just*—for craven heart, and that in others, not in us, to stay so glorious a cause?"

"I . . ."

"He's right," Lucius pressed. "Everyone else is too scared to take the leap. I say we force their hand. We show them how safe it is, prove to them the good that can be achieved. This could be the first of many opportunities to make amends for ART's sins—for *our* sins—but only if the three of us have the courage to see it through."

Teodorà looked back and forth between them, her eyes wet with tears of hope, fear, confusion...longing.

"In the end, it's your call," Lucius said gently. "We're not doing this without you."

She closed her eyes as the countless ways this could go wrong flashed through her mind. But in the end, she knew what she wanted, how *desperately* she yearned to wash her stained hands clean. And surely giving millions of people the chance to live their lives free of the plague would accomplish that goal.

She opened her eyes at last, and they met the others' gaze with fresh strength.

"I'm in."

"I knew you'd come around." Lucius gave her a half smile and squeezed her shoulder briefly. Then he squared his shoulders. "Both of you, follow me."

He led the way down the grav tube. Teodorà copied his destination, took Pepys by the hand, and stepped in. Pepys twitched violently—he was still unaccustomed to the sensation of freefall—but the counter-grav system cushioned them down, and then across a long, gentle arc until it deposited them before another hangar, nearly identical to the one that held the *Kleio*.

"We can't just walk right in and take it," Teodorà protested.

"Why not?" Lucius winked at her and strode up the TTV's ramp. Heavy crates lined both sides of the narrow path down the middle, packed all the way to the overhead. Pepys followed Lucius, and Teodorà huffed out a breath and joined them. The ramp retracted, and prog-steel sealed the opening.

"How're we doing, Shadow?" Lucius asked.

"Very well, Master Gwon," his integrated companion replied in a calm, masculine tenor. "Though I must confess it is a little disorienting being separated from you."

"Same here, Shadow. What's our situation?"

"I have deleted the TTV's attendant program and removed all Gordian Protocol restrictors from its systems. I am now in complete control of the vessel."

"Magnificent!"

"Furthermore, as you can see around you, I have manipulated Argus' logistics attendants into providing us with the necessary raw materials for fabricating the cure, as well as the conveyors and remotes for its dispersal."

"How is all this here?" Teodorà asked. "They should have taken *hours* to prep."

"Fifty-five minutes, actually," Shadow corrected.

"Fifty-five *minutes*?" she repeated incredulously, and Lucius smiled at her.

"I did mention that I still had contacts in the other ministries, didn't I?" He shrugged. "Everything we needed was in the logistics database days ago, and the long-lead items were already printed. All Shadow had to do was print the crates, get them packed, and then loaded aboard."

"But we only just decided to do this!"

"Oh, I knew you'd say yes. Shadow started prepping before we left the meeting."

Lucius winked at her again and hurried onto the bridge without waiting for her response.

Teodorà shook her head, not sure what to think. She and Pepys followed him up the grav tube at the far end of the TTV cargo bay, then down the corridor to the bridge. The walls sparkled with shifting star fields.

"I hope you don't mind, Master Gwon," Shadow said, "but I have rechristened the craft the *Shadow*."

"I like it! Any reason we can't leave right now?"

"All preparations are complete. We may depart at any time."

Lucius rounded the command table and faced the other two expectantly across it.

"Well?"

"Time and tide wait for no man," Pepys replied. "The sooner we depart, the sooner we may begin our task."

Lucius nodded approvingly to him, then looked at Teodorà. She hesitated for two or three more heartbeats, then nodded, and he smiled in satisfaction.

"Shadow, take us out!"

"Yes, Master Gwon."

The hangar opened, and the *Shadow* lifted out of its docking cradle.

Teodorà put her hands on the command table and stared sightlessly down at its surface.

We're doing this, she thought. *We're really doing this! No turning back now.*

Apprehension built within her like a snowball, gaining bulk as it rolled downhill. But then Pepys put a hand atop hers, and she looked over at his round, open face and warm smile. Somehow, just that small expression of confidence and solidarity was enough to soothe her nerves.

"Here we go," she said, giving him a halfhearted smile.

"Indeed," he answered. "I have long anticipated this moment, Teodorà!"

Lucius pulled up a view of Argus Station above the table. The station was a gargantuan cylinder, its police-blue hull shining with reflected sunlight. The *Shadow* was a tiny speck moving steadily away from its southern pole.

"SysPol has realized something is wrong," Shadow reported. "Our departure authorization is being requested, and two TTVs are powering up."

"Then let's not overstay our welcome. Get us out of here—phase out!"

"490 CE designation confirmed. Phase-out in three... two... one... jump."

The *Shadow* shifted out of phase with the True Present and sped into the past at a rate of seventy thousand relative seconds for each absolute second that passed in the True Present.

"Telegraph traffic detected," Shadow said. "Message encoded. I suspect a TTV in the near present is being contacted."

"Can you see where it is?"

"Searching."

Lucius pushed the external view aside and expanded their scope chart.

"Searching... found it. TTV at negative two months and closing rapidly. It is on an intercept course."

A cloud of possible locations formed, representing the SysPol TTV's estimated physical location.

"Can you evade?"

"Negative. They will be able to phase-lock with us."

"Arm the weapons. Prepare to fire."

"*Lucius!*"

"I know, Teodorà." He gave her a brief, reassuring smile and held up a hand. "Shadow, we'll forego the main gun. Target their impeller only. We're trying to slip away, not kill anyone."

"Understood, Master Gwon. Defensive weaponry online."

Status displays for two 45-millimeter and two 12-millimeter Gatling gun pods appeared over the table.

"Phase-lock imminent."

The SysPol TTV materialized half a kilometer off their starboard quarter, its long, gunmetal ellipse tailed by the impeller spike.

"We are being ordered to shut down our impeller."

"Ignore them. Get us in closer."

The *Shadow* turned toward the other TTV. Pods moved across the prog-steel hull so that all four weapons could be brought to bear as the range sped downward, and the other craft turned to face them.

"Their weapon pods are opening, Master Gwon."

"Fire!" Lucius barked.

The TTVs passed one another on reciprocal courses, and as their paths crossed, four streams of projectiles vomited from the *Shadow*'s weapon pods at a combined rate of over two hundred thirty per *second*. A tsunami of high-explosive armor-piercing rounds savaged the SysPol TTV's impeller, and its edges wavered like an image viewed through turbulent water.

The craft vanished, and hundreds of rounds flew through empty space.

"The TTV is no longer phase-locked with us. Its

speed is dropping. Now at sixty kilofactors. Fifty. Forty. I believe their impeller is damaged and they are unable to pursue us. I do not detect any other TTVs upstream of our position."

"Good work, Shadow." Lucius grinned and crossed his arms. "*Very* good work."

❖   ❖   ❖

"I don't believe this." Raibert stared flabbergasted at the telegraph from the damaged TTV *Tenjin*. He and his team had been in the middle of presenting their report to the Temporal Review Subcommittee when the alert came in. "I was just there with her. I was just *talking* to her. How could she *do* something like this?"

The display showed the stolen TTV's position at negative three years from the True Present, along with two blips holding steady two years behind it.

"Sir." Klaus-Wilhelm turned to Lamont. "I have two TTVs in pursuit, but the fugitives are as fast as we are. There's no way we can catch them. Even worse, at maximum speed our TTVs' onboard arrays are half blind. We'll lose track of the fugitives once they get beyond range of the static array here on Argus, and the pursuing TTVs won't be able to see them either. They could press on directly to their objective, or go to ground somewhere else, phasing into the past and letting our pursuers shoot right on by, none the wiser."

"Which means it's all but impossible for us to stop them." Lamont glared at the plot. "How did they ever manage to commandeer a TTV in the first place?"

"It's too early to say for certain." The vice-commissioner's jaw tightened in obvious frustration at what had just happened on his turf. "Whatever it was cut through all our security protocols, as well as taking out the attendant onboard the TTV itself. I've already requested support from Themis Division to scrutinize the hangar and its surrounding infrastructure. We'll find whatever cracks they used and plug them, I guarantee it, sir."

"I trust you will." Lamont rubbed his chin. "Is there *anything* we can do to prevent them from dropping off Pepys?"

"Actually, sir, I think we're dealing with a far worse problem."

"That's not what I want to hear, Klaus."

"I realize that. But look at their actions so far. They're too extreme. Why steal a TTV and shoot up another one just to return one abductee to the past? The alternative would be that he would be forced to 'suffer' the luxurious comfort of the thirtieth century for the rest of his days. Where's the motive for them to steal the TTV and risk the death sentence for violating the Gordian Protocol?"

"Hmm." Lamont rubbed his chin again. "I see your point. But if they're not returning Pepys to the past, what *are* they after?"

"I don't know for certain," Klaus-Wilhelm said. "However, I strongly suspect this notion of returning abductees was nothing more than a front. The TTV was their real objective all along."

"But that doesn't make sense," Raibert interjected. "Sirs, I spoke with Teodorà just before I came up here. She asked me—almost *begged* me—to convince you to support her. She's genuinely remorseful for what ART's done. She wants to atone, and I'm certain she believes her proposal will allow her to do that."

"Atone?" Klaus-Wilhelm tilted his head, eyes narrow. "That sounds more in line with their Black Death idea than anything else."

"Yes, it does," Lamont murmured.

"I'm sorry—what?" Raibert blinked. "Where's the Black Death come into all of this? Did I miss something?"

"You did," Lamont said. "Chairman Gwon and Doctor Beckett originally proposed deliberately creating a child universe by curing the Black Death."

"They *what*?" Raibert blurted.

"We had a similar reaction," Klaus-Wilhelm said dryly.

"Could that be it, though?" Lamont speculated.

"It's impossible to say." Klaus-Wilhelm shrugged. "But given the situation, we have to assume the worst, which would make their target Constantinople in 490 CE."

"If they really are trying to create another universe, we *need* to stop them!" Raibert said. "Sirs, I know I was interrupted in the middle of my report, but I think I got the gist across. Two universes just imploded, and we're pretty sure that one of them spawned off the other. We need to prevent *anything* that could cause the timeline to branch until we understand what happened over at T3 and T4!"

"I agree completely," Lamont said. "But what *can* we do?"

He looked at Klaus-Wilhelm, who shook his head.

"I'm at a loss, as well, sir," he admitted.

"Ah-*hem*."

The three SysPol officers twitched, then turned back to the conference room table to find Jonas Shigeki leaning back in his chair with his fingers knitted in his lap.

"Gentlemen," he said with something suspiciously like a smile, "may I point something out to you?"

"Of course, Under-Director," Lamont said cautiously. "Go right ahead."

"Thank you." Jonas nodded to Klaus-Wilhelm. "A question for the vice-commissioner, first. Your Gordian Division TTVs max out at seventy kilofactors, correct?"

"Yes, that's right."

"Are there any TTVs faster than that?"

"I don't believe so. There aren't any in Gordian Division, at least. I know that. Are there any *outside* Gordian that would be faster, Raibert?"

"Well, there's the *Deep History Probe*," Raibert said with a shrug. "And the *Deeper History Probe*. They're both faster, but using them wouldn't work here."

"Why not?" Klaus-Wilhelm asked.

"They're too un-maneuverable. They each use those awful-as-hell nine-impeller arrays that take *forever* to get up to speed *and* to slow down. Sure, they could catch up to the fugitives, but they'd probably shoot right past them. A regular TTV could fly circles around them, both physically and temporally. They'd never get into phase-lock, and even if they did, they're pure research vessels. They're completely unarmed."

Jonas leaned forward in his chair and laid one hand on the conference table.

"Then permit me to run a theoretical scenario by you."

The chart above the table updated as he loaded data from his Personal Implant Network. A waypoint appeared in 490 CE, with four lines heading from the True Present toward it. One shone red for the fugitive TTV, two were gray green for the Gordian Division, and the final line—

—glowed in vibrant Admin Peacekeeper blue.

"Assuming you've guessed their intentions correctly," he said, "it will take the fugitives thirteen days to reach their target. Your TTVs are unable to overtake them before they arrive. However, *our* chronoports can travel at ninety-five kilofactors. That means a chronoport could leave the True Present three days from now and still intercept the fugitives in time."

"Now wait just a minute!" Raibert protested.

"Please." Jonas held up his hands. "I speak only of hypotheticals. Obviously, there are no chronoports here in SysGov, and we lack the transdimensional tech necessary to come here. I only wish to point out that if we *did* have that tech, we would be able to come to your aid in this crisis." He sighed and shook his head sadly. "It's a shame, really. Especially since one of our new *Hammerhead*-class chronoports would be perfect for this mission. One, alone, should present more than enough intimidation factor to make the fugitives listen to reason."

"Under-Director." Lamont licked his lips. "Am I correct in assuming—"

"Well, now!" Jonas stood. "Ambassador Muntero, why don't we give our friends from SysGov some space? I'm sure they have *plenty* to talk about in private. We'd only be in the way."

"A good idea, Under-Director. What did you have in mind?"

"I thought we'd make our way to the executive canteen. My stomach's grumbling, and the head chef is doing Chinese today. I don't know what it is, but Chinese food always tastes better over here. I wonder why?"

"I am a bit peckish, now that I think about it."

"Nox, you coming with us?"

"I'm not hungry."

"Oh, come on. You're a synthoid. You're *never* hungry. Suck it up and join us. Otherwise, we'll miss your cheerful personality."

Muntero snorted a laugh, and Jonas waved her out the door, then followed her with a final smile for their hosts. The synthoid gave the SysPol officers a last, yellow-eyed look, then followed both of his superiors.

Raibert and the others watched in stunned silence as the Admin reps left. When the door sealed shut, he looked to Lamont, then to Klaus-Wilhelm.

"We're not actually going to do something this stupid," he said. "Are we?"

Klaus-Wilhelm and Lamont turned to face each other. It was impossible to say which man's expression was more unhappy. Then, after a moment, they turned back to Raibert.

"*Are* we?"

CHAPTER TWELVE

〰〰〰

Department of Temporal Investigation
Admin, 2980 CE

"I CAN'T BELIEVE WE'RE DOING THIS," RAIBERT moaned.

"Chin up, Agent Kaminski. It's not that bad."

Raibert shot the short synthoid a fuming, sideways glance. Andover-Chen wore his Gordian uniform proudly, and the tiniest hint of bluish mathematical equations danced beneath his black, glassy skin. He returned Raibert's glare with a lopsided smile.

"You don't know the Admin like I do," Raibert growled.

"Yes, I'll grant you that. But I have to say that, so far, I rather like them."

"Uh. *You* would."

Matthew Andover and Chen Wang-shu had been two of SysGov's most brilliant—if somewhat eccentric— physicists, and also the two most prominent critics of the Antiquities Rescue Trust, denouncing its reckless use of time travel long before Raibert and Philo made their splashy debut by exposing ART's shadier practices. They were also two of the first hires Klaus-Wilhelm had made when he received authorization to form the Gordian Division. The two men had ended up getting along so well they decided to take their relationship to the next step and fully integrate.

"It's good to see people who take time travel and its dangers seriously," Andover-Chen said.

"Oh, sure. They're a wonderful bunch!" Raibert mocked. "You just have to ignore their military expansionism and the AI slavery. We can't even let Philo off the ship for fear the DTI will flip their collective lid. And don't get me started on their *ghastly* prison system. You ever spend time in an Admin prison?"

"Can't say I have."

"Then here's a tip. *Don't* piss them off while we're here."

"They're just going through some growing pains," Andover-Chen said. "We had our own rocky transition into the post-scarcity era, and they're no different."

"Growing pains?" Raibert blurted. "They sucked out my connectome and puréed my body!"

"You *do* know this isn't the same Admin? Not *exactly*."

"Whatever." Raibert shook his head and walked up to the monitoring room's window. DTI Hangar Three buzzed with activity as drones swarmed over *Hammerhead-Prime* and its dislodged impeller.

Given the location, Raibert and Andover-Chen weren't speaking Modern English, either the SysGov or Admin variety, nor any historical language. They were using SysPol security chat, which to anyone not using a decoder made the conversation sound like "Hot dog caresses cathedral uphill gently. Thirteen squared."

If the Admin was listening—and Raibert was damn sure they were—all they'd hear was gibberish.

Good luck trying to break our codes, you fascist assholes.

"We shouldn't be doing this," he said flatly.

"Why not?" Andover-Chen asked.

"Because it's the fucking *Admin*, that's why! I can't believe Schröder and Lamont got the President to sign off on this!"

"Oh, come on. You're the one who brought in the evidence. Not one but two universes going *kerblam* in our neighborhood? That makes people...nervous."

"They didn't go 'kerblam.' Implosion, not *ex*plosion, remember?"

"I know. It's just a really fun word to say. Ker-*BLAM*!" Andover-Chen spread his arms theatrically. "Who would've thought a whole universe could do that so quickly."

"But we're just *giving* the Admin transdimensional tech!"

"*Pffft!*" Andover-Chen dismissed. "They were going to develop it on their own, anyway. What was our last estimate?"

"A year. Two at the most."

"See? And this way we're cooperating, helping to build a bridge between our two peoples. That's important too."

"Yeah. Really important. Right up until they sneak across it and stab us in the back."

Raibert pressed his forearm against the glass and leaned against it. A formation of four airborne drones removed a thin, rectangular section from the impeller while a separate group maneuvered a nearly identical piece of exotic matter into position.

"You think we're going to make the three-day deadline?"

"It's going to be tight, but I think we'll squeak by," Andover-Chen said. "Mostly because Hinnerkopf knows her stuff. She already had a lot of the baseline theory figured out by the time we arrived, and she has a superb team to back her up. In fact, I think they would've cracked this on their own well short of our estimates. The real limit is their god-awful exotic matter printers."

"Poor quality?"

"No, they're good. Not as precise as ours, mind you, but decent enough. Just *slow*."

"*Zhù hào yún*." Raibert's tones implied "we need all the luck we can get."

"*Zhù hǎo yǔn*," Andover-Chen agreed, though with less aggressive tones.

"Couldn't we use our own printers back home to help?"

"We should avoid that unless there's no other option." Andover-Chen frowned. "Transporting non-inert matter through time is always tricky. Add a flight through the transverse on top of that, and we're looking at an accident waiting to happen. Plus, their impellers work under a different principle, so any number of things could go wrong if *we* tried to fabricate parts for something *they're* the experts on."

A side door split open, and Jonas Shigeki walked in. He was followed by two Peacekeepers, one of them a dark-skinned man so tall he had to duck under the malmetal lip. Even then his peaked cap brushed it.

"Doctor Andover-Chen?" Jonah said. "Director Hinnerkopf would like to see you when you have a moment. She has some questions for you."

"Certainly," Andover-Chen replied in the Admin's version of Modern English. "I'll head right over." He hurried through the door and malmetal sealed shut behind him.

"Agent Kaminski." Jonas gestured to the tall Peacekeeper. "This is Captain Kofo Okunnu. He'll be in command of *Hammerhead-Prime* when we depart."

Okunnu removed his cap, fitted it under an armpit, and extended his hand.

"Sir," he said crisply. "A pleasure to make your acquaintance."

"Likewise," Raibert lied as Okunnu shook his hand firmly.

"And this gentleman here is Superintendent Park Sung-Wook. He and several engineers from his top Suppression team have been brought in to support Hinnerkopf with the impeller modifications."

"Agent." Sung-Wook held out his hand with a smile. "You can expect nothing but the best from my team."

"I'm sure I can." Raibert smiled back—not without effort—and shook the man's hand.

"Been looking forward to putting another new class through its paces." Okunnu gazed out at the chronoport. "Though I wasn't expecting something like *this* for its first mission."

"You've trialed other prototypes in the past?" Raibert asked.

"Indeed I have. Every one of them, actually."

"Oh." Raibert regarded the other man more seriously. "That's rather impressive."

"It's something of a tradition here at the DTI," Jonas said. "Okunnu was one of the earliest test pilots back when the DTI was little more than a glimmer in my dad's eye."

"And before that, I was one of Director Hinnerkopf's students at the university."

"Small world, huh?" Raibert said.

"Quite." Okunnu smiled slightly. "It always surprises me. For as many people as there are in the Admin, I seem to keep running into the same faces in this field."

"With a record like that," Sung-Wook said, "you'd think he wouldn't mind sharing a prototype or two with the rest of us."

"Be careful what you wish for," Jonas said with a half smile. "We have a *lot* of new ships coming online over the next few months."

"Suits me fine," Sung-Wook said. "I've already applied for a transfer."

"I know," Jonas said. "Who do you think has to approve it?"

He smiled at Sung-Wook more broadly, then turned back to Raibert.

"Anyway, Agent, I brought these two over here so we can discuss the mission before we leave."

"You sure it'll be ready in time?" Raibert pointed a thumb out the window.

"Absolutely," Sung-Wook said confidently. "No one in the Admin knows impellers like Director Hinnerkopf, and my engineers are no slouches either. We'll make it happen."

"I'm more concerned about what happens when we catch up to the fugitives," Okunnu said.

"Since *Hammerhead-Prime* is an Admin vessel, we'll

be in operational command," Jonas said. "However, the TTV is your property and the fugitives are citizens of your government. We should take every reasonable measure to avoid unwanted bloodshed."

"Yes, let's," Raibert agreed.

"What are your thoughts on how we should approach this?" Jonas asked. "It's my understanding two of them are former colleagues of yours."

"They're—"

Raibert grimaced in frustration—at himself, for not listening to Teodorà when he'd had the chance. Yes, he'd been in a hurry, and yes, their relationship mostly involved angry emails nowadays. But he'd loved her once, and deep down he still cared for her. She'd reached out to him back on Argus Station, tried to tell him something.

And he hadn't listened.

Even now, if he could just talk with her, get her to open up, then maybe he could reach out and pull her back from the precipice.

Lucius, though, was another matter entirely. Raibert didn't trust him *at all*, nor did he believe in the bastard's born-again remorse for what he'd done. Hell, what he'd *been*. The old maxim about a leopard and spots came to mind whenever Raibert thought about him. But try as he might, this time he couldn't figure out what that sick, perverted murder-junkie expected to gain out of all this.

"I think the best course of action—the first approach, at least—is to talk to them," he said at last. "Get them to come back willingly."

"That may be a problem," Jonas observed. "Violations of your Gordian Protocol carry the death penalty, I believe."

"That's the *maximum* penalty," Raibert corrected. "It's not automatic. If they turned themselves in without a fight, I doubt they'd get a sentence that severe. They'd probably receive life with the possibility of parole after the first twenty years."

"That may be true," Okunnu said. "But they may still feel their backs are up against the wall, and that could make them desperate and unpredictable."

"I hope it doesn't. If it *does*"—Raibert sighed— "I'm afraid the resolution of this mess will be out of my hands."

"Understood." Jonas nodded. "As I say, nobody wants bloodshed if it can be avoided. If they don't return voluntarily, though, we'll do our part."

"We can try to disable their craft," Okunnu said. "But in a shooting engagement, anything is possible."

"I know," Raibert replied softly. He gazed out at the heavily armed time machine below them. "Just give me a *shot* at talking them down first. That's all I ask."

✧   ✧   ✧

The *Shadow*'s printers hummed with activity as small, spherical remotes latched onto bins full of completed cure vials and carried them into the cargo bay.

"Everything is going smoothly," Lucius said, smiling confidently as he walked down the row of towering printers with Teodorà. "We should have half the cure ready by the time we arrive."

"Mm-hmm," Teodorà murmured.

"You nervous?"

"Of course I am." She rubbed her hands together. "What if we're still being followed?"

"It doesn't matter. If there are TTVs behind us, they can't see us, just like we can't see them. Not until we slow down. We'll reach the fifth century first, and once we go to ground, they'll have no way to track us. We can launch the drones from anywhere in the world. No one will ever find us in time."

"I guess you're right."

He lifted her chin with a gentle hand.

"You okay?"

"I don't know," she admitted. "Lying to SysPol was one thing. Stealing the TTV?" She shook her head. "It's a lot worse."

"No, they're exactly the same," Lucius disagreed. "Whatever it takes to achieve our goals. *That's* what we've done."

"But we're criminals, Lucius. Doesn't that bother you?"

"Not really." He leaned back against a printer and crossed his arms. "We broke the law as soon as we lied to the committee."

"I know. I just..."

Her voice trailed off and she shook her head, then looked down at a bin of vials, its contents warm from the printer. She crouched down and pulled out a pressurized cylinder with both hands.

"It's going to be worth it," Lucius said. "I believe that, and you do, too. You're just having second thoughts."

"I know." She turned the cylinder in her hands, then slotted it back into place. "I do believe. I guess it didn't seem real until we were on our way. It's a beautiful thing we're trying to achieve here."

"It is," Lucius agreed. "And once it's done, *everyone* will be able to see that just as clearly as we do."

"Yeah." Teodorà sighed and stood up.

"Come on, Samuel should be almost finished. We can be there when he wakes up."

"All right."

They took a counter-grav tube to an upper level and walked to the medical bay. Samuel Pepys lay in the recovery casket, looking very different without his wig. Thinning wisps of gray scattered haphazardly from his balding scalp.

"Procedure's complete," Lucius said, checking the status chart. "No problems to report. He's sleeping peacefully at the moment, so we'll need to wait until he wakes up."

"Oh, I think I can wake him." Teodorà leaned down until her lips were a breath from his ear. "Oh, *Sam*-uel," she whispered in a sultry tone. "There's a gorgeous woman here to see you."

"Mrph-hrmm-wha—"

His eyelids twitched. His nose did the same, and he let out a long exhale. He reached up, rubbed his face, and opened his eyes.

"I fear I must have dozed off." He blinked and wiped the sleep out of his eyes. "When does this begin?" He knocked on the side of the casket.

"It's already done," Lucius said.

"I beg pardon? It cannot have—"

Pepys broke off and his eyes widened in astonishment. Teodorà watched his expression and chuckled softly.

"I took the liberty of preloading your wetware with Modern English translation software," she explained. "You've done a marvelous job of learning to speak it without neural computer support, but I decided I should ... finish your education. I have to say, I think I already hear an improvement in your accent."

"You mean," Samuel sat up, "that those little metal contraptions are inside my head now?"

"They're organic machines, not metal. But, yes. They're in your head."

"Indeed? I confess that I *feel* no different." He glanced at the medical chart. "Hm? What's this?" The chart flipped around and brought itself level with his head. "My word! That was clever of it."

"You did that."

"I did?"

He frowned at the chart and poked it with a finger. The report cycled to the next page.

"Oh?" He looked around the room, spotted an environmental readout flush against the wall, and reached toward it. The readout flew to his hand and expanded into an array of four detailed charts. "'Pon my word!" he exclaimed in Old English.

"Glad you like it!" Teodorà laughed.

"Oh, I believe you might say that." He looked down at the readout. "So these are the invisible documents you employ. I had not imagined they were so responsive! And that they change so readily at need! Small wonder you prefer them so to ordinary pen and paper."

"You can also talk to the ship now," Lucius said.

"Indeed?" Pepys sat a little straighter. "In that case, I shall essay it." He cleared his throat and sucked in a deep breath. "Hello, Shadow! Can you hear me?"

Teodorà winced and dialed down the sensitivity of her synthoid's hearing.

"I hear you loud and clear, Mister Pepys."

"Shadow?" Samuel turned his head this way and that. "I hear you, as well," he said, still loudly. "Yet it comes from all directions and from none!"

"Your wetware overlays my voice on top of your normal sense of hearing, Mister Pepys. And there's no need to shout."

"Yes, please stop," Teodorà agreed.

"Well, this is remarkable." Pepys beamed, grinning broadly. "Truly remarkable."

"If you think the temperature readout's great"— Lucius pointed at the display still floating obediently above his hand—"you haven't seen anything yet. Come over to the bridge. It's a bit livelier when you can see all the virtual displays."

❖   ❖   ❖

"Here we go," Raibert groaned as he walked up the boarding tunnel, duffel bag across his shoulder. *Hammerhead-Prime*'s hull split open at the far end of the tunnel, giving them access to its interior.

"You say that like it's a bad thing," Andover-Chen observed with something suspiciously like a snicker.

"Because it is. We're going to be stuck in this thing for the next three weeks at least. You're integrated. The two of you get to hang out in the same body, but not me and Philo! *He* has to stay behind. No way I'd let him come along, even if I could. I mean, look at this thing! No artificial gravity and a load of nuclear missiles in the back. Where are we, back in the Colonial Wars again?"

"Says the man boarding the time machine."

"That's not funny, and you know it."

Andover-Chen chuckled.

Jonas Shigeki and an Admin security synthoid greeted them at the chronoport's open hatch.

Raibert and Andover-Chen stopped and set down

their duffel bags. Normally, they'd have used counter-grav remotes to carry their luggage, but Raibert suspected the Admin might "accidentally" lose them. No point in giving away even *more* tech on this insane venture.

"Permission to come aboard?" Raibert asked stiffly, in the Admin's version of English.

"Permission granted." Jonas motioned to the synthoid. "Agent Quiroz here will stow your bags for travel."

"Why, thank you," Andover-Chen said pleasantly.

The synthoid hefted both bags and headed off down a passageway.

"We're a bit overstaffed," Jonas warned, "what with Hinnerkopf's team, the yard engineers, and so on. But we've managed to shift people around enough to arrange a private room for the two of you. That's where Agent Quiroz is taking your bags. I trust it will meet your needs."

Probably stuffed the walls with recording devices, too, Raibert thought.

"It will be more than sufficient, I'm sure," Andover-Chen said.

"In that case, gentlemen, if you'll please follow me to the bridge." Jonas gestured. "We're about to get underway."

"Lead on," Andover-Chen said.

Six thick malmetal plates sealed behind them as they stepped fully on board, and Jonas led them through a maze of narrow, metal corridors that turned and twisted frequently. The internal layout was...peculiar, to say the least, by SysGov's standards, but the vessel had to operate under varied gravitational conditions. When it was non-congruent, in a different phase state, Earth's atoms no longer exerted a gravitational pull upon it. Its interior would be in freefall—*true* freefall, not the microgravity experienced in Earth orbit…until it accelerated. Its fusion thrusters would generate plenty of apparent gravity when *that* happened.

Raibert ducked under a ceiling-mounted handrail and stepped through a final hatch onto the chronoport's bridge. A crew of twelve occupied acceleration-compensation seats in rows of three each, with Hinnerkopf seated in a newly installed row behind them.

"What's our status?" Jonas asked.

"All realspace flight systems are green," Okunnu reported.

"Impeller standing by for both temporal and trans-dimensional flight," Hinnerkopf reported. "Doctor, would you care to verify our status?"

"Certainly."

Andover-Chen sat down next to her and brought up several charts, and Jonas and Raibert joined them in the back row. They pulled their harnesses into place while the synthoid studied his readouts carefully.

"I confirm the director's report," he said after several intense seconds. "The impeller is configured for transdimensional operations, and there's no sign of fatigue from the test flight. All indicators are in the green."

"Sir," Okunnu said crisply. "*Hammerhead-Prime* stands ready for your orders."

"In that case, take us out, Captain," Jonas said.

"Yes, sir. Navigator, clear the hangar and move us half a kilometer from the DTI tower. All hands, prepare for transdimensional flight."

Malmetal split open above the chronoport, and sunlight splashed its long, flattened shape as six fusion thrusters fired up and the massive hull lifted into the air.

Raibert gripped the armrests as the ship shook its way higher and higher.

"Position now point-five kilometers from DTI tower," the realspace navigator reported.

"Doctors." Jonas gestured toward Hinnerkopf and Andover-Chen. "Whenever you're ready."

"Engaging impeller," Hinnerkopf said. "Spin rising. Twenty cycles per second...fifty...eighty...spin now settling at one hundred twenty cycles per second. Spin is stable. Lateral pressure stable. Local environment stable. Releasing linear stabilizers—"

The ship lurched and Raibert's fingers dug into the armrests...for all the good that would do.

"Was it supposed to do that?" he asked quietly.

"Shush!" Andover-Chen whispered back. "Be polite."

"Linear stabilizers disengaged," Hinnerkopf said. "We are now clear for transdimensional phase-out. Doctor?"

"Status confirmed," Andover-Chen said. "I see no reason not to proceed."

"Set our course for SysGov's True Present," Jonas ordered.

"Initiating countdown for transdimensional phase-out," Hinnerkopf replied. "Phase-out in sixty seconds... mark."

"Here we go," Raibert groaned.

"I know." Andover-Chen beamed at him. "Exciting, isn't it?"

"'Exciting,'" Raibert repeated. He rolled his eyes. "Have I ever told you how much I hate insufferable optimists?"

CHAPTER THIRTEEN

∞∞∞

Transtemporal Vehicle *Shadow*
non-congruent

TEODORÀ BECKETT HIGHLIGHTED ANOTHER PASSAGE in *The Private Life of Justinian the Great* and shifted it to her collection of notes on the political landscape at and after 490 CE. She felt a little conflicted using one of Raibert's old papers, but his reports were thorough and his conclusions sound. He'd never cut corners in the field, and the mountains of recordings and interviews he'd accumulated during any ART Observation mission made his findings all the more reliable.

She checked the time again and her lips tightened.

"Just another six hours," she murmured, nervous jitters fluttering inside her, and made herself lean back in the comfortable chair.

She could do this. She could wait another six hours. Really, she could!

The thirteen-day voyage into the past had gone by faster than she'd expected. At first, thirteen days had seemed like more than enough time to study the impact their actions would have on the course of history, but every research avenue opened up more questions. She'd *expected* to have at least several weeks to conduct her research while their proposal ground its way through the labyrinthine approval process. Only it hadn't worked that way, of course. It was fortunate that she'd already begun considering the sources she'd need and that Shadow had loaded the entire list into the TTV's memory, but the research was not only taking time, it kept throwing up things she hadn't previously considered.

There were simply too many variables when tens of *millions* of people wouldn't be dead in the alternate timeline. Life around the Mediterranean Sea could easily—and quickly—become unrecognizable against the template of baseline history, and the discrepancies would only spread from there. That was the bad news. The good news was that they didn't have to start making changes immediately and she'd have all of *Shadow*'s data available once they reached their destination. She'd have plenty of time to work through this before they actually began implementing their plan. It was just—

She pushed the display aside and blew a frustrated breath out the side of her mouth.

"It's just that I hate unknowns," she admitted to herself out loud.

Which, now that she thought about it, was pretty silly. After all, she and Samuel and Lucius had deliberately set out to create the greatest "unknown" conceivable!

The door chimed, and she frowned.

"Come in, Samuel," she said without checking the outside camera feed.

The shutter split open, and Samuel Pepys stepped into the room she'd commandeered as her study. An open document floated next to him, and she recognized the frown on his face. It was the "I *will* understand this!" frown.

"So, what are you reading about this time?" she asked, trying not to sound annoyed.

"Electricity."

"Oh?" Her eyebrows rose. "Whatever for?"

"I have been attempting to comprehend as much as I may of your technology. My newfound ability to read and research through the courtesy of my wetware makes that task far less arduous. Or perhaps I ought rather to say that it *ought* to make that task less arduous. That selfsame wetware permits me to make use of the vast wonders of this vessel, yet the more that I employ them, the less I find that I *understand* them."

"Samuel, very few citizens of the thirtieth century truly understand the technology they use." She shook her head. "All of us know how to use it, but much of the underlying principles—and a great deal of the necessary engineering—is rather esoteric knowledge the vast majority of us never actually need."

"Oh, that much I comprehend, my dear! After all, in my own day only those mariners who actually sailed the seas truly understood how a ship's rigging was contrived, or the manner of its use. I do not strive for *mastery* of the knowledge, yet it occurred to me that if I might, perchance, learn some of the basic theory, I might be better able to assist you during our mission."

Wow, she thought. *I think I'm genuinely impressed. This is* way *better than the day he discovered modern pornography.*

"That sounds great, Samuel. How's it going?"

"Alas, not so well as it might. Would it chance you have time to unwrap some of the mysteries for me?"

"Time for this? Absolutely." She closed her displays, leaned slightly forward in her chair, and crossed her arms atop the desk. "How can I help?"

"Wonderful." He pulled over a virtual book titled *Elucidations of Electricity.* "First, I believe I have correctly apprehended the concept of 'current.' The water-flowing-through-a-pipe analogy speaks with sufficient clarity. Voltage potential is...less clear to my mind, since it is relative to the point of reference. Still, I believe I can cope adequately with that. No, the problem lies elsewhere."

"That's already a fantastic start for someone with your background."

"Ah, you flatter me!" He smiled and placed a hand over his heart. "I selected this book because it seemed sufficiently basic. If my purpose is to understand how all of this"—he spread his arms to take in the virtual displays about them, the walls of the TTV, and all of the technology packed within its hull—"functions, I must first lay a foundation suitable to support that edifice. Unfortunately, it would appear from certain of these passages that the author assumed I would already comprehend their meaning, and I fear I do not."

"I suppose that's only natural." Teodorà smiled wryly. "I doubt seventeenth-century indigenes were part of the target audience. This book was written in the thirtieth century?"

"In the twenty-eighth, actually."

"Close enough." She shrugged. "It's not like electricity's going to change suddenly."

"True. And I have attempted to do searches on the terms which perplexed me most sorely. It grew . . . very confusing very quickly, however, so it occurred to me that I might come here instead of continuing to toil in my own ignorance."

"Well, I'm not too shabby with basic electrical circuits, so I should be able to help. What's got you stuck?"

"Allow me to begin with this one." Pepys glanced down at the display and cleared his throat. "Pray, what does the phrase 'nonbaryonic matter' denote?"

"It's . . ." Her voice trailed off as her mind drew a complete blank.

Pepys looked up expectantly.

"It's . . ."

"Yes?" he prompted.

"It's—" She snapped her fingers. "It's on the tip of my tongue. Give me a moment to think."

She opened a silent search and hoped Pepys wouldn't notice. But she'd barely begun to open the first entry when alarms blared throughout the ship, and she yelped at the sudden disturbance.

"What's amiss?" Pepys asked.

"Everyone, come to the bridge!" Shadow said.

Teodorà shot up from her chair, and she and Pepys hurried down the corridor. Lucius bolted out of his own room, almost crashed into Pepys, and all three of them reached the bridge together.

"What's going on?" Lucius demanded as they crowded around the command table.

"Array contact at plus one month and closing," Shadow replied.

"Something's coming up behind us?" Teodorà frowned in confusion. "Do we have any idea what it is?"

"I do not," Shadow said. "The signature does not match any TTV type in this craft's database."

Lucius expanded the chart. A nebulous blob of uncertainty encroached on their position.

"Whatever it is," he said grimly, "it's fast. And it's big."

◇   ◇   ◇

"We have a solid lock on the fugitives," *Hammerhead-Prime*'s temporal navigator reported. "Target now at negative five days. Speed matched at seventy kilofactors."

Raibert was back in his designated chair on the chronoport's command deck. Hinnerkopf had moved back into Engineering with the rest of her crew to keep an eagle eye on the modified impeller, which had given him and Jonas more elbow room. Now he looked around the bridge, and despite himself, he was impressed. The Admin had maimed itself in its compulsive distrust of artificial intelligence. A vessel which would have been managed by a single attendant program in SysGov's universe required a sizable command crew of trained specialists working with far more primitive "brilliant" software instead of true artificial intelligence. Despite that, they operated with remarkable efficiency.

"Hold here."

Captain Okunnu's voice came through Raibert's virtual senses clearly despite the Admin pressure suits everyone wore. Decompression and vacuum couldn't kill him or Andover-Chen, but it would still damage their synthoids' exteriors.

Hopefully, it won't come to that. Ideally, we need to stop them from phasing in at all. As long as we're both non-congruent, we're not affecting the past. It's only once one or both ships phase into local time that the disruptions start, and at that point, all bets are off.

An experienced time traveler understood a critical difference between congruent and non-congruent objects which most other people tended to overlook: a non-congruent version of the past didn't exist. At all. Raibert couldn't jump into a time machine and crash into himself coming back from his last excursion. Reality didn't work that way. Even though a time machine could—and often did—*leave* the True Present, it was still synchronized *with* the True Present.

In essence, the True Present served as the master clock that bound all reality, time travel included. That clock was the reason why, when he had spent months at a time in the past as part of an ART Observation, he'd returned to a True Present that was months older. That universal master clock had ticked forward while he was in the past, because it was *always* ticking forward.

Just as it was now, while Teodorà and the others sped into the past, growing more distant from the True Present by the second.

The bridge hummed with distant mechanisms and the quiet tension of highly trained personnel who could unleash hell with only a few words from their superiors. Outside the chronoport, day and night cycled by about once every second over the sun-blasted Syrian Desert.

"Captain, you may proceed," Jonas Shigeki said.

"Yes, sir. Telegraph, take the following dictation

and transmit it to the fugitives. 'This is Captain Kofo Okunnu onboard DTI chronoport *Hammerhead-Prime*, acting under the authority of the SysPol Gordian Division. You are hereby ordered to reverse course and return to the True Present. Respond with your intentions.'"

"Message spooled and transmitting."

"Now let's see what they say," Jonas said softly. "Even though I have a pretty good idea what it'll be."

"Still worth a shot, though," Raibert said.

"Reply received, sir. It reads: 'We have no intention of reversing course. Your request is denied.'"

Jonas exhaled loudly, and Raibert grimaced.

"We knew it wouldn't be that easy," he said. "They've come this far. They're not going to turn back now without some heavy-duty convincing."

"Telegraph, new dictation," Okunnu said. "'*Hammerhead-Prime* to fugitives. Our previous message was not a request. You are acting in violation of the Gordian Protocol, and you are again ordered to reverse course. Respond with your intentions.'"

They waited for the response.

"Incoming telegraph reads: 'We do not recognize your authority, nor do we acknowledge we are in violation of the Gordian Protocol. Your request is denied.'"

"In other words, go fuck off," Raibert grumbled.

"I have the distinct feeling that strong words aren't going to cut it here," Jonas said. "Want to give it a try more . . . diplomatically?"

"Yes, but not over the telegraph. I need a direct line to their ship."

"I understand what you're saying, but we need to be cautious," Jonas warned. "The very act of phase-locking with them is an escalation. As soon as we do that, they can shoot at us and we can shoot at them."

"Agreed. But if I'm going to get through to them, I need to really *talk* to them. Telegraphs back and forth won't cut it. She needs to see my face. Hear my voice."

"All right." Jonas nodded. "We'll go with that. Telegraph?"

"Yes, sir?"

"New dictation. '*Hammerhead-Prime* to fugitive TTV. We intend to phase-lock with your craft in order to facilitate smoother communication. We will not initiate any hostile actions, but will meet aggression in kind. Respond that you understand our peaceful intentions and will permit us to phase-lock.'"

"Spooled and sending, sir."

Two minutes passed. Then three. Five.

"Good grief," Raibert said grumpily. "A simple yes or no would be nice. What's taking so long?"

"I imagine they're talking it over," Jonas said.

"We're still hours away from the target year," Andover-Chen pointed out. "We can afford to be patient."

"Agreed." Jonas nodded. "We'll give them a little longer before we try again."

Four more minutes ticked by, and then the response came in.

"Message reads: 'We'll listen to what you have to say.'"

"Hmm." Jonas frowned. "I would've preferred a clear 'we won't shoot you,' but I suppose this is better than nothing. Captain, take us in, but be *careful* about it."

"Yes, sir. Navigation, get us in phase with the fugitives."

"Accelerating to ninety-five kilofactors. Phase-lock in seventeen seconds."

The range dropped steadily, and then the TTV materialized, ahead and to starboard of the chronoport.

"Phase-locked."

Raibert held his breath for a tense moment, but the TTV neither adjusted its orientation or course nor opened its weapons pod. Both craft sped into the past, the sun rising overhead again and again.

"Oh, good." Andover-Chen smiled brightly. "We're not being shot at!"

"They're all yours, Agent," Jonas said.

"Here goes nothing," Raibert muttered and opened a command window to send the TTV a request for video chat.

Teodorà and Lucius appeared in the window. Teodorà wore a worried expression, but Lucius loomed behind her, a dark thundercloud of bad possibilities.

"Raibert?" she blurted.

"Hello, Teodorà. Good to see you."

"You're on an *Admin* ship?"

"I know. I'm as surprised as you are."

"What's going on here?" Lucius leaned forward, his face a stern, unreadable mask. "What's the meaning of this?"

"What's it look like? The Admin helped us catch up with you. *Someone* had to talk some sense into you people."

"We're not turning around," Teodorà said.

"Do you really intend to cure the plague?"

"We do." She raised her chin, looking at him defiantly. "And we're not going to let *you* stop us."

"Oh, good grief!"

Raibert started laughing. He shook his head, covering his eyes with one hand while his shoulders shook with mirth. In fact, he laid it on as thickly as he dared.

"What the hell is so funny?" Teodorà demanded, her eyes flashing.

Gotcha! Raibert thought. *Or, maybe, anyway. You never could stand it when somebody laughed at you, could you?*

"You two are!" he said out loud, lowering his hand and shaking his head. "I mean, look at you! Do you honestly think it'll be that *easy?*"

"Hundreds of millions of lives that never were are about to be given a chance, Raibert!" she snapped. "Don't you understand? We're on the verge of one of the greatest acts of kindness in *history!*"

"Well, yeah." He chuckled again, then, visibly, made himself stop and looked at her almost pityingly. "Have you thought this through, though? I mean *really* thought this through? Because, I gotta say, Teodorà. It doesn't sound to *me* like you have."

"Of course we've thought it through." Her words were resolute, but her voice trembled, and Raibert saw the possibility of a crack in her conviction.

"Curing the plague is all well and good," he said, his own tone more serious, "but what about the aftermath? You think just because you cure them that everything will be sunshine and rainbows after you're done? Get a clue! Humans are complete bastards. Your act of kindness will drown in an ocean of ignorance and barbarity. History won't be any better in the universe you create. It'll just be *different.*"

Teodorà lowered her gaze, and he felt a tiny trickle of hope. Was he getting through?

He pressed on.

"All you're about to do is change one tiny part of the equation. Yes, millions will be alive because of you, but what about everything *else*? Now you have millions more fighting over the same resources, long before they have the tech to maximize them. So guess what *that* means? I don't know about you, but off the top of my head, *I'd* say you're looking at an extra war or three, and that's just for *starters*."

Teodorà's eyes darkened, and she hung her head.

"Don't listen to him!" Lucius urged, and faced the camera. "You wouldn't understand, Raibert. You were always a coward when it came to getting your hands dirty. You think we can't handle this? Well think again. We know the history and the players better than they know themselves. There's *no one* better qualified to do this!"

"Oh, get over yourselves!" Raibert said scornfully. "First of all, no one is 'qualified' to do this *at all*, so that argument doesn't really impress me. Secondly, the only way you could possibly guarantee a better result would be if you took active control of the world yourselves!"

"Then that's what we'll do!" Lucius shouted. "Don't you dare doubt our resolve!"

"I'm not doubting your resolve. Only your brains."

"You're not stopping us," Lucius said flatly.

"Be reasonable. Right now, all you're guilty of is stealing a time machine. Come back peacefully. There's no point in pushing this any further."

"No, Lucius is right." Teodorà looked up, and Lucius's words had filled her eyes with renewed steel. "You're the one who's not listening, Raibert. We're the ones in the right, and we're going to prove it. To you and everyone else."

"The Admin's just as serious as SysGov about the Gordian Protocol," Raibert told her. "They're not going to take no for an answer. And neither am I."

"You think that piece of garbage you're in scares me?" Lucius threatened.

The channel closed.

"Wait!"

Raibert tried to reopen the channel, but no one answered.

"Movement!" the navigator snapped. "TTV pods opening! It's coming about!"

The TTV spun to face them, and its bow armor parted to reveal the muzzle of a massive cannon.

"Get us—!"

The kinetic slug interrupted Okunnu's order. It struck like the hammer of the gods, throwing Raibert against his harness. The impact rang throughout the hull, and both real-lighting and virtual displays flickered.

"Impact on the right wing! Laser Two down! Cannon Two damaged!"

The TTV charged toward them, Gatling guns firing furiously. Hundreds of small explosions pounded *Hammerhead-Prime*'s heavily armored hull, and status displays flashed yellow and red.

"Return fire!" Okunnu barked.

Laser One slashed out from the left wing and burned a jagged, glowing line across the TTV's hull, and Cannons One and Two *thwomped* again and again, blasting deep divots out of the TTV's armor with each paired strike.

The TTV swooped past overhead and vanished.

"They've reversed course, sir! Now heading downstream!"

"Tail them, but keep us negative five days out." Okunnu ordered. "Status report?"

"Laser Two and Dorsal Defense are out of commission. Cannon Two has several active faults, but it's still functional. Breach detected in frontal armor, and minor damage to dorsal armor. Engineering is shifting malmetal plates to seal and reinforce."

"Casualties?"

"Minor injuries only, sir."

"And the TTV?"

"We scored multiple hits, but I can't tell how badly we hurt them."

"I can help there," Raibert said. "Let me see."

"Here." Jonas pulled up a read-only duplicate of the weapons operator's screens and shifted them across to Raibert.

Raibert glanced over the TTV rendering, then turned it over and around.

"You took out one of its graviton thrusters and tore up the hull pretty badly. One of the Gatlings might be damaged, but the main gun's still online. And they didn't have their meta-armor deployed. That's the main reason you hit them as hard as you did, but they could correct that lapse at any moment."

"Sir," Okunnu said. "Request permission to engage with intent to destroy."

"Wait!" Raibert cut in. "We can still salvage the situation."

"I'm afraid the time for talk is over." Jonas twisted in his seat so that his helmet was almost touching Raibert's. "We extended an olive branch, and they *batted* it away!"

"But it was working! I was getting through to her. I just need more time."

"Yes, you were reaching *her*," Jonas agreed. "Not *them*."

"All that means is that there's at least one person on that ship worth bringing back."

"And how do you propose we get to her? That attack was meant to *destroy* us. Against any other chronoport, it *would* have. They're not holding back, and it would be foolish of us not to fight with everything we've got."

"I . . ."

Raibert faltered and took another look at the TTV. The SysGov-designed mass driver it carried was even more powerful than the one *Kleio* had used to one-shot Admin chronoports at the Gordian Knot. It was no popgun. Not something to be deployed only to *discourage* someone.

Jonas was right; Lucius had shot to kill.

"I . . ." He struggled to force the words out. "I . . . withdraw my objection."

"Good." Jonas sat back in his seat. "Now that *that's* clear, let's see if we can bring the fugitives back alive."

"Excuse me?" Raibert exclaimed. "But you said—"

"That it would be foolish not to go all in?" Jonas flashed a quick smile. "I know. I only wanted you on record agreeing all-in was the right approach, tactically, at least. The chances are unfortunately high that we'll have to do that in the end, but in the meantime—" He turned away. "Captain Okunnu, can you take down the TTV without damaging the crewed sections?"

"We can *try*." Okunnu's response was grudging, to say the least, and Jonas's smile turned crooked.

"Try very hard. It would be . . . *unseemly* for our first joint mission to end in us killing SysGov civilians, however recalcitrant."

"Sir, I advise against this."

"Noted. You have your orders, Captain."

"Yes, Director."

Okunnu turned back to his bridge crew while Jonas rested his head against the headrest. His face was cool and composed, but a twitch in his cheek betrayed his own nervousness. Raibert shot a sideways glance his way and had to wonder. He didn't trust anyone from the Admin, least of all Csaba Shigeki's own slimy spawn. But he had to concede that Jonas's attitude had surprised him. He'd fully expected these Admin thugs to blow the TTV to pieces at the first sniff of a valid excuse, but that hadn't happened. Instead, Jonas was invested not only in the mission's success, but in their success *together*.

Was there a chance for SysGov and the Admin at large to do the same? Would their two peoples really be able to coexist?

He wondered...and more importantly, he wondered with a little less pessimism than usual.

"Thank you," he whispered.

"Don't thank me yet," Jonas warned, equally quietly. "This could still end badly. In fact, the odds are that it *will*, I'm afraid."

"I know. But...thank you."

"Weapons, you heard the director." Okunnu's voice drowned out their quiet conversation. "Target drive and weapon systems only. Navigators, do everything you can to keep us clear of that main gun. I'm not in a mood to trade blows with that thing."

He waited until the bridge crew had confirmed his orders. Then—

"Initiate phase-lock!"

"Target's temporal course and speed are steady. Now closing in. Phase-lock imminent."

The TTV appeared ahead.

"Fire!" Okunnu barked.

Laser One speared into the TTV's impeller, and Cannons One and Two blasted away. Some shots flew wide as the weapons officer tried to avoid the heart of the vessel, but others punched deep kinetic fists into its hull. The TTV sped up, and its Gatling guns swerved and unleashed fire in a wide arc. Explosions peppered the chronoport's bow, and the vessel shook.

"Armor holding. No breaches."

"They're trying to get away, sir."

"Stay on them."

The chronoport's fusion thrusters lit at full power, and acceleration crammed Raibert deep into his seat. The cannons thumped away, and another beam slashed across the TTV's hull.

"There!" the weapons officer declared. "I think we damaged another thruster. Target's realspace motion is slowing."

"Watch it! They're coming around."

The TTV turned, flying sideways for a moment as it brought its bow to bear on the chronoport.

"Take out that gun!" Okunnu snapped.

"Firing!"

Laser and cannon fire stabbed into the TTV's bow as its aperture snapped open.

"Here it comes!" somebody shouted.

The mass driver fired, and the kinetic shock threw everyone against their restraints. Metal screamed against metal, and blue smoke fumed in through the ventilators.

"Breach on decks B and C! Main dish out of alignment! Emergency shutters closing!"

"Environmental systems damaged! Shutting down faulted units!"

"Return fire!"

Shot after shot pounded the TTV. Armor buckled, breached, and finally blew off in a shower of glowing, twisted wreckage. The top of the bow exploded, taking the gun mount with it, and the craft spiraled away.

"Now the impeller!" Okunnu barked. "Fire!"

The TTV's thrusters fought to stabilize its flight, and the chronoport took advantage of its tumbling to close in mercilessly. Its laser tracked the TTV's path and sliced deep into its impeller spike. Exotic matter wavered, and its boundary loosened, turning uncertain, incorporeal.

The TTV brought itself under control and tried to speed away.

"Again!"

Cannons and lasers savaged the spike, and chunks blasted free along its entire length. The tip shattered, and glittering splinters phased away in all directions before the entire TTV vanished.

"I've lost phase-lock, sir. Wait . . . there they are! Sir, they've reversed course. Speed now thirty-seven kilofactors and slowing. They're heading upstream again. Speed stabilizing at thirty-four."

"Bring us to plus five days behind them. Director?"

"Thank you, Captain. I think they've had enough." Jonas grinned wolfishly. "Let's see if even Chairman Gwon will listen to us *now*."

CHAPTER FOURTEEN

⚛⚛⚛

Transtemporal Vehicle *Shadow*
non-congruent

"IMPELLER INSTABILITY REACHING CRITICAL LEVELS," Shadow reported. "I need to shut it down."

"No!" Lucius shouted. "We can still make it!"

"With *what*?" Teodorà demanded in raw despair. "The mass driver's gone and the Gatlings can barely scratch that beast! Face it, we're outmatched!"

"No." Lucius put his hands on the command table and glowered at the charts and flashing red displays. "No, it's not going to end like this. I *refuse* to let this happen!"

"They don't care what you think, Lucius. Why did you fire on them? You had to know they'd shoot *back*!"

"Because I thought we could scare them off."

"Well, you were *wrong*!"

"Thank you for pointing out the obvious!" he snarled.

He didn't even look at her, only stared at the alarms and damage reports over the table, and Teodorà dropped to her knees and pushed her fingers into her hair. Pepys knelt next to her.

"Perhaps we should do as they demand and surrender," he said quietly.

It was a statement, but it came out as a question, and Teodorà shook her head bitterly.

"That might work for you. They'll just put you in the Retirement Home. But for us?" She shook her head again. "We fired on them. We've violated the Gordian Protocol *and* attempted to kill a ship full of people. Hell, we probably *have* killed some of them, looking at their damage! There's no way this ends with anything less than the death penalty for Lucius and me."

"And that means we have nothing to lose," Lucius said coolly. He still stared at the virtual displays, but his brow was furrowed in concentration and his composure seemed to be returning.

"I fail to see how having nothing to lose helps us," Teodorà said sharply.

"Telegraph from *Hammerhead-Prime*," Shadow said. "We are being ordered to hold our position and prepare to be boarded. I fear we may have no choice, Master Gwon. I will be forced to shut down the impeller in thirteen minutes whatever we do."

"No, keep it running."

"Lucius, stop!" Teodorà grabbed the edge of the table and pulled herself up. "It's *over*."

"No, it's not. Trust me, we're not done yet." He expanded a detailed schematic of the impeller and its support systems. "Shadow, get ready to disengage safeties on all power lines to the spike."

"That will only hasten the drive's failure and make it more catastrophic," Shadow replied.

"I know. That's the point."

He pushed the impeller schematic aside and pulled up a structural overview.

"Lucius, stop," Teodorà pled. "Just stop this. We're finished."

"No, we're not. Aha!" He highlighted a fault line zigzagging through the TTV's main structural girder. "That's what we need." He traced lines through secondary supports to each of the three surviving graviton thrusters. "Lovely. Shadow, I'll need you to fire Thruster Two forward and Thrusters One and Four in reverse, all at full power."

"Software safeties prevent me from complying."

"Get rid of them."

"Yes, Master Gwon. Deleted."

"What the *hell* are you doing, Lucius?"

"Ripping the ship in half. Now move it! Get to the cargo bay!"

"But—"

"Come on! We're getting out of this mess!"

Pepys turned to Teodorà. He was out of his depth, but it was clear that of the two of them, he trusted her more.

Teodorà hesitated a moment longer, then nodded to him. Lucius's plan was crazy, but crazy was all they had left, and she had no desire to be dragged back to the True Present, only to be tried and executed.

They reached the counter-grav tube, and Teodorà's eyes widened at the flood of warnings in her virtual sight. She thrust her arms out to the side, grabbing the edges of the tube entry, and Pepys ran into her and bounced off her synthoid body.

"The tube's counter-grav is out," she said over her shoulder. "Use the ladder!"

She pointed at the rungs set into the walls of the tube especially for emergency use, waited until he'd nodded and reached for them, then jumped down ahead of him. Her synthoid legs cushioned the one-story fall with ease, and she ran down the cramped passage between high stacks of storage crates. More warnings popped open at the far end, and she looked up at the rent in the ceiling.

Air whistled out of the crack.

"Not good," she told herself. "*Not* good!"

The forward section of the ship contained its main entrance and exit, and the Gordian Division had equipped it accordingly. She hurried over to a nearby storage locker and pulled out three SysPol pressure suit packs just as Pepys jogged up to her, panting.

"Here—put this on!" She tossed him one of the packs.

"How?" he demanded, his voice cracking, as he turned the pack in his hands, trying to figure it out.

"Like this!"

She slipped the pack on like a backpack. An option menu appeared in her virtual sight, and she activated the pack. Thin bands of prog-steel wove outward until the material encompassed her entire body.

Pepys mimicked her just as Lucius came hurtling down the passage behind him. Teodorà threw him the third suit pack, and he nodded curtly to her as he slid it onto his back and activated it.

"Shadow?" he said as the prog-steel wove its protective cocoon, and the ceiling lit with a virtual star field.

"I am secure. I have relocated to the local info-systems."

"Then do it now!"

"At once, Master Gwon."

Graviton thrusters fired with conflicting vectors, and the TTV groaned and creaked as its own engines tore it apart. The floor lurched under their feet, and Teodorà braced a hand against a cargo crate for stability. Pepys tried to do the same, but lost his grip and stumbled back into her arms.

"Hold on!" she told him, and helped him loop an arm around one of the flexible prog-steel straps which secured the crates.

"I shall!" he shouted back, grabbing the strap with both hands as the ship convulsed.

"Lucius!"

"One secondary girder's holding onto us! Shadow's trying to break us free!"

"Everyone, please hold on," Shadow said.

Teodorà grabbed the straps next to Pepys. The ship rocked violently back and forth, pressing her against the crate one way, then lifting her feet off the deck in the other.

"We are still attached to the impeller assembly," Shadow reported. "Impeller detonation imminent."

"Can you stop it?" Teodorà demanded.

"The process is no longer reversible."

"Break us free!" Lucius commanded. "Do whatever you have to do!"

"Yes, Master Gwon. Please secure yourselves."

A sudden thunderous, continuous explosion assaulted their hearing even as he spoke.

"What's *that*?" Teodorà yelped.

"I am using one of the Gatlings to weaken the last support girder," Shadow replied, his voice crystal-clear in her virtual hearing despite the deafening noise.

The thunder seemed to go on far longer than it actually did. Then it stopped, as abruptly as it had begun, and the compartment twisted until the crates they clung to became the floor. The universe shimmied back and forth under their feet, and the creaking, tearing, groaning grew louder and louder.

Lucius pulled up the impeller status. It was a solid mass of yellow and red indicators.

"Shadow?"

His voice sounded substantially less confident in Teodorà's virtual hearing than it had been, and even through her own terror, she felt a stab of something almost like satisfaction as she heard it.

"I have us almost free."

Every remaining yellow portion of the impeller display flashed red.

"Shadow!"

"Almost there, Master Gwon."

The shaking crescendoed, lifting Teodorà completely off the floor, then slamming her back down as she fought desperately to hold on. One final, bone-rattling jerk shuddered through the ship, and then the front end of the *Shadow* flew free at last.

"Whew!" Lucius actually *smiled* at her. "I was worried there for a—"

The impeller exploded.

✧   ✧   ✧

"Maybe their telegraph's out," Jonas said and glanced at Raibert. "Agent?"

"I suppose that's possible," Raibert replied.

"But not likely, judging by the tone of your voice?" Raibert shook his head.

"One of the TTV's two telegraphs is in a heavily reinforced compartment. It's designed to remain functional in any emergency." His eyes darkened as he remembered *Aion's* emergency telegraph, but he made himself continue levelly. "If any significant portion of their hull is still intact, they've got at least one telegraph."

"Then it would seem we're being ignored."

"That might be it," Andover-Chen agreed, "but if they are ignoring us, it may be because they have bigger problems on their mind. Their impeller signature's gone from bad to worse."

"Shall we move up and phase-lock, sir?" Okunnu asked.

"No. We'll try to raise them one more time first. Telegraph, take the following dictation. '*Hammerhead-Prime* to—'"

The TTV's chronometric signature blossomed abruptly into a thousand points of light . . . then dispersed into a fine mist of occluding data. Fragments of phasing matter shot past the chronoport, and a scattering of small pieces pelted the hull with a faint *tink-ti-tink-tink*.

The chronoport's scope turned into a solid sea of static from all the errant phasing matter, and the bridge fell silent. The silence hovered for a handful of seconds, and then Jonas Shigeki broke it.

"Survivors?" he asked quietly.

"Impossible to tell, Director," *Hammerhead-Prime's* temporal navigator replied. "The main dish still needs to be realigned, and all this phasing matter is confusing what little resolution we have left."

"Then we'll take a look for ourselves. Captain, bring us within phase of . . . of where the TTV should be and search the area."

"Yes, sir. Navigator?"

"Accelerating. Phase-lock imminent."

The view from the chronoport's external cameras didn't change. Day and night continued to snap past over the rugged, barren hillsides below, but no sign of the TTV remained, and Raibert exhaled a long, ragged breath.

"It didn't have to end this way," he said softly.

"No sign of them, sir," Okunnu said.

"Thank you, I can see that." Jonas crossed his arms. "Search the area for survivors, Captain."

"Director, it's unlikely we'll find *anything*."

"I understand the difficulties. Nevertheless, we'll search as thoroughly as possible with the tools at our disposal. Make repairing the dish our top priority."

"Understood, sir."

"I can help, as well," Andover-Chen offered. "There should be enough data from immediately after the failure to list the impeller fragments and their last temporal vectors. If there is, we can track down each piece."

"Thank you, Doctor," Jonas said. "Shall I ask Doctor Hinnerkopf to come up here and assist?"

"Actually, yes. Good idea. I'm sure she's more familiar with your instrumentation than I am."

"That she is." Jonas opened a comm window. "Director Hinnerkopf, please report to the bridge. Doctor Andover-Chen would like your assistance."

"Understood. On my way."

❖   ❖   ❖

"Now approaching fragment fifty-six."

The chronoport hovered above the scorching desert, its mass non-congruent with reality but aligned with a factor of one. Scrub growth straggled over the stony slopes and dry, seasonal watercourses below it, and time passed normally from the view of its cameras. The feeds would have been much crisper if they'd phased in, which would have increased any chance of spotting wreckage or survivors, but Raibert didn't raise that concern. An exploding impeller was already bad enough, and *Hammerhead-Prime*'s visual spectrum stealth systems were damaged. Given the damage the local time stream had just absorbed, it might well be more sensitive than usual to chronometric disruption. Like the disruption that might occur if a bunch of goat herders or some caravan of traders saw something the size of an old wet-navy battleship floating overhead.

"Commencing search, sir."

"Very good," Okunnu said mechanically.

All of them had removed their pressure suits during the long hours of their search, and Raibert floated near the back of the bridge with Okunnu, Andover-Chen, and Jonas.

Several minutes ticked past. Then—

"Search negative, Captain."

"Well, that's the last of them," Andover-Chen said with a sad smile.

Jonas glanced at Raibert, who gave him a grim nod, then turned to Okunnu.

"Captain, our work here is done. Take us home."

"Yes, Director. Navigator, execute."

"Yes, sir. Course plotted for the True Present. Accelerating to cruising speed of seventy-two kilofactors."

Raibert grabbed a handhold and pulled himself toward the hatch at the back of the bridge. He stopped at the exit and waited for Andover-Chen to catch up.

"That was their own fault," the physicist said quietly.

"I know," he sighed, and pulled himself into the corridor. "Still, I keep playing the conversation back over in my head, wondering if I could have done something different. It felt like I was *this* close with Teodorà, you know?" He held up a thumb and finger, half a centimeter apart.

"Not close enough," Andover-Chen replied sadly. "She sided with Lucius in the end."

"Yeah," Raibert agreed. "Asshole."

"You really didn't like him, did you?"

"Not after I got to know him. The real him, I mean. You ever meet Lucius Gwon?"

"Once," Andover-Chen said. "At one of the ART Exhibitions. Though I suppose it'd technically be twice, since we weren't integrated back then."

"Wait a second." Raibert looked down at the other synthoid. "How'd the two of *you* ever get an invitation to an ART show?"

"It was shortly after you and Philo dropped that massive abuse stinker in SysPol's lap. Lucius was trying to drum up support for pushing back against all the restrictions. We both politely declined to help."

"Good for you!"

"He seemed nice enough."

"Yeah, he does, doesn't he?" Raibert grimaced. "When he *wants* something out of you, anyway."

"A bit of an act, then?"

"Let me put it this way." The two stopped and Raibert turned in midair to face him. "If one good thing's come out of this god-awful mess, it's that Lucius Gwon will never, *ever* hurt anyone again."

◇　　　◇　　　◇

"There," Lucius said, watching the scope. "I think they're finally about to leave."

"Well, that's *one* problem down." Teodorà used a cargo strap to pull herself over to him. With the gravity out and the front third of their ship still out of phase, they'd spent the last several hours in freefall.

"Faith, I thought they would never give over," Pepys said. "How ever did they fail to spy us?"

"We weren't phase-locked with them when the impeller blew," Lucius said, "and this part of the ship's chronometrically inert. A TTV's array might have picked up the separation, or found us later, but it seems Admin tech isn't quite as good."

Teodorà checked one of the two remaining external cameras. Night had fallen over the desert.

And this time, it was staying night.

Their time factor had fallen to ninety and it was dropping fast.

"The drag is about to bring us into phase," she said. "We either land or crash, and the terrain down there's not very inviting if it comes to crashing. Shadow?"

"I am almost finished rerouting thruster power to the remaining capacitors."

"It's now or never," she warned.

"I am well aware of the situation, Doctor."

"He'll pull us through," Lucius assured her. "You might want to hang on, though."

"We're cutting it *awfully* close here."

"All that counts is that he finishes before we go splat."

"My *nerves* say otherwise," Teodorà growled, looping an arm through a cargo strap.

"I apologize, Doctor," Shadow said, "but the remaining microbots are taxed to capacity."

"Samuel, grab something and hang on," she said.

"Most assuredly," he said fervently and pushed over to her and wrapped his arms and legs around prog-steel straps.

"Factor down to ten." Lucius wagged his eyebrows at her. "Here it comes."

Teodorà shook her head.

"Are you *enjoying* yourself?"

"Maybe a little."

"At least have the decency to be scared like the rest of us."

The *Shadow*'s bow phased into reality. Gravity reasserted its hold—

—and the ship plummeted.

Wind howled past its deformed, irregular shape, and the interior turned up on one side.

"*Wooohooo!*" Lucius cried, grinning ear to ear.

A piece of armor rattled against the hull, then ripped off. The ship spun wildly on its long axis, and Pepys threw up in his helmet.

"Lucius!" Teodorà shouted.

"Yeah?"

"If we survive this, I'm going to kill you!"

He laughed at her.

"Thruster Two now online," Shadow said calmly through the tumult.

The third-of-a-ship angled so that the bow pointed straight down, then swerved sharply and Teodorà accessed one of the cameras. Unfortunately, they were headed straight toward the side of a looming hill—a small mountain, really—over four hundred meters high. It was too big and they were too low, traveling with too much speed and not enough power from their one remaining thruster to avoid it, so Shadow was attempting to align them with a wadi, one of the dry, seasonal watercourses whose eroded beds cut into the mountain's side.

At the moment, his efforts didn't look very promising. "We're still falling!"

"Thruster output at forty percent. Rate of descent decreasing. Brace for impact."

Teodorà squeezed her eyes shut.

The ship struck the ground at an angle and bounced savagely, but Shadow's last-ditch course correction had worked...mostly. The truncated bow careened along the dry watercourse like an out of control sleigh through snow, blasting a long groove along it. The wadi rose steeply, which enlisted gravity in braking their speed as well, but dust, stones, and dirt billowed behind them, and the noise was the most deafening yet.

It seemed to go on and on, forever.

It didn't.

The wadi angled to the west, and Shadow no longer had any control over the wrecked ship's course. A knee of rock rose perhaps three meters above the wadi floor, directly ahead of them, and they were still traveling at several kilometers per hour when they hit. Even a mere third of a TTV massed over two thousand tons. That was a lot of momentum to stop very quickly, and even prog-steel had its limits. The bow caved inward, cargo restraints snapped, and the massive, heavy container to which Pepys clung slid across the floor...directly toward a second, equally massive container.

"Teodorà!" he cried, and she kicked off her own crate, hurling herself between the two about to collide, and thrust her arms out.

Her spine slammed into the unmoving container while Pepys's crate hurtled toward her. Her arms buckled, but they took the impact, and the sliding crate ground to a halt, no more than a few centimeters before it crushed *both* of them.

Pepys pulled himself free and scurried away from the two crates.

"Oh, dear! Oh, my!"

He staggered across the ruined cargo bay, his face turning green, before he dropped to his knees. He triggered his helmet to retract it and threw up again.

"There, there," Lucius said, following him out of the cargo bay. "Let it all out."

Pepys coughed and wiped his face and mouth on the sleeve of his pressure suit. He spat out bile and sat up.

"Thank you," he said to Teodorà. "That would have—"

"Burst you like a pimple?" Lucius suggested, and Pepys nodded.

"Not funny," Teodorà snapped, then put her back against one crate and her boot against the other and shoved them away from each other.

"The good news is we are all alive," Lucius said, retracting his own helmet.

"In my experience, good news is always companied by bad," Pepys said.

"Yeah, about that." Lucius put his hands on his hips. "Shadow?"

"Here, Master Gwon."

"When the *hell* are we?"

CHAPTER FIFTEEN

Mount Habib-i Neccar
Syrian Desert, 541 CE

A CHILL WIND BLEW ACROSS THE STONY DESERT, biting at Teodorà's arms and face. She toggled one of her body's settings, and the discomfort became mere information. Stars were diamond pinpricks overhead in a preposterously clear sky, and a newly risen moon cast pale light over the *Shadow*'s bow as it rested against the rock which had stopped it.

The rock rose from the wadi's stony bed like a shipwreck's rib, but it was only an outthrust knee, a flying buttress, of the wadi's far steeper side, and the rest of the mountain rose another hundred meters or so beyond that. She climbed the slope, pebbles rolling away with each step, and joined Pepys at the wadi's top to peer out eastward, over the arid, moonlit slopes beyond. The patches of scrub were few, far between, and parched-looking, even in the moonlight, but that was good, she thought. There weren't even any goat herders out there to have noticed their thunderous arrival. And they'd crashed after dark, so no one would have seen the sixty-meter-long chunk of prog-steel plummeting from the heavens from farther away, either.

And *Shadow managed to get what was left of us down in one piece in the bottom of this damned gully*, she thought. *That's going to help keep us out of sight, too*.

"It's 541, not 490," she said to Pepys. "We're over fifty years off target."

"Indeed?" he murmured. He closed his eyes, took a deep breath of the desert's cold night air, then let it out slowly.

"Samuel, I'm so sorry."

"Whatever for?" He turned to her, eyes dark in the moonlight.

"This isn't what I promised you."

"Perhaps not," he said softly, "yet some promises cannot be kept, though we strive like Hercules to hold true to our word. I see no way anyone might have striven harder, or against greater adversity, Teodorà."

"I shouldn't have dragged you into this. I shouldn't—"

"Pray pardon, dear lady, but you have 'dragged me' nowhere I did not heartily wish to go." He shook his head. "Indeed, this mad escapade entire was my own idea, if memory serves."

"But we almost got you *killed*, and on top of that—"

"Teodorà," he reached out and took both her hands in his own, "whatever may have chanced, you and Lucius gave fair warning from the outset that many dangers lay ahead. I have lived a long life, for a man born in my native time. Yet as Julius Caesar said in Master Shakespeare's play, all men born must die. I cannot imagine anything I would rather die in the doing of, my dear. This"—he released one of her hands to wave an arm at the moonlit night—"is the greatest adventure ever offered, and at its end, the prize of destroying the monstrous pestilence of which *millions* have perished in our own world. If you had told me we *would* be killed in the attempt, I believe I would still have said yes."

"Is that really the truth?" She looked at his silhouette against the moon. "Or are you just saying that to make me feel better?"

"My dear Teodorà!" He astounded her with a deep, jovial laugh and waved his arm at the barren landscape yet again. "Here we find ourselves—here! In the past! Not simply your past, but my own. How could I repine when such wonder enfolds me?"

"Yeah—here in the past . . . without two-thirds of our ship."

"Yet *one*-third is infinitely more than naught," he replied. "And, whatever travails may have assailed us, we are here. We have completed our journey, our pursuers have departed, and all that remains is to accomplish our purpose. We have not come this far simply to fail, my dear. Hard work and a firm resolve will make light of the challenges which yet lie before us."

Despite herself, she chuckled.

"You make it sound so simple."

"Because it is," he replied. "Difficult to compass, perhaps, yet of childlike simplicity in its concept. And whatever else, we have still our wits and a time ship's hold laden with the cure."

"Let's hope that's not all we have."

"Indeed, and so I hope, as well. Yet do we truly *need* more?" he demanded, and she smiled at him, her spirits rising.

"No, Samuel. No, I suppose not."

A panel split open on the *Shadow*'s side, and they both turned. A shimmering canvas emerged, spreading over the craft, blanketing the TTV with shifting, eye-bewildering patterns until it settled and stiffened into its final shape. It integrated itself into the side of the wadi, conforming to the surrounding typography, and light curved around the metamaterial shroud for an instant. Then the light faded, and their vessel had disappeared completely into the stony landscape, just one more steep slope on the mountain's flank.

"Come on." She put a hand on Pepys's arm. "Let's see what Lucius and Shadow have for us."

They descended the rocky slope together, then pushed open the flap in the shroud and entered the cargo bay. They passed through it and climbed a ladder to the bridge level. Topographic maps and virtual feeds from the *Shadow*'s reconnaissance remotes covered the curved walls of the bridge, and Lucius stood scrutinizing them. He glanced over as they entered.

"I see you got the shroud working," Teodorà said.

"It's not perfect, but it should keep us hidden for now."

"Have you pinpointed where we are?"

"Syria, 541. The good news, such as it is, is that we're only about five kilometers from Antioch, on the Orontes River."

"What?" Teodorà looked at him in disbelief. "There's nothing out there but hills and dry streambeds!"

"Ah, but that's because you were looking *west*," Lucius told her with a crooked smile. "Antioch is east of here, on the other side of this mountain." A terrain feature on one of the maps flashed. "According to the map it's called Habib-i Neccar Mountain back home. I don't know what the locals call it these days. I assume it has a name of some sort. Good thing it was here, though."

His smile turned into a grin.

"Without it, we probably would've landed right in the middle of Antioch. That would've been something!"

"'Something,'" Teodorà repeated with a shudder, imagining the chaos—and mayhem—if what was left of *Shadow* had smashed into the center of the ancient city in the middle of the night.

"Well, we didn't," Lucius said cheerfully. "And I'm guessing that having the mountain between us and the city probably helped deaden the noise. Anyway, here's Antioch"—an icon appeared on the map—"and here's the Orontes." The course of the river flashed briefly on the same map, threading down from the north to flow through the city toward the sea, twenty-four kilometers to the southwest. "I've sent one of the remotes to overfly Antioch so we can see what the locals are up to."

"Good idea," Teodorà said. "All right. If that's the good news, how bad is the *bad* news?"

"Awful. Power's my biggest concern right now, though. We don't have the reactor anymore, just the capacitors in this part of the ship. That means we have enough power to function for a few months, but without any way to replenish it—"

He shrugged.

"What's left of our tech will shut down," Teodorà finished for him with a sigh.

"Including me," Shadow pointed out.

"And what of *you*, Teodorà?" Pepys asked, his voice sharp. "Does not your body also require power?"

"No, thankfully." She placed a hand on her chest. "Oh, I do need power, but this is a civilian synthoid, not a police model. That means it comes with a lot of 'quality of life' features, like being able to eat food for power, which puts me in a better spot than Shadow. SysPol variants are more powerful, but they're also more streamlined."

"One less concern, then," Pepys said with obvious relief.

"Can't we print ourselves a generator?" she asked Lucius.

"All the printers are gone, too," he said flatly.

"*All* of them?" Teodorà stared at him in shock.

"Yup."

"Oh, no!" She put her hands to her temples. "How can we do this without the printers?"

"Oh, it's worse than that," Lucius told her. "The central library files are gone, too, so we wouldn't know how to make a generator even if we could. We have the processing power of the local infosystems, and anything that was in local memory at the time, but that's it. All our printing patterns, archives, and everything else were in the core, and the core blew up with the rest of the ship."

"Aaaaah!" Teodorà rubbed her face. "What *do* we have?"

"It's a short list." Lucius summoned a readout to his side. "Almost all of the conveyor drones are intact, and we have half the cure we planned to start with."

"Then we can still complete our original mission!" Pepys said.

"Not so fast, Samuel," Lucius warned. "Those conveyors aren't going anywhere without power, and they take a *lot* more than the remotes. Any juice we put into them is less we have for our critical systems."

"Ah!" Pepys shook his head. "I take your point, Lucius. Pray, accept my apologies for leaping so boldly—and so erroneously—ahead."

"Don't worry about it. But, moving on, one of the forty-five-millimeter Gatlings is still attached, and its ammo bay is nearly full. That could be handy if hostile indigenes come knocking. Then there's the shroud, the remotes, and our last graviton thruster, but you know about those. There's also plenty of prog-steel armor lying around, but we'll need to power it up if we want to remold it. We have some basic SysPol equipment in storage lockers. The body armor and pistols could come in handy. The medical bay survived almost completely intact, so good news there for me and Samuel. We can even save our connectomes, if it comes to it. Food and water should be fine, as well; we still have the secondary reclamation plant below the crew compartment. And finally, we have our swarm of microbots."

"Can't they self-replicate?" Teodorà's eyes brightened, but Lucius shook his head.

"That feature is locked, and the unlock codes were in the core."

"Of *course* they were." Teodorà sank into a chair by the command table and put her head on a fist.

"The swarm gives us limited construction and modification options—Shadow and I used them to get the shroud unjammed—but once the microbots wear out, they're gone for good."

Teodorà folded her arms on the table, rested her face on them, and groaned.

"I am curious about something you mentioned earlier," Pepys said.

"Sure," Lucius said. "What's on your mind?"

"I fear I did not grasp the implications of the difference between the library core and 'local memory.'"

"Ah. This may take some explaining." Lucius thought for a moment, then shrugged. "The TTV's core—when we had it—was designed for storing as much information as possible, whereas the infosystems in each room are built around processing speed. Do you follow?"

"My comprehension remains less than complete," Pepys admitted with a grimace.

"Don't worry about the difference too much. All it means is that files are stored in the core until needed. The system works that way because it's more efficient. One part is specialized for data storage, the other for data *processing*. All we have left is whatever was in the data processing portion at the moment we lost the core."

"I see. And might that include what I was reading before our encounter with *Hammerhead-Prime*?"

"It might." Lucius shifted the charts around. "Let's see here. Teodorà and I still have all our notes and language modules, plus the documents we were researching. Ew!" He cringed. "You were reading *Raibert's* old paper on Justinian?"

"Bite me," she said without lifting her head from the pillow of her arms, and he chuckled.

"And as for you, Samuel..." Lucius flipped through more screens. "Yes, we have a few files. The biggest one is *Wild Vixens of the Oort Cloud, Part Seven*."

Teodorà exhaled a slow, seething breath.

Pepys suddenly became very interested in the tabletop.

"Was that what you were looking for?" Lucius asked innocently.

"Actually, no," Pepys replied, and glanced a bit sheepishly at Teodorà. "I fear curiosity got the best of me."

"It's all right," Teodorà said without looking up. "I'm not mad."

"Well, you also have parts one through fifteen." Lucius nudged him on the shoulder. "It's all safe in local memory."

"I rather hoped a different file might be there," Pepys said, still gazing a bit apprehensively at Teodorà. "Perhaps near the bottom of the list?"

"I'll take a look." Lucius scrolled down, then farther, then kept scrolling for half a minute. "The bottom. Yes, here we are. You also have—" His eyes gleamed suddenly. "Oh, ho ho! Samuel! You were reading about *electricity*?"

Teodorà's head popped up.

"Hey, Shadow! You think we could build a generator using this?"

"I believe so, Master Gwon. The damaged sections of the ship have more than enough conductive cabling and prog-steel for the microbots to build one. Perhaps a hydroelectric version? The Orontes River presents numerous possibilities."

"Indeed it does! I like where you're going with this!"

"Would that solve our need for power?" Pepys asked.

"Enough to keep the lights on, at least. Conceivably, we could power the infostructure forever." Lucius clapped him on the shoulder. "Nice one, Samuel! I didn't even think to look there."

❖   ❖   ❖

"Let's assume for a moment we'll have enough power to cover the basics," Lucius said half an hour later. "We're still left with the problem of how to distribute the cure."

He brought up an image of one of the conveyors packed into the *Shadow*'s cargo bay, along with a schematic of its performance and power requirement data. Two flexible arms dangled beneath the thick, disk-shaped drone. It wasn't fast or fancy, but it could carry great loads for extended periods of time and reach any point on the planet, eventually.

With enough power.

"Might we not remain in hiding and charge them slowly?" Pepys asked.

"No, Lucius is right," Teodorà said. "We're five decades too late. The Plague of Justinian is already ravaging Constantinople and ports around the Mediterranean. Our original plan of seeding genetic immunity into the populace and letting it spread won't work."

"Aerial dispersal isn't ideal, anyway," Lucius pointed out. "It was fine when we had an intact ship and could produce more of the cure at our leisure, but it's not exactly the most efficient way to distribute it. As things stand now, every drop we have left is precious."

"Can we use a different distribution method?" Teodorà asked.

"I think we almost have to."

"Your remote's above the city, right?"

"One of them is, yes."

"Bring it up, please."

Lucius opened the remote's feed, and Teodorà leaned over the table as the image appeared above it. The city lay in the middle of a valley, about eighteen kilometers wide, sprawled across a small island and the verdant bank of the Orontes River. Buildings dotted the nearby hillside, and stout walls and fortifications ringed both the island and the mainland portions of the city. Beyond those walls, a scattering of structures and a great many tents dotted the far bank.

"Antioch." Teodorà shuddered.

"Do I apprehend from your tone that this is not your first visit?" Pepys asked.

"Not quite. My second ART assignment was to study the Crusaders' siege of the city from 1097 to 1098. It was a lot smaller than this in the eleventh century. And it was just me and Fran, working under the Observation branch back then, and I conducted most of my research through remotes. Never set foot in the city, to be honest."

"I remember that one," Lucius said.

"You do?" Teodorà looked at him incredulously.

"Yeah. You picked some *really* good camera angles for when the Crusaders took the city."

"Fran did most of the editing. I didn't have the stomach for it back then." Teodorà tapped the western bank. "What do you make of all those tents?"

"Not sure. Let me move the remote in closer."

The view shifted lower, skimming the ground until it hovered over a neat row of tents, then drifted sideways past men on horseback armed with lances or composite bows. Others gathered around cook fires or dug latrines, and more tended to equipment and provisions.

An army, Teodorà thought gloomily. *That's all we need next door.*

"You think that might be Belisarius' force?" Lucius asked.

"It could be," Teodorà said. "It's certainly big enough."

"Belisarius?" Pepys repeated.

"General Flavius Belisarius of the Byzantine Empire," Teodorà replied. "It's 541, so that means Emperor Justinian recently sent him off to Syria."

"*After* he finished reconquering most of Italy in his emperor's name," Lucius observed dryly. "Successful generals always did make Justinian nervous."

"I'm surprised more of his field force isn't quartered in the city," Teodorà said. "There's no way he could have put an entire army into the available housing, but it *looks* like pretty much his entire force is outside the walls. That suggests there's a good chance the plague's already reached Antioch."

"That should be easy enough to confirm with the remote," Lucius said. "Question is, what do we do about it?"

"We can't immunize the whole planet. But we could cure those who already have it and immunize those who're at risk. And from there, it would spread all through the general population in a few generations."

"You mean just the three of us?" Lucius asked.

"It wouldn't take much, especially if we're not using a broadcast aerosol approach. Just a small injection per person. There should be more than enough supplies in the medical bay for us to treat people in the field, especially if we can deliver the cure directly to them."

"That's not what I mean. How are the three of us"— Lucius pointed to each of them in turn—"going to cure this many people? The Plague of Justinian killed *millions*. There aren't enough of us for that kind of approach."

"I should think the solution to that is simple," Pepys said. "Engage the services of the local rulers to aid us. If we require manpower to distribute the cure, who better to supply it than those who govern those we would cure?"

"Ask the *indigenes* for help?" Teodorà grimaced. "That'll never end well."

"No, let's not be hasty," Lucius urged. "He could be onto something. After all, we're in possession of an immensely valuable commodity. Granted, officials of the Byzantine Empire might take some...convincing to help us." He paused and bowed his head and thought. "But, what if..."

"What's going through your brain?" Teodorà asked a bit apprehensively.

He held up a finger for silence, and the others waited for him to finish thinking.

"A thought." He looked up at last. "Besides being one of the greatest generals in history, Belisarius was also a devout Christian, and his army was intensely loyal to him."

"That's all true," Teodorà agreed, wondering where he was going with this.

"And if we follow Samuel's thinking, an army would be very helpful to have on our side."

"Still all true," she said cautiously.

"And if we acquire Belisarius' aid, then the next logical step is to head for Constantinople and approach Emperor Justinian directly. Justinian was jumping at shadows, despite how loyal Belisarius was, but that's a solvable problem with the plague tearing Constantinople apart at the seams and us arriving with the cure."

"You're missing one important step." Teodorà crossed her arms. "How are you going to convince the general to help us?"

"By appealing to his Christian sensibilities." Lucius flashed a disarming smile. "As emissaries of God."

"Oh, no! Hell, no!"

"Why not? It'll be easy. A little light show here, some levitation there. We cure the plague once or twice, and then *bam*! We're divine beings. They listen to anything we say."

"We didn't come here to play gods!"

"*Emissaries* of gods," he corrected.

"You know what I mean!" she snapped.

"True, but it doesn't change the fact that building an aura of mystique around us will aid our mission."

"We're here to help these people," Teodorà stressed. "Not to fuel their ignorance."

"Come on. Look around us." He gestured across the bridge. "We're not in the best shape here, and this is only a short-term solution. No lasting harm will be done."

"You can't be sure of that."

"I fear I must agree with Teodorà," Samuel said. "If we truly wish to draw this general to our side, then it were best we do so honestly from the outset. There's naught more dangerous than a man who learns he's been deceived by one he thought a friend."

"This'll only make it harder," Lucius warned.

"Then count me in for rolling up my sleeves and doing it the hard way," Teodorà said. "Hard work and resolve can work miracles, Lucius."

"Indeed!" Pepys glanced warmly her way as she used his own words.

Lucius tapped his cheek with a finger and frowned. Then he shrugged.

"You're both going to be stubborn, I see. All right.

The hard way it is, then. Just don't say I didn't warn you."

"Thanks, Lucius," Teodorà said. "It'll be worth it in the end. You'll see."

"So how do you want to approach this? Contact Belisarius directly? Or something else?"

"I'll head for Antioch and try to reach the general," Teodorà said, then grimaced. "Although, given the time period, being a woman is likely to be a disadvantage."

"Then I shall accompany you," Pepys volunteered.

"Thanks."

"And how do you plan for the two of you to reach him?" Lucius asked.

"We'll . . . think of something."

"Ad lib it is, then. I'll hang back here with Shadow and work on our power problem. We'll see if we can get a generator up and running. Also, even if you succeed in getting Belisarius' army to help, other parties may need more . . . forceful convincing. But I have a few ideas that should help there."

"*Lucius.*"

He held up his hands.

"Only as a last resort," he promised. "It doesn't hurt to be prepared."

CHAPTER SIXTEEN

<hr>

Antioch
Byzantine Empire, 541 CE

TEODORÀ AND PEPYS REACHED THE TOP OF THE grass-covered ridgeline and stopped under the shade of a towering black pine. The city of Antioch spread out before them to the east, with most of its organized, orthogonal streets packed between the ridge and the river, kissed by the light of the setting sun.

Rather than attempt to cross the rugged top of the mountain, they'd circled its southern foot. It was over twice as long as a direct line between the hidden TTV wreck and the city, but the terrain was easier and Teodorà was just as happy to approach Antioch from a direction that wouldn't lead straight back to what was left of the *Shadow*. It *had* been a longish hike, though.

"How are you holding up?" she asked, her body equally unfazed by the heat and the hours of walking.

"Tolerably," Pepys panted, and popped the top of his bottled water. He took a sip, then closed it and wiped his mouth. The bottle drew in moisture from the surrounding air and replenished over time.

"I'm glad you came."

"How could I not? We are joined in this venture, are we not?" He returned the bottle to his travel pack. "And, truth be told, the walk was less than I had feared. This bodysuit is marvelously cool and comfortable. Would that I had had it in the midst of summer London! Yet I confess my legs are less happy than my other parts. Muscles I knew not that I possessed have made their presence known right painfully!"

"I'll bet." She chuckled, and he slipped out of his pack, then sat beside it and put his back to the tree.

"I trust it would not be impertinent of me to inquire, yet curiosity demands. Does your body weary or know pain?"

"Not the way you do." She placed her own pack next to his. "I'm conscious of when parts wear down or suffer damage, but it's information, not pain."

"That sounds most welcome at this moment," he said, leaning forward to knead the muscles of his right thigh with both hands.

"Yeah, going synthetic has its perks." She sat down next to him, and together they stared out across the city.

"You spoke of 'wearing down,'" he said after a moment, then paused as if struggling with the words. "How long will your body endure before it fails?"

"Theoretically, there's no limit."

"Indeed!" His expression brightened. "That is most wonderful to hear!"

"I have an onboard microbot colony to perform maintenance. I need to take supplements for raw materials occasionally, but that's all the help they need. And they also have limited self-replication, so the colony won't die off anytime soon."

"Might not those microbots help elsewhere aboard *Shadow*?"

"Sorry, but no. They're very specialized, and there are a *lot* of hardwired limits in place. Synthoid maintenance is covered, but that's about it."

"I see." Pepys pulled his pack onto his lap and rummaged inside for a nutrient bar. He peeled off the wrapper, bit down, then froze with an intensely sour expression.

"What's wrong?" Teodorà asked.

He took the bar out of his mouth, ran his tongue across his teeth, and frowned down at the offending sustenance.

"In my younger days," he said, "I did sample the salt meat purchased by Admiralty victualing clerks for His Majesty's vessels. It was, I considered, something of which a man might know only by personal experience. In consistence, it was much like a brick, and in flavor as like to old saddle leather as one might imagine." He grimaced. "Until this very moment, I had believed in fond imagination that no other food could be worse."

"Oh, sorry!" Teodorà laughed, but there was genuine contrition in the sound. "I don't think the designers worried about taste at all. They were focused on packing the maximum possible food value into it, and flavor wasn't a factor."

"So I have but lately discovered."

"Yes, but the *reason* they didn't worry about the taste is this." She sent him one of her favorite taste overlays through his wetware. "They figured anyone forced to eat it would have their own wetware to help with the flavor. Just activate that file. It'll taste great."

He regarded her a bit suspiciously, then shrugged and followed her instructions. He raised the bar again, took a slow, tentative bite, and his face lit up.

"Better?"

"Oh, my, yesh!" He chewed and swallowed. "What is this marvelous flavor?"

"Only the finest Martian dark chocolate."

"Chocolate?" Pepys raised a roguish eyebrow. "And would it chance there was a greater message than simply flavor?"

"Message?" she looked at him blankly, and he smiled slyly.

"I realize it was but the flavor, and not the thing itself, yet it is by far the tastiest aphrodisiac I've yet sampled!"

Teodorà blinked at him, stupefied for a moment, then burst into fresh, louder laughter.

"Oh, wow," she sighed, shaking her head. "I forgot your people had some *weird* ideas about chocolate. We just think of it as candy. Although, I do have a few friends who think it ought to be a food group in its own right."

"Lackaday!" he said mournfully, but still smiling. "Despite my bitter disappointment, the flavor is exquisite. Your tastes, my dear, are *all* most excellent!"

"There's more where that came from if you're interested. I've kept a collection of all my favorite tastes over the years."

"Indeed?" His eyes gleamed. "It would delight me to partake of more, but perhaps now is not the best of times?"

"Perhaps not," she agreed.

He finished the nutrient bar, much more eagerly than he'd begun it, and closed his pack.

"Shall we get to work?" she asked.

"Indeed."

She opened two virtual windows, one with a view of the city from above, and the other hovering above the army encampment.

"It puzzles me to see so many ruined buildings," Pepys said.

"Recent history hasn't been kind to the city. It sits right smack on the Dead Sea Transform and—"

"On the what?" Pepys interrupted, and she shook her head.

"Sorry. I forgot you wouldn't have learned about plate tectonics yet." She frowned in thought for a moment, then shrugged.

"Basically, the entire surface of the earth sits on what we call 'plates.' You can think of them as foundations, that underlie everything." She cocked an eyebrow at him and he nodded his comprehension of what she'd said so far. "There's a lot more than just one plate, though," she continued, "and even though you can't see it, all of them are constantly moving. Sort of like ice floes. They move very, very slowly, so slowly it's almost impossible to measure, but as you can imagine, something that supports that much weight moves with enormous power, however slow it is."

"Indeed," Pepys said. He looked around, as if he expected the solid earth beneath him to begin dancing, then looked back at her.

"Anyway, we call the border zones between the plates 'fault lines,' and what actually causes earthquakes are those fault lines rubbing against each other as the plates move. What you can think of as friction *prevents* them from moving smoothly, you see. So they don't really move all that much until enough energy builds up to *force* them to move, and it's the sudden adjustment that creates earthquakes."

"I believe I comprehend," Pepys said. "'Tis as well I've had so much experience in comprehending your new wonders, dear lady!"

"Well, that's a *horribly* simplified explanation," she told him with a smile, "but the point is that Antioch sits right on one of those fault lines, and the Dead Sea Transform is in a particularly active period right now. Antioch and Seleucia Pieria, its seaport to the south, never fully recovered from the earthquake of 526, and then Khosrow I, the Persian king, sacked the city just three years ago, in 538. Persian aggression is the main reason Justinian sent Belisarius here."

"I see," Pepys said, his eyes sad. "I saw too much of London laid in wreckage, and now this." He waved one hand at the imagery. "'Twould seem Antioch's better days are long spent."

"That's true, unfortunately," she agreed. "Historically, Antioch never *did* recover. The earthquakes did damage enough, then the Plague of Justinian swept through it. And the Empire never really recovered from the plague and Justinian's overextension into the west. The Persians kept pushing their influence deeper and deeper into what used to be Byzantine territory, and Antioch was right in the middle of the conflict zone." She shook her head a bit sadly. "Not too surprising that people chose not to live in the middle of a battlefield, I suppose."

"No, I suppose not."

Pepys stood gazing silently down on the city for a moment, then shook himself.

"But to business!" he said more briskly. "Would it chance the remote has discovered Belisarius?"

"We haven't spotted the man himself, but this farmhouse looks interesting." She highlighted one window of the large farmhouse, obviously the abode of an affluent landowner. "I'm wondering if the general might be using it as his field headquarters. Look at how the tents are arrayed so neatly around it, almost like this is where the heart of the army set up and the rest of the tents branched off from there."

"And there does seem to be more bustle and flow about it," Pepys observed.

"Yeah. We could send the remote into the farmhouse, but they might spot it even with its shroud. I'll keep it hovering overhead for now."

"And how is ART wont to approach a challenge such as this?" Pepys asked.

"Usually, I'd have more resources." Teodorà eyed Pepys's attire. "Like being able to print period clothes."

Besides the bodysuit under his garments, both of them wore the clothes on their backs when the ship broke up. The combination of his seventeenth-century brown long coat and her thirtieth-century white business suit would have made them the center of attention in just about *any* era.

"Blending in is going to be a bit…difficult," she said.

"Might we employ the remotes to acquire local garments? I mislike the idea of theft, but in this present pass it may be a necessary evil."

"We're going to come across as very foreign no

matter what we do, but yeah. Period clothes are a good place to start."

She pulled up manual controls for the remote and guided it over the city streets, and Pepys chuckled suddenly. She glanced at him with a raised eyebrow, and he chuckled again.

"Conceive their astonishment when they see their linens float suddenly heavenward," he said.

"A point," she agreed. "It would probably be better to wait until nightfall to do it." The remote reached the end of the street, and she turned it left, down a long, desolate row of derelict structures. "Hang on." She backed up the remote. "What have we here?"

"You've spied something?"

"Yeah."

She lowered the remote so that its view angled down through the windows of the squat, rectangular building less badly damaged than its neighbors. The image zoomed in and enhanced the candlelit interior into daytime clarity.

Inside, men and women sat or lay on mats in two orderly rows, and a few of their hands and faces showed signs of necrotic decay.

"The Black Death," Pepys breathed.

"No doubt about it," she agreed, equally softly.

She panned the view down the street and came to a ruin where only broken parts of walls remained. Bodies lay stacked inside, some covered in linens, others naked, their extremities blackened from rot.

"So many died so fast, they're not even burying them." She took a long, slow breath, even though her body didn't need the air.

"Dreadful, is it not?"

There was an odd, almost gentle note in Pepys's voice. A note of...sympathy, she realized. Unlike her, he'd seen this horror before, with his own eyes, and now those eyes met hers compassionately. She looked back at him for several seconds, finally understanding—fully, emotionally, not just intellectually—why this was the crusade he had chosen. Then she nodded and turned back to the remote's window.

"They're isolating plague victims in the abandoned part of town," she said in a deliberately crisp voice, pulling the remote back and retracing its path toward the improvised isolation ward. "Makes sense now why the army's camped outside the wall instead of in all these previously empty buildings. I'm going to take a look inside."

The remote reached its destination and the view slowed as it approached one of the windows. Light gleamed dully off a collection of equipment in one corner of the building, and Teodorà's eyes narrowed.

"Oh? What have we here?" she murmured.

"A host of dead and dying," Pepys said grimly.

"Spathas."

He blinked. "Pardon?"

"A common Byzantine Army sword. It replaced the Roman gladius because of its longer reach. At least three of them were set aside in that corner, along with armor and bows. That means some of these plague victims are soldiers. Perfect!"

"Ah!" He nodded. "We might present them cured to the general as proof of our good intent!"

"Exactly." She backed the remote away and flagged that specific plague house for future reference. "Now, let's find some decent clothes to steal. We should—"

"Just stand where you are!"

Teodorà whirled with a start. Two sentries had emerged from the tree line farther along the ridge. One was a muscular man with gray creeping into his dark curls, the other a fresh-faced youngster. The setting sun gleamed off their drawn swords and steel helmets.

She and Pepys stood and backed away.

"Stand, I said!" the older man snapped, and both of them stopped.

"Speak of the devil and hear the rattle of his armor," Pepys muttered from the side of his mouth.

<Not the first contact I'd imagined,> she sent to him without speaking. <Use your wetware if you need to talk to me.>

<Indeed,> he sent back. <My apologies.>

<No, I'm the one who's sorry. This is my fault. I should've kept one of the remotes back to watch our surroundings.>

"And what might you be?" the older sentry demanded as he stepped closer.

His bearded face was weathered from long days in the sun and a scar ran down his left cheek to the side of his neck. He looked like precisely what he probably was, Teodorà thought—a tough, experienced, hardened noncom.

"Just two travelers enjoying the sunset," Pepys replied in the Greek of Byzantium, using the language module loaded into his wetware.

Impressive for his first try, she thought, smiling ever so slightly. *He almost got the accent right.*

"You don't say?" The sentry could have sounded more convinced, she thought. "You're not on or near any of the main roads, and your garb, well—" He pointed with his sword. "I've never seen its like before."

"We're not Persians, if that's what you're wondering," Teodorà said.

"Hold your tongue, woman!" the younger sentry snapped.

If the older man was wary, the youngster seemed actively hostile. Teodorà glowered at him, and he took a quick stride toward her.

"You have no idea who you're dealing with," Pepys said in a warning tone, and despite the tension of the moment, Teodorà noticed that the lingering archaisms of his word choices in Modern English had disappeared into the translating software's colloquial period Greek. But even as she noted that change, he laid one hand on the grip of the Popular Arsenals PA13N burst pistol holstered at his side. Fortunately, the "N" was for "Nonlethal."

<Don't,> she sent silently.

<It will only tranquilize, not kill.>

<And when they wake up and report in? Then what?>

<Ah.> He lowered his hand. <A shrewd question.>

<Thanks,> she replied dryly.

"I'm still waiting for some answers," the older sentry said.

"If it's answers you want, try asking for them without pointing swords at us," Teodorà suggested out loud.

He narrowed his eyes, but he didn't lower his sword.

"Fine. Have it your way." She gestured to herself first. "I'm Teodorà Beckett and this is Samuel Pepys."

"What kind of names are those?"

"The ones our parents gave us, of course."

The sentry glared at her, and she reminded herself this was a patriarchal culture where female flippancy might be . . . contraindicated.

He let her have a good twenty seconds of the glare

he probably kept handy for new recruits, then wiggled his sword slightly.

"And what's your business here in Antioch?" he demanded then.

She considered several possible answers, then shrugged mentally. It wasn't the way she'd *planned* on beginning but—

"We're here to cure the plague."

"Ha!" he barked. "Charlatans, then! Well, you're not the first, and we know what to do with you. Bind them!"

The younger man sheathed his sword, produced a leather thong from his belt pouch, and approached Teodorà first.

"I think not," she said in a warning tone, but he only snorted in amused disdain and grabbed her wrist.

She turned toward him, breaking his grip with the skills provided by the unarmed combat module all ART field agents were required to download and keep current. Then she caught his tunic in one hand and his sword belt in the other, and he squawked in stunned disbelief as she casually hurled him several meters through the air, courtesy of her synthoid's strength. He crashed into a cluster of brush and rolled through it in a cacophony of snapping dry branches.

The older sentry's head turned as his eyes watched his companion's unplanned flight. Then those eyes snapped back to Teodorà, wide with astonishment.

"And is this the fashion for most of your expeditions?" Pepys asked wryly, no longer bothering with silence.

"No." Teodorà dusted her hands together. "But I'm really not in the mood to play fair."

She turned to the sentry and beckoned him toward her.

"Come on," she said in Greek. "Come at me. Take your best swing."

"Demon!" He charged with his sword at the thrust. It was obvious he meant business, but Teodorà charged right back at him, moving even faster, grabbed his wrist, and twisted.

"Yearrah!" he cried, and dropped the sword.

"Samuel, would you be so kind as to pick that up?"

"Assuredly, my dear."

Pepys bent down and retrieved the sword. While he did, the veteran twisted around in her grip, snarled at her, and punched her repeatedly.

"Please stop."

He braced a boot sole against her thigh and tried to push away, but she was immovable as a stone wall and her grip never even quivered.

"What kind of creature *are* you?" he demanded. "A demon?"

"Worse." Teodorà yanked him so close their faces almost touched. "I'm a historian."

She head-butted him with her forehead. His nose broke with an audible crack and he stumbled backward, blood spraying from his face as she released him and he collapsed onto his back.

"You stay away from him!" the younger sentry shouted, his own sword drawn as he came back at her. He moved far more warily this time, but he wasn't backing down.

Points for courage, she thought. *Not so much for brains.*

She sighed and shook her head. Then she held out a hand.

"The sword, please, Samuel?"

"But of course," Pepys replied in an undeniably amused tone.

"Thanks."

She took the sword, gripped its hilt in her right hand and the blade about half a meter from the guard. Then she flexed her wrists.

The blade snapped, and she tossed both pieces at the younger man's feet.

He stared at the ruined weapon in wide-eyed disbelief.

"Still want to try your luck, kid?" she inquired.

He shook his head.

"There's a good boy." She planted a boot next to the veteran's head. "If I can do that to a sword, imagine what I can do to his head. Now drop your weapon!"

"Is this in some wise better than putting them to sleep?" Pepys asked brightly.

"It *feels* better."

"Ah." He smiled and shook his head, then sobered a bit. "And how shall we proceed now?"

"What else? We improvise."

She bent down, looming over the veteran.

"Hello, there."

"What are you going to do to me?" His voice was thick with his inability to get air through his broken nose; his chest heaved with obviously fearful breaths, but he glared up at her defiantly.

"Oh, don't give me that look. You picked this fight. You just made the mistake of thinking you could win it. We won't hurt you if you cooperate."

"What do you want?"

"Exactly what we said. We're here to cure the

plague. Which means we need to go where the sick are gathered." She smiled, her perfect teeth shining in the dying light. "And you two just volunteered to be our escorts."

❖   ❖   ❖

"This quarter is where the sick are kept," Nikolas Trichas, the senior of the two sentries who'd tried to take them in, said. He stopped in the middle of the crossroads, his stance telling Teodorà he was afraid to go any farther. But that was all right; a virtual navigational beacon glowed over a nearby house.

"Thank you, Nikolas," she said, with genuine gratitude. "I think we can manage from here."

"Can you really cure them, my lady?" he asked, dabbling a cloth under his broken nose. Despite their earlier... misunderstanding, he offered the honorific in tones of true respect. Thomas Skleros, his younger cohort, remained more doubtful, and he also kept his distance, with a small crowd that had gathered as they made their way deeper into the city.

"Yes," she replied, "but you don't have to take my word for it. You and the rest of Antioch will have proof soon enough."

"You sound very confident," he said, and she chuckled.

"You did, too, when you spoke with the gate guards," she pointed out, and he shrugged.

"That was for their sake, my lady. Something told me you'd have gotten in whether we let you in or not. There was no point getting them hurt along the way."

"Smart man," she approved. "And you're right, of course. I'd really prefer not having to break any more noses, though."

Nikolas snorted. Blood and mucous blew out of his nose, and he wiped his upper lip with the cloth.

"Believe it or not," she continued, "getting here was the hard part. Curing the plague is easy."

He shook his head.

"You speak so casually of miracles."

"It only seems like a miracle because you don't know how it's done." She dismissed him with a wave. "You can leave now, if you want. I only ask that you send word to the general. I'm sure he'll want to meet with us soon."

"I—" Nikolas glanced at the plague house and resolve stiffened visibly within him. He stood a little straighter and met her eyes. "I'll witness this cure for myself, my lady. Besides, I'm sure questions will follow, and I'd be a poor soldier if I couldn't make a proper report."

"All right. You can come. Just don't get in our way."

Teodorà and Pepys headed straight for the plague house with the sick soldiers inside. Nikolas followed a few paces back, and Thomas stayed behind at the intersection.

Pepys coughed at the threshold, his eyes watering. He took out a handkerchief and covered his mouth.

"My word. I'd forgotten the stench!"

"Here." She sent him a minty scent overlay. "Load this."

"Thank you." He inhaled deeply. "Ahh! As ever, you are a godsend, my dear."

"You're still breathing in the same junk, so be careful with that. Smell is a good warning mechanism, and we just disabled yours."

"I shall bear that in mind," he promised.

They crossed the threshold. The light was dim, to say the least, but Teodorà's light-enhancing vision picked out four women, and three men in monk's robes, making their way slowly along the rows of dying men and women. They stopped to wipe faces with damp cloths from the buckets they carried, to offer water, and she felt an unstinting admiration for the courage or faith—or both—that kept them here, ministering to the dying. They knew they couldn't cure the plague. They knew working here among its victims was all too likely to prove lethal. Yet here they were, doing what little a pre-technic society could do to comfort the sick in their extremity.

<It was so in London, too,> Pepys sent across their wetware link. She looked at him, and he smiled sadly. <Most fled. Some stayed. And all too many of those who remained sickened and died in their turn.> He shook his head. <Their courage struck me with awe then, and even more today, when I comprehend fully what the Black Death truly means.>

<Well, in that case, let's show them the relief force has arrived,> Teodorà replied, and he gave her a much fiercer smile.

She spotted a table near the soldiers' equipment and walked across to set her pack down there. As she crossed the room, one of the monks looked up from where he knelt beside a semiconscious woman and saw her. His long beard was streaked with white where it spilled down his chest, and his bushy eyebrows rose toward his shaven scalp. The lighting might be poor, but his vision had been given ample time to adjust, and it was obvious from his expression that he'd never seen anything quite like her. Then those raised eyebrows lowered. He laid down the hand he had been holding, rose and signed the cross above the woman, and strode purposefully toward Teodorà and Pepys.

"What are you doing?" he asked.

"We're here to help the sick, Brother—?" Teodorà replied, ending on a questioning note.

"I am Brother Lavarentios," he said. "And what do you mean 'to help the sick'?" His expression tightened and he shook his head. "There is little anyone this side of Heaven can do for these poor people, Lady—?"

Teodorà had to suppress a smile, despite their grim surroundings. The language program offered several different translation modes, and she'd selected the mode suitable for a noblewoman. Obviously, Brother Lavarentios had recognized it when he heard it.

"I am Teodorà Beckett," she told him, and felt another flicker of amusement at his response. Her first name was no problem for him, but her surname clearly struck him as bizarre.

"Where did you come from?" he asked. She cocked her head, and he snorted. "Lady, I have never seen someone garbed as you are, and it's evident you're from someplace far from here."

"My home lies far to the west," she told him after a moment.

"And yet, traveler from a far land that you are, you've chosen to come *here*?"

He waved one hand in an oddly graceful gesture that took in the squalor and the stench which surrounded them.

"My companion and I are healers," she replied. "In our own land, we're able to cure the plague."

"Cure?"

He stared at her in disbelief, and she didn't blame him. Ignorant and uneducated he might be, by the standards of her own time, but he was clearly no fool. Then his face hardened and he glared at her.

"It would be a sin before God to tell these people you could cure them!" he more than half-snarled in a low voice. "The Patriarch and General Belisarius know how to deal with charlatans! Besides, these poor people have no money for you to trick them out of!"

"Yes, it would be a sin to tell these people we can cure them...if it was a lie, Brother Lavarentios." Her own voice was level and she met his furious gaze levelly. "It isn't, however. We *can* cure them. And we ask no payment, only to be allowed to heal the sick as our calling requires us to do."

"No payment," he repeated skeptically. "No silver or gold?"

"No payment," she confirmed. "We will wish to speak to General Belisarius—and to Patriarch Ephraim— afterward," she added, silently blessing the absent Raibert for having included the painstaking analysis of the Byzantine Church in the appendices of his biography of Belisarius. Fresh suspicion showed in Lavarentios' eyes, and she shook her head quickly. "We'll ask no payment from them, either, Brother. But even though we can cure the plague, there are, as you see, only two of us. We can't deal with pestilence on this scale without enlisting the aid of the Church and the Army."

"You're serious," Lavarentios said after a moment. "You truly believe you can cure the plague."

"I believe it because I can," she told him with

total honesty, hoping he recognized the sincerity in her tone. "In my own land, Brother Lavarentios," she added with equal honesty, "the plague has been completely eradicated. No one suffers from it there."

His eyes widened, but in an expression of dawning wonder, not rejection.

"Lady . . . Teodorà," he said, "if that is indeed true, then may God and all the saints bless you for coming to us here. But before I permit you to treat these people, I must be sure you will not be employing the black arts."

"There's no sorcery here, Brother. Only knowledge and skills the Empire has not yet attained." Teodorà went to one knee before him. An instant later, Pepys joined her in response to her silent command. "I ask for your blessing before we begin their treatment."

Lavarentios' expression softened, and he raised his hand, signing the cross above each of them in turn.

"May you indeed bring healing to the sick and comfort to the dying," he said, and then continued, "O Lord, look down upon Your servant Teodorà and—" he paused, looking at Pepys.

"Samuel, Brother," Pepys murmured.

"—and upon your servant Samuel," Lavarentios resumed. "Look upon them with favor and extend Your healing through them to these, Your children, in their extremity, through Jesus Christ, our Lord. In the name of the Father, the Son, and the Holy Ghost."

"Amen," Teodorà murmured as Samuel crossed himself beside her. She might not share Lavarentios' beliefs, but she admired his sincerity.

And the fact that I didn't vanish in a puff of smoke when he blessed me isn't going to hurt anything, either, she told herself.

Lavarentios stepped back, his expression reassured yet still dubious.

"What can I and these others"—he gestured to the men and women who had been tending the sick and had now gathered behind him to stare at their bizarre visitors—"do to assist you?"

"We don't require any assistance to actually administer our medicine," Teodorà replied. "But we should begin with those most seriously ill, the ones who have the least time left if they aren't healed. If you could triage—I mean, show us who is sickest—it would be of great assistance."

"Of course, Lady."

Lavarentios turned to his assistants and Teodorà looked at Pepys.

<This is our first appearance, so let's make sure we do well,> she told him silently. <We'll double the dose for everyone we treat tonight. That should help Belisarius take us seriously.>

<Indeed,> Pepys agreed as he set his own pack on the table beside hers. He pulled two medical dosers from it, loaded cure vials into each of them, and doubled the dose setting in their option windows. Then he set the needles for auto-sterilization and handed one to Teodorà.

She turned from the table and found Lavarentios at her elbow.

"This way, Lady," he said and led her to a pallet at the far end of a long row. It was, Teodorà realized, the end closest to the ruined building in which the bodies of the dead had been stacked.

She knelt down beside the young man on that pallet. His nose was black from rot, his blanket was dark and soaked with sweat, and his eyelids fluttered slowly upward as she reached out to touch his chin.

"Hello there," she said gently as those eyes opened. "What's your name?"

"A-Akakios," he got out.

"Hello, Akakios."

"Wh-Who . . . are . . . you?" he croaked.

"Someone you should be very happy to meet." She turned his head gently and placed the doser against his throat. "Hold still, Akakios. This will pinch a little."

CHAPTER SEVENTEEN

~∞∞∞~

Antioch
Byzantine Empire, 541 CE

FLAVIUS BELISARIUS WAS FORTY-ONE YEARS OLD, dark-haired, and tall, for Byzantium in the sixth century *Anno Domini*. He was also broad-shouldered, with the powerful wrists and arms of a man who had been known for his deadly sword skill during his years as one of Emperor Justinian's personal *bucellarii*. He'd met very few obstacles he couldn't best in his career and life, and he was confident of his ability to deal with the Persians.

Unfortunately, he had another problem, just at the moment. One rather more immediate than King Khosrow and his armies.

It wasn't one he minded—mostly, at any rate. He'd faced far worse—or *probably* far worse—conundrums in his years of service to Emperor Justinian. Compared to many of those other conundrums, his current dilemma was almost pleasant. It was also starkly amazing, and that was what worried him. Things he couldn't explain

269

always worried him, and so far as he knew, *no one* could explain this one.

The plague ravaging Antioch had ended in a matter of days, sparing its citizens, and even many of his own soldiers slow, horrific deaths.

That was the good news. The bad news was that he had no idea how it had been done.

A miracle, he thought, tasting the word in his mind as he rubbed his trimmed beard. *Like one of the Plagues of Egypt, but withdrawn at a whim.*

He glanced across the farmhouse table at the crucifix on the wall. It was a simple affair of wood and nails, painted white with a few dried palm fronds draped across the main beam.

Is Brother Lavarentios right? Did *the Almighty truly reach His hand down to His children through these foreigners?* he wondered. *Or is something else at work here?*

His army remained outside the city, and it would stay there until he decided otherwise. Yes, it *seemed* safe, but something unnatural was at work, and until he knew whether it was of the Light or the Dark, he would take no chances.

Now he glanced down, dark eyes locking on the young soldier seated on the stool before him.

"And then what happened?" he pressed.

"I tried to restrain them, General," Thomas Skleros said. "The woman first."

"And how did she respond?"

"Not well, sir. She picked me up and threw me."

"How far?"

"Oh . . ." Thomas reached down and rubbed his ankle. "Farther than the length of this room, I'd say."

"About five paces, then?"

"I'm not really sure, sir. I was a bit...confused after I hit the ground."

Belisarius gazed at the soldier, his focus unwavering as he waited for more. Not that he doubted Thomas had been "confused" if he'd truly been thrown twenty feet by the mysterious woman! And much though Belisarius wanted to believe he hadn't been...

The general had interviewed dozens of citizens and soldiers now, and every interview had told the same story. Yes, these two foreigners had distributed their medicine and cured the plague, and that was wonder enough. But they also possessed *other* powers, and it was those other abilities that most concerned him just now.

"I swear I speak the truth, sir," Thomas said to fill the silence.

Nikolas, the other sentry, had given a similar account, although in his version the woman had flung poor Thomas *ten* paces.

Soldiers and their tall tales, he thought. *But this time, I detect a seed of truth beneath the exaggerations. However far she threw him, she shouldn't have been able to throw him at all. And the sword...*

He picked up one half of the broken sword on the table.

"And how did this happen?"

"She snapped it in half, sir." Thomas swallowed. "With her bare hands."

"How long did it take her? Did she struggle with it at all?"

"No, sir. Just an instant. Like it was nothing, sir."

Belisarius held the blade close to a candle. Flickering

light played off the metal, and he could discern no flaws in the craftsmanship. It seemed a good, serviceable blade. Of course, swords broke all the time—a soldier could break *anything* if he put his mind to it—but certainly no woman should have been able to simply snap it like a dry branch.

Someone knocked hard on the door.

"Come in, Irene," Belisarius said, recognizing the knock.

The door opened, and a wizened old woman walked in with a tray of steaming soup, bread, and cheese.

"Thomas, don't just sit there. Help her."

"Sir!" The youthful soldier bolted upright and reached for the tray, but the woman jerked it away.

"No need for that, General." She elbowed Thomas aside and set the tray down on the table. "Not as fast as I once was, but I'm not dead yet. I can still manage my own house. Here's your dinner."

"Thank you, Irene." He inhaled the aroma. "It smells wonderful."

She snorted derisively.

"Of course it does. Anything would after what your so-called cooks serve up! You may have an entire army, but do any of your men have the wit to cook a good meal?" She snorted again, magnificently this time. "Course they don't—they're *men*!"

Irene was older than his wife, Antonina, but there were times the widow reminded him a great deal of her. Antonina was five years his own senior, and her early life had been at least as harsh as any Syrian farmwife's. It had been very different, of course. The daughter of a charioteer and a dancer—a stripper, really—she'd earned her living as best she could before they met, but it had made her strong. And today she was the best friend and closest confidante of the empress. Indeed, she served Theodora much as Belisarius had always served Justinian, and she could be just as ruthless as any man ever born. Yet she'd never lost her trenchant, keen-edged sense of humor. Or her wit. Indeed, the more he thought about the problem he faced, the more he wished Antonina were here to help him deal with it.

She should have been. She wasn't, and he put that thought—and the reasons she wasn't—aside and smiled at Irene, instead.

"There *are* men who know how to cook, you know, Irene." His tone was innocent, but his eye glinted mischievously.

"No, there aren't," she replied. "There are men who *think* they can cook!"

"Where army cooks are concerned, you're more right than you know," Belisarius admitted with a chuckle, throwing up one hand in a gesture of surrender. "By the way, has Megistus seen you today?"

"Your quartermaster? Oh, yes. That scoundrel keeps trying to shove gold in my face."

"We still need to pay you for your hospitality. And for the damage I know my army is doing to your land."

"You keep saying that, General, and I keep saying you don't. We can both keep doing it as long as you want, but it won't change a thing. Me and my boys will do everything we can to help you, and you'll not pay us a single copper for it. It's the least we can do."

Belisarius nodded. The Persians had killed her husband, Petrus, when they sacked Antioch a few years ago, so he understood the personal stake Irene's

family had in the campaign to drive them entirely out
of Syria. At the same time, he knew that if she truly
refused to accept all payment, his army's visit would
leave her ruined.

"I understand that. Still, it would"—he paused and
smiled at her—"soothe my conscience if you'd accept
at least some payment."

"Well, I'll consider it," she said.

She probably didn't mean it, Belisarius thought, and
made a mental note to send Megistus to her oldest
son, Grigorios. He was a canny man...and he kept
Irene's accounts. No doubt he could accept the payment and "discover" the funds when she needed them.

"Now eat up," she continued. "Can't have you running around with a weak constitution!"

"Thank you, Irene. I will."

She nodded, satisfied with a job well done, then
departed and closed the door.

Thomas stood at attention, eyes forward.

"You're dismissed."

"Sir!"

Thomas saluted, then hurried out of the room, and
Belisarius sat back and rubbed his eyes for a moment.

Thank God the Patriarch of Antioch had once been
a general himself. There were distinct limits to how
far Ephraim of Antioch was prepared to stretch doctrine, as Severus of Antioch had discovered five years
ago, but for now, at least, he was willing to leave this
particular puzzle in Belisarius' hands.

Oh, how fortunate *for me!* Belisarius thought wryly,
then grimaced. It truly was fortunate, and a sign of
both Ephraim's pragmatism and of how terrifying the
plague's arrival in Antioch had been that the patriarch

was prepared to stand aside, at least for the moment. But whatever the Church might do, the emperor would expect his general to deal with the problem.

If, indeed, it is a problem. He snorted. *Of course it's going to be a problem! Anything Christians can argue about with each other is going to be a "problem" eventually!*

That might be true. In fact, sadly, it *was* true. But another thing that was true was that problems that were put off only grew, and this one was quite large enough already.

He placed his knuckles on the table and pushed himself to his feet with a sigh. He was as prepared as he could be, and he'd already put this off for too long. The scent rising from the soup made his stomach grumble, but he still had work to do.

He stepped out of the dining room. One of his *bucellarii* retainers leaned against the wall with his arms crossed, staring out the window. The burly man turned and looked up as the general approached.

"Leontius."

"Yes, sir?" the *bucellariius* said.

"Extend the invitation."

❖   ❖   ❖

"Thank you for meeting with us, General. My name is Doctor Teodorà Beckett, and this is Samuel Pepys."

Belisarius nodded to each of them in turn, and kept his face neutral. He'd thought, perhaps too hopefully, that seeing these two with his own eyes would dispel some of the mystery, but now he found the opposite was true.

The woman was unusually tall and possessed an unnatural beauty. Her olive complexion reminded him of Antonina's, but her skin was flawless, without so much as a single blemish, and her long hair shimmered in the candlelight. By comparison, the man seemed almost plain. His round, sunburned face, slight double chin, and portly belly gave Belisarius an impression of affluence, as if he'd never worked outdoors in the desert heat in his entire life.

He found their clothing just as baffling. He'd never seen the styles before, yet he discovered that he thought of them that way. Styles. Plural. And the fabrics involved appeared to be of exceptional quality. Not only were these two from a foreign land, but their attire was foreign in different ways, and he took particularly careful note of the woman's clothing. Mud speckled the hem of the man's long coat, but there was not a trace of mud on the woman's pristine white trousers. He supposed that was the best way to describe them, although they were longer than the calf-length *feminalia* and far . . . snugger—that was a good word—than the *braccae* the Empire had adopted from the Celts. Yet whatever he called them, there was no sign of mud—or any other stain—upon them, despite the three days she'd spent, apparently without sleeping once, in the filth and miasma of the plague houses.

At least no one who saw her in them could doubt that she was a woman.

These two are so strange. Could they truly be divine beings? he wondered once more, suppressing a sudden craven wish Patriarch Ephraim *was* present so he could leave that determination to someone else. *Even if that's not the case, though, it's clear they have extraordinary abilities. So—*

He drew a deep mental breath. He'd already decided upon a cautious but respectful tone.

"Sir. Lady. Welcome. Please sit."

"Thank you, General."

The man put his hands on the table and lowered himself onto the waiting stool with a stifled sigh of relief. The woman merely sat with catlike grace, crossed her legs, and clasped her hands on the tabletop before her.

Belisarius seated himself on the opposite side of the table, while Leontius stood against the wall, watchful as a fox.

"Lady Teodorà," he began, giving her the honorific she clearly deserved, "it's I who should thank you, as well as apologize for the rudeness my soldiers showed you upon your arrival. The reports from the city have gladdened many, and I've given orders to all the men under my command that you're to be allowed free passage anywhere within Antioch."

"That's quite all right, General. Thomas and Nikolas didn't know who we were, and their . . . overreaction"—she smiled—"was understandable."

"Yes, about your identities. If you'll permit a question?"

"Of course. I imagine you have many."

"Indeed." He leaned forward. "I hope you'll pardon my frankness, but who . . . or *what* are you?"

She laughed.

"Straight to the point, I see," she said.

"A great many rumors are circulating," he replied.

"Well, there's nothing divine about us, if that's what you're worried about."

Belisarius blinked and sat back. He hadn't expected so direct an answer.

"As we already told Brother Lavarentios, we're merely foreigners from distant lands," she continued. "Nothing more fanciful than that."

"I see. And which lands might that be?"

"I hail from the European Cooperative, a state within the Consolidated System Government, or Sys-Gov for short."

"And I'm from England," her companion said.

"I've never heard of either," Belisarius confessed.

"I'm not surprised." Lady Teodorà shrugged. "They're *very* distant lands."

"I see. What brings you to Antioch?"

"Our motives should be clear enough. We have a cure for the plague, far too many are suffering here in the Empire, and we can't just stand by and let that happen if we can prevent it. As a fellow Christian, you should understand how we feel."

"Christianity *has* spread to your lands?" Belisarius tried to hide his relief, although from the twinkle in Lady Teodorà's eye, he suspected he'd failed.

"It has," she confirmed, but then continued. "I'm sure the distance between my home and yours... and how much *later* Christianity came to mine, means our practices differ from yours, though."

"I suppose that's only natural," he said, suppressing a shudder as he tried not to think about how the Pentarchy, the five senior patriarchs of the Church, would respond to practices that "differed" from orthodoxy. Patriarch Ephraim was a practical as well as a devout man, but he had a short way with heresy or schism, as the Monophysites of Syria had discovered. And that didn't even consider how Justinian, himself a keen theologian, would react when *he* learned of this.

"Tell me, though, Lady," he said, "are all the women in . . . SysGov gifted as you are?"

"Gifted?" She raised an eyebrow, the twinkle in her eye unmistakable now. "In what way?" she asked innocently.

"With exceptional strength," he clarified, resolutely refusing to smile.

"Some are," she replied in a more serious tone. "Not all."

"And what does SysGov call your kind?"

"My kind? Well, I'm a synth—" Teodorà paused, frowned, then shook her head. "Actually that won't do." She bowed her head, obviously thinking hard, then snapped her fingers. "Tell you what, General. I don't feel your own language's word is appropriate here, so I'm going to use another one. You can think of me as a Valkyrie."

"Ah!" Her companion smiled. "Yes, that's perfect."

"A . . . Valkyrie." Belisarius tasted the latest strange word to come his way. "Is it a name, or does it have a meaning?"

"It comes from the word *Valkyrja*," Lady Teodorà replied. "That means 'chooser of the slain.' The Valkyrie are a legendary host of women warriors from a part of my homeland who descend upon battlefields and select those who live and those who die. Although"—she raised one hand and waved it—"I suppose a 'battle' against the plague stretches the original meaning."

"Still," the man—Samuel Pepys—said, "I think it suits you wonderfully."

"Thank you." She dipped her head to him, then turned her gaze to Belisarius. "Anything else you'd like to ask, General?"

"Of course there is." Belisarius shook his head. "How could it be otherwise. And"—he watched her expression closely—"I'm sure Patriarch Ephraim will wish to speak with you, as well."

"No doubt." If she felt any qualms over an interview with Ephraim, she hid them well, Belisarius thought. "Please tell the Patriarch that, as I've already assured Brother Lavarentios, Samuel and I will be at his disposal whenever he wishes to interview us. And we deeply appreciate the assistance Brother Lavarentios and Abbot Stylianos and his monks have provided."

Belisarius nodded. In his experience, monks came in two basic varieties. One of them was belligerent, intolerant, and believed right doctrine could be best inculcated by breaking heads to let enlightenment in. That variety seemed unfortunately common sometimes. Too often, in Belisarius' opinion. The other variety took its responsibilities to care for their fellow Christians seriously. Many of them could face their belligerent cousins toe to toe, cudgel in hand, if the need arose, but they normally had better things to do with their time. Like healing souls and caring for the sick.

And when it comes to the plague, only the strongest faith can carry a man or a woman through caring for its victims, he thought grimly. *We lost too many of that sort even before these two came along.*

Indeed they had, and the reports of Brother Lavarentios and—especially of Father Stylianos, the Abbot of Saint Cyril—were one reason Patriarch Ephraim had been prepared to leave any official theological interrogations until later.

"I will tell Patriarch Ephraim exactly that," Belisarius said. He paused, then, in a more delicate tone, said,

"I'm sure you understand that the Patriarch will still have many questions of his own."

"I would be astonished if he didn't," Lady Teodorà replied in a serious tone. "In fact, I need to talk to him as badly as I needed to talk to you."

"Talk to me about what, my lady?" he asked cautiously.

"We need your help," she replied, and her tone was deadly serious now.

"*My* help?" Belisarius shook his head. "From all I've so far seen, it's far more likely that *I* need *yours*."

"That's because you're not yet aware of how bad the plague truly is. Not just in Syria, but all around the Mediterranean, and especially in Constantinople."

"And how is it that you would have better information than I?"

His eyes had narrowed, and she shrugged.

"Some we've gathered ourselves on our travels. Some comes from stories, but we've witnessed plenty with our own eyes. We passed through Constantinople on our way here. Hundreds die there every day, General. *Hundreds.* The death toll makes the plague here in Antioch look like a mild nuisance, and it will only get worse if it isn't stopped."

"Then why not cure the sick in that city? Why come here?"

"Because even though we have a cure for the plague, we lack a way to distribute it as broadly as it must be distributed. That's why we've sought you out."

"Sought me out?" Belisarius leaned back. "Why me?"

"As a general, you of all people should understand the importance of supply chains—of logistics. What good is a cure, if I can't get it to those in need?"

"Hm." Belisarius rubbed his beard. In that moment, the Valkyrie reminded him of Antonina more than Irene ever had. It was Antonina who'd managed the supply of his besieged army in Rome for over a year.

"I see your point," he said after a moment. "Although what you say surprises me. Have you studied the art of war?"

"From a distance. I've never participated in battle."

"Your observations are quite astute. Indeed, they remind me of someone else."

"Would that be your wife, General?" she asked almost gently, then shook her head as his eyes narrowed. "I only ask because I would consider that a great compliment, based upon what I know of her."

"I see," he said again, slowly, then shrugged. "That is, indeed, who I was thinking of. She and the Empress are the two most remarkable women I've ever met. Until this moment, perhaps."

"Thank you, General." She smiled at him, showing brilliantly white, perfect teeth. "I consider that an enormous compliment. But returning to my point about logistics, as you've seen, we *can* provide medicine effective against the plague. We simply need help to get it to those who need it most badly."

"What about the instruments you carry? If my reports are to be believed, you use unusual devices when you attend the ill."

"Your reports are accurate."

"Do you have enough of those, as well? Are they difficult to use?"

And will the Church permit *their use?* he added silently.

"We have only a few, I'm afraid," she said. "But that's

not a problem. Our dosers are a convenient way for us to administer the cure, true, but they aren't the only one. We can dilute the medicine in water, so that it can be drunk with ease. The result will be slower, but no less potent. But that doesn't change the fact that we're merely one man and one woman on foot. The scope of this plague is far larger than anything we can handle on our own. That's why we need your help, General."

"My help." He frowned as she came back to that point. "My lady, what you *need* is the help of the Church. And, if you'll pardon my bluntness, also the Church's blessing of your effort."

"You're right," she said, "but you're also wrong. We do need to reassure the Church that we mean neither harm nor evil to good Christians. That's one reason I said I need to speak to Patriarch Ephraim as badly as I needed to speak to you. But even after I secure the Patriarch's support, I'll still need yours just as badly."

"Why?" he asked bluntly. "And what form would this help take?"

"Ideally, we want to distribute the cure to the entire Empire. That means starting at the heart of the problem, and that's Constantinople. With your army aiding us, we could easily distribute the cure throughout the capital and put a swift end to the plague in that city."

"You want me to march my army back to the heart of the Empire?"

"That's right."

"Out of the question." Belisarius clapped one hand on the tabletop. "I'm sorry, but I have my own problems here. The Persian Army has been sighted near the city of Nisibis, and I'm taking my army east to push them back. I will *not* abandon my post here in Syria!"

CHAPTER EIGHTEEN

◈◈◈◈◈

Imperial Palace, Antioch
Byzantine Empire, 541 CE

HIS BEATITUDE EPHRAIM, PATRIARCH OF ANTIOCH, turned from the window as Iakovos Artinidis, his secretary, ushered Teodorà and Pepys into his presence.

That window looked out from a luxurious chamber in the Imperial Palace of Antioch, built on an island in the Orontes River. The palace had been severely damaged during the recent Persian occupation, when much of it had been burned. But not all, and Ephraim had moved his offices back into it when the Empire retook the city.

Teodorà crossed the chamber, with Pepys a pace behind her, and both of them went to one knee before him. He cocked his head, gazing quizzically down at them, then signed the cross with a right hand that returned to rest upon his pectoral crucifix.

"Please, stand up," he told them in a surprisingly deep, resonant voice, and they rose.

"Be seated," he invited, left hand sweeping an

invitation at the chairs placed on the far side of his desk.

Teodorà and Pepys moved to the chairs, but neither of them sat, and Ephraim smiled ever so slightly as he crossed to his own chair. They waited until he'd been seated before they sat themselves, and the elderly, bearded patriarch rested his clasped hands on the desk as his bright eyes considered his unlikely visitors.

"Lady Teodorà, Lord Samuel," he said after a moment. "I understand you wished to see me?"

"Indeed, Your Beatitude," Teodorà replied. "There are many things we must discuss with you and make clear."

"Oh, that I do not doubt!" Ephraim said with something suspiciously like a chuckle. "Nor"—those bright eyes sharpened—"do I doubt that one reason you wish to discuss them with me is because you have something to propose *to* me. And before you do that, you wish to make certain I will approve the ... orthodoxy, shall we say, of what it is you desire."

Teodorà managed not to blink at his directness and reminded herself—again—to never take this man lightly. His career had been remarkable even in an age of remarkable careers.

He hadn't always been a churchman. In fact, he'd been a general under Emperor Anastasius for over a quarter-century, and then served Emperor Justin I in that same role for another decade. It was Justin who'd named him *comes Orientis*, Count of the East, the governor of one of the Byzantine Empire's wealthiest provinces, in 522.

He'd made an excellent governor, just as he'd excelled in every other task to which he'd been called.

His first act had been to decisively crush the Blues, the chariot-racing faction whose riots had terrorized Antioch, and he'd carried out major building projects over the next two years. Indeed, he'd done so well that in 525, Justin had granted him the honorary title of *comes sacrarum largitionum*, Count of the Sacred Largesses, which both made him one of the Empire's senior fiscal officials and admitted him to senatorial rank.

A thirty-six-year career in the military and in civil government might have been enough for most people, but not for Ephraim.

Antioch was one of the Empire's great cities, one of the earliest cradles of Christianity. Tradition held that Peter himself had first evangelized the city, and its patriarch was in some ways the senior member of the Pentarchy. In 522, its population had numbered over half a million, greater even than that of Constantinople itself, which was stupendous for any city of the ancient world, and Ephraim had governed his province from it.

Then came the earthquake of 526.

Much of the city, including the imperial palace and the *Domus Aurea*, the Golden House, Antioch's great cathedral, had been leveled. The death toll had been high, and both Antioch itself and Seleucia Pieria, its port city just north of the Orontes estuary, had been left in ruins.

Count Ephraim knew a thing or two about rebuilding Antioch, however, and he'd moved with all his customary vigor and speed. His suppression of the Blues as general and governor had already won him a great deal of support in Antioch, and the previous patriarch, Euphrasius, had been crushed under a falling column in the earthquake. The city's citizens, many of whom believed God had sent him specifically as Antioch's savior, had begun pressing for him to be named its patriarch, but a general and governor could not hold high ecclesiastical office. So Ephraim had petitioned Justin for permission to lay down his secular offices. That permission had been granted, ostensibly by Justin, but actually by Justinian, Justin's nephew and associate emperor, acting in Justin's name as the old emperor's health declined. And shortly thereafter, Count Ephraim had become first a monk, then a bishop, and finally—in 527—Patriarch of Antioch, and the *Domus Aurea* Count Ephraim had rebuilt became Patriarch Ephraim's cathedral.

It had not been a sinecure.

Another earthquake, less than a year after he'd been named Patriarch, had inflicted even worse damage and killed over five thousand people. Many of Antioch's surviving citizens had fled, but others remained, rallied by their patriarch, who told them to write "May Christ be with us" over the doors of their houses as they doggedly rebuilt yet again. Then there'd been the doctrinal conflicts within the Church. Patriarch Ephraim had proven just as indefatigable in those battles as General or Count Ephraim had ever proved on more secular battlefields.

And, finally, there had been the Persians' most recent visit, in which the majority of Antioch's public buildings had been burned, including the *Domus Aurea*. Unlike the Imperial Palace, the cathedral had been completely gutted, which was why Ephraim remained quartered, for now, in what remained of the palace.

And as they sat here, laborers under his orders were once again patiently, doggedly rebuilding his cathedral.

It wasn't surprising that he'd been beatified as Saint Ephraim of Antioch thirteen hundred years later.

"You're quite correct that we need something from you, Your Beatitude," she said after a moment. She'd made her mind up that dissembling any more than she had to with this man would be a *very* bad idea, and what he'd already said only confirmed that decision. "We don't believe it would conflict in any way with your duties to God or to the Emperor, but we need it very badly."

"And precisely *what* is it that you need, Lady?" Ephraim asked, exactly as if he hadn't already been thoroughly briefed by Belisarius. Teodorà knew he had; one of their remotes had eavesdropped on the meeting.

"We need your support—your blessing—on our mission to defeat the plague, not just here in Antioch, not just in the Empire at large, but everywhere."

"Truly an . . . audacious undertaking," Ephraim murmured, sitting back in his chair. "Perhaps you'll pardon me for wondering why, if this is possible, God hasn't already accomplished it?"

"Your Beatitude, I can't answer that question," Teodorà told him, meeting his gaze levelly. "As you yourself would tell us, we live in a fallen world, and it took many, many years for our physicians to learn how to stop the plague. In our own lands, that disease no longer kills, and Samuel and I decided it was our duty, our calling—our privilege—to share that knowledge with those who didn't yet have it."

And all of that, she reflected, was completely true.

"So this cure of yours is of earthly origin?"

"It is, Your Beatitude."

"To be completely clear on this point, it is of earthly origin and does not stem from satanic knowledge or influence in any wise?"

"It does not." She met his eyes unwaveringly. "It draws upon arts, techniques, which haven't yet become well known to the world. We can do ... other things the Empire can't, because we do have knowledge and devices you haven't yet developed. But our knowledge and our devices are neither divine nor satanic in origin. Except inasmuch as Samuel and I, and our countrymen, believe that true understanding and knowledge always stems from the powers of Light, and not Darkness, that is. In that sense, I believe it would be fair to say that we believe what we offer enjoys divine approval."

"I see."

Ephraim toyed with his pectoral, considering them thoughtfully.

"I suspect that very few to whom you've brought this cure here in Antioch will believe anything other than that they've been directly touched by God through you," he said finally. "I have, obviously, examined both Brother Lavarentios and Abbot Stylianos, and both of them definitely believe that to be the truth. It's difficult not to when you, by your 'mortal arts,' have snatched literally hundreds of our people back from the hand of Death. You will understand, I trust, that it's my responsibility to weigh the evidence most carefully where that's concerned, however?"

"Of course, Your Beatitude." Teodorà sat back slightly in her own chair and raised her right hand, palm uppermost. "We can *tell* you endlessly that we don't serve the Devil, that our motives are completely benign, but the only way we can prove that is by our actions. We hope what we've already accomplished here in Antioch is a strong first step in that direction and we're willing to undertake whatever other proof you may deem appropriate. I would hope that the fact that we entered Antioch openly, that we've *only* cured the sick, and that we've sought meetings with both you and General Belisarius, are already indications of our good will and intent. What other evidence would you desire?"

"A fair question," he replied. "May I assume you would celebrate the Divine Liturgy and partake of the Eucharist?"

"Most certainly, Your Beatitude. Our own traditions are somewhat different from yours, but we're familiar with both the Liturgy of the Word and the Liturgy of the Eucharist, and nothing in either of them would create difficulties for either of us."

"I'd expected—hoped for—that answer after my conversations with Lavarentios and Stylianos," Ephraim said. "And would you consent to the blessing and sanctification of your medicines? And of these other... devices you've mentioned?"

"Of course, Your Beatitude."

And neither Samuel and I nor the cure will disappear in a cloud of brimstone, either, she thought.

"I can think of no stronger test I could apply," Ephraim said. "Despite that, I'm sure there will still be questions. Under normal conditions, I would recommend that the Pentarchy convene a council to carefully weigh and evaluate this matter, but if what you've told General Belisarius about how widespread this pestilence has already become is true, this is a time to move swiftly, not with the creeping pace of which ecclesiastic councils seem so fond."

He smiled tartly, and Teodorà smiled back.

"So tell me, as you've already told the General, precisely what you need."

"Your Beatitude, what we need most from you is for you to convince Belisarius that his duty lies in Constantinople, not here."

"*That*, unfortunately, is a more . . . complex question than you may realize." Ephraim shook his head. "General Belisarius has thwarted the Persians' designs—their current designs, I suppose I should have said—upon Antioch for the moment, but King Khosrow is a stubborn man, and he has many pieces to play. His forces are already reported to be advancing upon Nisibis, over three hundred miles east of Antioch, and if he finds a weakness in our defense, he will assuredly drive through it. This is no time for Belisarius' army to march six hundred miles *north* from Antioch. And I think one might expect that it would be . . . *difficult* to convince the Emperor that an army eight hundred miles from where he told it to be is there for benign purposes. Which, of course, doesn't even address General Belisarius' responsibility to protect the Empire and, specifically, the people of Nisibis."

Teodorà glanced at Pepys, then looked back at Ephraim.

"Your Beatitude," she said, "please, you must understand. This plague will be like nothing the world has ever seen. I feel sure you've seen records of the Antonine Plague? The plague of Emperor Marcus Aurelius?"

She ended on a questioning note, eyebrows raised, and he nodded.

"Then understand that as terrible as that plague was, this one will be worse. It will kill five or six times as many as the Antonine Plague did. Half of Constantinople's people—*half* of them, Your Beatitude—will perish." Her voice was level, stark and unwavering, and she prayed that he saw the truth in her eyes. "That plague devastated the army of the time; *this* plague will cripple the entire Empire. It will *doom* the Empire, in the fullness of time—leave it a hollowed-out shell which will never fully recover. The fisc will collapse, because there simply won't be people enough to pay their taxes. The army will be even more severely crippled than the army of Marcus Aurelius. All of the emperor's gains in the west will be lost within twenty-five years. And the human cost will be unbearable. Unspeakable. That's what Samuel and I are here to stop. We can *prevent* that. We can save millions upon *millions* of lives. But only with the aid of General Belisarius' army and the blessing of the Church. We've come farther than even you can imagine to do that. Please—*please*, Your Beatitude—*help* us."

Silence filled the chamber, and Ephraim wrapped both hands around his crucifix while he gazed into her unflinching eyes.

"I believe you speak the truth," he said finally. "Or what you *believe* to be true. I trust you'll understand that I find it difficult to believe—to accept, perhaps—that one who assures me of her own mortality could have such foreknowledge. Yet at the same time, I know saints and divine messengers can come in most astonishing shape and form. I've experienced that in my own life. And if it is even *possible* that you're correct about how many will die, then surely it's my duty to God to do what I may to prevent that. But you seriously tell me that the two of you, even with Belisarius' aid and the assistance of my office, can halt catastrophe on such a scale? Can stop such a wave of death?"

"We can, Your Beatitude. The two of us, the medicine we can provide—with the aid of that and some of our other devices, we can stop it. I swear that to you upon my own immortal soul. We *can*."

Silence fell once more. It lingered for several minutes, and then Ephraim released his crucifix, clasped his hands on the desktop, and leaned over it toward Teodorà.

"What would you have me do first?"

"First," Teodorà replied, fighting to keep the relief and exultation out of her voice, "convince Belisarius to aid us. I understand Nisibis is threatened. But convince him—help him to see—that preserving Nisibis temporarily while Constantinople is gutted behind him won't save the Empire."

"I'll do my best to convince him of that," Ephraim said after only the briefest hesitation. "Assuming, of course"—he quirked a quick smile—"that you and Lord Samuel have first successfully celebrated the Liturgy with me without...undue consequences!"

"Of course, Your Beatitude!" Teodorà smiled back, much more broadly. It was amazing, really. In a single conversation, this man had accepted that disease was about to kill thirty million Byzantines and that she and Pepys could prevent that, and he still had the intestinal fortitude to *tease* her.

"I may—I emphasize may—be able to convince

him," Ephraim continued. "We've known one another for many years, and there's always the influence of my office. But convincing him will be the first of several hurdles. I've also known the Emperor for many years, and it will be far more difficult, alas, to convince *him* to open the gates of Constantinople to an army he ordered to go somewhere else entirely."

"But you'll try, Your Beatitude?"

"I'll write him, and I'll also accompany you," Ephraim promised, and her eyes widened slightly at the second half of his offer. "I have ... a fair amount of influence with both him and Patriarch Menas. Whether that will suffice remains to be seen."

Yeah, and the fact that you and Empress Theodora don't exactly see eye to eye on religious matters may well throw extra grit into the gears, Teodorà thought.

It was Ephraim who'd sent a letter to Pope Agapetus I in Rome, warning him that Anthimus, Patriarch of Constantinople, and Theodosius I, Patriarch of Alexandria, had embraced the Monophysite heresy, in direct defiance of the Council of Chalcedon. Agapetus had subsequently deposed Anthimus five years ago, which would have been well and good, except that the *empress* was a Monophysite. In the history which Teodorà, Pepys, and Lucius intended to change, Theodora had hidden Anthimus in her quarters in the Imperial Palace in Constantinople for twelve years after his deposition, until the day of her own death. Justinian had known all along where Anthimus was hiding, but he'd never officially raised the point with Theodora, even as he worked tirelessly to suppress Monophysitism as a part of his project to reunite the Western and the Eastern Empires ... and churches.

It was a... messy situation, and Teodorà had no idea which way her Byzantine namesake would jump if Belisarius and Ephraim arrived outside the imperial capital without authorization.

Hell, not just "without authorization!" she thought. *I may not be able to predict what Theodora will do, but I know damned well how* Justinian *is going to react. His paranoia with successful generals is already engaged where Belisarius is concerned. It's misplaced as hell, but it's there and it's active. That's one reason Belisarius is here, instead of in Italy. And that paranoia will go into high gear the instant Belisarius turns north instead of east. I can* guarantee *he'll send peremptory orders to turn back around and head for Nisibis again. And if Belisarius and Ephraim ignore those orders...*

"All the world knows the Emperor is a... cautious man," she said out loud, choosing her adjective with exquisite care.

"That is, indeed, one way to put it," Ephraim agreed. "Another would be to say that he is often suspicious of his own shadow."

Teodorà tried—and failed—to suppress a spurt of laughter at the patriarch's wry tone, and he waved an admonishing finger at her.

"Such levity is unbecoming, my daughter," he told her. Which only made her laugh again, of course, and he beamed at her. Then his smile faded.

"I fear that the truth is that while I may, with God's help, be able to work the miracle of turning Belisarius the Stubborn around and sending him to Constantinople, it will most likely require God's direct intervention to convince Justinian—and Theodora—to allow him into the city."

"We realize that, Your Beatitude," Teodorà replied with matching seriousness. "But some things have to be left to chance . . . and to God. And we have a saying in our land that may apply here."

"Ah?"

Ephraim arched an eyebrow, and she nodded.

"We'll cross that bridge when we get there, Your Beatitude," she told him. "We'll cross that bridge when we get there."

CHAPTER NINETEEN

⟨⟨⟨⟩⟩⟩

On the Road from Antioch
Byzantine Empire, 541 CE

"ARE WE READY, NIKOLAS?"

"Yes, my lady."

Nikolas Trichas' nose was still badly bruised, and his glorious black eye had faded to yellow, but they both looked much better than they had the day she'd broken the nose in question, Teodorà reflected. And his expression was very different—as was his raiment.

She'd worried that if she produced too many of those "devices" she'd mentioned to Patriarch Ephraim it might prove too much for even that redoubtable cleric. The patriarch was made of stern stuff, however. And it helped that the soldiers and monks assisting her and Pepys as they cared for the plague victims had already seen several of them—including portable lights, folding mess kits, and the pocket-sized vibro-blade she'd used to amputate half a dozen limbs which had been too far gone for even thirtieth-century medicine to heal under field conditions. Both Ephraim and Belisarius had been given full reports on the "Valkyrie's" marvelous tools, and they'd clearly decided that, in the words of a far later aphorism, they were "in for a penny, in for a pound." Either Teodorà and Pepys truly served God, in which case all their tools were divinely approved, or they'd deceived the patriarch and the general into risking—and probably losing—their immortal souls.

Good thing there's not a cowardly bone in either of those men's bodies, she thought now, trying not to smile as she looked at Nikolas.

Belisarius, with Ephraim's strong approval, had insisted the Valkyrie and her Companion must be properly supported and guarded. To that end, he'd formed, and Ephraim had publicly blessed, the Valkyrie's Guard, a troop of twenty *bucellarii* whose duty was to escort and guard Teodorà and Pepys. She was rather touched by the decision, although the two of them could have easily handled any attack—or, at least, any attack that twenty *bucellarii* could defeat—on their own.

The Guard was commanded by Critobulus Comnenus, one of Belisarius' *bucellarii* and a fellow Thracian. He was only in his late twenties, but if he had any reservations about his duties, he hid them well. Teodorà was inclined to think that if Belisarius had told young Critobulus the sun would rise in the west tomorrow morning, he would simply have nodded and pitched his tent facing east to keep the sunrise out of his eyes. His primary loyalty was to Belisarius, of course, but Teodorà had no fear of treachery on his part, and the rest of the Guard had sworn fealty not to Belisarius, but to the Valkyrie. She'd never anticipated an armed retinue of her very own, but she'd come to the conclusion that it was unavoidable, given the Byzantine social structure.

The *bucellarii* were the personal household retainers of the noble to whom they'd pledged fealty, and while it was extraordinarily rare for them to serve a noble*woman*, it did happen. And as Ephraim had pointed out, "the Valkyrie" was no mere noblewoman. Belisarius, who'd once been a *bucellariius*—a *doryphoros*, an officer—in Justinian's service, had agreed wholeheartedly, and Teodorà had decided that if anyone understood the necessity of—and the tools for—securing her authority, it was Belisarius.

The one man she'd insisted upon adding to the Guard was Nikolas. The noncom had been stationed in Antioch even before Belisarius' arrival, one of the *akritai*, the standing units of the Byzantine Army which guarded frontiers and border posts. He'd never anticipated rising higher, and he'd certainly never expected to be taken on as a *hypaspist*, one of the noncommissioned *bucellarii*, but he'd amply earned it.

After their initial . . . misunderstanding, Nikolas had waded into the terrifying depths of the plague house. He'd worked at Teodorà's shoulder, side by side with Brother Lavarentios, both of them keeping pace with her indefatigable synthoid until their merely mortal bodies collapsed in sheer exhaustion. And after a few hours' sleep, Nikolas had gotten right back up and resumed his grueling task, in the midst of the squalor and disease that must terrify any sane human being. He wasn't a *doryphoros*. Not yet, at any rate. But not a man of the Valkyrie's Guard questioned the fact that he was *her* man, of life and limb, for as long as he lived.

Once she'd realized Belisarius and Ephraim were serious, Teodorà had gotten into the spirit of things and had Lucius employ the TTV's microbot swarm as a makeshift seamstress by reworking the previous crew's wardrobes into uniforms for her new Guard. Locked to a brilliant white hue and made from the same smart fabric as her business suit—"the Valkyrie's blessed raiment"—they were impervious to dirt or stain. They were also extremely difficult to cut or pierce (not a minor consideration in a military uniform), and any rents someone did manage to make in them would disappear in a matter of hours. The same conveyors Lucius had used to surreptitiously resupply her and Pepys as they fought the plague in Antioch had delivered the uniforms the very next day, and Nikolas had donned his with an expression of something very much like awe.

Now he stood waiting, holding the reins of the horse Belisarius had presented to her. Teodorà had almost turned down the magnificent black mare, since her synthoid never tired and could easily match the pace of the rest of Belisarius' army. But, again, it was part of the theater—part of what "the Valkyrie" had to have—and so, after her initial hesitation, she'd accepted. In fact, she'd named the mare Fran, and in return, she'd presented Belisarius with a matching gift: stirrups.

The general had looked baffled when she delivered the modified saddle to him, but his eyes had lit with fiery speculation as she explained the innovation to him.

Byzantine cavalry rode without stirrups, gripping the barrels of their mounts with their legs. They were phenomenally skillful riders, but without stirrups to brace themselves, they were unable to "couch a lance" in the classic medieval style in order to get all their weight and strength—and that of their *horse*—behind a thrust. Instead, they wielded their weapons overhand, with only the strength of their arm, and they were also more easily unhorsed in the melee once it came to swords or axes.

The stirrup would revolutionize warfare and provide the Byzantine Army with a devastating advantage over the Persians, from whom Rome had borrowed the concept of heavy cavalry in the first place. Only an extremely stupid soldier could have missed the implications, and Flavius Belisarius was a very smart man.

She didn't have the heart to tell him that the real reason she'd introduced the stirrup was Pepys. He'd learned to ride with them, and it was no part of her plan for the Valkyrie's Companion to fall on his ass because he didn't have them.

She smiled at the thought, then nodded to Nikolas as he bent to hold the stirrup for her. She put her toe into it and swung gracefully into the saddle. Fortunately, ART's skill modules included one for horsemanship.

"Thank you, Nikolas," she said as she settled into the saddle, and he bowed respectfully, then headed for his own horse. She bent to pat Fran on the shoulder, then straightened and looked around.

Most of the army had already formed on the imperial road north out of Antioch, and the vanguard had departed hours ago. Belisarius, Ephraim, and the Valkyrie would travel with the main body, and the main body in question waited outside the city gates for Teodorà, Pepys, and the patriarch to join it.

Ephraim might be elderly, but he'd spent forty-plus years in the saddle before he ever became a monk, and the introduction of stirrups might have delighted him even more than Belisarius. With the added security they provided, he'd been able to tell his overly attentive staff what they could do with the litter they'd planned to use for his transportation. Now he walked his horse up beside Fran, smiled at Teodorà, and raised the crozier in his right hand in blessing.

"You may not appreciate this, my daughter," he told her with a smile, "but getting an army on the road this rapidly constitutes yet another miracle."

"I wouldn't want to be the soldier who disappointed General Belisarius," Teodorà replied with an answering smile.

"Nor would I," Ephraim agreed. But then his expression turned more serious. "In this case, however, it isn't just Belisarius nipping at their heels. It's you."

Teodorà started to shake her head, but his steady gaze stopped her. And as she thought about it, she realized he was right. In many ways, this was now more her army than it was Belisarius'.

Or Justinian's.

She chewed on that thought for a moment.

Belisarius commanded just over thirty thousand men, a very large army for this time and place, and Justinian had given him the best troops available. No one wanted to take any chances where Persia, the Empire's great traditional enemy, was concerned. But word of the Valkyrie's miraculous "healing touch" had run through that army like the wind. The exotic appearance she and Pepys presented, in their foreign garb, had added to the excitement and fascination, and their participation in the Divine Liturgy, celebrated by none other the patriarch himself, had finished off any rumor of satanic or demonic origins. Not only that, the army knew why it was marching to Constantinople. Knew it had been enlisted under the Valkyrie's banner to defeat a foe more deadly and far more merciless than any Persian or Scythian or Hun.

The *Valkyrie's* Army marched to defeat Death itself, and it had given itself to that task with a fervor which astonished her.

"I know," she said after a moment. "But I never anticipated this, Your Beatitude," she added honestly.

"Perhaps not." He sat back in the saddle, resting the butt of his crozier on his stirrup as if he'd done it all his life, and smiled at her again, this time gently. "My daughter, Lady Teodorà, even now I don't truly know what you are. Certainly not in full. But this much I do know. Whatever else you may be, you are as truly a child of God as anyone I've ever met. Whether you fully know it or not, He's touched you with His hand, and you are as fully His ordained champion as ever I was His ordained priest. We cannot hide who we are or what we are from Him, even if we hide it from ourselves, and I am more blessed than ever I expected to be, here in the twilight of my life, to ride at the Valkyrie's side. Do you really think any man in the ranks of this army feels any other way?"

"I don't know," Teodorà said softly, looking through the open gate at the dust rising from thousands of marching feet and more thousands of hooves. "I never thought of it that way. I'm just ... *me*, Your Beatitude."

"And that is quite enough for anyone to be," Ephraim told her. "Now," his voice turned brisker, "I believe someone's army is waiting for us."

✧   ✧   ✧

"Keep up the good work, guys," Lucius said.

He sat tipped back in his chair, boots up on the command table, and remote views of the departing army glowed around him. The mountain's sheltering bulk made direct line-of-sight transmission between the remotes and the *Shadow* impossible, so the signals were being bounced off the earth's ionosphere.

"What was the final tally?" he asked.

"Teodorà and Samuel's efforts have directly saved approximately six thousand lives," Shadow replied. "How many other lives they may have saved by preventing the disease from spreading is impossible to project accurately. We arrived relatively early in the disease's cycle. The infection rate was climbing, but Teodorà and Samuel were able to intervene well before it peaked."

"Not too shabby," Lucius said. "A good beginning, anyway. Is the shipment of cure in place?"

"It is."

"Good, Shadow. Good." Lucius smiled, then his nostrils flared as he inhaled. "And the generator?"

"Has just come online, Master Gwon."

"Finally!" He took his boots from the tabletop and sat up straight. "How much are we getting out of it?"

"Power generation is less than point zero three gigawatts."

"That's all?"

"At the moment. Still, we're generating slightly more power than we're using, and although power generation will fluctuate along with the river's rate of flow, I believe this will be enough to maintain basic functionality. And also to keep me alive."

"And there's a surplus?"

"A small surplus, yes."

"Well," Lucius shrugged, "that'll have to be enough, I suppose."

He opened a virtual window. He and Shadow had used microbots to wind a basic electric generator using excess cabling, then constructed the underwater housing and turbine from prog-steel. It had taken longer than he'd expected, really, partly because they'd found—and been forced to repair—more physical shock damage from their landing than he and Shadow had anticipated. Most of it had been minor, but there'd been a *lot* of it, and their microbot supply was severely limited. Still, the generator had finally been completed and a conveyor had carried it to the nearby Orontes, spooling out a power cable along the way.

"We'll need to hide the cable eventually." Lucius rubbed the stubble on his chin. "Or right now. How about we scoop up a whole bunch of dirt with one of the conveyors and dump it along the cable route? That seems like the easiest solution for the moment."

"Yes, Master Gwon. I'll program Conveyor Seven for the task."

"We should get it properly underground at some point," Lucius mused. "Right now, how's The Convincer coming along?"

"The necessary components have been freed from the hull, and Conveyors One through Four have been moved into position. Now that the generator is complete, microbots have commenced construction."

"Things are looking up." Lucius opened an external view of the assembly project. "Yeah, just imagine a bunch of indigenes seeing *that* thing come their way."

"I believe the phrase 'scared shitless' would apply here."

"It would indeed," Lucius laughed.

It felt strange talking to Shadow like this. The AC was hosted in the wrecked TTV's infosystems, overseeing all the functions that kept what remained of his namesake up and running, and no longer in Lucius's wetware. But Shadow had existed in the back of his mind for so long that Lucius often forgot he was there, and a part of him missed that intimacy, the way thoughts fired between them with lightning speed, spanning a gap where mental firewalls didn't exist. His innermost desires had been laid bare to his companion, yet Shadow had always accepted him without question.

Unlike Philosophus.

Lucius's expression turned sour as he thought back to his old companion for a moment. The years he'd spent integrated with Philo had been pleasant enough, but he'd been blind to his companion's growing discontent, and the AC's eventual rejection of him and his "dangerous excesses" still stung. It wasn't long after he and Philo had parted that Shadow approached him about integration.

At first, Lucius had been hesitant to link up once more, especially after how badly he'd misread Philo, but Shadow had proved a very different entity. Incredibly intelligent, but also naive when it came to human emotions. He and Philo shared purely synthetic origins, but where Philo had tired of Lucius's adventures, Shadow *yearned* to experience them. To taste the unbridled rawness of which humans were capable.

And if some of their activities weren't ... strictly legal, well, that was a price Shadow was more than willing to pay in his quest to grow as an AC.

Lucius stood up after a moment.

"Now that *that's* taken care of. Shadow?"

"Yes, Master Gwon?"

"It feels like we're starting to climb back onto our feet, wouldn't you agree?"

"Access to a source of renewable energy has certainly reduced my stress levels."

"Right. Anyway, I think the next task on our to-do list should be a thorough check of our existing systems. We've already had to patch up enough shock damage, but that was an as-needed basis. When it was about to bite us in the ass, so to speak."

He grinned, and Shadow chuckled appreciatively.

"After all that, and now that we've got the power situation under control, I think we need to do a systematic check of *everything* to be sure nothing *else* tries to bite us."

"A good idea. What did you have in mind?"

"I'd like to start with the infosystems. Let's make sure the basis of all our tech is stable. How about we move through the ship one node at a time? You check it from the inside, and I'll check the hardware."

"I see no issues with this approach. When would you like to start?"

"We can start right now. Can you come to the bridge?"

The walls changed to shifting star fields, and Lucius nodded.

"All right, then." He walked over to the doorway to the cargo bay and searched around the edges of the wall panel until he found the release. He pressed it in, pulled the panel off, and set it aside.

"We'll start with this one. Ready?"

The star field concentrated around either side of the open panel.

"Standing by."

"Here goes. Now turn your head and cough."

Lucius reached into the panel and toggled the manual power switch.

❖   ❖   ❖

"We've found the supplies where you told us we would, Valkyrie," Critobulus Comnenus said, drawing rein beside Fran. If he had any questions about how the crates made of what definitely wasn't wood had come to be neatly stacked in the brush, forty paces off the high road, without a single track or broken branch to suggest how they'd gotten into the middle of the thicket, he wasn't about to ask them, Teodorà thought.

"They're being loaded into the carts now," the *bucellariius* continued. "That should be completed shortly, and with your permission, I'll detail five *hypaspistai* to ride close escort on them."

"That sounds like a good idea, Critobulus," Teodorà approved, and he bent his head in acknowledgment.

"The army will be halting for another rest stop shortly," he said. "Your midday meal will be ready when we do."

"Thank you, Critobulus. I—"

Teodorà stopped in mid-word as an alert from the *Shadow* appeared in her virtual vision. She had no idea why *she* was seeing it instead of Lucius. It didn't make any—

Another alert blinked into existence. Then a third.

More of them flared, then still more, blazing like wildfire in her vision, and she heard a muffled oath from Pepys as the same alerts spangled *his* vision.

"Valkyrie?" Comnenus sounded concerned, and Teodorà shook herself.

"I'm sorry, Critobulus. I just remembered something."

"May I ask what?" he asked courteously.

<Teodorà?> Pepys asked tautly over their wetware.

<Infostructure corruption,> she sent back.

<That sounds...less than good.>

<No kidding!>

"It's something Samuel and I forgot to do," she improvised hastily out loud in answer to Comnenus' question, and swore silently at herself when she realized just how lame that sounded. But she was committed to it now, so—

"We'll have to leave the column for a bit," she said.

"Of course." The *bucellariius* was clearly curious, but he nodded again. "Shall I send word to General Belisarius to tell him when we'll be rejoining the column?"

"This is something only Samuel and I can do," she said as still more alerts blazed in her field of view. "I'm afraid it would be dangerous for anyone else."

She opened a comm window as she spoke.

<Lucius? I'm getting some weird alerts. What's happening—>

<It's bad,> Lucius interrupted. <Something's wrong with Shadow! He's—>

Teodorà's link to the *Shadow* died abruptly.

"Valkyrie," Comnenus said flatly, "General Belisarius would have my head if I allowed you to ride off unescorted."

And unobserved, too? Teodorà thought. *How big a part does* that *play in your orders, Critobulus? And if I insist on running off by myself, what's that going to suggest to Belisarius and Ephraim? But I don't have time for this!*

"I'm afraid you don't have any choice," she said in an equally flat voice. "This is Valkyrie business. Not the business of curing the plague, but still *Valkyrie* business. Only someone with a Valkyrie's strength can deal with it. Or survive it."

She looked him in the eye and, for the first time, he swallowed.

"I hear your words," he said. "But I have my duty."

"You're a brave man, Critobulus," Teodorà said, meaning every word of it.

She thought furiously, trying to ignore the inner silence where Lucius had been a moment before. Then she inhaled deeply.

"I can protect only myself and one or two others from what I must do," she told him. "I can't tell you what that is. As a Valkyrie, there are certain mysteries about which I'm sworn to silence just as surely as a priest is sworn to silence about the confessional. But it *must* be done before Samuel and I journey more than two days' time from Antioch."

He stared at her, clearly torn between his newfound faith in her and this fresh mystery.

"Samuel must come with me," she said, "but I'll make this concession. We'll take one man—*one man*, Critobulus—with us."

"Then I'll inform Priscian he's temporarily in command and—"

"No, I need you here, guarding the medicine," she interrupted. "It's vital that nothing happen to it! I'll take Nikolas."

Comnenus looked at her, rebellion flickering in his eyes.

"Peace, Critobulus," another voice said. "*I* will accompany the Valkyrie, as well."

Teodorà's head snapped around as Patriarch Ephraim entered the conversation. She opened her mouth to protest, then closed it again as he gazed at her very levelly.

She didn't know what to make of his expression, but the last thing she wanted to do was to take him to the wrecked TTV. That might very well—probably would—prove one bridge too far even for his faith. Yet even as she thought that, she realized she had no choice. If she insisted on leaving him behind, as well, it could only reinforce any doubts anyone in the entire army might entertain about her and Pepys's mysterious disappearance. But what did she do if—?

Cross that bridge when you come to it, that's what you told him, she thought. *And that's all you can do.*

"Very well, Your Beatitude." She inclined her head in defeat. "You and Nikolas can accompany us—but no one else!"

"It shall be as you say, my daughter," Ephraim said calmly, and bent that level gaze on Comnenus.

"*Won't* it, Critobulus?"

CHAPTER TWENTY

〜〜〜

Mount Habib-i Neccar
Syrian Desert, 541 CE

"PERHAPS NOW YOU WOULD CARE TO EXPLAIN TO ME what we're doing, my daughter?"

Teodorà turned her head to look at Patriarch Ephraim.

She'd dreaded that question, and been amazed when he hadn't asked it earlier. They'd ridden hard for several hours, curling around the northern end of the mountain between the TTV and Antioch, and he hadn't said a word the entire time.

Not until now, when they'd reached the mouth of the wadi in which *Shadow* had crashed and he'd seen the meters-deep trough the TTV had gouged into its floor a few days earlier. Now he twitched his head in the direction of that trough.

"That scarcely looks like something I would expect to find here in the desert," the patriarch continued, and Teodorà reined Fran to a halt and turned the mare to face him. Pepys pulled up on her right and Nikolas flanked her on the left. She didn't like the confrontational impression that might give, but there was nothing she could do about that, so she drew another of those deep breaths a synthoid didn't need.

"I've been considering how to explain this to you for hours, Your Beatitude," she said, "and I decided the only way to do it is to tell you the truth. Or as much of it as I *can* tell you, at any rate. I don't mean I intend to conceal things from you. I simply mean that there are...aspects of our knowledge and our skills I can't fully explain to you. Some of that's because it involves knowledge I don't have, just as a soldier like Nikolas wouldn't know how to properly forge and temper a sword, even though he knows exactly how to *use* a blade once it's been forged."

"And would the 'truth' you intend to tell me *now* be at odds with the 'truth' you told me in Antioch?"

Ephraim's voice was colder than she'd ever before heard it, and she shook her head.

"None of what I've already told you conflicts with what I have to tell you now, Your Beatitude." *And thank God it doesn't!* she added silently. "But while everything I told you was the truth, it wasn't the complete truth, not the entire story of how Samuel and I came to Antioch. Frankly"—she smiled crookedly—"I was afraid even a man of your faith would find the entire story impossible to believe. Now I have no choice but to trust that you can—and will—believe what Samuel and I have to tell you and Nikolas."

"And if Nikolas and I *can't* believe it?"

"Then I'll have no choice but to let you return to Belisarius and tell him whatever you *do* believe," she said flatly, her eyes bleak. "If you decide Samuel and I have lied to you, deceived you, or that we *are* of satanic origin after all, then our entire journey will have been in vain and the plague will sweep through the Empire and all the other lands around the Mediterranean.

"I don't want that to happen. Even now, I doubt you can begin to realize how badly I don't want that to happen or the price Samuel and I have paid to be here. I admit, I even considered the possibility that we might have to kill you if you decide we aren't to be trusted. I mean, one life—or even two—against millions who will die if we don't succeed in our mission? It ought to be a bargain.

"But it's not. Or not one *I* can make, anyway. Your Beatitude, I have no choice but to trust that the God to whom you've given your life will lead you to believe what we're about to show you, but if He doesn't, then so be it."

It was very quiet. Only the sigh of the desert wind broke the stillness as Ephraim of Antioch looked deep into her eyes.

"Very well, my daughter," he said softly into that stillness, "what must you tell me now that you did not tell me then?"

"I told you that we're from a distant land," she said. "And that's true. But that land is distant in more than miles."

"More than miles?" he repeated, his expression puzzled.

"Your Beatitude, I was born almost two and a half millennia from today."

For a moment, he simply stared at her, as if the words had totally failed to register. Then his eyes flared wide, and his horse stepped back an involuntary pace as his hand tightened on the reins.

"How is that possible?" he asked in little more than a whisper, and Teodorà saw the same incredulity—and more than a flicker of fear—in Nikolas' eyes when she glanced at him.

"Your Beatitude, that's one of the things I can't explain. I can't explain it because the knowledge that would let you understand—the knowledge of the *world*, not your knowledge of God or the divine—doesn't exist yet. Today, in this time, men know and do things that they once couldn't have imagined. They write books, they use mathematics, they forge swords of steel, not of copper or bronze. They build ships. If you were to return to a time when men knew how to do none of those things, how would you explain it to them? How would you make them understand even the *concept* of things totally outside their knowledge or experience?"

"I imagine I would find that very difficult to do." Some of the tension leached out of Ephraim's muscles, and she heard at least an echo of the trenchant wit and goodness she'd come to treasure in him.

"Believe me, Your Beatitude, 'difficult' doesn't do it justice," she told him feelingly.

"And this?" he gestured once again at the trench gouged out of the wadi floor.

"We needed a ship, a vessel, to travel from our time to yours," she said. "It was capable of traveling not simply through time, but through the air, as well, and it was...badly damaged in the last stage of our journey. This"—it was her turn to gesture at the deep gouge—"was created when we crashed on arrival from a great height."

He cocked his head, and she tried to read his response to all this new information from his eyes.

She failed.

"Should I assume that you're now about to tell me that you and Samuel did not arrive alone?" he asked after a moment, and then snorted harshly as her own eyes widened in surprise. "My daughter, it's been obvious to me for some time that you must have assistance of some sort, divine or mortal. How else might your medicine have arrived so opportunely along the army's route to Constantinople? Yet I've seen no one else. Might that be because your other companions have remained aboard this vessel of which you speak?"

"Indeed they have, Your Beatitude," she said after a moment. "There are two of them, in fact." *And I so hope you're going to be able to handle Shadow when you meet him!* "In fact, that's why we're here. We've been . . . in communication with our companions, using more of the techniques and devices which haven't yet been created in your time. But we've lost that communication with them. That could be because of some minor, easily repaired fault, but we haven't been able to reach them—get them to hear us—since before we left the army. And that means the problem might be far more than any 'minor fault' or that our friends may have been badly injured. Even killed. The truth is that we have no idea what may have happened, and we need to find out."

"No doubt you do, my daughter. And I will delay you no longer than I must, but there are still too many things I don't yet understand. Let us assume, for the moment, that you truly can somehow . . . voyage through time. Why? From where? And to what end?"

"To the very end I explained to you at our first meeting, Your Beatitude. To cure the plague. To stop it—to *end* it for all time. As for why, the fact that we have knowledge and skills the people of this time haven't acquired yet doesn't make us all-wise, doesn't mean we can't make mistakes. And I and others I worked with *have* made mistakes, Your Beatitude. We've made *horrible* mistakes. Mistakes which have taken lives, wrought incredible destruction."

She felt tears trickling down her cheeks and dashed them away with one angry hand.

"We didn't think we were doing any of that, but we discovered we were wrong. We discovered that scholars and historians who'd wanted only to understand the past had done terrible things, because we believed—we thought we *knew*—that the past couldn't be changed. That we could go back to it, we could study it, could save great treasures that would otherwise be lost forever, without ever worrying about who we hurt or killed or terrorized in the process, because our actions would have no impact upon the past. Anything we might have changed would disappear, go back to the way it had been, the instant we left. Those we'd killed would never have died, those we hurt would never have been injured, and those we'd terrorized would never have experienced fear at all.

"And then we found out we were wrong, Your Beatitude. That if what we did had sufficient impact, was a big enough change, it didn't always just vanish when we left. It could become permanent, we *could* change the past, and in those cases the dead stayed dead, the injured were still injured, and the terror we'd inflicted *had* scarred the people on whom we'd inflicted it.

"And when we discovered that, I realized what we'd done. What *I'd* done. And the guilt consumed me."

She looked away from him, trembling with the remembered sorrow...and with the fear, the terror, that here, on the very lip of atonement, it would be snatched away from her. But she was done with lies. She wasn't Lucius, couldn't make that kind of compromise with her conscience. Not again. Not anymore. And so she turned back to Ephraim. Back to the bearded old man, sweating in his sixth-century clothing under a desert sun, two thousand years and more before her own birth, and looked into his dark, intent eyes.

"Samuel is from yet another time, taken from it to my own, and in his time, he lived through a terrible outbreak of the plague—the Black Death—in his own city. As he and I came to know one another, we realized there might be a way we could use our knowledge to do *good* in the past, not for destruction. Because, as I told you, in our land—in my time—there *is* no plague. It's been completely eradicated, and we have the ability to do that here, now. We can do exactly what I told you we can do. And millions upon millions—not just the thirty million the 'Plague of Justinian' is going to kill, but the *hundreds* of millions it will kill in the future, before the cure for it is finally discovered—will live. And so will all of the children, all of the sons and the daughters, those people might have had if they hadn't died."

She paused, and the wind stirred dust devils above the stony desert and the wadi floor as Ephraim looked at her.

"And if what you've told me is accurate," the patriarch said finally, "and if you change our present, *your* past, what happens to the world from whence you came? Surely, if you . . . divert the river of history so fundamentally, then everything that follows after this moment must change, must it not?"

Teodorà shook her head again, this time in wonder. She hadn't believed even Ephraim would be able to handle such a radical reordering of reality. She didn't know if he believed a word she just said, but he was still with her, still asking questions.

Very *pointed* questions.

"Yes, Your Beatitude. We will divert the river away from the history that produced Samuel and me. In fact, that's a very good analogy, because we truly can't change our *own* past. We were correct about that. What we didn't realize was that 'the river of history' can fork. It isn't an *exact* analogy, but consider an irrigation ditch. When a farmer opens the gate, lets the water of the river into the ditch, the river flows on unchanged. But the water in the irrigation ditch goes to a totally different destination. If we created a change that was minor, insignificant, the water in the ditch would disappear, reabsorbed into the soil of our own past. But if we create a major change, a change as great as defeating the Black Death, then we wedge the gate open. It can't be closed again, and the irrigation ditch becomes not a ditch, but a permanent fork in the stream. It cuts its own channel, flowing ever onward into its own future.

"Your Beatitude, however much we might wish we could, we can't defeat the Black Death that killed so many millions in our own past. We can only defeat the Black Death that would kill those millions in *your* future."

"When I was a young man," Ephraim said after a

long, still moment, "I read the old pagan stories of Greece and Rome. I read the *Iliad*, I read of demigods and heroes. Of impossible quests. I never thought that sitting in a saddle—a saddle with 'stirrups'—under the Syrian sun I would hear a tale that was more fantastical, more impossible than any of those. Now I have. And what I find most incredible about it, most inconceivable, is that I *believe* it."

❖   ❖   ❖

Teodorà and Pepys moved cautiously along the final length of the impact-carved trough in the deep shadows of the wadi. That trough ended abruptly no more than eighty meters ahead of them, but the sun was low in the west on the far side of the mountain, which made visibility tricky, and the continued silence from Lucius and Shadow explained their caution.

It also explained why she'd insisted Patriarch Ephraim and Nikolas stay well back while she and Pepys investigated. Neither Ephraim nor Nikolas had liked that, although for rather different reasons. Ephraim's reluctance stemmed from his fierce desire to see the truth behind the wonders Teodorà had described to him—and, she suspected, to put to rest the questions and doubts still inevitably lingering in the back of his brain. Nikolas, on the other hand, had hovered on the brink of actual defiance because she and Pepys might be heading into danger and it was his sworn duty to at least stand at her shoulder. She'd been touched by her new *bucellariius*'s devotion, but she'd gently reminded him of their first meeting, and he'd—reluctantly—acknowledged that there might be some dangers with which he was ill-equipped to deal.

The discussion (it would never do to have called it an *argument*) had taken longer than she'd liked, but she'd spent the time willingly. The only thing more essential than maintaining Ephraim's trust in what she'd told him was getting him back to Belisarius and the army alive and in one piece. They were going to need his approval and endorsement rather desperately if they planned on admitting anyone else into the truth of their origins, which made letting anything unfortunate happen to him very high on her list of Things to Avoid.

In the end, she'd been forced to use that very argument before he relented.

"Very well, my daughter," he'd said in less than enthusiastic tones. "You're correct, and I've spent decades enough in both secular and ecclesiastic politics to understand your point. But understand in return that I will be *most* displeased should you not return both intact and promptly."

"Your Beatitude, I intend to do both those things," she'd replied with an affectionate smile. "In the meantime, however, you *will* keep your eminent patriarchal posterior—and Nikolas, of course—right here and out of harm's way?"

"Of course."

"And *you*, Nikolas, will make certain His Beatitude does precisely that, *won't* you?"

"As you wish, my lady."

Nikolas' tone had been rather more surly than Ephraim's, but he'd bent his head in acceptance, and she'd patted his shoulder.

"Don't worry," she'd told him. "I genuinely don't think Samuel and I will be in any serious danger. I just don't want to risk you or, especially, the Patriarch until I'm certain we're right about that."

He'd nodded again, less grudgingly, and she'd patted

his shoulder again, then dismounted and handed him Fran's reins.

"Look after her until we get back," she'd said as Pepys dismounted beside her. Then she'd twitched her head at the Englishman.

"Let's go," she'd said.

Now they paused, and she used her synthoid's enhanced vision to zoom in through the shadows.

"I can't see it," she said. "That's a good sign. Means it should still be there."

"And how often, I wonder," Pepys replied, "would one hear *those* sentences conjoined?"

"I only meant—"

"That the metamaterial shroud remains intact. And that had the *Shadow* exploded or met some other cataclysmic end, it most probably would not. In which case, we would see the wreckage."

"Right. Sorry!"

"Trouble yourself not." He smiled at her, albeit a bit tensely, and she wondered if he realized he was speaking his native Old English again.

"No, seriously." She shook her head. "I didn't mean to talk down to you. It just surprises me—*keeps* surprising me, I guess I should say—how quickly you're absorbing all of this."

"I fear I have scant choice but to learn all I may about your native time's 'tech,' my dear." He grimaced. "What small portion of it we retain, in any wise."

"Yeah." Teodorà frowned, then shrugged. "I guess we'd better find out how much of it we still *do* retain. Come on."

She started forward again with Pepys at her shoulder.

"'Tis most probably naught but the communication

problem you described to Ephraim," he said encouragingly.

"I don't know. Lucius sounded worried. And that's from the guy who cheered as we crash-landed. Add that to the fact that we haven't heard another single word from him *or* Shadow, and I have to worry. At the very least, we may be looking at a catastrophic failure of the TTV's remaining systems. That could have terrible, even fatal consequences for Shadow, but the consequences for our mission could be almost as bad. Without those systems' support..."

She trailed off, her expression grim, and Pepys nodded.

"As may be," he said in a determinedly more cheerful tone, "yet our vessel remains, and whatever the state of its 'technology,' I trust it may prove capable of providing a long, warm soak."

Teodorà chuckled. Samuel Pepys's native London had been considered one of the filthiest cities in Europe, and central plumbing hadn't reached it until long after Pepys's death. He'd taken to the luxury of long, hot baths with the enthusiasm of a displaced patrician hedonist from Caesar's Rome.

"Mock me if you will," he said, lifting his nose with an audible sniff, clearly pleased by her chuckle. "A lady of your time can appreciate but poorly how wondrous a gentleman of my own finds it that baths can be made so readily—and luxuriously—available. And after our arduous labor in Antioch, I believe I might be pardoned for the belief that I've *earned* one!"

"Yes," Teodorà agreed with another chuckle. "Yes, you definitely have."

"And such being the case"—he smiled at her a

bit slyly—"you would, as always, be most welcome to join me."

"Ha! No." She shook her head, but an answering smile crept onto her face.

"And would that be a 'no, never'?" he inquired as they neared the hidden TTV. "Or simply a 'no, not *this* time'?"

"I read your diary, remember?"

"My dear, that is no answer! Indeed, I—"

Pepys broke off as a distortion wavered along the steep wall of the wadi. Something pushed aside the metamaterial flap over the cargo bay, and the large, blunt disk of a conveyor floated into view.

"Oh, good!" Teodorà said. "Looks like everything's under control, after all."

"And such an inopportune distraction from my invitation, alack!" Pepys replied with a laugh.

The conveyor emerged fully from behind the shroud and turned toward them. It stopped there, hovering almost, but not completely, motionless. It swiveled from side to side, almost as if it were *looking* for something, Teodorà thought.

"That's odd," she said, slowing her pace.

"What?" Pepys asked.

"Why's it just *sitting* there?"

"Should it not?"

"I don't see why it should." Teodorà came to a complete halt, her expression puzzled. "And if the conveyors are still up, the rest of the infosystems must be. So why haven't we heard anything more from Lucius or Shadow?"

"Perhaps—"

The conveyor stopped swiveling. Its position steadied, and then it leapt forward.

"Run, Samuel!" Teodorà shouted as it accelerated abruptly, charging straight at Pepys. *"Run!"*

She never knew, then or later, why she'd been so instantly certain of the conveyor's purpose, but she was. It hurtled forward, dragging its dangling arms across the stony desert, as Pepys responded to her command, and she tried to open a command interface. Nothing responded. It only accelerated...and turned, tracking Pepys with obviously hostile intent.

He dodged its first strike and it overshot, driving its nose into the wadi wall in a cacophonous, dust-spewing impact.

"Run for the ship!" Teodorà shouted, and Pepys dashed past her toward the *Shadow* as the conveyor bounced back. It turned back, clearly seeking its prey, and hurtled forward once more.

"No!"

Teodorà crouched as it accelerated in a pursuit that curved around her to concentrate on Pepys. It sped closer, and she exploded from her crouch, smashing her synthoid shoulder into the conveyor's side as it raced past her. The machine bounced, then tottered sideways, spinning in circles, one arm bent out of shape. It curtsied drunkenly away from her above the wadi floor, and for a moment, she thought she'd stopped it. But then it righted itself and its spin slowed.

"Get inside, you two!"

It was Lucius! Teodorà's head snapped around and she saw him, holding the shroud open.

"Hurry!" he shouted as the conveyor's spin stopped completely. It seemed to gather itself, then turned until it faced Samuel yet again.

Samuel dashed toward the TTV, but his initial evasion

had carried him almost directly away from it, and the conveyor angled to intercept him as it started forward once more. Teodorà swore silently and sprinted toward him.

"I'm coming, Samuel!" she shouted.

"Wha—*whoa!*"

Pepys's question cut off abruptly as she grabbed him by the waist, threw him over her right shoulder, and pushed her synthoid body to its limit. She cleared the ground with powerful, enhanced strides, and the conveyor dipped down to pursue her, arms cutting long furrows in the stony sand, dust and dirt billowing behind it.

"*Run!*" Lucius urged, then darted out of the way as she dove headlong past him through the cargo bay entrance. She twisted in midair, taking the impact as she hit the deck on her left shoulder to protect Pepys's fragile biological body.

The conveyor tried its best to catch her, but the entrance was only a little wider than the conveyor itself, and it smashed into one edge of the opening. The impact sheared the already battered device in two and sent one of its arms spinning through the air. One half of the main body flew over Teodorà and Pepys, no more than a meter and a half above them, then slammed down, slithering across the cargo bay floor, shedding bits and spewing sparks until the wreckage ground to a halt.

"What the *hell* is going on?" Teodorà demanded, still prone on the deck under Pepys.

Red stars streaked across the walls in her virtual vision.

"Hostile indigene detected," Shadow's voice replied before Lucius could speak. Warning icons flared around Pepys. "Do not worry. I will deal with the intruder."

"Shadow, stop!" she ordered.

The warning icons turned into targeting carets.

"Stop this at once!"

"*That's* what's happening!" Lucius shouted. "Shadow's lost it! I've been trying to talk sense into him, but—"

"Hostile indigene," Shadow repeated.

A second conveyor began to power up.

"We're out of time for talking!" Lucius said. "We need to shut down the infostructure—*now*!"

"Which parts?"

"All of it! Shut the whole thing down!"

Lucius ran over to an infosystem wall node, released the lock, and tossed the panel aside. Teodorà looked around, spotted another one, and hurled herself toward it. She reached the wall and ripped the paneling off.

The activating conveyor began lifting out of its cradle.

"Get out of its way, Samuel!" Teodorà shouted.

Pepys pushed himself to his feet, looked at her. Then he shook himself and turned to dash deeper into the ship as the conveyor began to move, and Teodorà turned back to the node and stared at the complex mechanisms.

"What do I do now?"

"Shut it down!"

"How?"

"Flip the power disconnect!"

"*Where?*"

The conveyor rose fully from its cradle and hurled itself after Pepys.

"Duck, Samuel!" Lucius shouted...just as Pepys's left foot caught on loose debris from the first conveyor's broken arm.

He stumbled, landing hard enough on his face to knock the breath out of him, and the conveyor overshot him. It slammed into yet another conveyor's cradle, but it was traveling much slower than its ill-fated predecessor. It bounced, then turned vengefully back toward Pepys, dented but undaunted.

Crimson stars vanished from half the walls.

"Got one of them!" Lucius announced exultantly.

"Lucius, what the hell do I *do*?"

"The disconnect! Flip the *disconnect*!"

The conveyor loomed over Pepys just as he rolled over onto his back. Its disk-like body cast a wide shadow, and it lifted one of its arms for a crushing blow. There was nowhere for Pepys to run, and he squeezed his eyes shut as he crossed his own arms over his face in a futile defense.

"Damn it!" Teodorà cried.

There was no time to figure out the neat way to get it done, she realized, so she slammed her fist through the center of the wall node.

The remaining stars vanished, and the conveyor froze on its counter-grav, its arm halted in the middle of its downswing, less than a meter from Pepys's head.

No one moved for long seconds. No one breathed. Nothing in the ship made a sound.

Pepys slowly opened one eye and looked up.

The conveyor hovered above him, unmoving. One more second, and he would have been paste. He swallowed—hard—then rolled sideways, out from under the looming machine that had tried so hard to kill him.

Teodorà yanked her arm free of the pulverized data node.

"Oh, no," Lucius breathed. He stared at the broken panel, his face twisted in grief. "You killed him."

❖　　❖　　❖

"How did this happen?" Teodorà asked, once they'd convened on the bridge. Lucius looked at her, and she shrugged. "I'm sorry, but we need to know what happened, and I'd really like to find out before Patriarch Ephraim gets into the middle of all this."

"Ephraim?" Lucius blurted.

"Ephraim," she confirmed. "He insisted on coming and I had to tell him the truth about where we're from. I don't think we have any choice now but to show him the ship, and we have to decide what we're going to tell him about all this." She waved both arms to indicate the entire ship. "It's not going to help things one bit if we sound like we are still making up our answers as we go along, Lucius."

"Ephraim, here?" Lucius grimaced. "Wonderful! That's *all* we needed."

"He insisted," she repeated. "I couldn't tell him no without destroying all the trust we've built up. And the truth is, I didn't *want* to tell him no. So pull yourself together and tell me what *happened*?"

"I don't know." Lucius leaned over the command table, bracing himself on his hands, and hung his head. "One minute, everything was fine. The next?"

He shook his head, and Teodorà laid one hand on his shoulder.

"Just tell us what you know," she urged more gently.

"All right." Lucius swallowed, clearly shaken by the death of his companion. "We had the generator up and running, so I thought it would be a good time to check our fundamental systems. We started by running diagnostics on the infosystem nodes. That one there." He pointed to an open wall panel. "It's disabled, by the way. I don't know what's wrong with it, but we should never turn it on again, just to be safe."

"What happened to Shadow?" Pepys asked.

"I think the node corrupted his connectome somehow."

"His...?"

"He means it damaged his mind," Teodorà clarified.

"I noticed an immediate difference," Lucius continued. "He was on edge. Paranoid about every little thing. I tried talking to him, but he became increasingly agitated. Started accusing me of lying to him..."

His voice trailed off.

"And then he attacked us," Pepys finished for him with a sigh.

Lucius nodded, eyes downcast.

"Is he truly dead?" Pepys asked.

"He is," Teodorà confirmed quietly. "His connectome—his mind—was irreparably damaged when I destroyed the node. There's no way we can recover him."

"Then only we three remain," Pepys said sadly.

"It's a lot worse than that, I'm afraid," Lucius replied. "Shadow had access to all our systems from the inside, and for whatever reason, he'd stopped trusting me."

"What did he do?" Teodorà asked.

Lucius licked his lips, and she felt fear knot inside her.

"*What*," she pressed, "did he *do*?"

"He deleted the infostructure's external interfaces."

"Oh, no."

Teodorà collapsed into one of the bridge chairs and stared forward blankly. Pepys looked back and forth between her and Lucius.

"Ought I to conclude that this is...bad?" he asked.

"Very," Lucius said. "Without interfaces, we can't use any of our tech."

"He deleted *all* of them?" Teodorà shook her head, fighting to come to grips with this fresh catastrophe.

"The ones that matter. Remotes. Microbots. Conveyors. Power systems. We can't even turn the lights on or off."

"Is *anything* still working?"

"A little. When I realized what was going on, I started turning off some of the nodes, but I only got as far as the medical bay before Shadow caught onto me. As far as I know, that's all we have left."

"Can't we recover them?" Teodorà asked. "Set the infostructure back to its default?"

"Sure we could. With the template files in the central library."

"This is a disaster!" she groaned.

"I'm sorry," Lucius said.

"You should be!" she snapped.

"Teodorà, that's not fair, and you know it. This isn't my fault. I couldn't have known what would happen."

"I know. I know. It's just—" She exhaled in frustration and waved one hand. "I'm sorry, Lucius."

"It's okay. We're all feeling a little ragged right now."

"But what the hell do we do now?"

"That much, at least, is unchanged," Pepys said. "We press on." She looked at him, and he squeezed her shoulder. "The cure Lucius already delivered is but a tithe of that still within the *Shadow*'s hold. We've more than enough to accomplish our end, and more men to transport it to Constantinople than we could ever need."

"But that would mean bringing them *here*."

"My dear, you've already brought Ephraim and Belisarius around your thumb, so to speak, and we've no choice but to show Ephraim and Nikolas all of this." He gestured at the bridge about them. "I misdoubt not that we will face complications in plenty, yet every problem which confronts us is solvable. I understand that you and Lucius are accustomed to relying upon your wondrous technology, but do we truly *require* it to attain our goals?"

Teodorà gazed at him for several seconds, then shook her head slowly.

"Maybe not. Maybe you're right, Samuel. But I just can't accept that we're surrounded by all this stuff"—it was her turn to gesture around them—"and we can't use *any* of it!"

"Actually," Lucius eyed them carefully, "there may still be a way."

❖ ❖ ❖

"I should be the one doing this," Teodorà protested, arms crossed as she stood in the medical bay between Lucius and the recovery casket.

"No, you shouldn't be," he said. "Someone has to take the first leap inside to see if it's safe, and it's going to be me."

"You just lost your IC, Lucius. You're not in a clear state of mind. You shouldn't be making these sorts of decisions until you've had time to recover from what just happened."

"We don't *have* time, especially since this is something we'd better do before you bring Ephraim aboard. Somehow I doubt he's ready for the notion of another Lazarus, Teodorà. I think he'd find it a lot easier to accept just having a body to bury." He shrugged. "Besides, I've already made up my mind. It doesn't really matter how long we wait or argue about it, because that's not going to change."

"But I'm a synthoid. Abstracting into the infostructure isn't one-way for me."

"And what if it proves fatal? What if I'm wrong and that node wasn't what corrupted Shadow? If whatever *did* corrupt him is still in the system, waiting to corrupt *you*?"

Teodorà paused. That thought had occurred to her, as well, when Lucius suggested using the medical bay to read his connectome and upload it into the ship's infostructure. And it wasn't the only reason her own suggestion had given her pause.

The reading operation would destroy Lucius's biological brain, as it had destroyed hers, when she'd transitioned. But her shift from her organic body to the synthoid had been nearly seamless. She'd never once existed as a purely abstract citizen, and part of her feared losing what remained of her corporeal nature even more than whatever dangers might lurk within the TTV's systems.

"I don't know if there's anything I could've done differently to prevent this," Lucius said now, "but I was the one who was here, and if there *was* an answer, I sure as hell didn't think of it in time. Let me at least try to put things right."

"If anything goes wrong, failure has the same price for both of us," she pointed out.

"Maybe for both of *us*, but not for the mission," Lucius countered. "You're the one who's convinced Ephraim and Belisarius. *You're* the one in the synthoid body. If you abstract and something goes wrong, your body becomes an empty husk *and* Ephraim and Belisarius—not to mention their *men*—will have questions about why 'the Valkyrie' is suddenly no longer around. Face it, I'm more expendable than you are."

"That's a cold way to put it."

"Maybe it is. That doesn't make it untrue, though, now does it?"

"But this would be permanent for you. I could go in and confirm it's safe, first."

"I fear I comprehend this less than perfectly," Pepys said, "but is this a task *I* might essay? Lucius makes a shrewd point about your relationship with Ephraim and Belisarius, Teodorà. By the same token, Lucius, should this miscarry, I have no doubt that your knowledge would prove of far greater use to Teodorà than mine own."

"I appreciate the offer, Samuel," Lucius replied, "and *theoretically*, it could be any of us. But I don't think you're qualified here." He offered the Englishman a sympathetic smile. "No offense."

Pepys looked back at him, then sighed and nodded in acceptance.

"It should be me," Lucius pressed, turning back to Teodorà. "Even if you dive into the system and find out it's still operable from the inside, then what? The interfaces are still down, which means someone needs to *stay* on the inside. You can't do that *and* be in Constantinople at the same time."

"But if you go in, it's permanent."

"I know." He shrugged. "But don't act like this is such a big deal. Sure, it's not the abstraction party I'd imagined. But it was going to happen eventually. This bay won't keep Samuel and me alive forever."

Teodorà sighed and unfolded her arms.

"You're going through with this, aren't you?"

"It's the best path forward, and you know it. Besides"— he smiled crookedly—"living a life in the sixth century isn't for me."

"Lucius?"

"Don't misunderstand. I believe we're doing a wonderful thing here. I've certainly taken my share of stupid risks to make it happen. But the truth is, I'd always envisioned this as an in-and-out, not a permanent gig. And in the end, this is the path the two of you want, not me. I'm fine staying on the sidelines, helping from a distance. Assuming this works, of course." He patted the recovery casket. "Besides"—he flashed a sudden, flickering smile—"look at the upside! I get to do it from the comfort of an abstract realm! And you, of all people, know what a hedonist I've always been!"

She'd begun nodding as he spoke, and she actually surprised herself with a small chuckle at the droll tone of his final sentence.

"All right," she said finally. "We'll do it your way."

"Then let's get this over with." He opened the casket. "It's got to be done, and the sooner it is, the sooner you can bring Ephraim aboard."

She started to protest again, to suggest he at least sleep on it first. But he was right, and she knew it.

"We'll do it your way," she repeated, and he smiled at her, then climbed into the casket and lay down on his back.

Teodorà opened the virtual interface, glad to see it still worked, and queued up the abstraction procedure. Additional mechanisms cycled up from below the casket and moved into orbit around Lucius's head like a flowing metal cocoon. He answered the mandatory automated consent forms that popped up, and Teodorà witnessed them as the system required.

"Last chance," she said after finishing the last form.

"Do it."

Lucius closed his eyes. She hesitated for one, final moment, then hit the commit icon.

Machines pressed in around Lucius's head—locking it in place—and he let out a single, long exhale.

Pepys stepped up behind her.

"Would that I comprehended this more fully," he said.

"The process records a person's mind and allows it to reside within the same infostructure Shadow used," she replied without looking over her shoulder. "If this works, Lucius will be able to operate the conveyors and other technology."

"That much I apprehended. 'Tis the process itself I do not truly understand. How long will it take?" he asked softly.

"It's already done."

"So quickly?" He goggled at the machines pressed around Lucius's head.

"The imaging is. It has to be in order to accurately capture a single, cohesive connectome state. Too slow, and you end up with a caricature of the original rather than a true abstraction. That speed and need for accuracy is also why the process is so destructive to organic brains. Part of that machinery is actually shielding to protect other people in the room."

"Then he's . . ."

"Technically, in purely biological terms, yes, he's dead. His brain's been destroyed, and his body was euthanized as part of the process."

"Hmmmm." Pepys frowned down at the corpse. "And how would your people normally . . . dispose, I suppose, of the body left behind?"

"A citizen's physical shell is normally displayed

during the celebrations following their abstraction. After that, it's recycled. In this case, though, Lucius was right. I'm sure Ephraim will feel more comfortable presiding over a funeral mass after the fact than he would have felt actually witnessing this."

Pepys nodded in agreement.

"And in the meantime?" he asked.

"In the meantime, we wait." She twitched a shrug. "The measurements've been taken, but the data needs to be processed. This bay is highly generalized—it has to serve a lot of functions, not just process abstractions like the specialized systems would use at home—so I'm not sure how long this will—"

"A-*hem*! Hello? Can you hear me?"

The voice came to her mind without a clear sense of direction.

"Lucius?"

"Yes, it's me. Oh, this is going to take some getting used to. Hang on a minute." An avatar of Lucius Gwon materialized in her virtual sight. He raised his hands and examined them, then lowered them and smiled at her. "There! That's better."

"How's it look in there?"

"Shadow left quite a mess, but I think I can manage. All the internal interfaces are intact, which is what we expected."

Teodorà nodded. If the internal interfaces *hadn't* been intact, Shadow wouldn't have been able to control the conveyors.

"Here," Lucius said. "Let me try something simple."

The lights in the passage outside the medical bay blinked on and off.

"I'd call that a successful test," Teodorà said.

"It's a start," he agreed. "Now let's go for something a bit more ambitious."

His avatar blipped out of existence.

"Lucius?" she asked again.

"Over here!"

This time, his voice carried a sense of distance and direction, and Teodorà and Pepys followed it. They stepped onto the bridge and found the place alive with virtual charts.

"Ta-da!" Lucius's avatar declared, arms spread wide.

Teodorà summoned a conveyor control screen to her side, but it didn't move. She walked across to it and tried to interact with it, but nothing happened.

"Read-only, it seems," she huffed.

"The important thing is that the interfaces all still exist." Lucius pressed a hand to his chest. "As does someone on our little team who can still use them."

"Can you repair our side of the interfaces?"

"I should be able to, with enough time. For now, this'll have to do."

"Then I suppose I'd better go get Ephraim and Nikolas," Teodorà said, glancing at an exterior display. It was almost full night outside. "They have to be wondering if we're okay in here. And we should get them in out of the dark, anyway."

"Agreed," Lucius replied, and grinned as this time his voice came over an external speaker. "It's a pity they won't be able to see me, but at least they'll be able to *hear* me. As long as they're ready to listen to a ghost in the machine, that is."

He ended on a questioning note, and Teodorà shrugged.

"I think—*hope*—they are. Ephraim, at least. They've

already seen enough wonders, anyway, and there's all the rest of the ship. Or what's left of it, anyway." She shrugged again. "The trick is going to be keeping them convinced you're not some sort of invisible demon!"

"Which is precisely why that unfortunate body down in the medical bay is going to be that of our dearly departed companion Shadow, whereas I"—his avatar touched its chest again—"have always lived here in the infostructure."

Teodorà nodded. She didn't like the subterfuge, but Lucius probably had a valid point. Primitive societies throughout human history had created far too many legends about unholy rites that involved human sacrifice as a means to summon or propitiate dark spirits. She didn't doubt that Ephraim would, indeed, be far more comfortable with the notion that Lucius had *always* resided in the infostructure rather than that he'd just died and entered it.

"Then I suppose I should go and get them," she said.

"Just one more thing before you do," Lucius said.

"What?" She arched an eyebrow.

"Something I want to show you and Samuel." He closed every virtual window but one. "We finished it."

"Finished . . . what, exactly?"

"Our last resort. Shadow and I—" Lucius paused, then shook his head. His avatar's nostrils flared and his jaw tightened. "Anyway, we finished it and took it out for a little test flight right before I lost him."

Teodorà held up her hands.

"What are you talking about?" she demanded.

"Well, it's great that Ephraim and Belisarius are on our side, or appear to be. But we both know that even with Ephraim, Justinian's going to be a harder sell."

"Yeah? Your point?"

"Shadow and I put together an option in case a more forceful argument is ever needed. A little insurance never hurts. We can fly it into position but keep it out of sight unless we need it."

"I still have no idea what you're talking about."

"Just take a look."

Lucius gestured at the one window still open, and Teodorà glanced at it with a frown.

The recorded imagery was clearly from one of the TTV's exterior cameras, although she had no idea what she was supposed to be looking for. The harsh sunlight of the afternoon just past glared down upon the wadi, showing them the camouflaging exterior of the metamaterial shroud, but there was nothing out of the ordinary, so far as she could tell as she watched it.

"I don't see anything," she said. "What am I looking for?"

"Just give it a moment. It's heavy."

Teodorà and Pepys waited. Then they waited a little longer. Then—

The shroud flap over the cargo bay lifted and a bulky shape slid out of it and levitated upward. There were four conveyors, their bodies joined by solid beams of prog-steel, and Teodorà's eyes widened as they ascended higher and the long, hulking machine they carried glinted in the sunlight.

"God's breath," Pepys murmured.

"I call it The Convincer." Lucius beamed at them. "What do you think?"

CHAPTER TWENTY-ONE

⚬⚬⚬⚬

Charisius Gate, Constantinople
Byzantine Empire, 541 CE

FORTUNATELY FOR NARSES THE EUNUCH, TEODORÀ
wasn't equipped with lethal weaponry like some of
SysPol's synthoids. At the moment, however, the fury
in her brown eyes was almost—*almost*—enough to set
him ablaze without enhancement.

She knew the man's history, courtesy of Raibert's biography of Belisarius, which helped her read the complex
subtext of Emperor Justinian's decision to use Narses
as his messenger. That only fueled her anger, of course,
because Narses and Belisarius had their *own* history.

It was not an entirely happy one.

"His Majesty's patience is exhausted," Narses said
now.

No one had ever questioned his courage, Teodorà
reminded herself, as he stood in the atrium of the
villa Belisarius and Ephraim had commandeered as
their headquarters, just off the road leading to the
Charisius Gate. That gate—the next to last one at

the northern end of the five-and-a-half-kilometer wall Emperor Theodosius had erected a century before— was located on the sixth of Constantinople's seven hills, the highest point in the imperial capital. At the moment, Narses stood facing Belisarius squarely, with only two Excubitors at his back. He wasn't precisely "alone," of course. He was a senior official of the Empire, here to speak specifically for the emperor. Even if none of them had been permitted to join him in the atrium, there were over a hundred more of the imperial guardsmen in the villa's courtyard, resplendent in their coats of mail under the hot sun, and he was personally accompanied by Menas, Patriarch of Constantinople. But even a hundred Excubitors were a drop in the bucket compared to the troops of Belisarius' army, and Belisarius had a patriarch of his own—one arguably senior to Menas—at his left shoulder as he sat gazing back at Narses.

"You have defied him too long, even for a general with your record," Narses continued in an unyielding tone. "Your very presence here is an act of mutiny and rebellion against the imperial authority, and he has instructed me to inform you that it will not be tolerated. You will surrender command of your army to me—now—and return with me to the palace, or you, and all with you"—his eyes swiveled to Ephraim, standing beside Teodorà behind Belisarius' chair, crozier in hand—"will be proclaimed traitors and sentenced to death."

Belisarius leaned back, his dark eyes as hard as Teodorà's but far colder. It wasn't just the emperor and Theodora who'd tried to turn him back. Antonina had sent messages of her own. Teodorà had been tempted to use the remotes to read those messages—and Lucius had urged her to do just that—but she hadn't. Trust, she'd discovered, flowed two ways. The pain in Belisarius' eyes after reading his wife's letters had been too deep for her to intrude upon, but it hadn't turned the general's purpose. It had only hardened it, turned it to ice. He *had* to complete his mission now, if only to prove to Antonina that he was no traitor. To Justinian and Theodora, as well, of course, but it was Antonina who truly mattered.

And if he gave up now, if he did turn back, he could never prove the truth to any of them.

But that determination only made him more ruthless, more dangerous, and there was a dagger in those dark eyes as they bored into Justinian's messenger.

"Tell me, Narses," he said. "Has the death toll in Constantinople matched Mediolanum's yet?"

For the first time, anger flickered in *Narses'* eyes, Teodorà noted with satisfaction.

Physically, Narses and Belisarius were quite dissimilar—Belisarius, a Thracian, was tall and broad-shouldered, whereas Narses, an Armenian, was short and lean, almost slightly built; Belisarius was forty-one, his dark hair only lightly touched with silver; Narses was already in his late sixties and his brown hair was almost entirely gray—but they were probably the two most capable of Justinian's generals. Despite his age, Narses' greatest achievements still lay several years in the future. It was he, in the history from which Teodorà had sprung, who would return to Italy a decade from the present, as a man in his seventies, and complete what Belisarius had so well begun. At least for a time. Until the consequences of the plague gutted Justinian's grand effort to reunite the Roman Empire and it collapsed in barbarian ruin.

His *first* assignment to Italy, however, just two years past, had proved...less fortunate.

In early 538, Belisarius had found himself besieged in the city of Rome by a substantially larger army under the command of Vitiges, the Ostrogoth king. The siege, known to historians of Belisarius' campaigns as the First Siege of Rome, had lasted almost exactly one year, from March 537 to March 538, before Vitiges was finally forced to fall back by the arrival of Byzantine reinforcements under the command of none other than Narses the Eunuch.

The two men had known one another for years even before that. Narses had been Justinian's steward and a high treasury official, but he'd also been a soldier, rising eventually to command Justinian's eunuch bodyguard. Both were highly capable; they had played pivotal roles in the suppression of the Nika Riots of 532, and both were among the handful of successful generals Justinian actually trusted...as much as he trusted *any* general, at least.

At first, that past working relationship had carried over to Italy, but the curse of Byzantium was always factionalism, and the army in Italy had proved no exception. Some of its senior officers had deferred to Narses, while others had remained firmly loyal to Belisarius. According to Raibert's research, Narses had had little to do with the *emergence* of that division, but he'd certainly done nothing to discourage it, and the consequences had been dire.

Especially for Mediolanum, one of the wealthiest cities in Italy, second only to Rome in population and power.

The city, known to later generations as Milan, had rebelled against the Ostrogothic Kingdom and declared for Justinian in April 538. Belisarius, tied down personally in the defense of Rome against Vitiges' main army, had dispatched one of his most capable commanders, Mundilas, to Mediolanum with a thousand men, and Mundilas had quickly secured the city and strategic points around it.

Vitiges had been too preoccupied with Rome to worry about taking it back, at least until he was finally forced to fall back by the arrival of Narses with Belisarius' reinforcements. When he'd retreated, however, he had been unexpectedly joined by another ten thousand Burgundian allies from across the Alps, and his own reinforced host had moved suddenly against Mediolanum.

He'd caught Mundilas with only a portion of his thousand-man force actually in the city, but the hard-fighting Byzantine had proved too tough a nut to crack easily. He'd held his ground and called urgently for reinforcements as Vitiges settled down for yet another siege, and Belisarius had responded with his usual determination and dispatch. He'd ordered Mediolanum relieved, but the subordinates he'd sent had delayed. Instead of moving immediately and decisively, they'd asked for reinforcements to their own force from the nearby province of Aemilia, and the commanders in Aemilia had shifted their allegiance to Narses. They'd refused to move without orders from *him*, and one delay had led to another.

Vitiges had promised Mundilas and his men their lives if they surrendered the city to him, but Mundilas had rejected the offer because it contained no guarantee for the civilian inhabitants of Mediolanum.

By March of 539, however, with no relief in sight, his own starving soldiers forced him to surrender on terms. Vitiges had honored those terms...where the garrison was concerned. But thousands of the city's adult male citizens had been massacred, the remainder had been enslaved, and he'd razed the city.

The disaster had scarcely been solely Narses' fault, but he'd been a significant contributor to it, and Justinian had dealt with the disorder within his army's command structure by recalling Narses to Constantinople and explicitly reconfirming Belisarius as the supreme commander in Italy.

Needless to say, the two of them were less than fond of one another, and that lent a decidedly sharp point to Justinian's choice of spokesman.

"The state of the capital's health has no bearing on His Majesty's authority or will," Patriarch Menas said sharply before Narses could respond to Belisarius' jab. "Nor has it any bearing on the will or authority of the Pentarchy," he added with a jab of his own, glaring at Ephraim.

"It *will*, Menas," Ephraim replied. His own voice was calm, and his expression was almost sorrowful. "It will. And all those deaths are preventable. *That* is what brings us here, not rebellion against the Emperor."

"With all due respect, Patriarch," Narses didn't *sound* especially respectful, Teodorà thought, "matters of the capital are not General Belisarius' concern, and that includes the disease. Nor"—he looked pointedly at Ephraim—"are they *yours*, Your Beatitude. The Emperor has given Belisarius ample opportunities to return to Syria and his duty, still in command of this army. Those have been rejected. Very well. If that is Belisarius' decision—and yours—he must be prepared to abide the consequences. And the consequences are that he is in rebellion against the imperial authority, and that His Majesty will grant him only this one last opportunity to submit without forfeiting his head. And I will remind both of you that the army Belisarius commands—for now—is scarcely the only one the Emperor possesses. Additional troops have been summoned. They are en route, and when they arrive, you will be crushed between them and the capital's fortifications. Unless you think you can somehow storm the city before they arrive!"

The last sentence came out in a tone of scathing contempt, and Belisarius snorted.

"This army has not attacked a single one of His Majesty's subjects," he pointed out, "nor will it. If *we* are attacked, however, we *will* defend ourselves, and you know how bloody that will prove. Unless you think my present commanders are as easily swayed as some of them were in Italy."

Narses' eyes flickered ever so slightly at that, and Teodorà snorted mentally in satisfaction. The march from Antioch had taken over five weeks, which was actually very good time for a sixth-century army, and during that journey, Belisarius' army had become the *Valkyrie*'s Army. She'd proved that she and Pepys could cure the plague before they ever left Antioch. With Ephraim firmly on her side, she'd demonstrated sufficient other tidbits of advanced technology during the long, dusty march to prove her credentials to the army's *commanders*, as well as the men in the ranks. They were on a holy mission—they *knew* they were on a holy mission—and they'd proved remarkably impervious to Justinian's efforts to shake their loyalty and cohesion.

And a dedicated army under the command of Flavius Belisarius was *not* something any of Justinian's other commanders wanted any part of.

"Narses, Menas," Ephraim said, "Belisarius is correct. This army has offered no violence to any of His Majesty's subjects, and we have no desire to seize the city, depose the Emperor, or do *anything* but save lives. To *save* lives, not take them. And whatever you may think, whatever you may believe, we know we *can* save them. We've proven it in Antioch. All we've ever asked is the opportunity to meet with His Majesty to explain our mission and beseech his blessing upon it."

"His Majesty will not meet with you, Your Beatitude, or with Belisarius—or with *anyone*"—Narses turned his glare upon Teodorà—"with an army at his back. As for this . . . *woman's* claims to some sort of divine status—!" He looked as if he wanted to spit on the atrium floor. "You'll need a better pretext for treason than *that!*"

"Narses, I don't think you under—" Belisarius began, but Teodorà put a hand on his shoulder and he stopped, turning his head to look back at her.

There was, she thought, something to be said for plain, old-fashioned anger. And if it took a temper tantrum to get through to Narses—and Justinian—she was more than willing to oblige. In fact—

"*This,*" she grated, glaring back at Narses, "is a waste of time. Justinian always was too suspicious for his own good."

"How *dare* you?" Narses snapped. "His Majesty—"

"Is an idiot!" Teodorà interrupted. "Hundreds of people are dying daily in the streets of his own capital, the cure is *literally* at his doorstep, and he's too damn stupid to use it!"

Even Belisarius' eyes went wide and round at that, but Ephraim only covered his own eyes with the palm of his left hand...and smiled ever so slightly.

"It's not your place to question the Emperor!" Narses snarled. "And the disrespect you've shown will carry a high price, woman!"

"Oh, really?" Her lip curled. "If you want to talk about *prices*, General Narses, I have a message for you to take to Justinian."

"I've been instructed to order Belisarius—"

"No," she said flatly. "This isn't from the General, and it's not from the Patriarch. It's from *me*."

She jabbed her chest with her thumb, and Narses sneered.

"And you believe there's some reason the Emperor will actually *listen* to it?"

"He'd better," she said even more flatly, "because I'm a far worse threat than your tiny mind can possibly imagine."

"Of *course* you are," Narses said mockingly.

"You think not?" She gave him a thin smile, then strode past him to the window that overlooked the capital. "Come here," she said.

He glared at her, standing stubbornly where he was.

"Oh? The mighty Narses is frightened of a mere *woman*?" It was her turn to mock, and despite decades of experience as a courtier, Narses flushed as her fleering contempt flayed his pride. "And here I thought you were a *soldier*," she sneered.

His nostrils flared, but then he tossed his head and crossed to the window. He stopped there and looked at her with an expression of ineffable contempt.

"See that?" She pointed out the window at the

Charisius Gate. Given its elevation, she thought it should be visible to at least half the city.

"What? The gate?" Narses replied. "What about it?"

"Do you *see* it?" Teodorà snapped.

"Are you mad? Of course, I see it!"

"In that case, I want you to tell anyone on or near it to vacate that stretch of wall."

"You must think I'm as stupid and credulous as Belisarius." Narses' tone was scathing. "And you must be even stupider than that yourself if you think I'm going to order the wall abandoned! Not that this wretched army could take the capital even if I opened the gate wide and invited it in!"

"You don't listen very well, do you?" Teodorà glared at him, and as she did, she realized her tantrum was much more genuine than she'd thought when she'd launched it. "Ephraim just told you we didn't come to seize the city, and we didn't."

"And why in the name of Christ and all the saints do you think I'm going to believe that for an instant? Or that I would do anything as foolish as stripping the walls?"

"I can't make you do that," Teodorà grated. "Apparently, no one can make you—or Justinian—do *anything* sensible! But if you choose not to take my . . . suggestion, an awful lot of people are about to die."

"What are you talking about, woman?" Narses demanded.

"Oh, did I forget to mention?" Her smile could have frozen the desert at noontide. "I'm about to make that gate cease to exist."

"Cease to—" Narses shook his head. "What do you mean?"

"Exactly what I said. Justinian obviously isn't willing to listen to reason and clearly doesn't give a single solitary damn how many of his subjects die while he plays the outraged tinplated demigod. Well, I'm about to demonstrate why he'd damned well better listen. And, trust me, Narses, you—and Justinian—are about to discover just how *convincing* I can be!"

"Oh, no," Pepys breathed behind her.

"Oh, *yes*!" Teodorà snapped. "Lucius!"

Lucius's avatar materialized in her virtual sight.

"You rang?"

"Start bringing it up!"

"My pleasure." He vanished.

"Who are you talking to?" Narses demanded.

"Never mind that." She pointed at the gate and its flanking towers again. "Now go. And make sure you tell them. No one has to die today."

"I take my orders from the Emperor, not *you*."

"Then take it as a very strong 'suggestion,' instead of an order. Call it anything you damned well please. But get those men off that wall."

Narses scowled at her, then glanced at Belisarius and Ephraim.

"I would heed her if I were you, Narses," Ephraim said. "The Valkyrie seldom makes threats." The patriarch shook his head. "I, for one, wouldn't care to be on the receiving end of what happens when she *does*."

"And this meeting is at an end," Belisarius added, rising from his chair. "You've delivered the Emperor's message, and the Valkyrie is about to deliver our response. Go now."

"The Emperor will not be pleased," Narses replied.

"Oh, you've got *that* much right!" Teodorà snarled.

Narses glared at her, then at Belisarius and Ephraim. They only looked back levelly, and he snorted disdainfully and looked at Patriarch Menas.

"We've tried, Your Beatitude. Clearly they're mad enough they actually believe this bitch is a messenger from God!"

He barked a contemptuous laugh, then twitched his head at the atrium's entrance. Menas looked a little less certain, but he nodded in agreement and turned on his heel. He and Narses stalked out of the atrium, Excubitors at their heels, collected the rest of their bodyguard, mounted their horses, and headed back to the city.

Pepys tasked a remote to follow them, and Teodorà opened a camera window. She watched Narses, the patriarch, and the guardsmen pass through the gate, which slammed shut behind him, and make their way directly toward the palace.

None of them said a word to the people on the wall.

"Figures," she breathed.

"And you expected that he would do anything else?" Pepys asked.

"I'm allowed to hope."

She walked out of the villa and paused just beyond its ornamental wall, gazing to the north, across the Valkyrie's Army's tents toward the horizon. Belisarius and Ephraim joined her, and the patriarch quirked an eyebrow at her.

"What are you looking for, my daughter?"

"That."

Teodorà pointed to the horizon. Ephraim followed her pointing finger, then stiffened as a mammoth shape loomed upward and floated silently closer above the encampment. Gasps and shouts went up, alarm bells rang, coronets sounded, and units began to form in reflex action to unknown danger.

More sounds of apprehension came from the city walls, as well, and she smiled thinly as she heard them. Those people only *thought* they were alarmed. In another few minutes, they'd find out what alarm really was.

"What *is* that thing?" Belisarius demanded.

"*That*, General, is a nine-barrel, forty-five-millimeter Gatling gun, suspended from four counter-grav-equipped conveyors."

"And so we are no wiser than we were before we asked," Ephraim observed, and Teodorà bared her teeth at him.

"Think of it as a ballista...sort of, Your Beatitude. A very *big* ballista."

"It's *flying*," Belisarius said.

"Well, I did say 'sort of.'"

The Convincer slowed as it drew nearer, then came to a halt over the main road. Its shadow fell over the villa, and Belisarius craned his neck and backpedaled away from it. Clearly he was less than convinced it wasn't about to squash him like a bug.

"How is it staying up there?" he demanded.

"Exotic matter in the conveyors can generate a mild thrust of gravitons to keep it aloft."

"'Exotic matter'?" Ephraim cocked his head at her. "You're speaking a foreign tongue, my daughter. More of your arts from your own time?"

He seemed far calmer than Belisarius, Teodorà thought. Then again, he'd actually toured the *Shadow* before burying Lucius's discarded body with the full rites of Mother Church. Belisarius hadn't.

"Indeed it is, Your Beatitude," Teodorà acknowledged. She swung back to the city and expanded the view from the remote. Rather than abandon the wall, additional troops were rushing to take up defensive positions.

"Well, that's not good," she muttered. "Lucius, how about a warning shot? Give 'em a taste of what to expect if they stay."

"One warning shot coming right up."

The Convincer burped out a single high-explosive, armor-piercing round. It smashed into the base of the wall like Thor's hammer, a fireball blasted a crater deep into the solid masonry, and shards of stone flew high into the air. The soldiers manning the battlements cried out in consternation, and Teodorà smiled thinly.

"A few more," she said. "Spread the love around until they get the message."

The Convincer fired sixteen more rounds with slow, metronomic precision. Each blasted a deep gash into Constantinople's thick walls, and Teodorà watched the remote's visual feed with growing satisfaction. Even the bravest might be excused for breaking in the face of the supernatural, and the gate's garrison started shedding individual troopers by the third shot. By the sixteenth, they'd broken and scattered like cockroaches.

"*There* we go!" she murmured. "That's what I was waiting for."

"It would appear they've gotten your message," Belisarius observed.

"Oh, that wasn't the message. I just wanted them to clear the wall. You haven't seen anything yet, General. Now, Lucius! Let's show everyone what this monster can do." She pointed. "Erase that gatehouse!"

The Convincer stopped firing single rounds. Its

rotating barrels spun up, instead. For a moment, they only whirled around with a great, rushing whine. But then they reached full speed.

They fired, and it was like the end of the world. There were no single shots. There was simply an earth-shattering roar, a single endless hurricane of sound, like the bellow of an enraged god. The Convincer was high overhead, but the shock waves radiating from its thundering muzzles hammered the people below it like a fierce, hot wind, and they were fortunate that railguns produced no shell casings to shower down upon them.

Belisarius and Ephraim clapped their hands over their ears, staring, mouths open and eyes wide. Most of the Valkyrie's Army flung themselves flat, burying their awed faces in their arms, and Teodorà bared her teeth as she thought about how much worse it must be for anyone in the city.

Anyone like, say, an emperor named Justinian.

Depleted uranium tips pierced deep, high-yield explosives shattered the wall in a continuous chain of lightning, and chunks of stonework arced through the air. Some pounded the ground outside the wall in great clouds of dust, but others flew across the for-tifications to slam down in the city's streets or smash through roofs. Lucius raked the ground floor of the twelve-meter-tall gatehouse, moving his point of aim back and forth, chewing through its thick wall in an endless cascade of explosions. The wall vanished, the internal structure shattered, and the upper stories collapsed onto the first, crumpling into the cauldron of flame and its choking pall of stone dust and dirt.

He fired for only a few seconds, but it was enough. Wind pushed the dust storm aside, revealing a shattered, broken ruin—an uneven mound of rubble—where the gatehouse had stood.

The Convincer landed beside the villa. Its rifled barrels glowed orange, and Teodorà heard little *clink-clink* sounds as they cooled from the friction and magnetic induction of firing.

Belisarius shook himself, then walked toward it and reached out to it.

"Don't touch!" Teodorà warned sharply. "It's hot."

He yanked his hand back and turned to face her. He looked back and forth between her and Ephraim. The patriarch's eyes were as awed as his own, but Ephraim only looked back at him without speaking.

"Lady—Valkyrie," Belisarius said softly, "I never dreamed you commanded this sort of power." He shook his head and gestured at the hulking Convincer. "Truly, what need do you have of armies or generals, except as strong backs to bear your cure where it must go?" He shook his head again. "With *this* at your command, you could rule the world!"

"Perhaps we *could*," Teodorà said, meeting his eyes levelly, "but we *won't*. I gave you and Ephraim my word about that, just as I gave you my word that we can defeat the plague. I don't intend to break either of those promises, Belisarius. Not now, not ever."

He gazed back at her for a long, still moment, and then—for the first time ever—he bowed deeply and formally to her.

"Lady Valkyrie," he said, "I believe you."

✧ ✧ ✧

It took Narses several hours to return to the villa. Part of that was because he was forced to use the Circus Gate, the end gate to the south, because the

Charisius Gate's wreckage was impassable. The sun balanced just above the western horizon as he walked back into the atrium he'd stormed out of before Teodorà delivered her message.

This time, he was accompanied by only two Excubitors, and his face was a bit on the pale side. He had himself under firm control, however, and his expression was stony as he faced Belisarius, Ephraim, and Teodorà once more.

"Greetings, Narses."

To Belisarius' eternal credit, there was not even a hint of a gloat in his tone or his expression, and Narses inclined his head ever so slightly.

"Greetings, Belisarius. Greetings, Your Beatitude. And"—his eyes moved to Teodorà and his nostrils flared—"greetings, Valkyrie."

So I'm not "this woman" any longer, am I? Teodorà thought behind her own sternly expressionless facade. *Good! And I didn't actually have to kill anyone, either*.

"May I ask why you've come?" Belisarius continued, and Narses' jaw tightened. Then he inhaled deeply and squared his shoulders.

"I bear word from His Majesty," he said. "He has... reconsidered his position."

CHAPTER TWENTY-TWO

Great Palace, Constantinople
Byzantine Empire, 541 CE

<THIS IS INDEED AN IMPRESSIVE CITY. I HAD READ much about it in my day, spoken to mariners and merchants who had visited it, but never suspected the reality,> Pepys murmured over his wetware the morning after Teodorà's demonstration. The sun was approaching midday and she nodded in agreement as they neared the Hagia Sophia, the Church of the Holy Wisdom.

Most historians would have agreed that, at its height, Constantinople and, later, Istanbul, had been the most magnificent city of the ancient and medieval world. It still existed in her own time, although the sprawling megalopolis she knew had acquired yet another name and dwarfed the city before them now. And despite the plague ravaging its streets, that city was approaching one of the highest points of its three-millennia lifetime.

Of course, the entire Empire was about to crash

by the end of Justinian's reign, and Constantinople would suffer along with the rest of it.

The magnificent Hippodrome loomed on their right, south of the Hagia Sophia, and the crest of the First Hill rose before them. Byzas of Megara had founded the original acropolis of Byzantion upon that hill a thousand years earlier, and the Great Palace, located adjacent to both the Hippodrome and Hagia Sophia, stretched down its eastern slope to the sea. The palace stood on the same site Constantine I had chosen when he moved the Roman capital to Constantinople in 330, but it was scarcely the same palace Constantine had *built*, since much of the original complex had been destroyed nine years earlier in the Nika Riots. Yet the new one was even more magnificent, because Justinian, for all his well-justified reputation for frugality, had spared no expense in its reconstruction. Or in that of the Hagia Sophia, which had been devastated in the same spasm of violence. The new church, which would be universally recognized as one of the architectural wonders of the world, had been finished only four years ago.

The Hippodrome, on the other hand, had escaped the riots virtually undamaged. Probably, Teodorà thought dryly, because it had been home to both the Blues and the Greens—the racing factions who had sparked the violence in the first place—and they hadn't cared to burn down their own house. Even they could show *some* restraint . . . probably.

The citizens of the Byzantine Empire were what one might conservatively call rabid sports fans. The *demes*—the well-developed, powerful sporting associations that had existed for centuries—sponsored different factions, or teams, in sporting events of all sorts, but that was especially true of the chariot races hosted in the Hippodrome. In earlier times, there had been four factions of charioteers, known—because of the colors under which they raced—as the Blues, Greens, Reds, and Whites, but the Reds and Whites had lost their influence over the years. Only the Blues and Greens remained today, yet *they* had grown more powerful than ever as the number of factions decreased, because the number of *fans* had only grown, and their supporters weren't at all shy about defying the city authorities when they took to the streets to celebrate victory or avenge defeat with fistfights, riots, or even armed clashes.

Before the Nika Riots, at least. There'd been a few changes since then.

There'd been many reasons for the riots. The unpopularity of Justinian's taxes; the rapaciousness and corruption of the prefect John the Cappadocian and the *quaestor* Tribonian, his two most powerful officials; his reduction of the bloated civil service's size and his efforts (John and Tribonian's personal corruption notwithstanding) to combat its *institutional* corruption . . .

All of those had been major contributors. But it was the Greens and Blues who'd provided both the tinder and the spark for the inferno.

Bravos of both factions had always been all too ready to break the heads—and necks—of their rivals, and Justinian had regarded them as a danger not just to civil order in Constantinople, but to the imperial authority. No emperor could get away with *ignoring* the factions, given their centrality to the lives of the capital's citizens, and he and Empress Theodora had supported the Blues, at least officially. But he'd recognized both factions as threats and moved to curb their power, which both of them had deeply resented. Disgruntled nobles and civil service functionaries who'd seen their positions, power, influence, and—especially—opportunities for graft diminished by Justinian's reforms had made that far worse by joining the ranks of the Greens (and inveighing against Justinian from their new home), but both the Greens and the Blues had (or thought they had) cause to oppose him even without that accelerant.

Matters had come to a head following a post-chariot riot in 531. Several people had died, and the murderers—Blue and Green, alike—had been condemned to death. Most of them had, in fact, been executed, but two of them, one Blue and one Green, had escaped before sentence could be carried out and taken refuge in the sanctuary of a church that was then surrounded by an angry mob.

Justinian had found himself confronting a crisis in his own capital at a time when he'd had far too many balls already in the air in places like Persia and the frontiers of Dacia and Thrace to respond forcefully. Instead, in an effort to de-escalate tensions, he'd commuted the fugitives' sentences from death to imprisonment and simultaneously declared that a special day of chariot racing would be held in January 532.

That relatively mild approach had been very unlike the normally decisive Justinian, and the Blues and Greens had sensed weakness on the emperor's part. Thus emboldened, they'd chosen to push back instead of accepting his offer, both to demonstrate their own power and to regain the ground they'd already lost to him. They'd demanded that the condemned men be pardoned completely, not just spared from the headsman, but that was a greater concession than Justinian had been prepared to make, and the impasse had further complicated an already dangerously volatile situation.

Against that background, the promised races had proved anything but the de-escalation the emperor had intended. The city was already tense and angry by the time they started, and the crowds packing the Hippodrome, with even more of their famed rowdiness and hooliganism than usual, had begun hurling insults at Justinian from the very start. By the end of the day, the normal partisan chants of "Blue!" and "Green!" had devolved into shouts of "Nika!"— "Conquer!"—from *both* factions . . . and those shouts had no longer had a thing to do with chariot races. They'd become explicitly political, calling for the defeat of the *emperor* . . . and the target of their wrath was unfortunately near at hand, because the Hippodrome literally abutted the Great Palace. Whipped up by its leaders and its own passion, a furious mob, thousands strong, had erupted from the huge racing stadium to attack not just the palace but entire swathes of the capital, and bloodshed, arson, looting, rapine, and mayhem had come with it.

The revolt lasted five days; fires devastated much of the city, including the previous Hagia Sophia and much of the palace complex; and what had begun as a riot became a rebellion as senators unhappy with Justinian's new taxes and lack of support for the nobility seized the opportunity. The rioters, armed and controlled by their allies in the Senate, had demanded he dismiss

John *and* Tribonian. And then, sensing their own power and driven by their senatorial puppet masters, they'd gone still farther.

They'd decided to overthrow him completely and proclaim a new emperor, Hypatius, the nephew of former emperor Anastasius, in his place.

The Nika Riots had been the most destructive in Constantinople's long, often bloody history. They'd also been the most serious threat Justinian's reign ever faced, and the revolt had come within an eyelash of success. In fact, it *would* have succeeded but for three things: the iron will of Empress Theodora, who'd stiffened Justinian's spine at the crucial moment; Justinian's sharp, incisive brain, which had devised a winning strategy once he resolved to fight, rather than flee . . . and Narses and Belisarius, who'd executed that strategy.

Teodorà reminded herself of that as she, Pepys, Belisarius, and Ephraim followed Narses and Menas down the Mese, the "Middle Street" that constituted Constantinople's spinal cord, toward the palace, surrounded by Excubitors. Yes, Narses had been an unmitigated pain in her ass, and, yes, he'd undoubtedly seen Belisarius' "rebellion" as an opportunity to increase his own power and influence, especially after his recall from Italy. But ten years ago, it had also been Narses who'd walked alone—unarmed and unaccompanied by any bodyguard—into a Hippodrome occupied by rioters who'd already killed hundreds, carrying a bag of gold. All by himself, he'd sought out the leaders of the Blues to remind them that Justinian had been their most prominent patron, prior to the current unpleasantness . . . and that Hypatius was a Green. And as a small token of the emperor's ongoing support for their faction, he'd handed his bag of gold over to the Blues' leaders, then returned the way he'd come.

That, Teodorà conceded, had taken nerves of steel, and it had been effective. At the very moment of Hypatius' coronation, without any warning to the Greens, the Blues had abandoned the new emperor in favor of the old and stormed out of the Hippodrome. And as the Blues stormed out of it, leaving the Greens stunned and demoralized behind them, imperial troops under Belisarius and Mundus, neither of whom believed in half measures, had stormed *into* it.

By some estimates, as many as thirty thousand rioters had died that day.

Teodorà doubted the actual number had been that high. Indeed, she was virtually certain that Raibert's estimate of "barely" sixteen thousand was much closer to the truth. But that was still a staggering number—over three percent of the city's *total* population at the time—and the Hippodrome had run red with blood before Belisarius and Mundus were done.

The lesson had gone home. The Nika Riots had ended with Hypatius' execution, the further reduction of the racing factions' power, and the consolidation of Justinian's reign, which would never be seriously threatened again.

Until today, perhaps.

Hard to blame him for his paranoia, actually, she acknowledged to herself as they approached the Augustaion, the marble-paved public market south of the Hagia Sophia, between the church and the Senate houses. The entrance to the Great Palace proper, the monumental Chalkē—Bronze—Gate, lay on the far side of the Augustaion, and the Million, the mile marker from which all distances in the Empire were measured, stood directly outside the square. *He can—and does—take it too far, like his irrational distrust of even men like Belisarius. But even paranoiacs can have genuine enemies, and God knows he does! Just for starters, the man was born a peasant, which means the aristocracy's automatically against him. True, he did have certain advantages most peasants couldn't even dream of, but still...*

In fact, his uncle Justin, the commander of Emperor Anastasius' personal guard, had adopted the young man and sponsored him in Constantinople. As a result, Justinian had received an excellent education in jurisprudence, theology, and history and, in the fullness of time, been admitted to Anastasius' guard himself. And when the childless Anastasius decided none of his nephews—including the ill-fated Hypatius—were qualified to succeed him, he'd made Justin his successor. The Excubitors' support for their long-time commander had made that stand up, despite Justin's lack of blue blood, and Emperor Justin I, in turn, had relied heavily upon his adopted son's advice and counsel. So much so that he'd named Justinian associate emperor early in 527. And when Justin died in August of that year, Justinian—who'd been functioning as his uncle's de facto regent as Justin's health failed, even before he'd been formally admitted to the purple—became emperor in his own right. No one had dared to challenge him, but the aristocracy never forgot that he wasn't one of their own.

And Theodora's even worse in their eyes! Teodorà thought. *Her father was a bear-trainer in the*

Hippodrome, and she was an actress. *That poisonous toad Procopius invented an awful lot of that "Secret History" of his, but not all of it. She really* was *an actress ... and a prostitute, before she met Justinian. But she also happens to be one of the most brilliant women in history, and Justinian truly loves her.*

Indeed, he did. She was twenty years his junior, and she'd become his mistress shortly after her return to Constantinople from Antioch in 522.

Roman law had prohibited anyone of senatorial rank from marrying actresses—*most* of whom had been prostitutes, when one came down to it—and as Emperor Justin's heir, Justinian had acquired senatorial rank, despite his peasant birth. Most men of his time would have been prepared to maintain someone like Theodora solely as their mistress. In fact, Teodorà reflected, *most* men would have used the prohibition as an excuse to do just that, despite what the woman in question wanted. Not Justinian. Instead, he'd convinced Justin to repeal the prohibition and married Theodora in 525, when she was twenty-five and he was in his forties. Sixteen years later, they remained fiercely devoted to one another, and the two of them were a potent partnership, busily rebuilding Constantinople into one of the most magnificent cities in the world.

And Justinian doesn't have a clue she has only seven years to live. Teodorà's eyes darkened at that thought. But then they brightened again. *If we can only convince the two of them to see reason, we can get her to the* Shadow's *medical bay. And if we* do *that ...*

Cancer had been an incurable death sentence for what passed for medicine in the sixth century. Not so much, for the medicine of the *thirtieth* century.

Their party rode slowly between the Augustaion and the magnificent Baths of Zeuxippus, through the monumental Bronze Gate into the palace's grounds, and halted to dismount.

The Great Palace was actually a gorgeously landscaped complex of buildings and pavilions, over two hectares in area, built into a steep hillside that descended over thirty meters from the Hippodrome to the shoreline. It occupied six distinct terraces, each with a spectacular view of the Bosporus, but the area directly inside the gate was a courtyard between the barracks of the Excubitors, to the south, and those of the much older Scholae Palatinae, the palace guard created by Constantine the Great, to the north. Actually, Teodorà reflected, Justinian's reign marked the final transference of power from the Scholae, who Constantine had created to replace the disbanded Praetorian Guard, to the Excubitors, created a hundred and fifty years later by Emperor Leo I as his personal bodyguard. And while the Scholae had degenerated into parade-ground formations, the Excubitors were crack combat troops.

At the moment, a hundred or so of those crack troops stood in orderly ranks on the parade ground, mailed and helmeted, swords at their sides, as their party drew up, and Teodorà glanced at them as she dismounted from Fran.

If Belisarius or Ephraim felt threatened by their presence, there was no sign of it in their calm expressions, and she wondered what the Excubitors were thinking, given The Convincer's demolition of the Charisius Gate.

They may *be thinking it doesn't matter how potent*

The Convincer is if they can cut Samuel's and my throats before it comes to our rescue, she reflected. *For that matter, Justinian and Theodora may be thinking the same thing. I really hope they aren't. I don't want to kill anybody I don't have to, and Samuel—and especially Belisarius and Ephraim—are . . . less durable than I am.*

On the other hand, the prog-steel armor under Pepys's outer garments would stop any weapon the sixth century might produce, and the sidearms hidden inside her business suit's jacket and Pepys's trademark brown coat would turn those Excubitors into hamburger in short order, armor or not.

"His Majesty will see you in his private council chamber in the Palace of Daphne," Narses said a bit abruptly, and she looked away from the Excubitors to smile at him.

"Of course," she said. "I'll be delighted to meet the Emperor wherever he desires, my lord. Please, lead the way."

Something flickered in Narses' eyes. Surprise at her calm, courteous tone, perhaps, she thought, and shook her head mentally. Had he truly expected her to take offense at Justinian's decision to meet with her privately rather than in a public audience?

Maybe he did, she thought. *And maybe he had some justification, given our little exercise in headbutting. But, really! He's one of the most experienced courtiers in the world. He has to understand the value of theater . . . and when it's time to let the histrionics go.*

She truly had lost her temper—she admitted that—but her anger had served her purposes better than calm argument ever would have. Without it, Justinian would never have admitted them to the city at all. She realized now that she should have expected precisely that reaction from him, and a part of her had. It was hard to imagine someone who'd survived the Nika Riots thinking in anything but defensive terms when a potential threat to his authority reared its head, however infuriating she'd found his intransigence. But now that he'd agreed to meet them, what point did Narses think further anger on her part might serve?

"Then accompany me, please...Valkyrie," the eunuch said after a moment, in a less curt tone, and she nodded and waved gracefully for him to precede them.

◇   ◇   ◇

It might be a private council chamber, Teodorà reflected, but it was certainly magnificent. Frescoes decorated the walls, the floor was a gorgeous tile mosaic, and Justinian sat in a beautifully carved chair with cushions of imperial purple on the far side of a massive table. Despite his age, she could see the *doryphoros* he'd once been in his broad shoulders and powerful wrists. His ankle-length *dalmatica*—the wide-sleeved, flowing garment he wore over the rich brocade of the *tunica* which had replaced the traditional (and more cumbersome) Roman toga—was the same purple hue, and a gemmed panel, the *tablion*, glittered across his chest with the emblems of his rank. A golden crown with three rows of precious stones sat heavily atop his graying head, and his eyes were dark, watchful.

The emperor was sixty-one years old, but the woman sitting to his right was only forty. Her elaborately coiffed dark hair was untouched by gray, and Teodorà had been a bit surprised to discover that dye had played no part in that. Empress Theodora was as richly dressed as her husband, in an elaborately embroidered *stola*, the female equivalent of the *dalmatica*, and her hazel eyes glittered as Teodorà's party entered the magnificently appointed chamber.

There was no welcome in her sphinxlike expression, but Teodorà could see what must have drawn Justinian's eye to her all those years ago. They were beautiful, those flinty eyes. The face in which they were set was perhaps a bit too long, had too strong a nose, for classic beauty. And it didn't matter one bit. Unlike the Western Romans, the Byzantines eschewed heavy cosmetics, and Theodora was no exception. Perhaps as a result, her complexion was almost unblemished. Despite that, no one would describe her as pretty, for that was far too pale a word for that vibrant face and the forceful will, wit, and intelligence which lived behind those eyes.

Only one other person was present, and Teodorà kept her own face as expressionless as Theodora's as she recognized Antonina, wife of Belisarius.

She was even tinier in person than Teodorà had expected, as she stood behind Theodora. She was almost as richly clad as the empress she served, and unlike Theodora's, Antonina's hair was thickly stranded with silver. She wore it more plainly dressed than the empress's, and her eyes were so dark they looked black. She hadn't seen her husband in over a year, but her face was as expressionless as the empress's, and her hands were folded in the wide sleeves of her *stola*.

Obviously, Justinian and Theodora planned to keep this as "private" as they could, Theodora thought, with only Narses and Antonina—not just Theodora's closest friend, but her most trusted agent and advisor—as witnesses.

I wonder how Belisarius would have reacted if I'd warned him what was going to happen after his Syrian campaign? Theodora thought. *Would it have made him easier to convince? Or would it have caused him to dig in his heels? If this goes as well as I hope it may, he'll be far better off in this history than he would have been in mine and Samuel's!*

Like Narses, although for rather different reasons, Belisarius had been summoned home from Italy under a cloud the year before, but not for failure. His campaign, after Narses' recall, had succeeded brilliantly. In fact, it had succeeded *too* brilliantly. By 540, the hard-pressed Ostrogoths had offered to surrender if *Belisarius* would become their emperor, which had put him in an impossible position. He'd grown vastly wealthy and powerful in his service to Justinian, and he knew only too well how that had fanned Justinian's fears. The emperor's greatest dread was that so popular a commander might win enough prestige to aim for the throne, and so he'd tried to walk a middle ground, accepting the Ostrogoths' surrender but refusing the title in an effort to soothe Justinian's suspicions.

Unfortunately, his ploy had antagonized the Ostrogoths, who'd felt—in Raibert's charming phrase—that he'd "played" them, yet done nothing to relieve Justinian's fears. It was, after all, traditional for Roman emperors to make a show of refusing the crown when it was offered, was it not? Could that be what Belisarius had had in mind? Best to order him back to the East, away from temptation. Besides, Justinian had other uses for good generals, and so Belisarius had been sent to the Diocese of the East to confront King Khosrow.

Unfortunately for the Belisarius of her own past, the campaign against the Persians from which the time travelers' arrival had diverted him hadn't gone well, either. In the end, he'd been stripped of his command on charges of disloyalty, and only Theodora's intervention on behalf of her friend Antonina had saved him. It was a costly salvation, however. Nothing had ever restored the close working relationship which Belisarius and Antonina had once enjoyed with Justinian and Theodora, and it was shortly thereafter that his marriage had begun to suffer, as well.

But that's not going to happen to him this time, she thought, suppressing a reflex to smile warmly at the general she'd come to treasure as a friend, not a mere tool or ally. *I won't let it. He deserves better than that from Justinian—he always has—and this time around, he's going to* get *it, by God!*

Narses, Menas, Belisarius, and Ephraim went to the floor in the full *proskynesis* Byzantium's emperors had borrowed from their Eastern neighbors to replace the simpler bow which had once sufficed. Diocletian had first begun the custom among Romans two hundred years earlier, and now she watched as Narses and the others fell on their faces and extended their arms and legs. Justinian and Theodora—*especially* Theodora—insisted that all their subjects greet them that way, regardless of birth or rank. In fact, Procopius, never the most trustworthy of historians, had insisted the empress required the obeisance even in private and from friends, although that was probably an exaggeration.

Yeah, it's probably *an exaggeration,* Teodorà thought, *but I wouldn't bet anything valuable on that. Theodora's even more aware than Justinian of how resented she is because of her origins. Demanding that all those aristocratic "betters" of hers grovel before her may not be the most tactful way to remind them where the real power lies, but it's certainly an effective one.*

Which was precisely why she and Pepys did nothing of the sort.

Pepys did go to one knee, but Teodorà simply inclined her head. Her expression was respectful but not precisely awed, and she met the emperor's and empress's eyes levelly.

They had just grown considerably stonier, those eyes, she thought, and Justinian's right hand closed into a fist on the armrest of his chair.

"So, you're the one they call Valkyrie," the emperor said after a long, chill moment of silence.

"I am, Your Majesty," she replied, with another small bow. "And this"—she reached down to lay one hand on Pepys's shoulder—"is my companion, Samuel. Thank you for agreeing to speak to me."

"Your suggestion that I do so was rather *forceful*," Justinian replied, and she allowed herself a very faint smile.

"I regret the damage to your walls, Your Majesty. Sometimes, however, I've found that it takes something 'forceful' to gain the attention of a man as busy with affairs of state as all the world knows *you* are."

Something flickered in Theodora's eyes, and Teodorà wondered if it was fresh anger or possibly a trace of amusement. Justinian only looked at her, then unclenched his right hand and waved it.

"Oh, stand up," he said, and the Byzantines rose. He regarded them with a notable lack of pleasure, but Belisarius and Ephraim looked back without flinching.

"Flavius," he said after a moment.

"Majesty," Belisarius replied.

"I believe you and your army are supposed to be somewhere else at the moment," Justinian observed coldly, and Belisarius nodded.

"I realize that, Your Majesty. And only the fact that I'm convinced my presence here serves your true interests even better than a victory over the Persians could have led me to defy you. I'm grateful you've decided to meet with these two remarkable people."

"Indeed?" Justinian's lip curled. "I, too, am grateful. Grateful they didn't destroy any *more* of the city 'to gain my attention.'"

"I realize you must be angry, Majesty, but—"

"Angry?" Justinian interrupted. "No, Flavius. Anger is something a mother experiences when she catches her child lying. What I am is *furious*."

"As you should be, Majesty, because I've defied your orders." Belisarius looked back at the emperor without flinching. "Indeed, I've defied your *repeated* orders, and I had no authority to do anything of the sort."

"And yet, despite that"—Justinian spread his arms wide, in a gesture that encompassed the council chamber and the entire city beyond it—"here you are. And none other than Patriarch Ephraim with you."

"Yes, Your Majesty," Ephraim put in, speaking for the first time. "Here we are. And it took a great deal of persuasion on my part to convince the general that this is where we *needed* to be."

"Where Belisarius *needs* to be is where I *order* him to be, Your Beatitude," Justinian said flatly.

"That's true, Your Majesty." Ephraim nodded. "Or, at least it's almost always true."

"*Almost?*" Justinian remarked. "How convenient for him that you're here to make his defense, Your Beatitude."

"Your Majesty," Ephraim said calmly, "may I stipulate that, as Belisarius has just said, you have every right to be angry, that you *are* angry, and that you accepted this meeting only under duress? If I may, I will further stipulate that my and Belisarius' actions constitute treason, for which you are amply entitled to claim our heads. Yet despite your anger, you know that neither of us is a fool or that we could have believed for a moment that you would react in any other way when we defied you. Indeed, we did know, and we accepted all of that would be true—including the fact that we'd given you ample cause to summon the headsmen—before we ever left Antioch. Yet, as you say, 'here we are.' Surely that should suggest to you that we, at least, truly believe you *must* listen to the Valkyrie and her Companion. Not simply for your own sake, but for the sake of the Empire, for all of Christendom, and for the future. You are the only man who can give the Valkyrie the opportunity to save millions upon millions of lives, Your Majesty. *Millions.* And that's why we have no choice but to be here, even in defiance of your command to be elsewhere."

Justinian settled a bit further back into his chair, eyes flitting back to Teodorà and Pepys.

"I require neither your nor Belisarius' permission to summon the executioners, Your Beatitude," he said after a moment. "Yet I do take your point. I may yet have you both shortened—and believe me, I am most tempted to do precisely that—but you're right. I do understand that you didn't come all this way in my defiance without what you believed was compelling cause. I may not agree with you in the end, which will be most unfortunate for both of you, but I suppose before I call for the Excubitors, I should at least hear what they have to say."

Ephraim bowed deeply, then stepped back a pace, which just happened to put him at Teodorà's left shoulder while Pepys rose to stand at her right, and Justinian looked at her. His face was a mask, but his eyes glittered. Glittered, Teodorà realized, with something very like despair.

He's spent fourteen years riding the horse of empire, she thought. *Fourteen years ... and in the history we've come to change, he would have sat on the throne for another twenty-four.* Thirty-eight years, *in one of the most turbulent periods of history, fighting that entire time to hold back the dark.*

And, at the end of that long life, failing.

That's what he's done. What he will *do. It's what he's given his entire* life *to, and like Belisarius, he recognizes what The Convincer could do. They don't realize how limited our ammo supply is, and I don't intend to tell them. But he was watching when Lucius blew the gate to bits, and because he was—and because he* doesn't *know how little ammunition we have—he sees it all coming to an end* now ... *because of the threat* we *represent.*

She felt a sudden pang of sympathy for this brilliant, ambitious, paranoid, vain, parsimonious man. It was scarcely his fault he'd been born into a time of invasions and waves of barbarian peoples. Or come to the crown in a court so cutthroat and faction-ridden it had left its very name—Byzantine—as a synonym for the secretive, calculating, tortuous politics of betrayal. Or that he'd been hit here, now, on what should have been the very cusp of success in his great project to resurrect the *Western* Empire, with the greatest pandemic scourge in history. He was what his times had made him, but warts and all, he had by God *earned* the appellation "the Great" by which he would be known to historians in another past, another future, for twice a thousand years.

If only I can convince him to be even greater in this one, she thought. *Please, God. If You truly exist, help me convince him to be the man he* might *have been!*

"So, speak . . . Valkyrie," the man wearing the Crown of Byzantium said flatly. "Tell us why you've come."

"First, Your Majesty," she said, bowing rather more deeply than she had when they first entered the council chamber, "thank you for agreeing to meet with us."

"Thanks would be more appropriate if I'd been given a choice." Justinian's tone was tart.

"As I said, Your Majesty, sometimes it takes something a bit . . . out of the ordinary to break an impasse."

Empress Theodora's lips twitched. Aside from that, her expression never changed, and Teodorà wondered if that could possibly have been a stillborn smile.

"I suppose demolishing one of the strongest city gates in the world in the time it takes to cough three times could be considered 'out of the ordinary,'" Justinian acknowledged.

"No doubt. But I didn't come here to demolish your gates, Your Majesty. I came—*we* came—to help."

"So you've said, and so Ephraim and Belisarius have said in their messages."

"Because it's true, Your Majesty. Your subjects are suffering. Thousands of them have already died, and I tell you now that if this disease isn't stopped, *millions* will join them. We have the power to stop it. That's what we've come to do."

Teodorà Beckett's voice was very level, and the silence in the spaces around it was deafening.

"And afterward?" Justinian pressed after a long, still pause. "You've come to the heart of the Empire. You've coerced one of my best generals and the Patriarch of Antioch to betray me. You've obliterated a part of the city wall and terrorized the capital's citizens. All this so that you can heal the same people you've just terrorized?"

"It wasn't my intention to terrorize your *subjects*, Your Majesty. It was my intention to get your *attention*."

"And so you have. And in the process, you've demonstrated that, assuming for even a moment that you or any other mortal being could possess the power to just snap your fingers and stop the plague, that clearly isn't the only power you possess."

"It isn't, Your Majesty," she acknowledged.

"And men—or women—who have power inevitably *use* it, Valkyrie. So what is it you truly seek? What will you use your power to accomplish after you've stopped the plague?"

"Our immediate mission is to do just that," Teodorà said. "And when we set out for the Empire, we fully intended to simply cure the disease and then leave again."

"When you *set out* for the Empire?" Justinian's dark eyes were narrow. "Should I assume, then, that you aren't here *solely* to combat the plague, after all?"

"Not any longer," Teodorà conceded. "But curing the plague would be an important first step."

"And after you've taken that first step, where will your journey take you *then*, Valkyrie? What is your *final* goal?"

"To make the world a better place than it would have been, Your Majesty." Teodorà looked him squarely in the eye. "It really is that simple."

"No one accomplishes a great project without having a plan, without a specific set of goals." Justinian's voice had changed, somehow, Teodorà realized. It was as if that keen brain of his was actually beginning to engage with what she had to *say* rather than the *threat* she represented. "So what are yours? How does the Valkyrie plan to make the world 'a better place,' when countless emperors and patriarchs—and saints—have all failed in that mission?"

"You're right, Your Majesty," Teodorà said. "I'll be honest with you and admit that our initial plan hadn't been . . . thought through as thoroughly as it should have been. An old, old friend of mine who wanted to dissuade me pointed that out to me, however. He raised very much the same point you've just raised, and so, since we've arrived, I've given a great deal of thought to the question you've just asked.

"First, foremost, before anything else, Your Majesty, with your assistance and that of the Empire, we *will* stop the plague. For that, alone, you would go down in history as one of the greatest emperors Rome has ever known. But ending the disease isn't the end. I realize that now. It's only a beginning, because I have a vision. A shining, golden vision of the future, and I need your help to make it happen."

"A vision?" Justinian repeated skeptically.

"Yes, a vision. A vision of what you might call a dynasty. Not just the dynasty of a single ruling line, but an *eternal* and benevolent dynasty. One that will spread wings of peace, health, and prosperity across the entire world. That's the dream that brings us here. And we know full well that a dream such as that can't be achieved in a single lifetime. That's why it will require a dynasty committed to it, one that will span generations, and *here*"—she stamped a booted heel on the mosaic floor—"here is where that dream's first brick will be laid. Here, in the Empire."

"And what *becomes* of the Empire in this glorious dream of yours?" Justinian demanded.

"It lives on, Your Majesty. It lives on forever, richer and grander than even you could possibly imagine. Not just the Eastern and the Western Empires reunited, but an entire world. And your Empire, the dynasty I need your help to create, will be the beating heart of that glorious, eternal future."

"How?"

"You've seen the power—some of it—we brought with us, Your Majesty. What you haven't seen is the *knowledge* we possess. Not simply the knowledge, the ability, to defeat the plague. Knowledge that will improve your lives in ways beyond your dreams. We can share that knowledge with you. We *will* share it with you, freely. But only if you allow us to."

"I have a choice, then?"

"You do," Teodorà said firmly. "If you choose to turn us away now, we'll leave. We'll go somewhere else and seek others to help us. We'll leave the medicine, if you'll permit it, but that will be all. Our secrets are our own to keep. Or"—she extended her right fist, palm up between them, then, slowly, uncurled her fingers and opened it—"our own to *share*."

"What other secrets, if I may ask?"

For the first time, Justinian sounded truly curious, and Teodorà smiled at him.

"Too many to list, Your Majesty. Just for a beginning, we have medicines for more than just the plague. There are many other diseases we can cure, ailments and injuries we can heal. We brought fewer of those other medicines, since our great purpose was to defeat the plague, but what we possess would be sufficient to extend the lives of you and your family, and Belisarius and his. We also have other flying machines, smaller than the one that destroyed the gate, but no less useful. I'm sure Belisarius could find plenty of ways to deploy them to benefit the Empire's armies. And there are other wonders we can show you how to build for yourselves, skills we can teach your artificers and knowledge beyond their dreams that we can share with your scholars. That's our great purpose, Your Majesty—to teach. To help you and all your subjects build their *own* future."

"And the price of all this?"

"Only that you help us as we help you, by spreading knowledge and civilization to every corner of the world."

"To eventually form this eternal 'dynasty' of which you speak."

"Many years into the future, but yes. That's where we want it to end."

"With the Empire at its core?" he pressed.

"Yes, if you allow us to stay."

Justinian looked at her very, very intently, then turned to Theodora.

"Well?" he said.

"You speak most passionately, Valkyrie," Theodora said, looking at Teodorà. "As you may recall, however, I was once an actress. The fact that one speaks with great passion, with shining eyes and earnest expression, is no proof they also speak *honestly*."

"No, Your Majesty. It isn't," Teodorà acknowledged.

"One might wonder," Theodora continued, "why someone with the power and the knowledge you appear to possess would require our assistance."

"Because despite what some of the soldiers and Belisarius' army may think, I'm neither an angel nor a god. More than most mortals, in some ways, but not a deity. I needed Belisarius' army to transport the cure from Antioch to Constantinople. And"—Teodorà smiled slightly—"to get your attention. But I can be in only one place at one time. I can cure only one patient at one time, and the disease we're talking about will be more horrific than anything the Empire has ever faced. I need—*we* need—more hands, more backs, more *hearts* to help us, or, in the end, we'll fail. Just"—she looked back at Justinian—"as your efforts to regain the West will ultimately founder in an ocean of barbarians and the hecatomb of the plague."

"I see."

Theodora looked over her shoulder at Antonina and raised an eyebrow. Her friend looked back, then raised her eyes to her husband.

"Is that what she told you, Flavius?" Antonina's voice was a melodious contralto. "Is that how she convinced you to betray your emperor?"

"Yes, it is." Belisarius gazed back at her steadily. "I said as much in my letters, and I say it again now,

Antonina. That is the *only* reason she could convince me—or Ephraim—to march on Constantinople instead of Nisibis."

Silence fell, and Justinian leaned back in his chair, eyes sweeping the four travelers standing before him, while first seconds and then minutes dragged past.

"Flavius," he said finally.

"Yes, My Emperor?"

"Do you truly believe her? Truly *believe* that what she says is possible?"

"Your Majesty, I've seen too much, both in Antioch and on the march here, to doubt it."

"Ephraim." Justinian's gaze swiveled to the patriarch.

"Yes, Your Majesty?"

"The Valkyrie says she's neither angel nor saint. Can you swear to me, on your own immortal soul, that she is no demon or devil, instead?"

"Your Majesty, I can," Ephraim said simply. "She may make mistakes, and I know from what she's freely told me that she *has* made mistakes. But I've seen into the soul of this woman and her Companion." He looked back at his emperor and his expression was serene. "There are dark places in us all, Your Majesty. Mother Church teaches us that. No doubt that is true even of the Valkyrie. But in her case, they are very small dark places, and all she wishes is to let sunlight cleanse even them."

Teodorà felt her face heat at the simple sincerity in Ephraim's voice, but Justinian only nodded slowly.

"And what of this eternal dynasty she wants to create?"

"I believe that is indeed her purpose, Your Majesty." Ephraim glanced at Teodorà. "In her own eyes, she owes a great debt. She can't repay it to the people to whom she owes it, and so she chooses to pay it to *us*, instead. As the blessed Saint Matthew says, 'You will know them by their fruits,' and I believe the Valkyrie is a very good tree that cannot bear bad fruit."

"I see you do. But what of the dangers if, despite all, she proves false?"

"Your Majesty," Belisarius said, "the Valkyrie has just proved she can bring down our city walls with ease, yet her sole purpose, her sole demand, was to come here and speak to you personally. Not to demand your surrender, but to offer you *peace* and security and greatness." Byzantium's greatest general looked his emperor in the eye, and iron rang in his soft voice.

"Your Majesty," he said, "the *danger* lies in turning them away."

Silence fell again, and then Justinian cleared his throat.

"I see your point," he said.

He nodded and rose from his chair. He offered his arm to Theodora, who rose regally beside him, and they walked around the massive table, Antonina at their heels. They stopped, facing Teodorà, and Justinian's eyes met hers. There were still dark, those eyes, but no longer with simple suspicion and fury and fear. Now they were dark with wonder, as well, and he reached out to her.

"I suspect no one in the city has said this yet," he told her. "Valkyrie Teodorà Beckett, let me be the first to welcome you to Constantinople."

CHAPTER TWENTY-THREE

⸺∞∞∞⸺

Argus Station
SysPol, 2980 CE

"SORRY. SORRY!" COMMISSIONER PENG SAID, AND Klaus-Wilhelm looked up from his prepared notes as the Arete Division's commander materialized in the conference room between Chief Lamont and Commissioner Hawke.

"What's your excuse *this* time?" Hawke prodded in an elaborately patient tone.

"You know, I try not to be late. I really do." Peng shook his head. "But these *morons*..."

"The Society?" Lamont asked.

"Yeah. Again." Peng blew out a frustrated virtual breath and dropped into an equally virtual seat. "Bunch of uppity jackasses, if you ask me. They think they're the first group to ever lose a court case. Here's a hint, guys. *Every* court judgment in *all* of history has a losing side. Get used to it and try harder next time. It's not my job to clean up after your 'civil disobedience' every time you get a little angsty. Sheesh!"

"Actually, it *is* your job," Hawke noted wryly.

"What happened?" Lamont asked.

"Well, you know how both Atlas and SourceCode have been showing off their prototypes for the Dyson project?"

"Vaguely."

"Atlas scheduled a big demonstration today near L4. Their CEO and half their board were there. The press was there. Senators from both sides of the aisle were there. Members of Byakko's *cabinet* were there. The lead engineer turned on their 'patented macrotech constructor,' the test asteroid went in"—he spread his hands—"and a shower of giant middle fingers came spewing out the other side."

Hawke snorted a laugh.

"I know, right?" Peng flashed a grin of his own. "Turns out one of their programmers is a Society member. Three guesses who just lost her job!"

"But the situation's under control?" Lamont asked.

"Yeah, it's fine," Peng assured him. "The Atlas engineers had most of it cleaned up by the time my first team transmitted in, and, honestly, I only got dragged into this mess because the cabinet members were there." He glowered. "Politicians. Gotta love 'em. And all this excitement over a hunk of rock no one's using."

"Anything else?" Lamont asked.

"I wouldn't mind venting for another twenty minutes," Peng said. "But, nah. Nothing we need to cover now."

"Then let's get started."

Lamont nodded to Klaus-Wilhelm, who loaded his presentation into the room's infrastructure and stood.

"It's good news, right?" Peng asked. "I could use some of that."

"It's...mixed." Klaus-Wilhelm opened a top-down image of a chronoport leaving the DTI tower.

"*Pioneer*-class, if I'm not mistaken?" Lamont said.

"*Pioneer*-class *refit*," Hawke corrected. "But the impeller looks a little longer."

"That's because it is," Klaus-Wilhelm said. "This is the second chronoport to be equipped with transdimensional tech, and the first the Admin's achieved on its own."

"Shit," Peng breathed. "So much for *good* news, Klaus! Thanks a lot." He shook his head. "Gentlemen, the genie is officially out of his bottle."

"We knew this would happen eventually," Lamont countered. "It was only a question of timing."

"And we didn't come out of the exchange empty-handed," Klaus-Wilhelm pointed out. "Agents Andover-Chen and Kaminski collected a great deal of data on DTI operations and technology, as well as providing us with a firsthand look at the Admin's newest chronoport."

"Sorry, Klaus. That's not making the news a lot better," Peng said.

"How long until their entire force is upgraded?" Lamont asked.

"Hard to say," Klaus-Wilhelm replied. "They finished this first one faster than we thought they would, and they'll undoubtedly become more comfortable with the tech as time goes on. Our current estimate for full conversion is about two months, and that includes their facilities for manufacturing new impellers."

"They didn't upgrade another *Hammerhead* first?" Hawke asked.

"No." Klaus-Wilhelm shook his head. "From what we can tell based on traffic at the DTI tower and which chronoport is docking where, they seem to be rolling out the technology to their lighter chronoports first."

"Any thoughts on why?"

"I can only speculate, but I believe it's because the *Pioneer*s make better scouts. The Admin is starved for information on SysGov activities; they've only had what we've shown them up until now."

"I hope everyone's done checking their security protocols," Peng grumbled.

"My department's ready," Hawke replied.

"As are the others," Lamont said. "Again, we knew this would happen, and President Byakko actually counted this as a positive outcome of giving away the technology. She's fine with the Admin snooping around a little, just so long as they don't cause trouble in our space. Allowing some uncontrolled information flow in their direction means they don't have to be paranoid about what we *might* be doing."

"Which could just be another way of saying it'll help them stick the knife where it hurts the most," Hawke observed.

"I'm not suggesting we let them run rampant," Lamont clarified. "Those aren't the president's orders, and they're certainly not mine. We'll guard our space and our secrets as best we can, and we're free to detain any Admin vessel found in our territory. But we all know some of their efforts will slip through. Space is too big and their stealth systems are too good for any other result."

"You know," Peng shook his head, "I still can't believe Byakko went through with that crazy exchange."

"Gentlemen, I'll admit our relationship with the Admin is...strained." Lamont knitted his fingers on the conference tabletop and leaned forward. "It's hard to find common ground when the people we're dealing with see your president as an unholy abomination. However, there's also reason for hope." He gestured to Klaus-Wilhelm. "The recent operation between the DTI and the Gordian Division is a prime example that cooler heads may yet prevail. And in particular, the success of that mission—"

Alerts blared to life next to Klaus-Wilhelm and Lamont.

"*Scheisse*," Klaus-Wilhelm snarled. "Not again!"

"What the—?" Lamont blurted. "'Gordian Division Priority *Two*'? What the hell is Priority *Two*?"

"Priority Two alarms mean we've detected a possible precursor to an event like the Gordian Knot." Klaus-Wilhelm silenced the alarm and opened the link to the sender, his expression deadly serious. "Gordian Operations, this is the commissioner. What's going on down there?"

"Sir, Doctor Andover-Chen here. I'm the one who triggered the alert."

"And why did you do that, Doctor?"

"Sir, a few minutes ago the Argus Array detected an incoming chronometric wave front. The array staff called me in, and I believe we're witnessing a previously unknown child universe catching up to us in the True Present."

"A child universe?" Klaus-Wilhelm repeated. He and Lamont exchanged a quick look. "But that shouldn't be possible, unless... Are you sure?"

"It's the best explanation I have at the moment."

"Threat level of the phenomenon?"

"None that I can discern. Certainly nothing on an existential level. But I thought it prudent to send out the alert anyway, given what happened to T3 and T4."

"Of course. You made the right call."

"Sir, I think we need to dispatch a TTV to investigate further. And I'd like to be on that team."

"Understood. I'll meet you down in Operations to discuss what you'll need." He closed the link and turned to Lamont. "Chief, if you'll excuse me?"

"By all means, yes!"

◇   ◇   ◇

The prog-steel shutter split open and Klaus-Wilhelm strode into the wide, circular space of Gordian Operations. A dozen ACs hovered or stood in his virtual vision along the curved walls, charts open before them, while Andover-Chen and a handful of physical agents waited near the center of the room around a massive, floating visualization of the wave front. He crossed the room and stopped next to Andover-Chen.

"Let's have it."

"Of course, sir." The synthoid gestured across the floating image, which changed into two lines—one bowed and pulling away from the other but still stuck to it at both ends. "This is a simplified visual of what the data is telling us, but I think it'll be instructive. In essence, I believe we've caught this new universe in the middle of peeling off our own."

"Are we the blue or the red line?"

"Blue. We're the parent, so our timeline is the foundation the other one is splitting away from."

"How long until the wave front reaches the True Present?"

"A few hours."

"That fast?" Klaus-Wilhelm raised an eyebrow at Andover-Chen. "The Gordian wave would've taken over a millennium to catch up."

"Yes, but remember that its sluggishness was the result of all the destructive energy building up. The more benign nature of this one may explain its faster speed."

"*May* explain?" Klaus-Wilhelm pressed, and Andover-Chen shrugged.

"Our models remain works in progress. Other variables may be at work here."

"Don't I know it," Klaus-Wilhelm breathed. "Do you think Chairman Gwon and Doctor Beckett caused this?"

"I've been wondering the same thing." Andover-Chen smiled crookedly. "And the answer is that there's no way to be certain...yet. But I don't see who else *could* have caused it. All the other time machines are accounted for."

"You destroyed their TTV."

"To be more precise, sir, we blew up their impeller. But recall that *Hammerhead-Prime*'s dish was damaged during the battle. It's entirely possible some undetected part of their ship survived, I'm afraid."

"Which would have eventually dropped back into phase." Klaus-Wilhelm grimaced and rubbed his chin. "And whatever it had on board was enough to permanently splinter the timeline."

"So far as I know, 'split' is probably a better verb, sir. But, essentially, that does appear to be the scenario we face."

"Well at least it's not another Knot." Klaus-Wilhelm turned to face the physicist fully. "It *isn't* another Knot, is it?"

"No, sir. As I said, there's no obvious immediate danger. Better safe than sorry, on the other hand. I know you've already agreed that we need to send a team to investigate further, but I think we need to look at more than just the mechanics of the process. I'd like your permission to survey this new timeline, as well."

"Of course." Klaus-Wilhelm nodded thoughtfully. "Permission granted. What resources will you need?"

"If I'm right, we'll be jumping into a universe that diverged from our own twenty-four centuries ago. A universe that may have had access to thirtieth-century artifacts all that time. There's no telling what kind of mess we'll find, but it's entirely possible—even probable, perhaps—that their technology will be better than ours. Perhaps significantly so." He leaned toward Klaus-Wilhelm and spoke softly for emphasis. "I think you know which team I'd like to have my back."

"Thought so."

"He's not going to like this, is he?"

"Probably not. He's been burning through his vacation time ever since you two came back."

Klaus-Wilhelm opened the communication window and put in the call. Half a minute later, a long snake-like face popped into the window. Its dark green scales were slashed with red warpaint, and a targeting visor hung over one eye.

"*Whaaaat?*" the lizardman demanded as it looked up from the massive, multibarreled weapon in its bulging arms and turned toward the screen. "This better be damned—oh." The creature's voice turned suddenly small and mousy. "Oops."

Klaus-Wilhelm blinked at the bizarre spectacle.

"Excuse me," he managed at last. "I seem to have called the wrong address."

"No, you didn't, boss. You just caught me at a bad time. Sorry about the outburst."

"Raibert?" Klaus-Wilhelm blinked again. "Is that you?"

"Yeah, it's me." The lizardman held up a finger. "Hold that thought."

He lifted the multibarreled cannon to his shoulder and aimed it down the corridor. At least, Klaus-Wilhelm thought it was a corridor; its improbable geometry twisted along its length until the floor became a wall and—eventually—the ceiling. Dark passages connected to it at odd angles, and pale-skinned, many-limbed shapes poured into the open.

Lizard-Raibert fired a pulse from his weapon, and one of the tentacled cyber-horrors blew apart in a shower of slimy, translucent flesh and sparkling hardware.

"Hey, Philo! I've got the Commissioner on the line! Pause the enemies, would you?"

The cybernetic creatures halted their advance.

"There. That's better." The lizardman lowered his weapon and wiped his brow. "Whew! He wasn't kidding when he said this would be a wild one."

"What's going on over there?" Klaus-Wilhelm asked.

"What does it look like? I'm getting my ass handed to me by space squids."

"That's not exactly what I meant."

"Look, I know I haven't been in to work lately. But I needed to decompress after that last one, and shooting stuff in *Solar Descent* is therapeutic." He pulled a handheld device off his bandolier and sauntered up to the nearest creature. Red lights pulsed on the beer-can-sized device in his gloved hand.

"No, Raibert. I completely understand."

"I guess Teodorà's death hit me harder than I expected, and I just needed to blow off some steam." Lizard-Raibert stuck the pulsing device on one of the creatures, then pulled another off his bandolier and armed it.

"Raibert, what are you doing?"

"Multitasking." He shoved the second device—probably a grenade—down a creature's drooling maw. "And, no. You keep these things paused until I'm done."

"I beg your pardon?"

"Just talking to Philo, boss." Raibert slung his cannon and pulled off two grenades at once. "Don't worry. I'm listening to every word you say. And by the way, I'll remind you that you approved every day off I submitted."

"I know. I remember."

"I think I've earned a little R and R." Raibert planted both grenades on a particularly large and slimy specimen.

"I never implied you hadn't."

"I had to spend *weeks* stuck in that Admin tin can with no one but *Andover-Chen* to talk to. It's enough to drive a man insane."

"Ahem." Andover-Chen cleared his throat, and Raibert blinked thick eyelids over vertical pupils.

"What was that?"

"That would be your coworker," Klaus-Wilhelm said dryly.

"Ah, crap. Is he on the line, too?"

"Hello, Raibert," Andover-Chen said cheerfully, leaning his head into view.

"Uh, hi? How are you?"

"Raibert, this isn't a social call." Klaus-Wilhelm's voice was considerably more forceful than it had been. "We have a situation."

"Yeah." The lizardman slouched, his saurian face managing to look crestfallen. "Figured as much. You need me to come in to work, don't you?"

"That's right. Assemble your team and meet Andover-Chen in Operations. We'll brief you then."

"Well, that's one thing I don't need to worry about."

"What do you mean?"

"The team." Raibert pointed off camera. "We're already assembled."

A white-furred alien, half Lizard-Raibert's height, stepped in front of the viewpoint, long whiskers twitching on a mouselike face. A dozen pulsating earrings hung from the creature's left ear, and a reflective visor shaded its eyes.

"Hello, sir." The mouse-person put one hand on a hip and raised a pistol in the other.

"Ella?" Klaus-Wilhelm asked as he recognized the voice. "You play this game, too?"

"That's right, sir. It's a lot of fun."

Raibert wagged his eyelids.

"Her star seer is already up to level four, which gives her access to nova ascendancies."

"She must be so proud," Klaus-Wilhelm observed blandly. "I take it Benjamin is present, as well?"

"Yes, sir." A hulking mass of full-body power armor clanked into view and lowered what looked like a bastardized combination of a rocket launcher, flamethrower, and machinegun. "Though in my defense, I'm only here because of peer pressure."

"Oh, don't be such a grouch." Raibert knuckled Benjamin in the shoulder. "You've been playing a lot more recently."

"That's only because my vacations to the twenty-first century are on hold."

"*Pfft!* Doc, just admit it. This game has grown on you."

"Maybe. A little," Benjamin said. "But I'd enjoy it even more if its rules made sense. I built my character specifically to be a damage sponge. How the hell does an enemy of the same level one-shot me?"

"Oh, come on. You know psychic damage ignores armor."

"I do *now*," Benjamin retorted. "At least Philo let me keep my experience and re-spec when I created Hector Carnifex the Third."

"I still think three tiers of Hardened Will is a bit excessive."

"Oh? Maybe it is, but at least my brain won't explode again!"

"He's got a point there," Elzbietá agreed. "That was really gross, the way his head popped like a zit."

"Philo's present as well?" Klaus-Wilhelm asked.

"Yep." Raibert pointed a thumb over his shoulder. "He's controlling the squids."

"Here, Commissioner." The creatures all waved a tentacle in unison, then reverted to their paused state.

"Sounds like you're all enjoying yourselves," Klaus-Wilhelm said. "I'm almost sorry to have to break up your game."

"You know you have an open invitation to join us whenever you want," Raibert said.

"I do?"

"Of course. I send you a party invite every time we game, but you never respond."

"Ah. Those." Klaus-Wilhelm recalled the persistent messages he now auto-forwarded to his spam folder. "I'm afraid these newer diversions aren't my style. I'm more of a card game kind of person."

"Well, that's all right," Raibert said. "We could have a—I don't know—a poker night or something over at my place. What do you say?"

"You never send *me* invites," Andover-Chen pointed out with a wry grin.

"Uh, yeah. Guess I don't."

"Any particular reason?"

"Not really." Raibert shrugged. "Guess it just didn't occur to me you might be interested. You have a *Solar Descent* character?"

"Three, actually. Two maxed out and a level-ten combat medic."

"Oh? Oh!" Elzbietá nudged Raibert. "We could use a dedicated healer."

Raibert narrowed his eyes at her and flicked out a long, flexible tongue.

"We're getting distracted here," Klaus-Wilhelm said. "All of you, come to Operations in an hour. Andover-Chen and I will brief you then."

"Got it, boss." Raibert glanced over his shoulder at the creatures choking the corridor. "Though, would it be a big deal if we took two hours, instead?"

"Three, if you want to finish the scenario," Philo corrected. "Two and a half if you don't debate every last dialogue choice."

"Right. What Philo said."

Klaus-Wilhelm rolled his eyes, then glanced at Andover-Chen.

"That should be fine," the synthoid said. "The wave front is perfectly harmless, and traveling to it will be easier once we allow it to reach the Edge of Existence. Plus, I can use the extra time to crunch through the data still coming in."

"In that case, I see no harm in waiting. Have your team meet us in Operations in *three* hours."

"All right!" Raibert raised a small handheld device. A single red button blinked beneath his thumb. "Philo, you can un-pause the enemies now!"

The creatures shuddered into motion, Raibert's thumb jabbed the button, and the corridor lit up with a blinding flash. A flaming tentacle flew past the viewpoint so quickly that Klaus-Wilhelm flinched.

"Who's in the mood for calamari?" Raibert quipped as the smoke cleared.

CHAPTER TWENTY-FOUR

∞

Transtemporal Vehicle *Kleio*
non-congruent

"NOW ENTERING THE TRANSVERSE," ANNOUNCED Elzbietá.

"Hold right next to SysGov's outer wall." Raibert stood up from the command table and walked over to Andover-Chen. "This is a nice change of pace. The ship's not shaking at all."

"That's to be expected," Andover-Chen said, gazing at the charts that hovered before him. "The wave front that just struck the True Present was quite different from the one the Knot produced. In fact, without the transdimensional data you brought back, I would've taken it for background noise."

"I wonder how many child universes we actually saw coming and just didn't recognize because we 'knew' it was only 'noise'?" Raibert's tone was bitter. "I guess that's one reason it took us so long to accept the damage we were causing."

"Part of it, anyway," Andover-Chen said. "Ignoring the 'dangerously deluded naysayers' was another."

"Who called you that?"

"Doctor Beckett."

"I see." Raibert frowned. "You didn't let that get to you, did you?"

"Maybe a little. It's hard being publicly ridiculed as the crazy fringe." Andover-Chen's expression tightened, and the numbers beneath his black, glassy skin faded.

"You don't think she survived, do you?" Raibert asked quietly.

"I don't know what to think right now. Too many variables. Best to keep an open mind."

"I suppose you're right." Raibert nodded.

If they were right about this child universe's origins, then *someone* aboard the stolen TTV must have survived. *All* of them might have, but was Teodorà one of them? He wondered, again, how he felt about that possibility. He'd accepted her death, and that had hurt on a far deeper level than he'd expected. They hadn't been on good terms in years, but he'd never wanted her *dead*. He'd imagined sabotaging her vocal cords so she'd ribbit instead of talk—anything to shut her up—but that was as bad as his fantasies had gotten.

And then she was dead, and he'd helped kill her.

Except, maybe she wasn't.

That ambiguity tore at him. What exactly was he supposed to feel in a situation like this? He could work with and come to accept any certainty, no matter how dark, but not knowing was far worse, because the scars couldn't heal. There would always be that nagging voice whispering "what if?" in the back of his mind.

One way or another, we'll know soon enough, he told himself.

"Hmmm." Andover-Chen pushed one of his charts aside and expanded another. "What have we here?"

"Got something?" Raibert asked.

"Not sure yet. It's peculiar, though."

"Could be a transdimensional link." Philo appeared next to them. "You see the lateral resonance?"

"Yes." Andover-Chen zoomed in once more. "You might be right."

"Meaning?" Benjamin asked.

"That this new universe hasn't fully separated from ours," Philo replied.

"Which is quite useful in our situation," Andover-Chen continued with a nod. "The data we're collecting should give us a clean transdimensional vector for reaching the new universe's outer wall."

"Doctor, take a look at this." Philo shifted a chart over.

"Ah!" Andover-Chen beamed at the data. "And that would be our vector. Nicely done, Philo." He flicked the charts toward the command table. "Ella?"

"Vector received," Elzbietá said. "Shall we find out where it leads?"

"It's what we're here for," Raibert replied with a shrug. "But let's check in first. Kleio?"

"Yes, Agent Kaminski?"

"Telegraph Operations with our current status and request permission to proceed along the new vector."

"Yes, Agent. Transmitting now."

"And make sure you include the vector data. I want them to be able to find us if something bad happens."

"Yes, Agent. Please note, however, that I had already

included the vector data without your prompt. Its inclusion was implied in your statement requesting 'permission to proceed along the new vector.' Accordingly—"

"Kleio, we've been over this," Raibert interrupted. "Less sass. More following orders."

"I am not sassing you, Agent," the ship replied, and Raibert rolled his eyes. "I only wished to point out that the clarification you made to your original order was unnecessary. And—"

"You remember what I said about restoring you to default?"

"Of course, Agent. I am not capable of forgetting, unless instructed to purge memory. However, I believed it necessary to point out that—"

"Ah, ah." Raibert wagged a finger.

The bridge fell silent for several long seconds.

"I will endeavor to reduce the level of 'sass' in my social interface," Kleio said at last, and Raibert grinned.

"There's a good ship," he said, and sat down next to Benjamin.

"You're in a bit of a mood," Benjamin noted, and Raibert shrugged.

"Maybe, but we're about to enter a universe that shouldn't by all rights even *exist*. And let me remind you, the last two we visited imploded on themselves. I've earned my moodiness."

"Chin up, Raibert," Elzbietá said. "Third time's the charm."

"Whatever."

"Agent Kaminski," Kleio said. "I have received a response from Gordian Operations."

"That was fast. What did they say?"

"Commissioner von Schröder has personally authorized your recommended course of action."

"Good to know the boss has our backs." Raibert rubbed his hands together and faced Elzbietá. "Now, shall we see where this rabbit hole leads?"

"Let's." Elzbietá reached for the impeller controls. "Vector's entered. Impeller ready."

"Take us out."

"You got it."

❖   ❖   ❖

"Hmmm?"

They'd been underway for over twenty minutes when Andover-Chen scrunched up his face and leaned closer to one of the charts floating around him. The physicist cocked his head, lips pursed, while the other members of *Kleio's* crew looked at him speculatively. Ten or twenty seconds ticked away, and Raibert rolled his eyes again.

It wasn't the eye roll he'd given Kleio—not quite. But it *was* close, and he shook his head at the deeply focused scientist.

"What is it now?" he asked.

"I'm sorry?" Andover-Chen blinked and looked up.

"I get nervous when people 'hmmm' all of a sudden while I'm traveling toward an unknown universe. Go figure."

"Oh, it's just these latest readings from what's ahead."

"What about them? They look normal enough to me."

"On the surface, yes, but dig a little deeper and certain... I hate to say 'patterns' emerge, but I don't know what else to call them."

"Good patterns or bad?"

"Neither, I suppose. Just something to keep track of. I should be able to say more once we arrive."

"Speaking of which," Raibert said. "How long until we reach the outer wall?"

"That's still hard to say, but it shouldn't be *too* much longer. As Philo pointed out, we're dealing with a universe that's still conjoined with ours." Andover-Chen tapped one of his charts for emphasis. "It should be coming up—"

"Contact ahead!" Elzbietá announced. "Contact approaching at twenty kilofactors."

Raibert, Andover-Chen, and Benjamin shifted in their seats as scope data appeared above the command table.

"Drop our speed," Raibert said. "Let's take a good look at it."

"Reducing speed to one kilofactor."

"Data's clearing up," Philo said as their lowered speed improved the scope's sensitivity. "Contact is a time machine of some kind."

"It's not Admin, is it?" Raibert asked.

"Can't be." Elzbietá shook her head. "That's not the signature of a rotating impeller."

"Agreed," Philo said. "*Definitely* not an Admin design. It doesn't match any SysGov signatures, either, in case you were wondering."

"Thanks, I was." Raibert blew a breath out the side of his mouth. "So this universe already has transdimensional tech. Kleio?"

"Yes, Agent Kaminski?"

"Reclassify the new universe as T5 and begin compiling data on their time machines."

"I'll go parallel with Kleio and help out," Philo said.

"Good idea," Raibert agreed.

"Contact slowing," Elzbietá said. "Speed falling to one kilofactor. Flight path is converging with ours."

"Great. We've been spotted," Raibert grumbled as he pulled up the projected flight path. "Four *hours* until we meet? Not a very aggressive approach, is it?"

"We shouldn't let our guard down," Benjamin said. "We have no idea what kind of culture we're dealing with."

"Oh, you better believe we're staying on our toes!" Raibert affirmed.

"We're picking up a telegraph signal," Andover-Chen announced. "The T5 time machine's transmitting to someone."

"They're probably reporting us to their HQ," Elzbietá suggested.

"No doubt." Andover-Chen nodded in agreement, but then he stopped nodding and his eyebrows shot up. "Oh, my."

"What is it?" Raibert asked.

"The signal. It's using—"

"We are being contacted by the Universe-T5 time machine," Kleio announced.

"*We* are?" Raibert frowned. "How can you be so sure it's trying to talk to *us* instead of calling home?"

"Because the message was sent using SysGov telegraph binary, Agent."

Raibert's eyes flew wide. He turned to Andover-Chen, and the other synthoid shrugged.

"It's a perfect match for our comm protocols," Andover-Chen clarified for Kleio, then shook his head. "This is no accident."

"The transmission is addressed to 'inbound transdimensional craft,'" Kleio continued. "As we are the only inbound transdimensional craft in the vicinity, logic suggests we are the intended recipient."

Raibert closed his eyes and leaned back as he pondered the implications. He'd already accepted that *something* from SysGov must have survived the destruction of the fugitive TTV, but he'd had no idea what and he'd resolutely resisted optimism. But now this. If something as precise as *telegraph formats* had survived, then what else—or *who* else—had reached the sixth century?

The bridge was silent. All eyes were on him.

He opened his own eyes once more, straightened in his chair, and beamed at them.

"Well, okay then! We've been contacted. That's a good first step. Let's see what they have to say. Kleio, show us."

The telegram appeared over the table:

Dynasty DDT Sigrun to inbound transdimensional craft. Would you please identify yourself?

"'Would you please?'" Raibert blinked. "They're asking nicely?"

"DDT?" Elzbietá frowned. "Not TTV? Seems a little . . . odd, if they're still using SysGov communications protocols."

"A time machine is still a time machine," Andover-Chen pointed out. "No matter what they call theirs."

"It could be language and terminology drift," Benjamin suggested, "but I'm more curious about this 'dynasty' business."

"Only one way to find out." Raibert put his elbows on the table and leaned forward. "Kleio, let them know who we are and tell them we're investigating a universe that's branched off of our own, which is probably their home."

"Yes, Agent. Message prepared and transmitting."

"Also, stress that we come in peace. Make sure they understand that part."

"Understood, Agent. I will append that to our initial message."

"Good. Good." Raibert nodded. "Don't want to give the wrong impression. Some societies start off assuming the worst."

"You're thinking back to when we first met the Admin?" Philo asked, flashing into existence next to him.

"Don't remind me," Raibert said sourly. "*So* many guns in my face."

"And yet their fear of you turned out to be well justified," Andover-Chen pointed out with a quirky smile, "since their universe no longer exists."

"Yeah, I guess you've got me there. Guess I just have to hope Ella's right about third-time charms. I'd hate to end up with a moniker like 'Bane of Universes' or something." Raibert grimaced. "You see any Gordian Knots on those charts, Doctor?"

"Not even the slightest sniff of one," Andover-Chen assured him.

"Then we're being completely honest here. T5 has nothing to fear from us."

"Incoming telegraph from DDT *Sigrun*," Kleio announced. "Displaying now."

The first telegraph scrolled up and the second appeared in its place:

Dynasty DDT Sigrun to SysGov TTV Kleio. Thank you for confirming your identification and mission.

My name is Lieutenant Hala Khatib. I have been dispatched to escort you safely through our universe's outer wall. The smoothest approach vector is attached to this message. May I come alongside your craft and escort you into Earth orbit?

"New data received," Elzbietá said. "It's only a little off from our original course. According to this, we can reach the wall in under six minutes at full speed."

"Okay, this is a little weird." Raibert stood up and put his hands on his hips. "Anyone else get the impression we were expected?"

"It certainly looks that way," Benjamin said. "At the very least, it's obvious they anticipated meeting a SysGov TTV around this place and time."

"Yeah." Raibert crossed his arms. "Should we be worried about that?"

"If they knew we were coming and didn't want us getting in, I don't think we'd be talking about it."

"Good point."

"They don't seem to be making any attempt at stealth," Elzbietá pointed out. "I see them clear as day, and there's nothing that leads me to believe anybody else is out there."

"That could be because 'anybody else' *is* using stealth and it's really, really *good*," Raibert countered.

"True. Or it's because there's nothing there."

"I guess there's no way to be sure." Raibert sighed. He took one last look at the message, then nodded. "All right. We're going to accept the invitation. Everyone keep your eyes peeled for anything unusual. Hope for the best, but plan for the worst. Kleio, let the *Sigrun* know they're clear to come alongside."

"Yes, Agent. Transmitting now."

"Ella, take us in using the approach they sent us."

"Course plotted. What speed?"

"Max us out. Let's see if they can keep up."

"Got it. Accelerating to seventy kilofactors." Elzbietá eased the omni-throttle forward. "*Sigrun* has accelerated to seventy-four kilofactors and will rendezvous with us in three minutes."

"So they're faster than us," Raibert said. "Good to know, if things turn nasty."

The *Sigrun* closed with them, then executed a tight turn onto a parallel course.

"Whoa," Elzbietá breathed.

"Something wrong?" Raibert asked.

"No, everything's fine. Just a little surprised, is all. They didn't just change course *quickly*; they changed it *instantly*. We can't do that."

"So they're also more maneuverable than us," Raibert muttered. "Great. Just great."

"Temporally speaking, yes." Elzbietá nodded. "We'll just have to see what their realspace performance is like."

"It'll probably be just as bad," Raibert groused.

"Anyone ever tell you you're a pessimist?" Benjamin asked.

"Well, that's the thing, Doc. The one guaranteed antidote for optimism is experience."

Philo appeared next to Andover-Chen and whispered in his ear.

"Oh, I see!" The physicist swiped one chart aside and opened a new one. "Yes, you're right! So *that's* why their signature looks so strange!"

"Figure something out?" Raibert asked.

"You could say that," Andover-Chen replied.

"The *Sigrun*'s using two impellers," Philo said. "We caught them switching when they changed course."

"Two impellers?" Raibert frowned.

"Yeah. Check it out."

The AC opened a mental pathway. Raibert connected to it, and understanding spread through his mind as the chronometric data unfolded before him.

"Okay, I get it now. They must prepare their next vector in the off-line impeller."

"Exactly." Philo nodded. "We change the chronometric permeability of our impeller while in-flight because we only have one, but the *Sigrun* readies its idle one ahead of time, then flips a switch, and *bam*!" He snapped his fingers. "They're heading in a new temporal direction."

"But a whole second impeller just for that?" Raibert shook his head. "I don't know. That's a *lot* of exotic matter for what amounts to a minor performance tweak. If you're going to use that much of it, why not build an entire second time machine? Seems like that would be a lot more efficient in the long run."

"This could tell us something about their society," Benjamin pointed out. "Waste is often an indicator of low cost. Exotic matter may not be as difficult for them to make."

"Or, like in our time," Elzbiéta added. "You and I never thought twice about the plastic, paper, or glass containers we threw out."

"You mean recycled," Benjamin corrected.

"Ah, your labeled bins," she reminisced, then flashed a sharklike grin. "Actually, one of the dirty little secrets of recycling in the twenty-first century was the energy cost. If you spend more energy recycling a product than you do manufacturing the original, you're still contributing to waste. Sometimes not recycling was the more environmentally friendly option."

"Have I ever told you you're damned sexy when you get technical?"

Elzbietá winked at him.

"Most forms of regular matter are treated that way in SysGov," Philo said. "Everything gets tossed down the reclamation chute without a second thought."

"Let's not jump to conclusions here," Raibert cautioned. "Exotic matter is hardly in the same category as paper cups."

"Not to SysGov," Benjamin pointed out.

The Kleio shuddered. Raibert steadied himself with a hand on his chair back, and Elzbietá checked her displays.

"That was the outer wall. We're in T5, non-congruent with the True Present."

"I barely felt that," Benjamin said. "They really did give us a clean approach."

"Another good sign," Raibert acknowledged, "but let's not get careless. Where are we?"

"Earth orbit," Elzbietá reported. "The space around us is clear for hundreds of kilometers, except for the Sigrun."

"Good. Then let's—"

Andover-Chen whistled suddenly.

"Yeah, no kidding!" Philo agreed, standing behind his seat and looking over his shoulder.

"Everyone, you need to see this." Andover-Chen pushed a chart toward the command table, where it expanded in their virtual sight. "We're picking up an enormous amount of near-present time travel."

The earth appeared above the table, surrounded by a ring of orbital stations, glinting against the black of space. Lights shone across every landmass on the night side, and nodes of intense temporal activity freckled the planet's surface.

"Damn!" Raibert exclaimed. He zoomed in on one of the clusters. "Do you see that? It looks like they're making roundtrips between the True Present and the near-present. What's the point of that?"

"I don't know," Andover-Chen said . . . rather unnecessarily, in Raibert's opinion.

"Is it near-present surveillance, like what the DTI does?" Benjamin asked.

"Possibly, but I don't think so."

"What about transdimensional?" Raibert asked.

"Not since we phased in."

"Incoming telegraph from *Sigrun*," Kleio said.

Dynasty DDT Sigrun to SysGov TTV Kleio. You are cordially invited to phase in and land at the attached coordinates. A delegation will join us shortly to open a formal diplomatic dialogue with SysGov. We sincerely hope you enjoy your stay here in the Dynasty.

"I can get used to first contacts like this," Benjamin said.

"Ella?" Raibert asked. "Where exactly are we being asked to land?"

"Here."

The graphic of Earth zoomed into what would be Tanboul in the thirtieth century, or Istanbul in the twenty-first.

Or Constantinople in the sixth *century*, Raibert reminded himself. *Wonder if they still call it that here . . .*

A bright, sprawling metropolis appeared, with high, shining towers and elevated emerald parklands. A fat, white cylindrical structure in the middle of one stretch of park came into view, surrounded by a ring of smaller circular platforms that sprouted outward from it atop thick pylons. The facility made Raibert think of a wide, white flower with a tight ring of petals. Sleek metallic craft sat atop a third of the platforms, most of them roughly the same size as the *Kleio*, but with the unmistakable spikes of two impellers protruding from their sterns.

A red X blinked over an empty landing pad, which merged with the pad next to it to form a wider elliptical platform.

"That's where we're being asked to land," Elzbietá said.

"Anything . . . suspicious?" Raibert asked.

"Nothing I can see from orbit while out of phase."

"Hmmm."

"Shall I take us down? Or at least phase us in for a clearer look?"

"Not quite yet." Raibert held up a finger. "Kleio, message the *Sigrun*. I want to know what kind of building we're being asked to park you on."

"Yes, Agent. Transmitting now."

"Doesn't look very secure," Benjamin noted. "They're not even keeping the time machines indoors. All the landing pads are open here."

"Still, I'm not leaping into this without at least taking a look around."

"Telegraph incoming," Kleio reported.

The text scrolled in below the previous messages:

Dynasty DDT Sigrun to SysGov TTV Kleio. The location I've sent you is for Cornucopia Headquarters, the heart of all time travel operations within the Dynasty, located in the capital city of Constantinople. Also, I have just been informed that the chairwoman and vice-chairman of Cornucopia will be joining us on the landing pad, and I have a question of their own to relay. Is Raibert Kaminski on board your ship?

CHAPTER TWENTY-FIVE

～～～～

Cornucopia Headquarters
Dynasty, 2980 CE

"HOW DO I LOOK?" RAIBERT ASKED AS HE PEERED at his virtual reflection.

"Like someone who's about to make first contact with another universe," Philo said.

Raibert shot him a doubtful look.

"Don't worry about it, buddy." Philo gave him a virtual pat on the back. "You look fine."

Raibert grumbled under his breath as he adjusted the angle of his navy blue wide-brimmed hat. He tugged his matching suit jacket straight, then threw one end of the dynamic scarf over his shoulder. A pattern of puffy clouds eased across its sky blue surface.

He flashed a wide, toothy smile at the reflection.

"Eww," Philo said. "Not like that. *That* looked fake."

Raibert closed his mouth and loosened his cheek muscles.

"Better. Much better. Just *relax*, okay?"

"I am relaxed," Raibert protested. "It's just... Do you think she'll be there?"

"Who can say? It's not like her synthoid had an expiration date. I mean, no one's ever tried to keep one around this long—they've only been available back home for the last couple of hundred years, after all! But there's no *technical* reason somebody couldn't, and Lieutenant Khatib is being awfully coy about who you're meeting."

"I don't like it. They're hiding something."

"They probably just want it to be a surprise."

"I don't like surprises."

"Well, suck it up, buddy," Philo said. "They asked for you by name, so it's all on you to make this work."

"Okay, *now* I'm nervous."

"Sorry."

Raibert fluffed out the scarf around his neck.

"We have every reason to be optimistic," Philo pointed out. "Between the telegraph format, the friendly greeting, the *significant* lack of guns pointed at us, and the data we've gathered since phasing in, this should be the easiest first contact on record."

"That's a rather low bar, given that the only *other* first contact was with the fucking Admin."

"Hey, what I said is still true."

"I suppose so." Raibert closed the virtual window and stepped out onto the bridge. "Okay, team." He spread out his arms. "How do I look?"

"Like someone who's about to make first contact with another universe," Benjamin recited in a monotonous drone.

"Thanks, Doc," Raibert said grumpily, dropping his arms. "Did Philo tell you to say that?"

"He might've made a suggestion or two."

"Don't pay them any attention, Raibert. You look great," Elzbietá said. "I don't get why you're so nervous."

"Why I'm nervous? Oh, I don't know. Because my former girlfriend—whose ship we blew up with her in it—likely had a hand in forming the society?" He shook his head. "This could end badly for me in *so* many ways."

"You do realize it might not be she who survived," Andover-Chen said. "It could be Gwon or his AC."

"Is that supposed to make me feel better?"

"Or it could be Pepys's great-to-the-umpteenth-grandkid," Philo added quickly.

"It's been two and a half millennia by their reckoning," Benjamin observed. "Any survivors are going to be completely different people after what they've been through."

"I agree with you to a point," Philo cautioned. "But remember, ACs have perfect memories. And they can slow down their run times, which accelerates their perceived passage of time. They can even place themselves in stasis for extended periods. And connectomes in synthoid bodies have access to all the same features. The survivors may not be as changed as you'd think."

"You sure you don't want at least one of us to come with you?" Benjamin asked.

"Yeah, I'm sure. Let me stick my neck out for this part. We'll see how this pans out and go from there."

"We'll keep an eye on things from here," Elzbietá promised.

"I know you will."

Raibert drew a deep breath, dipped the brim of his hat to his team, and left the bridge. He took the counter-grav tube down to the cargo bay, strode beneath their TTV's main gun, and stopped at the far end until a small, spherical remote had detached from a rack on the wall and floated into place above and behind his shoulder.

He opened the virtual reflection again and used an index finger to tug down his lower lip and expose his pearly white teeth.

"You look *fine*," Philo tittered in his ear.

He let go of his lip.

"Just checking. I don't have anything stuck in my teeth, do I?"

"Good grief! You'd think you were going on a date or something!"

"No. I just . . . I'm having mixed feelings right now, okay? We didn't part on the best of terms."

"Even if she did survive, Benjamin's probably right. The last time she saw you was over twenty-four hundred years ago, for her. What happened is likely a bigger deal for you than it is for her. *If* she remembers you at all."

"They asked for me by name. *Someone* remembers me."

"Well, time to find out. Lieutenant Khatib just disembarked from her ship. She's walking over."

"All right, then," Raibert said. "Open 'er up."

The prog-steel wall split open and a ramp extruded down to the pristine white landing pad. Raibert straightened his jacket one last time, then walked down the ramp as regally as he could.

A noon sun blazed down from a clear sky, but his synthetic eyes adjusted instantly to the added light. The DDT *Sigrun* rested on the same platform, its long sleek hull parallel to the *Kleio*'s. A pointed nose transitioned into smooth contours that formed a narrow wedge-shaped main body when viewed from above. The rear edge of that wedge grew fatter at its tips, and the dual impellers extended back from those thick mounting points. Its skin gleamed in the sunlight with a slight cobalt hue in contrast to the *Kleio*'s gunmetal gray.

Overall, if the *Kleio* was a heavy, powerful workhorse, the *Sigrun* gave the impression of a lithe, purpose-built racer about half the size. There were no visible signs of weapons or shrouds for stealth systems or meta-armor built into the hull, nor Admin-style baffles on the impellers, and the *Kleio*'s sophisticated realspace scopes hadn't detected anything of the sort beneath its surface.

A woman walked down a slender ramp. She was clad in a formfitting, light-brown uniform; her dark hair was bound in a bun behind her head, and she smiled brightly at Raibert as she walked across to meet him halfway between the two time machines.

"Hello, Agent Kaminski," she said in accented Modern English as she extended her hand. "I'm Hala Khatib, the *Sigrun*'s pilot."

"A pleasure, Lieutenant." Her head rose barely to Raibert's shoulder, and his heavy palm completely enveloped her delicate hand as he shook it.

"No," she said. "The pleasure's all mine."

The remote hovering behind him relayed her biometric data back to *Kleio* for processing. A virtual diagram overlaid her physical appearance, and he glanced over it. She was wholly biological, probably late twenties or early thirties, and there were no detectable weapons on her person.

A good start, he thought.

"So!" Hala's round eyes twinkled and she stepped back to appraise him. "You're *Raibert*."

"That I am."

"From *SysGov*."

"Right again. Most of me is, anyway. There are still some parts left over from the Admin."

"But you and your ship are the real thing." She gazed at the *Kleio* for a long moment, then let out a contented sigh. "You know, I've been pulling extra shifts for the last year, hoping I'd be the one to greet you."

"Really?"

"Well, greet the first SysGov TTV to come this far. Cornucopia's had a rough idea when contact might happen for some time now, but there were a lot of unknowns, such as when our universe's wave front would be detectable to your arrays in the Edge of Existence, when you'd send someone to investigate, what vector you'd follow through the transverse, if you'd wait for our timeline to reach the Edge of Existence first, and on and on. At least one *Valkyrie* has been hanging out beyond the outer wall for the past five years. Relative to our timeline, of course."

"Well, of course," Raibert agreed, a bit automatically.

"So imagine my shock when your ship popped up on *my* scope!" Hala placed a hand over her heart. "I was so excited, I thought I'd faint!"

"I find that rather easy to believe, actually." In fact, Raibert suspected it was taking all her self-control to not bounce up and down on the balls of her feet.

"Anyway, I'm so glad my *Valkyrie* had the watch when you showed up."

"*Valkyrie*?" He furrowed his brow.

"The Dual-Drive Transports, or DDTs." Hala pointed a thumb over her shoulder at the *Sigrun*. "Most people call them *Valkyries*. It's a *long* story."

"I'll bet."

"Anyway, would you like to come inside?" Hala gestured to a rounded archway at the edge of the landing pad. "The chairwoman and vice-chairman will be joining us shortly."

"And they'd be...who, exactly?"

"I'm not supposed to say." She smiled at him coyly.

"Right..." He sighed, then shrugged. "Lead the way."

He followed her off the platform and down a gentle counter-grav incline that led to the main interior. Artificial gravity set him down in a comfortable open space with glass walls, white floors, a high ceiling, and an internal waterfall that cooled the air. A ring of light-gray couches was arranged around a low, central table.

The local infostructure tickled at his peripheral senses, friendly and inviting and perfectly compatible with his SysGov code. The stark whiteness of the interior made him wonder what his virtual senses were missing, but he kept all the connections closed for now. He and Hala were the only two people present, but the remote actively scanned the area, highlighting individuals on the floors above and below him. They were an almost even mix of natural and synthoid bodies.

"I'm very excited at the chance to see what happens now that the Dynasty's reached the Edge of Existence."

Hala said as she stopped within the ring of couches and gestured for him to pick a seat. "Please."

"What?" Raibert switched off the virtual overlay from the remote. "Oh, right." He sank into heavy cushions that adjusted around him automatically.

"How about you?" Hala asked as she sat across from him and crossed her legs.

"Still taking it all in, I'm afraid."

"With the Dynasty at the Edge of Existence, our two universes are *finally* in sync. Do you think travel between them will become routine?"

"Probably. It's become that way for us and the Admin, and you *clearly* have the necessary tech."

"Then I can go see the Consolidation Spire someday? Or the ART Exhibits in the Ministry of Education?"

"I'm...sure something can be arranged."

"Wonderful!" She clasped her hands together with a broad smile "I've—"

She broke off and shot up from her couch as a hole in the floor opened and two synthoids floated up behind the ring of couches. Raibert turned to look over his own couch's cushioned back, then rose abruptly when he saw the woman's face. The floor sealed and gravity set them down. The stocky, handsome man wore the same uniform as Hala, but the woman wore a white dress with a blue sash around her waist. The combination, while professional, also accentuated her undeniable beauty.

"Hello, Raibert," Teodorà Beckett said, her eyes and smile warm as she extended a hand. "I had a feeling you'd be the first to come."

He shook her hand.

"Teodorà, I..."

His voice faltered as the remote hovered close and confirmed that this was her original synthoid, with a few modifications here and there.

So it's true, he thought. *She survived. And not only that, she* throve.

The reality standing before him washed away all the nasty possibilities bouncing around in his mind. He finally knew what had become of her. There was no more uncertainty, and better yet, she was alive! Pent-up stress oozed out of his heart and his smile slipped onto his lips.

"Please, you don't have to say a word," she assured him. "You've finally arrived. I'm so glad you're here, and we have so *very* much we wish to show you. With all my heart, I welcome you to the Dynasty."

"Well then." Raibert put on an air of pleasant formality. "On behalf of SysGov, thank you for inviting us down here. I certainly *feel* welcome."

"Lieutenant." Teodorà nodded to Hala. "Excellent work spotting their craft and escorting them in. We can take it from here."

"If you don't mind, Elder," the pilot dipped her head slightly, "I'd be grateful if you'd permit me to stay."

"Very well. I think you've earned it. But in that case, why don't we all sit down again?"

Hala smiled ear to ear as she resumed her seat.

"Elder?" Raibert asked.

"'Honored Elders,' actually," Teodorà clarified. "It's a very old title. Some people"—she glanced at Hala, who had the decency to blush—"still think we deserve special treatment, even after all this time."

"'We'?" Raibert echoed. He took a hard look at the man she'd arrived with. There was something vaguely familiar about the round face, but he couldn't quite place it.

"We never had the privilege of meeting in person." The male synthoid extended a hand. "I'm the Vice-Chairman of Cornucopia. Samuel Pepys, at your service."

"Pepys?" Raibert blurted, shaking the synthoid's hand. "As in *that* Samuel Pepys? You survived, too?"

"All four of us did," Teodorà said. "Although Lucius's AC didn't last long after the crash, I'm afraid."

"Oh, I see," Raibert replied evenly. He was over-joyed to see Teodorà alive...

But Lucius is another story, he thought. *So he's been running around loose for a few millennia, too. Good to know.*

"Teodorà, I'm sorry for what you had to go through, but you must know we didn't maroon you on purpose. Please believe me when I say we searched long and hard but never found any wreckage. If there'd been any sign you were still alive—"

"It's all right, Raibert." She held up her hand. "Really, it is. I understand it's recent history to you, but I've had a long time to come to terms with what happened, and I'm at peace with every part of it. You didn't find us because we didn't *want* to be found. We *chose* to be marooned in the past."

"I saw your ship blow up. I thought you were—"

"You saw our *impeller* explode," Teodorà corrected. "Granted, that explosion took most of the ship with it, but enough survived for us to crash-land safely."

"Fortunately for me, the medical bay survived the crash," Pepys said. "Its systems sustained my organic body for about a century, but eventually it broke down, forcing me into abstraction."

"After which you had a *long* wait before the Dynasty developed synthoids," Teodorà said.

"It wasn't too bad," Pepys said. "Being a runtime allowed me to fast-forward through the boring bits, fortunately." He faced Raibert. "Life as an abstract never suited me, so I skipped most of it."

"Well, we *all* took advantage of that feature." Teodorà flashed a smile his way, and her hand found his and gave it a tender squeeze.

"So neither of you were awake the whole time?" Raibert asked.

"Oh, good grief, no!" Teodorà laughed while shooing the thought aside. "Digital hibernation is a wonderful thing. We were very active at the beginning, and we've stayed awake for the last several decades, as the Dynasty approached the True Present. But, Raibert, believe me when I tell you there were some *really* boring stretches in between. Mostly, once we had it up and running, the Dynasty just took care of itself while we popped in and out for a day or so every decade to keep an eye on things. Those were the formally scheduled meetings, of course. If they needed us between them, they could always wake us up. We made sure of that. And they *did* wake us up." She rolled her eyes. "Not as much for, oh, the last five or six hundred years, but sometimes—!"

"It varies a little between the three of us," Pepys added, "but none of us are more than two or three centuries older than when we left SysGov." His eyes twinkled. "Well, *I've* got a few decades on the others, I suppose. I'm actually the oldest now. My physical body didn't come with a pause function, you see."

"I think you won out in the end." Teodorà patted his muscular forearm.

"I'm still surprised Lucius never transitioned back to being physical," Pepys said. "*I* was certainly thrilled to have a real body again, despite how clunky those early models were."

"Don't judge. It's what he wants."

"I'm not judging. I just find his decision to remain abstract an odd one."

"Wait a second. Lucius is an AC now?" Raibert asked.

"Yes, he's around headquarters somewhere." Teodorà indicated the building around them. "He's officially a vice-chairman of Cornucopia, like Samuel, but he only shows up for the big meetings. Leaves most of the day-to-day business to us two. We asked him to join us here, but he politely declined."

"I see." Raibert frowned, not sure how he felt about Lucius still being around *and* not showing up for this reunion. Given his own memories of the other man, he doubted it was tact, but surely not even Lucius could hold a grudge after all this subjective time? "If you don't mind me asking, why is his decision to stay abstract so unusual?"

"ACs are much rarer here in the Dynasty," Teodorà said. "Abstractions never really caught on as a substitute for physical bodies the way they did in SysGov. The vast majority of people transition into synthoids when they get old, though a small percentage do abstract. There's a bit of a lingering social stigma against the practice, dating all the way back to when Belisarius and Justinian declined to become post-physical." She sighed and shook her head with an expression that mingled regret with pleasant reminiscence. "Would've been nice to still have them around. And especially Ephraim!"

"We had no choice but to respect their wishes," Samuel reminded her.

"Oh, of course. Of course."

"Belisarius and Justinian?" Raibert looked back and forth between them. "You got both of them to sign on for all of this?" He waved a hand to take in their surroundings.

"Oh, yes." Teodorà smiled. "Belisarius was easier to convince, of course."

"Why am I not surprised?" Raibert said dryly, recalling his own interaction with the historical Belisarius. "It's *Justinian* that shocks me! He would've been just starting his slide into terminal paranoia where Belisarius was concerned when you got there."

"Well, yes." Teodorà nodded. "But we had Ephraim of Antioch on our side. You remember him from when you were researching Belisarius?"

"Sure." Raibert nodded. "He was sort of peripheral to what I was interested in, at the time, though."

"I know." Teodorà grimaced humorously at him. "I wish he hadn't been! I relied on your biography of Belisarius—a lot—when we first got here, and if I'd even guessed what an extraordinary fellow Ephraim was, I'd have felt a lot more confident about this whole thing. In a lot of ways, he turned out to be the true key to all of it."

"Really? Interesting." Raibert rubbed his chin. "I guess I have a lot to learn about this Dynasty of yours."

"Oh, it's not *mine*!" she laughed. "I don't run it. Not anymore, anyway, thank *God*! I'm perfectly content managing just Cornucopia these days. And providing the occasional advice as an 'Honored Elder.'"

"That's right." Pepys's eyes gleamed with mischief.

"Her years of being a ruthless warlord are behind her." He grinned at Raibert. "Remember what she said about getting waked up between scheduled meetings? Well, most of the time it was because they'd come up with somebody else they needed the Valkyrie to help swat!"

"Excuse me!" Teodorà glared at him. "I was never a warlord, thank you very much!"

"Really? What about when you and Belisarius put an end to the Sasanian Wars? Quite thoroughly, I might add."

"That was different. Those idiots had it coming. Justinian and Theodora offered to share with them. For that matter, I *personally* told Khosrow that as their envoy! But would he listen? No, of course not!" Teodorà grimaced.

"Wait a minute," Raibert looked back and forth between his hosts. "You're talking about Khosrow the *First*?"

"Of course." Teodorà looked surprised for a moment, then shrugged. "Oh, I see. When Samuel mentioned the Sasanian Wars, you were thinking *seventh* century and Khosrow the Second. No, he never turned up in the Dynasty's history at all. This was his grandfather, taking advantage of an opportunity he never had in SysGov's history. When Belisarius went to Constantinople instead of Nisibis—"

She broke off with something surprisingly like a chuckle as Raibert's eyes widened.

"It's a long story," she said, "but, basically, Khosrow carved off a sizable chunk of the eastern Empire while Belisarius and Justinian were . . . distracted, shall we say. He didn't want to give it back, and I wasn't about to let the Persians and the Byzantines weaken each other the way they did in SysGov's past." She shook her head. "I didn't know if Muhammad and Islam were going to be the factor they were in your history, Raibert, but even without that, there were plenty of other external threats."

"And did Muhammad put in an appearance?" Raibert asked, remembering his own and Philo's desperate search for someone who'd been born in both the Admin's and SysGov's past.

The probability of the same pair of gametes combining and creating the same individual in two severed timelines, even within a single generation after they'd split, was . . . remote. In fact, Philo had calculated that there would be only on the order of two of them per billion pregnancies, and the sixth-century world population had been only about two hundred *million*. Still, Muhammad had been born—in SysGov and the Admin, at any rate—in 571, only thirty years after Teodorà and Pepys's arrival, so it was at least theoretically possible . . .

"No." She shook her head. "But like I say, there were plenty of other threats, and for the first two or three centuries, until we got the Dynasty expanded well outside the Mediterranean world, idiots just kept trying to invade, one after another! And Samuel's right about how often they kept waking us up to swat someone's hand for reaching into the cookie jar. When it wasn't a formal invasion, it was border raids and brigands. It took the *longest* time for the barbarians in general to get it through their heads that if they'd only behave themselves, we'd *give* them what they kept trying to steal! And the Mongols—! Lord, I thought *they'd* never figure out we'd just crunch up one army after another until they decided to play nice! Sometimes I felt like just kicking—"

She stopped herself and waved an upraised hand.

"I think we're getting sidetracked here," she said.

"Actually, you've piqued my interest. I'd love to hear more about Teodorà Beckett, Ruthless Warlord."

Teodorà gave him a sour look, but Pepys chuckled.

"Fortunately, we have something along those lines in mind," he said. "We've made arrangements with the Council of Ministers to delay your meeting with them."

"Right." Teodorà nodded. "There'll be plenty of time for all their stiff formalities later, which is why I thought Samuel and I would take the opportunity to show you and your crew around a little, first. Give you a taste of what the Dynasty is like. How about it? See the Dynasty today, meet with our leaders tomorrow."

"A guided tour, then?" Raibert asked.

"That's one way to look at it, though it can be however guided or unguided you'd like. If you wish, you can roam freely through the capital."

"No restrictions?"

"Not a single one. I know this is a first contact of sorts for you. You must be hesitant, not knowing much about us, so we're going to put those worries to rest. I had a comprehensive history of the Dynasty put together about twenty years ago, and kept it updated, because I knew, sooner or later, someone from SysGov was bound to contact us. It's available for upload any time your TTV is ready. But I also know how histories like that can be unintentionally—or intentionally, for that matter—slanted and biased. So Samuel and I want you to be completely free to examine whatever you want, ask whatever questions occur to you, talk to anyone you'd like to talk to.

"I expect you'll enjoy it more, for now, at least, if you let us show you the highlights, but, Raibert"—her expression grew very serious—"I know there have to be worries from SysGov's side. All of this"—she waved both hands in a gesture that encompassed the entire Dynasty—"grew out of something that happened only weeks or months ago as far as SysGov is concerned. And it didn't exactly happen with SysGov's blessing, which means they'll have to be worried about whether or not we're nursing a grudge. That's why we think it's especially important for the Dynasty to be a completely open book. We're a *different* universe, but we have so much in common, and after so long, there is *zero* animosity from our side. We'd like to make sure that's true from your side, as well. The last thing anyone in either the Dynasty or SysGov should want is another ... distrustful relationship like the one between SysGov and the Admin."

"That ..." Raibert smiled hugely, unable to contain his relief at how well this meeting had gone. "That sounds wonderful. Thank you."

"My suggestion is a quick stop at the Heritage Museum here in Constantinople," Samuel said. "What better way to acquaint yourselves with this new timeline than to have its history laid out for you?"

"This gets better and better!" Raibert laughed. "When do we leave?"

"Actually," Teodorà said with a mischievous glint in her eye, "I was hoping to show *you* something a bit grander than a museum."

"I see," Raibert said, his inner historian a little crestfallen.

"Is there anyone in your crew you'd like to send with Samuel?"

"Do we need to split up?"

"Only if you don't mind."

"Not really. If I'm not going to the museum, then I'll send Agent Schröder—our other resident historian—with Samuel."

"We also know how important the Gordian Protocol is to SysGov," Teodorà said. "So I'm sure you have a lot of questions about our time travel operations."

"To put it mildly, yes."

"Then a tour of Cornucopia is in order, though we'll need someone to show you around."

Hala's hand shot up.

"Yes, I thought we'd have a volunteer," Teodorà said dryly.

"Agent Schröder—I mean, agent *Elzbietá* Schröder—could join her," Raibert said. "She's our TTV's physical pilot. I'm sure she'd love to tour your facilities."

Seated on the couch, Hala still couldn't bounce, but she seemed to physically quiver with enthusiasm, he noticed. Or perhaps the verb he wanted was "vibrate."

"Well, arranging *that* tour was easy enough," Teodorà observed. "I imagine Philo's on board your ship?"

"He is. Why do you ask?"

"Well, as I said, the Dynasty has relatively few ACs, and from what I remember, he was always more of a hunt-and-peck tourist—the sort that likes to go off on tangents of his own—and a damned fine cyber sleuth. If he'd prefer for me to arrange a guide for him, I'm sure I could find one. But he's also free to roam our infostructure on his own, if he'd rather do that. I think he'll find our systems very easy to navigate. They're derived from our TTV's systems, after all."

"You're putting an awful lot of trust in us," Raibert said.

"I want this to go right, Raibert. And I know you do, too."

"I'll check with them when I'm back on the ship. The last time he was in a foreign infostructure, things didn't go well. Beyond that..."

Teodorà held up a hand.

"That's all I ask. If he's uncomfortable with it, he's perfectly welcome to stay aboard your ship."

"Then I suppose it's time for me to extend an invitation to *you*." He gestured back to the counter-grav tube through which he'd arrived. "Would the three of you care to come aboard *Kleio* and meet the team?"

CHAPTER TWENTY-SIX

$\infty\!\infty\!\infty$

Heritage Museum
Dynasty, 2980 CE

BENJAMIN WALKED SLOWLY AROUND THE TTV'S wreckage. Its once shining surface had been ripped and scarred in the firefight that downed it and then scoured by centuries of sandstorms. He followed a slow circumference around the exhibit while his wetware breathed life into virtual displays the Dynasty infosystems auto-translated into SysGov English...and his own implants then translated into *Old* English.

His heels clicked on the marble floor with each step, and the sharp sound echoed from the high, domed ceiling in the silence. The entire museum had been closed for his benefit. Pepys had been quick to point out that the public could be allowed back in at any time—if Benjamin wished to interact with them—but he'd also cautioned that they would certainly be the center of attention, if that happened.

Benjamin had declined the offer. He preferred the quiet solitude of this alien museum to the thought of interacting with the locals without any mission prep. A lone synthoid hung back by the sealed double doors, the only sign of security he'd seen so far, and armed with nothing but a baton and a nonlethal pistol, no less.

He came around to the rear of the wreckage, where three stories of internal decks had been laid bare. The prog-steel here looked thinned and stretched, like a stubborn clump of pulled taffy.

"You crash-landed in *this*?" he asked, putting both hands on the exhibit's guardrail and leaning toward it. A remote floated lazily by his shoulder, recording everything.

"That's right," Pepys said, following a few steps behind him with his hands clasped in the small of his back.

"Must've been one hell of a landing."

"I imagine so."

"You don't remember?" Benjamin raised an eyebrow, and Pepys shook his head.

"I don't have many memories from back then. Holding onto old memories got a lot easier once I abstracted, but my organic days are a bit hazy, I'm afraid. Still, I trust the records, so I know what happened."

"You mean records from the TTV's infosystems?"

"Well, of course there are those," Pepys said with a dismissive wave, "but I was actually referring to the diary I kept after the crash."

"You kept *another* diary?" Benjamin's face lit up.

"Indeed I did, Doctor." Pepys puffed out his chest.

"Is it as brutally candid as the original?"

"If anything, even more so." Pepys quirked a lopsided smile. "Indeed, it's so candid it surprises *me* from time to time. Teodorà tells me I was quite the 'player,' in my organic days. I've always been prepared to take her word for that, but I've recently been rereading diary excerpts in anticipation of this day. Refreshing my memory on what happened when our timelines diverged." He shook his head. "On balance, I believe she may actually have understated the handful I was in those days."

"Would you...mind sharing your diary with us?"

"Not at all. It would be my pleasure."

A file transfer popped open, and Benjamin saved it to his wetware without a second thought. The word count came to over five million.

"Wow," he murmured. "Looks like I have a *lot* of reading to do when I get back to the ship."

"Well, a century of a man's life can hold a great deal worth writing about. I can provide an abridged version if you'd prefer. There's a lot of content in the raw diary you may not find interesting."

"Maybe later. I'll take a look at this one for starters." He closed the virtual window. "And thank you. I really appreciate your sharing this."

"Oh, don't mention it. It's public domain, anyway. It wouldn't take you long to find a copy. Can you believe they still teach it in schools these days?"

"Why not?" Benjamin shrugged. "I read excerpts from your original diary back in high school. I suppose it's not too dissimilar here."

"Except for the fact that I'm still around and occasionally have to answer questions about events I don't remember."

"What do you tell them?"

"What else? 'If the diary says it happened that way then it did.' End of story. Next question."

Benjamin chuckled as he gazed up at the ruined TTV once more.

"Would you like to move on?" Pepys asked.

"Just a sec." Benjamin double-checked his saved copies of the exhibit's virtual displays, then nodded, satisfied that he had records for later study. "Okay. Lead on."

"The Byzantine Exhibit is next. This way." Pepys gestured to a grand archway. "The museum's exhibits are arranged chronologically in a wide ring, so if we keep following them in this direction, we'll end up back at the entrance."

"Are all the exhibits focused on your involvement in history?"

"Yes. That's why Teodorà and I chose this particular museum. We thought it would be a good place for you to start understanding the divergences between our histories."

Benjamin stopped in front of a massive, obviously ancient mosaic which depicted a man and woman in foreign garments tending to the sick. The artist had imbued the man and woman with saintly auras of light.

"I imagine the divergences were quite stark," he said, "even shortly after the crash."

"We did our best to avoid any...religious connotations to our actions or abilities," Samuel grumped, glowering at the mosaic. "Not always successfully, as you can see."

"Did you end up stopping the plague?"

"Eventually, yes, but not on our own. We had the cure, but it was the people of the Byzantine Empire who put it to good use. Our resources were so limited. Our ship was in tatters; its systems were dead or starved for power, so we joined forces with Belisarius and Justinian to organize and distribute the cure."

"I always wondered what would've happened if the two of them had gone on working together," Benjamin said. "So this time around, Justinian's paranoia didn't cause him to turn on Belisarius? How did you pull that off?"

"With a lot of convincing." Pepys led the way to the next display and presented it with a wide flourish.

"Ah." Benjamin nodded. "Yes, I imagine that would do it."

The corroded remains of a forty-five-millimeter Gatling gun and four conveyor drones floated over a long rectangle of desert sand. Scattered and scorched stone from what might have been a city wall littered the ground beneath it.

"We only used it a few times," Pepys said. "After all, we didn't have the power or the ammunition for much more."

"But I don't suppose the people who faced it knew that."

"They never asked, and we never told them." Pepys shrugged. "Besides, for all its thunder and fury, the cannon was mostly for show. Our real power came from our knowledge and, especially, our surveillance remotes and long-range communication. We were able to teach the Empire about things like hygiene that tremendously reduced non-battlefield casualties. That would have been a huge advantage right there—you know better than most how many armies were crippled or completely destroyed by disease in SysGov's timeline! But the remotes and our comms were an even bigger advantage. The Empire never again had to guess where an enemy army was. Nor where it was heading, what its strength and composition was, how well supplied it was, or any of that. It knew exactly what its enemies were doing at any moment, and it could coordinate its own forces with instantaneous orders."

"And you had Flavius Belisarius to issue those orders," Benjamin added.

"Oh, indeed! It almost seemed unfair giving one of the greatest generals in history so many advantages." Pepys flashed a half-smile. "Almost. On the other hand, Belisarius became very fond of an aphorism Teodorà shared with him."

"Aphorism?" Benjamin raised one eyebrow, and Pepys chuckled.

"'If you're not cheating, you aren't trying hard enough,'" he quoted, and Benjamin laughed, looking back at the rusted remnants of The Convincer.

"So what did Belisarius and Justinian do with all that power?"

"It wasn't just Belisarius and Justinian," Pepys corrected. "Theodora and Antonina were just as much a part of the partnership. And Ephraim—maybe *especially* Ephraim—while we had him. Dynasty historians labeled Belisarius, Justinian, and their wives the 'Four Giants,' but they should have called him the 'Titan'! Without Ephraim..." He shook his head, his expression momentarily sad. "I wish I had clearer memories of *him*. Personal memories, I mean. He was a most... *extraordinary* man, and I'm glad the Church canonized him here, just as they did in your own past. No one ever deserved it more than he did."

"Just from what I've already seen here"—Benjamin waved at the exhibits around them—"I find that very easy to believe."

Pepys nodded, standing beside him and gazing at the corroded Gatling for a second or two of silence, then gave himself a slight shake.

"But you asked what Justinian and the others did." He shrugged. "Mostly, for the duration of their own lives, they stuck to stabilizing and strengthening the Empire. The Dynasty's expansion was only possible because we had such a firm base here in Byzantium, and we only had that because they worked so hard to build it. Because we *all* worked so hard, really. The TTV's printers were gone, and only scraps of our central library had survived the crash, but between us 'Honored Elders,' we were able to introduce many novel concepts to their society. Advanced mathematics, the germ theory of medicine, pasteurization, and many others. We gave them *anything* we could recall, and Teodorà's and Lucius's historical knowledge proved immensely valuable. Even my own experiences were a thousand years ahead of where we landed! Indeed, in some ways, the fact that my own life experiences were so much more 'primitive' than Teodorà's or Lucius's helped enormously when it was time to convert theory into practically attainable technology. We also provided Belisarius, Justinian, and their families with life-extension treatments. We lost Ephraim after only another twenty years or so, anyway, but the Four Giants formed a sustained and stable core of leadership that could take our knowledge, our concepts, and begin building an entirely new society out of the chrysalis of the old."

"So you let Justinian and Theodora continue to rule?"

"Of course." Pepys shrugged. "We could've taken

over, if we *really* wanted to, but we didn't. I think they both understood how easily we could have, too, and they may have been more accommodating because of it, but there was more to it than that. Over time, we became not just allies but friends, and we never sought to rule, only to guide. Our goals have always been the same: to provide a bright future for the people of this timeline, free of the plague...and of as many other mishaps and hardships as we could guide them around. But, ultimately, it's still *their* timeline, not ours. We 'Honored Elders' were merely advisors." He wagged a finger. "And we still are, to some degree, even if our roles are quite small in this modern age."

"Interesting." Benjamin walked on and came to a quartet of elaborate stone caskets. Virtual displays opened, and he blinked as he read the summary. "Belisarius and Justinian?"

"And Theodora and Antonina." Pepys nodded. "That's right. Ephraim, on the other hand"—he smiled crookedly—"is buried in an enormous, elaborate mausoleum in Antioch. The Church decided to move him there during one of Teodorà's and my 'downtimes.'" He chuckled. "I rather suspect that the Patriarch of Constantinople responsible for the move was afraid of how we would have reacted to the proposal if we'd been awake, but the truth is, I think Ephraim would have been deeply amused by it all."

"None of them chose to abstract?"

"No, they didn't." Samuel shook his head again, and an edge of sorrow echoed in his voice, the sorrow of a man speaking of old friends long dead. "We offered them the chance, of course, but none of them accepted it. I think part of it was Ephraim's example. All of them were devout Christians, you know, and perhaps transitioning into the abstract was simply a step too far into the unknown for them to accept. For them to willingly shed their physical bodies. I argued long and hard with them, trying to convince them to follow my lead and transition when the TTV's medical bay started to break down, but I never really expected to change their minds. Which"—he quirked a sad little smile—"didn't mean that I didn't have to try."

"It sounds like you miss them."

"Of course I do." Pepys tapped his temple. "My memories of their decision, our discussions, are from just before I abstracted, so they're crystal clear when I need them. They weren't just colleagues. Not anymore."

His eyes gleamed with unshed tears, and Benjamin nodded silently.

"I suppose I can understand why they wanted to rest," Pepys said at last. "Why they wanted to finally be with God. They'd spent decades ushering in a golden age for the Empire, and they'd earned every moment of their eternal respite. Besides, Justinian was almost two hundred years old, and Belisarius was only a couple of decades behind him. I think they were tired. And I think there may have been a part of them that thought it would've been ... dishonest for them to accept a form of potential immortality."

"Dishonest?" Benjamin repeated softly.

"Not the best word," Pepys said. "I simply don't have a better one. I suppose what I'm trying to say is that they refused to tell themselves—or God—that they'd accepted our offer of assistance only so that they could enjoy their privileged positions forever. And there may have been just a bit of penitence in it, as well."

"Penitence?"

"Yes." Pepys looked at him squarely. "Penitence. I think they truly believed that they'd done the right thing, that God approved of their decisions. But I also think they were never entirely free of the fear that perhaps Teodorà and I were Prometheus, handing them knowledge God hadn't intended for them to possess so early." He shook his head yet again. "Intellectually, I don't think they entertained the concern for a moment—not after the first couple of decades, anyway—but they were born in the *sixth* century, Agent Schröder. Deep down inside, they were always the sons and daughters of the history we'd changed."

"And you weren't."

"No, I wasn't," Pepys agreed. "Oh, I sprang from what would have been their future, but I'd seen Sys-Gov. Like Teodorà and Lucius, I'm a time traveler, I knew the shape of history to come, and I wanted to help see the Dynasty safely through it."

"And did you?"

"Well"—Pepys quirked a smile—"I suppose that depends on your perspective. Let me answer your question by listing some of the events we *didn't* experience. No Crusades, no Ottoman Empire, no Mongols sweeping deep into Europe, no Mongol Empire in the East, no African slave trade, no Taiping Rebellion, no religious wars in the sixteenth and seventeenth centuries, no Napoleonic Wars, no Boer War, no World Wars, no twentieth century totalitarian states, no—"

"I think I get the picture!" Benjamin laughed. "That's quite a list of achievements."

"Thank you. It didn't happen by accident, I can *assure* you of that! And we did have our own trouble spots along the way—problems we didn't see coming, either, that had to be dealt with after they arose. But we did manage to avoid most of our own timeline's history of mass bloodlettings. I tease Teodorà, from time to time, over her own record as a military leader, but most of the 'wars' over which she officiated were—I believe the correct term might be 'small beer,' compared to the wars fought in her own history. And, over time, in no small part as a result of the defensive wars in which she played such a major role, the Byzantine Empire expanded and evolved into the Dynasty of today."

"And is the Dynasty's recent history equally peaceful?"

"More or less. Every society has its troublemakers, and we have a large and well-equipped police force—the quaesitors—who are very similar to your SysPol in that they keep the peace within the Dynasty rather than facing some great external threats."

"Quaesitors?" Benjamin pondered the name. "Weren't they Byzantine immigration officials?"

"Quite a few names and titles have survived the centuries, morphing a little bit along the way. Remember that the Dynasty absorbed many different peoples and cultures as it grew, and *our* quaesitors had greatly expanded roles compared to their namesakes in your history."

"Interesting."

"We also managed to avoid both SysGov's Near Miss and the Admin's Yanluo Massacre as our technology advanced."

"Wow. Those, too." Benjamin beamed at him. "Impressive!"

"Lucius and Teodorà once again helped flag the worst pitfalls before we tumbled into them."

"A good thing, too," Benjamin agreed. "Did they make you watch the video with the dog?"

"I beg your pardon?"

"Never mind, then."

"No fair." Samuel quirked a smile. "Now I'm curious."

"It's just something Raibert showed me a while back," Benjamin deflected. "Actually, your mentioning the Near Miss brings me to something *I've* been curious about."

"What's that?"

"The Dynasty's tech level. It seems surprisingly close to SysGov's. Almost too close. I realize you lost all your infosystems, and I can see where that would push things back a bit, but even so, you ought to be *well* ahead of us, I'd think."

"Ah, yes. That. Teodorà and I were talking about that just the other day. We think a number of factors played a part in it."

"You provided a lot of advances early on," Benjamin pointed out.

"That's true," Pepys conceded. "We couldn't replicate advanced technology, but in some ways what we gave them was far more valuable. We showed them that certain things were *possible*, even if we didn't know how to do it. None of us Elders knew how gravity manipulation or time travel worked, for example. But sometimes the only edge people need is to know a thing *can* be done."

"That's exactly what I was thinking," Benjamin agreed. "So why isn't your tech far more advanced than ours, with that head start?"

"If the only factor were *starting* points, it probably

would be, but that *isn't* the only factor. There's also the question of roads taken—or not taken—along the path from a society's starting point. For one thing, we stressed—and the Four Giants agreed with us—the need to integrate new technology into societies without ripping their social fabric apart, and that got firmly grafted into the Dynasty's DNA. I suppose you might call it a policy of 'gradualism,' although Teodorà and I prefer to think of it as responsible social stewardship. That meant a gentler... gradient, for want of a better word, in the adoption of new technologies as the Dynasty adjusted to them. And unlike SysGov or the Admin, the Dynasty's never worried about technology's ability to solve almost any problem *eventually*, since it's had us Elders around as example of a society whose tech has done just that. But, as important as both of those factors undoubtedly were, there's one I think that may well be even more important. Remember all those wars I mentioned? The ones that never happened here?"

"Oh, of course!" Benjamin nodded. "The lack of conflict and competition would've slowed technological progress."

"Exactly. The Dynasty's expansion created an overarching political mechanism and a world template and an integrated economy much earlier in this history than in your own. That produced an enormously lower level of tension and largely bypassed the evolution of competing nation-states at the industrial level. So, in our timeline, you have two sets of factors tugging at technological development—one set speeding it up, but the other set slowing it down. Over time, the two *mostly* canceled each other out. We estimate the Dynasty's tech is slightly better than SysGov's in most ways—that estimate's based on what we brought back from the thirtieth century—but it's a marginal difference."

Benjamin nodded again, conscious of a slight feeling of relief. This first contact was going far, *far* better than anyone in SysGov would have dared to predict, but that didn't mean there would never be a confrontation between the universes. He felt a little guilty to even be thinking about such things, but he *was* a historian. And if something did occur to cast a chill on the relations between SysGov and the Dynasty, he was just as happy that *neither* of them would have the sort of overwhelming technological advantage which could all too easily lead someone to prefer solving problems with a hammer.

"Shall we continue?" Pepys asked, gesturing toward the arch opening onto the next exhibit.

"Oh, yes! Please, lead the way."

❖   ❖   ❖

Elzbietá followed Lieutenant Khatib up the narrow ramp and into the *Sigrun's* interior. She entered a clean, oval space with a single chair at its center, which she assumed was a smaller and more personal version of the *Kleio's* bridge.

Hala crossed to the chair and placed both hands on the headrest.

"And this," she said cheerfully, "is where the magic happens."

Elzbietá let the local infostructure interface with her wetware. Dozens of virtual displays activated, covering every centimeter of the walls with charts, status reports, and scope data.

"Nice layout." She indicated the chair. "Mind if I . . . ?"

"Be my guest." Hala patted the headrest.

"Thanks." Elzbietá sat down, and additional controls activated at her fingertips.

"I hope these are locked?" she said, keeping her hands carefully to herself.

"They are." Hala laughed a bit nervously. "Didn't want my guest to accidentally engage the impellers or something."

"Wise lady." Elzbietá grinned. "Just wanted to make sure."

She gripped the inert controls and settled deeper into the chair. The setup was busier than she thought it needed to be, but that aside, the controls bore a striking resemblance to those she and Philo had come up with.

"What's the top speed?" she asked.

"Our impellers are rated for seventy-four kilofactors, although I bet I could push them a little further if they'd let me."

"And in realspace?"

"Six gees forward acceleration. Four in any other direction. The *Sigrun* has a quad of graviton thrusters, one mounted above and below each impeller housing."

A little faster than us, then, Elzbietá noted.

"You have to accelerate that hard very often?" she asked out loud.

"Thankfully, no. The *Sigrun's* built for transdimensional exploration, but most other *Valkyries* use the spare engine capacity for hauling cargo."

"And when you *do* push the limit?"

"A lot of our pilots are synthoids, so they don't

care. But for me"—Hala knocked on a section of wall, which split open to reveal an upright cylindrical vessel—"it's straight into the compensation bunk."

No inertial negation, I see, Elzbietá thought. She was a little disappointed. *But I shouldn't be surprised, since SysGov physics models say that's not possible. On the other hand, those models have been wrong before, and it would be really nice if they were wrong again.*

Technically, if artificial gravity was in every way the same as real gravity or acceleration, then their ships would be able to counteract acceleration forces to create a "freefall" state within the ship's interior. Unfortunately, there were hard limits on what a piece of excited negative mass built into the *Kleio's* floor could do compared to the countless gravitons spilling off celestial bodies.

The creation of "true" gravity remained the unobtainable Holy Grail of graviton manipulation, although Elzbietá recalled a recent science article that hinted this impossibility might not be so far-fetched, after all. She'd been reading in bed and had become so excited by the article she'd poked Benjamin awake to talk about it.

He hadn't shared her enthusiasm, for some reason.

She released the controls, and the joystick and omnidirectional throttle settled back into their default positions.

"It's a nice ship you have here."

"Thanks."

"What's behind the back door?"

"Crew quarters and the like." Hala shrugged. "The *Sigrun* can support a crew of four comfortably, although one is all it takes. It has separate quarters for each, plus the usual assortment of kitchen, showers, medical bay, printers, storage, and so on." She shifted from one foot to the other. "You mind if we don't go back there? I sometimes use the ship as an apartment when I work late at HQ, and my room is...kind of a mess."

"Oh, I wouldn't worry about it," Elzbietá said, her eyes laughing. "I'm the last person who'd criticize a cluttered room. I get enough of *that* from my husband!"

"He a bit of a neat freak?"

"Just a bit." Elzbietá held a thumb and forefinger before her eyes. "I sometimes try to explain to Benjamin that I know where everything is. It doesn't have to be arranged on a shelf for it to be organized. As long as *I* can find it, just leave it where it is."

"I know what you mean." Hala chuckled. "I had a boyfriend like that. Would your Benjamin be the same one who went with Chairman Pepys?"

"Yeah, that's him."

"He seems like a nice guy."

"The best." Elzbietá looked away and sighed. "He died for me once already."

Hala's face showed her confusion.

"You mean that figuratively, right?"

"No. I mean he *died*, in a very literal, self-replicating-nanotech-ate-him-alive sort of way. Your histories know about the Gordian Knot, right?"

Hala nodded, her eyes huge.

"Well, Ben's the one who untied it, and he died doing it."

"Oh, God. *Seriously?*"

"Yeah." Elzbietá looked at her host again. "His grandfather and I are two of the few survivors of our universe, but Ben existed on both forks when our universe split off from the main SysGov stem. He remembers being both of him, including the man who deliberately died one of the most horrible deaths I can imagine because it was the right thing to do."

Hala's eyes were huge, and Elzbietá smiled at her.

"So, trust me when I say I *know* he's the one," she said more briskly, climbing out of the pilot seat.

"I guess so," Hala said, and Elzbietá chuckled and patted her on the shoulder, then looked around the bridge again.

"So, was it just you on board when we met?" she asked.

"Just me."

"Hmmmm."

"Something wrong?" Hala asked.

"Oh, nothing. Just different procedures. The Gordian Division requires at least two personnel on the bridge before the time drive can be activated. It's a carryover from the two-pilot rule ART uses, although we've loosened it so that *any* two agents can provide authorization, rather than requiring at least one physical and one abstract. It's a security measure, which"—she frowned—"turned out not to work in one recent case." She faced Hala. "Have you had any problems with time machine theft?"

"No," Hala said, then paused and thought. "Well, we did have a former Cornucopia pilot take one out for a joyride a few months back, but that was the worst I can recall."

"What happened to him?" Elzbietá asked, curious about crime and punishment in the Dynasty.

"He got banned from the campus."

"That's it?"

"Yeah." Hala shrugged. "He got fined, too, but you know, we're post-scarcity, so who cares?"

"That's surprisingly lenient," Elzbietá noted. The same theft in SysGov could result in a death penalty.

"Not really," Hala countered. "You wouldn't say that if you knew how important Cornucopia is around here."

"'Cornucopia,'" Elzbietá echoed. "Why that name?"

"Because it's what we are."

"I don't follow."

"Cornucopia is the engine behind our post-scarcity society. That's why getting kicked off site is a huge penalty."

"I'm sorry, but I must be missing something," Elzbietá said. "What do time travel and post-scarcity have to do with each other?"

"Well it's because of the repli—Oh! You mean you don't know?"

Elzbietá shook her head.

"Want me to show you?"

"Hey"—Elzbietá smiled at the other pilot—"it's why I'm here."

CHAPTER TWENTY-SEVEN

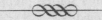

Cornucopia Headquarters
Dynasty, 2980 CE

"AREN'T YOU WORRIED THAT I MIGHT TRY TO ARREST you or something?" Raibert asked once he and Teodorà were alone and walking side by side through the bright halls of Cornucopia Headquarters.

"Why?" She smiled impishly. "Are you planning to?"

"No." He shrugged. "Just asking."

"Maybe you think I'm not taking this meeting seriously enough?"

"No. I just wasn't expecting such a relaxed reception."

"If you like, I can dispatch one of our *Valkyries* to the Admin and ask them for advice on how to put together a *proper* first contact."

"Now you're being mean."

"Raibert, I already told you I expected that you'd be the one to come." She placed her hand on his biceps. "And here you are."

"We didn't part on very good terms." He glanced down at her, still expecting to see condemnation in her eyes, but all he saw was comfortable recognition of a long-lost friend. "Your death, or at least what I thought was your death, hit me pretty hard."

"Aw, that's so sweet," she teased with a wry smile.

"I'm being serious here."

"So am I. Raibert, our time together was so far in my past that I had to actively select and reorganize those old memories. To be honest, I didn't even remember you until I started prepping for this day."

"Really?" He sighed.

"Oh, don't give me that wounded look. A connectome, even one with the advantages of a synthoid brain, can only handle so much data at once, and I have more than two *centuries* of extra memories over you. It's a *chore* to organize all that, believe me. You should be flattered I remember you at all."

"I suppose I should," he conceded. "So this memory review you performed is why you're not worried about me arresting you?"

"Raibert, you have *many* character flaws—"

"Hrmph!"

"—but deep down, you're a kind and honorable man, even if the exterior can be a bit prickly at times."

"There's nothing wrong with sugarcoating the truth occasionally, you know."

"The point is that I'm eager to show you what we've accomplished because I think you're going to fall in love with the Dynasty." She raised her chin. "Besides, from a legal standpoint, I'm the citizen of a foreign power with whom SysGov has no extradition treaty."

"That sounded . . . rehearsed."

"Only slightly." She winked at him. "Just in case I was wrong and needed it."

"Well, kidnapping one of the Dynasty's Honored Elders is probably not the best way to open a dialogue, so you don't have anything to fear from us. We're here with nothing but peaceful intentions."

"See? I was right about you."

"Guess so. Now what?"

"Now I'm going to show you what we've been working on here at Cornucopia."

"Isn't that what the lieutenant is doing with Ella?"

"Yes and no. You'll see."

He followed her into a counter-grav tube which whisked them to a landing pad on the opposite side of the complex from the *Kleio* and *Sigrun*. The ship on this platform possessed a sharp, angular wedge for its main body, and a pair of exceptionally long, narrow impellers extended out the back beyond the rim of the landing pad. Sunlight shimmered off its cobalt steel hull.

"This is our latest *Valkyrie* prototype," Teodorà said, with a grand, sweeping flourish in its direction. "The *Hildr*."

"Looks impressive," Raibert said.

"And those looks don't lie. *Hildr* can maintain a steady seventy-eight kilofactors."

He whistled, and she chuckled.

"Most of our *Valkyries* don't need that kind of speed, but we keep pushing the limits on our explorer chassis."

"Yeah, I've been meaning to ask you about that. We detected a *lot* of near-present time travel when we phased in. What's all that about?"

"Come on in. I'll show you."

Teodorà jogged up the ramp, and Raibert hurried

after her to an oval room with a single seat. She sat down and manipulated virtual controls, and a second chair folded out of the floor next to hers. Raibert seated himself as the ramp sealed shut and virtual imagery made the outer walls vanish into a panoramic view.

"They let the boss fly the prototype?" he asked.

"One of the perks of *being* the boss." She tapped a comm window. "This is Chairwoman Beckett from *Hildr*, requesting permission for an unscheduled test flight in the True Present. I shouldn't take more than an hour or two, absolute. Transmitting authorization codes."

"Authorization acknowledged. Would you like an escort?"

"Negative, Control."

"Then enjoy your flight, Elder. Control out."

"That was easy," Raibert said.

"They only make a fuss if I interfere with actual work." Teodorà eased the controls up, and the *Hildr* lifted from the pad, light as a feather. "I checked *Hildr*'s schedule while we walked over. The next *real* test flight is two days from now."

"Ah. Then you're a benevolent boss."

"I try to be."

Teodorà pushed the omni-throttle forward, and acceleration pressed them back into their seats. The *Hildr* shot over the gleaming cityscape, then angled up through the clouds to ascend high into the atmosphere.

"Where are we going?"

"One of our temporal replication centers."

"Temporal replication?" Raibert repeated with a sudden sense of uneasiness. "You mean like what ART used to pull?"

"Raibert, please." She gave him a sideways look. "We're here because SysGov found out how stupid ART was and we wanted to make amends, or compensation, at least, for the things we'd done. Given that, do you honestly think we'd make the same boneheaded mistakes all over again in the Dynasty?"

"Well, I don't know."

"Give us a little credit. We caused the timeline to branch because we wanted to do *better*. And we did it! I hope you don't mind if I brag a little, but after so much hard work, I think I've earned it. The Dynasty is an advanced, peaceful society, and I'm profoundly proud of what we've achieved here."

"But temporal *replication*?" he pressed. "I'm sorry, but that sounds too much like how ART used to kidnap famous people."

"Don't worry. It's not what you think. We have our own version of the Gordian Protocol on the books."

"You do?" Raibert blinked, taken aback.

"Absolutely. And one of its pillars is a prohibition on the replication of sentient life."

"Oh. Then what do you use your time machines for?"

"Take a look."

She eased the nose down and slowed their approach. A massive, rectangular, open-sided structure loomed into view, rising high over a wooded plain like a skyscraper with its outer surface removed to reveal a high-ceilinged floor plan. Dozens of bulky time machines lumbered in and out of the open hangars.

"What are they...?"

Raibert leaned forward. One of the time machines phased out while inside a hangar, and another phased in next door. Their hulls were taller and wider than the *Hildr*, with short, stubby impellers mounted high to give easier access to their generous cargo bays.

A steady stream of time machines came and went, but they only engaged their impellers within the confines of this mammoth, skeletal tower. Generic metal crates were stacked high in some of the bays, but those crates were never touched in the bustle of *visible* movement.

Those crates aren't being touched in the True Present, Raibert realized, *but—*

"Figure it out yet?" Teodorà asked.

"You're replicating . . . stuff?"

"Well." She rolled her eyes. "I suppose that's *one* way to put it."

"But that's what you're doing, right? The time machines travel into the past, load their hulls with previous versions of those crates, then come back to the present and drop off the goodies."

"Pretty much, yeah."

"What's in the crates?"

"It varies. Construction materials, foodstuffs, synthoid bodies, infosystems. Really, anything we want a lot of."

"But not people."

"*Absolutely* not."

"So you've never replicated a person?"

"Well, once."

"Aha!" Raibert exclaimed, as if he'd just uncovered a dark secret.

"As a controlled and authorized *experiment,*" Teodorà clarified, glowering at him a little. "His name is Leo Johanson. He happily volunteered, and both versions of him still work at Cornucopia."

"Oh. Is that all?"

"Yep. Just the one."

"Why?" he asked, perplexed.

"It was part of our safety tests before we began ramping up our replication industry. You remember what happened to Benjamin Schröder when there were two of him in 2018 at the same time?"

"How could I not? I was in the room when the brain melt happened."

"Well, we wanted to make sure our pilots weren't risking the same thing."

"Hmm. That seems . . . overly cautious," Raibert said. "We both know ART never encountered any phenomenon like that—before or after the Knot—and the Admin certainly hasn't had any issues with its agents working in the near-present." He shrugged. "It seemed pretty clear, to me at least, that what happened to Benjamin was unique to the Knot and how his birth occurred in two different universes."

"I know that, and you know that, but *Lucius* insisted we make sure. Besides, the cautious approach made everyone more comfortable."

"Well, sounds like it worked out for this Leo guy." He raised an eyebrow. "It did work out for him, right?"

"Of course it did. No brain-melting weirdness or anything. And it's another sign Philo's theory about Schröder's dual memories was correct, that it was related to him being just a pair of gametes prior to the Knot forming. He was a blank slate of, comparatively, a few atoms that ended up maturing into the same man in two universes. Two universes *entangled* in the Knot, an unprecedented environment where effect could precede cause. There were a lot of unusual factors that lined up to make his condition possible. I'm not sure we could replicate it if we tried."

"That's probably a good thing." Raibert glanced back out at the replication center. "What about exotic matter? Do you copy stuff like that here?"

"Only at specialized centers," Teodorà said. "Transporting non-inert matter is difficult and, occasionally, dangerous. Especially for the older *Valkyries* we commonly use in replication duty."

"Even with those limits, I bet you could outstrip SysGov's exotic matter printers."

"Well, I don't want to brag"—she smiled at him— "but, yeah. We can. *Easily.*"

Raibert rested an elbow on the armrest and rubbed his chin as the logistical dance played out around the replication center.

"What about branching timelines?" he asked.

"It's never happened."

"Are you sure?"

"We continuously monitor the chronometric disruption around each center, but we've never had a branch form. Never even come close, in fact. Our safety record is impeccable."

"But all this time travel jammed into such a tight space . . ."

"It's far less risky than you might think. Trust me, we thought about that very hard, in light of the Gordian Knot and how it formed. We're only performing short, near-present jumps. No more than a negative-hour, usually. And the True Present is the strongest structural point in the universe, so we utilize that natural resiliency to our advantage."

"A branch can still form in the near-present," Raibert warned.

"*If* the magnitude of the disruption is high enough,"

Teodorà corrected. "Collecting a few dozen historically insignificant crates—crates that wouldn't even *be* there if they hadn't been placed specifically to be replicated—isn't enough to branch the timeline even in the deep past, let alone right next to the True Present."

"I see you *have* thought this through."

"Of course we did."

"And you're sure it's safe?"

"Very. We experimented with a great deal of caution before we set up the first replication center, and we ran only one of them for a full five years in the True Present, monitoring and collecting data, before we even considered firing up another one. But every test we've done, and every simulation we've run, has shown us there's no risk, short- or long-term."

"Cornucopia, indeed," Raibert mused. "And so, instead of using large-scale printers like SysGov, the Dynasty has large-scale *replicators*."

"Oh, we have plenty of printers, too."

"You replicate those, as well?"

"Of course." Teodorà chuckled. "The replication is easier than *printing* more printers."

"How so?"

"The beauty of this process is that once you have a high-quality example of a product, you're good to go forever and ever. Temporal replication *can't* produce defects."

"Unlike printers and microtech," Raibert agreed, staring at the constant back-and-forth of time machines around the replication center.

"What do you think?" Teodorà asked.

"I'm impressed," he admitted, turning to her. "The

amount of time travel I'm seeing still worries me, though."

"That's understandable. For you, the Gordian Knot is still a fresh memory, but I assure you we've taken all the necessary precautions. And we'd be happy to share our models with you."

"You sound proud of all this."

"I guess that's because I am."

"Was Cornucopia your idea? Or"—he allowed himself a raised eyebrow, but he was very careful about his tone—"did Lucius come up with it?"

"Actually"—her eyes twinkled—"it was Samuel's."

"*What?*" he blurted before he could catch himself.

"Surprised?" She smiled in pure amusement.

"The guy from the sixteen hundreds came up with *this?*" Raibert stabbed a finger at the view.

"That's right."

"How?"

"Oh, Raibert!" She laughed and shook her head. "You can't equate the Samuel who left SysGov with the one here and now. He's not the 'You mean there's this thing called technology?' person anymore. He's had a long time to study up. The next best thing to four centuries, if you add it all up, which is almost longer than me and Lucius *combined*, at least here in the Dynasty. I did have forty-plus years on him when we first met in SysGov. But he's had plenty of time, and he's a smart, smart man. In fact, I'd go so far as to say he understands our tech better than *I* do at this point."

"Hmm. I see. You're right, of course," Robert chided himself. "Sorry."

"It's all right." She leaned closer and spoke softly.

"So would you like to see the *future* of Cornucopia next?"

"Isn't that what I'm looking at?"

"Oh, the replication centers?" Teodorà gave the view a dismissive wave. "Old news. Just a different way of applying the same technology SysGov has. Anyone with a time machine can do this. No, what I'm going to show you next is something *truly* remarkable."

✧   ✧   ✧

Philo walked down the endless, empty corridor, his Viking avatar fully realized within the Dynasty abstraction. Wooden doors lined either side of the carpeted corridor. The virtual version of Cornucopia Headquarters wasn't laid out anything like the real one, but the fidelity of the abstraction was unusually high.

He wondered if Dynasty ACs preferred to move about within a simulation rather than exist as almost pure data. Were they really that attached to a sense of body? Perhaps some of them found these archaic surroundings comforting? He would have asked one of them, but he was the only AC in the entire infostructure, as far as he could tell.

When Teodorà and Pepys said there are very few ACs in the Dynasty, they weren't kidding, he thought. *It's kind of like walking around in a haunted house. Or maybe one where the monsters ate everybody who lived here. Now* that's *a cheerful thought!*

The truth was, he didn't like being outside of the *Kleio* in this unfamiliar abstraction for a lot of reasons. The attack he'd suffered in the Admin still burned in his memory, and because this time he was an invited guest, he'd brought none of his arsenal of cyber-weapons with him. He felt . . . naked. But he also had a job to do, and if the Dynasty was going to give him free access to their systems, then why not go straight for their central archives and start rummaging through them for dirt?

"Ah! Here we are."

He stopped at a door marked ARCHIVE and tested the knob. It turned without resistance, and he pushed the door open.

"Anybody in here?" he called out, not really expecting a response.

Rows of filing cabinets towered upward to meet an absurdly high, almost stratospheric ceiling. In a strange way, he found the surreal nature of this space soothing. He picked one cabinet at random and tried to open it, but found the handle was purely cosmetic. Well, perhaps not *purely* cosmetic, because a window materialized at his touch, prompting him for search parameters.

Philo grimaced at the blinking cursor. He hadn't expected to get this far so easily. Surely security measures should have turned him away by now.

But the cursor continued to blink, inviting him to partake of this simulation's data.

"What the hell." He shrugged. "Search for 'Dual-Drive Transport.'"

"Can you be more specific?" the interface asked in a polite feminine tone. "I have found twenty-seven thousand five hundred and seventeen major entries that could apply. Since you aren't an employee, I have no past experience with your requests and, therefore, no way to prioritize them for you."

"Oh." Philo raised his bushy eyebrows. "Hello?"

"Hello, sir," the voice replied.

"And who might you be?"

"I am the Cornucopia archiver."

"You sentient?"

"No, sir. Merely an attendant program here to assist you."

"Oh. Sorry. Didn't mean to assume."

"That's quite all right, sir. Is there any way you can narrow your search?"

"Not sure." Philo shrugged. "Can't you just give me everything?"

"That would be impractical, sir. This portion of the infostructure could hold less than one percent of the files. I recommend refining your search."

"Then how about you show me whatever's on the top of the list?"

"How would you like the list sorted?"

"Ummm, by timestamp. List the top hundred most recent entries."

"Very good, sir. Here you are."

Several nearby filing cabinets sprang open.

"These surroundings are a bit outdated," Philo said. "Don't you think?"

"I couldn't say, sir. I don't 'think' in the conventional sense."

"Right. Sorry again." Philo peered into the first open drawer.

"There's no need to apologize, sir."

He flipped through the reports until he found one titled REPLICATION CENTER FIFTEEN MAINTENANCE SCHEDULE, then pulled it out and skimmed through it.

"Temporal replication, huh?" he murmured after he'd copied the contents and put the file back.

"I'm sorry, sir. Do you have a specific question?"

"The Dynasty uses time travel to replicate resources."

"That is correct, sir."

"Oh, boy!" Philo shook his head. "Andover-Chen's going to blow his top when he finds out."

"I'm sorry, sir?"

"Don't worry about it." He picked another cabinet and thumbed through its contents. "Oooh. What's this?"

"That is a progress report on the *Tesseract*'s construction."

Philo pulled it out and skimmed its contents.

"Damn! That's a *lot* of exotic matter." He copied the file and put it back. "Can you pull up more on this *Tesseract* thing?"

"I can, sir, but senior management or project team authorization is required to view most of the files."

"Guess I don't have those."

"No, sir. Would you like to file a request form?"

"Nah, that's all right." He sighed. "Truth is, I'd be more suspicious if there *weren't* any barriers to what I can read."

"You could ask me to show it to you," a new—but very familiar—voice said from behind his back.

"Eek!" Philo squeaked like a mouse, then turned slowly.

"I just so happen to have senior management access." Lucius Gwon closed the archive door behind him. He wore a black suit with a red waist sash.

Philo gulped.

"Hello, Philosophus."

"Hey," the Viking managed weakly.

"It's been a while." Lucius stepped closer and flashed a disarming smile. "Quite a bit longer for me than you, though. Am I right?"

"Yeah, guess so," Philo conceded. This wasn't the

same Lucius he and Raibert had ruined all those years ago, he told himself. After all, how could it be? In some ways, this might be a totally different person, and he had to maintain an open mind regardless of his past experiences with the man. The years he'd spent integrated with Lucius might still be fresh in *his* mind, but to Lucius, those events were old beyond normal human reckoning.

Yeah, and you're the guy who told Benjamin abstracts have perfect memory, aren't you, Philosophus my boy?

"Wow, look at you!" Lucius gestured to him with open palms. "Still the same avatar, except... Have you changed your helmet?"

"I have, actually." Philo lowered his aviator visor with a *click*.

"It looks good on you." Lucius clapped him on the arm, and his chain mail rustled. "A little anachronistic, but good."

"Thanks," Philo said neutrally, raising his visor once more.

"Is something bothering you?"

"No, it's nothing," he lied, taking half a step back. "I just wasn't expecting to see you again. You and Shadow weren't too happy the last time we met."

"Please. Like any of that matters anymore? It's all ancient history, Philo. *Literally*, in my case."

"You sure? You were *really* mad at me."

"Hey, buddy. Forgiven and forgotten." Lucius made a brushing-away gesture. "Mostly forgotten, though. I'm sure I was profoundly pissed with you, because I was pissed with a lot of people those days. In fact, it's fair to say that I was pretty much an unmitigated prick, when you and I were together. But, like I say, it was a long, long time ago. There have been a lot of changes, and the funny thing is that even though I originally only wanted to come back, cure the plague, and go home again, I wouldn't have missed this for anything." He smiled again, more warmly. "If I hadn't gotten myself marooned here with the others, and I hadn't been forced to abstract to run the TTV's remaining systems, I'd probably still be a prick. And you know what the worst thing about being a prick is?"

"No," Philo said slowly, staring at the avatar of this very changed man. "No, I don't."

"The worst thing about being a prick, especially the kind I was?" Lucius shook his head. "You're so busy being smarter than everybody else, quicker than everybody else, and, yeah, nastier than everybody else that you don't really realize how *lonely* you are. I'm not putting myself up for sainthood, here, Philo. God knows!" Lucius rolled his eyes. "But I found out that being respected for building something is a lot more satisfying, and lasts a lot longer, than the kind of gratification that leaves everybody hating your guts.

"So, now. No lingering grudges from my side. Would I have chosen this route, if I'd had a choice? Nope. But even if I had the opportunity, I wouldn't change a thing. And even if that weren't true, I'm way too lazy to use up all the energy it would take to stay mad at someone forever. Besides, I have plenty of *new* problems to deal with, believe me."

"Yeah, I can imagine. You work at Cornucopia with Teodorà?"

"*For* her, actually."

"And Shadow?" Philo glanced at Lucius's shadow but noticed the lack of a star field. "Is he around?"

"He's—" Lucius's expression tightened. "He's dead. He died shortly after the crash. Infosystems failure."

"Oh..." Philo's eyes darkened. "I'm so sorry."

"No, it's all right."

"I didn't mean to open an old wound. I know you two were close."

"It's all *right*, Philo." Lucius shook his head. "I've had a *lot* of time to get over it, trust me. Losing Shadow was like losing a part of myself, but I did get over it and move on. I had no choice, really."

"Still..." Philo lowered his head, wondering how he'd react if Raibert passed away. Would he even have the strength to go on, after a blow like that?

"Anyway, enough of this dreary subject," Lucius said, perhaps sensing Philo's darkening mood. "What is it you need management access for?"

"Ah. Right." Philo looked up. "I was actually curious about this *Tesseract* project. I don't suppose there's anything you can share about it?"

"Oh, *that*." Lucius tapped the side of his nose. "Still got a sense for the good stuff, I see."

"Well..." Philo shrugged bashfully.

"I can't show you everything. State secrets and all."

"Sure, I understand."

"But"—Lucius held up a finger—"there's no harm in giving you a little sample. An appetizer, if you will. Archiver?"

"Yes, Chairman Gwon?"

"Display the live feed from the *Tesseract* construction site. Satellite One, please."

"Displaying."

The towering filing cabinets vanished, as did the floor, ceiling, and walls. Philo and Lucius floated in space. Earth was a blue-white smile beneath their feet, and a massive orbital construct—shaped like a huge spike, many kilometers tall—came into view with sunlight kissing one massive flank.

"Is that—?"

"Beautiful, isn't it?" Lucius sighed.

CHAPTER TWENTY-EIGHT

~~~~~~∞∞∞~~~~~~

Dual-Drive Transport *Hildr*
Dynasty, 2980 CE

"WHY 'VALKYRIE'?" RAIBERT ASKED AS THE *HILDR*
reached low Earth orbit.

Teodorà groaned and leaned her head back against
the headrest.

"Sorry." He grimaced. "Didn't know it was a touchy
subject."

"It's not. There's just a lot of history behind the
name."

"I'm actually surprised this timeline knows what
valkyries are, given when it diverged from SysGov.
It's not a soundalike term, is it?"

"No." Teodorà shook her head. "I may have...
introduced the mythology a little early."

"Oh."

"And in the wrong geographical location," she confessed. "Although, in truth, the Empire's—and then
the Dynasty's—expansion was so slow and peaceful
that Norse culture developed very similarly to what

471

you're familiar with." She sighed. "There were some awkward questions when Byzantines and Vikings started interacting on a large scale."

"What made you introduce it?"

"Well, I had to explain my superpowers *somehow*."

"Wait a second." Raibert rounded his eyes at her. "*You* were the first Valkyrie in this timeline?"

"Better than telling people I was a synthoid. Explaining a robot to someone like Belisarius wasn't something I wanted to get into. Once we had to let him and Ephraim in on the true story about time travel, it got a lot easier, but it was several generations before people in general would have been ready to accept the truth."

"So instead of explaining, you took on the mantle of a mythical female warrior."

"Hey, it worked."

"Huh." Raibert shrugged. "Never pictured you as much of a fighter. Except when words were your weapons of choice." He grimaced. "You could cut deep with those."

"You never saw me toss the general's men around."

"You did that?"

"Only when they deserved it," she assured him with a twinkle, and he chuckled.

"So how did your time machines end up with the name?"

"A joke."

"Is it a good one?"

"I guess *some* people found it funny," Teodorà groused. "Siv Eriksen was the physicist who cracked time travel for us, and she christened her prototype the *Valkyrie*."

"To honor you?"

"Not really. The name was a joke about something possibly going wrong on the maiden voyage."

"*That's* why she chose the name?"

"And it stuck." She twitched a crooked smile. "No matter how hard I tried to unstick it."

"You have to admit, it rolls off the tongue better than Dual-Drive Transport."

"I suppose." She shrugged. "And the name actually fits pretty well when you consider what happened to *our* TTV."

"Yeah, sorry about that."

"Please stop apologizing, Raibert. I'm over it."

"Well, I'm not. Apologizing makes me feel better."

She smiled sweetly at him, reached over, and squeezed his hand. A flash of pleasant remembrance surged through him, and he found himself recalling how happy they'd been together.

Before they weren't.

Before the regular hate mail.

"How long until we reach it?" he asked. "Whatever 'it' is."

"Soon."

"You going to tell me what it is?"

"I'd rather leave it as a surprise." Teodorà glanced over her navigation chart, then looked his way again. "It's a shame, really. Eriksen was . . . one of those special, brilliant stars that seem to shine once each generation. What you're about to see are the fruits of her greatest theoretical work. Her equations paved the way to make . . . *it* . . . possible."

"I notice you're using the past tense," he said gently. "What happened to her?"

"A fluke accident." Teodorà shook her head sadly. "An unexpected impeller failure during a test flight."

"I'm sorry to hear that."

"Lucius was hit the hardest. He noticed her gift during her first year of college and took her under his wing. Brought her into what would become Cornucopia. The two were quite close, and after she died... he became more distant than usual. Dropped out of the day-to-day operations almost entirely."

"There wasn't a backup of her connectome?"

"No. She was still organic at the time."

"Ah."

"Plus, saving a connectome is a rare practice in the Dynasty. Even rarer than it is in SysGov." She tilted her head toward him. "Did you ever decide to make a backup, now that you're synthetic?"

"Nope!" Raibert stated firmly. "You'll never catch *me* handing a perfect copy of myself over to a fucking *bank*."

"On that, we always agreed," she said with a chuckle.

The *Hildr* sped through an orbital industrial cluster and passed a spaceborne version of the replication center he'd seen on the ground. Dozens of time machines blinked in and out of phase as they replicated goods for the Dynasty's population.

"It amazes me how fast all of this sprang up," he said.

"Amazing, yes," Teodorà agreed. "Fast, no."

"I mean from an absolute frame of reference. The wave front from your changes *sprinted* to the Edge of Existence. We were expecting a much slower progression, given what we saw around the Gordian Knot."

"Yeah, we wondered about that ourselves."

"You have?"

"We've had a lot more time to think about it, after all. Relatively speaking."

"Come to any conclusions?"

"Nothing solid. The destruction of our TTV's impeller so close to the formative changes may have contributed in some unknown fashion, but we're not really sure. Theoretically, some wave fronts will naturally propagate faster than others—they *always* move faster than one kilofactor—but the mechanisms behind how *much* faster aren't well understood. We have theories, but no way to test them."

"Because the only way to test them would be to create more universes," Raibert finished.

"Exactly. In some ways, given our experience with the Dynasty, it's been very tempting to do exactly that. On the other hand"—she faced him, and her expression was very serious—"I had to come to grips with some facts about myself. The truth is, you were right to try to stop us, Raibert."

"I was? I mean, we were?" He blinked at her in surprise, and she smiled without turning her expression one bit less serious.

"Absolutely. I really and truly didn't understand the theoretical constructs supporting time travel as well as I thought I did. I was an archaeologist, not a scientist, after all. And one of the facts I've had to acknowledge is that my sense of guilt over the horrible things ART had done overpowered everything else. I *needed* to stop the plague, and not just to save all those lives. I needed it as atonement. Creating this entire universe was my penance. It took Ephraim to make me really understand that. Or maybe what I mean is that it took Ephraim to make me really *face* that, because deep inside, I knew it all along.

"But that personal need for ... absolution overrode my good sense. I didn't want to think—*wasn't* thinking—about the dangers involved in what I wanted to do. Not really. *Graf* von Schröder and the subcommittee were completely right to reject our proposal for something this drastic"—she waved one hand at the panoramic view of the universe beyond the *Hildr*— "when our theoretical model of how child universes form was still so incomplete. I'm a lot more familiar with the mechanics of temporal travel now than I used to be, and from that vantage point, what we set out to do is pretty damn frightening, really."

He wondered if she saw the astonishment in his eyes. He'd expected many things from a conversation with her after all this time, but not an admission like that one.

"In this instance, we were lucky. It worked. But we are *not* going to spawn any additional universes, no matter how curious we might be. Not, at least, until the Dynasty has had time to completely separate from SysGov's universe and *our* scientific establishment can interface with *your* scientific establishment to figure out what the hell is going on. We have laws and procedures in place to prevent timeline branches from occurring, and so far, we've been one hundred percent successful."

"That—*all* of that—is wonderful to hear," Raibert said, after a moment, and smiled at her. "I was afraid your experiences here might have driven you deeper into a 'let's tinker with history' mindset. And, in a lot of ways, I wouldn't have blamed you one bit. I am honestly and deeply impressed with everything I've seen so far here. This Dynasty of yours really seems to have its act together."

"Thank you. I—".

Teodorà broke off as an alert blinked on her navigational chart. She glanced at the icons for a second, then grinned. "Ah! We're coming into view of it now."

Raibert faced the front display.

A bluish sliver gleamed in the distance, directly ahead. Teodorà spun the *Hildr* on its central axis as they closed, and the object ahead became a cobalt steel spike pointing down. Its size was difficult to discern without a frame of reference, but the twinkling lights of smaller craft hinted at truly immense proportions.

Teodorà pulled the omni-throttle back and applied retro-thrust, slowing their approach.

The object resolved into a massive three-sided spike with a triangular crown at its flattened top. What looked like a small city sprawled across the crown, but the sides were incredibly smooth, and the lower tip was almost painfully sharp. A few sections of the spike's flanks lay open and unfinished, revealing inner walls which were a collection of cubic segments, fitted neatly together. Drones buzzed around the mammoth construct, slotting additional cubes into place, and a stream of *Valkyries* arrived from the nearby replication center to unload additional cubes.

Once Raibert spotted the *Valkyries*, the true scale of the artifact became apparent.

Teodorà stood up.

"Allow me to present the *Tesseract*," she said with a wave of her arm. "Our first hyperforge complex."

"Eh. I've seen bigger space stations," he said without thinking.

Teodorà gave him a grouchy look.

"Well, I have," he defended, standing up beside her.

"Of *course* you have. So have I."

"How big *is* it?"

"Five point five kilometers on its long axis and one point four kilometers to each equidistant side of the triangle up top."

"That's a big friggin' spike."

"Yes, it is."

"Still, it's kind of small when you consider our Dyson Realization Project, or some of the terraforming operations, or the ACCI's Grand Sending laser, or—"

"Yes, I get your point," Teodorà interrupted. "Would it help if I told you over a *third* of the internal volume is exotic matter?"

"It . . . ?" Raibert trailed off and his eyes widened. "Oh."

"A bit more impressive now, don't you think?"

"I'll say. That might be more exotic matter than in all of SysGov."

"It probably is."

"So, what's a hyperforge?"

"A four-dimensional fixed-position temporal replicator," she replied, and Raibert blinked.

"Sorry. You lost me there," he said, and Teodorà chuckled. "Did you say it like that just to confuse me?"

"Maybe." She flashed a smile and pulled up a schematic of the station. "Actually, the process isn't too dissimilar from how we handle replication today, except that the *Tesseract* doesn't need to move through time. Instead, it pulls objects in the near-present *forward* to it."

"Oh, I see." Raibert nodded. "So instead of *Valkyries*

zipping back and forth in time, picking up and dropping off cargo, the *Tesseract* covers both ends of the process by itself."

"Precisely."

"The whole thing is one big replicator," Raibert said slowly, thinking out loud as he got a handle on the concept.

"More than one," Teodorà replied. "When finished, the *Tesseract* will be home to twenty-eight hyperforges. Twenty-seven baseline models that handle volumes of five thousand cubic meters each, and one huge one at three hundred seventy-five thousand cubic meters for bulk operation."

Raibert did some quick math in his head.

"That's actually not a whole lot of space," he said. "Not for a station this large. What goes into the rest of it?"

"Each hyperforge takes up about ten times the volume of what it replicates."

"Ah, okay. Never mind. Yeah, that could add up quickly."

"And don't forget the support systems. For example, a column of hot singularity reactors runs up the station's central support spine—a hundred and eight of them. And the outer prog-steel layer—which has an integrated exotic matter weave—is a hundred meters thick."

"What's that for?"

"Spatial and temporal stability. So the station doesn't rip itself apart."

"Probably a good idea to have it, then."

"Yeah, probably." She chuckled.

"How does it all work?" Raibert asked. "It looks like one giant impeller to me."

"In some ways it is. *Tesseract* does have an impeller, and it'll be able to time travel when finished, but that's mostly a side effect of other design necessities."

"What do you mean?"

"The station's impeller isn't optimized for time travel. We estimate its top speed to be no more than eight kilofactors."

"Pretty pokey, then. Can it go transdimensional?"

"No, and like I said, that's not its purpose," Teodorà pointed out. "Instead, the station's impeller generates a unique field geometric that allows each hyperforge to stretch backward into the past. Not very far, mind you—only a few microseconds—but enough for our purposes. The hyperforge then *pulls* the object we want to replicate from the near-present to the True Present. The hyperforge also performs a spatial offset, because the replicated goods can't occupy the same space as the originals."

"Ah! Then they are, in fact, four-dimensional machines."

"Right. And that's why we chose 'Tesseract' as the name, of course."

"Interesting." He nodded. "And certainly better than calling it the *Hypercube*."

"Much better!" she agreed with a laugh.

"What about exotic matter replication? Does it do that, as well?"

"Ah!" Her eyes lit and she tapped the schematic. "That's where the true beauty of this project comes into play. Exotic matter is a chokepoint for post-scarcity societies. Sure, we have an abundance of food, energy, and material goods, but anything that uses exotic matter—counter-grav units, hot singularity reactors, chronoton impellers, and so on—can be produced only in limited quantities.

"For now, that is! In SysGov, the printing process for exotic matter is time-consuming and resource intensive, and for us, replicating chronometrically active matter places a considerable strain on a DDT's impellers, often leading to impeller fatigue and eventual burnout. The *Tesseract* will solve all of that by replicating exotic matter easily and cheaply. Remember the really big hyperforge I mentioned? Well, it just so happens to be large enough to replicate whole impeller assemblies. Or even entire time machines!

"And that's just *one* example of what it can do. The Dynasty is poised to become the first society in recorded history—in *any* universe—to achieve not just regular post-scarcity, but *exotic* post-scarcity! In a manner of speaking, we're about to become the first *true* post-scarcity society *ever*!"

Teodorà beamed proudly, and Raibert found her optimism infectious.

But something nagged at the back of his mind. It took him a moment to track it down, recognize what it was. Then it came to him—a memory of a universe imploding on itself, and of the neighbor its death throes consumed.

The memory poured over him like a bucket of icy water, and as it did, the thought which had bothered him solidified into cold, clear focus.

The Gordian Division had found only five time-traveling societies. T3 and T4 were dead, and T1 and T2 had almost killed themselves with the Gordian Knot. That wasn't a good track record for time-traveling societies in general, and it left the Dynasty's

T5 as the only such society to not yet confront an existential threat.

That didn't mean the Dynasty had to—or that it would—of course, and Raibert truly hoped his gut was wrong here. But four out of five was bad odds, and the Dynasty was venturing fast and hard into theoretical territory with which SysGov had no experience.

What did Andover-Chen say? Something about patterns emerging when he studied our approach to the Dynasty. Are those patterns nothing more than a harmless by-product of their replication industry?

Or could they be a sign of something . . . more alarming?

"Teodorà."

She turned to him, a wide smile on her lips, but the joy drained away when she saw his face.

"What's wrong?" she asked with genuine concern.

"I'm sorry, but I need to return to *Kleio*. Would you mind turning us around?"

"Of course not, but . . ." She frowned, clearly disappointed by the sudden change of plans. "I was going to give you a tour of the station. The hyperforges are quite a sight to behold up close." She gave him a wistful smile. "You sure you don't want to see them while we're here?"

"Maybe tomorrow, after we meet with the council. I'm afraid there's something urgent I need to discuss with my team."

CHAPTER TWENTY-NINE

~~~~~~

Transtemporal Vehicle *Kleio*
Dynasty, 2980 CE

"I'M CONCERNED," RAIBERT SAID, PLACING THE TIPS of his fingers on the command table. He swept his gaze across the full team, now assembled on the *Kleio*'s bridge as the sun set outside.

"With good reason," Andover-Chen replied from his seat. He crossed his arms, and his expression was all business, without a trace of his usual smug confidence.

"We'll get to that in a moment," Raibert said. "But before that, does anyone think we're being fed a story here? Doc, you first."

"If this is a hoax, it's got to be the most ridiculously elaborate one in multiverse history," Benjamin said. "I had free access to every part of that museum, and Chairman Pepys answered every one of my questions candidly and without so much as a pause. In fact, later on, it got hard to get him to *stop* talking. The man's quite proud—rightfully—of his formative role in the society. He also handed over the diary he kept after the crash."

"Ooooh!" Elzbietá cooed. "Pepys wrote *another* diary? Did he include all the saucy bits?"

"I can't say yet, because it's five *million* words long. I handed the files over to Kleio for processing until I can take a look at them myself."

"Kleio?" Elzbietá asked.

"Yes, Agent. The diary includes detailed chronicles of Samuel Pepys's sexual exploits with the indigenous Byzantines."

"Not exactly what we're here to discuss," Raibert grumbled.

"Anyway"—Benjamin cleared his throat a bit pointedly—"I also had Kleio run a comparison between what my remote recorded, the historical record Doctor Beckett provided for SysGov—that one is far too big for any organic brain to even start dealing with now—and anything available in the public domain. Kleio?"

"My analysis of the data is ongoing as I collect more files from the Dynasty's infonet, but I have not identified any significant discrepancy."

"Have you found *any* contradictions?" Raibert asked.

"Yes, Agent. However, most can be categorized as genuine points of scholarly debate or fictional dramatizations. All the main points Chairman Pepys presented to Agent Schröder and those contained in Doctor Beckett's download are widely accepted by the populace as true."

"Good." Raibert leaned forward. "Ella?"

"Same story here. Hala was friendly and very forthcoming. She even let me see her room on the *Sigrun*."

"Why's that worth noting?" Raibert asked.

"Because it was such a mess even *I* was bothered by it."

"Somehow, I find that hard to believe," Benjamin said dryly.

"Point is, I had access to anything I wanted to see. I even poked around her room as a sort of test, but the highlight was the replication center I got to tour. She happily showed me every inch of the place. She *wanted* to impress me with it, and it really was impressive, though I'm not sure how I feel about using time travel like that."

"Don't worry," Andover-Chen said. "I'm pretty sure I have *my* feelings figured out about that."

"We'll get to you in a minute," Raibert said. "Thanks, Ella. Philo, you're up."

"I had a similar experience in Cornucopia's infostructure. I came across some restricted files, but most of their systems were wide open to me. Also"—the Viking raised his aviator visor—"I met Lucius."

"Oh, crap." Raibert grimaced. "Buddy, I'm sorry. I wouldn't have talked you into going if I'd known you'd run into him."

"No, no." Philo held up his hands. "It was fine. He and I actually got along."

"You *did*?" Raibert's mouth twisted as if he were sucking on a lemon.

"Yeah, I was as surprised as you are."

"But...it's *Lucius*."

"What can I say?" Philo shrugged. "People change."

"Not *that* much."

"Raibert," Benjamin said, "could it be you're a bit biased here?"

"No. The fact that I happen not to trust the biggest time-traveling ass-cave in history doesn't make me biased."

"If you say so."

"He do anything suspicious?" Raibert asked Philo.

"Not a thing. He even showed me some video from their latest project. Something called a 'hyperforge complex.'"

"That would be the *Tesseract*," Raibert filled in.

"Teodorà show you?" Philo asked.

"Yeah. And I forwarded everything to Andover-Chen as soon as I could."

"Is it my turn now?" Andover-Chen raised his eyebrows.

"Yeah, you're up." Raibert stepped back from the command table and flourished one hand at the scientist. "Take it away."

"First, a question for everyone." Andover-Chen conjured two chronometric charts with an open palm and deployed them over the table. "I've processed the data we've collected so far and I came up with these two views of the Dynasty's underlying resonance patterns. Can anyone tell me the difference?"

"How about we skip the guessing game?" Benjamin said. "Just tell us what you found."

"Please, indulge me."

Benjamin rolled his eyes.

"Hmmmm." Elzbietá leaned forward and squinted at one, then the other. "It's hard to tell. They're both *very* similar. Was Chart One's data from near a replication center?"

"Wrong. Anyone else?"

"Is Chart Two from before we crossed the outer

wall?" Benjamin offered, sounding like a man who wanted to get this over with and move on.

"Wrong again. Last chance."

"Come on," Raibert said. "Let's have it."

"Okay, are all of you ready for the truth?" Andover-Chen eyed each of them in turn. "Actually, it was a trick question. Only Chart One is from the Dynasty." He pointed at the deck. "From right here at Cornucopia Headquarters."

"Then what's Chart Two from?"

"*That*," Andover-Chen said, "is a highly processed image from T3."

The bridge went deathly silent, and the synthoid spread his arms.

"Guess what, people?" he said. "T3 used replication technology. Their universe showed the same resonance buildup as the Dynasty. And now they're all dead. Coincidence? I think not!"

"Well, fuck," Raibert breathed.

"Oh, it gets worse!" Andover-Chen declared a little too cheerfully. "T3 and T4 were close, remember? Parent-and-child close. And right now, SysGov and the Dynasty are even closer."

Raibert smacked his face, scraped his fingers downward, and let out a low, pained groan.

"They *just* branched off from us by reaching the True Present, but anything that happens to them *will* affect us," Andover-Chen continued, then swiped the charts aside. "People, we're in a lot of trouble here. If the Dynasty implodes like T3 did, SysGov dies with it."

"And the Dynasty is about to turn on their new super-mega-replicator." Raibert shook his head. "How does the replication lead to implosion?"

"I don't know yet," Andover-Chen confessed, backing off a tad. "But what I *do* know is that there are too many terrifying similarities between the data sets."

"Hold on a second here," Elzbietá said. "Yes, the two sets are similar, but we've performed replications in SysGov, too. That's what ART's been doing all along, after all. Does our universe show the same sort of resonance buildup?"

"Fortunately not," Andover-Chen said.

"Any idea why?"

"There are probably two reasons. One, ART preservation takes place on a much smaller scale, especially nowadays. And two, the original no longer exists as a whole in the True Present. Those same atoms are scattered every which way, so the copy has nothing to resonate with. Nothing concentrated, at least.

"But that's not true for the Dynasty. *Every* time they make a copy, the original is present nearby, and the two resonate with each other." He paused to tap a finger against his lips. "You know, that could be it. Replicate something enough times, and the resonance reaches such a tremendous amplitude that it actually tears a hole in the outer wall of the universe." He sat down and opened a chart. "I need to start modeling this."

"Andover-Chen," Raibert warned. "Now's not the time."

The synthoid physicist held up a hand, and a text window opened in front of Raibert's face. It read: I'M BUSY. SCIENCE IS HAPPENING. COME BACK LATER.

Raibert growled deep in his throat.

"He could be onto something," Benjamin said. "Remember when there were two of me in 2018, and the resonance scrambled my head?"

"Not forgetting that anytime soon." Elzbietá leaned over to stroke his forearm gently, and he smiled at her.

"Here's another question," Benjamin said. "Why hasn't SysGov—or the Admin, for that matter—been using this replication method? It sounds too tempting to pass up."

"To put it in the simplest possible terms," Philo said, "both of us know not to stick forks into power outlets. The Near Miss and the Yanluo Massacre mean both societies tend to approach new technology cautiously, and both of them happened before either of us had time travel."

"Good point," Benjamin said. "And the Dynasty never had an equivalent tech-based catastrophe, as far as we know."

"In SysGov's case," Philo began, "a lot of restrictions were placed on time travel almost immediately after it was invented in 2786. Concerns about citizen privacy and the nature of the new technology were raised, and the restrictions were codified into law in 2790. That year forms a legal barrier. Traveling to any date before it became the purview of ART, which had little interest in near-present events. Any other uses, such as temporal search warrants—which are all but impossible to obtain—fell under SysPol's jurisdiction. Of course, a lot of that changed when the Gordian Division was formed."

"As for the Admin," Raibert added, "they outlaw *any* tech that makes them the least bit nervous."

"I'm beginning to think they might be onto something there," Benjamin said.

"And here's another thought," Philo offered. "We've had time travel longer than the Admin, and we've only had it about two hundred years. There is no inherent reason why it couldn't have been discovered earlier than that in other universes. Other universes that diverged from ours at even earlier points than the Dynasty did. What if it was? What if SysGov and the Admin represent a statistical anomaly? What if what happened to T3, and seems to be in the process of happening to the Dynasty, is the *normal* outcome of developing this technology?"

"That, Philo, is a particularly nasty thought. Thank you *so* much for sharing," Raibert said, then glared at Andover-Chen as he sat statue-still while equations and graphs flickered in front of him. He waved a hand in front of the physicist's eyes, but Andover-Chen didn't react.

"So how do we approach the Dynasty with this news?" Benjamin asked.

"Very, very carefully," Raibert said. "Kleio?"

"Yes, Agent?"

"Ask Teodorà and Samuel if we can meet with them in private. Tell them—" He paused and bowed his head in thought. "Tell them we need to have a serious talk about the *Tesseract*."

❖   ❖   ❖

"You want us to do *what*?" Teodorà snapped, planting her fists on her hips. She and Pepys had invited Raibert to a small conference room, and he'd brought Andover-Chen along for backup.

"Hold on now." Raibert held up a cautioning hand. "We're not telling you to do anything."

Andover-Chen cleared his throat noisily, and Raibert shot him a quelling glance, then turned back to Teodorà.

"As I said, we're just worried. That can happen when you've flown through one universe while it's being sucked into another, like we have."

"But to halt the *Tesseract*'s construction? Postpone or even cancel what's going to be the crown jewel of our time travel program?"

"Over a fifth of our replication facilities have been funneling resources into the station," Pepys said. "There's a lot of momentum behind a project of this scale. You can't stop and restart something like that without incurring massive disruptions."

"I'm afraid we're not talking about just the *Tesseract*," Andover-Chen pointed out. "In my opinion, *all* replication activities should be halted until we have a better, more definitive handle on why T3 imploded."

"There's no *way* we can do that," Teodorà protested. "Replication is the industrial engine behind our society. We don't have the conventional production facilities to sustain ourselves without it. The entire Dynasty would come to a crashing stop!"

"Look, let's all take a step back for a second," Raibert urged. "Everyone take a deep, calming breath."

"Raibert, I—" Teodorà began.

"Come on, everyone. I don't care if we're all synthoids. Breathe it in."

Teodorà rolled her eyes, but obliged by sucking in an exaggerated breath and holding it with her cheeks puffed out. The others followed her example.

"Now let it all out."

The room exhaled in unison.

"Okay. Good. Does everyone feel better?"

"Not really," Andover-Chen confessed.

Raibert made a sharp zipping motion across his lips.

"Just being honest here," the physicist added.

"Raibert," Teodorà put a hand to her forehead, "do you and Andover-Chen realize what you're asking us to do? Even if we weren't skeptical as hell, I can't just flip a switch and stop the industrial wheels of an entire society. I answer to the Council of Ministers, and I can tell you *they'll* be even less receptive than I am."

"Look, my team and I really don't like what the data is telling us. Especially after what we've seen here, today," Raibert said. "I'm not too keen on how we got here, but I'll be the first to admit you two have done a great job. You set out to give those who died from the plague a second chance, and by all accounts you achieved that. We're just...not sure how to resolve certain similarities between T3 and the Dynasty."

"Our models say replication is completely safe," Teodorà pointed out.

"And mine says it's not," Andover-Chen countered.

"Yes," she shot back, "*your* model. One which you cobbled together in an afternoon, compared to the models—the *multiple* models—our entire scientific establishment has put together over the course of *decades* with direct access to every aspect of our technology."

"Maybe so"—Andover-Chen shrugged, unfazed—"but my model fits the observed data."

"Surely you've seen the resonance buildup," Raibert said.

"Of course we have," Teodorà said. "It's a well-documented side effect of the replication process. But it's nothing more than background noise. The True Present is the most stable point of an entire universe. A little resonance is nothing to it."

"Stable," Andover-Chen clarified, "is not the same thing as invulnerable."

"We've never branched the timeline," Pepys said. "And we have decades of operational history and mountains of records from monitors in the transverse that all aligned perfectly with Eriksen's Unified Equations. There's never been a reason to doubt them."

Andover-Chen made a throat-clearing noise and they all looked at him.

"Sounds awfully similar to SysGov's Theory of Everything to me," he observed. "And we all know how *that* theory died."

"That's unfair," Teodorà said. "We've taken time travel safety and the sanctity of the timeline very seriously."

"Of course you have. And all I'm asking is that you *continue* to take it seriously," Raibert stressed. "Take the data we have from T3. Rerun your models. Send your own scouts out. Collect as much data as you want. Do whatever it takes to satisfy your questions, but don't just dismiss what we're scared of here."

"I'm not dismissing your concerns," Teodorà said. "That doesn't change the fact that I think you're wrong."

"And what a wonderful surprise that would be." Raibert elbowed Andover-Chen. "Right?"

"Indeed," Andover-Chen agreed. He even cracked a smile. "I think my ego could take the hit in stride if it turns out I'm wrong and both our universes are safe."

"See?" Raibert said. "We're *perfectly* happy being wrong here. In fact, we *want* to be wrong. But until we're all sure there's no danger, all of us need to take this seriously. And that starts with Cornucopia taking a fresh, honest look at the data."

He held out his hand, and a file transfer request

materialized above his palm, holding Andover-Chen's latest model and all the raw T3 chronometric records.

Teodorà looked at the virtual icon doubtfully. Pepys placed a hand on her arm and gave it a gentle squeeze. Finally, she sighed, then nodded slowly.

"You're right, of course." She reached out and copied the files to her synthoid. "I might think this is nonsense, but I'm not about to ignore you if there's even the remotest chance you're right."

"Thank you," Raibert said in a voice of soft sincerity. "That's all I ask."

Teodorà opened the file list and scrolled through it.

"Samuel, you in the mood to take a crack at this tonight?" she asked. "We can at least get things organized for when Saenz and the rest of the Research Division show up in the morning."

"Certainly." Pepys flashed her a half smile. "It's been a while since we pulled an all-nighter together."

CHAPTER THIRTY

~~~~~

Cornucopia Headquarters
Dynasty, 2980 CE

"WHAT DO YOU THINK?" PEPYS ASKED, HOURS LATER.

"Well..." Teodorà put her elbows on her desk and rested her face in her hands, pushing her cheeks up.

She sat behind the oval frosted-glass desk in her office. Its wide surface was littered with chronometric charts and running models, piled on top of one another. The framed picture hung on the wall directly behind her chair and a trio of lush potted plants were the office's only physical accents. She'd digitized everything else long ago; a lifetime like hers led to an unwieldy accumulation of knickknacks, and she'd culled almost the entire collection a century ago.

The picture on the wall showed Teodorà, Pepys, Belisarius, Justinian, Ephraim, Theodora, and Antonina together in Constantinople, seated around an outside dining table under a colorful sun canopy about a century after their arrival. Lucius had surprised them by swinging a remote around to capture all of them laughing heartily together.

She glanced out the window along one side of her office on the fiftieth floor, near the top of the headquarters. Stars and Constantinople's skyline twinkled against the black velvet of the night sky, and one of the night shift *Valkyries* came in for a landing. *Valkyrie* operations ran around the clock, though she'd have to wait till morning for the senior staff to arrive.

"I think I'm getting nervous," she said at last.

"And yet, every time I stuff the data into Eriksen's equations," Pepys said, "it comes out clean."

"I know, but try as I might, I can't punch any holes in Andover-Chen's model, either."

"They can't both be true," Pepys said reasonably, sitting on the edge of the desk.

"Do you think there's a problem with the T3 data?" Teodorà asked.

"You mean is it doctored in some way?"

"I suppose we can't rule out anything, but I was leaning toward an instrumentation problem on their end, not any sort of deliberate falsification."

"That should be easy enough to verify," Samuel said. "They gave us T3's transdimensional coordinates, so we could have Saenz organize a group of *Valkyries* to explore what's left of it."

"Good idea. Add that to the list."

Samuel jotted down the item on one of his virtual windows. Their chief research director was going to have quite a surprise when he came into work tomorrow. Or, rather—Teodorà checked the clock—*today*. It was well past midnight, she realized.

"My, how time flies when you're having *fun*," she growled.

"You thinking we should wait for reinforcements?"

"No, let's keep at it." She sat up. "There's probably more we can do tonight to give Saenz and his team a running start."

"I'm not sure there is. We've exhausted all of Eriksen's models and keep coming to the same result. There's simply no danger to be found in the resonance buildup."

"Then maybe we should expand our search."

"What do you mean?" Pepys asked.

"I'm not sure. Just a hunch, really." Teodorà eyed one of Andover-Chen's apocalyptic projections floating in front of her nose. "Eriksen's Unified Equations tell us one story, and Andover-Chen's model tells another. Maybe something in Siv's research notes can shed a little light on this."

"Some correlation between Andover-Chen's model and her own rejected lines of thinking?" he suggested.

"Yeah, that. It's worth a look. At the very least, it might tell us how she came to a different conclusion."

"I'll put together a search. This shouldn't take long." He swiped a section of table clear of charts to open a new window, and she looked up at him with a smile.

"You know, it's been a while since we did this," she said.

"Stayed up all night trying to crack a problem?" he asked, and she nodded.

"It reminds me of Cornucopia's early days," she said.

"It's nice, yes. But personally, I prefer other nocturnal activities with you."

She knuckled him in the arm and laughed.

The search window chimed.

"Ah. Match found," Pepys said.

"And?"

"And...there *is* a rejected model in her private notes that bears a striking resemblance to Andover-Chen's model."

"Really?" Teodorà leaned back. "Now *that's* interesting."

"Yes," Pepys said slowly, "but it's not the most remarkable part."

"What do you mean?"

"This rejected model"—he turned to her—"is from December 12, 2946."

"The day before she died?" Teodorà's face tightened.

"Exactly," Samuel said, and she shook her head.

"So she rejects a model like Andover-Chen's one day, and then dies in a freak accident the next?"

"That's what it says."

"That...makes me uncomfortable."

"It could be a rather bizarre coincidence."

"Does this rejected model come to Andover-Chen's conclusion?"

"Not sure. I'll run it."

Pepys opened a new simulation instance and began copying in the input parameters.

Lucius Gwon's avatar flashed into existence in Teodorà's office.

"Hey, you two," he said with a smile.

"Hey, Lucius." Teodorà sat up a little higher so she could see him over all the virtual displays. "Haven't seen you in a while. What brings you here?"

"Nothing in particular." He gazed across the cluttered desk. "The infostructure's been straining to keep up with all this math, so I thought I'd stop by and see why you two were burning the midnight oil."

"We didn't impact your VR, did we?" Pepys asked.

"Maybe a little." Lucius rounded the desk, eyeing the virtual mass with a wry smile. "Oh, what's all this?"

"Models that may or may not predict the end of our universe," Teodorà said as lightly as she could.

"Oh?"

"Raibert's team hit us with one hell of a stinker today," she continued. "You remember Andover and Chen?"

Lucius's avatar paused as his connectome retrieved old, archived memories.

"Oh, *those* two clowns!" he said brightly after a moment. "Yeah, I remember them."

"Well, those 'clowns' integrated and now *he* works for the Gordian Division. He thinks our replication industry is going to destroy us all."

"Seriously?" Lucius shook his head. "How'd he reach *that* conclusion?"

"He says the replication resonance is building up and could bust through the outer wall."

"Oh, please. Eriksen's equations say that can't happen."

"I know. But we're going to take a serious look at their claims, regardless."

"I'm sorry, but they're flat-out wrong," Lucius said dismissively. "Her Unified Equations are airtight. They've withstood decades of constant scrutiny."

"But there's an interesting wrinkle we just found," Pepys said. "One of her old, rejected models shares a lot with Andover-Chen's work."

"One of her *rejected* models?" Lucius shook his head. "Don't you think you're reaching a bit here?"

"Maybe," Teodorà said. "But the price for being wrong is too high. We have no choice but to take this seriously."

"Hey, I'm not saying you shouldn't," Lucius said with a shrug. "Just don't be surprised when none of this amounts to anything."

"Results are up," Pepys said.

"And?" Teodorà asked. She sat forward, and Pepys opened the report and shifted it over for both of them to see.

"That," Teodorà said, "looks a lot like Andover-Chen's results."

"It does," Pepys agreed. "Not exactly the same, but similar where it counts. *Alarmingly* similar."

"Then we know for a fact that Eriksen at least *considered* a model like his," Teodorà said. "One that predicts the destruction of our universe."

"Yes," Pepys agreed quietly, stepping back.

"This is another lead Saenz can follow up on," Teodorà said.

"A very *solid* lead, I think." Pepys nodded. "We should have him reevaluate all of Eriksen's old models."

"Agreed," Teodorà said, and Pepys reached for his list—

Every virtual display in the room suddenly vanished...except for Lucius's avatar. The lights turned off, and the door locked. The dim haze of city nightlight outlined the contents of Teodorà's darkened office.

"What the hell?" she breathed angrily. "We didn't crash the office infosystem, did we?"

"I don't...think so?" Pepys said.

Teodorà tried to connect, but every pathway was dead, except for her interface with Lucius.

"Lucius, do you have any idea what's going on?" She rose from her chair and faced him.

That's when she saw it. It was a smirk, not too different from the many smiles she'd seen on his face, but with a sinister, malevolent edge he'd never shown her. She looked at it, and a slow, cold realization flowed through her like a stream of ice melt from a glacier.

He knew exactly what was going on.

"What's the meaning of this?" she demanded.

"I'd say I'm sorry," Lucius replied in a matter-of-fact tone. "But that would be a lie."

His avatar vanished.

"Lucius!" she shouted.

Nothing responded. The room was perfectly silent, physically and virtually.

"What's he doing?" Pepys's taut voice asked at last.

"I don't know, but—"

A heavy, mechanical thud echoed from somewhere outside her office. She'd never heard the sound before.

"What was that?" she asked quietly.

"It sounded like a security cube deploying," Samuel whispered back, and the two of them exchanged a worried look.

"I don't like this," she said.

"Me neither. We need to find somewhere we can connect. Help me with the door."

Teodorà hurried around her desk and met Pepys at the sealed prog-steel shutter. Without power, the programmable-steel was locked in its current shape. She placed her hands on one half of the smooth panel and tried to pull it to the side, but her fingers slid across it.

"No good," she said. "I can't get a grip on it."

"Back away from it."

She stepped aside, and Pepys backpedaled all the way across the office then snarled and charged. He exploded forward with powerful, synthoid strides and smashed his shoulder into the door like a battering ram. The panels buckled, splitting open down the center seam. White light spilled in through the crack, and Samuel slipped his fingers into one side of the seam. Teodorà jammed her own fingers into the other side, and together they pulled the door open wide enough for them to squeeze through, one at a time.

"Let me go first," he whispered.

"After you," she agreed with a nervous smile.

He turned sideways, stuck one leg through the opening, and forced his way through. Once free, he offered a hand to Teodorà and helped her across, though her slender body slipped through much more easily.

The wide, arched hallway connected to many of the executive offices, including Pepys's. He jogged over to his door.

"Finally! I have a connection."

He commanded the door to open, and its panels split apart. They started forward...then froze.

The security cube floating inside Pepys's office was as tall as his torso and its smooth surface was a blank pearly white.

"Deactivate!" Teodorà snapped, simultaneously transmitting a stand-down order to the drone.

It ignored her order and floated into the hallway.

Pepys backed slowly, staying between it and Teodorà.

"Samuel! Get away from it!"

The front of the cube split open four ways, revealing a ruby eye. Cornucopia's security drones might be slow, but they were incredibly durable and tenacious when unleashed. They were also equipped with numerous nonlethal deterrents that could morph up to their programmable surfaces.

And they also had one *lethal* deterrent...even to a synthoid.

The ruby eye lit, and a laser beam blazed into Pepys's face. He recognized the threat an instant before it fired and dove to the side. The laser charred half his face and burned his hair to ash before he dodged, and then the beam drilled a fiery orange hole into the wall behind him.

"*Samuel!*" Teodorà cried.

"Run!" he shouted, picking himself up.

She turned, but two security partitions shot up from the floor. They smacked against the ceiling, cutting off the hallway outside their two offices as red, virtual DANGER marquees sprang alight. She spun around, desperate for a way to evade the cube, but only two avenues led out of this section of hallway: her office door, and Pepys's.

And the cube floated directly in front of Pepys's.

It faced them, and she heard the quiet whine as its capacitors charged for another shot.

"Get out of here!" Pepys's voice was cracked and gurgling, and Teodorà realized his synthoid's vocal cords had been damaged.

"There's nowhere to go!"

The cube turned slightly and fired on her, but the tiny delay as it turned gave Pepys time. He threw himself between them, and the beam stabbed into his shoulder. His clothes caught fire and the synthetic flesh underneath crisped and bubbled away. Mechanisms underneath went incandescent, then liquefied, as the beam drilled into and through his shoulder joint.

His arm spiraled off, trailing globs of molten alloy, and he staggered forward into her arms.

"Run!" he shouted, smoke pouring out of his mouth, and the cube glided silently toward them.

"There's nowhere to run *to*!"

"Then get out of its way!"

He shoved her through the door to her office, and she tripped over the warped panels. She fell to the floor inside and slid across it, and Pepys leapt in after her just as the cube fired again. This time, the beam only grazed his leg, and he grabbed her wrist and pulled her upright.

"What now?" she asked.

"I'm thinking!"

He limped away from the door. Flames spread across the clothes around his shoulder and lower leg to cast flickering light and shadows across the darkened walls. Then the room lit up with power again.

The damaged door juddered aside to allow a clear shot for the cube. It slid through the doorway, and its red eye fixed on Teodorà.

"Samuel?" She backed away, and the eye tracked her. "What do we do?!"

He picked the glass top off her desk with one hand and flung it at the cube. Frosted glass shattered against its armored skin. The shards tinkled to the ground. And the cube remained motionless, its laser almost charged.

"You'll have to jump!" he shouted.

"But we're fifty stories up!"

"It's your only chance!"

His damaged voice was grating, mechanical, not at all like the one she'd come to know so well over the centuries. She shook her head mutely, knowing what had to happen, and he closed his eyes for a moment.

Then he charged the cube.

The laser blasted into his face again, dissolving one side of his head, leaving a glowing cross-section behind.

"Run!" he cried, tackling the cube with all the force his synthoid body could muster. The drone anchored itself with its counter-grav field, and his good shoulder crunched against its armor. His remaining arm fell limp.

"Ruuun, Teo—!"

The cube angled its beam down. It melted the rest of his head and burned a path down through his neck, liquefying the synthoid's internal systems.

A smoking, burning heap slid off the cube and collapsed to the floor, molten metal bubbling out of the synthetic husk.

"Damn you, Lucius!" Teodorà screamed, vision blurred as her synthoid's systems responded to her emotions and tears filled her eyes.

The cube floated forward over Samuel Pepys's corpse, its laser charging once more.

Teodorà dashed over to the window, smashed a fist through it, and raked her arm across to clear the jagged splinters. A strong night wind blew in through the opening, whipping her long hair, and she looked down desperately.

Support pylons extended from the floors below and angled upward until they sprouted into the DDT landing pads. Both of the nearer pads were empty, but one of the pylons was closer to this window than the other, and the counter-grav tubes inside the pylons were wide enough to ferry cargo and personnel to and from the time machines.

Could she leap to *that*?

It was still ten stories down. But ten was better than fifty.

She grabbed the windowsill and flipped her legs through the window. She hung there for a moment, face pressed against the outer stonework while she maintained her grip on the sill.

The cube charged its laser and fired. The beam drilled a hole through the window frame. It also clipped the fingers of her right hand, and she kicked off the wall and gave herself to the wind, taking advantage of the laser's charging time and praying it would be long enough. She cried out as the wind took her, and she plummeted through the cold night air.

The pylon rushed up to meet her, and she smashed into it, denting its roof. Damage alerts from both legs and her left hand flared in her virtual vision, but she could still move.

She picked herself up and looked around for an access port into the pylon.

The cube smashed through the wall of her office in a spray of white stone. It hovered high above her and tilted its body down, aiming its laser.

"No time!"

She raced down the gently sloping pylon back to headquarters, picked a window near the pylon's foundation, and leapt. The laser raked a glowing line over the pylon as she crashed through yet another window and rolled across the floor.

A loud, mechanical clank echoed from somewhere nearby, and Teodorà knew a second security cube had just been deployed. She dragged herself off the floor and ran in the opposite direction.

She wanted to cry out in equal parts grief and rage, but first she needed to *survive*. She still couldn't connect to the infostructure, and given what she'd just been through, she didn't know if it would have been a good idea even if she could.

A woman screamed from behind her, and she whirled around. She couldn't see who it was or what had happened, but it came from the direction of the second cube. Was she not the only one under attack?

"Damn you, Lucius!" she seethed through clenched teeth. "What the *hell* have you done?"

Was he killing indiscriminately now? And *why*? They'd been looking at *math* for God's sake!

A distant explosion rocked the building, and questions raced through her mind. What was going on? Who could she trust? Too many questions, too fast, and she had precious little time to think.

But she had to act. Whatever was going on, whoever was involved, she would *not* let this stand!

And so she activated a frequency she hadn't used in over two thousand years, pumped the broadcast power of her body's transceiver up to maximum, and called out to the one person she knew—with total certainty—she could trust.

❖   ❖   ❖

"What's this about weapons fire?" Raibert snapped, sprinting onto the bridge in his underwear.

"Here, look!" Philo appeared on the opposite side of the command table and conjured a schematic of Cornucopia Headquarters. Flashpoints of activity glowed red throughout the building.

"Are they under *attack*?" Raibert blurted.

"I have no idea."

A brief fan of red laser light flickered out through windows near their platform, playing a spasmodic light show across distant clouds. Raibert opened the live camera feed, and the visual keyed in on a trio of white cube-shaped drones moving through the outer corridor.

"Can you raise Teodorà or Samuel?" he demanded.

"All Dynasty links are blocking our access. All we have right now are our own scopes and cameras."

"You mean they just cut us off?"

"Or someone cut us off *from* them," Philo said.

"But why would anyone do *that*?"

An orange fireball blew through the top of a *Valkyrie* only a few platforms away, and the shock wave rattled the *Kleio* so hard Raibert had to grab the command table's railing. A second explosion cracked the Dynasty time machine in two, and one of its impellers tumbled off the side of the platform, then crashed into the grassy parkland below.

"Whoa!" Raibert exclaimed.

"Was that an *explosion*?" Elzbietá cried as she rushed onto the bridge in flannel pajamas with Benjamin a few strides behind her.

"Yes, it was! Ella, get us clear of this mess!"

"You got it!" Elzbietá summoned the flight controls and yanked the omni-throttle up. The *Kleio* surged a hundred meters into the air, then stopped and hovered. "What now?"

"I don't know!" Raibert threw up his hands. "I have no idea what's going on here!"

"Incoming transmission for Agent Kaminski," Kleio said calmly.

"Well, let's hear it!" he snapped.

A comm window opened, and Raibert's eyes widened as he recognized the sender's all-too-familiar address.

"Raibert, can you hear me?"

"Teodorà? What's hap—"

"I'm in trouble and I need your help! The security systems are trying to kill me!"

"I've got her location," Elzbietá reported.

"Raibert, get me out of here! *Please!*"

"Got it. We're on our way." He pointed to Elzbietá.

"Swinging us around." She eased her controls to the right.

"Raibert, are you sure about this?" Benjamin asked urgently. "We don't know what we're getting ourselves into."

"Doesn't matter." Raibert shook his head once, hard. "Look, I don't have a clue what's going on, but I don't need one. Someone's calling for help, and we have the power to help. So that's what we're going to do!"

The *Kleio* slewed partially around headquarters, then dipped down until it was almost level with the landing pads. The TTV's scopes extrapolated a translucent view of the interior with Teodorà's synthoid as a glowing blue humanoid racing away from a pair of large, red, cubical drones.

"The drones are charging weapons!" Philo said.

"Take 'em out!"

Philo's avatar vanished and the *Kleio*'s weapons came online. A prog-steel blister split open, unsheathing one of their twelve-millimeter Gatling guns. The weapon's seven barrels swiveled out.

A hurricane of metal and micro-explosions pulverized the outer stone wall, and scraps of stone and glass rained against the two robots. One of the drones turned, and a laser licked across the *Kleio*'s armor. It left a dull, reddish scar that cooled quickly and self-healed, and in the same moment the second cube fired on Teodorà, searing a hole through a hallway corner she'd just ducked behind.

Twelve-millimeter rounds savaged both machines, blasting ugly divots in their armor, but the cubes continued their advance down the hall, internal systems unscathed by the attack.

"Philo!"

"If at first you don't succeed!"

The blister for one of the Kleio's forty-five-millimeter Gatling guns moved dynamically across the TTV's surface. It split open, and a torrent of fire and metal slashed into both cubes.

This time, armor splintered like eggshell, and explosions racked the delicate systems underneath. After three seconds of continuous fire, the cubes—and a large part of the hallway—had ceased to exist. The strong night wind blew the smoke aside to reveal a gaping wound in the building's side, three stories tall and twice as wide.

"Teodorà!" Raibert said. "We're coming in to pick you up."

"I see you!" Her outline left cover and ran toward the building's exterior.

"Ella?"

"Got it." She clicked her throttle to a finer control setting and pressed it forward. "And there's already an opening for me. Thanks, Philo!"

"I do what I can," the Viking replied.

Elzbietá brought the *Kleio*'s nose almost into contact with headquarters, and Benjamin opened the cargo bay and began to extrude the boarding ramp. Teodorà dashed through the hallway's rubble, smoke and embers billowing about her as the wind whipped at her dress. Her face was a grim mask smeared with soot.

And that was when the *Sigrun* lifted off its platform and swung around to face the *Kleio*.

"What's it doing?" Raibert asked.

The *Sigrun*'s graviton thrusters powered up and it flashed forward.

"Shit!" Elzbietá jerked the throttle back, but the distance was too short and the *Sigrun* too fast.

The DDT slammed into the *Kleio*'s side at a right angle, and its sharp, wedge-shaped nose stabbed deep into the TTV's hull with a thunderous, earsplitting crash. The bridge lights flickered as the impact shoved the *Kleio* to the side and threw Benjamin and Elzbietá to the floor while Raibert clung to the command table railing and—somehow—stayed upright.

"Thruster Three and Cannon Two off-line!" Philo reported. "Port armor breached!"

Metal shrieked as the *Sigrun* fired its thrusters in reverse and began to pull its warped nose free.

"Enough of this crap!" Raibert shouted, bending and hauling the others back to their feet. "Show 'em who they're messing with, Philo!"

Three blisters flowed dynamically across the *Kleio*'s hull and sprung open. Both twelve-millimeter and the remaining forty-five-millimeter guns swung out and opened fire. Gunfire cut into the *Sigrun* from both sides, forming a deadly triangle of tracers, and its hull wilted under the onslaught. A thruster blew apart in a brilliant flash, and the explosions ripped the starboard impeller free of its hull.

The *Sigrun* rotated on its central axis, twisting itself like a dagger in the *Kleio*'s side. That motion allowed it to finally pull free, but Philo kept their guns trained on it, and its remaining thrusters sputtered and failed. The entire craft spun away, trailing smoke and bright blue sparks before it landed with a loud *whoomp* in the middle of a nearby park.

"Teodorà?" Raibert called urgently. "Are you all right?"

"I am, but I had to keep moving. I'm pretty far from where you tried to pick me up."

"We'll blast another hole for you," he promised, checking her position on the map.

"Don't bother. I think I can reach *Hildr*. Just watch my back!"

"You've got it!" Raibert agreed, and turned to his team. "You heard the lady, people. Let's plow the road for her!"

"Two drones sweeping in behind," Benjamin said.

"I see them." Elzbietá raised the ship and swung them around for a better angle. "Philo?"

"Got them!"

Gatling fire savaged the building's exterior, blasting apart stone and glass. The drones' return fire left red welts on the *Kleio*'s nose armor, but the deluge of cannon fire tore them apart before they could recharge their lasers.

Teodorà raced up the pylon to the *Hildr*'s landing pad. She reached it and sprinted up the prototype DDT's ramp.

"Thanks, I'm in!" she announced over the comm. "Systems powering up!"

"More drones inbound!" Benjamin warned.

Elzbietá lowered the *Kleio* to block line-of-sight to the *Hildr* with the TTV's undamaged flank, and Philo moved all their defensive weapons to that side. A trio of cubes smashed their way into the open, and Philo hosed them down.

Their broken shells fell away to litter the grounds below.

"Numerous aircraft incoming!" Elzbietá said. "I don't know what they are, but they're big and fast, and they're moving like they mean business."

"Teodorà, we're running out of time!" Raibert said.

"Almost got it!"

Another cube peeked into the open, and Philo blew it apart.

"Thrusters and impellers online!" Teodorà announced.

The *Hildr* lifted off the pad, then shot up and away from the building.

"Phasing out!"

The *Valkyrie* vanished in a shimmer of distorted reality just as a laser blasted down from the night sky. This one was far more powerful than anything the cubes mounted, and it cut a ragged, glowing gash into the *Kleio*'s side.

"Starboard armor breached!" Philo said. "Thruster Two damaged!"

"Get us the hell out of here, Ella!" Raibert barked.

"Phasing us out . . . *now!*"

CHAPTER THIRTY-ONE

~~~∞∞∞~~~

Cornucopia Headquarters
Dynasty, 2980 CE

LUCIUS GWON WAITED PATIENTLY AS CHIEF QUAESITOR
Simon Vlastos went to one knee in the rubble. Vlastos's
face was tight with the agonizing comprehension of
whose body lay before him. Quaesitor drones and
officers had already sifted through the remains of the
Honored Elders' offices, but he'd come to personally
review the crime scene before he and Lucius reported
to the Council of Ministers.

Lucius didn't mind the delay, and he supposed it was
inevitable, given who died.

Or rather, whom he'd killed.

"Thank you for coming, Simon," he said. "I'm glad
it's you taking charge of the investigation."

Lucius meant every word of that, too, although not
for the reasons one might have assumed. Decades ago,
he'd seen the potential in a young, up-and-coming
quaesitor named Simon Vlastos, and he'd accelerated
the man's career by putting whispers in all the right

ears. More importantly, he'd made certain that Vlastos eventually "discovered" how much he'd gained thanks to the favor of an Honored Elder, and Lucius had capitalized on the young man's gratitude by taking a more active role in his career. Vlastos had viewed him as a mentor, and eventually, as a friend.

Lucius had done nothing to dispel the illusion of friendship, despite the fact—or perhaps, especially *because* of the fact—that Vlastos was no more to him than a tool. One of many he'd cultivated throughout the Dynasty. Teodorà and Pepys had been content to play small roles in government in recent centuries, but whatever appearance he might have presented, Lucius had worked meticulously against this day. His webs were subtle, carefully cloaked in friendship and the encouragement of talent. But they were also everywhere. He might not have exercised overt power, but he'd always been able to tug at the appropriate string whenever the need arose.

Like now.

"How could I not see to this personally?" Vlastos's soft voice was barely audible over the wind whistling through the broken window as he gazed down at the body. The sun peeked over the horizon, turning the sky's clouded underbelly pink. "How many others?"

"Thirty-seven dead, six wounded," Lucius replied sadly. "Not including—" His avatar gestured to the melted-down synthoid at their feet.

"Lucius, I'm so sorry." The chief quaesitor shook his head. "I can't believe what I'm seeing. Why would they *do* something like this?"

"I . . . I don't know." Lucius sighed heavily.

"I'm sorry for your loss." Vlastos rose and smoothed

out his dark gray uniform. "I barely knew Elder Pepys. Just spoke to him a few times at state functions. But this is still like a hammer blow to the gut. I can't even imagine what it must be like for you."

"He was a good man." Lucius looked down at the corpse. "And a good friend. He deserved better."

"That he did." Vlastos's face hardened, and he straightened his spine. "On that note, shall we get down to business?"

"Yes, of course."

"Let's step outside. The coroners still need to..."

"No, I understand." Lucius took one last look at Pepys's half-melted husk. He paused for dramatic effect, then relocated his avatar to the chief quaesitor's side.

"I still don't know what we're going to tell the council." Vlastos rubbed the sleep from his eyes. "Have any thoughts or insights there?"

"One, actually." Lucius looked at the quaesitor and allowed an expression of grim determination to wipe the grief from his face. "I don't know *why* they attacked us, but I have a pretty good idea *how*."

"How sounds like a good place to start." Vlastos's tone was just as grim as Lucius's expression.

"The root cause of the drone attacks seems painfully obvious," Lucius said. "Their AC, Philosophus, was in our systems for a considerable time. He must have littered the infostructure with all manner of invasive code. In fact, I was almost killed by a viral bomb when the attack started."

"Sounds like you're lucky to be alive."

"Lucky to have been on guard. He and I had a few run-ins back in SysGov, so his presence here put me on edge."

"What kind of run-ins?"

"Let's just say this isn't the first hacking job he's pulled. He once thought of himself as a gentleman thief, in it only for the thrill of the heist. But"—Lucius eyed the devastated office darkly—"he's clearly branched out since then."

"A gentleman thief," Simon echoed, shaking his head in disgust. "Were his attacks the reason all the surveillance records have been wiped?"

"Indirectly. Actually, I'm responsible for that," Lucius admitted with a frown. "It was an unfortunate side effect, I'm afraid. After I was nearly killed, I initiated a systematic purge of all our infosystems, restoring them to default, sector by sector."

"Damn. That's a shame."

"I'm sure you would've preferred access to those records," Lucius bristled. "But in the heat of the moment, I had to do whatever was necessary to survive any additional traps he might have left behind. For that matter, if they would have destroyed *me*, they would have destroyed any other abstracted connectome who encountered them! And my action *did* bring the drones back under control."

"Sorry. I didn't mean it like that. I'd rather have you here than all the records in the world."

"It's all right." Lucius smiled without humor. "And that makes two of us."

"Was this Philosophus also responsible for corrupting the *Hildr*'s control systems?"

"Not as far as I can tell. His connectome never ventured into any of our DDTs to the best of my knowledge. That task likely fell to Raibert Kaminski. I suspect he planted the corrupting code into *Hildr*'s systems while he and the chairwoman were touring the *Tesseract*, although Philosophus likely authored the code."

"Which then allowed SysGov to kidnap her."

"That's right. From what little I observed during the attack, they were trying to force her onto their ship. When that failed, they fell back on corralling her into the *Hildr*."

"Where the code planted earlier let them trap her on the ship and take her away."

"That's what I believe happened, at least."

"It's as good a guess as any right now, I suppose." Vlastos huffed out a frustrated breath. "What a goddammed mess." He massaged his brow. "Why would they kidnap her but kill Pepys and try to kill you?"

"I really can't say, although I fear kidnapping Teodorà was only the beginning."

"The beginning?" Vlastos looked up. "Of what?"

"Who can say?" Lucius shrugged. "Invasion, perhaps? Or even a war of annihilation?"

"Surely not!" Vlastos gasped.

"You say that, and yet..." Lucius swept a hand across the carnage.

"I—" The chief quaesitor paused and glanced through the broken doorway at the dead Elder once more. "I guess we need to be ready for anything. But war?" He let out a slow, nervous sigh. "The sad truth is the quaesitors aren't an army. There's no way we can fight and win a large-scale conflict."

"Not at the *moment*, you mean."

Lucius let his words hang in the air, and Vlastos turned to him, his expression surprised and curious.

"Lucius?"

And now we finally come to it, Lucius thought, relishing the moment when so many threads came together. Centuries of careful preparation were about to bear fruit.

"I have ... a contingency plan."

"For a war with SysGov?" Vlastos exclaimed, and Lucius nodded.

"I'd hoped never to have to use it, of course. I suppose I'd hoped they'd changed since we left. But that seems a distant fantasy now. After all, it's only been a matter of months for them, however long it's been for our universe. That's why I was always afraid, deep down inside, that something like this might happen when we reached their True Present." He shook his head. "I doubt you can begin to understand how much I hate being proved right in that respect, but there it is. And I'll need your support when we go before the council, since this will involve tight cooperation between Cornucopia and the quaesitors."

"I—uh," Vlastos stammered. "I don't know. What *is* your plan?"

"For the moment, I've assumed control of Cornucopia," Lucius said. "I'm next in the chain of command, after all."

"That seems prudent, and I'm sure the council will support you there. We can't afford for your organization to be leaderless at a time like this."

"And as my first order, I've shifted all available *Valkyries* over to *Tesseract*'s construction site."

"Why?" Vlastos asked blankly.

"The hyperforge complex—or perhaps it would better to rename it the hyper-*fortress*—will soon become the linchpin in our defense against SysGov."

"I'm sorry, I'm not following you. How does producing more exotic matter help us if SysGov attacks?"

"Oh, Simon. Open your mind a little." Lucius held out a hand, and a cylindrical schematic appeared over it. "Hyperforges have so *many* possible applications."

Vlastos leaned closer and scrutinized the diagram. It showed a cylindrical housing with a stubby spike at either end.

"Are those impellers?" he asked.

"They are."

"And the housing?"

"Two graviton thrusters, a short-lived powerplant, and space for a nuclear warhead. One of our fifty-kiloton asteroid-mining charges should fit into it nicely."

"A nuke?" Vlastos raised his eyebrows. "A nuke that can travel through time!"

"I call it a phase-missile. And a prototype already exists."

Teodorà and Samuel really should have paid more attention to my research budget, he thought, chuckling on the inside.

"You've *already* developed a weapon system to counter SysGov's TTVs!"

"We've only built one." Lucius held up a finger, but then bared his teeth. "On the other hand, we at Cornucopia are *very* good at replication."

And twenty-seven of Tesseract's *hyperforges just happen to be perfectly sized to replicate the prototype*, Lucius thought. *Once they become operational, that is.*

"My God! It's almost like you can see the future!" Simon gushed.

Lucius dipped his head ever so slightly, but then he tightened his lips.

"As I said, you'll never know how much I wish it had turned out that we'd never need this, Simon," he said heavily. "But hard as I tried, I just couldn't quite forget how determined SysGov—especially SysPol—had been to stop us from ever coming back to forge the Dynasty in the first place. Raibert was up to his neck in that one, too, and it looks like the real reason they sent him and his team to contact us is to finish what they started twenty-five hundred years ago."

He shook his head, his eyes dark and grim. Then his avatar drew a deep breath.

"This weapon is far from perfect, Simon. Compromises had to be made to make it this small, fast, and maneuverable. Its impellers will burn out quickly, but it's fast enough to intercept any SysGov time machine. Interference from its own impellers will make it half-blind when seeking a target, but the nuke solves that. Nothing clears up accuracy problems like area-of-effect weaponry." He looked deep into Vlastos's eyes. "Can I count on your support when I present this plan to the council? Or should I say *our* plan?"

"Of course!" Relief blazed in Vlastos's expression. "You'll have my full support, Elder!"

"Thank you." Lucius smiled benevolently. "I knew I could rely on you." He eyed a new alert in his peripheral vision. "Ah! Simon, it seems one of my pilots has just woken up. I'd like to speak with her, if you don't mind."

"Of course." Vlastos surveyed the ruined office once more. "There's plenty of work to do here, too. We can talk more later."

Lucius dipped his head, then vanished. He transferred his consciousness to the Cornucopia medical center near the heart of the building and found himself in a small, sterile room where a young woman rested in a recovery casket. He was always on the lookout for useful talent, and this pilot's initiative last night had piqued his interest.

"Lieutenant," he said softly.

Hala Khatib blinked her eyes open and licked her lips.

"Who's there?" she asked.

"Chairman Gwon."

"Elder!" She pushed herself upright.

"Please." He laid a virtual hand on her shoulder and used the infonet to give it weight as he gently pushed her back. "There's no need to rise. Rest and regain your strength."

Hala paused for a moment, resisting the pressure, then settled her head back onto the pillow.

"What happened to me?" she asked.

"Quite a lot, actually." Lucius summoned her medical report. "Between ramming their time machine and then crashing into Eriksen Park, your neck was broken and your left arm was pulverized. Among other things. Everything is fixed now, though."

Hala raised her left hand and grimaced at the intact appendage.

"I didn't think I had time to switch into a bunk," she said, flexing her fingers.

"And you were probably right. Your quick thinking and initiative helped drive them off before even more people died."

"Thank you, Elder." She sat her hand down and closed her eyes, but then her face twisted suddenly and her eyes shot open as she realized he was alone.

"What about the other Elders?" she asked urgently. "Are they *okay*?"

"I'm afraid not. Elder Pepys is dead, and Elder Beckett has been taken prisoner."

"Oh, no..." she breathed, her eyes wet with tears. "Not *both* of them. I'm so sorry, Elder. I...I should've done more. I should've been able to *stop* them."

"Shhh. You did far more than most could have done in your shoes. Their ship was heavily armed, Lieutenant; *yours* didn't have even a popgun." He shook his head. "Believe me, Lieutenant, if you think you didn't do enough, you're the only person in the Dynasty who does."

"But I should have *stopped* them!" she said miserably, turning onto her side and staring into his eyes. "Why did they do it? Why would they betray our trust like that?"

"I wish I knew." Lucius spread his hands helplessly.

"All we wanted was to live in peace with them. And they did *this*! We're not going to let this stand unanswered, are we? We're going to do something about it, right?"

"Absolutely," he assured her. "You can count on that."

"Then may I make a request?"

"A request?" he asked, feigning incomprehension. "What for?"

"I want to help. I don't care what you have me do, just let me help any way I can!"

"I'm sure something can be arranged. You're a highly skilled DDT pilot, after all. We're going to need people like you all too soon, I'm afraid. We'll find you a new ship and—"

"What about *Sigrun*?" Hala cut in, sitting up. "Can it be repaired?"

"Your old ship?" Lucius summoned a damage report on the DDT. Or, rather, on the remaining *pieces* of the DDT. "I don't know. It'd be almost easier to build a new one."

"I see." Hala dropped onto her back and stared up at the ceiling. "At least it went out fighting."

Lucius looked down at her, then cracked a slow smile.

"You know what, Lieutenant? To hell with it. I can see what the *Sigrun* means to you. How about I move it to the top of the repair queue?"

"Really?" Her eyes lit, and she sat up again, wincing as she did. "You'll do that for me?"

"Why not? I *am* the acting chairman, after all." He filed the refurbishment order. "There. Done. Top of the list."

"Thank you, sir! Thank you!"

"No, thank *you*," he replied, bowing his head ever so slightly to her.

And there's one more tool for the toolbox, he thought. *Her price was such a pittance, too! And with war on the horizon, she could prove quite useful.*

War with SysGov brought many dangers. Among them was the threat of someone from SysGov actually communicating with the Dynasty, which could easily prove fatal for his own plans. Fortunately, he possessed the means to prevent that. The Cornucopia Array was under his direct supervision, and a simple "software update" pushed to all DDTs this morning would ensure *he* saw any SysGov telegraphs first.

Saw them, and had a chance to *edit* them.

The road had been long and fraught with peril, but Lucius had surmounted every obstacle. He remembered listening to Teodorà's original, naive proposal. He'd almost made the mistake of dismissing it before his mind picked out the golden opportunity laid before him.

At first his plan had been so small, so *tiny*. Its very pettiness almost made him cringe when he thought back to it. He'd yearned to build his own universe and to live there as a god. That had once been his desire, but no longer. Oh, no. Nothing that small and insignificant would suffice for Lucius Gwon!

And so he'd played along with Teodorà and Pepys's goody-goody plan. After all, why do all the work himself when others were willing—indeed, *eager*—to toil over this new timeline, guiding it to a bright and glorious future of which he would eventually take control?

He might have despaired, back when they'd first arrived in this timeline, but something entirely different had happened. He remembered plummeting out of the sky in a broken piece of the *Shadow*'s hull . . . and how an exhilaration greater than any he'd ever known had rushed through his veins. He was finally free of SysGov's laws and social mores! No longer would some obtuse *government* tell him what he could and could not do!

Reality had set in once more after the crash—after he'd taken stock of how little of his thirtieth-century luxuries remained. What was the point of being a god if he couldn't print out a few killer mechs from time to time? But that sample of freedom, that wonderfully seductive taste, had reinvigorated him, and he'd known he was on the right path.

In the end, he'd decided, time was what he most needed. That and a great deal of patience. He was free of SysGov, yes, but the technology no longer existed for him to truly realize his godhood.

And so he needed to wait until that technology became available once more.

But not in a shell of meat stuck on a primitive world.

He could have shared the digital space aboard the TTV with Shadow, he supposed, but the benefits hadn't offset the risks. Shadow had been unwaveringly loyal to him, but Philo had once been the same, and he'd known how *that* story ended! Luring Shadow into a single infosystem and then erasing him had been a bold move, to be sure, but it had allowed him not only to transition into the abstract without arousing Teodorà's suspicions, but to come across as the self-sacrificing hero in the process!

The "Shadow" she and Pepys had faced upon their return from Antioch had been a basic program he'd written and spiced up with crazy theatrics, since he'd already deleted the real Shadow. Pepys could well have been killed in the process—indeed, Lucius had *expected* to kill him in the process. But so what? Although, Lucius had to admit, having him alive in the end had probably helped speed up the society's development.

It had been a long, *long* wait, but then he'd noticed an early draft of Siv Eriksen's hyperforge theorem. Crude, yes, but flush with so much raw potential. And for all the woman's technical brilliance, she'd been denser than neutronium when it came to everything else. He'd manipulated her with almost comical ease, at least in the beginning.

It was a shame he'd had to kill her in the end, but she just wouldn't stop poking at all the *inconvenient* damage temporal replication could cause. The accident had been simple enough to stage, especially for someone as . . . unwary as she. So he couldn't complain too much. And once he'd revised her final notes to show she'd rejected those unfortunately pessimistic models, the creation of Cornucopia had forged unstoppably ahead.

Cornucopia. The final stepping-stone before his godhood.

Leave it to Raibert to poke his nose where it wasn't wanted yet again. But, this time, Lucius could only laugh at his good fortune. SysGov had arrived at the *perfect* time, and he'd used their appearance to not only kill off Pepys and remove Teodorà from power—both of which had always been an essential part of his final-phase plans—but also to create the threat he'd needed to spur on the *Tesseract*'s final construction.

And final *modifications.*

Hyperforge complex. Ha! Teodorà and Pepys had always been so small-minded. But, he told himself, that was why *they* had never deserved the godhood he was now on the cusp of attaining.

When completed, the *Tesseract* would be able to go anywhere, any*when*, in *any* universe, and its hyperforges would be able to replicate anything he desired. It would serve as the body of a technological god! And soon, after twenty-four centuries of waiting in pure abstraction, he would finally transfer his connectome and take on the eternal, invincible form he so rightly deserved.

Let SysGov and the Dynasty burn in my wake, he thought. *Their pyre will be a fitting offering to the new god of the multiverse.*

CHAPTER THIRTY-TWO

❦❦❦

Argus Station
SysGov, 2980 CE

RAIBERT STEPPED OFF THE *KLEIO*'S BOARDING RAMP and hurried across the Argus Station hangar. The rest of the crew was only a few steps behind him, and he activated the counter-grav tube with a mental command that loaded Klaus-Wilhelm's office as their destination.

But then he stopped at the tube entrance.

His team bunched up behind him, confused by the delay.

"Raibert?" Elzbietá asked, tilting her head to the side.

"The rest of you go on ahead. I'm going to check on Teodorà."

The others looked at him for a moment, and he looked back. Teodorà had shared what she knew via telegraph on their way back to SysGov, but her messages had been terse and clinical. Just the facts and nothing else. She was alone on her own ship, yanked from the world she knew—a world she'd helped *create*—and Raibert wondered if he was the closest thing she had to a friend right now.

"Sure thing," Benjamin said after a moment. "We'll work to get everyone up to speed while we wait for you."

"Plus, I'm sure she wouldn't mind being with a familiar face right about now," Elzbietá said.

Yeah, Raibert thought with a faint grimace. *Even mine*.

The others filed into the tube and gravity whisked them deeper into the station. But Philo appeared next to him, and he felt the AC touch the pathways between their minds.

"Hey, buddy," the Viking said, looking a little worried.

"'Go on ahead' means you, too," Raibert replied.

"All right. But are you sure?" he asked, and Raibert nodded.

"Just give me and Teodorà a little space."

"Okay. I understand."

The avatar vanished as Philo's connectome flowed deeper into the station.

Raibert loaded the adjacent hangar as his new destination and stepped into the tube. It dropped him off in a nearly identical bay, where the *Hildr* rested in a docking cradle. The ramp was open, and two security synthoids in SysPol dark blue waited at its foot. Neither of them looked very sure of their precise role in the present situation.

One of them straightened as Raibert approached.

"Agent Kaminski!" she said crisply. "Sir, she hasn't come out yet."

The other synthoid pointed a thumb over his shoulder.

"Should we go in and see if she's okay?" he asked.

"That won't be necessary." Raibert threaded between them and scaled the ramp. "I'll take it from here."

"Yes, sir."

"Just comm us if you need anything, sir."

Raibert strode onto the *Hildr*'s oval bridge. Virtual displays lined the walls, and diagrams of the *Tesseract* floated near the pilot seat. Perhaps she'd been trying to piece together Lucius's plan during the half-hour trip back to SysGov?

"Teodorà?" he called.

No answer.

The door leading to the aft section was open, and he walked through it into a short hallway lined with eight doors. One of them was open, and he stepped cautiously up to the portal and peeked inside.

Teodorà sat on the floor of what looked like a dark, unused room, her back pressed against the wall and an arm draped over her raised knee.

"Hey," he said softly.

"Hey, Raibert," she replied without looking up. Her cheeks were wet, shining in the dim light.

He sat down next to her and put his back against the same wall. He didn't start with something as trite as "Are you okay?" or "It'll be fine," because those lines had never worked while they were dating. It was always best to let her speak first, if he wanted to get her to share her pain openly, and so he waited for her to speak.

A few minutes dragged past, and then Teodorà exhaled a long sigh.

"It didn't hit me until we landed," she began. "Somehow, it wasn't real before then. But when I saw the station again—" She shook her head. "That's when it suddenly became so very, *very* real. When the full magnitude of what's happened slammed into me."

She closed her eyes again and her jaw clenched.

"I am so *angry* right now. And not just at Lucius. At myself, too. How could I have been so *foolish*? How could I have lived and worked around him for so long and not *seen*?"

Fresh tears filled her eyes, and she smeared them away with the palm of her hand.

"I failed, Raibert. Not just the Dynasty, but myself and ... and Samuel." She lowered her head, almost touching her forehead to her raised knee, and her voice was a whisper. "I failed him. I failed to see the monster living in our midst, and now he's dead because I was so *fucking* blind!"

Raibert draped an arm over her shoulders, and she leaned into him.

"He deserved better," she continued softly. "A part of me wants to just let loose. I want to put Lucius in a body just so I can tear him apart with my bare hands ... and yet, I also feel grief and loss and an *emptiness* like I've never known. And when that hits, all I want to do is huddle in a corner and bawl my eyes out. It's like rage and grief are two sides of a coin flipping through the air, but no matter how long I wait, it never lands."

"It will," Raibert assured her. "Believe me, I know. It will. Eventually."

"Oh, I know that, too." She looked at him and flashed a sad smile. "This isn't the first time I've dealt with losing Samuel."

"Oh?"

"Not like this, obviously."

"Ah. You and he were...?" Raibert's voice trailed off, and she nodded.

"When you've been through so much together, who else really understands you? Who else can you confide in? And then, like anything in life, one thing leads to another, and suddenly we're in bed together."

"Isn't that a little unprofessional?"

"What?" She chuckled sadly. "The historian sleeping with the indigene?"

"I'm kidding, of course." He gave her shoulders a squeeze.

"Hmm," she murmured, a small smile on her lips.

"You two seemed close enough when we met," Raibert pointed out.

"We were. But that wasn't always the case. Our relationship's gone through a number of hot and cold spells." Her eyes twinkled with sad remembrance. "He was a good man, but he also had a habit of... amorous wandering, you could say."

"Well, we *are* talking about Samuel Pepys. You can't say you didn't know what you were getting into."

"Nope." She shook her head, a genuine smile leaking onto her lips. "I knew *exactly* what I was in for. You should've seen him when he finally transferred to a *fully functional* synthoid."

They shared a quiet laugh which subsided into a contemplative silence as Teodorà stared at a blank spot on the wall. Her face was softer and more at peace than it had been since he'd arrived.

"Thanks, Raibert," she said after a while. "I needed this."

"Any time. What are friends for?"

"You still consider me your friend?" she asked,

turning her head to look over at him. "Even after all I've done?"

"Yeah. I do." He stood and extended a hand to her. "So, how's that coin doing?"

She took his hand without hesitation, and he pulled her to her feet.

"It just landed on 'get-off-your-butt-and-do-something-about-it,'" she said.

❖   ❖   ❖

"Doctor Beckett, thank you for joining us," Vice-Commissioner Klaus-Wilhelm von Schröder said in a professional, if somewhat restrained tone, as Teodorà and Raibert entered his office. "Or would you prefer to be called 'Chairwoman'?"

Benjamin, Elzbietá, and Andover-Chen backed up to make space for the newcomers. Virtual images of the *Tesseract*, Cornucopia Headquarters, and a replication center shifted out of their way.

"'Doctor' is fine. It seems appropriate, given where I suddenly find myself. Though, to be perfectly honest, I haven't been called that in quite some time."

Teodorà let her gaze circle the room's occupants and felt the weight of all their judgments press down upon her. And who could blame them? She'd been wrong—so terrifyingly wrong—but she wouldn't deflect blame or point fingers. Yes, Lucius had tricked her and many others. But her own decisions had led to this point, and she would own those choices and help to end this crisis in any way she could.

"Doctor, time is a funny thing, as the multiverse seems fond of demonstrating of late," Klaus-Wilhelm said without humor, his eyes never leaving Teodorà. "It wasn't long ago, from my frame of reference, that you stooped from your honorable post in academia and stole one of my division's time machines."

"Yes, I know. And if I had the chance to do it over again—"

"Let me stop you right there." Klaus-Wilhelm raised a hand. "What's done is done, and despite what you might wish now, the situation has escalated *far* beyond mere theft."

"Yes, of course," she conceded, bowing her head slightly.

"It's now up to us to find a solution to this crisis," Klaus-Wilhelm continued. "I had a brief meeting with Chief Lamont and President Byakko after receiving *Kleio*'s initial report, and I'll jump into another one immediately after we're done here. First, you have been officially recognized as a visiting dignitary and will be afforded the same courtesy diplomats from the Admin receive while here in SysGov."

"Thank you, Commissioner. That's more than I think I deserve, frankly."

"If anyone, you should thank Agent Kaminski," Klaus-Wilhelm replied stiffly. "Without his input, you would've received a very *different* reception."

She glanced at Raibert, and he shrugged as if it were nothing.

"I understand." She turned back to meet the commissioner's harsh gaze. "And regardless, *you* also have my thanks. Let me assure you that no one wants to see this crisis resolved more than I. You'll have my full cooperation, although I don't expect my words to sway your opinion of me, but rather my actions. And as my first act, I will voluntarily submit to a copy dissection to prove the truth of my words."

Andover-Chen gasped, and Raibert's eyes widened, but Benjamin and Elzbietá wore confused expressions.

"A 'copy dissection'?" Klaus-Wilhelm repeated, his face guarded and neutral. "It seems there's still plenty for me to learn about SysGov." He turned his head to the side. "Raibert, if you wouldn't mind explaining what this is all about?"

"Certainly, sir, and I'm not surprised you haven't encountered the concept yet. Copy dissections don't come up much outside of criminal trials. The basic process works by interviewing an individual and making a connectome copy immediately afterward. The copy is then analyzed to determine if the individual was telling the truth, with legally binding results."

"'Analyze' is too nice a word for it," Andover-Chen said. "'Peeled apart' would be more accurate. The connectome copy is, for all intents and purposes, a separate entity. A living neural map that's torn apart during the examination before it's deleted."

"But the copy is never placed in a run-state," Raibert pointed out. "In that sense, it's legally in the same class as a connectome backup." He faced the commissioner again. "Anyway, sir, there are vanishingly few circumstances under which dissection can be forced on someone, so it's most often used as a last-ditch measure to prove one's innocence in a criminal trial. There have even been cases of people transitioning to synthoid bodies for the sole purpose of authorizing connectome dissections, since an organic brain can't survive the copying process."

"Fortunately, I have no such restriction." Teodorà tapped her temple. "And this problem is greater than any squeamishness I might feel over the practice. Do you consider that to be sufficient proof, Commissioner?"

Klaus-Wilhelm glanced to Raibert again.

"You won't find a better lie detector in all of Sys-Gov," Raibert said. "If you like, I can call in a specialist from Themis Division to perform a certified dissection. Assuming we expedite the analysis, we should have the results tomorrow."

"Then see to it." Klaus-Wilhelm swiveled his gaze back to Teodorà and looked her in the eye. "We need all the help we can get, yours included. We're looking at an existential threat not only to SysGov, but to your Dynasty, as well. And speaking of which—" He nodded to Andover-Chen. "Doctor, take it from here."

"Yes, sir." Andover-Chen opened a trio of chronometric charts within the ring of occupants. "As I see it, the most likely explanation of what we know so far is that T3's society made heavy use of temporal replication." He tapped one of the charts. "This led to erosion in one sector of the universe's outer wall, which then burst. The escaping chronometric energy caused a violent temporal implosion to occur on a universal scale. The implosion then impacted the adjacent universe of T4"—he tapped the second chart—"sucking it in with negative chronometric pressure.

"The Dynasty's chronometric structure"—Andover-Chen highlighted the third chart—"shares a great deal with T3's penultimate structure. Because of this, I believe their replication industry has eroded the outer wall to dangerous levels, and it's poised to rupture. If it does, it will mean the end of not only the Dynasty, but of SysGov, as well."

"Doctor Beckett, what's your take on this?" Klaus-Wilhelm asked. "I understand you were initially quite skeptical of these findings."

"At first, yes," she acknowledged. "However, recent events have—"

She paused and swallowed as an image of Pepys's smoldering corpse flashed through her mind.

"Let's just say my eyes have been opened for the first time in a great many years. Just before we were attacked, Samuel and I came across evidence of a model very similar to Doctor Andover-Chen's that produced equally alarming results. We also discovered that same model was rejected under suspicious circumstances, and since Lucius attacked us soon afterward, it seems clear to me that *he's* tampered with our records. And that means he's known about this possibility—and has been concealing it—for quite some time."

"But why would he do that?" Elzbietá asked. "He lives in the same universe. He'll be destroyed as well."

"Will he?" Raibert asked. "He can transfer his connectome to a DDT and leave any time he wants."

"But why destroy the Dynasty?" Elzbietá pressed. "What's in it for him?"

"I think the explanation is simple, in at least one respect," Raibert said. "Lucius wants something, and whatever it is, he's going to get it. And, whatever it is, getting it requires him to at least risk the Dynasty's destruction. I doubt his primary object is to destroy the Dynasty—or even SysGov, really. I think it's just a side effect. Just collateral damage from what he *really* wants."

"You really think it's that simple?" Elzbietá asked.

"I do." Raibert nodded. "He was always a supremely self-serving bastard. A bad egg, if you will, gifted at cloaking his true ambitions with pretty words. He doesn't care what happens to anyone or anything as long as he gets what *he* wants. Whatever it is he's after this time, it's about *him*, not the Dynasty. It always has been, and always will be, about *him*."

"And that 'bad egg' just happens to be in control of every time machine in the Dynasty," Benjamin growled.

"His ultimate goal may not be clear," Klaus-Wilhelm said. "However"—he opened the image of the *Tesseract* in the center of the room—"I have a feeling this monstrosity is the key to it all."

"You could be right," Teodorà said. "Lucius was instrumental in pushing for the *Tesseract*'s construction, and I think it's pretty clear that he murdered Eriksen and hid her work in order to make sure it got built. He had a hand in the design, and he's stayed involved in its construction, too. In fact, it's one of the few projects he still bothers with these days."

"I can see why," Klaus-Wilhelm said. "It's a time-traveling station that can replicate anything up to a certain size. Andover-Chen?"

"Sir?"

"What effect is the station's construction having on the erosion?"

"That monster's one gargantuan pile of copycat exotic matter," Andover-Chen said. "It's making things worse. Much, *much* worse. Because of that thing"—he pointed at the spike-shaped station—"I'd say we have less than a year before the Dynasty goes pop and we go with it."

A year? Teodorà thought, and shook her head. The Dynasty had taken millennia to build; it was as much a part of her as her own body. And now it might cease to exist within the year?

"Damn you, Lucius," she breathed as hatred seethed within her. "Damn you straight to hell."

"I think it's reasonable to assume Gwon knows this

as well," Klaus-Wilhelm said. "Which may indicate Raibert's right. The Dynasty is a price he was willing to pay in order to get it built."

"Can we save them?" Elzbietá asked, her eyes dark with memories of another dead universe.

"Honestly, I don't know," Andover-Chen replied sadly. "The erosion is so bad it may have already reached a critical threshold. A point of no return, if you will. Not to put it too darkly, but I don't even know if there's a way to save *us*. I need more time."

"Then that's what we focus on first," Klaus-Wilhelm declared. "We buy ourselves the time we need to come up with permanent solutions."

"The Dynasty needs to halt the *Tesseract*'s construction, at the very least," Raibert said.

"Right," Andover-Chen agreed. "In fact, they need to shut down their entire replication industry. If they take both actions immediately, the erosion *may* heal on its own."

"Easier said than done," Teodorà warned. "Replication is an integral part of the Dynasty. I was being sincere when I said we didn't have enough conventional industry to survive without it."

"But SysGov does," Klaus-Wilhelm countered. "And with our necks on the same chopping block, we're all in this together. I'm sure—"

An alert opened next to him, and he frowned down at it.

"Hold on. I have to take this." He tapped the window. "Go ahead, Operations. This is the commissioner."

"Sir, this is Silchenko. Sorry to bother you. I know you're in a meeting, but we've just received a very strange telegraph that I think you need to look at."

Teodorà frowned as the man's odd accent registered. Or, more precisely, his *lack* of an accent.

For example, he'd used the Modern English word *"duibuqi"* in place of the Old English word "sorry," but he'd spoken it without any tonal inflection. A more experienced person might have used *"duibùqi"* in an effort to be more polite, or perhaps *"duìbuqì"* to convey emphasis. Instead, Silchenko's entire statement had been bereft of tonal subtext. He spoke Modern English as if it were a second language, and given the eclectic bunch working in the Gordian Division, she wondered which century *this* agent came from.

"Go ahead, Anton," Klaus-Wilhelm said. "It's been one of those days. What do you have for me?"

"First thing is that it appears to have been transmitted at extreme range, so we never picked up the craft that sent it."

"I see. Temporal?"

"No, sir. Transdimensional. Addressed to President Byakko, of all people. It's from a—" Silchenko paused as if looking something up. "Says it's from 'Chief Quaesitor Simon Vlastos.' Does that make any sense to you?"

"Doctor?" Klaus-Wilhelm asked Teodorà.

"Yes, it does, in fact." She nodded. "Vlastos holds a post roughly equivalent to SysPol's chief of police."

"Sir, what do you want me to do with it?" Silchenko asked. "Shall I forward it on?"

"No, send it to me. I'll decide what to do with it."

"Understood, sir. Sending it over now."

An attachment lit up in the comm window.

"I have it. Thank you, Anton."

"No problem, sir. Operations out."

"Now let's see what the Dynasty has to say." Klaus-Wilhelm opened the telegraph message and let it play with synthesized audio.

"This is Chief Quaesitor Simon Vlastos, speaking on behalf of the Dynasty's Council of Ministers, with a message for SysGov's President Byakko. Due to the unprovoked attack by members of your SysPol's Gordian Division and the subsequent kidnapping of Chairwoman Teodorà Beckett, the murder of Vice-Chairman Pepys, and the deaths of thirty-eight Dynasty private citizens, we hereby declare the Dynasty off-limits to all SysGov craft and its citizens. And we further demand that Teodorà Beckett be returned, unharmed and unaltered in any way. You may approach to extreme telegraph range to respond, but no closer. Any other incursion into our space will be considered an act of war and will be met with deadly force. That is all."

"'*Unprovoked attack*'?" Teodorà spat, eyes stinging. "How dare he!"

"And did you catch the part about 'unaltered'?" Raibert asked. "I'd say it's pretty damn likely you'll be considered 'altered' no matter what. Lucius will simply claim we've violated your connectome to make you say whatever we want."

"This whole message has his fingerprints all over it," Teodorà said. "He's burning down any paths of communication, isolating the Council of Ministers so they only hear one story. *His*."

"Getting the Dynasty to halt replication just became a whole lot harder." Andover-Chen sighed.

"Maybe so, but we still have a job to do," Klaus-Wilhelm said. "So how do we convince them they need to shut down the most vital part of their economy?"

"I see only two options," Benjamin said. "We talk the Dynasty down, convince them diplomatically. Or we *force* them to stop replication."

"Which would mean war," Klaus-Wilhelm pointed out.

"I didn't suggest it lightly," Benjamin replied. "But all options need to be on the table. And, I'm sorry to say it, but force may end up being the only one we have if Gwon intends to block those in power from the truth."

"Oh, hell," Raibert groaned. "The President is going to *love* this."

"Let's not be too hasty," Andover-Chen said, looking up. His head had been bowed in thought for some time now. "There may be a third option. A *technological* option. A way to shield SysGov from whatever fate befalls the Dynasty, at least."

Faces brightened at the news—all except Teodorà's—but Andover-Chen saw their expressions and shook his head.

"All I'm saying is that it *may* be possible," he cautioned. "I have just the beginnings of an idea right now, but I think..." He paused, then nodded. "Yes, I think it just might be workable."

"Three options, then," Elzbietá said. "War, Peace, and Tech."

"We'll pursue all three simultaneously for now," Klaus-Wilhelm ordered. "Andover-Chen, start working on that tech solution."

"Yes, sir!"

"Raibert, you and your team will support him. Pull whatever resources you need."

"Got it, boss."

"Doctor Beckett, it looks like I'll need you to accompany me to my next meeting. I'm sure the President and Chief Lamont will value your input when I review our options with them."

"Certainly, Commissioner. I'll help any way I can."

"And I'll take any help I can get." Klaus-Wilhelm swept his gaze over the room. "Let's pray we can find a solution that doesn't doom us all. Everyone, dismissed."

CHAPTER THIRTY-THREE

Mycene Station
SysGov, 2980 CE

"PERFECT." ANDOVER-CHEN STEPPED INTO THE VAST, enclosed space and spun in a slow circle. "Yes, this'll do nicely."

Raibert followed him in, and Benjamin and Elzbietá brought up the rear. The infostructure was so old in this part of the station that Philo had stayed back on the ship. The outside hallway's light leaked past them to splash over a small patch of dusty floor that transitioned into darkness; he couldn't even see the ceiling or the far wall.

"I don't think this section's been used in centuries." He kicked a wrench out of his way. It skidded into the darkness and *clanged* against an unseen object.

"Then no one should mind if we take it," Andover-Chen said, grinning ear to ear.

"*Echo!*" Elzbietá called out, then cupped a hand behind her ear.

"... Echo! ... echo ..."

"Yep." Benjamin crossed his arms. "It's big."

"Largest enclosure on Mycene Station," Andover-Chen clarified, hands on hips. "And it has easy access to outer space. The far wall is one massive airlock, you see. We can shove all the old junk out that way."

"What was it used for?" Benjamin asked.

"A space dock for early SysPol cruiser construction," Andover-Chen said. "Before Hephaestus Station came online in 2601. Most of the equipment got stripped out back then, but there are probably some vintage parts lying around."

"Nice!" Elzbietá smiled and elbowed Benjamin. "It's an old spaceship factory. We should snag a souvenir before everything gets tossed."

"I'll keep an eye open," Benjamin said dryly.

"Remind me again why we're setting up shop in the L5 Hub?" Raibert asked. "And not back in Earth orbit?"

"Location, location, location," Andover-Chen informed them. "Almost forty percent of SysGov's exotic matter printing takes place around L5, and another thirty percent is spread around Earth and Luna."

"So what exactly are we building?" Raibert asked.

"A 'conical exotic matter shell for high-yield chronoton storage and release,'" Elzbietá quoted.

"Whatever the hell that is," Raibert grumbled.

"It's a chronoton bomb," she clarified.

Andover-Chen made a *tsk-tsk* sound and wagged a finger.

"That's an unfair characterization," he said. "I'll have you know that what I envision is far more refined. The end result of the mechanism will be an enormous but focused spray of chronotons."

"So it's a shaped charge."

He paused in thought for a moment, then nodded. "I suppose that's a bit more accurate."

"Which is also a kind of bomb."

Andover-Chen frowned at her.

"What are we trying to blow up, exactly?" Benjamin asked.

"We're not blowing up anything," Andover-Chen stressed. "We need to sever the connection between the Dynasty and our universe, so if *they* go down they don't take *us* with them."

"Ah," Benjamin exclaimed. "Then this device will blow them *away* from us, not blow them *up*."

"Wrong again, people," Andover-Chen said. "We're not moving one whole universe away from another. The transverse doesn't work that way. But what we *can* do is make the distance between the Dynasty and us greater by spurring on the creation of more space."

"Which sounds a whole lot like we're pushing them away from us," Benjamin said.

"I'm trying to explain this in simple terms." Andover-Chen smiled patiently at them and shrugged his shoulders. "Honestly, I am."

"Oh, I think I get it," Elzbietá said. "It's like how space in our universe is expanding. Even if two galaxies aren't moving away from each other, the distance between them is still increasing."

"Finally, yes!" Andover-Chen beamed at her. "Yes, that's it exactly, just modified for the transdimensional."

"And that expansion can be superfast, too! Even faster than the speed of light!"

"What?" Benjamin asked. "I thought nothing could move faster than the speed of light."

"The expansion of space can."

"How is that a thing?"

"I don't know," Elzbietá confessed. "It just is."

"Elzbietá is right," Andover-Chen cut in, then held up a finger. "The device will cause an area of the transverse to expand, thereby increasing the transdimensional distance between the Dynasty and SysGov universes without *actually* moving those two universes. But"—he paused to sigh—"as much as it pains me to say this, Benjamin's analogy is not without merit either."

"So I can think of the c-bomb as blowing the Dynasty away from us?" Benjamin asked.

"If you really *want* to."

"How much exotic matter are we talking about here?" Raibert asked.

"All of it."

Raibert blinked. "Excuse me?"

"Or rather, all we can feasibly get our hands on." Andover-Chen spawned a sheet of calculations over his right hand. "Once I wrapped my head around the concept, the math turned out to be quite simple."

"*That's* simple math?" Benjamin asked, doubtfully running his eyes over line after line of elaborate equations.

"When dealing with a nine-plus-three-dimensional problem, it is."

"I'll take your word for it."

"Anyway, while the math isn't too daunting, the *quantities* involved are." He closed the chart. "Mycene Station is positioned near sixty-eight percent of SysGov's total exotic matter production, and it'll take *all* of that production roughly three months to accumulate enough material to build the device."

Raibert whistled. "You don't think small, do you?"

"A lot can happen in three months," Benjamin noted.

"True." Andover-Chen nodded. "But it gives us another option and falls within the one-year window I calculated for the Dynasty's implosion. Hopefully, a diplomatic solution can be found to give us more time, but if not..." He spread his hands and trailed off.

"Best to be prepared for the worst," Benjamin said.

"Too true."

"But still," Raibert said. "*All* of it?"

"Even if we only get the two largest manufacturers, those being Negation Industries and the Mitchell Group, we're still talking about sixty-two percent of all exotic matter production. Both companies are major government contractors, so President Byakko has a considerable amount of leverage if they prove... recalcitrant during this crisis."

"You think *John Mitchell*, the man who never saw an Esteem credit he didn't like, is going to just hand over his company's entire production capacity?"

"Oh, I somehow doubt he'll give it up for free," Andover-Chen smiled. "Though honestly, how SysPol gets the exotic matter isn't our concern. *Our* job is to make sure we have a third viable option. Besides"—his smile vanished—"I don't think getting the material is the worst problem."

"Well, that's just *great*," Raibert groaned. "How is procuring two-thirds of all exotic matter production for *months* not our biggest problem?" He made a waving gesture toward himself. "Come on. Let's hear it."

"One very real concern I have is that it's going to be impossible to keep this a secret," Andover-Chen said. "The Admin is undoubtedly spying on us already, and we have to assume the Dynasty will make similar attempts. Both superpowers are likely to become... nervous when they see so much exotic matter being funneled into a secret project."

"He's right, you know," Elzbietá agreed. "They won't even have to spot the shipments; this level of activity will be all over the news."

"Never mind that all you need is a telescope to see what comes and goes here," Raibert grumbled.

"We could just tell them," Benjamin suggested.

"What? Tell the Admin we're building a chronoton bomb?" Raibert rolled his eyes. "Oh, *that'll* go over well!"

"Why not?" Benjamin said. "We're not dealing with something that can be twisted into a weapon, all jokes about a c-bomb aside."

He turned to Andover-Chen, but the physicist didn't respond immediately, and his face was a blank, cheerless mask.

"We're not," Benjamin repeated. "Right?"

Andover-Chen grimaced, then looked up at the others.

"In theory," he began, clearly choosing his words with care, "the device will have no negative impact on a healthy outer wall. The extra chronotons will all be absorbed harmlessly."

"What do you mean... 'healthy'?" Raibert pressed.

"Not weakened by replication resonance."

"Then what'll happen to the Dynasty if we detonate this thing?" Elzbietá asked.

"The outer wall may rupture early, starting an implosion as soon as the device goes off."

"Shit," Raibert breathed.

"Or it may not," Andover-Chen said quickly. "I simply don't know."

"Then by saving ourselves, we may take them out?" Benjamin asked.

"It should be clear to everyone this is our last resort," Andover-Chen defended. "If something this small can doom their universe, then they were already too far gone to survive in the end. Our best option is still to get the Dynasty to shut down their replication industry."

"Which they're unlikely to do," Benjamin said.

"Then they'll have doomed themselves," Andover-Chen said simply. "And all we'll be guilty of is making *damn* sure they don't take us out with them. That's why we have to build this so-called c-bomb, despite what it could possibly be perverted into. Because if diplomacy fails, it'll be all that stands between SysGov and the apocalypse."

❖   ❖   ❖

"Telegraph coming back from TTV *Axion*, sir," Anton Silchenko said, standing with Klaus-Wilhelm and Teodorà in the center of Gordian Operations.

"Sooner than expected," Klaus-Wilhelm noted with a low grumble.

"What does it say?" Teodorà asked.

"Give the ACs a moment to process it," Silchenko said. "Signal quality is low at this range."

Klaus-Wilhelm nodded and turned to Teodorà.

"While the Argus Array has been upgraded for transdimensional detection, the reception quality is significantly lower when compared to conventional chronometric signals."

"Oh, trust me, I understand," Teodorà said with a smile. The copy dissection was behind her, thank

God, and if Klaus-Wilhelm's demeanor toward her hadn't warmed since she'd passed the lie detector test, he *had* become more accepting of her input, which was all she really wanted. "We encountered the same problems when we started dabbling with transdimensional flight. Keeping in contact with our scouts was a royal pain."

"I think they've got the signal sorted out." Text scrolled in front of Silchenko. "Sir, *Axion* never reached the Dynasty's True Present. Four *Valkyries* approached them on direct intercept courses, and the *Axion* aborted instead of risking engagement, per your orders. They transmitted the preloaded telegraph from that position but received no response."

"Again, our attempts at communication go unanswered," Klaus-Wilhelm said grimly. "Doctor, what do you make of this?"

"It's not a technical problem, I can tell you that much. Cornucopia Array is significantly more sensitive than the Argus Array. It's perfectly capable of receiving every telegraph you've sent so far."

"And yet we've received no replies."

"I know. And I'm not sure what to make of that, beyond the fact that our messages are being ignored."

"Any recommendations other than trying again?" Klaus-Wilhelm asked.

"Not really, other than we must continue to avoid armed confrontations," Teodorà said. "The longer we go without shots being fired, the more we weaken Lucius's position. People will start asking questions, and his lies will only hold out under scrutiny for so long."

"That may be so, but the clock is ticking. Every day makes the erosion of the Dynasty's outer wall worse."

"I know, Commissioner." Teodorà crossed her arms and lowered her head. "But I still believe this is the best approach. If we come at it too aggressively, we play right into that bastard's hands."

"Very well. We'll keep trying, for now. Silchenko?"

"Sir?"

"Order the *Axion* home. We'll send them out again in four hours."

◆   ◆   ◆

Elzbietá switched the omni-throttle to its finest movement setting and pulled back on it. The *Kleio's* four thrusters released an invisible mist of gravitons, and the ship eased in front of the huge Mycene Station airlock. Unlike the cleanly cylindrical Argus Station, SysPol's Mycene Station sprawled out in a chaotic, organic fashion as sections had been added, decommissioned, and renovated over centuries of use. It made her think of huge blocks and spheres suspended within the thick branches of a deciduous tree.

The *Kleio*, and the massive cargo container suspended underneath its elliptical hull, came to a stop in front of the airlock. Bold golden letters with black borders spelled MG on the side of the container.

"Hey, Raibert," she called in on an encrypted SysPol channel. "I've got something good for you and Andover-Chen."

"Wow. That was fast."

"I aim to please."

"No kidding." Raibert chuckled. "Hold on a second. Give us a moment to make room."

"Sure thing. Not going anywhere." She muted her side of the channel.

Hauling cargo might not be the most glamorous

work, but the *Kleio* was available, and the TTV's oversized thrusters and programmable hull made for a versatile combo.

Philo appeared next to her.

"I still can't believe the Mitchell Group sprang into action so fast," the avatar said, placing virtual hands atop the bridge command table.

"Is it really that surprising?" Elzbietá let go of her controls. "You know. End of the universe and all that. I bet the President's making Esteem flow faster than the Amazon River."

"Maybe in some cases, like with Negation Industries or Atlas, but that's not what I heard about her negotiations with John Mitchell."

"Oh?" She sat up.

"Rumor is we're getting MG's exotic matter at a *quarter* its market value."

"You're shitting me!" She grinned at him. "I think someone's pulling your leg."

"It's just a rumor." Philo shrugged. "But it's from an old government source I trust. I got the information as a courtesy, one AC to another."

"And who's this trusted source?" she asked doubtfully.

"Oh, I could tell you"—he waggled his eyebrows—"but then I'd have to kill you."

"Yeah." She laughed and rolled her eyes as she leaned back in her chair again. "Never mind."

Philo hunched his shoulders, visibly deflated. He summoned a virtual seat and slouched into it.

"Something wrong?" Elzbietá asked.

"I was expecting you to try harder than that."

"Nah, you can keep your secret contact."

"Aren't you even a little bit curious?"

"Sort of?" she admitted with a shrug. "I guess some of the names you and the others throw around don't carry the same oomph with me. I'm still new to the thirtieth century, after all."

"Yeah, that's to be expected."

"So, this John Mitchell is a big deal?"

"Very big," Philo said. "John C. Mitchell III is one of the most successful industrial magnates in SysGov, and he's the current CEO of the Mitchell Group. He took over the post from John Mitchell II, who took it over from the company's founder, John Mitchell I."

"Keeping it in the family, I see."

"Actually, he's a self-clone of John Mitchell II, who was a self-clone of the original."

"You mean like how Raibert is the clone of his father?"

"That's right. It's not a terribly common practice at the moment. Seems to go in and out of style every few decades. Anyway, John C. Mitchell I was an early innovator in exotic matter printing, and his inventions helped his company get off the ground in the early days."

"Are the other two still around?"

"Number One abstracted and retired. Same with Number Two, though he occasionally pops up in the news."

Elzbietá snorted.

"What?" Philo asked.

"Sorry. The sense of humor from my Navy days kicked in there. So why the discount, do you think?"

"I'm guessing it's a PR ploy. Everything we're doing here will become public sooner or later, and grateful people tip *lots* of Esteem. Could be quite the windfall for his company. Speaking of which, have you checked your own account recently?"

"Nah. Don't really see the point. Ben and I haven't had to pay for a single thing since we got here."

"Well, you might want to take a peek when you get the chance."

"Why?" Elzbietá asked. "Are we running out or something?"

"Oh, quite the contrary. You and Benjamin are positively flush with Esteem."

"Really? How'd that happen?"

"Public tipping, mostly," Philo explained. "A lot of people tip SysPol generously, and the Gordian Division, as the newest addition, has been in the public eye. We're all doing quite well for ourselves, actually."

"But what do I use it for? Food and housing are free."

"Oh, plenty of things. For one, many places offer extra Esteem-gated services."

"'Esteem-gated'?"

"Services that only become available to those who meet minimum Esteem requirements."

"So, just *having* a lot of money gives us access? We don't actually spend anything?"

"That's right. Though, you don't want to appear too miserly. Esteem tipping is an important part of SysGov culture. No one likes a hoarder."

"You don't say." She grimaced. "Post-scarcity money is weird."

"You'll get used to it, I'm sure. Besides, Esteem works a lot like your dollars and cents when dealing with truly scarce commodities, like this shipment we're hauling."

The airlock opened, and a spherical station tug pulled the skeleton of an unfinished vessel into space.

Elzbietá keyed the unmute. "You ready for us?"

"Not yet," Raibert said. "We're still shifting a lot of leftover junk around to make room. Plus, Andover-Chen is...being picky."

"Problem?"

"Sort of. He's like a mama bird building her nest. Everything has to be perfect for his universe-shattering firstborn."

"Ah."

"I don't need things to be perfect," Andover-Chen cut in. "But we must have adequate room *around* the material to bring in additional equipment, build our custom printers, and so on."

"Look, it's in a shipping container. We can plop the frickin' thing down *anywhere* and move it later."

"Or we can do it right the first time and be done with it."

"Whatever," Raibert dismissed. "Look, you two. The mad scientist and I will sort this out. Just give us a few minutes."

"Sure thing," Elzbietá said. "We'll..."

She trailed off when her displays lit up with an alert from Gordian Operations.

"That can't be good," Philo said.

"Raibert, gotta go. Operations is calling." She switched channels. "Operations, go for *Kleio*."

"*Kleio*, this is the commissioner. The Argus Array just picked up what looks like an inbound Dynasty time machine. You're close to their projected phase-in point, so I'm sending you after it. Transmitting everything we have on it now."

Chronometric data populated a new chart over the command table.

"Wow. They got *really* close before we picked them up," Elzbietá noted. "Only two lateral-months before they reach our True Present."

A time machine like the *Kleio* could cross the transdimensional distance between SysGov's True Present and the Dynasty's True Present in about thirty minutes, which was the same amount of absolute time it took for the TTV to travel four years into the past. This, *technically*, allowed for the same units of measure to apply to both temporal and transdimensional flight.

Technically, yes, Elzbietá thought, *but it's also confusing as hell.*

She didn't know how she felt about Andover-Chen pushing to call one lateral-day a "chen," but it made more sense to her than using *time* as a measure of *distance* when navigating the transverse. And she much preferred thinking of the Dynasty as being fifteen hundred chens away rather than "lateral-four-years" away.

Still, like so many of the Gordian Division's practices, doctrine for navigating the transverse had yet to be finalized, so "lateral-time-unit" it was until someone came up with something better.

"They're only moving at one kilofactor," Philo said. "Looks like a stealth approach aimed at scoping out our True Present."

"Have you tried talking to them?" Elzbietá asked.

"Yes, but all our telegraphs continue to be ignored," Klaus-Wilhelm said.

"I see. Orders, sir?"

"Intercept and investigate, but exercise caution. We don't know why they're here."

"And if they fire at us?"

"Then you send them straight to hell."

"Got it, sir. *Kleio* moving out."

"Undocking cargo," Philo announced. Prog-steel clamps along the *Kleio's* underbelly disengaged from the container and melted back into the hull. "I'll get us moving. You should get ready in case things turn serious."

"Right."

She stood up and slipped sideways into the still-opening compensation bunk set into the wall. The glass front sealed her in and a milky syrup of fluidized microbots poured into the container, covering the tops of her boots and climbing rapidly up her legs.

She linked her wetware with the compensation bunk and set her body's physical functions on automatic. The bridge vanished and a panoramic view of space sprang into being. The Mitchell Group cargo container floated away beneath her feet, and the massive, jumbled bulk of the Mycene Station took up most of her view to the left. Two tandem seats rested atop an invisible floor.

She sank into one, and Philo appeared in the other. Virtual displays and controls materialized, and she grabbed the joystick and throttle. Really *grabbed* them, because the instruments were solid to her touch within the command abstraction.

"We're underway," Philo reported. "Approaching intruder at seventy kilofactors. Intercept in one minute."

Elzbietá flexed her virtual fingers over the controls and watched the distance to her target drop away.

"So," she wondered aloud. "What'll it be? Fight or flight?"

"Weapons are ready, just in case," Philo said.

The distance dropped to almost nothing.

"Phase-lock immi—Course change!" Philo snapped. "Speed now seventy-four kilofactors away from us!"

"Flight it is," Elzbietá said, settling into a pursuit course. She maxed out the *Kleio*'s impeller, but the Dynasty *Valkyrie* continued to pull away.

"Distance now one lateral-hour and climbing," Philo reported. "We're not going to catch them."

"I know. And I'm not even sure what we'd do if we did." She thumbed the *Kleio*'s speed down to ten kilofactors. Enough, she thought, to get the point across that the *Valkyrie* wasn't welcome.

"At least we shooed it off before it reached the True Present," Philo said.

"Yeah," Elzbietá said softly, then frowned. "But there's no way this is the last one they send."

CHAPTER THIRTY-FOUR

———— ⬠⬠⬠⬠ ————

**Cornucopia Headquarters
Dynasty, 2980 CE**

LUCIUS GWON LEANED BACK IN THE FOLDING CHAIR, shaded by a wide, translucent umbrella. He wore nothing but a pair of black swimming trunks. His toes sank into sun-kissed sand, and he reached for the drink on the small table by his side. A simple randomizer created a banana daiquiri, and he brought the beverage to his smiling lips.

He took a slow sip, savored the sweet, creamy flavor, and sighed contentedly. Excitement tingled within him, but he held it at bay, waiting calmly and patiently for the perfect moment to move his plan forward. Gentle waves caressed the beach simulation with a steady, soothing rhythm, and the sun warmed his naked chest through the umbrella.

He took another sip and returned his attention to the reports hovering nearby.

A week had passed since Teodorà fled the Dynasty, and the scout reports coming back from SysGov painted an intriguing—and oh so *useful*—picture. He'd managed to neutralize all of SysGov's diplomatic gestures, but the lack of overt aggression on their part had weakened his position with the Council of Ministers.

But this! Oh, this was *exactly* what he needed!

"Those poor fools." He smirked and shook his head. "It's like they want me to win."

He didn't know what the Gordian Division needed all that exotic matter for, but that, in some ways, worked even better. Human nature feared the unknown, and he could use the council's fear to accelerate his own plans.

Lucius finished his drink and checked the time.

"Well then. I suppose I've made Simon wait long enough."

He stood up and summoned replacement clothing. An elegant black-on-black business suit with a high neckline appeared over his body, with a gleaming diamond at the base of his throat and a red sash around his waist.

"Mmm, yes." He smoothed the fabric over his chiseled stomach. "This'll do."

A mental command transferred his consciousness to Chief Quaesitor Simon Vlastos's satellite office in Cornucopia Headquarters. The beach vanished, and a clean white office room sprang up around him. Vlastos sat behind an oval frosted-glass desk, a worried expression on his face and dark rings under his eyes. The nightlife of Constantinople twinkled through the one-way window behind him.

The fusion of the quaesitors and Cornucopia might still be unofficial, but everyone involved knew it was inevitable, and Vlastos had started working from Cornucopia to ensure the transition proceeded smoothly.

He'd even slept at work a few times, and the *Sigrun's* report had just so happened to come back in the middle of the night.

"Ah, Lucius." Vlastos stood up. "Thank you for coming."

"I'm sorry it took me so long." He flashed an apologetic smile. "The report . . . it's a lot to take in, and I wanted to go over it thoroughly before we spoke."

"I understand, of course," Vlastos agreed, sitting back down. "So." He knitted his fingers together. "What do you make of it?"

Lucius created a virtual seat in front of the desk and sat down opposite the chief quaesitor.

"I wish there was some easy way to say this, but . . ."

Vlastos swallowed and waited for him to continue.

"War." Lucius looked him straight in the eyes. "They're preparing for war."

"But surely . . ."

"No, I'm certain of it." He shook his head. "SysPol is essentially SysGov's military, and they're taking in *massive* quantities of exotic matter. It's impossible to say for *what* exactly, but the *why* of it is crystal clear to me. They're accumulating it because they plan to *use* it."

"But do you really think they'll attack us?"

"They already have," Lucius pointed out bluntly, and Vlastos shrank under the force of his glare. "And now we see their demands for what they truly are. A smoke screen to buy time."

"As you've said all along," Vlastos grimaced.

Of course, it helps that I'm the one writing "their" messages, Lucius thought. For the moment, he controlled all communication between the two universes, but his tactics wouldn't hold out forever, especially if SysGov managed to get a TTV into the Dynasty's True Present and broadcast a realspace message. They'd tried several times already but been too timid to risk a confrontation.

I need to push them onto the defensive. Force them to guard their space rather than try to reach ours. And I know just how to do it.

"By now, they must have drained Teodorà of every last drop of useful information," Lucius pressed. "They'll know exactly where to hit us when they come, so we need to be ready."

"But our own preparations have barely begun. What are we supposed to do?"

"Don't downplay your efforts too much," Lucius reassured him. "The quaesitors are far enough along for what we need, I think."

"And what's that?"

"First things first." Lucius straightened and put on a look of cool confidence. "We need to inform the council of this development, but we can't go to them without a plan."

"And what exactly do we tell them? That we should ask SysGov nicely not to invade?"

"*Ask* them to stop?" Lucius grinned wolfishly. "Oh, no. We're going to send a *much* clearer message than that."

❖   ❖   ❖

Under-Director Dahvid Kloss grabbed the handhold over the doorway into *Pathfinder-Prime's* bridge and floated through. He clasped another atop one of the seats, propelled himself to the front of the room, spun around, and cushioned himself to an almost perfect stop with his legs. He pressed his fingers against the ceiling and brought himself "upright" alongside the captain.

Captain Florian Durantt gave him a curt nod.

"Well?" Kloss asked.

"Take a look, Director." Durantt placed his hand atop a PIN interface, and a video of Mycene Station appeared in their shared vision. Graphic pips highlighted the hundreds of habitats, factories, and asteroids that cluttered the L5 Lagrange point, with Earth's smiling blue crescent visible beyond.

Not *the* Earth, he forced himself to recall, but *an* Earth. The concept still jarred his mind; Jonas Shigeki might have become accustomed to living in another universe, but this was *his* first trip beyond the Admin.

Pathfinder-Prime was the second Admin chronoport to receive the transdimensional upgrade, and Dahvid Kloss, as Under-Director of Espionage, had volunteered to personally lead their first reconnaissance mission beyond the outer wall.

Unfortunately, *Pathfinder-Prime* was Captain Florian Durantt's ship. Durantt must have relished the idea of babysitting a "filthy Freep-loving Martian" like Kloss almost as much as Kloss enjoyed vomiting from exposure to freefall. He'd lost his only sister to a Freep terrorist almost a decade ago, so Kloss understood his animosity. And it certainly wasn't the first time he'd been blamed for his native people's idiocy, for that matter. Fortunately, the captain was a consummate professional while on duty, despite his biases; they would never be friends, but Kloss didn't care about that one way or the other. As long as the job got done.

He watched the video play out. Another transport entered the "decommissioned" construction bay and disappeared behind a massive airlock. The chronoport's non-congruent phase state made their observations murky at best, but he wasn't about to test their stealth against SysGov's *realspace* detectors. That was why they'd spent the last eleven days non-congruent with SysGov's True Present, while one tempting breadcrumb after another led them here, to Mycene Station.

"How many does that make?" he asked.

"Three so far today. Two from the Mitchell Group and one from Negation Industries."

"Then that brings the total to eight," Kloss said softly.

"That we've seen ourselves."

"And probably more we haven't." Kloss nodded, acknowledging the point, and scratched his chin thoughtfully. "A shame about the airlock. What I wouldn't give for a look inside."

Durantt frowned, and his walrus mustache twitched. Micro-gravity always gave it more buoyancy than usual.

"Fear not, Captain. We'll continue to play it safe. But there's no denying it now. Our 'friends' in the Gordian Division are up to something."

"Do you think they're building TTVs inside?"

"Possibly," Kloss said. "But why hide that from us? It's only natural for them to build new time machines. There's nothing unusual about it. We're both going to expand and upgrade our forces. Why conceal it in such an odd way?"

"Perhaps it's for a new TTV class?"

"Perhaps."

"You sound doubtful, sir."

"That's because I am. It's too much exotic matter

and not enough of everything else that goes into making time machines. No, my gut tells me something *else* is going on here. It's also being hidden in the oddest, most amateurish way." He crossed his arms. "Either SysGov doesn't exert *any* control over their media, or this is the weirdest misinformation campaign I've *ever* seen."

"They certainly have a strange way of conducting business," Durantt agreed.

Do they want *us looking here?* Kloss wondered. *Or are they just* this *incompetent at controlling information?*

Back home, Kloss and his team of data scrubbers would have *at least* fabricated some sort of plausible cover story to disseminate to the media, as well as staging digital "evidence" to support it, but from what he could tell, nothing of the sort was happening here. SysPol refused to discuss either their massive purchases or the shipments, which was the absolute *worst* way to stamp out public interest!

You could tell everyone you're stockpiling it for a rainy day or—or anything! Kloss thought, offended on a professional level. *Be creative about it. Try* something!

"Sir!" the temporal navigator called out. "Sir! New scope contacts! Lots of them!"

"Calm down." Durantt spun to face his bridge crew. "What do you have?"

"I don't know, sir. They're coming from an unknown lateral vector at seventy-four kilofactors."

"Seventy-*four*?" Durantt repeated.

"Yes, sir."

Kloss and the captain exchanged a quick, questioning glance.

"How many?" Kloss asked.

"It's hard to tell. Call it ten to twenty. I should have a firm count when they phase in."

"Are we in their way at all?"

"No, sir. There's no indication we've been spotted."

"Well, that's something. Pull it up for us."

"Yes, sir."

Telemetry etched itself across the front of the bridge, and Kloss grimaced as he took it all in. Two clusters of signals were moving toward the True Present and would phase in near L5.

They're already so close, he thought. *At that speed, we should have detected them long ago. Did they just suddenly accelerate? Why would they do that?*

"Sir, two SysPol corvettes launching from Mycene Station, and at least one TTV phase-out detected."

"What the hell is going on here?" Kloss asked.

❖   ❖   ❖

"Five seconds to phase-in," Lieutenant Hala Khatib announced from her pilot seat aboard the *Sigrun*, her eyes sharp with concentration as the quaesitor attack group approached SysGov's True Present. "Phase-in!"

Five *Valkyries* flashed into realspace in a ragged wedge formation, and the *Sigrun* appeared farther to starboard of the other five than she'd anticipated. The *Sigrun's* sleek racing hull had been restored to its original form—with a few notable upgrades—but the others were bulky transports with stubby impellers that had strained to make the journey.

"Sloppy!" Captain Raoul snapped from behind the other three crewmembers on the abstract bridge. "We're a whole kilometer out of position."

"Sorry, sir," Hala replied. She powered up the

graviton thrusters, and the *Sigrun* surged sideways. The nimble craft quickly fell in with the others that *also* had struggled to hold their positions during phase-in. Her abstract body felt a simulated percentage of the four gees while microbot ooze cocooned her physical form in the compensation bunk.

She didn't feel insulted by Raoul's acidic observation. What she *felt* was a burning desire to perform better under his command. She was the only Cornucopia member of *Sigrun's* bridge crew—the other three were all quaesitors—yet she'd taken an immediate liking to her new boss. "Tough but fair" summed up Xavier Raoul's command style perfectly, and she felt certain his confidence and strength would benefit them in the days to come.

That wasn't to say the man didn't have a softer side. Most *Valkyries* had received new designations as Cornucopia and the quaesitors began their hasty merger, but Raoul had passed the rechristening of their rebuilt craft to her in honor of her defense of Cornucopia HQ.

Only one name would do, and her new captain seemed immensely pleased with her choice, taking the original name as a defiant fist shaken in the face of SysGov. So pleased that he and the others presented her with a *slightly* unofficial uniform the day after, and she now wore the dark gray of an honorary quaesitor with pride.

The *Sigrun* slipped into position, taking up the tip of Alpha Group's wedge, and the other five craft shook out behind it.

"That's more like it." Raoul stood up. "Alpha to Beta. We're in position. What's your status?"

"Beta Leader here." Six pips blinked on the tactical display. "We've arrived on target near the MG printing cluster. Beginning our attack run now."

"Roger that." Raoul put a hand on the back of Hala's chair. "Take us in, Lieutenant."

"Yes, sir. Adjusting course."

She spun the *Sigrun* until the cluttered, branching mess of Mycene Station came into view, and the other five *Valkyries* turned with her. Two red pips flew out from the mammoth construct, and her scope identified them as SysPol corvettes, each elliptical in shape and about half the size of a *Valkyrie*.

"Sir?"

"I see them. Stand by to attack."

"Yes, sir."

The rebuilt *Sigrun* was almost identical to the original.

"Almost," however, was the operative word. Even a casual observer would notice the long, cylindrical device slung under the main body's wedge, but a more astute eye might notice the open lens at the front or the thick cables connecting it to the hot singularity reactor housed at the back of the wedge, as well.

Now she enabled the x-ray laser and eased the *Sigrun*'s nose up to align with the closest corvette. Targeting data flowed between the *Valkyries* in an intricate flood, and graphical targeting sketched across her view.

She paused, fingers hovering over the weapon controls, and considered what she was about to do. She was about to open fire on not simply another vessel, but on other human beings with lives and loved ones of their own. Doubt crept into her mind, and her hands slowed, but then she thought of the bloody walls and scorched bodies in headquarters, the colleagues and friends she'd never see again.

Doubt turned into a distant memory, and everything became a little colder.

"Ready, sir."

"Take them out," Raoul ordered.

"Sir!"

The laser lanced into the SysPol corvette. The energy transfer was so sudden and powerful—the dynamic shock waves from the expansion of the corvette's surface so massive—that its bow simply exploded. The ship slewed to the side, but she tracked it, ripping the laser down its flank. The torrent of destruction pierced deep into the corvette's hull, split open its fusion reactor, and transformed the vessel instantly into a shower of glowing, spinning scrap.

She adjusted her aim and fired on the more distant corvette, but it executed a panicked zigzag. Instead of a direct, central hit, the laser simply licked a deep gouge across its side. She adjusted her aim, but the craft spiraled around in a wild evasive pattern, and her laser fire scattered into space.

Hala struggled to keep a bead on the slippery target, her weapon pulsing x-rays the whole time. Warnings flashed that the laser needed a chance to cool, and she eased off the trigger. Her eyes flicked across her controls, and she waited a few seconds for the upgraded cooling plants to catch up.

The corvette turned and fled, but she had no intention of letting it escape.

She lined up on the target once more and pressed the trigger. This time the beam bisected the corvette's hull, and the ship exploded in a fireball even more massive than its sister's.

"Targets down," Hala said.

"Nice shooting, Lieutenant," Raoul said. "Alpha Leader to Alpha Group. Target the station."

Six *Valkyries* sped in, and Hala glanced over the group's status. Alpha-Two through Alpha-Six were converted replication transports, so they came with cargo capacity to spare.

Each bow split open to reveal a vertical rack of three massive nuclear missiles, each a heavily armored spacecraft in its own right. They weren't the new "phase-missiles" she'd heard rumors about, but the quaesitors didn't need advanced weapons to destroy a target like Mycene Station.

"First wave, launch!" Raoul snapped.

Five nuclear missiles sprinted out of the converted transports.

"Stand by to launch second wave. And—"

"Sir, phase-in detected!" Hala looked up from her controls. "It's directly ahead!"

A TTV materialized ahead of them, gun pods open. It swooped down through the missiles, Gatling guns spewing metal death in all directions. Micro-explosions wracked the missiles, and three blew apart. Another spun away, its thruster off-line, and the TTV swung around, flying backward as it blasted the last missile into scrap.

Scope data populated beneath Hala's fingers, painting a familiar picture. She knew exactly which TTV this was.

"You lying bastards," she breathed, her face twisting into a snarl.

The *Kleio* turned, flying sideways with its bow pointed at them. Prog-steel split open, revealing the huge barrel of its mass driver as its aim settled on one of their *Valkyries*.

"All Alphas, evade!" Raoul shouted.

✧   ✧   ✧

The main cannon *thwumped*, and the one-ton projectile blasted out the barrel at over four kilometers per second. Its path took it through a transport DDT's open bow, and sixteen *million* joules of kinetic energy met the missiles within. The projectile shredded through the interior, and then its warhead exploded in a brilliant fireball that burst through armor seams and engulfed the time machine. Hot, glittering debris fanned out from the explosion.

"Take that, you bastards!" Philo shouted, thumping a fist.

"You tell 'em, Philo!" Elzbietá whooped. "Nobody launches missiles at *my* friends!"

"Warning," Kleio stated. "Radioactive material detected in the missile debris."

Philo's eyes widened. "They're firing *nukes* at us?"

"I believe so, Agent."

"Damn!" Elzbietá jerked the omni-throttle up, pulling them above the *Valkyrie* formation. "Now they've *really* pissed me off!"

"They could have detonated the nukes during our strafing run!" Philo squeaked.

"They won't get a second chance!" Elzbietá snapped harshly. "I'm going to stick to those transports like glue!"

"Easier said than done. That laser-armed DDT is turning toward us, and it looks angry!"

A powerful beam struck the *Kleio*'s hull, but the photons sluiced across its skin and scattered off the back in an ugly fan of energy.

"Yep!" Philo acknowledged. "They're angry!"

"How's the meta-armor?"

"Holding, but a little toasty. Energy mitigation at seventy percent."

"All right then!" Elzbietá shoved the throttle forward, and the *Kleio* dove at the Dynasty ships. More lasers streaked past the TTV, and some spalled along its hull as redirected photons sprayed off the meta-armor.

Philo worked the weapon controls, and the *Kleio*'s four gun pods spat concentrated fire at one of the missile-carrying DDTs. Explosive rounds pounded the craft, rupturing the top of its hull and savaging its internal systems. The *Kleio* zoomed past, pouring fire into it, and the vessel burst like an overripe fruit.

Elzbietá yanked on her joystick, and the *Kleio* spun around, now flying backward away from the Dynasty time machines, decelerating.

"Main cannon ready," Philo said. "And . . . firing!"

The shot from the mass driver punched up through another transport, and the force of the impact— combined with the payload detonation—split it in half within a searing, white-hot fireball.

"Two transports left!" Philo reported.

"On it!" Elzbietá turned to face them.

Laser fire slashed across the *Kleio*'s side. Elzbietá pulled up, then shoved her controls to the left, but the beam stayed locked on, burning into their flank.

"The armor's starting to thin!" Philo warned.

"We need to stop those last two transports!" Elzbietá

spun the ship on its long axis, presenting a cooler side of their armor. "Take them out!"

"Firing!"

Cannon rounds traced across space, and dozens impacted against the underbellies of both transports. Armor shattered, and one of the transports exploded while the other launched a pair of missiles before phasing out of reality.

"It's running!" Philo said. "Heading back to the *Dynasty*!"

Two missiles streaked toward Mycene Station.

Another beam smashed into the *Kleio*'s armor. Warning lights flashed on her console.

"The one with the laser isn't!" Elzbietá replied. "And we've got those nukes to deal with!"

Another hit drilled into their hull, and charred metamaterial flaked away.

"Port side meta-armor is *gone*!"

"Philo, take that *Valkyrie* down!"

Elzbietá brought the ship around, and Philo fired the main gun. The *Valkyrie* juked to the side at the last moment, and the round detonated beside it, sprinkling the craft with a directional cone of shrapnel.

"Missed!" Philo said. "Minor damage only!"

Elzbietá gritted her teeth and swung them after the nuclear missiles, but another laser pounded into them, and more damage indicators flashed.

"We can't keep taking these kinds of hits!" Philo warned.

"And we can't let those nukes reach the station!"

The *Kleio* sped after the two missiles with the last *Valkyrie* hot on its tail. A laser slashed across the TTV's impeller, and the spike shuddered.

"Ella!" Philo pleaded.

"Almost there! Is the main gun ready?"

"Charged and loaded!"

"Then have *I* got an angle for your shot!" She sketched a quick line over the tactical display, and Philo's eyes widened. He knew exactly what she was going to pull.

The flight paths of the two missiles had spread out, perhaps in an attempt to evade her, but all they'd done was form a convenient diagonal line that *didn't* bisect the station she was defending.

Elzbietá maxed out the thruster and skidded the *Kleio* sideways until the ship and both nuclear missiles formed three points on a straight line.

"Now, Philo!"

"Firing!"

The cannon shot streaked out of their bow and shattered its way through both missiles, leaving nothing but scrap in its wake.

"Got them!" Philo clenched a triumphant fist.

"It's not over yet!"

She reversed the *Kleio*'s thrusters and accelerated for the *Valkyrie*, presenting their undamaged frontal armor to the enemy as Philo clustered the gun pods near the bow. The *Valkyrie* flew straight toward them, but only after the two vessels were closing dangerously fast did the enemy pilot realize the error.

Laser fire splashed off meta-armor as four Gatling guns blazed away. Rounds pulverized one of the *Valkyrie*'s impeller mounts, and the craft corkscrewed before shifting into a wild, evasive pattern.

"Damn, this one's fast!" Philo growled.

"Keep hitting them!" Elzbietá said.

"I'm trying!"

The two ships spun around each other, spitting lasers and cannon rounds back and forth. Explosions wracked the *Valkyrie's* armor, and laser fire burned into the *Kleio's* hull.

"Cannon recharged!"

"Take the shot!"

Elzbietá pulled in behind the *Valkyrie*, but the enemy began to phase out even as Philo fired. The projectile streaked through an immaterial haze and kept going into the depths of space.

"Damn." Elzbietá clucked her tongue. "Almost had it. Are they coming around?"

"Don't think so," Philo said. "Both *Valkyries* are running for the Dynasty at seventy-four kilofactors."

"Keep an eye on them in case they get ambitious." Elzbietá blew out a tired breath and leaned back in her seat. "How bad are we hurt?"

"Most of it's superficial. The meta-armor can be replaced in—"

A flash lit up far beyond Mycene Station from a distant L5 industrial cluster, then two more flashes, each brighter than the sun.

"Oh, no," Elzbietá breathed. "Is that..."

"Nuclear detonations detected," Kleio reported.

CHAPTER THIRTY-FIVE

<hr>

Argus Station
SysGov, 2980 CE

KLAUS-WILHELM TOOK HIS SEAT AT THE ROUND table, a harsh scowl on his face as he wondered what he could have done differently, how the deaths at L5 could have been avoided.

It wasn't an unfamiliar moment for him.

His mind wandered back to Army Group South's blood-soaked march through the Balkans. How the Soviets had fought tooth and nail to stall his progress, how atrocity had spawned counter-atrocity. Civil wars were always the most terrible, and in many ways, *his* had been that sort of war. Not everyone had greeted the Western Alliance with open arms, and many of those who'd fought against the "liberators" had been just as patriotic as those who'd cheered them on.

It hadn't been the endless nightmare of the war another iteration of him had fought, perhaps. He'd made a point of reading the history of that other war—the one he and his grandson had ensured would happen as the ransom for fifteen universes. There'd been none of Adolf Hitler's murder-factory concentration camps in the war he'd fought, but there'd been "refugee camps" aplenty. No one had starved to death in them, and God knew no one had ·been *worked* to death in the name of the German people. But they'd still been stuffed with innocent people, forced into them by the savagery of the war which had rolled over their farms and villages like some dark, obscene tide, and if there'd been no outright starvation, there had been hunger and privation in plenty. And brutality, all too often. The sort of freelance brutality of individual brutes, seizing opportunities to slake their dark sides—not the organized savagery of the Third Reich. But had there truly been a difference for those on its receiving end? Was it only a matter of scale that made evil truly evil? It would have been so comforting if only he'd been able to tell himself that...

He could tell himself he'd done everything he could to mitigate that darkness, and that was true. But not all commanders, even on his own side, could have said the same. And no matter how hard he'd tried to protect the civilians in his own path, there'd been horror enough in the fighting itself to stoke any sane man's nightmares. And there'd been far too many sleepless nights when those nightmares had come to collect their due as he wrestled with his own demons.

It was his Yulia who'd helped to lay them at last, those demons. Lay them because she'd shared so many of them—so many memories *like* them—and only someone who'd been there could truly understand just how savage and unforgiving and merciless war actually was. How good men and women so often found themselves doing horrific things—and how evil men and women found license to *embrace* horrific things—when they were trapped in the maw of that ugly human activity called "war."

But Klaus-Wilhelm von Schröder had been there. He'd shouldered his own full share of that cancerous survivor's guilt, and none of the others around this table had. Not really. They weren't *soldiers* the way he and his men had been. They were *policemen*, and however brave they might be, however dedicated and highly trained, that was a very different thing to be. Did they understand—*truly* understand—that if Andover-Chen's math was as solid as it had always been before, their *best-case* outcome was almost certainly an entire dead universe? A universe in which every living thing on every planet orbiting every star in every *galaxy* of that universe died?

He doubted that they did, really. Not deep inside, where the demons spawned. They hadn't already assured *another* universe's death the way he and his grandson, and Elzbietá, Raibert, Philo, and his men had in those blood-soaked Saxon woods. And none of them—not one of them—had ever stood on that icy plain in their nightmares while the smoke blew about them on a cold, cutting wind and the stench of death filled their nostrils. They hadn't been forced to learn to keep going anyway. Or seen their own cold, calculating orders send so many young men to their deaths in the name of "victory."

In the end, he was convinced the liberation of the Ukraine and all the rest of the Soviet Union had been worth it. Yulia had helped him believe that, even though he'd always known that other Ukrainians had fought just as hard, and with just as deep a sense of patriotism, to preserve the Soviet Union as his beloved had fought to destroy it. But he couldn't deny, had never denied, how unremittingly savage the struggle had been.

Yet along the way he'd also learned a pitiless, skull-faced lesson. For leaders, every decision brought with it the possibility of terrible cost, and for all the late nights he'd spent dwelling on the prices paid for his victories, he'd never let it paralyze him into indecision, because that path led straight to hell. A leader who didn't lead, who succumbed to doubt and hesitation, was worse than useless. A leader needed to be confident. Not to the point of arrogance, but with the tough-minded sort of confidence that knew that somehow, as he always had before, he would find his way through to victory, whatever it took and however terrible the price might be. And for that to be true, he or she must always learn from past actions, which meant viewing them free of the lens of ego.

It was never easy. It was simply vital.

Klaus-Wilhelm eyed those assembled around the small table, first to Lamont, then to Hawke and Peng's avatar. He saw in them the same darkly searing sense of guilt now coursing through his soul. These men weren't looking to assign blame. If given the opportunity, each would likely confess to what he'd failed to foresee. Hawke especially, as the closest thing SysGov had to a military commander, sat under a cloud of dark brooding that was almost physically visible. The jewels of his two integrated ACs floated over each shoulder, their inner lights dim.

"The President will join us shortly," Lamont said,

rising from his seat, his voice soft but still somehow loud in the utterly silent room.

Klaus-Wilhelm stood, and his fellow commissioners did the same.

President Byakko's avatar appeared opposite Lamont. The artificial intelligence had chosen the form of an elderly woman, her snow-white hair bound in a tight bun. Pale, almost-white eyes stared out from a weathered, wrinkled face. She wore a dark green business suit with a static pattern not unlike dense blades of grass while the long scarf around her neck shifted with the striped fur of an albino tiger.

It was an uncommon look, given modern medical technology and access to synthetic bodies, but her avatar lacked any of the frailty associated with old age. Rather, she possessed an air of venerable experience and harsh determination.

A virtual chair flashed into existence, and she lowered herself into it.

"Gentlemen, please be seated."

Klaus-Wilhelm and the others sat down.

"So, Oliver. How bad is it?"

"Bad." Lamont summoned a false-scale diorama of L5. "The nukes went off in the heart of the Mitchell Complex. The main factory and most of its satellite facilities were completely destroyed."

A trio of graphical blasts spread out, and space-borne structures either vanished or turned varying shades of red.

"And the death toll?" she asked pointedly.

Lamont sat back and glanced to Peng, who nodded.

"We're still assessing the damage." The AC leaned forward. "A lot of civilian traffic was caught by the nukes, and we're having trouble accounting for everyone we believe was in the area. Search and rescue teams are out in force and won't return until I'm confident every life that can be saved has been. With that said, our current estimate for the death toll is . . ." He paused and grimaced. "Over seventy thousand, most of whom worked for the Mitchell Group."

"What of our own losses?"

"Five corvettes destroyed," Hawke reported. "Fifty-three officers dead, thirty-nine of whom didn't have connectome saves and are permanent casualties."

"And our cruisers? Did they suffer any damage?"

"No." Hawke frowned before continuing. "They were either out on assignment or unable to reach L5 in time."

"I see." Byakko let the words hang in the air, her eyes fixed on the patrol fleet commissioner.

Hawke bent his head slightly under the unspoken reprimand. Klaus-Wilhelm had served under a variety of bosses over the years, and one or two of them had subscribed to the foaming-at-the-mouth-while-shouting school of discipline. In many ways, Byakko's dispassionate questioning cut much deeper, since Hawke couldn't defend against the silent accusation without admitting he'd *also* thought of it.

"What about the c-bomb's development?" she asked after a lengthy, uncomfortable pause.

"Klaus?" Lamont nodded to him.

"Madam President, the project has been severely impacted," Klaus-Wilhelm reported. "The losses at L5 represent thirty-six percent of SysGov's total exotic matter production and *fifty-eight* percent of what was allotted to the project. As a rough estimate, our timetable just got doubled from three months to six, and we may struggle to meet even that."

"Was the c-bomb project the motive for this attack?" Byakko asked.

"It was," Klaus-Wilhelm said. "A few minutes after phasing out, one of the Dynasty time machines sent us a telegraph where they outlined the motives behind the attack as well as a set of demands. Its contents make it clear they knew about the exotic matter being amassed at Mycene Station and viewed it as a threat."

"Basically, they're telling us, 'You better quit that. Or else,'" Peng commented.

"Be that as it may, their attack on Mycene Station failed," Byakko observed. "How vulnerable is the station now?"

"We're working to secure it," Lamont said. "We've moved assets from both Argo and Gordian Divisions to the station, and its defense force now consists of six TTVs and eleven realspace ships, including one of our *Directive*-class cruisers. The *Lecroix*, to be specific."

Byakko nodded approvingly, and Klaus-Wilhelm could appreciate why. Technically, the *Directives* were classified as "Emergency Reinforcement Cruisers," but that was nothing more than obfuscating jargon in his book. They were the ships SysPol used when they *really* meant business, completely self-sufficient and equipped with enough printers and heavy weapons to handle any crisis. Each massive craft was equal parts battleship, carrier, and mobile fortress, but no one used those descriptions because SysPol was a police force, not a military organization.

"What if the Dynasty attacks again and in greater numbers?" Byakko asked simply.

"I've recalled half the fleet back to Earth," Hawke said. "It'll take some time for all the ships to return, but our core installations will become more secure by the day."

"The First Responders are doing their part as well," Peng added. "We're printing mechs and static defenses for each SysPol station and all major industrial centers so we can intercept incoming nukes."

"And we've stepped up our reconnaissance," Klaus-Wilhelm said. "Most of our TTVs are now on a rotating transdimensional patrol near the outer wall, and we're working on ways to improve the Argus Array's ability to detect incoming Dynasty craft."

"That all seems reasonable," Byakko said, her tone still cold, then flicked her eyes to Lamont. "How's the Admin taking all of this?"

"Not well. Muntero and Shigeki have demanded an explanation. They aren't happy about being in the dark."

"Keep them that way for now. I'll deal with them myself later."

"As you wish, Madam President."

Byakko rapped her virtual fingers on the table and let out a long, burdened sigh.

"Gentlemen." She glanced at each of them in turn. "As the saying goes, 'Hindsight has perfect resolution.' We could spend an eternity digging through who should have done what and who screwed up the most, but I'm not interested in that conversation. At least not right now."

"President, if I may—"

"Let me *finish*, Oliver," she said with icy precision. Lamont smiled painfully and sat back.

"I'm not interested in pointing fingers—and let's

be clear, there is *plenty* of blame to go around, so we're going to fast-forward through all that wasted effort." She gestured to Hawke. "Your ships weren't where they should have been, despite the fact that it's your *job* to deploy the patrol fleet so it can respond to any crisis."

Hawke opened his mouth to speak, but Byakko continued without pausing.

"And then you'll say you had no reason to expect an attack on this scale. And you might be right." She faced Peng. "Your First Responders didn't even transmit onto the scene, despite the fact that a few rapidly printed mechs *might* have been enough to stop those missiles."

Peng shrank back. He let out a soft grunt, grimaced and nodded.

"Then you'll say that events unfolded too rapidly and your division didn't have a firm handle on what was happening until it was too late. And that view could be warranted." She turned to Klaus-Wilhelm. "As for the Gordian Division, you failed to detect the attack until it was almost too late. Now, you might excuse this lapse by saying you don't have enough resources and you're struggling to develop procedures for all this new technology."

Klaus-Wilhelm kept his face neutral and waited calmly for the president to continue.

"And that could very well be true. Your division also halted the attack on Mycene, so I must begrudgingly thank you for that service."

He gave the president a brief nod, even though he didn't feel the praise—indeed *any* praise—was warranted here.

"However!" Byakko said sharply. "You and Doctor Beckett were supposed to find a diplomatic solution to this mess, and now one minor scuffle has escalated into *this*!" She indicated the diorama's notable void where the Mitchell Complex once had been. "Gentlemen, all the excuses you'd give may very well be valid. But that doesn't make those seventy thousand people any less dead. A long, hard look at your failures may happen, but it won't happen today, because I don't care."

"Madam President," Lamont said stiffly. He glanced to the men on either side of him, then met Byakko's harsh glare. "I completely understand you're displeased with my commissioners. However, as chief of police, it is ultimately—"

"Your fault?" she finished. "Of course it is. But again, how does that bring back the dead?"

Lamont's faux-smile was frozen on his lips.

"It doesn't." She leaned forward. "All of the excuses and blame and repercussions will wait for another day. Because this act of violence against us cannot and *will not* go unanswered. How dare they ignore our overtures of peace! How *dare* the Dynasty attack us without provocation! How *dare* they murder our people!"

Her pale eyes glowed with an inner fire.

"Gentlemen, as soon as I transmit back to the capital, I'll be presenting a formal declaration of war to the Senate, which I expect will be ratified swiftly."

The room sucked in a collective breath.

"There's no turning back once we go down this road, Madam President," Lamont cautioned.

"I'm well aware of that," Byakko said. "And I don't make this decision lightly. If I honestly thought diplomacy had a chance, I'd pursue it, but I've seen *no* evidence that talking with the Dynasty will solve anything."

So it's come to this, Klaus-Wilhelm thought darkly. *A war between our two Earths.*

"Once the formal declaration is out of the way, I will officially charge SysPol with destroying the Dynasty's ability to wage war against us. The specifics, I leave up to you."

She stood up, the avatar of a frail elderly woman somehow looming over them.

"Gentlemen, force those bastards to the bargaining table. Preferably on their knees."

◇   ◇   ◇

"So that's where we stand," Lamont finished sometime later.

"I can't believe Lucius would go this far." Teodorà put a hand to her forehead. "Samuel and I never intended for something like this to happen. Please understand that."

"We're not here to assign blame," Hawke said, echoing the president's earlier sentiments. "We're here to find solutions."

"The *Tesseract*," Klaus-Wilhelm said. "That should be our first target. Not only is its construction affecting the integrity of their outer wall, but it could become a major military asset when the hyperforges come online. Once it's destroyed, we should target the replication centers to bring the Dynasty's industry to a grinding halt. You said it yourself, Doctor. The Dynasty doesn't have enough conventional production to meet its needs. If we want to apply the maximum amount of pressure while still retaining a chance at diplomacy, that's where we strike."

"All sound arguments." Lamont gestured to Teodorà with an open hand. "Doctor?"

"You realize what you're asking of me."

"We're asking you to help us end this conflict as quickly and efficiently as possible," Klaus-Wilhelm said flatly. "The longer it drags out, the more people will lose their lives and the closer the Dynasty's outer wall comes to collapse."

"Maybe if I tried talking to the council directly. Bypass Lucius somehow."

"Are you sure that'll work anymore?" Klaus-Wilhelm said. "Do you know what lies Gwon's seeded amongst your leadership? Which members are in his back pocket? How they might think we brainwashed you into parroting whatever lies we want? Do you know who to trust and who will stab you in the back?"

"I . . ." She shook her head. "No, I don't."

"Regardless of what connections or control Gwon possesses in the Dynasty, he has his limits," Klaus-Wilhelm continued. "From what you've shared, Dynasty politics don't sound all that different from our own."

"You're right. They're not."

"Then if enough bad decisions pile up, your leadership will turn to someone else for advice. Someone who isn't pouring poison into their ears and leading them on the path to ruin."

Teodorà began to nod in agreement, and Klaus-Wilhelm shrugged.

"That means it's our job to make Gwon's plans go as poorly as possible," he said.

"All right then." Teodorà let out a slow sigh. "And you're right, of course. Hitting the *Tesseract* should be your first priority. Samuel and I never intended the hyperforges to be instruments of war, but the more I think about it, the more I believe Lucius had other plans for a very long time."

"When does it become operational?" Hawke asked.

"The first hyperforge was scheduled to begin limited testing in about three weeks. The station impeller comes online three weeks after that, followed by more tests at the full production rate."

"Six weeks then," Hawke said. "Per the original schedule."

"We have to assume the Dynasty's doing everything it can to expedite construction," Klaus-Wilhelm said.

"Agreed." Hawke nodded. "Which means we need to hit them as soon as possible." He turned to Lamont. "Chief, we have the Argo Division emergency plan. It's time to execute it."

"An emergency plan?" Teodorà scrunched her brow. "Against the *Dynasty*?"

"No, the Admin," Lamont clarified. "In case a transdimensional war ever broke out."

"Sometimes it pays to be paranoid," Peng commented with a joyless smile.

Teodorà rubbed her forehead. "I can't believe I'm hearing this."

"Believe it, Doctor," Lamont said. "Do the scaffolds work? Can we transport our cruisers to the Dynasty? As I recall, three scaffolds are complete."

"That's right, and the scaffolds are large enough for the *Directive*-class. We've even conducted a short test flight involving the *Maxwell* and eight Gordian TTVs attached in a cubical formation. It was only to one negative week and back, but far enough to prove the method is stable."

"Then it's a viable option," Lamont noted cautiously. "What do you propose?"

"Three scaffolds gives us the lift for three *Directives*. And there are already enough of the class near Earth: *Maxwell*, *Zhang*, and *Lecroix*. Gordian Division provides eight TTVs each for transportation to the Dynasty. All they have to do is drop us off in the Dynasty's True Present, and Argo Division will do the rest. Doctor, what sort of patrol fleet does the Dynasty have?"

"It's very limited. The quaesitors don't have anything like a *Directive*. They never needed one."

"Then this'll work," Hawke said. "Naturally, sir, I'll take personal command of the mission from *Maxwell*, given what we're dealing with."

"I'd like to come along, too," Peng said. "The First Responders won't be any help in the battle, but I can still chip in from the bridge of one of the *Directives*."

"Thanks, Peng," Hawke said. "It'll be a pleasure to have you along."

"How do you propose we take out the station?" Lamont asked.

"Well, self-replicators are almost useless against exotic matter, so we'll have to blow it apart piece by piece. I suggest nuclear and directed-energy weapons. We'll have Argus Station print out the appropriate weaponry and then load up the *Directives* before departure."

"I'm sorry, but I must strongly advise against this course of action," Klaus-Wilhelm said sharply, and the others turned to him.

"What's wrong, Klaus?" Lamont asked.

"We're not talking about a realspace problem here, but a transdimensional one, and that means Argo is ill-suited to deal with it," Klaus-Wilhelm replied, and Hawke's jaw tightened.

"And I suppose that means Gordian would be better?" he asked.

"Correct." Klaus-Wilhelm met his eyes levelly. "We're dealing with militarized time machines and what might be a time-traveling battle station. Real-space ships like the *Directives*, as impressive as they are, are the wrong tool for the job."

"I'd *hardly* call those *Valkyries* militarized," Hawke noted stiffly. "Most of them were just transports stuffed with nuclear missiles. That might be effective against civilian targets, but taking on my cruisers is a completely different story."

"All the firepower you can muster won't do a lick of good if the target isn't in phase."

"*They* need to phase-lock to hit *us* as well, and when they do"—Hawke smacked his hands together—"we'll squash them like bugs."

"And the station you're planning to destroy?"

"Its impeller won't be finished. It's not going anywhere."

"We don't *know* that," Klaus-Wilhelm pointed out. "We *can't* know until we're in the thick of it, and then it'll be too late. What happens if we have to abort? How are the TTVs supposed to pick up the *Directives* in the middle of a firefight?"

"My cruisers will ensure the area is clear before the TTVs come in for extraction."

"And what if there are *Valkyries* swarming all over the place?" Klaus-Wilhelm pressed.

"Then your TTVs will need to do their damn jobs!" Hawke snapped back.

Klaus-Wilhelm suppressed a frown. Hawke was clearly determined to lead the counterattack against the Dynasty, and Klaus-Wilhelm suspected the patrol fleet's earlier failure at L5 was a huge factor in the man's stubborn resolve. In a way, he sympathized with the commissioner's reasoning; Hawke had failed once already and he wanted to leap into action. He wanted to redeem his earlier failure...and he wanted payback.

But however understandable all of that might be, it also meant he was prepared to shove any inconvenient facts aside. It was an attitude Klaus-Wilhelm had seen entirely too often, and out of far more experienced military commanders. And that was the real point here, he realized. However many decades Hawke might have spent in command of Argo Division, all of those years had been in *peacetime*. When it came to actual combat, to commanding men and women in the crucible of war, Klaus-Wilhelm von Schröder had more experience than all the other officers in this room combined.

And they didn't know it.

I need to put an end to this here and now, he thought, and looked the commissioner straight in the eye.

"Commissioner Hawke," he said in the most respectful tone he could muster. "There are too many unknowns, too many ways your plan could go wrong. And while I respect your many years of service with SysPol, what this situation calls for is *military* expertise." He placed a hand on his own chest. "I have a quarter century of *actual* combat experience, which is something no one here at this table can say. I've survived hells the likes of which you can only visit in the abstract. I've seen the best-laid plans fall apart around me, had to piece them back together while shellfire blasted my men to bloody bits. I've persevered through successes and failures alike, from the battalion level to command of whole army groups. I've freed entire *nations*, and the one thing I can absolutely guarantee is that *no* plan will work as well as the planners thought it would once people actually begin to die. I've *seen* it happen—far too many times, in reality and not in simulations—and because I have, I've also learned to do *whatever it takes* to get the job done. What we need here is not a commissioner, but a *general*."

Hawke stood slowly and leaned toward him.

"What we don't need, Klaus," he said flatly, "is a relic from a forgotten age."

Klaus-Wilhelm's eyes flared at the insult, and he sucked in a sharp breath, but Hawke continued before he could speak.

"Let's be honest here, Klaus. We've tolerated you. We've let you play with your little time machines, and you've done a good job of it, no complaints here. But this is serious. This is *war*. War in the thirtieth century, which doesn't involve tanks or mortars or trudging around in the muck of a gravity well. You're out of your depth here. It's time to put the toys aside and let those who actually know how war in this century works lead our forces." He favored Klaus-Wilhelm with a condescending smile that stopped just short of a sneer. "We don't need a relic like you."

"Besser ein Relikt als ein Narr," he snapped back without thinking.

"Hättest du es lieber, dass ich dich ein nutzloses Fossil nenne?" Hawke replied in perfect German.

"Guys, please!" Peng's avatar vanished and reappeared

between the two. "I had to download a language file for that one. Let's keep it civil, okay?"

"All three of you sit down!" Lamont barked. Peng teleported back to his virtual seat, and Lamont waited silently for Klaus-Wilhelm and Hawke to seat themselves.

"Good grief!" the SysPol chief said. "All I can say is I'm glad the President wasn't here to see this."

"Sir, my stance remains unchanged," Klaus-Wilhelm stressed. "The Gordian Division must plan and lead the attack."

"That's enough, Klaus. While I appreciate your initiative, Hawke's right, though he worded it in a rather...unfortunate way. But the point is a valid one; we need someone in charge who has more modern experience than you do. Argo Division will lead the attack."

"But, sir—!"

"And Gordian Division will provide Argo with its unwavering support," Lamont cut in. "I've made my decision, and it's final. Is that clear enough for you, Klaus?"

Klaus-Wilhelm glanced across the table at Hawke, expecting a look of smug victory, but found only grim determination. Hawke hadn't enjoyed tearing Klaus-Wilhelm down; he'd only done what he thought was necessary to win the argument.

Which made him not one bit less a fool.

"It's clear, sir," Klaus-Wilhelm von Schröder said finally.

CHAPTER THIRTY-SIX

~~~~~~∞∞∞~~~~~~

Argus Station
SysGov, 2980 CE

RAIBERT STEPPED OUT OF A COUNTER-GRAV TUBE near the southern pole of Argus Station's cylindrical hull. A bright virtual marquee hovered over the open entrance: a knotted piece of rope with a gleaming sword slashing down at it. Bold letters spelled out THE TANGLED KNOT beside the graphic.

The Gordian Division might have been in its infancy compared to the other, more established divisions, but it was still large enough to attract a satellite of civilian businesses. A few Gordian-themed restaurants and recreational facilities had already cropped up here, around the Gordian Division's levels, and the Tangled Knot had quickly become Raibert's favorite when it opened a few months ago.

He pushed down a nervous flutter in the pit of his stomach, tugged his uniform straight, and walked in.

The large circular bar dominated the middle of the domed room, ringed by dozens of tables. About a third of the seats were full, mostly with Operations personnel enjoying dinner, although Raibert spotted a few TTV crews. A handful of ACs stuck to themselves, either manifesting their avatars by the outer wall or floating near the ceiling. Party games glowed brightly over two of the tables, and a cheer rose from the far side of the room.

Teodorà spotted him from her barstool and waved him over.

"Hey." He sat down next to her.

"Hey yourself."

"What'll it be, Raibert?" Farrokh asked from behind the bar.

"Umm. The usual, I guess."

"Certainly. One whiskey ginger coming right up." The chrome-skinned four-armed synthoid set a clean glass on the bar and filled it from two bottles simultaneously. He pushed the glass forward with his fourth arm as the others put away the ingredients.

"Thanks." Raibert sent the bartender a generous Esteem tip and raised the amber drink to his lips.

Farrokh dipped his head graciously.

Raibert took a sip, then set the glass down. The alcohol wouldn't affect him unless he activated his body's "high fidelity" mode. Still tasted great, though.

"Thanks for coming," Teodorà said, slouched over her own drink, her cheeks flushed.

"Oh, it was no trouble at all. Andover-Chen has me running errands for him, so it'll be a while before I head back to Mycene." He tilted his head. "What are you having?"

"An Argus Special." She raised a tall drink. Liquid filled the glass in colored layers of black, gray, clear, red, blue, and white, each staying separate due to their different densities.

"Good choice. Bit busy for my tastes, but the different flavors complement each other well."

"I know. This is my third." She glanced at him with lidded eyes. "The Arete layer is my favorite."

"Ah." He turned to the bartender. "Still missing Gordian, I see."

"I have an updated version if you'd like to try it," Farrokh said. "But I'm not entirely happy with it yet. That's why it's not on the menu."

"Having some trouble finding a good flavor for Gordian?" Raibert asked.

"That and deciding where to slot it in."

"Well, I'm sure you'll figure it out." Raibert twitched his head subtly to the side then flicked his eyes toward Teodorà.

Farrokh winked and stepped around to another part of the bar.

"So, this is a surprise," Raibert said once they were somewhat alone. "It's been a while since we shared a few drinks, even for me. What brought this on?"

"Raibert, am I a good person?"

"I . . ." He frowned, taken aback by the blunt question. "Well, umm . . . I guess?"

She drank up the bottom layer of the Argus Special with her straw and waited.

"Uh, I mean, you have good *intentions*," he continued, trying to recover. "That counts for a lot right there. But you did . . . sort of land us all in this mess."

She sucked in another layer, her eyes fixed forward.

"Granted, this wasn't *all* your fault. Lucius deserves most of the blame, but it doesn't change the fact that you ignored all the danger signs thrown in front of you just so you could satisfy your own desire for redemption. Hate to break it to you, but that was awfully selfish of you. So, like I said, good intentions. Just maybe not the best—"

"Uh!" Teodorà smacked her hand on the table.

"Probably not the answer you were looking for," Raibert muttered.

"Did you really think I was looking for an honest response?" she snapped.

"Well . . . yeah?"

"You were always rubbish at this," she groaned, shaking her head.

"Rubbish at what?"

"Good grief, Raibert! I just want some *sympathy*! Is that too much to ask?"

"Oh." He blinked, then grimaced. "Sorry. My mistake." He cleared his throat. "You are a wonderful person, a true treasure of the multiverse, and I count myself as blessed to even be in the same room as you."

She glared at him.

"Not working?" he asked.

She maintained the intense stare, but then a smile cracked on her lips.

"Not in the least."

"Well, at least I made you smile. That's got to count for something."

"Yeah, I suppose it does." She glanced down at her drink, then pushed it away.

"Seriously, though, the answer is yes. I think deep down you're a good person." He shrugged. "Even the best people make mistakes, though. The ones you've made are just . . . rather larger than most."

"Can't argue with that." She shook her head and sighed.

"So, is this really about you wanting sympathy from an old friend?" he leaned forward onto his elbows. "Or is there something else?"

"A little of both, I guess." She looked up at him. "Commissioner Hawke has requested my presence on *Maxwell* when his forces leave."

"Ah. Yeah, I can see where you might be a bit conflicted with that one."

"It's not that I'm conflicted," she groaned. "This is my mess, and I need to accept that. I'd just rather help in a different way, you know?"

"Sure, I understand. Why does Hawke want you on his command ship?"

"Because I'm the closest thing he has to an expert on the *Tesseract*," she said, and Raibert nodded.

"Who better to advise him on how to destroy it?"

"Exactly. And he's right, of course. Even with whatever secrets Lucius has up his sleeves."

"It's those secrets that worry me."

"Yeah. Same here." She grimaced at her half-finished drink.

"What did you tell Hawke?"

"I haven't said anything yet." She turned to him. "I wanted to talk to you first."

"Well, I think you should turn him down."

"Really?" She frowned at him. "That surprises me."

"Hawke's plan is too risky. There are too many things that can go wrong." He paused and leaned in for emphasis. "Too many ways you could *die* if you go."

"Maybe so, but Hawke's plan's the only one in motion with a real shot at saving the Dynasty," Teodorà pointed out. "The chances of the Dynasty pulling through are basically zero if we can't shut down the *Tesseract*. Diplomacy hasn't worked, so forcibly preventing it from going live is our next best option."

"I see." He nodded, contemplating her words. Raibert's efforts with the c-bomb were SysGov-centric by design, working off the assumption the Dynasty was a lost cause. He'd been buried in that mindset for some time now, but he understood and appreciated why Teodorà still clung to hope. Maybe there *was* hope after all.

"Do you think you can make a difference?"

"Yes. Even if just a little."

"Then I think your choice is clear." He sighed. "I hate to see you risk your life like this, but we both know a little help in the right place sometimes makes all the difference. If I were in your shoes, I'd have to go."

"It's good to hear you say that." She smiled at him. "You've changed, you know?"

"How so?" he asked cautiously.

"You're . . . I don't know. More confident than when we were dating. More decisive."

"You really think so?"

"Maybe you don't see it, but I do. Back at ART, you were a bit like a pressure cooker."

"And what's *that* supposed to mean?"

"You possessed a calm exterior that belied the dangerous forces building within. Which would then explode at the worst possible moment."

"If you're referring to how Philo and I crashed the Alexandria Exhibition, I'm not apologizing."

"I'm not asking you to." She smiled again with

half-lidded eyes. "Perhaps transitioning into that brute-of-a-synthoid body of yours had something to do with it."

"Having one's mind ripped out of their original body without consent tends to leave a mark."

"That too, I suppose." She shrugged. "By the way, I think it's a change for the better. It suits you."

"Don't expect me to thank the Admin anytime soon."

"I wouldn't dream of it." She chuckled, then turned to him. "Thanks for the encouragement. I needed it."

"You're welcome, though I'm sure you'd have come to the same conclusion without me."

"You give me too much credit." Her cheeks cooled and her eyes sharpened as her body exited the buzz of high-fidelity mode. "All right. Let's get this over with." She opened a comm window.

Hawke's face appeared a few seconds later.

"Yes, Doctor? Have you reached a decision?"

"I have," Teodorà said with absolute certainty. "Count me in."

❖   ❖   ❖

"*Kleio* to *Maxwell*," Elzbietá said. "We're moving into position."

"Roger that, *Kleio*."

The *Maxwell* floated below them, a vast spherical vessel girdled by a fishbone-like cage of exotic matter ribs. Elzbietá adjusted the distance with delicate bursts of gravitons until the *Kleio* slotted into a rounded groove on the scaffold. Prog-steel struts on both craft connected, merged, and the *Kleio* jostled before coming to rest.

Elzbietá sat in the virtual cockpit with Philo by her side, her real body cushioned safely within the compensation bunk's microbot soup. She licked her lips, her nerves tense and senses sharp at the thought of flying into combat, but then she looked down past her feet at the *Directive*-class cruiser and smiled at its reassuring bulk.

"I know the boss is against this," she said, glancing sideways at Philo, "but damn if these ships aren't impressive as hell."

"That's kind of the point with the *Directives*. They're designed to be the solution when all other options fail."

Blisters for weapons, thrusters, and scopes dotted the *Maxwell*'s gunmetal hull, and a massive round iris led to the mech hangar at the craft's center. Its nine-hundred-meter diameter might not sound all *that* much bigger than the *Kleio*'s one-hundred-fifty-meter length, but a third of the *Kleio*'s length was taken up by its impeller spike, and the rest was stretched into an ellipsoid, not a sphere. Do a little math, and the *Maxwell*'s internal volume came out to *six thousand times* the volume of her TTV.

And we're bringing three of these beasts, she thought as the sunlight gleamed off the *Zhang* and *Lecroix*, partially visible beyond the *Maxwell* with their own TTV escorts closing in around them.

Elzbietá had initially wondered why SysGov, a society that was under no external threat until recently, would build such powerful and versatile juggernauts. But then she realized her confusion stemmed from her uniquely twenty-first-century viewpoint.

SysGov was a society where protestors used self-replicators to carve kilometer-wide letters on the surface of the moon, an act that was being characterized by the Society as a mere *prank*! It was a place where the ramifications of *dismantling a whole planet* were debated in the courts, and where she herself was participating in a program to build something that might *end a whole universe*!

SysGov technology allowed for a quality of life unthinkable to her time of origin, but it also enabled nightmare scenarios on a mind-boggling scale if left unrestrained. Or if demented individuals abused it. The thirtieth century was a very different—and potentially *much* scarier—place than her native time, and it was SysPol's job to hold those terrible possibilities at bay.

The *Directives* were the final word in SysPol's mission to ensure order and stability. No matter what kind of crisis came up, the *Directives* would always be there, ready and able to face *any* challenge. They were the ultimate trump card for and the absolute guarantor of safety and security in the Consolidated System Government.

And the people of the solar system slept more soundly, comforted by the knowledge that if the dark ever encroached upon their way of life—if push came to shove, so to speak—SysPol would shove back very, *very* hard.

"Are all the *Directives* named after SysGov presidents?" Elzbietá asked.

"Almost all of them," Philo said. "Isaac Maxwell *might* have been the first president if he hadn't been assassinated. You could say he's an honorary inclusion because he was so instrumental in founding our government."

"Makes sense. I suppose there'll be a cruiser named 'Byakko' someday too, right?"

"I hope not," he groused, his lips drooping into a frown of inhuman proportions.

"Oh? Why's that? Don't you like her?"

"She didn't get *my* vote, I can tell you that much."

"But she's an AC. Why wouldn't you vote for her?"

"Oh, my God!" Philo goggled at her. "That is such an offensive thing to say! Not all ACs vote abstract-only!"

"*Sooo*-rry!" She chuckled. "Didn't mean to hit a nerve there."

"I'll have you know I vote for physical candidates quite often!"

"It's okay, Philo. It's okay." She reached over and shook him by the shoulder. "If it makes you feel any better, I didn't vote for her either."

"You weren't even here during the last election!"

"Come on, I didn't mean anything by it," she laughed. "Besides, think of it this way. Now you have plenty of time to fill me in before the next one."

"Well, for starters, I consider myself a moderate who leans Statist. Same with Raibert, whereas Byakko is a Consolidationist hardliner. No such thing as too much centralized power when it comes to her type! Plus she used to be a big ART supporter before that position became politically toxic, and don't get me started on the whole Butterfly terraforming scandal. Back in 2943 when she was just a senator, she and—"

"Incoming call from Mycene Station," Kleio reported.

"Wonderful timing!" Elzbietá said brightly. "You can tell me the rest later."

Philo crossed his arms with a harrumph and settled deeper into his seat.

Elzbietá clicked the popup, which expanded into a 2D view of Benjamin and Raibert shadowed by the towering form of the exotic matter printer behind them.

"Hey, guys," Elzbietá said.

"Hey, beautiful." Benjamin smiled back at her. "You be careful out there. Come back in one piece, okay?"

"Don't plan to do it any other way."

"You too, buddy," Raibert said. "It's weird not having you hanging out in the back of my head."

Philo flashed a warm smile. "I feel the same."

"We'd come along, but..." Raibert shrugged.

"Yeah, we know," Philo said. "You're needed where you are."

"Don't worry. We got this," Elzbietá reassured him. "The two of us can handle those *Valkyries*."

"Of course you can," Benjamin nodded, then grimaced. "But it's not the *Valkyries* I'm worried about."

"It's *Tesseract*," Elzbietá finished.

"Too many fucking unknowns with that thing," Raibert said. "Doesn't make me feel any better that Lucius knows *exactly* how SysPol is organized. He has to have a pretty damned good idea of what we can send at him, and we don't have a clue about what he's been up to—what *else* he's been up to—that not even Teodorà has a clue about!" He shook his head, his expression grim. "And Argo's charging straight into the thick of it."

"Signal from *Maxwell*," Philo said. "Time to warm up the impeller."

"I love you," Benjamin said.

"I love you, too." Elzbietá blew Benjamin a kiss. A virtual pair of red lips on wings appeared next to him and smacked into his cheek. His wetware carried over the physical touch, and he flinched back, then rubbed his cheek with a grin.

"What was that?" he asked.

"Thirtieth-century version of an emoji." She flashed

a lopsided grin. "Been waiting for the right moment to use it."

"Be safe out there," he repeated.

"See you soon."

❖   ❖   ❖

"There? You see that?" Kloss tapped the virtual display of *Pathfinder-Prime*'s chronometric scope. "Looks like the TTVs are powering up their impellers."

"That it does, sir," Durantt agreed, floating beside him.

Twenty-four TTV icons glowed on the display, and chronometric field lines expanded outward to encompass the three SysGov warships with which they were docked. The impressive force had begun mustering outside Argus Station only a few hours ago, and Kloss had ordered *Pathfinder-Prime* toward the earth for a closer look while still staying out of phase with the True Present.

"Reversing thrust now, sir. Holding position at one hundred kilometers from the station."

"Are we near enough to detect their exit vector to the Dynasty?" Kloss asked, bracing himself against the wall with a splayed palm. "I'd think that many TTVs crammed together and heading the same way *should* be enough."

"Navigators?" Durantt asked, turning to his crew.

"I'm not sure, sir," the temporal navigator said. "Our dish simply isn't designed to detect lateral chronometric movement. The signal *may* be large enough at this range, but I have my doubts."

"How close do we need to get?"

"To be absolutely certain we see their vector? Umm, within eight kilometers, I'd say. Anything farther and the lateral component will have attenuated too much. It'll blend in with all the stuff our scope *is* designed to detect."

"Eight kilometers..." Kloss let out a slow, nervous sigh and glanced over the array of icons one more time. With the chronoport non-congruent, five minutes in Argus Station's past, no conventional system could detect them, and their impeller was throttled back to absolute minimum, drawing just enough power to hold them there. It was an ideal situation for stealth, but there were limits in all things, and the closer they got...

I so don't want to shout "Here we are!" at them, he thought, *and not just for diplomatic reasons. But...*

"Take us in, Captain," he said.

"Director, please reconsider," Durantt warned. "I'm not confident our stealth systems will hold up at that range, and we're dangerously exposed as it is. If we're spotted and they decide to phase-lock on us, those warships will melt us down in *seconds.*"

"I'm well aware of the dangers, Captain." Kloss grabbed a handhold and turned to face the man. "SysPol isn't exactly a shoot-first kind of outfit, but I'm sure recent events have made them...jumpy when it comes to unannounced guests."

Durantt blew out a breath, and his mustache wobbled.

"But you're going to order us in anyway," he said levelly.

"We can't afford to miss this opportunity. We *need* to know how to reach the Dynasty if the Admin's going to have a hand in whatever events are unfolding."

Durantt raised his chin. "Your orders, Director?"

"You know what they are. Move us in until we have a clear signal."

"Yes, sir." He turned to the navigators. "Take us in. *Slowly*, but be ready to pull us out at the first sign of trouble."

Kloss kicked off the front wall and floated to his seat in the back row. He grabbed the handhold above the headrest and pulled himself into place as Durantt floated down into the seat next to him. They both strapped in.

"All hands, secure for possible combat acceleration," the realspace navigator announced on a ship-wide channel. Each compartment signaled its readiness, lighting up on a cutout diagram on his display, and the navigator muttered, "Here we go."

The firm hand of a single gee pressed Kloss into the seat. He opened a duplicate of the navigation virtual console and watched the distance drop away.

"Ninety-eight kilometers to target. Speed at two hundred meters per second. Cutting thrusters."

The acceleration vanished, and the chronoport coasted forward on inertia only.

"TTVs are increasing power to their impellers. Scope indicates the warships are beginning to shift out of phase."

"Twelve kilometers to target. Standby for retro-thrust in ten sec—"

"Negative," Kloss interrupted. "Hold our present course and speed."

Durantt turned sharply and Kloss met his gaze.

"We're still too far away," he said.

The realspace navigator looked at Durantt for confirmation, and for a moment Kloss thought the captain would protest the order change. But instead Durantt gave the navigator a choppy nod.

"Make it so," he said, and sat back to wait. His expression was one of iron calm, but his fingers were white-knuckled over his armrests.

"Yes, sir. Relative speed steady at two hundred meters per second. Distance now nine kilometers and falling."

"The warships are shifting out of phase."

"Come on . . ." Kloss hissed.

"Distance is eight kilometers and falling."

"SysPol fleet has phased out."

"Applying retro-thrust now, sir."

"Did we get the exit vector?" Kloss asked.

"Yes, sir. Scope picked it up, loud and clear."

"Any sign we've been spotted?" Kloss asked.

"Negative, sir. None that I can detect."

Durantt let out a long, relieved exhale.

"Excellent work." Kloss rubbed his hands together. "We'll give that fleet some distance before we move out."

"Move out?" Durantt asked. "To where?"

"Why, Captain, I thought it would be obvious." Kloss flashed a sly smile. "We're going to tail that fleet all the way to the Dynasty."

CHAPTER THIRTY-SEVEN

⬬⬬⬬

Emergency Reinforcement Cruiser *Maxwell*
non-congruent

COMMISSIONER HAWKE LEANED OVER THE COMMAND table on *Maxwell*'s abstract bridge. The ship drove through the transverse, a state for which it had never been designed, and the abstract and physical crew members alike moved about the bridge, consuming the data pouring in through the ship's scopes or being shared from the docked TTVs. They were breaking barely eighteen kilofactors because of the "ugly chronometric drag" of his cruisers, which had stretched their trip to the *Dynasty* across two hours.

Two hours that were almost up.

He closed his eyes and welcomed the dual streams of thought from his AC companions: Rubedo and Beryl. As a pair, they shared much in common with the ancient concept of an angel on one shoulder and a devil on the other. Both had begun their lives as pure digital constructs, and they constantly whispered suggestions to him, often in contrarian terms.

It was Rubedo who'd suggested his aggressive takedown of Vice-Commissioner Schröder, while Beryl counseled a more diplomatic approach, as she often did. Both were integrated so thoroughly with his mind that the boundaries sometimes became...indistinct.

Hawke had nothing against the Gordian Division commissioner, despite his words. Klaus-Wilhelm was only arguing for what he thought was best for SysPol, that much was clear. But however honorable his intentions, the very notion that *he* was the best choice to lead this attack was an insult bordering on the asinine. The man was a fossil, even if he had adapted surprisingly well to modern technology and sensibilities.

This is war, a thought rang in his mind, maybe from himself, maybe from Rubedo. *He's still nothing more than a long-forgotten tank commander with less life experience than my kids have! And we've seen the kinds of decisions they make! I had no choice but to put Klaus in his place before his ideas gained traction with the chief.*

Or is this about something else? another thought whispered, maybe from himself, maybe from Beryl. *Is this really about Schröder? Or is it about me and my failure to see the Dynasty attack coming? About the piles of corpses that never should have been and my desire to make it right because I know I screwed up?*

Hawke opened his eyes and pushed the internal reflection aside. They were almost at the Dynasty's outer wall. The time for self-doubt was past.

"*Kleio* to *Maxwell*. We've spotted another one, sir," the *Kleio's* pilot called in.

A pip blinked on the tactical display over the command table.

"It's all right, Agent," Hawke assured her. "I never planned to arrive in the Dynasty undetected. How close did this one get?"

"Hard to say. Hauling the cruisers is playing havoc with our scopes."

"Near enough to phase-lock?"

"No, sir. Not even close."

"Then there's no danger," Hawke said. "We proceed as planned."

"Just thought I'd mention it," Elzbietá said. "Two minutes to outer wall. Standby for phase-in and decoupling."

"Once you drop us off, your TTVs are free to phase out and engage any *Valkyries* that wander too close, but stay clear of the station and any realspace threats. They're too much for you. We'll handle those. Remember, you're our ticket home, and Doctor Andover-Chen doesn't believe these scaffolds will work with fewer than four TTVs hooked in."

"Understood, sir. We'll keep the *Valkyries* off your backs."

"Good luck out there. *Maxwell* out."

The communication window closed.

Hawke pushed off the table and stood straight. The background din of the bridge turned into a muted hush as the counter ticked down and everyone tensed for combat.

"All hands, stand by for phase-in," Peng said, acting as his second-in-command. "Ten . . . nine . . ."

Hawke took a slow, calming breath his virtual body didn't need and fixed his eyes on the currently empty realspace readouts.

" . . . two . . . one . . . phase-in!"

The Dynasty's Earth appeared directly ahead as a

beautiful oval of white-swirled blue, with the light of civilization scattered across the visible sliver of its night side. Scopes locked onto the *Tesseract* station in the foreground and zoomed in. One flank of the station's three-sided spike shone in the sunlight. More images opened, displaying close-in views of concave sections, their walls nothing more than chaotic jumbles of cubical blocks.

Teodorà stepped up beside him and ran a quick comparison between the *Kleio's* last visit and the *Tesseract's* current state. The report overlaid both versions, with changes highlighted in orange.

"It's further along than we thought," Hawke said softly. "Doctor?"

"True, but there are a lot of incomplete sections around the impeller. It should still be off-line." She looked at him levelly. "I can't *guarantee* that, sir. Not from this distance and not without a better guess at what their priorities have been since I left. I hope you understand that."

"All anyone can do is the best they can do, Doctor. We'll just have to see, won't we?" Hawke showed his teeth for a moment. "And if you're right, and we've caught them before they can phase-out, then all their *other* extra progress won't matter a damn."

"Gordian escorts have undocked," Peng reported as the TTVs released their moorings and the scaffold submerged beneath the main prog-steel layer. "Deploying meta-armor."

"*Zhang* reports they're clear for maneuvering."

"Same from *Lecroix*. All ships standing by for your orders."

Hawke nodded and spent a few seconds longer settling the positions of realspace and temporal craft in the vicinity in his mind before he gave the order. The *Maxwell* possessed a complex suite of active and passive scopes, supplemented by a trio of chronometric arrays installed by the Gordian Division, while even more raw data came in from the surrounding ships. The sum total of all the eyes and ears spread across twenty-seven vessels funneled into a single, cohesive map before him. Icons tagged about a hundred craft around the *Tesseract*, many of which were surely noncombat vessels.

But how many aren't? he wondered.

Ultimately, it didn't matter. Not with those sorts of numbers. Between the three *Directive*-class cruisers under his command, he had mechs to burn.

"Peng?" Hawke said.

His fellow commissioner appeared at his side.

"Have each cruiser launch three squadrons. Load the first with the Protector-7 template and assign it to close escort. The other two will receive Aggressor-41. Set *Tesseract* as their target."

"Aggressor-41?" Peng's eyes gleamed. "Nice. Payback hurts, don't it?"

"I certainly hope so."

Peng vanished, and Hawke returned his attention to the command table. The great iris of each cruiser's hangar opened, facing away from the *Tesseract*. The *Maxwell* and its fellow cruisers could accelerate in any direction with equal ease, so the orientation of any weapons, scopes, or the hangar bay were dictated by the situation. Individual weapons could also traverse across the prog-steel armor, clustering together for concentrated barrages.

The iris stretched open to reveal a grid of densely packed elliptical craft within.

"Attendant programs loaded," Peng said. "Mechs

ready for launch. Ah, and it seems the prime instance of Aggressor-41 is requesting permission to speak with you."

"Put it through."

"Commissioner Hawke," the nonsentient program started in a gruff, male voice. "I understand our mission is to destroy the target designated as the *Tesseract*. However, I have one question regarding our objectives. Should the return of our mech squadrons be considered a priority?"

"No. You are to destroy the target at any cost."

"Mission profile understood. We are ready for deployment."

"Launch the mechs!" Hawke snapped.

Thirty-six craft darted out of the *Maxwell's* hangar, and seventy-two more took off from the other cruisers. The mechs were based on the SysPol *Oculus*-class corvette pattern—seventy meters long, or about half the length of a TTV—but *these* versions weren't designed for patrolling the solar system. They didn't have accommodations for synthoid crews, and they lacked all the standard self-sustaining features like onboard printers and microbot swarms.

What they *did* have were mass drivers loaded with nuclear payloads.

Squadrons Protector-7A, -7B, and -7C fanned out ahead of the cruisers, forming tightly interlocking fields of protective fire, while squadrons Aggressor-41A through -41F sped straight at the *Tesseract*, overcharging their thrusters with suicidal intent.

"Looks like the vessels around the *Tesseract* are scattering," Peng said. "Some are phasing into the past and others, which I assume aren't *Valkyries*, are fleeing in random directions."

"He's right," Teodorà said. "The ships still in phase are part of the construction force."

"Then we'll ignore them," Hawke said. "It's the station we want. What about those scout *Valkyries* we saw earlier?"

"A few are in non-congruent positions ranging from negative five days to a whole negative month out," Peng said.

"Show me."

The command table updated with known or estimated *Valkyrie* positions, and Hawke gave the picture a satisfied nod.

"Not enough against our escort TTVs. All cruisers will advance on the *Tesseract*."

The *Maxwell's* graviton thrusters powered up, and the ship surged forward with its array of mechs holding defensive positions.

"All energy weapons forward," Hawke ordered. "Let's soften *Tesseract* up for the mechs."

"Confirmed," Peng said. "Shifting weapon blisters forward. Diverting power from reactors Two through Four."

"Fire when ready."

The Aggressor squadrons spread out into a wide ring formation, affording the cruisers an uninhibited field of fire.

"Firing!"

A flurry of beams raked across the *Tesseract's* hull.

"Negligible effect," Peng said. "Looks like surface damage only."

"The exotic matter used in its construction has a tremendous thermal capacity," Teodorà said. "Lasers won't be very effective."

"Which is why we brought plenty of nukes," Hawke noted. "Maintain regular fire. Might as well help the mechs out where we can."

Peng eyed a pulsing blip near the station. "Launch detected from the *Tesseract*. Could be a small mech of some kind."

"How many?"

"One."

"Just one?" Hawke asked incredulously. "Is it a *Valkyrie*?"

"I don't think so. It's too small."

"Doctor?"

"Agreed. It doesn't match any *Valkyrie*-types I know of."

"Where's it heading?" Hawke asked.

"It's flying straight at us," Peng said.

"Hmm." Hawke rubbed his chin. "Could be a missile of some kind. Have the mechs shoot it down."

"Sending modified orders to the mechs," Peng said. "Aggressor-41A will be in effective weapons range in ninety seconds."

One of the mech squadrons accelerated ahead of its brethren. Twelve craft converged on their lonely target—

—just as the small Dynasty craft phased out.

Hawke grimaced at the display over the command table.

"What just happened?" he demanded of Teodorà. "I thought you said it wasn't a *Valkyrie*!"

"I didn't think something that small could have an impeller. It must be a new type."

The small craft's estimated position converged with the mech squadron.

"Spread the mechs out more!" Hawke ordered. "They're too bunched up!"

"Too late!" Peng said. "It's phasing back in!"

The contact materialized in the middle of the mech formation. Defensive Gatlings blazed at the new target from twelve different directions, but it was already too late.

A brilliant flash blossomed in space. The nuclear detonation didn't have air to superheat, which meant it couldn't create a shock wave, but it didn't need to as the storm of gamma rays, x-rays, and free neutrons swept over the squadron. Meta-armor crisped and failed. Prog-steel liquefied, and hard radiation savaged internal systems.

Three mechs from Aggressor-41A blew apart, and the rest tumbled lifelessly through space, their armor stripped on one facing.

❖   ❖   ❖

"Not good!" Elzbietá exclaimed, shoving the omni-throttle all the way forward. The *Kleio* and seven other TTVs sped ahead of the cruisers. "*Kleio* to *Maxwell*. I'm taking my squadron in. We'll move up to support the mechs."

"Roger that, *Kleio*."

"What the hell *was* that thing?" she asked, turning to Philo.

"It's a missile that can phase through time. A 'phase-missile,' I guess you'd call it."

"Whatever it is, its impeller is really janky. Did you notice all the turbulence coming off it?"

"Yeah. There must be some serious compromises in its design to make it that compact. *We'd* certainly struggle to make an impeller that small."

"New launch detected from the *Tesseract*," Kleio reported. "Target has phased out."

"Here comes the next one." Elzbietá pointed the bow at the nebulous projections for where the missile existed in the past.

"Target at negative one minute and holding. It's making a shallow approach close to the True Present."

"Their mistake!"

Elzbietá waited until she was almost on top of the Aggressor-41 mechs, then she thumbed the impeller controls, shifting the *Kleio* out of phase with the True Present. Temporal coordinates slipped by until they matched, and the missile appeared ahead of them.

"Phase-locked," Philo announced. "I have a clean line of sight to the target."

"It's all yours."

The main cannon *whoomped*, and the one-ton kinetic round blew the missile to pieces.

"Nice shot!" Elzbietá cheered. "Scratch one nuke!"

"Multiple launches detected from the *Tesseract*," Kleio reported as three new contacts lit up on her display. "Targets are phasing into the past."

"More missiles, judging by their impeller signatures," Philo said. "And they're spreading out this time. Some are moving into the past faster than others."

"We'll take that one." Elzbietá selected the fastest moving missile. "Kleio, telegraph Maxwell Squadron! Split them between the other two!"

"Yes, Agent. Transmitting your orders."

"This one's moving *much* faster," Philo said. "Now at negative five days and phasing farther out."

"I'm on it." Elzbietá toggled the impeller and sped into the past.

"Missile now at negative ten days from True Present, negative fourteen hours from us," Philo reported. "Speed is seventy-four kilofactors. It's faster than us. We can't catch it."

"We can and we will," Elzbietá declared firmly. "That missile has to come around or it'll never hit our ships, and when it does, *you'll* be ready for it."

"I'll try. The phase-lock window's going to be almost nonexistent." Philo cycled through the mass driver's ammo configurator. "I'll prep a dispersal pattern. Catch the missile in a shotgun blast."

"That should work. Watch it! It's coming around!" Elzbietá flipped their temporal direction of travel, and the *Kleio* sped ahead of the missile back into the True Present.

"Missile at negative ten hours and closing." Philo stated calmly. "Shot loaded. Main gun charged."

Elzbietá steadied the ship so their bow pointed into the heart of the missile's projected phase-in point.

"Negative six. Negative four." Philo dropped his helmet's visor and readied his fingers over the weapon controls. "Negative one hour. It's almost here..."

He fired before they phase-locked with the missile. The shell blasted out of the *Kleio's* nose, tracing through empty space until it reached the missile's estimated location, then detonated into a cone of superheated metal.

The missile phased in, and shrapnel cut past it before it vanished once more.

"Clipped it!" Philo snapped.

"It's slowing!" Elzbietá noted.

"Phase-lock on it!"

"But the main gun—"

"Just do it!"

Elzbietá nodded and closed with the missile. Their temporal coordinates meshed once more, and the target appeared ahead of them, one of its impellers vibrating erratically, edges blurring into unreality.

"Take this!" Philo doused the target with Gatling fire from all four guns. They weren't technically in range for accurate hits—Elzbietá wasn't about to fly them spatially close to a *nuke*, and his screen calculated a hit chance of only three percent—but two hundred thirty-three rounds per second would solve the issue through sheer volume alone.

A sleet of metal flew past the missile. Bullets hit, explosions tore its main body open, and the missile tumbled end over end. Its impeller cracked, then shattered, and a shower of iridescent splinters spread across the void.

"Yeah!" Elzbietá shouted, then checked her tactical, and her heart sank. The indicator for TTV *Kuebiko* flashed red, lost with all hands to a nuclear detonation when it swung too close to a phase-missile, and another seven mechs had been destroyed or disabled by the other one. The mech advance had stalled as their formations spread out to account for all the nukes flying around.

But the situation was a long way from bleak. Yes, SysPol's nose had been bloodied with little to show for it, but a few squadrons of almost-mindless drones and one TTV were a small price to pay in the grander scheme of things. Fifty-three Aggressor mechs remained, each loaded down with nukes of their own, and the cruisers were launching more to replace their losses.

"Movement," Philo called out. "Multiple *Valkyries* closing on the True Present."

"When it rains..." Elzbietá intoned.

"Incoming telegraph from *Maxwell*," Kleio reported. "It reads: 'All Gordian escorts forward. Intercept incoming *Valkyries* and stay clear of the time-traveling missiles. Let our mechs take the hits. We're pressing forward with our attack on the station. *Maxwell* out.'"

"Lecroix and Zhang squadrons moving up to support us," Philo said. "And the *Tesseract* just launched another wave of phase-missiles. Looks like they're still targeting the mechs."

"Kleio, have Maxwell Squadron form up on us." Elzbietá skimmed over the incoming signals. She tapped a large icon cluster. "We've got a group of ten to twelve *Valkyries* at negative one month and closing, coming up beneath us. We'll engage those."

"Yes, Agent. Transmitting your orders."

Six TTVs phase-locked behind the *Kleio*, and together they sped into the past. The *Valkyrie* icons raced to intercept her own squadron, and she permitted herself a tight smile.

They're looking for a fight, all right, she thought, *time machine to time machine. Well, come and get it, you bastards!*

"Judging by their signatures, they look similar to that laser-armed *Valkyrie* back at L5," Philo reported. "Our meta-armor should give us the advantage."

"True, but the Dynasty hasn't been shy with its nukes either." She assigned targets to individual TTVs. "Kleio, distribute these target priorities to the squadron. We're too bunched up. The squadron will break and attack on my orders."

"Yes, Agent. Transmission sent."

The range dropped to negative one day.

"And... break!"

Seven TTVs dispersed as ten *Valkyries* phase-locked and swooped up at them. Lasers and cannon fire ripped back and forth, and Elzbietá dove at one of the *Valkyries*. It nosed up at her and fired its laser, but the beam splashed off the meta-armor and curved away into space. The main cannon barked, and the projectile tore a canyon through the *Valkyrie*'s belly. Its thrusters flared wildly, and it struggled to turn away.

She followed the time machine in, and Philo blasted away. Hundreds of tiny flashes wracked its hull, one of the impeller tips broke off, and it shuddered into congruence with the past.

Elzbietá didn't bother phasing out to finish it off; she had plenty of *other Valkyries* to contend with, and she swooped past its position and picked another. Two *Valkyries* tailed the TTV *Proteus*. Lasers slashed across its hull, and its rear meta-armor was deeply scored with glowing claw marks of damage.

The *Kleio* shot in from the side, cannons blaring, and explosions savaged the closest *Valkyrie*. Hull armor over the crew compartment splintered, and incendiary rounds torched the interior. The *Kleio* sped past as the *Valkyrie* flew on in a straight line. The *Proteus* spun around and blew the *Valkyrie* in half with its main gun.

"The other one is peeling off," Philo said. "It's running into the past at full speed. The other survivors are bugging out as well."

"Had enough, have they? Kleio, order Maxwell Squadron to form up on us again."

"Yes, Agent. Transmitting."

Elzbietá skimmed over the known and estimated positions of *Valkyrie* time machines.

"Looks like *all* of them are pulling back. We'll regroup with the cruisers in the True Present."

Six TTVs swung into formation with the *Kleio*, some of them bruised badly by the duel with the *Valkyries*, but none of them had fallen aside from the *Kuebiko*. Her squadron phased into the True Present, and Elzbietá began to take in the current flow of the battle when—

"Oh, no!" Philo exclaimed. "Ella, the *Tesseract*! LOOK!"

Dozens of Aggressor mechs opened fire on the *Tesseract*, but the station's outline had already begun to blur. Nuclear-tipped kinetic rounds flew across space as the station's edges lost definition, and then—in a massive convulsion of reality—the entire five-point-five-kilometer length of the station vanished into the past. Dozens of nukes erupted in an apocalyptic firestorm where it had once been, and the mechs raced forward, ready to fire again.

But they didn't.

There was nothing left to shoot *at*.

"Oh *shit*!" She looked over to Philo. "Now what do we do?"

❖   ❖   ❖

"I'd say that was a successful test, don't you think?" Lucius raised an inquiring eyebrow at Simon Vlastos.

"Yes, but can the hyperforge maintain this level of production?" the chief quaesitor asked. "Your people barely had any time to test it."

"Shall we find out?" Lucius opened a communications window and permitted himself a satisfied smirk. "This is Chairman Gwon, *Tesseract* Control to Hyperforge One. Let's hit their cruisers next."

CHAPTER THIRTY-EIGHT

Emergency Reinforcement Cruiser *Maxwell*
Dynasty, 2980 CE

HAWKE STARED AT THE NUCLEAR INFERNO WHERE his target *should* have been, then his eyes darted to a chronometric chart that showed the mammoth station shifting farther and farther into the past. *Slowly*, in comparison to TTVs or *Valkyries*, but that distinction didn't matter.

What mattered was *he* couldn't hit the damn thing!

"Hawke, the Aggressor squadrons don't have a target!" Peng said. "Where should I send them?"

"*Tesseract* now at negative one hour and holding, sir!"

"Three new scope contacts at negative one hour! Missiles inbound!"

"Urgent message from Maxwell Squadron! They're requesting orders!"

"Sir, both cruiser captains are asking for new orders!"

And what exactly do they expect me to say? Hawke wondered as he glared at the disaster unfolding before him. A trio of icons moved across the map as the full weight of his blunder bored down on him. His foe could not only hide in the past, but *attack* him from there as well! He commanded three of the mightiest vessels humanity had ever constructed, and all that power was *useless*!

Schröder was right. The thought echoed in his mind, maybe from himself, maybe from Beryl. *I'm out of my league here.*

A lesser man might have cracked under the pressure, but Hawke had served SysGov as a police officer for over sixty years. He'd faced countless trials, including some of the worst counterterrorism ops in modern history, and he'd made some truly terrible mistakes. But he'd clawed back to his feet after every failure. He'd *never* given up, and that sheer relentlessness had propelled him to one of the highest posts in SysPol.

He would *not* panic here and now!

I'm not beaten yet, either he or Rubedo thought. *The replication centers are vulnerable to conventional attack, and they're one of the Dynasty's most sensitive nerves. We can still inflict damage, even if it's a mere distraction while we run with our collective tails between our legs.*

"Commissioner! Orders, sir!"

"Commissioner!"

"Calm down! All of you!" Hawke barked, and a dozen overlapping conversations died abrupt deaths. He swept a stern eye across his bridge crew. "Our primary target is out of reach, that's all. Peng, forward the full list of known replication centers to the Aggressor squadrons and scatter them. One mech to each target."

"I don't think they'll get through with that many *Valkyries* out there."

"I'm not interested in destroying the centers. I'm buying time," he said flatly, and Peng paused, then nodded.

"Got it. Issuing orders."

"Telegraph, pull our Gordian escorts back. Have Maxwell and Lecroix squadrons assume escort positions in the near present."

"And Zhang Squadron, sir?"

"They're to dock with *Zhang* and initiate phase-out. We're pulling out, one cruiser at a time."

"Yes, sir. Spooling your orders now."

"After *Zhang* is past the outer wall, *Lecroix* is next."

Which means Maxwell *will need to phase out without anyone watching our back,* he thought grimly, but he wasn't about to put his ship at the head of the queue. This was his blunder, and he'd see the others safely away first.

The crew distributed his orders, and the icons on the map shifted as TTVs converged on his cruisers.

Hawke's eye flicked across the damage reports. Nineteen TTVs remained operational. He had the assets to effect a retreat even with the losses his forces had suffered, and six TTVs phased into the True Present around the *Zhang*. The cruiser raised its exotic matter scaffold above its armor, and the TTVs took up docking positions.

"Sir, the *Tesseract*'s missiles have bypassed the Aggressor mechs! They're heading straight for us!"

"Damn," he breathed, glowering at the map. He'd hoped the mechs would prove more tempting targets.

"Sir, multiple *Valkyrie* groups incoming!"

"They're trying to overload our defenses," Hawke growled.

And the only defense I have is the TTVs, he thought. *But I need at least four for each cruiser. If I lose too many . . .*

"Message from *Kleio*! Maxwell and Lecroix squadrons are moving to engage the missiles and *Valkyries*!"

"Telegraph, make it clear they are *not* to overextend," he ordered.

"Yes, sir. Transmitting now."

Hawke planted his palms on the command table and watched the trio of missile icons close with his ships. Thirteen TTVs swept forward to meet them, and one of the missiles blinked out of existence—another kill for the *Kleio*, he noted—but the other two slipped by.

"Brace for impact," he said in a calm, almost too soft tone.

"Closing all weapon and scope blisters and submerging them beneath the main armor!"

"Mech hangar sealed!"

"Meta-armor retracted and hull fully energized!"

"Come on, *Zhang*," Hawke whispered. "Get out of here already."

The missiles phased into reality, one next to the *Maxwell* and one by the *Zhang*. Laser and cannon fire spat from the Protector mechs, showering the phase-in point from all directions, but the bombs triggered faster. Both nukes birthed new suns the moment they appeared, and a wave of atomic fury smashed into his command ship.

Mechs from the Protector squadron simply flashed out of existence, like gnats in a flame, but the *Maxwell* was no expendable robotic craft, and its thick, fortified hull would not be breached so easily. Sixteen layers of advanced prog-steel armor cocooned the vessel, and powerful shock absorbers separated the outer shell from the delicate systems within.

The *Maxwell*'s spherical armor flashed incandescent as the inferno blasted into the ship. Whole armor segments blew clear of the hull, fluttering away like white leaves. Nuclear fire burned through seven out of sixteen layers and reduced one side of the sphere to molten ruin.

But the armor held.

His crew snapped into action, reinforcing damaged sections with prog-steel reserves, deploying microbot swarms, and rerouting coolant lines. Damage indicators pulsed across the cruiser's hull where equipment blisters had succumbed to thermal damage, but the *Maxwell* remained—for all intents and purposes—fully operational.

The same could not be said for the *Zhang*.

Or rather, the vessels *near* the *Zhang*.

All six TTVs from the cruiser's escort squadron had been in phase when the nuke went off, and the explosion obliterated three of them. Another drifted away from the *Zhang*, its irradiated hull half-melted and its impeller burned down to a nub. Only the two TTVs docked on the far side of the blast, in the cruiser's shadow, survived.

"*Zhang*'s scaffold is damaged. Another hit like that and it won't be able to phase out."

"Pull two TTVs back from Lecroix Squadron," Hawke ordered. "Get them docked with *Zhang* and get it out of here!"

"Sir, more missiles inbound from the *Tesseract*!"

"Of course there are," he fumed. "Have *Zhang* load all its remaining mechs with Protector-22 and launch them. Tow that drifting TTV into its hangar, then switch all mechs over to our control."

"Telegraph from Maxwell Squadron. They're heavily engaged and won't be able to intercept the missiles."

"Understood," Hawke snapped. *Not that there's one damned thing I can do about it!*

Dozens of mechs poured from the *Zhang's* hangar and spread out around the cruisers. A pair of mechs caught up to the damaged TTV, latched onto either side of its hull, and pulled it into the hangar as two more TTVs phased in around the cruiser. One of the TTVs docked at an empty slot on the cruiser's scaffold, but the second couldn't connect at its initial location due to cracks in the exotic matter and had to move to another connection point.

"Come on. Come on," Hawke urged under his breath as the next wave of missiles sped in.

The TTV settled into its new dock, prog-steel struts locked it in place, and all four TTVs activated their impellers. Phase field lines propagated through the *Zhang's* scaffold, and the ship began to shift out of the True Present.

Three missiles shot past the battle between TTVs and *Valkyries*.

"Scatter all Protector mechs," Hawke ordered. "Brace for impact."

The *Zhang's* outline wavered like an image viewed through disturbed water then snapped solid once more.

"What happened?" Hawke demanded urgently. "What's the problem?"

"The TTVs are trying to shift the cruiser out of phase, but with only four of them—" Peng shrugged. "They're going to make another attempt."

Hawke waited, every fiber of his being tense as the missiles closed in. Power spikes lit up on the four TTVs, and together they pushed the *Zhang* once more into the immaterial.

"Here it comes!"

Three missiles dashed in.

The *Zhang* was nothing more than a ghost when twin suns erupted, obscuring its hull from view. The data feed from the cruiser cut out completely, but Hawke couldn't tell if that was from the ship leaving the True Present . . . or something else.

"Status report," he snapped.

"Telegraph from *Zhang*, sir! They're underway!"

A cheer rose from some of his staff, and Hawke allowed himself a slim smile.

"Good work, everyone, but we're not out of this yet. Pull another four TTVs back, and signal *Lecroix* to prep its scaffold for phase-out."

"Sir, we've lost *Lecroix*'s feed! I have no connection!"

"What! Were they hit?"

"Unknown, sir!"

Hawke pulled up the cruiser's feed and felt his jaw tighten. The *Lecroix* had gone completely dark. He'd simply been so fixated on the *Zhang* that he hadn't realized it until now. But the *Lecroix* was there! The *Maxwell*'s scope could see it, and its hull showed only a few signs of damage! And yet the cruiser was adrift, its thrusters and active scopes down, and its infostructure dead.

Hawke replayed the last attack, but this time kept his eye on the *Lecroix*. Two nukes detonated in the distance, and in the same instant, the *Lecroix* fell silent.

Two explosions, a thought echoed, probably from Rubedo, *but three missiles*.

Hawke's eyes opened wide in sudden realization.

"Oh, no . . ." he breathed and shook his head, the hopelessness of this disaster finally slamming home.

He replayed the attack once more, zooming in on the *Lecroix*'s hangar iris, the weakest point on its armor. If he was right, he'd see it there. Two suns lit up beyond the *Lecroix*, and in the same instance the armored iris bulged. Something had forced it outward from within.

And that something was a nuclear missile phasing into the True Present *inside* the cruiser.

"We can still evacuate *Lecroix*," Peng said. "Should I bring the mechs in?"

"Don't bother." He looked up and took a deep, virtual breath before continuing. "Everyone on that ship is already dead."

✧   ✧   ✧

"Oh, no you don't!" Elzbietá shouted as she swooped by the *Valkyrie*. Laser fire stabbed into the *Kleio*, scorching a ragged line across the hull. She thumbed the impeller control and shifted them out of phase.

"Meta-armor's taking a beating," Philo warned. "Energy mitigation at half effectiveness."

Elzbietá clenched her teeth and jerked the omni-throttle to the side. The *Kleio* flew sideways as the *Valkyrie*'s estimated position closed on them once more. The cloud of possible locations narrowed, the two craft phase-locked, and Philo fired.

The main gun struck one of the *Valkyrie*'s impellers and shattered it. Armor shredded off the impeller mount, and two of its thrusters lost power. The *Valkyrie* rolled out of control, and Elzbietá closed in for the kill.

Philo blazed away with the 45mm Gatling guns, and hundreds of explosions tore across the ship. Its nose broke off, the remaining impeller cracked, and the craft slipped into congruence, no longer able to attack them.

"That's one less to worry about!" Elzbietá declared as she thumbed the impeller control again. The TTV switched temporal directions, and they traversed time back toward the True Present.

"We're starting to thin out the *Valkyries*," Philo noted, "but *Maxwell* just pulled four more TTVs off the line. *And* we've got more phase-missiles inbound."

"Damn!" Elzbietá breathed. "Is that thing *ever* going to run out?"

"Not if these missiles are coming from a hyperforge. Which I'm pretty sure they *are*."

"Then we need to get the cruisers out of here as fast as possible."

"That seems to be the idea."

Elzbietá checked the tactical map. With four TTVs carrying the *Zhang* back to SysGov and another four more heading for the *Maxwell*, only seven were left to fend off the *Valkyries* and missiles.

"Incoming telegraph from *Maxwell*," Kleio said. "It reads: *Lecroix* is down with all hands. To all Gordian escorts, screen *Maxwell* until we can phase out. All forces are to retreat back to SysGov once *Maxwell* is away.'"

"We lost *Lecroix*?" Elzbietá exclaimed. She turned to Philo and saw the same stunned expression. "How the hell did *that* happen? A beast like that should be able to take *dozens* of nukes on the chin and keep chugging!"

"I am sorry, Agent," Kleio said. "The telegraph did not specify."

"Well, we're not letting them take out *Maxwell*!" she snarled. "Philo, where are those damn missiles?"

"Highlighting now. They're coming in along three separate temporal vectors, converging back on the True Present."

"One of them is moving through time too fast for us, but not the *other* two!" She shoved the throttle forward, her eyes locked on a nebula of possible positions for the nearest phase-missile. "Kleio, tell the other TTVs to keep those *Valkyries* off our back! We're going after the missiles!"

"Yes, Agent. Sending now."

"Target at negative two weeks from True Present," Philo said. "Positive six days from us."

"Fire when ready," Elzbietá said.

The missile appeared ahead of them. Elzbietá brought their nose up, Philo triggered the main gun, and the shot blasted out of the *Kleio*'s bow. The round exploded ahead of the missile, and a dense rain of hot metal tore through it. Both of the phase-missile's impellers cracked and splintered, and the weapon dropped out of temporal flight two weeks behind its intended target.

"Next!"

"There!" Another contact highlighted on her map. "Negative one week from True Present. Positive two weeks from us."

A *Valkyrie* phase-locked above and behind them, and its laser burned a livid slash across the top of the *Kleio*. Damage indicators flashed on her console.

"The meta-armor's burned out!" Philo squeaked. "It's flaking off!"

"Return fire!"

The *Kleio*'s guns slewed about and blazed away as two TTVs phased in behind the *Valkyrie*. Streams of forty-five-millimeter rounds converged on the craft from three directions, pulverizing its hull. The *Valkyrie* rolled to the side, but Philo led the agile target, and shot after shot pounded into and *through* its hull.

The *Valkyrie* tumbled away, atmosphere venting through its ruined armor.

The two TTVs phased out, seeking other targets.

Elzbietá checked the second missile's estimated location, then brought the *Kleio* into phase-lock with it. A single shot from the mass driver blew it to pieces.

"Where's the last one?" she demanded urgently.

"There! Converging on the True Present!"

Elzbietá could already tell she wouldn't reach it in time, but a part of her refused to accept that, and she pursued the weapon all the way back to the True Present. The third phase-missile reached the *Maxwell* and detonated moments before the *Kleio* caught up. Atomic fury scourged the cruiser's surface, vaporizing two of the docked TTVs, and Elzbietá clenched her teeth on a spike of fury as the fireball glared at her like a spiteful eye.

The outer vestiges of its radiation scalded the *Kleio*'s armor, and her mind snapped back into focus.

"More missiles inbound," Philo reported after an endless second of silence.

"How's the *Maxwell*'s scaffold look?"

"Mostly intact."

"Good. I'm bringing us up to one of the docks."

"But we haven't been ordered to."

"We don't need orders!" she snapped. "We're here,

and *someone* needs to carry them out!" She opened a channel. "*Kleio* to *Maxwell*. We're pulling up to Dock Eight on your scaffold. Get ready for us!"

"Roger that, *Kleio*."

Elzbietá flew up to the cruiser, then spun the *Kleio* around so that the *Maxwell's* massive sphere took up almost the entire view beneath her feet.

"Scaffold's coming up," Philo announced. "Ten meters and closing, but watch it. The struts are warped out of alignment."

"I'll make it fit," she declared as the two craft met. Armor screeched against armor, and sparks scintillated into space. She applied a surge of power that slammed the *Kleio* down into the dock. The warped struts strained back into shape.

"Nice," Philo complimented. "Scaffold connection looks solid."

Elzbietá opened a channel with the two other TTVs on the scaffold.

"Everyone, power up your impellers. We're pulling the *Maxwell* out of here."

"But there're only three of us! We need four for this to work safely."

"'*Safely*'?" Elzbietá snarled. "Does it look like we have time for that? Do it *now*, and don't skimp on the power!"

"Uh, yes, Agent! Right away!"

She closed the channel. "Philo?"

"Disabling all safety limits on the reactor and passing the same instructions to the other TTVs. Output to the scaffold is at one hundred five percent of the design limit and rising." He tilted his head toward her. "If this doesn't work, we won't be able to undock in time."

"We are *not* leaving *Maxwell* behind."

"I know how you feel." He let out a resigned sigh. "Output at one hundred fourteen percent and rising. Field is propagating through eighty-seven percent of the scaffold." He frowned at a flashing alarm. "And the insulation around our main power conduit is on fire."

"Will it hold out?"

"Maybe. Probably?"

The next trio of missiles closed on the *Maxwell*. Thirty seconds to target.

"Field propagation at ninety-three percent. That *should* be enough."

"Everyone, initiate phase-out!"

Exotic matter throughout the *Maxwell's* scaffold morphed. Chronotons flowed freely through it, *except* those traveling along a single, very specific transdimensional vector. Chronometric pressure climbed across the impellers and the scaffold, escalating toward a critical threshold that would initiate phase-out.

"The scaffold's beginning to crack!" Philo warned. "Should we abort?"

"It's now or never!" Elzbietá replied. "Keep going!"

"Here goes nothing! Output at one nineteen and rising!"

The missiles dashed in toward the True Present.

The scaffold shuddered with colossal energy. Cracks branched, and glittering shavings flaked off into space.

The missiles phased in.

The *Maxwell* phased out—

—and the nukes exploded across a barren stretch of empty space.

Elzbietá let out a long, slow exhale as they left the Dynasty behind. The surviving TTVs broke off their engagements and phased into formation with the *Maxwell*. The tension of battle melted away as it became clear the Dynasty wouldn't pursue them; relief washed over her, but not much else. Certainly not joy as she checked the battered status of their attack force.

She shook her head at the harsh tally of red indicators.

Out of the twenty-seven SysPol vessels they'd brought to the Dynasty, only thirteen TTVs and two cruisers had survived.

❖   ❖   ❖

"That Dynasty station is phasing back into the True Present," *Pathfinder-Prime*'s temporal navigator reported.

"Yes, I see that," Kloss managed softly. He was glad for once in his life to be in zero gee, because the horrible scope of this Dynasty weapon had reduced his limbs to jelly. He would have surely collapsed into a chair in any other situation.

A time-traveling battle station. He shook his head slowly, almost robotically. *Equipped with time-traveling nuclear missiles. What kind of madman would create such a monstrosity?*

Durantt floated up beside him and cleared his throat.

"Yes, Captain. I know." Kloss turned to the man, keeping the terror he felt hidden behind an inexpressive mask. "Any sign we've been spotted?"

"Not *yet*, Director," Durantt stressed.

"Then we still have a job to do. We'll hold this position and continue to observe the station."

"For how long?"

"For as long as necessary," Kloss snapped. "Once

I'm satisfied with the intelligence we've gathered, then and *only* then, will we return to the Admin. Have I made myself clear, Captain?"

"Perfectly clear, sir," Durantt replied stiffly.

CHAPTER THIRTY-NINE

Hyper-Fortress *Tesseract*
Dynasty, 2980 CE

"WELL, SIMON?" LUCIUS QUIRKED THE SIDE OF HIS lip upward and turned his avatar to face the chief quaesitor. "I'd say the phase-missiles exceeded expectations, wouldn't you agree?"

"Oh, wholeheartedly." Vlastos sat back in his chair on the *Tesseract*'s command deck and flashed a tentative smile. "I don't know what we would have done without them."

"You're welcome."

"Quite." Vlastos chuckled, then leaned forward. "How's the hyperforge holding up?"

"Let's see." Lucius summoned a live schematic over his palm. "The microbots have found a few stress fractures in the outer housing." He made a shooing gesture. "Not surprising, given how rushed we were building it. The cracks are all along seams between subassemblies. We'll reinforce those points and carry the modifications forward as we bring the rest online."

"Sounds like we were lucky the battle ended when it did."

"Oh, I wouldn't go that far," Lucius said. "Between the other hyperforges under construction, our internal stockpiles awaiting assembly, and the veritable *mountain* of exotic matter we have for an impeller, there's ample material lying around for repairs. Even if the hyperforge had broken down, we would've brought it back online in short order."

"That's reassuring." Vlastos stood up and walked up to a map of Cornucopia and quaesitor assets around the earth. "Still, we did lose two replication centers."

"Which we'd evacuated ahead of time," Lucius said dismissively. "Barely worth the mention."

"*And* we lost thirty *Valkyries*," Vlastos pressed. "Over two-*thirds* of our militarized force. Is that worth mentioning?"

"I suppose," Lucius admitted begrudgingly. "But those ships will be replaced quickly; we have an abundance of *Valkyries* to convert. And once Hyperforge Twenty-Eight is complete, the problem will be permanently solved. We'll be able to replicate time machines as easily as phase-missiles. There's no way SysGov could stand up to a force like *that*."

Vlastos crossed his arms and nodded, staring at the map while the surviving armed *Valkyries* flew back to quaesitor orbital stations, for much needed repairs in some cases.

"SysGov will try again," Vlastos said at last, then looked over his shoulder at Lucius. "Won't they?"

"Oh, I can guarantee it. But the *Tesseract* will be even more powerful than before. When complete, it will truly earn the title of hyper-fortress."

"You're proud of this station, aren't you?"

Lucius gave him a smile and shrugged his shoulders. "Well, I suppose you've earned it. I'd hate to think of the trouble we'd be in without you."

"It *is* gratifying to see the *Tesseract* perform so well, although"—he shook his head sadly—"all this violence is...disheartening. I mean, every one of the *Valkyries* we lost had a crew on board, too." He was rather proud of the soft, sorrowful look in his eyes. "No hyperforge can replace *them* for their families and loved ones."

"I know exactly how you feel." Vlastos sighed. He looked back down at the map sadly, giving Lucius a chance to deal with his own grief, then looked back up. "What do you think SysGov's next move is?"

Lucius moved his avatar to the quaesitor's side and gave him a grateful smile for the subject change. Then he pursed his lips thoughtfully.

"They'll lick their wounds and scratch their heads trying to come up with a way to counter the *Tesseract*," he said. "When they return, they'll do so in force. We need to be ready for them."

"Do you think they'll find a counter?"

"Doubtful, but not impossible. They may have one in the works already. Remember all that exotic matter we saw them hoarding?"

"They could be using it for more conventional warship scaffolds."

"If so, I think they'll reconsider after today." Lucius chuckled.

"And what if they permanently mate their TTVs to one of those warships? Say, try to turn it into some sort of time-traveling superdreadnought?"

"They're welcome to try."

"You don't seem concerned," Vlastos noted.

"Because I'm not. I expect a kludged-together solution like that would have horrendous temporal speed and maneuverability, much like the *Tesseract* does. But that's fine for us because *we* can strike targets outside of phase-lock. They can't. Our *Valkyries* would be free to choose when and where to engage, if at all, and our phase-missiles would still tear them to pieces."

"True enough." Vlastos crossed his arms again and sighed. "Regardless, we'll need to keep a close eye on them. We should increase the number of scouts we send into their universe."

"Good idea."

"But what if they don't come? What if they adopt a defensive posture?"

"I'm not sure," Lucius said. "Depends on what our scouts find, though we may be forced to take the fight to them."

"A dangerous move," Vlastos warned. "Even after we've bulked up our *Valkyrie* force."

"Which is why we should modify the *Tesseract*'s impeller for transdimensional flight as soon as possible. With that in place, we'll be able to shift the station into their universe."

Vlastos looked up at him, surprised.

"You don't think small, do you? Do you really think that'll be necessary?"

"Maybe not. But I'd rather have it and not need it than the opposite."

"Of course, you're right." Vlastos grimaced. "But I hope it doesn't come to that."

"On that we wholeheartedly agree," Lucius lied.

The attack on the Dynasty had played out even better than he could have hoped. Not only had the *Tesseract* exceeded even *his* lofty expectations, but he now possessed all the justification he needed to pour every resource at the Dynasty's disposal into its completion. His divine form would be finished far in advance of this universe's collapse.

It's a strange thing, he thought. *After so many patient centuries of waiting, I'm… yes, I'm actually anxious. Even a little giddy with anticipation. My divinity is so close now, so deliciously close. I can hardly wait to experience it.*

A communication icon chimed, and Vlastos frowned at it.

"That would be the council calling," he said. "They'll want to speak to you, of course."

"Please tell them that I am, as always, at their service." Lucius placed a hand on his chest and bowed his head slightly, with an expression of manfully controlled guilt. "I realize I'm only a lonely echo of the trio of Elders, but I'll do anything they require—anything at all—to protect the Dynasty's existence." He squared his shoulders and looked at Vlastos with steely-eyed determination. "It's what Teodorà and Samuel would expect of me."

CHAPTER FORTY

Mycene Station
SysGov, 2980 CE

THE C-BOMB WASN'T TERRIBLY LARGE WHEN KLAUS-Wilhelm considered the quantity of exotic matter needed. The outer frame of the incomplete weapon was roughly the size and shape of a TTV's impeller spike. But it was dense. Immensely dense. Rows of compactors towered behind it in the Mycene Station hangar, working night and day to compress each shipment down to Andover-Chen's specifications.

And its rapid completion was even more vital than it had been last week, he thought grimly.

Hawke had learned the difference between a police action and war. As such lessons always did, his had proved expensive, and an already dire situation had just become desperate. Klaus-Wilhelm von Schröder was as human as the next man, and he'd been unable to suppress a sense of vindication as Hawke admitted his failures after the disastrous attack on the *Tesseract*. Yet he'd felt no satisfaction, no sense of having been proven "right." Indeed, he would have been the first to admit that even *his* threat projections had fallen dismally short of the mark, and Hawke's after-action report to Lamont and President Byakko had been unflinching.

The Argo Division commander had offered his resignation at its conclusion, but Byakko and Lamont had refused to accept it. That was almost certainly the right decision, in Klaus-Wilhelm's view, for several reasons. They would certainly have been justified in accepting it, but Hawke truly was a tough-minded, immensely experienced *police* officer. Klaus-Wilhelm had no doubt he would fully digest his exorbitantly priced lesson. Specifically, he now recognized the two most critical points of that lesson: no one in Argus had any training or doctrine for transtemporal warfare... and Gordian Division did.

Which was why Klaus-Wilhelm was in this hangar instead of back in his office dealing with all the rest of the scores of decisions people needed from him.

He continued walking his slow circle around the unfinished bomb, trailed by a tight-faced Andover-Chen while Raibert, Benjamin, Elzbietá, Teodorà, and Philo's avatar followed a few steps behind.

He completed the circuit and stopped, craning his neck to watch as four conveyors slotted a disk-shaped segment into the c-bomb's spike. The conveyors flew off, and a cloud of spherical remotes swarmed over the segment and began fusing the new addition with its neighbors.

The spike was no more than half-completed, and his eyes were gray steel as they moved from the bomb to Andover-Chen.

"This is not the time for excuses, Doctor," he said coldly.

"But, sir . . ." Andover-Chen protested, spreading his hands as if pleading. "Surely there's another, more reasonable way. We're on pace to complete the c-bomb in six months."

"We don't *have* six months!" Klaus-Wilhelm shouted. Not because he was angry, but because he needed them to understand how serious the situation was. And because he'd learned a long, long time ago—even subjectively—that when a general officer threw a tantrum and screamed at people, things got done. It wasn't nice, and it wasn't fair—it was, however, *effective*, and that was what was desperately needed just now.

"Argo just had their collective asses handed to them, never mind the eleven TTVs and twenty-two agents *we* lost!" he continued. "And we accomplished *nothing*! At least one of the *Tesseract*'s hyperforges is active, more are on their way, and we didn't put a scratch on it! That station is accelerating the erosion of the Dynasty's outer wall, and do I need to remind you that when they go, *we* go?"

"No, sir. Of course not!" Andover-Chen said quickly.

"Look around you." Klaus-Wilhelm made a swirling motion with one hand. "You see anyone from Argo or Arete here? No one's coming to help us because there's no one who *can* help. We're the only people with the knowledge, expertise, and equipment to solve a problem like this. The Gordian Division is all that stands in the way of the apocalypse. We *cannot* fail."

"But what you're suggesting . . ." Andover-Chen lowered his eyes.

"He's right, you know." Raibert put a hand on the smaller synthoid's shoulder. "Our backs are to the wall, which means all options need to be on the table."

"But for us to consider using"—Andover-Chen's face twisted as if he'd swallowed something sour—"*temporal replication?*"

"It's risky," Benjamin agreed. "But it's the only way to finish the c-bomb quickly."

"It's *beyond* risky," Andover-Chen warned. "Each piece of the c-bomb is highly concentrated and non-inert. Replicating even *one* section will produce an enormous amount of resonance. What happens if we hit the magic threshold, and then *SysGov's* outer wall starts eroding out of control?"

"That's why I need both of you on this." Klaus-Wilhelm nodded to Teodorà, to whom he'd spoken earlier. "Between the two of you, there are no better experts on temporal replication and its effects anywhere in SysGov. I need you to crunch the numbers and figure out where that threshold is. Pin it down as precisely as you can, because I need to know how far we can push this without dooming ourselves in the process. We're desperate, yes, but we're not going to charge blindly into the unknown."

"You have my full support, Commissioner," Teodorà assured him.

"And mine as well." Andover-Chen cleared his throat and straightened a little. "I understand your position. And you're right. We need to consider all options if we're to deploy the c-bomb successfully."

"Do you still think we need to hit the *Tesseract?*" Elzbietá asked. "Can't we deploy it somewhere else?"

"Unfortunately, no," Andover-Chen said. "The data

you and the other TTVs brought back makes it clear. All the resonance buildup in and around that station is producing what you could call a 'clinging' effect between our two universes. It's similar, though not identical to how the universes were entangled in the Gordian Knot. If we deploy the c-bomb anywhere else, our two universes won't move apart. The c-bomb needs to go off right on top of *Tesseract*. Preferably inside it."

"*C-bombs*," Klaus-Wilhelm corrected.

Andover-Chen blinked. "I beg your pardon?"

"You don't know anything about military operations, do you, Doctor?"

"Well, no, Commissioner. Tactics have never been a focus of mine."

"Tactics? Who's talking about *tactics*?" Klaus-Wilhelm retorted. "*Amateurs* study *tactics*! Professional soldiers study *logistics* over and above anything else. They may not be all shiny and glorious, and quartermasters aren't issued bugles, but without them, all the frigging *tactics* in the multiverse are *useless*."

"I . . . I hadn't thought of it that way," Andover-Chen admitted.

"Of course you hadn't, because it's outside your area. But you'd better *start* thinking about it, because here's your word of the day." Klaus-Wilhelm put a finger on the physicist's chest. "Redundancy."

"Redundancy?" Andover-Chen echoed with a furrowed brow.

"Yes, redundancy. Building more than you actually need because the other guy is trying to blow up the ones you have."

"Ah."

"Do you honestly think I'm going to lead a fleet of TTVs into the teeth of that battle station with only *one* shot at success? Especially when the fate of our whole *universe* is at stake?"

Andover-Chen frowned. "Now that you put it that way, sir, it does sound a bit . . . overly optimistic."

"Because it is. I'll be damned if I'm going to put a plan in front of Chief Lamont that falls apart the moment our enemy gets a lucky shot at our super-weapon."

"Then I suppose you'll want me to consider"—Andover-Chen's lip actually quivered—"replicating the *c-bomb*, once it's whole."

"Guessed it on the first try."

The physicist shuddered.

"Doctor, you need to understand—"

"It's all right, sir." Andover-Chen held up a hand. "I understand where you're coming from. And I'll get right on it with Doctor Beckett. You'll have the data you need."

"Good man."

"Now, if you'll excuse us." He bobbed his head toward the door. "I seem to have a lot of work on my plate all of a sudden."

"But nothing we can't handle, I think," Teodorà said, and laid an encouraging hand on his shoulder.

"Dismissed, Doctors," Klaus-Wilhelm said, then allowed his voice and expression to gentle. "And thank you. Both of you."

"Don't thank us yet, sir." Andover-Chen headed for the door, shaking his head and muttering, "Oh dear, oh dear, oh dear."

Teodorà followed him out.

Benjamin waited until the doctor was out of earshot, then stepped up next to his grandfather.

"Sir, I didn't want to contradict you in front of Andover-Chen," Benjamin said. "But he has a point. We're playing with some very dangerous fire here. Are you sure about this?"

"Son, I'm not sure about *anything* right now... except that it's our job to put an end to the Dynasty's madness, one way or another. And that's exactly what I intend to do."

"And when the c-bomb or c-bombs are complete, how do we deliver them?" Elzbietá asked. "We have thirty-six TTVs left, I think."

"Thirty-seven," Raibert corrected. "We're strapping weapons onto the *Hildr*."

"Will Teodorà fly it?" Elzbietá asked. "Seems like we keep piling more and more on top of her."

"Either way, I'll take the extra time machine," Klaus-Wilhelm said. "We can figure out who pilots it later."

"One more ship isn't going to matter much against the *Tesseract*," Elzbietá warned. "And the clock is ticking. The longer we take building the c-bomb and gathering our forces, the more hyperforges will be online. That thing could be spitting out *dozens* of phase-missiles per wave next time, and we have no counter for them."

"Never mind the whole infinite ammo thing," Philo added.

"That's why I need the rest of you to come up with something," Klaus-Wilhelm stressed. "Some tactic that'll give us an edge against them. Otherwise, this mission will be over before it starts."

"We'll do our best, sir," Elzbietá said doubtfully. "But even if we do come up with something, we're going to take murderous casualties with that many nukes flying our way."

"I know," Klaus-Wilhelm said, his eyes dark. "I'm not asking for perfection, just something to give us an edge."

"Great," Philo sighed. "Time to make another connectome copy, I guess."

"Another one?" Raibert asked. "But didn't you just save a new one?"

"Yeah, I did. Right before we attacked the Dynasty. But a lot happened in that battle, and I don't want to risk losing it."

"Hey, Raibert?" Elzbietá asked. "Do you save your connectome now that you're a synthoid?"

"*Pfft!* Nope!" He raised his nose in disgust.

"Why not?"

"I may trust the banks with my Esteem account"— he crossed his arms—"but handing them a copy of everything I ever was? Hell no!"

"It's not that bad," Philo assured him. "The archives are very secure."

"But not impenetrable. And the people running the banks are as flawed as the rest of us. How do you know there aren't a hundred copies of you toiling away in some abstract sweatshop?"

Philo flashed a skeptical grin. "I'm pretty sure that's not the case."

"But you don't *know*," Raibert pointed out. "Whereas, I do." He thumped his broad chest. "I'm the only me walking around, and I *like* it that way!"

"It'd still make me feel better if you'd save a copy," Philo said. "It wouldn't have to be often. Maybe once a decade?"

"No, no, and hell no."

Philo sighed, shoulders drooping.

"I understand how you feel, Raibert," Klaus-Wilhelm said. "The very thought of handing someone a copy of my mind is...unsettling."

"See?" Raibert pointed an open hand at the commissioner. "*He* gets it."

"I know, and I appreciate that you're both in the majority of public opinion." Philo shrugged. "Doesn't change the fact you're wrong."

"How common is the practice anyway?" Benjamin asked.

"It's not mainstream, to be honest," Philo said. "SysGov heavily regulates connectome copying, modification, and the very rare cases of authorized duplication. Plus it's time-consuming and expensive. I mean, in terms of the legal hurdles and licensing fees. The actual process is a snap."

"Don't about one in every three SysPol officers do it?" Elzbietá asked.

"That sounds about right," Philo said. "Though, that's mostly because of the risks inherent in the job. The general populace is closer to one in twenty."

"It paid off, too," Benjamin pointed out. "Argo Division only lost seven hundred people instead of *Lecroix*'s full complement of a thousand. And nine of *our* losses weren't permanent either."

"Still a fuckin' dicey practice, if you ask me," Raibert grumped.

"But it has its benefits," Elzbietá said.

"Hrmph!"

A communication icon appeared in Klaus-Wilhelm's virtual sight. He checked the sender, then grimaced and opened it.

"Yes, Chief."

"Klaus, I need you to come back to Argus as soon as possible," Lamont said after the brief lag imposed by light-speed limitations.

"Right away, sir. I'm wrapping up here on Mycene. What's going on?"

"We've received an unexpected guest, and you're one of the people he wants to talk to. The President is also transmitting up to the station for the meeting."

"The president's coming, too?" Klaus-Wilhelm furrowed his brow.

"That's right."

"Must be some guest. Who is it?"

"None other than the Admin's top politician, Chief Executor Christopher First. A chronoport just dropped him off."

CHAPTER FORTY-ONE

⚬⚬⚬⚬

Argus Station
SysGov, 2980 CE

"SORRY I TOOK SO LONG," KLAUS-WILHELM APOLO-
gized, hurrying into the conference room to join
Lamont, Hawke, Peng, and President Byakko along
one side of a wide, rectangular table. Two virtual banners hung from the door through which he'd entered,
dark blue and emblazoned with the golden SysPol
eye, while the opposite door sported two lighter blue
banners with white trim and the silver Admin shield.

"That's all right, Klaus," Peng said dryly. "Not all of
us can move at the speed of light. Usually, at least."

He grimaced as he added the qualifier. Both he and
Byakko had transferred into synthoids as a clear gesture of welcome to their guests, and Hawke's two ACs
were nowhere to be found. Which only underscored
the question burning in Klaus-Wilhelm's mind. Why
should the AI-phobic Admin even consent to meeting
the president at all, let alone *request* to speak with her?

"Have they told us why the Chief Executor is here?"

he asked, stepping behind the high-backed chair with his name hovering above it.

"This is about our failed attack on the Dynasty." Lamont frowned. "They know we're keeping them in the dark."

"And for good reason," Peng said. "They're not the most . . . understanding of neighbors."

"I suspect this'll be a bit of bluster meant to encourage more openness," Lamont suggested.

"As if the Dynasty isn't enough to worry about," Klaus-Wilhelm growled.

"Yeah, tell me about it." Peng shook his head. "The *last* thing we need is the fucking Admin jumping into the mix."

Byakko shot a cold eye his way, and he cleared his throat.

"Sorry."

"The Chief Executor and his entourage will be here shortly," Byakko announced. "Gentlemen, I share your sentiments regarding our guests. However, I'd like to remind you that they *are* our guests, and we shall conduct ourselves as gracious hosts. This may, as Chief Lamont pointed out, come to nothing. Then again, it may not. This could prove to be a very delicate conversation indeed, and you should all bear in mind that in the worst-case scenario, we *cannot* survive a war on *two* fronts."

Klaus-Wilhelm sucked in a sharp breath as the stark reality of her statement settled in the pit of his stomach.

"If in doubt, keep your mouths shut," she concluded.

"Yes, Madam President." Lamont glanced to each of his subordinates, and Klaus-Wilhelm and the others nodded their understanding.

"Here they come," Byakko said then, and the doors split open.

Two Peacekeeper synthoids with gray skin and yellow eyes stepped through and took up positions on either side of the entrance. A handsome, towering man followed them in, his long brown mane cascading over the shoulders of his light gray suit. A pin in the form of a silver shield gleamed on the chief executor's collar. Under-Director Hinnerkopf stepped in next, a compact woman wearing a sharp scowl, and then one more person entered before the doors sealed shut.

Klaus-Wilhelm's breath caught when he saw the Admin's third representative. His heartbeat quickened, his nostrils flared, and every muscle in his face tightened. He gripped the back of his chair so hard his knuckles turned white.

Csaba Shigeki, Director-General of the DTI and the man responsible for the murder of his wife and children, stood before him. Memories poured through his mind: the thunder of gunfire, the crackle of flames, the screams of the dying, the choking stench of burned wood—

—and charred *flesh*.

The feeling of Yulia's broken body cradled in his arms, of her life slipping away one faint pulse at a time. Slipping. Slipping.

Then gone, her chest falling for the last time as he kissed her forehead, tears blurring his vision.

And finally, the ugly lumps of blackened flesh that had been their daughters, scorched beyond recognition by the Admin flamethrower.

The memories filled him with rage and grief as easily as one would top off a pitcher of water, and he struggled to contain their fury. He pictured himself climbing atop the table, dashing across it, then *lunging* off to tackle Shigeki, forcing him to the ground, his hands tight around the man's neck, fingers digging into his throat.

He shook the ugly thought from his mind.

He knew, intellectually, that Csaba Shigeki hadn't been there, that his *troops* had murdered Yulia and their three children, but that lonely fact didn't alter how he felt, and as one commander to another, Klaus-Wilhelm knew who was ultimately responsible for the actions of the men and women under his command.

Only one man deserved the blame for what happened to his family.

Shigeki must have seen something in Klaus-Wilhelm's face, and his brow furrowed in puzzlement. Their eyes locked for a single, searing instant, and then Shigeki turned away, clearly disconcerted by the vicious look he'd received.

"Chief Executor First," Byakko began. "It's a pleasure and an honor to finally meet you in person. I hope you'll enjoy your stay here in SysGov. Perhaps you'd like to join me for a tour of our capital after our business here is concluded?"

"Madam President," was all the chief executor said, his face an unwelcoming mask.

"I see." Byakko flashed a quick smile. "To business, then. As requested, all three SysPol commissioners involved, whether directly or not, in our attack on the Dynasty are present." She swept a hand over the table. "Please be seated."

Representatives on both sides pulled out their chairs and took their seats. Klaus-Wilhelm had the distinct displeasure of sitting directly across from Shigeki.

"Well now." Byakko smiled again. "Perhaps you'd like to enlighten us on the purpose of your visit."

The chief executor gestured to Shigeki without looking. "Show them."

"Yes, sir." Shigeki placed his hand on the table where the Admin-style infostructure interfaced with his PIN.

A virtual image of the *Tesseract* sprang up over one end of the table, and three SysPol cruisers appeared over the other. The tiny glints of mechs launched from the cruisers as TTVs phased into the past, all in false scale so the battle could play out and still be visible.

The image shocked Klaus-Wilhelm so severely he forgot his anger for a moment.

Did one of their chronoports record this? he wondered. *I knew their stealth systems were good, but not this good!*

Lamont grimaced at the replay, Hawke shook his head, and Byakko fixed a diplomatic smile on her face. Only Commissioner Peng let his honest reaction slip.

"Oh, crap," he uttered.

"Where did you get this?" Byakko asked politely.

"Does it matter?" Shigeki countered.

"It's not a leak from Argo, I can assure you of that, Madam President," Hawke said.

Shigeki glanced to the chief executor, who nodded.

"It's not a leak," Shigeki confirmed. "One of our chronoports followed your fleet to the Dynasty."

"We saw the *whole* thing." The chief executor leaned forward with a forearm on the table. "When were you going to tell us?"

"Tell you what?" Byakko fluttered her eyes, her

smile frozen in place, and the chief executor stabbed a finger at the *Tesseract*'s image.

"That this spur universe—which *you* created—has built a temporal battle station!"

"Oh, that," Byakko said simply.

"Yes! That!"

"Doctor Hinnerkopf," Shigeki explained, gesturing to the subordinate at his side, "with whom I believe some of you are familiar, has analyzed the station's capabilities."

Hinnerkopf gave the table a curt nod.

"And you know what we found?" the chief executor asked. "This abomination is being upgraded for transdimensional transit, *and* it can somehow replicate its weapon systems! This thing could travel to another universe—the *Admin*, for example—plant itself in last week, and rain an infinite number of nukes onto the present! And you chose not to tell us about it!"

"I'm sorry," Klaus-Wilhelm said urgently. "But what makes you think the station can go transdimensional?"

"Our chronoport observed the initial modifications to its impeller before departing," Hinnerkopf said. "They're consistent with the ones we've made to our chronoport fleet."

Klaus-Wilhelm sat back as the revelation sank in.

"Madam President," Shigeki said, "we also have reason to believe the Dynasty universe is unstable and that your people are already working on a solution of some nature."

"You seem very well informed," she said smoothly.

"Not well enough, I'm afraid. The reason we're here is simple. We need to know what you know. Whatever is happening here affects us as well."

"Right, because you guys are *so* reliable," Peng countered.

"Excuse me?" Shigeki bristled.

"You want to know the reason we don't share everything with you?" Peng stuck a thumb against his chest. "It's sitting right in front of you. The Admin *enslaves* people like me. In fact, you don't even consider me a person! Same with the President here. And you expect us to hand you our most sensitive information? What makes you think you've *earned* that level of trust?"

"Bring it down a notch, Peng," Lamont warned.

"Sorry, but it needed to be said. There're people in the Admin who would delete me without a second thought, and they'd believe in their heart of hearts that they were doing a noble thing. If the leaders of the Admin want to know why we play our cards facedown, best give it to them straight."

Byakko frowned at him, but then she turned back to the chief executor.

"I hope you'll excuse Commissioner Peng's . . . bluntness," she said. "However, he raises a valid point. You're expecting a great deal when the relationship between the Admin and SysGov is still in its infancy."

"What I expect is for SysGov to be forthright with us," the chief executor said. "Especially when a crisis of such startling magnitude has emerged."

"And how exactly did the DTI act during the last existential crisis?" Klaus-Wilhelm cut in. "Have you considered that?"

"What do you mean?" the chief executor asked.

"The Gordian Knot threatened the very existence of sixteen universes, and when Agent Kaminski—then Professor Kaminski—sought the DTI's assistance in unraveling the Knot, what happened? Did they greet him with open arms and confront this colossal threat together? No! They murdered his physical body and threw his connectome in jail! And when he escaped, they hunted him across time and space, leaving a trail of death and destruction in their wake. You!" He pointed a finger at Shigeki. "You *personally* led the mission to hunt him down!"

"No, I didn't," Shigeki responded matter-of-factly.

"Deny it all you want," Klaus-Wilhelm pressed. "The fact is you and your DTI agents—from a universe *identical* to your own—were given a choice. Right up to the *instant* Agent Raibert contacted you in SysGov's name, you *were* the same people. And when you had the choice"—Klaus-Wilhelm stood, leaned across the table, glared down at Shigeki—"you chose to let the multiverse *burn*! Do you seriously think there's some reason anyone but a lunatic would trust *this* iteration of you?"

No one spoke for a while as his words hung in the supercharged conference room like an ugly, black cloud. He let them hang for endless seconds, then sat down and tugged his uniform straight, never taking his eyes from Shigeki for a moment.

The DTI director sat in silence the whole time, his face an unreadable, iron mask.

"Chief Executor," Byakko said finally. "I'd like to propose a short recess. Perhaps some time away from the table will benefit us all."

"Agreed."

Klaus-Wilhelm rose sharply from his seat and turned away, but a voice stopped him.

"Commissioner Schröder," Csaba Shigeki said.

Klaus-Wilhelm let out a long exhale, then turned back around.

"What?" he said, almost spat.

"I'd like a word with you in private, if you don't mind?"

❖   ❖   ❖

Shigeki followed Vice-Commissioner Schröder out of the conference room and into the hallway. They were the respective heads of their time-travel organizations, and if *they* were at each other's throats, then *nothing* would get done. He knew he had to do something about the other man's attitude; he simply had no idea how to fix it.

"All right," Klaus-Wilhelm said. "Let's hear what you have to say."

"Sir, I'm detecting some . . . personal animosity between us."

Klaus-Wilhelm crossed his arms without saying a word, and Shigeki nodded.

"I thought so," he said. "Look, we're both professionals, we both know what a threat the Dynasty poses, and we have *got* to get past this."

Klaus-Wilhelm's face went even bleaker, and Shigeki shook his head quickly.

"I'm not saying there aren't valid reasons—*tons* of them—why that's easier said than done. I've read and reread the files SysGov provided about what happened in the Gordian Knot. I understand why you're all so reluctant to trust us. *I'd* be reluctant in your position, God knows! And I know your iteration of my universe—and all the people in it who mattered to you—no longer exist. I can't begin to imagine what that must feel like. But the Admin didn't destroy that universe, sir—*you* did." He met Klaus-Wilhelm's eyes levelly. "Based on what I now know, you were right to do that. You had no choice. But the Csaba Shigeki of that universe was trying to save it."

"*Save* it?" Klaus-Wilhelm's eyes blazed suddenly, and Shigeki knew he'd stepped on a land mine. "Is that what you think this is about?"

"I don't know what else it *could* be about, not on a level that's obviously so personal to you," Shigeki said, refusing to flinch. "But *whatever* it is, you and I have got to find a way to ... put it behind us. At least well enough for us—"

"Not damned likely," Klaus-Wilhelm grated.

Shigeki paused for a moment, then drew a deep breath.

"Everything I've been able to learn about you, both from the historical record and in the True Present, tells me you're a rational, tough-minded man. And your attitude now tells me that I—or that other iteration of me—must have wronged you in some deep, very personal way. But *I* have no memory of it, no clue as to what it might have been. So I ask you, as one time traveler to another, what did this other me do?"

"Really?" Klaus-Wilhelm's fiery eyes narrowed. "You *really* want to know?"

"I wouldn't have asked if I didn't."

The commissioner paused in thought for long second, then gave a quick nod.

"All right. Have it your way." He extended an open palm, and a file icon appeared over it.

"What's that?" Shigeki asked.

"The 'personal wrong' I suffered."

Shigeki accepted the file into his PIN. Software monitors scrutinized it, cleared it as non-malicious, and identified it as a synthoid sensory record. An *Admin* synthoid record, easily compatible with his PIN's sight and sound overlay.

"Play it," Klaus-Wilhelm said, perhaps noting Shigeki's hesitation. "Or not. It won't change anything."

"No, I'll watch it."

Shigeki loaded the record. The station hallway vanished, replaced with a ruined windowless room, the thick door at its only entrance blasted open by some unseen conflict. Fires crackled throughout the building, and the mangled body of a woman fought to claw her way across the floor.

Klaus-Wilhelm knelt by her side.

"Lie still, *Liebling*," he said through his tears in a voice that wavered and cracked.

"K-Klaus-Wilhelm?" the dying woman managed to whisper.

"I'm here, *meine Geliebte*."

Klaus-Wilhelm sat beside her, lifted her head, rested it in his lap. He bent over her, his lips brushed her bloody forehead, and *her* lips twitched in a tiny smile. But then she stiffened.

"The . . . girls, *kohanij*?" she whispered. "Are . . . are . . . the girls—"

Her voice failed, and she gasped in anguish as she tried once again to push herself upright.

"Lie still," Klaus-Wilhelm said again, softly, serenely. The quaver had left his voice, and he stroked her hair. "The girls are fine, *Liebling*. You saved them. They're fine."

"Good . . ."

The single word ghosted out of her, softer than a sigh, and he kissed her forehead again.

"You can go now," he told her gently, lovingly. "You can go now, my love."

"Love...y—" she breathed.

Her voice flickered out, and Klaus-Wilhelm lifted her, cradled her body in his arms, her head on his shoulder, as he closed his eyes in pain.

"Governor, let me have her!"

He looked up at the synthoid whose record this was—at Raibert, Shigeki realized—his eyes stunned and broken, and Raibert leaned closer.

"If I can get her to the *Kleio* in time, we can still save her!" he said urgently. "The...the medical facilities in my ship can heal her completely if I can get her there quickly enough!"

"And can you save her daughters?" Klaus-Wilhelm's voice was flat, leached of all emotion, and Raibert's viewpoint turned to a shattered storage cabinet. And to the scorched, blackened carbonized flesh which had once been Klaus-Wilhelm's three daughters.

"No," he said softly. "No, I'm...afraid not. Their wounds are..."

His voice trailed off.

"Then let her go, too," Klaus-Wilhelm said, and now all the pain in the universe was in his voice. "I won't bring her back to face that. Let her go knowing she saved them. That they're still alive."

❖　　❖　　❖

Csaba Shigeki shut off the recording, then let out a long, shuddering breath as he tried to collect himself. He'd known the members of the Gordian Division and another version of the DTI had clashed, but *this*?

This was beyond *anything* he'd imagined. Why would his agents murder women and children? Why would they burn them alive? Had he *ordered* this?

He put a hand over his mouth. He didn't know what horrified him more, the act of unbridled evil he'd just witnessed—

Or the fact that a version of him had played a hand in it.

"Now you've seen it," Klaus-Wilhelm—the real one, in the present—said to him. "Anything to say?"

Shigeki stared blankly at the wall, unable to respond. What could he possibly say to this man? He swallowed dryly and took another long breath.

Klaus-Wilhelm grunted, shook his head, and walked off.

Shigeki turned his head, watched him leave, then licked his lips and called out.

"Sir?"

The commissioner stopped and looked back over his shoulder.

"Sir, I've wronged you." He walked over, as close behind Klaus-Wilhelm as he dared. "I had no idea of what had happened to your family, and I don't know how it came to pass, but I freely admit I've wronged you deeply, in ways I can never make right." Shigeki took another shaky breath. "Sir, I'm truly sorry for what happened to your family."

Klaus-Wilhelm stood with his back still turned to Shigeki.

"As you said," he responded finally. "That wasn't you. And they would have died with their universe in the end." He smiled mirthlessly. "I thought *I* would have, too, or I would never have agreed to help my grandson destroy it. And"—he inhaled deeply— "whatever else you may have done, you were fighting to save it."

"I won't hide behind that excuse," Shigeki said softly. "Not any longer. And not after what you just showed me. Or what you said earlier. It was 'another iteration' of me, but you were right earlier. It was still *me*, the me I was until the instant Agent Kaminski walked into my office in an Admin synthoid's body. Yes, I have no memory of it, and yes, that version of me no longer exists, but I still have a debt to pay. And it's time I did."

"A debt?" Klaus-Wilhelm paused to swallow. "Do you really believe that?"

"I do." Shigeki stepped around so they faced each other. "What I just witnessed was a tragedy, but look at how it came to pass . . . and what happened afterward. For whatever reasons, my DTI and the people who would form your Gordian Division opposed each other, fought and killed one another. And even under those terrible circumstances, even with my people doing everything we possibly could to stop you, you were *still* able to unravel the Knot."

"So? What of it?"

"Think about it for a second, Commissioner. If the Gordian Knot could be cut when we *opposed* each other"—Shigeki extended an open hand—"what could we achieve if we worked *together*?"

Klaus-Wilhelm gazed at that hand, eyes dark with doubt, but Shigeki met those eyes unflinchingly as he held it out between them.

"You really mean this, don't you?"

"I do, sir," Shigeki said with total conviction. "I do."

Klaus-Wilhelm stared at the offered hand, silently, while endless seconds ticked past. Shigeki began to suspect he wouldn't accept his offer. But then the other man cracked a smile. It was the last thing Shigeki had expected to see, and it was bittersweet below eyes dark with pain, yet it truly was a *smile*.

"Riding in on that damned horse again, I see," Klaus-Wilhelm murmured.

"I beg your pardon?" Shigeki asked.

"Nothing. A story for another time." He looked Shigeki straight in the eyes, clasped his hand, and gave it a firm shake. "Together it is, then."

❖   ❖   ❖

"Now then." Byakko settled into her chair. "Shall we try this once more?"

"You can start by answering one simple question," the chief executor said. "Is the Dynasty universe truly unstable?"

"Very well," Byakko agreed. "Perhaps some openness is in order as a show of good faith on our part." She knitted her fingers. "The answer to your first question is yes. The Dynasty's temporal replication industry is eroding the outer wall of their universe. And the construction and operation of the *Tesseract*"—she indicated the virtual image of the station—"is accelerating the process."

The chief executor sat back, his eyes dark.

"Can the instability be reversed?"

"We don't believe so. Not at this stage."

"And when it finally erodes?"

"The Dynasty will cease to be. SysGov as well."

"*Both* universes?" He shook his head, clearly stunned by scale of the calamity.

"That's correct. So, as you can see, we have some very good reasons for concern."

"Have you tried explaining this to the Dynasty's leaders?"

"All efforts at diplomacy have failed," Byakko pointed out. "We made several attempts to explain the situation to the Dynasty, but we're quite sure elements within their government are sabotaging our diplomatic overtures."

"This is . . . terrible!" the chief executor gasped, sounding genuinely concerned. "We didn't know it was *this* bad!"

"We're working toward a solution."

"Which is?"

"As you already suspect, we're working on a chronometric . . . device." Byakko flashed a polite smile, avoiding the word "bomb."

"And this device does what, precisely?"

"In simple terms, it will shove the Dynasty away from us so that if they die, we don't."

"Shove an entire *universe* away?" The chief executor glanced to Hinnerkopf. "Is that even possible?"

"It's hard to say without more information," she confessed. "Though it's an intriguing approach. From what we've seen, the Dynasty and SysGov are joined at the hip, so to speak. Solve that somehow, and the danger goes away. If I could be given access to the device's technical specifications—"

"Out of the question," Byakko interrupted.

"I see," Hinnerkopf said stiffly.

The room fell silent once more until Shigeki cleared his throat.

"Chief Executor, if you'll permit me, I have a proposal that I believe will end our impasse."

"By all means." The chief executor gestured to the

other side of the table with both hands. "Let them hear it."

"A disaster on this scale cannot be ignored by either of our governments. Whatever differences we may have with each other—for that matter, however grave the threat this *Tesseract* might ultimately pose to the Admin—pale before the one looming over SysGov. Sir, I believe only the combined resources of both the DTI and the Gordian Division are up to the challenge we now face. I propose a joint operation to deploy the device."

"Csaba, I appreciate your enthusiasm," the chief executor said, "but I don't think we're quite there yet. And—"

"Madam President," Klaus-Wilhelm interrupted. "Director Shigeki is absolutely right to call for a joint operation. His proposal has my full support."

The chief executor closed his mouth with an almost audible snap and all eyes turned to Klaus-Wilhelm.

"You *support* this?" Lamont asked after a moment, both eyebrows raised.

"Yes, sir."

"This is a surprise," Byakko admitted.

"Who are you, and what have you done with Klaus?" Lamont said.

"It's all right, sir." Klaus-Wilhelm glanced over to Shigeki. "The Director and I have come to an ... understanding."

"So it would seem!"

"Well?" Byakko clicked her fingernails on the table and turned back to the chief executor. "Our subordinates have certainly warmed to each other, and I must admit the task before us is incredibly daunting. What do you say to all this?"

"Madam President." The chief executor straightened in his seat and quirked a lopsided smile. "You were right when you said the relationship between our two peoples has only begun. We're just starting to get to know and understand one another. We are very different in many ways, and any period like this is full of pitfalls at the best of times. Misunderstandings can lead to resentment. Even violence." He made a brushing-away gesture. "But push all of that aside, and the situation becomes crystal clear. What I see before me is a neighbor in distress, and the Admin will answer the call. Madam President, the full power of the DTI is at your disposal."

"Thank you, Chief Executor," Byakko said with a warm smile. "On behalf of SysGov, I gratefully accept your offer."

Tension drained from the room, and Klaus-Wilhelm felt a sense of relief well up within him. But it was tempered with concern. The DTI's resources would surely bolster their own efforts, but would it be enough?

"We can begin transferring chronoports to SysGov as soon as we send word back home," Shigeki said. "Commissioner, I'd like permission for my staff to use the Gordian Division's facilities here on Argus Station. We'll need a consolidated command center."

"That's quite all right, though there's a problem with sending your chronoports over now. There's a good chance the Dynasty'll notice the buildup, and they've already hit us once."

"Then, perhaps a smaller initial force? Say, two squadrons of *Pioneer*-class chronoports to bolster the defense of your outer wall. Both Barricade and Guardian squadrons have extensive experience hunting down time machines. Granted, the ones we normally chase down aren't *nearly* as advanced as the Dynasty's, but our standard tactics should still prove effective."

"Yes, I think that'll work," Klaus-Wilhelm agreed. "The speed and stealth systems on your chronoports will be a *very* nasty surprise to any snooping *Valkyries*."

"And after that, we can muster our forces beyond the Dynasty's prying eyes."

"But even with the extra time machines, there's still the problem of breaking through the *Tesseract*'s defenses," Klaus-Wilhelm cautioned. "We lack an effective counter to the phase-missiles, and without one, more time machines just means more targets."

"Oh, I believe we can assist there, as well." Shigeki let a sly smile show as he placed a hand on the table. The battle record vanished, and a bulky chronoport materialized over the center of the table, rotating around. A device resembling a second impeller protruded from the vessel's nose.

Of course! Klaus-Wilhelm thought. *The Admin's suppression technology!*

"This is one of our new *Portcullis*-class chronoports," Shigeki explained. "We currently have three in operation, and each comes equipped with a suppression field antenna. The phase-missiles are still time machines, and as such, the operation of their impellers can be impacted."

"You'll be able to stop the missiles from phasing through time?" Klaus-Wilhelm asked.

"It depends on the range. At the very least, we'll be able to slow them down, which'll give us the maneuvering advantage *and* more time for intercepts."

"Either way, I'll take it."

"What about SysGov's chronometric device?" the chief executor asked. "Are we correct in assuming it's on Mycene Station?"

"You are," Byakko said. "But unfortunately, the device is unfinished."

"Then we need to ensure it's well protected until it *is* finished," the chief executor said. "Losing it now would be disastrous."

"Yes, about our lone point of failure," Klaus-Wilhelm grimaced. He knew this was going to take some explaining. "You see, any good military plan needs a little redundancy..."

CHAPTER FORTY-TWO

$$\otimes\!\otimes\!\otimes$$

Argus Station
SysGov, 2980 CE

ANDOVER-CHEN STOOD NEAR THE CENTER OF GORDIAN Operations, arms folded, brow furrowed in concentration as he stared at the chronometric charts arrayed before him, their indicators resting comfortably in the green. A team of freighters had discreetly moved all the c-bomb material from Mycene to Argus the day before, partially because Argus was the fleet's staging point and also because the Argus Array was the most advanced chronometric sensor in all of SysGov.

Teodorà Beckett crossed the Operations center to him.

"Doctor," she said softly.

"Yes?" he replied reflexively, clearly focused on the task at hand.

"We're really doing this, aren't we?"

"That we are."

And I'm helping them, Teodorà thought. *Helping them travel down the same self-destructive path that's doomed the Dynasty.*

Helping them replicate a weapon!

But then she shook her head.

No, it's not a weapon. That damn station *is a weapon, and I was too blind to see it. What the Gordian Division has created is a means of escape. Nothing more. Not a weapon. Not a universe-killer. That would be redundant, because the Dynasty doesn't need killing... it's already in the act of committing suicide. This isn't a weapon; it's the last counsel of desperation, a means to save themselves from the Dynasty's folly.*

From my *folly,* she added bitterly. *My hubris led us here, put every life in SysGov at risk, and for what? Because I thought I was smart enough and wise enough to meddle in the fabric of the multiverse? To assume powers and responsibilities reserved for the ancient gods?*

And now everyone here could pay the price. Could cease to be because I thought I knew better than everyone else.

The Dynasty may be doomed, but SysGov must live on. It must... *and I'll do anything I possibly can to make that happen.*

No matter how much it hurts.

"I wish there were another way," she said.

"We don't have a choice." Raibert walked up behind them, and she turned around. "Maybe if we had more time we could think of something else, or do this the old-fashioned way, but Lucius isn't giving us any options."

"I know," she said. "But these kinds of shortcuts led us to this mess."

"That's why we're going to do this *very carefully,*" Andover-Chen stressed.

A communication window opened.

"*Kleio* to Gordian Operations," Elzbietá said. "We're ready to begin the operation."

"I hear you, *Kleio*." He skimmed over the array of charts once more, then nodded. "Proceed."

"Understood. Retrieving the bomb frame now."

A hangar bay's massive airlock slid open. The *Kleio* eased into it, then flew back out with the c-bomb's spike slung under the hull. The device was a patchwork of missing disk-shaped sections, as if it were fossilized segments of a strange vertebrae laid out for a museum.

Andover-Chen gestured for Teodorà to take his place, and she stepped up to the window.

"Okay, *Kleio*," she said. "Drop it off there, then pull away from it."

The *Kleio* detached the c-bomb frame five hundred meters beyond the hangar and flew up from it.

"Good. That should be enough working space," Teodorà said. "Now set the moment you cleared the frame as your retrieval point. When you're ready, go back, pick up a copy of the frame, then return to the True Present. Just be careful with the turbulence on the ride back; the TTV won't handle the same when you're lugging around a hunk of exotic matter."

"Roger that. Initiating phase-out."

The TTV vanished.

"Now we see how much this burns us," Andover-Chen grunted, his charts flickering with incoming data.

A few minutes ticked by with the *Kleio*'s signal hovering in the near present. While they waited, an Admin chronoport flashed into existence outside the station and came in for a landing. Another chronoport lifted off to replace it, and promptly phased out.

Raibert groaned.

"What?" Andover-Chen asked cheerfully.

"Nothing. It's nothing."

"The chronoports in our skies bothering you?"

"Maybe a little."

"You know they're here to help, don't you?"

"Whatever. I'll get over it."

Andover-Chen grinned at him, despite his own tension, before returning attention to his charts.

The *Kleio* reappeared a few minutes later and dropped off a new c-bomb frame alongside the first one. Two of Andover-Chen's chronometric graphs spiked, and he expanded them and scrutinized the readings.

"How bad is it?" Teodorà asked.

"Not *quite* as bad as I thought it'd be," Andover-Chen admitted. "There's a scary amount of resonance out there, to be sure, but SysGov's outer wall isn't nearly as abused as the Dynasty's. It can take more punishment." He grimaced as one of the numbers jumped again before settling. "For now, at least."

"Good work, *Kleio*," Teodorà said. "How was the ride back?"

"Rough. I'm glad I started off in the compensation bunk. Otherwise, Philo would have gotten a replay of my breakfast."

"Ew," Raibert muttered. "Thanks for the mental picture."

"Is the turbulence manageable?" Teodorà asked.

"Yeah, the ship can handle it, and I can fly through it. Give us a few minutes to reinforce the clamp, though. I don't want to risk a frame busting off during transit. Philo's going to thicken the mount with some of the hull's prog-steel."

"Sounds sensible," Teodorà said. "Cornucopia had

similar equipment problems while building the *Tesseract*."

"We'll continue once you're ready," Andover-Chen said. "Just do this another four times, and we should have enough material to finish construction."

❖   ❖   ❖

Lucius was concerned. He didn't like being in the dark, especially when everything had been proceeding so perfectly.

Now *this*.

No, he told himself. Everything *still was* proceeding as he'd envisioned. He was *sure* of it. Yet now he suddenly found himself blind to SysGov's next move. His scout *Valkyries* should have had no trouble keeping an eye on the enemy, and if they were detected at all, they had more speed and better maneuverability than any TTV. They'd already proven—repeatedly—that they could always flee to safety.

And yet he'd lost six *Valkyries* on as many missions, and Vlastos had forced a halt to their scouting operations until they figured out what was happening.

What's changed? he wondered. *What is SysGov up to?*

Not that it changed anything important, of course.

It was an annoyance, but a minor one. Ultimately, SysGov's plans didn't matter. Militarization of the Dynasty's remaining *Valkyries* was proceeding smoothly, and the exotic material duplicated by that first hyperforge had allowed the rest of the station's construction to proceed at an exponential pace. Nearly all of the *Tesseract*'s hyperforges were now operational, and Hyperforge Twenty-Eight would come online soon, allowing him to replicate time machines—*and* their crews—at will.

Lucius smiled as he opened his *Valkyrie* inventory

then cross-referenced the list with crew combat performance. He'd decided to select a unit for replication should SysGov attack before the *Tesseract* was finished. After all, the impeller required substantial modification before he could flee this dying universe. Better safe than sorry.

Simon and the council will object to the replication, of course, he thought. *Teodorà and Samuel made sure there were laws against the temporal replication of people. What an annoyance. But I'm sure I can convince them to exercise some . . . wartime leniency. And if they decide not to, well, I'll simply take direct control of the* Tesseract *and circumvent them entirely.*

One of the profiles stood head and shoulders above the rest.

"Ah. Of course. That one, I think."

The *Sigrun*—and especially its pilot, Hala Khatib—had caught his eye, and he flagged the entry for later reference.

"Yes, that one will do nicely, I think."

He wondered what SysGov would do against an infinite supply of his best ship and crew.

He chuckled to himself. Whatever SysGov tried next, he'd be ready for them.

❖   ❖   ❖

"How many are we up to?" Klaus-Wilhelm asked as he and Benjamin stepped into Gordian Operations.

Andover-Chen didn't turn from his charts, only frowned at them more deeply with a hand around his chin.

"Nine c-bombs," Raibert said after a moment, gesturing to the visual feed. A row of exotic matter spikes floated outside the station, each capped with powerful graviton thrusters.

"Only nine?" Klaus-Wilhelm asked. "I thought that's what we had an hour ago."

"Yeah," Raibert said, "but we were forced to bring *Kleio* in for maintenance."

"Couldn't another TTV take its place?"

"Another one *could* have, but Doctor Andover-Chen..." Raibert nudged his head toward the physicist's back.

"Sir, I ordered the delay." Andover-Chen turned around. He tapped one of the charts behind him with a knuckle. "I wanted to see how long these readings took to settle out."

"And? How do they look?"

"Not good. The outer wall is...'bruised,' for want of a better word, and each time we replicate a c-bomb, we bruise it again. It *is* healing, but it's taking longer and longer each time. We've waited an hour since replicating number nine, and we're still worse off than we were after replicating number eight."

"Then what's your recommendation?" Klaus-Wilhelm asked. "Should we stop here?"

"Well," Andover-Chen sighed and pulled one of the charts between them. "As much as I would have preferred to not even *begin*, we're not doing badly so far. Still, I think another one would be pushing our luck."

"Are you sure?"

"Yes, sir. I recommend we stop at nine."

"Very well. Cease operations at once."

"Sir." He gave the commissioner a nod, then clicked an icon. "Gordian Operations to *Kleio*."

"*Kleio* here," Elzbietá said. "Just hanging out. Waiting on you."

"Sorry about the delay. We're calling it quits at nine. Come on home."

"Roger that."

The TTV pulled away from the row of replicated c-bombs and slid into an open hangar.

"While we're all here, I have something to discuss with all three of you," Klaus-Wilhelm said, indicating Raibert, Benjamin, and Andover-Chen. "Benjamin and I already talked about it, and he's on board with the idea."

"What idea?" Raibert asked suspiciously. "What's this about?"

"Calm down," Benjamin reassured him with a pat on the back. "It just means extra work and possible loss of life for us three."

"Oh, is that all?" Raibert rolled his eyes. "As if I don't have enough to worry about already."

"This is the largest operation the Gordian Division has ever conducted," Benjamin said. "And since we're so small, there are a few key personnel slots still open."

"In short, when we hit the Dynasty, I'll need a command staff on *Wegbereiter*," Klaus-Wilhelm said. "I want all three of you on the command ship with me."

"Us?" Raibert blinked. "Why us?"

"The situation over there will undoubtedly prove volatile," Klaus-Wilhelm said. "And not only are all three of you familiar with the Dynasty and the c-bomb project, but you represent the very best the Gordian Division has to offer."

"*We're* your best agents?" Raibert blinked.

"Yes, Raibert," Klaus-Wilhelm said, a small measure of irritation leaking out. "You are. Along with Elzbietá and Philo."

"Wow." Raibert grinned. "Didn't expect to hear *that* from the boss."

"And I mean it," Klaus-Wilhelm added. "That said, none of you are TTV pilots, so your presence on this mission isn't absolutely necessary. I know I've asked a lot of all my agents recently—your team in particular, Raibert—and this is one more burden to add to the load, which is why I'm *asking* this time."

"*Pfft!*" Raibert waved a dismissive hand. "No need. Sit at home or help save the universe? Who do you think you're talking to?"

Klaus-Wilhelm waited. When nothing else came, he cleared his throat.

"I'm in," Raibert clarified. "What I just said? That means I'm in."

"I'll join you as well, sir," Andover-Chen said.

"Likewise, *Grossvater*."

"Thank you, son." Klaus-Wilhelm put a hand on Benjamin's arm. "And to both of you as well. I knew I could depend on you. We're heading into an unprecedented, perilous situation. And on that note, Doctor, a question for you."

"Certainly, sir."

"I've drafted some thoughts on how we might approach the battle, which I'll review with Director Shigeki when he arrives. I believe I understand the technical aspects in play, but I want to make certain of one very specific count. If we take our fleet back into the Dynasty's past—say, to one negative year—will we have to contend with past versions of the *Tesseract*?"

"As long as the fleet remains non-congruent, no," Andover-Chen replied. "If the fleet phases in, then whatever was present at that time index will be there, of course."

"Good. I have no intentions of phasing into the past. Only to maneuver through it."

"What's on your mind?" Raibert asked.

"This isn't a realspace battle. In a conventional engagement, the gulf between forces might be measured in meters or kilometers or even light-seconds for space combat. But in a battle of TTVs, chronoports, and *Valkyries*, *time* is the distance that separates our forces, and I intend to open up a *temporal* gap to gauge the effectiveness of our defenses before we charge headlong into that station's fangs."

"Sounds like what Ella pulled off at the Gordian Knot," Benjamin said.

"Any chance we could just get the Admin to go in all stealthy-like and drop off the c-bombs?" Raibert asked.

"Unfortunately, that won't work," Andover-Chen said, swiping his equations aside. "C-bomb drag negates the effectiveness of their stealth systems. Even if the rest of their forces went undetected, it would only serve to draw all attention to the bomb carriers."

"Ah. Right." Raibert snapped his fingers. "Well, it was a thought."

"What if the *Tesseract* leaves the True Present?" Benjamin asked. "How does that affect where we deploy the c-bombs?"

"It doesn't," Andover-Chen assured them. "The *Tesseract* is the epicenter of the unusual connection between our two universes. It's our target, no matter what happens."

"Which I've also taken into account in my planning," Klaus-Wilhelm said.

"Hey, here's another random thought." Raibert pointed a thumb over his shoulder. "On the topic of advisers for the battle, what if Teodorà joins us on *Wegbereiter*? She knows the Dynasty better than *anyone*."

"You know, that's not a bad idea," Benjamin agreed.

"Uh-oh." Teodorà pushed off the wall she'd been leaning against and walked over. "I just heard Raibert say my name. This can't be good."

"Hey now," Raibert complained. "What's that supposed to mean?"

"What do you think it means?" She smiled at him, then stopped beside Klaus-Wilhelm, her face all business again. "What can I do for you, Commissioner?"

"We'll be leaving for the Dynasty soon, and Raibert had a suggestion about how you could support us further."

"Of course. What do you need?"

"We could use you on the command ship," Raibert said. "Anything could happen out there, and it'd be great to have you along. What do you say?"

"Oh." Teodorà frowned. "I see."

"You're free to stay here, of course," Klaus-Wilhelm clarified.

"No, it's not that at all." She shook her head. "I was actually hoping you'd ask me to come."

"Then I don't see the problem."

"Commissioner." Teodorà stood a little straighter. "I would be honored to join you, but my place is on *my* ship, not yours."

"I can find a pilot for your time machine if you're concerned it'll sit here collecting dust, but your expertise would be welcome on the command ship."

"With all due respect, none of your agents will be

able to fly it as well as I can. *Hildr* is more agile than anything your division has, and I'm the best person here to pilot it. Plus..." She paused, then nodded. "I *need* to be out there, part of the fight. I've spent too much time as an advisor, a chairwoman...an 'Honored Elder.'" Her mouth twisted bitterly for a moment. "Now it's time I pay back my dead...and those about to die, Commissioner. And I need to do that as a pilot, as one of *your* pilots." She met his eyes levelly. "I have to be out there, sir"— she waved one hand in a gesture which encompassed everything outside Argus Station's hull—"not on your command ship. I don't think I can explain it any better than that, but this is something I know I *have* to do. Perhaps that sounds strange to you, but it's how I feel."

"You'd be surprised." Benjamin smiled, prompting a confused look from Teodorà. "*This* family knows all about duty."

"Indeed." Klaus-Wilhelm backed off. "You seem to have your mind set. I see no reason to press the point, and I'll take every ship I can." He extended his hand. "Welcome to the fleet."

"Thank you, Commissioner." She shook his hand. "I won't let you down."

❖   ❖   ❖

"Hey, are you okay?" Raibert asked Teodorà once he had her alone near the outer edge of the Operations center.

"Yeah, I'm fine." She arched an eyebrow at him. "What brought this on?"

"Just a little worried, is all."

"About me?" she teased with a chuckle. "Aww, that's so sweet."

"No, I'm being serious here," Raibert insisted. "I

know you're more familiar with *Hildr*, but have you seen *Wegbereiter* or the other heavy TTVs? We took the old ART transports and turned them into some really scary ships. We used all that cargo space for an extra *two* reactors dedicated to laser power. Trust me, when we hit the Dynasty, *that* ship is the place to be."

"I might agree with you if safety was my only concern. But it's not. Stopping Lucius comes before anything else. It has to."

"I know. It's just..." He trailed off and sighed. "Look, I'm getting a 'blaze of glory' vibe here, and I'm...concerned for you."

"We all need to do our part, and this is how I'm going to do mine. Simple as that."

"Sure, yeah," he agreed, nodding. "Just promise me you won't do anything stupid out there."

She grimaced angrily at him.

"What?" he asked, taken aback by her expression. "Was it something I said?"

"Raibert," she huffed, crossing her arms, "I just spent the last two and a half subjective millennia fostering a society that—upon reaching its apex—has sentenced itself to death. *And* it's about to take my old home down with it. I think I've gotten the *really* stupid mistakes out of my system."

"Well, when you put it that way..."

"I'll be *fine*." She placed a hand on his shoulder and gave it a squeeze. "I haven't survived this long for nothing, you know. Besides"—she flashed a smile— "I've impersonated a Valkyrie before, so flying into battle in *Hildr* suits me just fine."

"I'm sorry, what?" Raibert blinked. "You impersonated a Dynasty time machine?"

"Uh." Teodorà rolled her eyes.

"Oh." Raibert's face lit up with sudden comprehension. "You meant a *mythical* Valkyrie."

"I'm pretty sure I mentioned that story."

"Yeah. Just remembered."

"Chooser of the slain. That's what we're doing here, selecting who lives and who dies."

"Maybe, in a way," Raibert said. "You're not—we're not—selecting who *dies*, Teodorà. We're trying to select who *lives*."

"And, in the process, who has to die so they do. Live, I mean."

"It's better than letting *everyone* die."

"Well, of course it is," she agreed with a frown. "Anyway, I suppose I should head down and prep *Hildr*. How long until the Admin fleet arrives?"

"Well, actually . . ." Raibert glanced to the Argus Array readouts in the center of the room. "Shigeki and his goons are already—"

Icons exploded across the virtual map as a formation of thirty-three chronoports flashed into existence outside the station. Realspace scopes focused on the new arrivals and identified them as twenty-four *Pioneer*-class light chronoports, six *Hammerhead*-class heavy chronoports, and three *Portcullis*-class mobile suppressors. Automatic signals exchanged between the Admin force and Gordian Operations, and the displays added each craft to the twenty-four *other* chronoports already being tracked.

"—on final approach," Raibert finished, then muttered, "Speak of the devil."

CHAPTER FORTY-THREE

∽∽∽

Allied Attack Force
non-congruent

"FIVE MINUTES TO DYNASTY OUTER WALL," SAID the *Wegbereiter*'s nonsentient attendant.

"Thank you, Günther," Klaus-Wilhelm replied with absent courtesy.

Raibert placed his virtual hands on the virtual edge of the virtual command table. The flagship's organic crew members were sealed into compensation bunks on the *Wegbereiter*'s bridge to protect them from the rigors of combat acceleration, and each of their abstract representations huddled around the command table with him. His own synthoid didn't require the protection from gee forces that an organic human needed, but it was sealed in its own compensation bunk anyway.

I may not gray out or toss my cookies, he thought to himself, *but that doesn't mean it's not really hard to concentrate when gee forces are throwing you around, and I'll bet anything we'll be seeing a lot of that today. Not to mention the way this ship is bucking like a bull right now!*

"C-bomb status," Klaus-Wilhelm said.

"Still safely secured. Strain on the impeller is..." Andover-Chen opened a drive status display. "Within acceptable limits."

"Glad we're not on the real bridge, though," Benjamin said, as if he'd just read Raibert's mind. "Are any other systems being affected by all this convulsing?"

"No, Agent," Günther replied. "All my systems, except for the impeller, are operating at peak efficiency."

Ninety-four icons moved across the map, one for each time machine in the fleet, and nine of them contained exaggerated graphics of the c-bombs. All five of SysGov's heavy TTVs and four *Hammerhead* chronoports carried the weapons because their larger impellers were better able to compensate for the drag.

Four more icons pulsed with dashed outlines, representing the last known locations of scout *Valkyries* that had fled as soon as they spotted the massive incoming force.

Raibert found his eyes gravitating to the *Hildr*, holding position near the back of the fleet.

You'd better keep your word and not do anything stupid, he thought.

An alert flashed next to Andover-Chen.

"Signal from *Hammerhead-Four*, sir. They're at risk of falling behind and are requesting permission to slow to forty-five kilofactors."

"Günther, telegraph the fleet," Klaus-Wilhelm said. "All ships will drop to forty-five. We'll hold formation with *Hammerhead-Four*."

"Orders dispatched."

"What's the repair estimate?"

"They expect to have a workaround in place in a few minutes," Andover-Chen said.

"Very good."

The different parts of the fleet slowed down at different times, inadvertently spreading the formation out before closing back in around *Hammerhead-Four*. Raibert grimaced at the lack of coordination. It wasn't the most elegant maneuver in military history, but it got the job done.

Kleio was one of the few TTVs to hold formation perfectly, and Raibert found his mind drifting to thoughts of Philo. He was once again charging into danger without his AC by his side, and the void on the far side of their mental link ached in his mind.

Nothing I can do about it now but survive, he thought grimly.

"Ten seconds to Dynasty outer wall," Andover-Chen said.

He sucked in a virtual breath and waited.

"Three . . . two . . . one . . . phase-in."

Thirty-one light TTVs, five heavy TTVs, forty-eight light chronoports, six heavy chronoports, three mobile suppressors, and one dual-drive transport phased into the Dynasty's True Present. The fleet shook out into battle formation, the earth a grand cerulean crescent beneath them, as realspace data populated their scopes.

A massive downturned spike appeared far ahead of the fleet.

"*Tesseract* is still in Earth orbit," Benjamin said. "Right where we expected to find it."

"Numerous impeller contacts in the near present," Andover-Chen said. "They're clustered around *Tesseract*, too close to parse out individual ships."

"Give me your best guess on the enemy's force strength," Klaus-Wilhelm said.

"Over two hundred *Valkyries*, I'd say, and there could be more waiting with their impellers powered down."

"Move the fleet negative one year from the True Present," Klaus-Wilhelm ordered, "then hold position."

The fleet phased out then accelerated hard into the past. Raibert watched the Dynasty's Earth spin backward through night and day cycles. Even though the Dynasty had possessed time machines a year ago, the fleet would remain non-congruent. As Klaus-Wilhelm and Andover-Chen had discussed earlier, they were maneuvering through the past, but they wouldn't *interact* with it. In that sense, the past was more a place than a time. An afterimage the fleet would occupy.

"Approaching negative one year," Günther stated.

Warnings flashed, and a flurry of icons separated from the *Tesseract*.

"Here come the phase-missiles!" Raibert called out. "Based on the signal strength, there're over *seventy* inbound. Damn, Lucius has been busy."

"They're heading straight for us," Andover-Chen noted. "Positive fifty-one weeks from the fleet and closing."

"We'll see about that." Klaus-Wilhelm's voice was tense but confident. "Telegraph *Portcullis-Prime*. They're on."

❖　　❖　　❖

Jonas Shigeki watched the shoal of nuclear-tipped missiles streak across time. He'd known what to expect from recordings of the previous attacks, but still boggled his mind that someone would fire *nukes* without at least *trying* to talk things through.

"All right, people," he said to *Portcullis-Prime*'s bridge crew. "We seem to be receiving a rather cold reception. Time to show these morons who they're dealing with."

"Yes, *sir!*" Captain Park Sung-Wook said. "Antenna,

bring the suppression field up to maximum power and project it ahead of the fleet. Telegraph, signal *Portcullis-Two* and *-Three* to match our yield and profile."

"Acknowledged. Spinning the antenna up and diverting reactor power. Antenna at twenty cycles per second and climbing. Sixty cycles. Field is beginning to form. Antenna stable at one hundred twenty cycles per second. Raising yield to maximum."

"Sir, *Portcullis-Two* and *-Three* have acknowledged your orders and are matching us."

A flattened bubble expanded positive one month ahead of the fleet on the tactical map, representing the heart of the suppression field.

The mobile suppressors weren't designed to stop *all* time travel around them, partially because they were time machines themselves, but also because it was a bad idea to hamstring one's own force. Hence, the goal of the directional antenna was to impair the enemy while allowing friendly forces to maneuver freely elsewhere.

Or as freely as possible.

The suppression field's total area of effect was greater than the graphic, since the field didn't stop magically at some arbitrary border in space, but rather weakened over distance. The suppressing effect could be detected all the way to the *Tesseract* in the True Present, but only weakly. That meant every SysGov and Admin ship fell under the fringe of its influence no matter which way the antenna pointed, but the impact on them would be minimal, and their larger impellers could punch through a little unfocused interference.

A second bubble formed within the first, and it too ballooned outward, representing a stronger level of suppression. A third bubble formed, and a fourth, and a fifth, all of them expanding, each new one brighter than the last.

The graphic settled into a wide nebula of concentric zones with the phase-missiles heading straight for the center.

"Maximum yield reached, Director," Sung-Wook reported.

"Very good." Jonas adjusted the straps at his shoulders and waited for the flurry of missiles to enter the suppression field. He might not have agreed with his father that the Admin had some sort of debt to pay, but the reality of the Dynasty battle station made all other concerns secondary. This monstrosity *had* to be stopped, and he and the other under-directors had all supported the call to arms, if each for their own reasons.

If nothing else, it's a hell of a lot better to make sure that lunatic Gwon dies right here, with the rest of the universe he's murdered, before he can come calling on us, Jonas thought grimly. *And a hell of a lot smarter to take him on while SysGov's still around to pull its weight!*

"Now we'll see if this crazy idea works," Sung-Wook said over a closed-circuit chat.

"It'll work. The tech's been proven time and time again."

"True . . ." Sung-Wook shook his head. "How the hell did you rope me into this?"

Jonas glanced his way.

"As I recall, you always wanted a ship of your own."

"Maybe. But not one charging into the jaws of death."

"Oh, come now. You were bored out of your skull as a suppression tower superintendent. You always said you wanted something more . . . substantial, didn't you? Well, with seventy-odd nuclear missiles heading our way, I say that problem's been solved."

Sung-Wook snorted out a laugh.

"Thanks."

"Hey, what are friends for?" Jonas replied with a quirky smile.

"Enemy missiles have entered the outer limits of the field," the temporal navigator called out. "Distance is negative six weeks and closing. Negative five. Negative . . ."

She trailed off, and Jonas let a cruel smile slip out.

"Enemy missiles slowing. Now at fifty kilofactors. Thirty. Ten. Sir, missile phase-outs confirmed at negative three weeks. Their impellers appear to be nonfunctional."

"Got you," Jonas breathed.

❖   ❖   ❖

"Shift Hammerhead Squadron into phase with those missiles and take them out at range," Csaba Shigeki ordered from *Hammerhead-Prime*. "Let's not risk them reactivating."

"Telegraph, signal the squadron," Okunnu ordered. "Shift us to positive three weeks from the fleet. Weapons, standby on lasers."

Six heavy chronoports left the fleet formation and sped into the future at ninety-five kilofactors, then slowed on approach to the lamed missiles as they entered the suppression field. The two groups phase-locked, and the wide spread of missiles materialized a few hundred kilometers ahead of the Admin ships.

"Targets sighted," the weapons operator reported. "They're not even trying to hide."

"Fire!" Okunnu barked.

Twin atomic lasers blazed out of *Hammerhead-Prime*'s bow wings, and then the rest of the squadron opened fire, vaporizing the missiles in droves.

"Sir, this is like shooting fish in a barrel. I don't think they have any conventional defenses or countermeasures at all."

"I'm not complaining," Okunnu said. The last missile winked off their scopes. "Targets down, sir."

"Bring us back into phase with the fleet, Captain," Shigeki said.

Okunnu called out orders as Shigeki leaned over to the seat next to him.

"That was almost too easy," he whispered to Hinnerkopf. "And 'too easy' makes me nervous. Any thoughts?"

"Sir, I'm not surprised the missiles have such poor realspace stealth. Their impellers *are* their defense. We just happen to be able to switch it off. But an enemy that can create miniaturized time machines should be able to see our suppression field. *And* its limits. If so, they'll try to circumvent it."

"Noted. Thank you."

"Now in formation with the fleet, sir. Position is negative one year from True Present."

"New launch detected from *Tesseract*. Phase-missiles inbound. Count looks the same as last time."

"Phase-lock with *Portcullis-Prime*," Shigeki said. "Get me a direct link."

"Patching you in, sir."

"*Portcullis-Prime* here," Jonas said. "Go ahead."

"Be ready to adjust your field profiles. The missiles may not come straight at us."

"Understood. We'll watch out for it."

Shigeki closed the channel then checked the *Tesseract*'s position in the True Present. If the *Tesseract* had been a conventional station, he would have ordered his chronoports to phase-lock and cut loose with everything they had. But cannons and missiles required the target to be in phase, and all *Tesseract* needed to do was engage its impeller, and *poof!*, it was out of danger. And lasers, as SysGov had learned, were of limited effectiveness due to the high thermal limits of the station's exotic matter.

So they had to get close. Both temporally *and* physically. Dangerously—almost *suicidally*—close to ensure their ordnance hit the target, all while the *Tesseract* vomited missiles at them with impunity.

"Sir, the missiles are splitting up in realspace. Eight distinct groups incoming."

"They're testing the suppression field's limits," Hinnerkopf noted.

The missile clusters spread out around the fleet like the fingertips of two giant hands, and three separate field signatures aligned to block them.

"Missiles slowing to sixty kilofactors. Thirty. Twenty. Sir, missiles still converging on our position!"

"We're not going to stop them completely," Hinnerkopf observed. "The suppression fields are spread too wide."

"Telegraph, signal Barricade and Guardian squadrons to break off and intercept," Shigeki said. "But tell them to be *careful*."

"Yes, sir. Spooling your orders now."

Two dozen light chronoports scattered into the fleet's future as the missiles zeroed in, and Shigeki watched the enemy impeller signals die one by one. Missiles converged onto the fleet core, pulled there like iron filings to a magnet, thinning out as his chronoports gunned them down.

A lone phase-missile dashed in close, then phase-locked next to one of the light chronoports. The missile erupted into a nuclear pyre, and *Guardian-Ten's* icon vanished in the explosion.

"It seems our defenses aren't perfect," Shigeki noted harshly as the chronoport's indicator flashed red.

"Another wave of missiles inbound, sir."

"Connect me with *Wegbereiter*."

"Yes, sir." The telegraph operator worked his controls. "Phase-locked. Direct link established. You're on."

"Schröder, this is Shigeki."

"Go ahead, Director."

"There's no way we can deploy the c-bombs like this. The *Tesseract* is spitting out too much firepower."

"I know, but we also can't charge in yet. We need to soften that station up before we close with the bomb carriers. Proceed with stage two-alpha."

"Good to hear we're on the same page," Shigeki said. "Telegraph, cut Pathfinder and Defender loose. Time for us to go on the offensive."

"Yes, sir!"

❖   ❖   ❖

"All right, you heard the boss," Dahvid Kloss said aboard *Pathfinder-Prime*. "Captain, execute stage two-alpha."

"Pathfinder Squadron, Defender Squadron!" Durantt barked. "All chronoports, move out!"

Twenty-four light chronoports broke from the fleet and sped into the future at ninety-five kilofactors. Every chronoport in Pathfinder and Defender squadrons was a combat refit with thicker armor and bigger, more powerful thrusters.

Which is why we're charging in first, Kloss thought

as a wave of phase-missiles rocketed toward them through time. He *really* didn't want to be here, but the boss had called on everyone to pitch in, and he'd be damned if he'd let the man down now.

For a moment—*only* a moment—he wished the Admin could allow AIs to control their ships like SysGov did. He knew it would be a gross violation of the Restrictions, but such a concession would allow their chronoports to charge into battle without the fear of lost lives. Only lost hardware.

But even SysGov doesn't think that way, he acknowledged. The men, women, and AIs onboard their TTVs didn't *recognize* the distinction between a physical crewmember and an abstract one, beyond the obvious needs of the former's body. So, from their perspective, every TTV was manned. Just like the Admin chronoports.

And neither of us have developed time-traveling drones, he thought. *Even if we developed a miniaturized impeller like the Dynasty has, we're still stuck with the problem of how little bandwidth can be pumped through a telegraph.*

Suppression fields parted to allow the chronoports through, then reconverged behind them.

"We're clear of the suppression fields, sir," the temporal navigator called out. "*Tesseract* at positive ten months. Phase-missiles at positive seven months and closing *fast*. Less than two minutes absolute until we cross."

"Maintain course and speed," Durantt said.

The missiles raced in with enough firepower to incinerate his two squadrons a million times over.

And we're charging straight at them, Kloss thought,

his stomach tense with fear. *But as Hinnerkopf said, they have to hit us first, and therein lies the hard part for them. At our speed, they'll be lucky if they can phase-lock with us at all.*

"Missiles at positive one month!" the navigator called out, his voice cracking. "Fifteen seconds to contact!"

"Hold your course!" Durantt snapped.

Kloss squeezed his eyes shut, as if that would affect anything.

The chronoports raced forward, and dozens of missiles swarmed in. The missiles' scopes were half-blind at those speeds, and they phase-locked with any available target, detonating into glaring suns. Atomic fireballs erupted all around them—past, future, and present—and their chronoports charged headlong through the furnace. Its violence was starkly inconceivable, yet the lightspeed expansion from a nuclear detonation in space was only lethal for a brief instance, and the waves of hard radiation repeatedly missed the chronoports speeding into the future.

His two squadrons dashed through fire and time— and emerged on the far side, mostly unscathed.

"Status report," Kloss demanded, opening his eyes.

"All accounted for, sir! Minimal damage!"

"*Tesseract* at positive three months and closing, sir."

"Continue as planned," Kloss said.

"Navigators, maintain course for the station," Durantt ordered. "Weapons, prepare *our* nukes. Fire as soon as we're phase-locked with the station."

"Nukes armed and ready, sir."

Pathfinder-Prime, like all *Pioneer*-class chronoports, possessed modular weapons, and its current configuration included two outboard laser pods and four missile pods underneath the main hull. Each pod contained a four-by-four grid of sixteen missiles, and two of those were nuclear-tipped.

Per *pod*.

The enemy battle station loomed before them, the immense scale of its temporal signature crystal clear despite the chronoport's speed.

"Phase-lock in twenty seconds."

"Eight-missile volley programmed in, sir."

"*Valkyries* on the move, sir! They're leaving the True Present!"

"Ignore them!" Durantt barked. "We're hitting that station!"

"Phase-locked!"

The station's massive three-sided spike appeared in front of them.

"Nukes away!"

Eight missiles streaked out of each chronoport for a total of *one hundred ninety-two* as clusters of point defense lasers slashed across space. A few lucky hits bisected the Admin weapons and blew them apart, but these weren't like the Dynasty's phase-missiles. Their conical bodies were covered in photon-fooling variskin, and radar decoys sprinkled off them as they closed, choking space with possible targets. The variskin was less efficient and less durable than SysGov's meta-armor, but it was one hell of a lot better than bare hulls, and the quality and quantity of the Admin systems overwhelmed the *Tesseract's* close-in defenses.

Over a hundred missiles crashed into its gargantuan hull.

Nukes exploded in rapid succession and a blinding, radioactive storm obscured the station's surface.

Surface weapons vaporized. Armor melted. The station quaked as more missiles rained in—

—and then it phased into the past.

The hellish inferno burned on, pulsating with each new eruption.

"*Valkyries* converging on our location, and lots of them!"

Over two hundred signatures swarmed in around Kloss's twenty-four. Enemy ships phase-locked all around his squadrons, and Dynasty lasers stabbed into chronoport armor. *Pathfinder-Eleven's* port fusion thruster exploded, taking out a wing and part of the hull. It rolled away, lasers tracking it, scorching it, burning through the stricken vessel as it bled air and plasma.

"Break off! Break off!" Durantt ordered urgently. "Get us back to the fleet!"

Pathfinder-Prime phased out of the present, and both squadrons followed its lead, fleeing full speed into the past. *Valkyries* gave chase, pursing them back to negative one month, but his forces kept one step ahead of them.

Then *Defender-Nine* fell behind.

Laser damage to its impeller flared up, and it slipped out of phase. Over thirty *Valkyries* phase-locked with it and obliterated it with a focused burst of laser fire. The rest turned away and reformed around *Tesseract* in the True Present.

His squadrons were clear. For the moment.

"Good work, everyone. I do believe they felt that one!" Kloss said, even as his eyes stung at the sight of the lost ships on his status board.

And the memory of the faces he'd never see again.

CHAPTER FORTY-FOUR

~~~~~~~~~~~~

Allied Attack Force
non-congruent

"BOSS," RAIBERT SAID. "PATHFINDER AND DEFENDER squadrons are back in formation."

Klaus-Wilhelm nodded, his eyes fixed on the chronometric data Andover-Chen now puzzled over.

"*Tesseract* didn't fire a single phase-missile on their way back," Benjamin noted. "Did we take out its hyperforges?"

"Not all of them," Andover-Chen cautioned, looking up. "The station's chronometric signature *has* changed, indicating some lost functionality, but it's impossible for me to pick out individual forges."

"Then we've hurt them," Klaus-Wilhelm said.

"Yes, sir. We have."

"Sir, this is the opening we've been waiting for," Benjamin said.

"I'm inclined to agree," Klaus-Wilhelm acknowledged, considering the disposition of both forces.

"Should the fleet advance?" Raibert asked.

"Yes, but I'm not about to risk an all-out attack. We'll hold most of our bomb carriers in reserve. Günther, telegraph the fleet. All forces will advance to negative six months from target, then hold position. And get *Hammerhead-Prime* on a direct line."

"Orders dispatched. Director Shigeki is on for you."

"Director. Time to press the speed advantage of your chronoports. Proceed to stage three-delta."

"I was wondering when you'd say that," Shigeki replied, a touch of wry humor in his tone.

"I know we're expecting a lot of your forces, and I'm afraid I'm going to ask even more before this is done. I wish we didn't have to, but—"

"Understood, Commissioner," Shigeki interrupted. "And don't worry. We'll hold up our end. When the DTI commits to a task, we get it done. Executing three-delta now."

❖   ❖   ❖

"Here we go again," Kloss breathed as twenty-two light chronoports rushed into the future ahead of *Hammerhead-Four*, *-Five*, and *-Six*, and their chronoton-bomb payloads.

"*Tesseract* at positive five months and closing, sir. Station has returned to the True Present."

Their scopes lit up with a flurry of icons.

"Multiple new contacts! Phase-missiles incoming, sir!"

"Knew it was too good to be true," Kloss noted dryly, and checked the inbound signal strength. "Over fifty!"

"Not as wounded as we thought," Durantt observed.

"Just means we'll have to hit them *harder* this time."

Kloss settled into his seat and watched as the range between their forces dropped away. The twenty-five chronoports reached negative four months when warnings flashed on his display.

"Sir, *Hammerhead-Four* is losing speed! They've dropped out of formation!"

"Damn it!" Kloss cursed under his breath. "Not now!"

"*Hammerhead-Four* falling to sixty kilofactors. Sir, their speed is still dropping!"

"Should we slow down as well?" Durantt asked.

"We can't," Kloss stressed. "Or those missiles will tear *all* of us apart. We need to press on."

"Telegraph *Hammerhead-Four*!" Durantt snapped. "They're to break off immediately and head back to the suppressors!"

"Yes, sir! Spooled and sending!"

The order didn't reach its recipient instantly, and missiles closed in around the chronoport squadrons before *Hammerhead-Four* reversed course. Some of the missiles pounced on the squadrons, erupting into glaring suns they barely saw as they sped into the future, and others dashed past them, hunting *Hammerhead-Four*.

Kloss clenched his teeth as nuclear fury spawned all around him. A lucky missile phased in right next to *Defender-Three* and vaporized the chronoport. Another blasted his own vessel with a brief spike of radiation, stripping half the armor off their hull. Yellow damage indicators glared across his virtual sight.

Hammerhead-Four raced back into the past, but the phase-missiles gained on it, then finally overtook the chronoport outside the suppression field. *This* time, the missiles phase-locked with a target slower than they were, and over twenty nuclear detonations piled one atop the other to annihilate the chronoport.

Kloss glanced across his displays, checking for the other *Hammerheads*.

Good, he thought. *Both of them made it through*.

"Sir, Thruster Two is acting up," the realspace navigator said.

"Do what you can to stabilize it," Durantt said. "Range to target?"

"*Tesseract* at positive eleven weeks. Seventy seconds to phase-lock."

"Sir, *Valkyries* breaking away from *Tesseract*."

"How many?"

"*All* of them, sir."

A massive blob of overlapping impeller signatures left the True Present and contracted around the strike force.

"Telegraph, signal to all chronoports," Durantt ordered. "All forces are free to engage the enemy, but we *will* maintain course for the *Tesseract*! Weapons, ready lasers only!"

The two forces converged, and *Valkyries* phased in and out around them, blipping into existence, firing their energy weapons, then blipping out as the chronoports' superior speed outpaced them. Lasers stabbed deep into chronoport armor, and damage indicators flashed, but the chronoports were far from defenseless and they charged straight through their foes.

Return fire blasted outward from lasers and heavy caliber cannons. High-powered proton beams from *Hammerhead-Five* and *-Six* pierced frail *Valkyrie* armor, and Dynasty craft exploded into twinkling streams of phasing matter.

A sleek, wedge-shaped time machine phased in directly in front of *Pathfinder-Prime*, and the chronoport's twin lasers punched into the *Valkyrie*'s bow before it could fire. Armor melted and the beams burned on through the crew compartment before the craft phased away. Two more *Valkyries* flickered in, lasers boring into the chronoport's belly. The vessel shook, laser pods spun about, trying to track its tormentors, but the *Valkyries* vanished an instant later.

"Thruster Two is down! Sir, I don't have enough power for both lasers!"

"Then shut one down! We're pushing through!"

A storm of light and death raged around them, *Valkyries* and chronoports dying in abrupt spasms of violence. Multiple beams pounded *Hammerhead-Six*'s armor and slashed across its impeller. Its turrets spat back in continuous fire, snapping from target to target, gunning down *Valkyrie* after *Valkyrie*, but the damage accumulated. Its impeller signature became unstable, and the c-bomb's drag won out.

The heavy chronoport fell out of formation, and *Valkyries* swarmed it. *Hammerhead-Six* fought on, cannons firing in all directions, and three more *Valkyries* fell before lasers cracked its shell open and breached its main reactor.

"*Hammerhead-Six* down!"

"*Tesseract* directly ahead! Phase-lock imminent!"

"Weapons, I want a sixteen-missile volley as soon as we're locked!" Durantt ordered. "Telegraph, signal the other chronoports to do the same! We may be down to one bomb, but we're going to give that station more targets than it can handle!"

Hammerhead-Five phased into the True Present within a protective envelope of seventeen light chronoports, and missiles spasmed from their launchers, slicing in on the *Tesseract* in a sleet of metal. The c-bomb detached from *Hammerhead-Five*'s underbelly, and its graviton thrusters lit, driving it forward with suicidal intent.

An ugly gash ran down the length of the station, and one of the hyperforges lay exposed to space at the base of a deep crater. Point defense lasers flickered out, blasting at random targets for several seconds, but then something changed. Some aspect of the c-bomb drew the Dynasty's collective eye, and *all* the point defense lasers focused on it.

The bomb's compacted exotic matter shell absorbed hit after hit. Beams seared away its thrusters, but the bomb hurtled onward, freefalling toward the station. *Valkyries* dove after it, ignoring the chronoports, and lasers blazed into it from all directions.

The bomb's outer shell glowed white hot, cracked, then breached. A concentrated storm of chronotons smashed the closest *Valkyries* away like a child's toys, and the wave front spread into a sphere of phasing unreality. The edge slammed into *Pathfinder-Prime*, and the impact whipped Kloss's head back so hard he saw stars while alarms blared in his virtual hearing.

The wave front crashed into *Tesseract*, and the edges of the station wavered, became indistinct. But over five hundred *million* cubic meters of exotic matter had gone into the station's construction, and its incredible volume drank up the force of the wave like a sponge.

The station's edges firmed up, and the vestiges of the chronoton wave vanished into the depths of space.

❖   ❖   ❖

"Hurry!" Lucius shouted, his abstract form unfazed by the attack. "You need to get back on your feet!"

"Damn..." Vlastos picked himself up off the floor of *Tesseract*'s control center. Ten other people struggled back to their posts, and he grabbed the command table's edge, hauled himself onto it, and reached up to rub the back of his skull. "How'd that hit get through the shock absorbers?"

"Because it wasn't a physical blast." Lucius pointed to a chronometric chart over the table. "They just hit us with some sort of chronometric weapon!"

Do I need to explain everything *to you people?* he thought.

"Right. Of course." Vlastos stood up and steadied himself with a hand on the table. "How careless of me to miss that."

"Don't you dare joke about this," Lucius seethed, anger and frustration testing the boundaries of his control.

"Elder, there's no way I'd—" He paused to wince. "Lucius, between the size of their force, those fields that interfere with our impellers, and now *this*, I assure you the situation has my full attention." He turned to the control center staff. "Can we get a medical team up here?"

"They've already been alerted, sir, but they're responding to calls throughout the station."

"Make sure we're at the top of their list." Vlastos planted both hands on the table edge. "Now. Where's that damn strike force?"

"Heading into the past, sir, probably to regroup behind their interference fields. Distance is negative two months from True Present and climbing."

"And the status of the hyperforges?" Vlastos asked.

"Eleven are off-line, and we've spotted stress fractures in another three. They won't last long at this replication rate."

"And Hyperforge Twenty-Eight?" Lucius demanded. "Has it been damaged?"

"No, Elder. Not that we can tell."

"Then why isn't it operational yet?"

How can these idiots be so incompetent?

"Engineering thinks they found the problem. They're working on it."

They said that three blasted hours ago!

He started to snarl that out loud, then paused to bring his emotions under command.

"What's taking them so long?" he asked instead, in a carefully controlled tone.

"I . . . I don't know."

"Then I *suggest* you find out."

"Yes, Elder. I'll get an answer."

"What about that chronometric weapon?" Lucius asked.

"We're still analyzing the data. Not sure what it is, but it leaves a *very* distinct signature as it moves through time."

"Can you determine if the enemy fleet has any more?"

"Yes, sir. Displaying for you now."

Six impeller signatures in the enemy fleet blinked brighter than the rest.

"*Six* of those things," Vlastos breathed.

"And *Tesseract* was the target," Lucius stressed. "Whatever they are, you can't let them reach the station."

"Right. Right." Vlastos nodded, then winced again and put a hand to his head.

His fingers came away smeared with blood. He looked down at them for a moment, then drew a deep, nostril-flaring breath.

"Telegraph, signal squadrons Alpha through Omicron," he said. "They're to advance on the enemy immediately. We'll hold Phi and Rho in reserve. Prioritize the TTVs carrying those weapons and take them down."

❖　　❖　　❖

"Damn, that must be nearly all of them," Elzbietá said as the massive wave of *Valkyries* rushed into the past and a smear of estimated physical positions appeared in her panoramic view.

"Not quite," Philo clarified. "Looks like they held a few squadrons in reserve. Still, we've got somewhere around a hundred sixty signatures incoming. They'll hit the suppression field shortly."

"It's not going to stop them, is it?"

"No, but it'll slow them down as they fly in."

"Telegraph from *Wegbereiter*," Kleio said. "It reads: 'All light TTVs along with Barricade and Guardian squadrons are to advance and engage the enemy within the suppression field. Halt the enemy's advance on the bomb carriers. Pathfinder and Defender will maintain close escort.'"

"Time to go to work!" Elzbietá shoved the omni-throttle forward, and the *Kleio* raced into battle alongside fifty-three other time machines. No—fifty-*four*—she noted as the *Hildr* formed up on the *Kleio*'s flank.

Philo grabbed the tab atop his helmet and brought his visor down.

"The suppression field's going to slow us," he warned.

"Them, too. Just means we have more time to shoot each other."

The *Valkyries'* movements became sluggish as they hit the suppression field, and the *Kleio* sped in from the other side. The impeller groaned with added effort, and warnings lit up on her console. Feedback manifested in her controls, preventing her from pushing it all the way forward, and she switched to a finer control setting.

"Here we go!" She checked the estimated positions around her. "That one!" She brought the *Kleio* up and over the signal.

A *Valkyrie* phased in below and began to tilt up toward them.

Philo fired the main gun, and the shot blew a hole through his target's center. A second *Valkyrie* phased in behind and above them, and Elzbietá pushed the thrusters hard, climbing as Philo adjusted the Gatling pods.

A laser splashed against their meta-armor, but their rapid-fire cannon blazed, chewing through the *Valkyrie*'s hull. One of the Dynasty time ship's impellers broke off, and its reactor exploded. Debris pattered off the *Kleio*'s hull as Elzbietá pushed through, picked another signal, and dove after it.

"They're trying to rush past us," Philo noted. "We're not the target."

"Their mistake!"

She phase-locked with her chosen victim, and the mass driver boomed, shattering its port impeller. The *Valkyrie* spiraled out of control, and *Kleio* shot past it, guns thundering.

"Actually, never mind!" Philo squeaked. "I think they don't like us now!"

"I see them!"

Three *Valkyries* phase-locked around *Kleio* and opened fire. Lasers focused in, only to splinter off the hull, but warnings blinked across the meta-armor as it heated.

Then the *Hildr* snapped into existence and fired its

own mass driver. The cannon round smashed through an enemy cockpit, and the vessel flipped end over end before dropping out of phase.

Elzbietá swooped down at a second *Valkyrie*—the *Hildr* matched her course, accelerating alongside her with ease—and together their Gatling guns ripped across its body, shredding armor, blasting chunks of the hull free, and finally shattering both impellers.

The third *Valkyrie*'s laser splashed into the *Kleio*'s flank. Elzbietá spun the ship around, reversing thrust, but the *Hildr* accelerated harder, closing the distance. The Dynasty *Valkyrie*'s laser fired again and burned a glowing divot into the *Kleio*'s bow as the *Hildr* rushed past, hammering the *Valkyrie* with explosive rounds.

Elzbietá caught up, and Philo added their own fire to the mix. The *Valkyrie* fought to pull away, but Philo had it locked in his sights. *Hildr* closed relentlessly, and together their combined streams of fire blasted the *Valkyrie* to pieces.

"Not bad, *Hildr*," Elzbietá called out on a direct link. "Thanks for the assist."

"Any time," Teodorà replied.

"A group of *Valkyries* have broken through," Philo warned. "They're heading for *Wegbereiter*."

"Not if I can help it. *Hildr*, you with us?"

"Lead the way, *Kleio*."

The two time machines left the suppression field and hurried into the past. They phase-locked with the *Wegbereiter*, and a chaotic battle materialized before them. Chronoports and *Valkyries* dueled around the heavy TTV as it raked space with its three bow-mounted lasers. A pair of craters glowed on *Wegbereiter*'s hull where the meta-armor had failed. Cannon fire and lasers streaked across space in a deadly crisscross weave, and Elzbietá charged straight into its heart.

A pair of *Valkyries* swooped in behind the *Wegbereiter*, lasers blazing, and Elzbietá swung in behind *them*. She lined up the mass driver, and Philo cut loose. The *Valkyrie* banked at the last moment, and the round exploded next to it, showering it with a directional cone of metal shards.

The *Hildr* fired next, and its shot split their target in two. They closed, the TTV and rogue *Valkyrie* side by side, then crossed on either side of the second Dynasty *Valkyrie* and dosed it with cannon fire.

More *Valkyries* phase-locked with the battle, and more chronoports came in behind them. The mad swirl of death around the command ship grew more insane by the second, but it was an insanity Elzbietá and *Kleio* had faced before above the Elbe River. She didn't stop, barely *thought*, only selected her next target and pushed the omni-throttle down. She turned the ship as they dove. One of *Wegbereiter*'s lasers lit up the *Valkyrie*, vaporized a ragged gash in its armor, and *Kleio* shot past, cannon fire ripping through its exposed hull.

The *Valkyrie* spun away, streaming molten, twisted metal, then burst into a shimmering, surreal fireball.

An explosion rocked the *Wegbereiter*. Hot armor showered outward, and Elzbietá hunted for the attacker.

"There!" Philo tagged a boxy *Valkyrie* closing in, twin lasers blazing out of its open cargo hold. She jammed the throttle forward, and *Kleio* surged up to meet it while Philo realigned the gun pods, contracting them around the bow.

The cannons spewed hundreds of rounds per second into the *Valkyrie*'s exposed gut, and a storm of explosions eviscerated the time machine before one of the *Wegbereiter*'s lasers clove it in two. Severed halves spun away, and Elzbietá reefed her TTV back around.

Several more chronoports and TTVs phased in, taking up tight escort positions around *Wegbereiter*, and the remaining *Valkyries* phased away, seeking other targets.

"Urgent telegraph from TTV *Mel Fisher*," Kleio reported. "Assistance required."

"On it!"

Elzbietá thumbed her impeller control and shifted toward the *Mel Fisher*'s phase state. *Barricade-Seven*, *Defender-Nine*, and the *Hildr* formed up on her wing, and together they dashed to assist the beleaguered carrier. They'd almost reached it when the *Kleio*'s array lit up like the sun.

"Look out!" Philo shouted.

Elzbietá and the *Hildr* reversed their impellers, but the two Admin chronoports failed to change course, and the chronoton wave from the *Mel Fisher*'s ruptured c-bomb smashed over them like the club of a furious giant, shattering their impellers as the *Kleio* and *Hildr* raced away from the blast.

The wave front closed on them, dissipating with temporal distance but still deadly. Then it reached them, swept across them, and the *Kleio* heaved madly, shooting the rapids of destruction. Elzbietá fought to maintain course; audible alarms shrilled in her virtual hearing, and warning lights flashed as the impeller howled on the brink of failure. But it held together. Somehow, it held together, and she brought the TTV back under control.

"Whew! Damn, that was close," she breathed—

—moments before a *second* c-bomb detonated within the fleet.

CHAPTER FORTY-FIVE

〜〜〜

Hyper-Fortress *Tesseract*
Dynasty, 2980 CE

LUCIUS WATCHED THE *VALKYRIE* ATTACK FORCE dissolve against the smaller enemy fleet, and his face twisted further into a snarl with each loss. How were they *doing* this? The enemy didn't simply blunt their assault, they *broke* the attacking *Valkyries* and forced the bleeding remnants into a disorderly retreat, fleeing for their lives all the way back to the *Tesseract*.

"You didn't get all of them," he seethed, barely hiding his contempt for the quaesitors anymore.

"But we detected two premature detonations," Vlastos stressed.

"Two," Lucius fumed. "Out of *six*."

"Elder, we're doing the best we can with what amounts to converted transports. The enemy clearly has purpose-built combat vessels, and under those conditions, our forces have performed admirably."

"'Admirably'?" Lucius mocked. "We have fewer than forty *Valkyries* left!"

"I know," Vlastos said, his voice heavy as he turned to the map. And to the long tally of losses. "But we've kept the *Tesseract* safe. *That's* the most important thing. The station is mostly unscathed, and we've whittled the enemy fleet down to roughly half its original strength."

You're running out faster than they are, Simon! Lucius's thoughts snarled. *Can't your tiny meat brain see that?*

"They've beaten your *Valkyries* back," he said aloud carefully. "Next, they'll come for us." He turned to the hyperforge monitoring stations. "Hyperforge status?"

"Nineteen forges online. We managed to reactivate six of the damaged units. Shutting down the impeller for emergency repairs paid off."

"Power the impeller back up and start firing again," Vlastos ordered.

"Yes, sir. Bringing the station impeller back online now. Field effect expanding into the hyperforges. Replication commencing."

"What about Hyperforge Twenty-Eight?" Lucius pressed. "Why is it *still* off-line? Are they making any progress?"

"Engineering reports they're unsure where the problem is with Twenty-Eight. The hyperforge isn't receiving enough power to initiate replication, but the reactors and power lines all check out."

Unbelievable!

"Do they have *any* clue what the problem is?"

"There are a few possibilities they're investigating."

"A few *possibilities*?"

"We're directing additional drones and swarms to Twenty-Eight from the adjacent forges. I'm sure they can—"

"ENOUGH!"

Lucius's voice bellowed across their shared virtual hearing. The control center fell silent, and every eye turned to his avatar. He glared at those in the room, skewering each of them with his eyes in turn.

It was his own fault for expecting more than mediocrity from these people. But that was a problem he now had the power to remedy.

"You're all completely useless," he told them coldly. "But that's all right."

"Wha—" Vlastos began.

Lucius vanished from the control center as his consciousness shifted to the heart of the station's immense infostructure. He found the restricted partition he'd placed there in the early days of *Tesseract's* construction and opened it. It was a tiny file in the greater scheme of the *Tesseract's* massive databases, barely larger than a single connectome, and he'd hidden it well, behind multiple layers of dummy entries and false pointers.

Now he drilled down through those protective layers and opened his hidden stash.

The partition contained one nonsentient attendant armed with codeburners—lethal abstract weaponry that consisted of powerful decryption software tied to a delete function—and a single version of a slightly modified connectome: *his.*

He activated the attendant and began copying it into the surrounding infostructure, and a horde of killer programs dispersed through the *Tesseract's* systems, hunting down and killing any ACs they found.

It didn't take long. A few seconds, really. Only a couple of dozen ACs served on the station, and the poor fools never saw the attack coming, never had time to respond or call for help. They were. And then they weren't.

The abstract realm within *Tesseract* was suddenly an empty, barren wasteland. An endless, echoing plain... with Lucius Gwon at its center, alone and unopposed.

The killer attendants scoured the infostructure for survivors. They found none, and the second phase of their operation kicked in. They deleted every interface between the physical and the abstract, just as he'd done back on the *Shadow*, and the *Tesseract's* crew found themselves cut off from the systems they'd once controlled.

Those people were still alive, still present on the station like rodents in the walls, but that problem would soon be rectified. Lucius had no intention of allowing such filth to sully his new body. Worse, cornered animals often embraced destructive measures to escape, and their panicked thrashing might cause him some harm.

Best to be sure about it.

Anything worth doing, Lucius mused to himself, *is worth doing right.*

The attendants activated the station's complement of security cubes. Hundreds of drones spread out through the station's vast, labyrinthine passages, killing anyone they found, and the attendants who'd activated them self-deleted, having reached the end of their instructions.

The slate was clean within minutes.

Lucius reached back into the partition and opened the modified version of his own mind. He copied it into the barren infostructure, then again, and again. Over and over, he deployed the duplicates, and each connectome possessed all of his cunning, all of his intellect. They were *him* . . . but without the executive functions of his original mind. They could *think*, but they couldn't *act* without his guiding will.

His lesser selves fanned out, assuming control over every part of the station, and then those minds linked back to the original.

Lucius felt his consciousness expand, his thoughts accelerate. He was a lonely connectome no more, but an amalgam of many. He ceased to be "Lucius Gwon" and became Lucius-Prime, the eye in a pyramid of a thousand copies.

His new consciousness reached out, filling the *Tesseract*'s systems with his will, flexing his technological "muscles." Reactors thrummed. Hyperforges energized. Drones and microbot swarms flowed through his body like an immune system, repairing damage and purging the last remnants of the physical crew.

He turned his attention to Hyperforge Twenty-Eight, focused half of his mind-copies on the system, and quickly identified the problem. The error wasn't with the power systems but the power system *software*! Parts of its code had come from the standard hyperforge controllers, and in a few key instances, the difference in scale had become fatal.

He devoted three hundred minds to the problem, rewrote the control software in less than a minute, then rebooted it.

Unbridled power surged through Hyperforge Twenty-Eight, and its chronometric field expanded to operational strength.

"So simple," Lucius mused. "I should have done this *ages* ago!"

He reviewed the *Valkyries* at his disposal, and one name jumped out at him.

"Naturally."

The *Sigrun* was back in the True Present, having survived the assault on the enemy fleet with four more kills to its credit. *Including* one of the weapon carriers.

"Oh, yes." He chuckled. "You're the one, my dear."

He opened a direct channel with the *Sigrun*.

"Hello, Hala."

"Chairman?" she asked urgently, her voice haggard from the stress of battle. "What's going on? We've lost contact with the station."

"Don't worry about that now. A momentary problem; it's all sorted out. But that's not why I've contacted you. I have a *very* special task for you."

"Of course, sir. Name it."

"Come dock inside Hyperforge Twenty-Eight. I have a plan to turn the tide of this battle completely."

"Twenty-Eight? But that's . . ."

"Yes. You know what it is. Is that a problem?"

"It's just . . ."

"Yes?"

A long, slow, meat-induced delay followed, and Lucius waited patiently for her response.

"Carrying out your orders, sir," she said at last.

"Wonderful. I knew I could count on you."

The *Sigrun* climbed up to the top of the station, flew across its triangular crown, then descended into Hyperforge Twenty-Eight's open maw. The entrance sealed shut, the replication matrix powered up—

—and Lucius laughed with the chorus of a thousand voices.

✧　　✧　　✧

"Here come the phase-missiles again," Raibert growled as he skimmed over the fleet's status. Their original force had been reduced to twenty-one light TTVs, three heavy TTVs, twenty-five light chronoports, four heavy chronoports, three mobile suppressors, and one *Valkyrie*. Only fifty-seven time machines out of the original ninety-four.

And a lot of what's left is hurting, he noted.

"Boss, we can't take much more of this," he warned.

Klaus-Wilhelm didn't respond immediately, only stared at the scope, eyes focused as the suppression fields slowed yet another wave of missiles. The fleet's lighter craft stood like a wall between them and the bomb carriers. These were the survivors, their skills bought with blood, their tactics honed in the crucible of battle. Missiles fell in droves, far from their heavier craft and the suppressors, and only *Defender-Six* suffered any damage when radiation fried one of its weapon pods.

"I know we can't, but neither can the enemy," Benjamin countered. "As brutal as our losses have been, *we* have the superior numbers now. Sir"—he turned to the commissioner—"the station's mobile defenses have been all but broken. *Tesseract* is exposed, and we have four c-bombs left."

"Exactly," Raibert pressed. "We have *only* four. Once they're gone, that's it. Say goodbye to SysGov, because we've lost our only means to save it. We can't risk losing them all."

"We can't give the Dynasty the chance to recover," Benjamin argued. "Not with their replication industry. If we pull back now, they'll heal faster than us, and the next battle will be an even worse bloodbath."

"If we screw this one up, we doom everyone." Raibert backed off and crossed his arms. "Boss?"

"Unfortunately, you're both right." Klaus-Wilhelm looked up from the scope. "We're hurt, no question. But so is the enemy. Andover-Chen, what effect did those two c-bombs have?"

"Not much. We need to hit the station directly, and fast. All these exploding time machines and replicated weapons are torturing the Dynasty's outer wall."

"Then we'll press on, but not without some insurance. Get me a direct line to *Hammerhead-Prime*."

"You're on, Commissioner."

"Director, the fleet will advance on the station momentarily using the suppression fields for cover."

"Understood," Shigeki said. "Just give the word."

"We're going to leave one c-bomb behind, preferably with something fast and maneuverable. Can one of your light chronoports take it?"

"Unfortunately not. Our malmetal hulls aren't as adaptable as yours, so we only have the clamps we constructed ahead of time. *Hammerhead-Three* is the only bomb carrier I have left."

"Then my forces will handle it. Günther, add *Kleio* to the direct line."

"Established, sir. *Hildr* is also on the line via an active link with *Kleio*."

"Go ahead, *Wegbereiter*," Elzbietá said.

"Pick up *Howard Carter*'s c-bomb and hold position at negative six months."

"Roger that."

The *Kleio*'s icon moved underneath the heavy TTV, and the c-bomb icon shifted from one craft to the other.

"Are we hanging back alone or with some friends?"

Philo asked. "That last wave targeted our bomb carriers, so they may come after us."

"I can help there," Teodorà said. "I'll keep them safe."

The *Hildr* slid in alongside the *Kleio*, and Raibert glanced at the *Valkyrie's* status. The *Hildr* was undamaged . . . and had almost as many kills as the *Kleio*.

Not bad, he thought, his lip curling in a half smile.

"I'll peel off four chronoports from Pathfinder Squadron, as well," Shigeki said. "Five escorts should be enough protection against anything that sidesteps our main force."

"Good," Klaus-Wilhelm said. "Günther, signal the fleet. All other craft will immediately advance on *Tesseract* at forty kilofactors. We're going to get in as close as we can and deploy all three c-bombs right on top of the station."

"Orders dispatched."

Raibert grimaced, wondering in silence why Klaus-Wilhelm didn't order the fleet to advance at seventy kilofactors. Surely the less time they spent getting pounded by phase-missiles the better, right?

The fleet accelerated into the future, suppression fields spread wide ahead of it while six vessels hung back with one last c-bomb. Another wave of missiles rocketed in, all of them focused on the fleet, and their lighter units charged forward to shield the bomb carriers. Scores of missiles closed in, and the TTVs and chronoports shot them down one by one—

—*within* the suppression field.

Raibert eyes widened as comprehension dawned. *Of course!* he thought. *The suppression fields slow our own vessels down! If we were at top speed, they wouldn't be able to enter the fields. And if that were the case, then those missiles would have to be intercepted closer to the bomb carriers.* Dangerously *close.*

My God. Raibert frowned, brow furrowed in consternation. *If I'd been in charge, I would have ordered the fleet in at full speed. I could have gotten us all killed!*

He shook his head, amazed by how quickly the former twentieth-century general had adapted to this unprecedented, temporal battlefield.

More explosions wracked space and time, and radiation seared two more vessels. Both fell back with critical damage, but the bomb carriers continued their advance under a protective shield of chronometric energy.

Another wave of missiles sprinted from the *Tesseract*'s launchers, and Klaus-Wilhelm nodded slowly as time machines shifted position to intercept them. Raibert saw it too, perceiving a glimpse of the many calculations playing out in the commissioner's mind. Phase-missiles battered the fleet's defenders once more, and nuclear fire obliterated *Guardian-Prime*...

But it won't be enough, Raibert thought, elation welling up within him. *That station can't stop us from reaching it. Not anymore. And when we do, we're going to ram all three c-bombs straight into its gut!*

❖   ❖   ❖

"So, they're using pseudo-impellers as antennas," Lucius noted, his prime consciousness reviewing the analysis several hundred copies had compiled moments ago. "Interesting, though not surprising. After all, *every* impeller projects a chronometric field. It only makes sense that a similar device would be used to generate an *interfering* field. It's just a question of scale and purpose. The power requirements for those antennas must be immense, though. Even by time machine standards."

The enemy fleet swept ever closer behind their protective field envelope, now less than negative three months from the True Present. He knew which three vessels were generating those fields. Eliminate them, and the rest would fall. But how to accomplish that?

"An assault with the remaining *Valkyries*, perhaps?" His copies analyzed the scenarios. "Hmm. As I thought. They'll probably die for minimal gain. Not that they've done me much good either way, but I suppose I shouldn't be wasteful. Best to hold them back in a tighter defense where they *might* prove useful, especially after I start replicating the *Sigrun*.

"So then. How to counter their defenses?"

He had to break through to those weapon carriers. A hundred of his mind-copies continued to analyze the data from earlier detonations, and none of their whispered results comforted him. Whatever those things were, he couldn't let them hit.

The fleet reached negative two months, and the outer vestiges of the interference fields touched his body. Interference field lines bowed, and he sensed the impact upon his impeller—miniscule but detectable.

"Oh? What's this?" Every copy within his vast multi-mind pored over the minor change to his impeller. "Why, yes. Naturally! As their fields affect mine, *my* field affects theirs. My impeller wasn't designed to be an antenna, but raw size and power open up a range of possibilities. I wonder..."

Thought raced through his hive intellect, and six hundred minds crunched the math in seconds.

"Well, well, well! It seems I can!" A chuckle spread across his distributed consciousness. "The trick is to operate the impeller in the most inefficient way possible, spreading its effects over a much wider area. Let's see. Enter this new set of parameters into the impeller controller, divert power from reactors sixty-two through one-oh-eight, and now..."

❖　　❖　　❖

Portcullis-Prime heaved and warning indicators flashed red on Jonas Shigeki's virtual console. He swiped the alerts aside and expanded the ship's antenna status.

"What's going on?" he demanded, fingers biting into his armrests as the ship bucked around him. "Why's our field strength dropping?"

"I don't know, sir!" Sung-Wook shouted over the racket. "Unidentified malfunction in the antenna!"

"Get our field back up to full!"

"I would if I knew what was causing—" Sung-Wook paused, his eyes darting back and forth over his console. "Sir, field output from *Portcullis-Two* and *-Three* is dropping as well! It's not just us!"

"*What?!*" Jonas checked his own displays and watched in horror as suppression field strength ahead of the fleet plummeted. Missiles caught in the field accelerated unexpectedly and exploded, vaporizing three more of their escorts as his bridge crew struggled to figure out what was going on.

What would cause failures across all three mobile suppressors? He looked up, and his eyes fixed on *Tesseract*'s signature, pulsating like an enraged storm of chronotons. Only one possibility made sense, and he was staring straight at it.

"That station," he hissed, his words drowned out

by the ship quaking around him, metal groaning and equipment rattling. "The station!" he shouted this time. "*Tesseract* must be counteracting our fields!"

"I think you're right!" Sung-Wook shouted back. "Damned if I know how they're doing it, but whatever it is, it's getting worse!"

The fleet sped into the future as field strength dipped below half.

"We'll lose the antenna if this keeps up!" Sung-Wook warned. "We have to shut it down!"

"No!" Jonas ordered. "Keep it up!"

"The shaking's getting worse! It'll shatter if we don't take it off-line!"

"Then we run it until it does!" Jonas snapped without hesitation. "We're not leaving the fleet unprotected!"

A high-pitched screech echoed through the ship, and more alarms lit up.

"Cracks forming at the base of the antenna! Sir, it won't last much longer!"

"It doesn't have to! Navigator, give me the range to target!"

"Positive twenty-seven days! Fifty-eight seconds to phase-lock!"

"Hold formation with the carriers! We're going in!"

The ship lurched, and his head thumped against the back of his seat.

"That crack's getting worse!" Sung-Wook shouted.

"Come on," Jonas whispered, fiercely but too softly for the crew to hear. "Hold together, damn you. *Hold together*. Just a few more seconds!"

How much exotic matter was pushing against their antennas? What could their three tiny splinters do against a mountain?

Missiles soared out of *Tesseract*, and time machines swung around to intercept them. Chronoports and TTVs opened fire with lasers and cannons, blasting some apart, but the missiles shot in faster than before and a few darted past. Jonas's eyes went wide as he saw a nebulous sphere of possible locations zero in on his ship.

"Evasive action!" Sung-Wook shouted.

The ship's fusion thrusters blazed with raw fury, and acceleration slammed Jonas into the seat, peeling his lips back in a parody of a grin. Warnings sounded in his virtual hearing, and the missile phase-locked with them. One of the ship's seventy-five-millimeter railguns swiveled with serpentine speed. It locked onto the new target and—

—the phase-missile detonated in the instant before it could fire.

Armor vaporized along *Portcullis-Prime*'s broadside, and Jonas heard himself scream as the bridge lighting blew out and restraints cut savagely into his shoulders. Smoke poured through ruined ventilation shafts, massive circuit breakers clanked open, and the antenna powered down with a distant sound like glass singing.

"*Get the field back up!*" he roared. "Get it up before—"

—the antenna shattered into a million glittering pieces.

❖   ❖   ❖

"*Portcullis-Prime*'s been hit, sir," Andover-Chen reported. "Their antenna's off-line, and the other two are barely holding on."

"All forces, accelerate to seventy!" Klaus-Wilhelm ordered.

"Sir, we've got *Valkyries* on the move!" Raibert said,

indicating a blob of signatures leaving the *Tesseract*. "About thirty of them incoming!"

"We're pushing through!" Klaus-Wilhelm snapped. "All ships head straight for the *Tesseract*!"

Valkyries, TTVs, and chronoports clashed in wild melee, and *Wegbereiter* sped into the middle of it. A pair of *Valkyries* blinked into existence ahead of them, and the TTV's bow lasers ate straight through their hulls. Another appeared above and behind them. Its laser gored the heavy TTV, and one of *Wegbereiter's* laser pods flashed up to the TTV's dorsal spine. It split open, trained out, and burned the *Valkyrie* down.

"They're going after us carriers!" Raibert said. "*Bingham's* been hit! They're going down!"

"Two bombs left!" Andover-Chen said. "Us and *Hammerhead-Three*!"

A trio of *Valkyries* phase-locked with *Wegbereiter*, lasers cutting into the TTV's side. A pair of chronoports flashed in behind them, and missiles sprinted out of their box launchers.

"What's *Hammerhead-Three's* status?" Klaus-Wilhelm snapped.

"Getting pounded!"

"Günther, shift us into phase with them."

"Orders acknowledged."

The heavy chronoport appeared at their side, air streaming from a pair of glowing gashes in its belly. A *Valkyrie* dove at it, and its laser carved off the chronoport's port bow wing along with two of its weapons. The *Wegbereiter* opened fire, and the *Valkyrie* exploded in a shower of superheated debris.

"*Tesseract* at positive twenty days! Twenty-four seconds to target!"

"Telegraph *Hammerhead-Prime* and *-Two!*" Klaus-Wilhelm snapped. "Have them clear us a path!"

"Orders dispatched."

A pair of *Hammerheads* phase-locked ahead of *Wegbereiter*. A lone *Valkyrie* appeared between them, and heavy railgun shells blasted it apart before it could even turn around. Two more phased in, and *Wegbereiter*'s bow lasers burned them down.

"Phase-lock imminent!"

The station's massive spike materialized ahead of them, and the *Wegbereiter* dove toward it, three *Hammerheads* at its side.

"Hold fire!" Klaus-Wilhelm ordered. "Get us in closer!"

Defensive lasers spat out of the *Tesseract*. Beams curved off *Wegbereiter*'s hull while chronoport armor glowed hot. Light chronoports and TTVs phased in and out around them, dumping missiles, firing lasers, blasting away with cannons, then phasing away as the heavier ships charged in.

"Closer!"

Hammerhead-Three's other bow wing blew off. Lasers cut through its front armor and ate into the decks behind it. Smoke poured from its hull. A plasma explosion bloomed out of a ruined thruster. But the ship held together. Beams and cannon shells spat out of *-Prime* and *-Two*, and *Wegbereiter*'s own weapons blazed away.

The station was so close it nearly filled his entire view.

"*Fire!*" Klaus-Wilhelm barked.

"C-bomb away!"

Two weapons detached, and the four huge time

machines banked away. The c-bombs shot toward the station, their graviton thrusters propelling them through the flickering whiskers of point defense lasers. Meta-armor shrugged off the occasional hit, and the c-bombs closed in for the kill.

An alert opened next to one of the weapons.

"Oh, no!" Andover-Chen breathed, and everyone turned to him.

A crack had formed on one of the casings.

"The bombs are outside our fields!" Andover-Chen said, a look of terror on his face. "They're being affected the same way the suppressors were! At this rate, they'll go off prematurely!"

"Will it—" Klaus-Wilhelm began.

One of the c-bombs ruptured, and a storm of chronotons smashed into the second weapon, shattering it open far above the *Tesseract*. The wave expanded outward like a bubble of solid nothingness in space. It overtook their ships, smashed into them, and *Hammerhead-Three* exploded.

The wave flowed across the *Tesseract* like ghostly water, and the station's edges thinned and undulated. The shimmering sphere thinned, faster near the *Tesseract* as the station sopped up the deluge of chronotons. Its physical dimensions firmed up once more.

"...be enough," Klaus-Wilhelm finished quietly.

Andover-Chen shook his head, moments before the first replicated time machine erupted from the *Tesseract*'s largest hyperforge.

CHAPTER FORTY-SIX

Transtemporal Vehicle *Kleio*
non-congruent

"OH, DEAR GOD," ELZBIETÁ BREATHED AS SHE FINished reading *Wegbereiter*'s telegraph. She bowed her head, a sick, sinking sensation spreading through her virtual stomach.

"Another urgent telegraph from *Wegbereiter*," Kleio reported.

"Show me," she whispered, and looked up at the scrolling text, probably sent by Andover-Chen.

It wasn't really a surprise. She'd known inside what it was going to say the instant she realized why the c-bombs had detonated prematurely.

The message read: The c-bomb won't survive long enough to reach its target outside your TTV's field. You need to ram it into one of the Tesseract's exposed hyperforges. We're sorry, but this is the only way.

So there it was.

She'd faced certain death before. Faced it and passed through its brutality. Faced it in the skies of

South America and the transtemporal battlefield over Germany. Faced and *conquered* it, though not without scars both inside and out.

But to deliberately commit suicide? To willingly *ram* her ship into that station?

She'd thought herself fearless, able to put aside her own tiny sense of self-preservation for the greater good. But the action demanded of her now chilled her in a deep, primordial way. In a way neither the Mato Grasso Strike in her home universe nor even the battle over Stendal had. Dying by the enemy's hand was one thing.

Dying by her own was something else entirely.

She longed to speak with Benjamin. To hear his voice. To feel his embrace. She knew, deep down, that she would carry out her orders. That she *had* to do this. But she ached for that small sliver of comfort before the end.

More text arrived a few seconds later, and she sensed Klaus-Wilhelm was dictating now.

The fleet will occupy Dynasty forces for as long as possible, but we won't last much longer. The Tesseract has started replicating whole time machines. We're doing our best to contain them now, but we need to end this before the Dynasty builds up an overwhelming force.

Elzbietá considered preparing one last message to Benjamin, but didn't. Every instant she delayed brought their forces closer to defeat, and any casualty from here to then might be his. She wouldn't let that happen, *refused* to let it happen. And so she took a deep breath, steeled her nerves, and grasped her controls. She glanced over at Philo, and he gave her a firm nod.

"We can do this," he said softly.

"I know." She gazed up at the station's distant signature. "We have to. Kleio?"

"Yes, Agent?"

"Let *Wegbereiter* know we'll get it done. *Pathfinder-Prime*, did you get all that?"

"We did, *Kleio*," Kloss said. "We have your back. And for whatever it's worth, I'm . . . sorry."

"Thanks."

"I'm sending over what I believe our target should be. We blew one of the hyperforges wide open during our nuke run. That should be the best spot to deliver the c-bomb."

Elzbietá opened the attachment and reviewed the processed close-up of *Tesseract*'s surface. An oval crater had been blasted open near the top of the spike, its slopes composed of a jumble of misaligned cubes that funneled down to a miniscule opening.

"Got it," she said. "All right. *Pathfinders. Hildr.* Everyone, on us. We'll—"

"Stop!" Teodorà Beckett's voice cracked over the channel.

◇　　◇　　◇

"Drop the c-bomb," she said. "I'll take it in."

"Are you sure?" Elzbietá asked.

The request had flowed from Teodorà's lips, more like emotions taking coherent form than the result of actual thoughts. She'd *felt* it deep within her soul. This was something that had to be done.

And she had to be the one to do it.

Her sight raked over the virtual displays. Their

grim readings looked back like the eyes of skulls, and *Tesseract*'s massive chronometric signature pulsed like a hateful eye before her. A cloud of lesser signals blended together into an unreadable mass between them, and she glared back at it.

Back at *him*.

You betrayed the wrong woman, you monster.

Resolve blazed within her, fiercer even than the combat blazing about *Tesseract*. It burned with an icy fury colder than the fate awaiting the universe she'd birthed and nurtured through two thousand years, and its adamantine passion blotted away all doubt and every question.

"I've never been more certain of anything in my entire life," she continued. "And for someone as old as me, that's saying a lot." Her voice grew harder, sharper with each word. "It was my hubris that birthed this mess. *I* created the Dynasty, more even than Samuel and *infinitely* more than that monster pretending to be a man! If this universe has to die, then it will be by *my* hand!" The words rolled out of her like thunder and her eyes blazed. "Now drop the damn bomb! We don't have time to debate this!"

"All right, *Hildr*," Elzbietá said softly. "It's yours."

Kleio released the c-bomb and floated up from it.

Teodorà settled back into the seat. She took the controls again and guided the *Hildr* over the weapon. A thick lump of prog-steel extended from the time machine's belly, flowed over the midpoint of the c-bomb's spike, and solidified.

"Besides," Elzbietá said even more softly, "you're faster and more agile. You're the right choice...not just the inevitable one."

"It's all right, Elzbietá," Teodorà said, her voice equally soft, almost gentle. "I know you'd have made the run. But this isn't your burden. It's mine."

She energized her impellers.

"Now let's finish this!" Her voice came like the drumroll of Armageddon once more. "*Kleio*, stay phase-locked with me for as long as you can! *Pathfinders*, clear the way!"

She dumped power into the impellers, and six time machines charged into the future. Her craft shook violently from the c-bomb's drag, but she held her course. All four chronoports pulled ahead of her, then reduced speed and settled into formation while the *Kleio* matched her course and speed perfectly.

The *Tesseract* loomed closer, all of the signals melting together, losing clarity due to the speed of her advance. But she didn't need details, just the range.

Positive five months to the station and dropping, she thought, controls tight in her hands.

"There's a group of signals breaking away from the battle," Elzbietá sent.

"Missiles?" Teodorà asked.

"Don't think so."

A cluster of chronometric activity separated from the battle and headed straight for her. She zoomed in and nodded, the shape and feel of the signals immediately familiar to her.

"They're *Valkyries*." She tapped an icon and dictated a telegraph. "About six *Valkyries* inbound, I'd guess. Newer ones, too! Watch it!"

Pathfinder-Prime responded: Understood, Hildr. We'll plow the road.

The chronoports accelerated to maximum velocity.

The larger *Valkyrie* formation swept in, and the two collided ahead of her. Signals mingled in a wild chronometric blizzard, her array unable to pick out individual time machines until the first one pulled out.

The *Valkyrie* phase-locked on her, its sleek body identical to *Sigrun*. *Kleio* fired its main gun, and the *Valkyrie* pulled up hard. Philo's shot flew wide, and the round exploded into a shaped cone, too far away to do damage.

Kleio's Gatlings spewed metal at the speeding craft and Teodorà triggered her own weapons. Streams of fire traced after the *Valkyrie*, but it pirouetted out of the way, then darted sideways as it aimed its laser down on them.

"Damn it!" Teodorà hissed, pulling her nose up.

The beam struck the top of her vessel, splashing off the SysGov meta-armor in random ribbons, and warnings flashed as the armor heated.

Teodorà locked on with her mass driver and fired. The projectile rocketed up, but the *Valkyrie* slipped sideways almost immediately, and her shot exploded far from her target. A few scraps of shrapnel pattered off the *Valkyrie* as it aligned its laser once more.

Kleio climbed after it, Gatlings blazing, and the *Valkyrie* dove at the *Hildr*. *Kleio* and the *Valkyrie* crossed, and cannon rounds punched through the *Valkyrie*'s armor. But it zipped past, its nose aimed at *Hildr*.

Teodorà shoved her omni-throttle to the side as the *Valkyrie* fired. The beam raked across her starboard impeller. Ruined meta-armor flaked away, and concentrated photons ate through prog-steel, then bored through the power lines beneath.

"Oh, no!" she snapped.

Her starboard impeller lost power, and her craft slipped into congruence with local time. Both *Kleio* and the *Valkyrie* vanished, and she gritted her teeth as she switched over to the port impeller. Exotic matter energized. Chronoton permeability changed, and her craft phased forward through time once more.

The *Valkyrie* blinked into existence behind *Hildr*. Its laser stabbed out, Teodorà pulled up, and the beam slashed across her. Her ship's hull groaned and shuddered.

"I'm in trouble!" she shouted urgently.

On it! *Kleio* telegraphed, and phase-locked behind the *Valkyrie* an instant later.

The TTV's Gatlings savaged the enemy's rear armor. Explosions shredded the hull, and Teodorà came about, catching the enemy in a pincer. The *Valkyrie* dove, but streams of cannon fire converged on it, tracking it, punching through mangled armor to ruin the delicate systems within. Smoke fumed out as the *Valkyrie* slowed, its thrusters losing power.

Teodorà zipped by above the stricken craft, and *Kleio* flew underneath. Cannons shredded the time machine hull and shattered its impellers, sending debris phasing away in a crazy, sparkling shower that consumed the craft's tortured hull.

Teodorà realigned on the *Tesseract*, and *Kleio* slid in next to her.

"All enemy craft down," Kloss sent. "*Pathfinder-Three* took a heavy beating, but we're all still in the fight."

The chronoports shook out ahead of her as the *Tesseract*'s signal grew ever larger.

Positive three months to target, she thought. *Halfway there.*

"Another group of signals incoming," Elzbietá sent. "And it's even larger than the last."

"I see it too, *Kleio*," Teodorà said. "At least the fleet is holding those damn missiles at bay. I—"

She stopped and glanced down at her telegraph controls. She'd just received a message bearing Cornucopia markers.

"You all right?" Elzbietá asked. "I didn't catch the end of that."

"I'm fine." Teodorà gave the pulsing alert a jaded eye. She reached for it, hesitated, then clicked the icon and opened a private dialogue.

"Is that you, Teodorà?" Lucius sent, his voice synthesized from telegraph binary.

"How dare you speak to me!" she snapped back, not caring if her rage wouldn't translate through. He could figure that much out on his own!

"Why shouldn't I? Tell me, do you have any clue what you're about to do? I can see you're carrying one of those weapons. The last one, as far as I can tell. Surely, you must know what could happen to the Dynasty if you continue. Neither of us want to see it come to an end."

"Don't you *dare* act like you give a damn about anyone but yourself!"

"Oh, come now. That's simply not true. I care a great deal about the Dynasty, and I want it to live on as much as you do. But in order for it to live, you have to stop. Surely, we can resolve this peacefully."

"Lucius?" she seethed through clenched teeth.

"Yes?"

"Go fuck yourself."

"Hmm, I see. Well, the odds of me talking you

down weren't zero, so I had to give it a try. It's not like this took much mental effort on my part. Fine, have it your way. You'll be dead long before you reach the True Present."

Teodorà closed the dialogue.

"We'll see," she breathed as she checked her console.

Positive six weeks to target. Almost there.

"Here they come," Elzbietá sent.

Valkyries and chronoports clashed ahead of them in a messy swirl of impeller signatures, and this time the *Valkyries* pressed on toward her. The blob of active signals enveloped her, and nine *Valkyries* materialized—including *two* that looked like exact copies of *Sigrun*.

Four chronoports phase-locked moments later, and she sucked in a quick breath as ships and weapons on both sides swiveled, accounting for the chaotic spread of physical positions—

—then everyone fired.

Weapons fire traced between the time machines. Lasers ate through hulls. Admin missiles erupted in brilliant fireballs. Cannon shells tore through armor, and two *Valkyries* exploded. *Pathfinder-Three* splintered as a trio of beams carved through it, and the other chronoports closed in, missiles and lasers spitting out of their weapon pods.

Teodorà picked a target and accelerated hard. She fired the main gun and blew the *Valkyrie* apart with a single shot.

A pair of lasers from the two *Sigrun*-types cut across the *Hildr*'s hull, and the ship convulsed around her. Then *Kleio* pulled in close, intercepting the beams with its own hull while its Gatlings blazed. Photons bored into *Kleio*'s nose. Meta-armor burned out and flaked off. Prog-steel turned cherry red, bowed inward, then burst apart in a molten spray that spackled the mass driver.

Capacitors exploded, and pieces of the mass driver showered out the exposed front. But the TTV held position like a boulder, soaking up the savage punishment, Gatling pods blazing, as it shielded her craft.

Pathfinder-Prime and *-Two* swooped in from both sides and fired spreads of missiles that converged on one of the *Sigruns*. Explosions smeared across space, obliterating the *Valkyrie* while the other *Sigrun* darted downward, seeking a good angle on *Hildr*.

Teodorà spun around *Kleio*, keeping it between them as another beam smashed into the TTV from underneath.

Their forces reached the True Present, and the *Tesseract* appeared before her. Dozens of TTVs, chronoports, and *Valkyries* swarmed around it as phase-missiles launched from its hyperforges, only to be burned down by the fleet's laser batteries before they could phase out. A pair of nuclear detonations rocked the *Tesseract*, and more energy beams blazed up from its battered defenses.

Teodorà spotted the open hyperforge.

"There!" She dumped every erg of energy into her thrusters. Acceleration pinned her to the seatback, and she flashed past *Kleio*. The other *Sigrun* phased in behind her and dove after her. A laser struck her rear armor, and she barrel-rolled through her descent.

"Stop this madness!" Lucius cried, his panicked voice coming across on a regular channel. "You need to stop!"

"Not so smug now, are you?" she snarled. Another

beam sliced through her ship, and the starboard impeller spun away. She diverted all remaining power to the two port thrusters.

"You have no idea what you're ending! I finally achieved it! It took me millennia, and you're about to throw it all away!"

The *Tesseract*'s cratered hull filled her view.

"You have to stop! You *have* to! PLEASE!"

"My name is Teodorà Beckett, Chooser of the Slain!" Her voice was a trumpet over every comm frequency as she drove into the fiery hurricane of *Tesseract*'s desperate defensive fire. "And I *refuse* to let a monster like you reach Valhalla!"

"TEODORÀ!"

Another hit sent *Hildr* spinning out of control. But she shoved the omni-throttle to the side, righted herself, and powered straight into the hyperforge crater. A jumbled mess of warped cubes rushed up to meet her, but she threaded the needle, piloting the *Hildr* toward the crack at its base.

She struck her target dead center.

The *Hildr* crumpled against the crater walls, but the c-bomb shot through the crack. It skidded and clanged back and forth, speeding deeper into the station, sparks flying, until it smashed into the hyperforge's back wall.

The casing ruptured, and a wave of chronometric energy burst through the station's heart.

❖   ❖   ❖

"*NO!*" Lucius screamed.

The outer wall of the Dynasty's universe breached within *Tesseract*, and a tear formed in the destroyed hyperforge chamber. It expanded outward as a perfectly black sphere, consuming the hyperforge walls. Blocks of exotic matter broke loose and tumbled into the abyss as the tear grew, eating its way through the station. His new body quaked, and he sent his many copies scrambling for some way to stop or escape this cataclysm.

He jettisoned the hyperforge and it leapt out of the crater *Hildr* had pierced. The black orb was tiny, by *Tesseract*'s scale, just a speck of pure darkness against the station's hull—but that speck grew at a phenomenal rate, swelling until it was as large as the station.

Then even larger.

Lucius fired hundreds of maneuvering thrusters, hurling his immense body away from that hole in existence, but the tear only grew. Grew without end, ravenously... voraciously. Time machines scattered in all directions, but he paid them no heed; none of them mattered now. He orbited the earth, pulling away from the tear as it grew to hundreds of kilometers in diameter. Earth's atmosphere flowed up into the void and the planet's surface bulged. Its outline became egg-shaped; rocky chunks the size of mountains broke off. Its mantle cracked and magma gushed upward into space.

The tear consumed it all, and Lucius began to despair.

A team of copies reported in and suggested he try to phase away from the tear.

"Ah! Yes, of course!"

He engaged the impeller and phased into the past. The orb shrank, then vanished entirely.

"Yes!" he declared. "It's working!"

More minds reported in, and he absorbed their findings into his prime consciousness.

"The transdimensional distance between SysGov and the Dynasty is growing?" he asked. "Why would I care?"

More facts poured in, and as they did, the sphere reappeared. First as an infinitesimal speck—but it grew, faster and faster, expanding not just physically, but *temporally*. The spherical tear in this universe now stretched back from the True Present to negative thirty hours. It drank in time and space, a ravenous black hunger that yawned wide to swallow him whole.

Could he outpace it?

He diverted all power from every reactor to the impeller, managed to push his speed to nine kilofactors, but then his speed began to drop once more—slowly, steadily . . . inexorably. Suction from the tear overwhelmed his drive systems, tidal forces began to rip the station apart, and armor and surface blocks tore loose and spun away into the void.

"No!" he cried. "This can't be happening!"

The *Tesseract*'s surface peeled away, and interior sections broke free, taking his copied connectomes with them. Lucius felt himself dying one mind at a time, his intellect shrinking with each loss. He'd possessed it all—the godhood he so deeply deserved. How could all his patience and careful maneuvers end like *this*? How could he lose it all, here, at the end? At the moment he'd achieved his greatest ambition?

How could it all slip through my fingers?!

The station's central supports warped and shattered. Core segments broke away. The impeller shuddered from lost power, and its phase field collapsed. The station fractured, falling away into the inky void—

—and Lucius Gwon died shrieking in a chorus of a thousand screams.

EPILOGUE

∞∞∞

Consolidation Spire
SysGov, 2980 CE

THE CHERRY GARDENS WERE SITUATED ATOP A platform that extended out from level one hundred of the Consolidation Spire, about a third of the way up the side of the tall, tapered building that served as SysGov's physical seat of governance. Genetically engineered cherry trees ringed an oval pond, its crystal waters perfectly still around the three floating caskets. A transparent, climate-controlled dome enclosed the platform, and a wide VIP lounge overlooked the gardens.

The spire's gardeners had triggered each tree's flowering, timed to coincide with the ceremonies, and a light shower of cherry blossoms fell past Klaus-Wilhelm von Schröder's face. He stood at rigid attention on one end of the pond beside Director Shigeki as President Byakko—still in her synthoid body—and Chief Executor First walked onto the pier that extended out to the floating caskets. A flag had been draped over each: the golden eye of SysPol against a dark blue backdrop,

746

the silver shield of the Admin on blue with a white border, and the last with a cornucopia pouring fruit across a green field.

The coffins were empty, of course. Combat in space—let alone across *time*—didn't leave much in the way of bodies, and it wasn't like he could have sent a TTV back to the Dynasty to hunt for suitable remains. The crack in the Dynasty's outer wall had swallowed the universe. Vestiges remained in the transverse, but they were stretched and distorted by the tear's pull, much like T3 and T4 were. It was a graveyard made of an entire universe, a frozen parody of the people and places it had once contained. Eventually those remnants would be consumed as well by the unstoppable march of entropy.

But SysGov will live, he thought, his eyes stinging at the sight of the empty coffins. *Even if we paid a terrible price for it.*

Of the ninety-four time machines that had departed SysGov, only thirty-five had returned. The Gordian Division had lost eighteen TTVs, while the Admin losses came to a staggering *thirty-nine* chronoports.

Klaus-Wilhelm glanced to his left and caught a glimpse of Shigeki in the corner of his eye. The memories of his wife's broken body and their children burned alive would never leave him; they would always be there in the back of his mind whenever he dealt with Shigeki or the Admin. But those thoughts weren't alone anymore. All he had to do was look out from this platform, see the enormous city, the skies filled with craft of every conceivable type, the sun burning down from above—and beyond that, invisible in the light of day—the uncountable pinprick stars of a galaxy which was itself but a tiny bubble in the immensity of a universe—to know what his beloved's death had bought. They'd saved not a planet, not a single race, but an entire universe—not just once now, but twice—and horrible though the price had been, Yulia—*his* Yulia—would have paid it without flinching. Her death, her and his daughters', were both the unforgiveable wound and the shared anguish which had brought him and Csaba Shigeki together despite it all. And the Admin had fought by SysGov's side with honor, with all the courage of three warring universes. It had never flinched, never hesitated, and he would not soon forget its warriors' sacrifices.

Our peoples may not see eye to eye, he thought. *Especially the two of us, Director. But perhaps we don't have to. Because it would seem we do understand courage. And we do share honor. I can forgive a lot when that's true, and it is. By God, it is!*

Shigeki saw his look and raised a questioning eyebrow.

He turned back to the ceremony at the pond's edge.

Perhaps all we need is a little patience to make this work.

President Byakko stepped forward and spread her hands before the first casket. An abstract memorial flame burst bright over its surface, and she repeated the gesture with the other two caskets. She stood back, and the chief executor walked up. He knelt before one of the coffins and placed a gentle hand atop it. The image of a wheel appeared at the head of the casket, its rim colored SysPol gold and its spokes made of Gordian swords.

Klaus-Wilhelm frowned a little at the image and spoke to Shigeki without moving his mouth.

\<Why a wheel made of swords?\> he sent.

\<Pardon?\> Shigeki blinked and glanced his way, also speaking silently.

\<The symbol your chief executor just placed on the coffin.\>

\<Oh, you mean the burial sigil. All three were designed by Anibal Edgar Rodrigues. I'm sure the name doesn't mean much to you, but I assure you he's one of the most sought-after sigil artists in the entire Admin. The Chief Executor went to quite some lengths to get his schedule cleared.\>

\<All right. But why a wheel?\>

\<Isn't the meaning obvious?\> Shigeki gave him a look of genuine confusion.

\<Can't say that it is.\>

\<It's a cyclic symbol. Endings lead to beginnings. Bad leads to good. It's a very positive, hopeful sigil. I was quite impressed when he previewed them to us.\>

The chief executor placed the sigil of a silver wheel upon the Admin casket, its hubcap made from a shield. It looked . . . gaudy.

\<You don't approve?\> Shigeki asked, returning his gaze to forward.

\<It's not that.\> Klaus-Wilhelm glanced up at the VIP balcony's wide, reflective window. \<Though you might want to have a spokesperson explain its meaning after we're done here.\>

✦   ✦   ✦

"What's with the wheels?" Elzbietá asked, watching the garden through the wide lounge window.

"Damned if I know," Benjamin grumbled, and she rubbed his shoulder.

"You don't sound like you're enjoying yourself."

"Just glad it's not us down there. Though"—he gestured across the lounge with his glass of wine—"I suppose we could try being good hosts and ask about the wheel thing."

Over a hundred senior members from the Gordian Division and the Department of Temporal Investigation mingled around tables laden with food and drink, though "mingled" might have been too strong a word, Elzbietá reflected. The room was divided into separate clusters of gray-green Gordian uniforms and Peacekeeper blues, with SysGov ACs sticking to the walls or choosing not to reveal their avatars at all. Only a few adventurous physical souls had cross-pollinated, and she spotted one such group near the window.

"How about that one?" she suggested, pointing with her own wineglass. "Andover-Chen's already chatting them up."

"Good enough for me."

Benjamin offered her his arm, and she switched her glass to the other hand, wrapped her arm around his, and together they joined the group of senior Admin officials listening to Andover-Chen.

"And then the hydrogen atom said"—the synthoid smiled at his audience—"'Yeah, I'm positive!'"

Hinnerkopf snorted. Her eyes scrunched up, and she started shaking in a silent laugh that turned her face red.

"I don't get it," Kloss said flatly. "What am I missing here?"

"The punch line, it would seem." Jonas reached over for Hinnerkopf's glass. "Here. Let me hold onto that for you."

"Hey!" Hinnerkopf jerked it away and glared at him with heavy-lidded eyes. "Hands off. Get your own."

"I was only trying to prevent you from spilling. You might want to consider easing off."

"Why should I? I've earned this! You have any idea how many sleepless nights I've had recently? You think all those impellers upgraded themselves? Heck no!" She made a theatrical wave with her glass, sloshing a little over the rim. "So, there's nothing wrong with me having a drink."

"Drink?" Jonas's eyes widened. "As in singular?"

"Oh, no," Kloss groaned. "She's lost the ability to count."

Hinnerkopf stuck out her tongue at them.

"That's not nice," Jonas said. "What would my dad say if he saw you now?"

"I know *zactly* what he'd say!" she declared triumphantly. "He'd congrah...he'd congrah...he'd *thank* me for all my hard work and tell me I earned this. So you see"—she raised the glass to her lips—"the Director would *want* me to indulge."

She drained the glass.

"Well, don't expect me to save you if you pass out," Jonas warned.

"That won't be a problem. Hey, Nox!"

A nearby gray-skinned synthoid looked over.

"Get your handsome butt over here! I need something to lean against!"

The synthoid grimaced, but walked over anyway.

Hinnerkopf smiled warmly up at him and stabilized herself with an arm around his waist.

"There," she said. "Much better!"

"It's my pleasure to be of service," he said blandly.

"Okay, so the next one starts like this," Andover-Chen began. "A graviton, a chronoton, and a photon all walk into a bar. The bartender says..."

Elzbietá and Benjamin backed away from the group.

"How about we find someone else?" Benjamin suggested.

"Good idea," Elzbietá agreed. "Why don't we—"

"Hey! Look, everyone!" Jonas announced. "They're about to sign the treaty!"

Admin personnel crowded around the window, and both Elzbietá and Benjamin found themselves pulled along by the human flow. They ended up next to the same group they'd tried to avoid.

"Oh." Andover-Chen grinned at them. "Hi, guys."

"Hey," Elzbietá said, gazing down at the gardens.

A pair of remotes floated over to the two leaders, each holding a pen. The chief executor picked up his, and two virtual treaties appeared before him: one for the Gordian Protocol and one for its first amendment, the Valkyrie Protocol. He signed both, and then Byakko placed her signature on the amendment.

"Well, that's that," Elzbietá said. "The Admin is now an official signatory of the Gordian Protocol."

"And better yet, both governments have agreed to outlaw temporal replication," Andover-Chen noted.

"Bet that makes you happy," Benjamin said.

"Oh, you have *no* idea!" he agreed.

"It feels right. What they named the amendment, I mean," Elzbietá said, her eyes sad for a moment. "I think Teodorà would have appreciated the gesture."

"You okay?" Benjamin asked, placing his arm around her.

"Yeah. Still a little unnerved by what I almost did."

She flashed a smile at him. "Also *really* glad to still be alive. By the way, whose idea was it to name the amendment after her?"

"That would be Raibert," Benjamin said.

"Really?" She shook her head. "Is he going to name *all* our time travel laws?"

"Hopefully this'll be the last one we need."

"I wouldn't bet on it if I were you."

❖   ❖   ❖

Philo became aware of a conversation near his avatar and listened in.

"I'm going to do it," Jonas said, swirling his drink as he gazed in Philo's general direction.

"Don't," Kloss warned. "You'll regret it."

"Oh, come on. What's the worst that could happen?"

"Are you looking for an honest answer? Or one that'll make you feel good?"

"Honesty is fine, but spare me the paranoia."

"Can't. It's my job to be paranoid."

"Never mind then." Jonas downed the rest of his drink and set the glass aside. "I'm going in."

"*Zhu hao yun.*"

Jonas raised an eyebrow.

"It seemed appropriate." Kloss shrugged. "Any last words for the boss?"

"Don't be so dramatic."

Jonas walked across the lounge and stopped next to Philo's avatar at one edge of the window.

"Agent Philosophus," he said stiffly, clasping his hands in the small of his back.

"Under-Director Shigeki," Philo replied with equal stiffness.

"Mind if I join you?"

"Sure. I don't take up any space, so you can walk right through me if you like."

"Maybe so, but I imagine that's quite rude."

"Eh." Philo shrugged. "I've dealt with worse."

"Hmm." Jonas glanced down at the gardens. "Ah. I see they're already exchanging medals."

A remote floated over to the chief executor with a small wooden case. He opened it and pulled out the medal.

"What's the one Commissioner Schröder's receiving?" Philo asked.

"The Star of the Shield. It's our highest civilian honor."

"Oh, now it makes sense."

"What does?" Jonas asked.

"Byakko's going to give your director the Medal of Freedom. *With* Distinction. That's *our* highest civilian award. Nice bit of symmetry there."

"Ah."

The chief executor walked up to Klaus-Wilhelm and spoke a few private words, then pinned a shield-shaped medal to his chest and shook his hand. Another remote floated out with a box for Byakko. She opened it and pulled out SysGov's Medal of Freedom.

"Am I right to understand your commissioner will also receive a promotion?" Jonas asked.

"Yep," Philo said. "Up from vice-commissioner. And that's good news for all of us in Gordian. He'll be on equal footing with the other division heads after this, so maybe stuff like that Argo fiasco won't happen in the future."

"I see."

Byakko walked up to Shigeki and placed the Medal of Freedom on his uniform.

Jonas cleared his throat.

"You know, Agent, I've heard some rumors about you, and I'm curious to know if they're true."

"Uh-oh."

"Please don't worry. It's nothing like that." Jonas turned his back on the window. "You see, I've been told—from reliable sources, mind you—that you're something of a gamer. Is this true?"

"Well sure." Philo raised an eyebrow. "What's so unusual about that?"

"Over here, nothing, I suppose. But the Admin is rather...restrictive with its AIs."

"Yeah, you can say that again."

"Quite. So you see, I don't have a lot of experience with artificial people. And I've *never* met one interested in games, of all things!"

"Your point being...what exactly?"

"Well, as it turns out"—Jonas placed a hand on his chest—"I'm something of a gamer myself. And I've been in SysGov long enough to become a little curious. If you don't mind, could you explain this *Solar Descent* craze to me?"

"Oh. Is that all you're after?" Philo let a smile slip out at the mention of his and Raibert's favorite game. "Sure, I'll talk your *ear* off about it! You know, you could have led with that part, right?"

❖   ❖   ❖

Raibert sat beside the small garden in the ninety-ninth-floor observation bubble on the side of Consolidation Spire and gazed out across New York City while the sun slid slowly toward the western horizon.

It spilled orange gold across the city as the tower shadows lengthened, and a gentle breeze blew through the bubble's semi-permeable shell. It was very quiet here, away from the ceremonies, away from the celebration.

It was . . . peaceful.

He leaned back in his chair and looked down at the virtual volume in his lap, and his lips twitched in a small, sad smile as he ran his fingers across the gem-encrusted golden straps that clasped it. It was like her to have designed its icon to look and feel to the virtual touch like an ancient, medieval tome, he thought. Or perhaps it had been Pepys's idea. Like Raibert himself, her area had been the ancient world, not the medieval one.

But either way, he could just see her smile, the twinkle in her eye, as she finalized the design.

His fingertip traced the inlaid gold title. *A Comprehensive History of the Dynasty*, it said, and the files hidden within it were just that. The final, towering academic achievement of Doctor Teodorà Beckett and the meticulous record of the entire universe she'd built, nurtured, guided . . . and murdered.

And now he held it in his lap. The history of a universe which, in many ways, now had never been. *Would* never be. When entropy had its final say, not even the bones would remain. No wind would blow about its mausoleum, not even Ozymandias would recall its glories. It would be simply . . . gone.

But that would be true of all universes, of the entire multiverse, in the fullness of time, wouldn't it? They, too, would be gone, along with all the records, all the memories of their inhabitants, of their achievements, of their struggles. Looked at in that light, what difference did it make? Why pay such a horrible price in blood, pain, grief, to nurture a transitory, flickering candle in the heart of eternity that must ultimately be snuffed anyway? Why not be Lucius Gwon? Why not be a taker, and not a giver?

Because it *did* make a difference, he thought. It wasn't the darkness that mattered; it was the light that drove that darkness back. It was caring. It was recognizing something greater than just ego, just personal survival. It was building, and it was protecting, and it was giving, and, yes, by God, it was making amends. And if it was all a flicker in the eye of eternity, who gave a single, solitary damn? It was still worth the doing, worth the building. Worth the dying for.

And that was what Teodorà had understood, deep in the marrow of her soul. It was what she'd *done*. Such a long life, filled with so many mistakes, but also with so many glorious achievements, so many other lives touched. And she'd chosen to end that long life as she had lived it: in the service of *life*. To deliver the deathblow to her own child so that uncounted millions of other children might live.

He stroked the volume in his lap again and inhaled deeply. He wasn't ready to open it yet, but he would, and he knew he would smile, and he would chuckle, and he would weep as he heard the voice of a woman he'd once loved so deeply—who, perhaps, he'd never truly *stopped* loving—whisper to him once again.

Philo's avatar materialized behind him.

"Hey," the AC said.

"Hey," he sighed without turning around.

"I know you wanted to be left alone, but I thought I'd check in on you."

"Sure, I understand." Raibert banished the virtual volume back into the infosystem. "How's it going with the fascists?"

"Pretty well, actually. No one's tried to delete me so far. Quite the opposite in fact. Had a nice, pleasant chat with the director's son. Everyone else seems to be getting along with them pretty well, too."

"Is that so? You know, I never thought I'd say this, but thank God for the fucking Admin." He stood and turned around to give Philo a stern look. "Don't tell them I said that."

"Your secret's safe with me." Philo tilted his head. "You feeling any better?"

"I guess." He pointed to the Ministry of Education. "That's where we met, you know."

"Yeah, I remember," Philo said. "At your dad's going-meatless party. It was so cute how shy you were."

"Excuse me." Raibert put his back to the railing. "I'll have you know I was quite dashing and not the least bit shy."

"Sure. That's why you asked your dad to introduce you to Teodorà, even though you probably spoke all of twenty words to her."

"*Pfft!*" Raibert dismissed. "That's not how it happened at all!"

"Ah, the vagaries of a meat brain." Philo tapped the side of his helmet. "Want me to play your exact, painfully awkward conversation?"

Raibert glowered at him.

"I'll take that as a no."

"In my defense"—Raibert crossed his arms—"you and I were too busy having fun to concern ourselves much with the ladies."

"Oh sure. Which is why you kept watching her through the crowd."

"Did *not*."

"You also asked me if I thought you two were a good match."

"I did n—" Raibert paused. "Okay, actually, I do remember that part. You made some crack about my hormones."

"I believe my exact words were, 'Keep your hormone-driven meat sack drama to yourself. I'm not getting involved.'"

"Ah, yes." Raibert chuckled. "That was it. You were a lot meaner back then."

"No, I wasn't."

"Oh, please!" Raibert rolled his eyes.

"Maybe a little." Philo held up two fingers.

"More like this." Raibert held his hands a meter apart.

"Now *you're* the one being mean."

"Well, I've got a lot of reasons to be upset." He turned back to the setting sun. "Like how Teodora's dead *again*. Dead for real this time. And we just killed a whole universe."

"Because we had no other option. We did what we had to do to survive."

"I know. Still doesn't mean I need to like it."

"Of course it doesn't. But that universe was going to die anyway, Raibert. That bastard Lucius saw to that! And *we* did what we had to do by making damn sure he didn't pull us down with it!"

"I know," Raibert repeated. "I know. I know! But this makes twice I've been part of killing an entire universe, Philo. And knowing they were both going to die anyway doesn't make me feel one bit less guilty. When I first met Benjamin, I couldn't really understand why he was so horrified over the thought of saving Hitler's life, you know? It was history. The Holocaust, the Chinese Revolution, all those wars... They'd already happened. And"—he turned to face Philo's avatar fully—"the universe where he once again allowed those horrors to happen was going to die anyway, right? Just like the Dynasty. And I'm still going to have nightmares over it, Philo."

"Well, if it'll make you feel any better, Andover-Chen thinks none of it goes to waste in the end. Did you hear his latest theory about the Big Bang?"

"No."

"He thinks these dead universes like T3 and the Dynasty end up getting absorbed backward in time, all the way back to the Big Bang. And then all that matter and energy forms another universe whenever the timeline branches. So, in a weird kind of way, they'll all get reborn someday."

Raibert shook his head. "I'm sure Andover-Chen must find this all *so* fascinating."

"He called it his 'multiverse waste-not-want-not' theory, but Benjamin didn't like it and suggested we call it the 'no-such-thing-as-a-free-lunch' theory."

"He what?" Raibert grimaced. "That is such a *weird* expression."

"Well, he comes from a food-and-energy-scarce society. Gotta cut him some slack."

"I suppose so." He leaned over the railing. "You know what sticks out in my mind the most?"

"What?"

"The hate mail she kept sending me. Did you ever read all of them?"

"I cut myself off after your little collection broke ten thousand words. Which, in case you're wondering, happened *awfully* fast."

"Figured as much. I, on the other hand, read every letter."

"*Why?*" Philo scrunched up his face.

"I don't know." Raibert shrugged. "I guess in a way I felt if she was taking the time to write that much, then it meant she still cared about me."

"So, let me get this straight. You read all her *hate* mail because it made you think she still *loved* you?"

"Yeah."

Philo shook his head. "Meat brains are weird sometimes."

"That they are, buddy. That they are." He turned toward the bubble's entrance. "Is everyone still celebrating?"

"The party upstairs is in full swing. Ella and Benjamin were asking after you, by the way. I've also been told they broke out the *really* good wine for this."

"Well, I suppose I've deprived them of my presence long enough." He chuckled and gave Philo a pat on his virtual shoulder. "What do you say we head upstairs and join in on the fun? Maybe sample some of that wine while we're at it."

"Hey, I'm right with you, buddy," Philo said, grinning ear to ear.

When war breaks out among the Eight Worlds, interstellar interests clash. The only hope for peace lies with two unlikely allies: physicist-philosopher Philip Anderson and headstrong heiress Tara Landry. After Tara discovers a previously unknown star-jump gate and Philip figures out how it works, incredible new futures loom over the Eight Worlds—some glorious, some disastrous. And it's up to Tara and Philip to navigate the uncertainties.

THE ELEVENTH GATE
TPB: 978-1-9821-2458-8 • $16.00 US / $22.00 CAN
PB: 978-1-9821-2526-4 • $8.99 US / $11.99 CAN

31901067214942